The Rain Maiden

The Rain Maiden

A NOVEL

Jill M. Phillips

Citadel Press   *Secaucus, New Jersey*

Published by Citadel Press
A division of Lyle Stuart, Inc.
120 Enterprise Ave., Secaucus, N.J. 07094
In Canada: Musson Book Company
A division of General Publishing Co. Limited
Don Mills, Ontario

Queries regarding rights and permissions should be
addressed to: Lyle Stuart, 120 Enterprise Avenue,
Secaucus, N.J. 07094

Manufactured in the United States of America

Library of Congress Cataloging-in-Publication Data

Phillips, Jill M.
    The rain maiden.

    1. Philippe II Auguste, King of France, 1165-1223--
Fiction. 2. France--History--Philip II Augustus,
1180-1223--Fiction. I. Title.
PS3566.H47927R3   1987   813'.54   87-11709
ISBN 0-8065-1008-0

TO L.

"What gift to give? I would as
  soon be blessed,
To lay all this at your feet with
  all the rest..."

"That I could drink thy veins as wine, and eat
Thy breasts like honey! that from face to feet
Thy Body were abolished and consumed,
And in my flesh thy very flesh entombed..."

—SWINBURNE

Prologue

GREY.

Rain-beaded stone tinctured by shadow-limbs of faded trees. Dismal dawn. Sky, ashen and oblique. *Paris*. Late winter. Everywhere, grey.

Adele of Champagne stood at the window looking out over the city. Her thoughts, unsettled, fluttered like the wings of a thousand birds. Meaningless shadows chased through her mind. Uneasiness. Distemper. Fatigue after a night of nightmare vigil. She shivered. It was cold and the chill bit into her bones achingly.

Once long ago she had been warm. Glowing with beauty and expectation she had come west from the wine country to marry Louis VII. Two renowned beauties had preceded her, both of them unable to bear the son he needed. Within a few years Adele had succeeded, and her future had glittered with promise and sunlight.

But the world was a greyer place now. She was no longer young. She was no longer beautiful. *Pity women*. They might sniff power but never taste it; dream of love but never know it; have beauty but never keep it. She looked down at her hands. From their wrinkled perch the rings glinted up, rich and teasing. Memory steeped in vinegar . . .

Oblivion was better. Death had its pleasures; the living could be just as cold. *She thought of Philippe*. Somewhere out in the royal *demesne* the young king of France was a widower and did not know it. Settling herself on the long stone bench, out of the way

of the window draft, she waited for his return and dozed fitfully.
A white wraith chased her through a foggy dream.

She started to a sudden rush of wakefulness—footsteps on the
stone stairs. He stood a few feet from her, tall and thin, his un-
ruly black hair curled against his neck just brushing the shoulder
of his rumpled surcoat. For a moment he looked at her without
speaking, and she studied his expression. It was an old face, be-
lying his youth—sallow, hollow-cheeked. His gaze leapt at her,
black-eyed and intense but his voice was fainter. "Mother?"

Her arms reached for him. "Oh Philippe..." Unaided the
tears came, choking off the sentence, but the tears told him the
answer. Involuntarily he stepped back, unwilling to believe. It
was a moment before he found his tongue. "When?"

"Just before dawn," Adele managed to say. "She was calling for
you."

"And the child?"

Adele gripped her hands together. "Two of them. Both boys.
Both dead." The admission brought new sobs and she covered
her face while Philippe stood by in stunned complacency. "If only
you hadn't been away," Adele wept. "She was in torment...she
swore she would not die until you returned. Time after time she
refused Absolution. It was only at the last that Sully forced her to
take it. She was wild, screaming foul things. It was as though she
had lost her mind."

With uncharacteristic gentleness he took his mother in his
arms, holding her silently for a few minutes. It was as tender as
they had ever been. "Mother," he finally said, releasing her, "I
want to see her."

"Not now," Adele clutched a little at his sleeve. "Sibylla is with
her."

Tension sharpened his features at the mention of his sister-in-
law. She was always at the apex of his anger. Headstrong and
interfering, always critical, never at a loss to flaunt her dislike of
him through witty epithets, Sibylla's presence at court had been
necessitated by his wife's dependence on her. After today she
would no longer be needed.

With a sigh he drew himself up to his full height, his eyes
never leaving his mother's face. His voice was dagger-sharp. "I'm
going to the chapel for an hour to pray. When I come back I

want to see Isabel. You can tell Sibylla that until my wife's funeral she is welcome here. Afterwards I want that bitch out of here for good. See to it!"

Sibylla stood beside the bed, shivering in the dully-lit chill of a rainy morning. The fire had gone out hours ago and no one had thought to replenish it. Outside the wind was shrill but inside all was silent. Sibylla's hands were folded and her lips moved in silent, habitual piety, but under her breast her heart was bitter.

Beside her stood Philippe-Auguste, twenty-four years old and this day a widower. His taut features betrayed nothing and his eyes were dry as he stared down at the small, still figure: Isabel, his twenty-year-old wife. Beside her on the bed lay two swaddled bundles: infants who had not survived her.

Sibylla stared across at her brother-in-law, hating him in silence. He was cold as ever. No tears. No show of grief. No evidence of any human feelings. All the loathing she felt for him rang in her voice. "Isabel called for you, she needed you with her. But you couldn't even do that for her. You couldn't even let her *die* in peace!"

He could not play a scene with her, as he had so often in the past—not now, not today. She had never understood his relationship with Isabel. Like the other members of her family Sibylla thought him insensitive, cruel. Of course they could not comprehend. They did not know. They did not understand. Only Isabel. *Only her.*

In a controlled voice he said, "You blame me for this, I know, Sibylla, but you are wrong. I can understand that you might wish to ease your own grief by accusing me, but you do me an injustice. I loved her." Then with less conviction he added, "She knew that I loved her."

Sibylla swept her dark hair back from her forehead and faced him with blazing hazel eyes. "You loved her? She *died* for want of love from you! I wish to God she had never laid eyes on you!"

Philippe slumped to the floor beside the bed. He covered his face with his hands and sat wordlessly for a few moments as Sibylla watched him, unmoved. He wasn't grieving! Sibylla knew better, she remembered, she *knew*. She was not so young that she did not remember the ugly pictures: Isabel's fits of hysteria, the tears, the sudden fevers, the bruises on her soft white skin. He had done this to her. He was a monster: he had driven Isabel to corruption and madness and death. "Will you still leave for the Holy Land in June?" she chided bitterly. "A living wife couldn't keep you here—will a dead one delay you, I wonder?"

"I am pledged to go," he answered sharply. "I took the cross three years ago. It was your sister's pleadings and demands that kept me here as long as this."

"She is dead—so now you bury her and pick up your plans where you left off. How typically politic of you. And how heartless!"

Philippe wasn't listening to her. He was staring at a memory, trying to fix it in his mind. *A girl with hair pale as the sun and eyes the color of the Seine. She was holding out her hand to him as he kissed it, kneeling before her, swimming in the scent of her perfume and watching as the wind made ruby ripples in her skirt*... "Christ she was beautiful," he whispered, fingering a strand of hair that streamed out, gold and silken over the bed and almost to the floor. "There was no one like her, no one. She gave me more pleasure than any pagan ever knew. To touch her—to have her was..." He grimaced in frustration, one fist pressed to his chin. "Now it is over, and I shall never have such fulfillment again. With anyone. *Never.*"

Sibylla's eyes were greedy with hate for him. "As always you think only of yourself! That is all she ever meant to you: a plaything for your lust! You never loved her, never cared for her, never brought her happiness. You degraded her, shamed her and made her miserable. She was so sensitive, vulnerable and fine—and you took away every gentle thing in her life...."

His voice was heavy, weary. "You're just a child Sibylla, you don't understand. You don't know how it was between us. She loved me! I made her happy!"

Sibylla's voice was steady. "You debased her! You treated her like a slut!"

Philippe jerked his head up to look at his sister-in-law; a black-eyed stare. "She was a slut," he answered quietly, "but it wasn't her fault. Or mine. It was her father and her uncle—*your family,* Sibylla—with their unnatural love for her, using her for their own pleasure and purpose, trying to influence her against me, trying to make her hate me." His lips trembled as though he was very close to tears and his voice throbbed with feeling, "None of you could face the truth: she loved me!"

"Yes," Sibylla conceded, "she loved you. But I can't imagine why she did. I know how you treated her, the things you did to her—she told me! I'll never forget, Philippe, and so long as I live I will never let you forget either!"

He hadn't moved or tried to silence her accusations but when she fled towards the door Philippe's voice turned her around. His voice was thick, his words dark with the undercurrent of intimidation. "Because of the circumstances I shall choose to forget what you have said to me. But I advise you Sibylla, and mark this down: you would do well to remember *who* I am...."

For only a second she stood there, rigid, unmoving, poisoned with hate. Her mind was whirling, chaotic; she wanted to strike, to hurt him any way she could. "You killed my sister!" she hissed at him. Then she ran from the room.

Philippe sat beside the body of his wife for a long while without moving. His emotions were a tangle of anger and frustration. He needed to cry, and wanted to; he wanted to scream his sorrow to the ceiling, to pound the floor with his fists—to curse the God that had taken her away from him. But instead he sat, very still, numb with self-control, remembering....

Slowly he got to his feet and looked down at Isabel. Still so lovely! Her head was tilted back and her eyes were closed but her lips were slightly parted as though waiting to be kissed. *His Isabel!* Wherever her restless soul was now, her beauty remained to haunt him.

He was instantly seized with the conflicting urge to touch her and the fear of doing so. Carefully he pulled aside the wool coverlet and stared down at her naked body. He had known her vibrant and flushed, pulsing and alive. He brushed his fingers (cautiously at first) across her flawless breasts, then let his hands cup them, the fingers prodding her cold flesh. The odd sensation of fullness and hardness stirred him, and he pillowed his face at her bosom.

Nestled in a little grave between her breasts was the silver chain hung with a silver band. Philippe drew it out, looking down at the ring he had given her. The ring of the Druid priestess. *A pagan relic to symbolize a Christian marriage...* Isabel had said, and she had always worn it. More than the ivory cross he'd given her, or the Byzantine wedding ring, or the pearls of St. Clotilde; more than anything that ring had symbolized *them*. Philippe and Isabel. Pagan and saint, both. Always. Forever.

With a free hand Philippe pulled the blanket off, tossing it to the floor. The sight of her blood-stained legs and belly sent a wave of nausea over his trembling body and he stumbled forward, collapsing onto the bed beside her. No one understood. No one. She had died for want of love from him, Sibylla had said. But he *had* loved her—loved her the only way he could love her; the only way she wanted to be loved: ruthlessly, jealously, passionately...

...*in imagination he fled from this place*... *he was sixteen again, bedding an unrepentant twelve-year-old in the shadow of a cathedral, bathed in twilight and silvery falling mists*... *and she—she was ripe and hot and wet with desire for him*... *Isabel, his beautiful child with the body of a woman and a soul as wise as the world*...

He grasped her hair, kissing it, burying his face in a sweet perfumed tangle, wetting it with his tears. In an agony of longing he pulled her closer and did what he had to do, whispering words she could not hear. She was his again—his for an instant as he fought to expel the obsession of a decade in a single sob of joy. Then just as suddenly he was alone once more, panting and sobbing against her unresponsive body; feeling as cold and lifeless as she. *My blood is filled with you, my body, my soul....*

She had always mastered him. First subtly; later with tears and passion and her fierce possessiveness. He had hated her more often than he had loved her, but her body was the only sanctuary he had ever known. "Let me go, Isabel...please let me go!" he wept against her.

Francorum Rex Dominus Superior
The King of France, Supreme

THE ACCESSION of Philippe-Auguste confirmed a seven hundred year continuance of monarchy in France. Two formidable dynasties had soured into dissipation before Hugh Capet, Philippe's ancestor, founded the Capetian line in 987.

The earliest French kings were bred of a heathen Rhineland tribe which overran Roman-occupied Gaul in the year 275 A.D., terrorizing the Imperial legions with their fearsome axes and shrill battle cries. They called themselves *Franks*, and eventually became allies to the Romans. It was this unlikely alliance which repelled the advance of Attila the Hun and his Asiatic hordes in 451.

One of the Frankish heroes of that famous battle at Châlons was Merovius, who gave his name to the first dynasty of Frankish kings. The Merovingians began as barbarians and scarcely evolved beyond that point. Legend consigned their beginnings to the mating of a mortal queen with a marine deity, but the fierce rulers who sprang from the line were real enough. Foremost was Clovis (the grandson of Merovius), first king of the Franks (481–511). From the age of nineteen he ruled as king at Tournai; within five years he had vanquished most of Gaul.

The importance of Clovis is not measurable by his kingship (he was more warrior than ruler) but the symbolism he brought to the French crown when he converted in 499, becoming the first Christian king in western Europe. He had married the Burgundian princess Clotilde a decade earlier; it was doubtless her persuasion which motivated his conversion, for despite their differences she held great sway over him.

Bishop Rémi of Rheims baptized Clovis and three thousand Frankish soldiers, charging them: *"Adore what you have burned, burn what you have adored...."* Several centuries later an apocryphal account of the ceremony had a dove bringing a phial of sacred oil from heaven with which to anoint Clovis in baptism. This symbolic transfiguration was the cornerstone by which French monarchy was apotheosized in the centuries to come. Exalted above all other monarchs, the King of France *alone* ruled by divine right.

But Clovis was still the barbarian chieftan at heart and at his death carved up his empire accordingly, making bequests to his four sons and charging them to maintain peace amongst themselves. That did not forestall the inevitable: division, destruction, and fratricide. After Clovis there were a few notable kings of the Merovingian line (Clotaire, Chilperic I, Sigebert, Dagobert) but not many. By the middle of the seventh century the Merovingians were a succession of addle-brained adolescents, the *rois fainéants*. The real power was concentrated among civil servants —the "Mayors of the Palace" who eventually succeeded the Merovingians as kings of France. Sending the remaining Merovingian claimants off to the cloister, they established a dynasty which later came to be called Carolingian.

Charles Martel ("The Hammer") was the greatest warrior of this line; the hero at the Battle of Poitiers in 732, he saved Europe from an Arab invasion. But it was his son Pepin the Short who became the first Carolingian king in 751. Pepin in turn fathered the most magnificent of his race, the man who gave his name to the dynasty, Charles the Great. The French called him *Charlemagne*.

He became sole king of the Franks in 771 and in the year 800 the pope crowned him Emperor of the West (a rough parallel to the later title of Holy Roman Emperor). Charlemagne's territories spread over a tremendous area: from the Atlantic coast east to the Danube; from the North Sea south to the Mediterranean. He was a constructive administrator, a wise judge of individual capabilities, an awesome builder, and possessed a keen, logical, and inquiring intelligence. A profound influence upon learning and the arts, Charlemagne brought about a cultural renaissance which would forever remove the barbaric stamp from western civilization.

By 843 the Treaty of Verdun had made piecemeal partition of Charlemagne's great empire amongst the heirs of his son. Wars and intrigues (political and personal) had their way, and the proud Carolingians subsided into mediocrity. Once again the real power of the realm was in the hands of civil servants—the skilled and ambitious Mayors of the Palace. Yet these men—descendents of the Counts of Paris—were a cautious lot and did not seek to establish themselves on the throne by means of a violent overthrow. They bided their time instead and waited for a subtler method.

It came as one of destiny's ironic occurrences. The last of the Carolingian kings, Louis V—only twenty years old and newly crowned—fell from his horse and unexpectedly died in 987. Such was the odd chance which created a new dynastic line, whose exponents were to rule France for the next eight hundred years.

Hugh Capet was crowned king in 987 and ruled for nine years. His character evidenced significant qualities which would appear again and again in the personalities of the best of the direct Capetians: patient determination, sagacity, passionate instincts bridled by reason, and a certain personal humility. Hugh wore his crown only once: on the day of his coronation.

Hugh quickly consolidated his position as king and secured a future for his line by having his son Robert crowned heir apparent. But despite Hugh's foresight and gift for administration, his power remained nominal. The royal *demesne* at the time consisted of only some four hundred square miles around Paris. (Despite the territorial ambitions of several of Hugh Capet's successors, the kingdom of France and its importance did not increase appreciably until Philippe-Auguste came into the full flower of his political genius.)

The mid-eleventh century found France's aspirations for growth inhibited by the power of the great fiefs which encircled it: Normandy, Brittany, Burgundy, Champagne, Anjou, Aquitaine and Flanders. A great-great-grandson of Hugh Capet was the first of his family to make a serious move in subjugating the surrounding political entities of the continent. Louis VI (called "Le Gros," for he was hugely fat) was an energetic and successful soldier but he failed miserably when he fiddled in Flemish politics and attempted to foist a Norman cipher upon them after the horrendous murder of Charles the Good had deprived the Flemings of a count. Louis the Fat did have some good instincts, however; his last act as king was to marry his shy young son to the heiress of the richest region on the continent: the Aquitaine. Thus, he affixed its wealth and power to the French crown.

This Louis (the Seventh, called "Le Jeune") became King of France in 1137, shortly after his marriage to Eleanor of Aquitaine. Unlike his vigorous father (and pitiably unsuited to the harsh potentialities of his office) sweet-faced Louis made the fatal error of falling in love with his beautiful young wife, allowing himself to be manipulated by her for many years. His emotional servitude might have lasted a lifetime but for two circumstances: Eleanor's youthful caprices evolved into mature adulteries; and the children she bore him were daughters. Thus, in 1152, mild-mannered Louis Capet finally asserted himself and contrived to divorce his wife.

A strong duality persisted within the character of all the Capet men: cool-headed rationalism, and a flawed sense of spiteful revenge. Applied judiciously these traits tended to balance one another. In the matter of Louis and his marital difficulties, it was clearly a case of spite outdistancing reason. When he divorced Eleanor he had reconciled himself to losing the Aquitaine. He would have done better to consider who would be the next husband to inherit it. . . .

By the second half of the twelfth century the primary juggernaut forestalling French power was an English king, Henry II, the greatest ruler in the western world since Charlemagne. A brilliant tactician, a wise diplomat, a clever negotiator, a bold and original thinker, his power bestrode Christendom.

Henry came to the throne in 1154 after the death of his uncle, King Stephen. From his mother he had inherited his right to rule England and the duchy of Normandy; from his father the counties of Anjou and Maine. Henry's parents were two of the more remarkable figures of the twelfth century and his own personality reflected their image. Matilda ("Maud the Empress") was a virile, headstrong, decisive woman. Daughter of Henry I of England, widow of the German Emperor of the same name, she had married Geoffrey, Count of Anjou—a generation younger than herself and the handsomest man in the western world. Geoffrey's glib charm cloaked a crafty, conniving, brutally tempestuous disposition. He and Matilda loathed each other, but sexually and politically they were well-matched. It was from this seething union that one of the legendary figures in English history, Henry Plantagenet, had his beginning.

After her divorce from Louis, Eleanor—beautiful, rich, accomplished, and now charmingly available—was sought after in marriage by many men. But she had already secretly decided who her next husband would be. She had fallen in love with him even before her separation from Louis when, as a seventeen-year-old, he had come with his father to Paris. In May of 1152, already carrying his child, Eleanor of Aquitaine married young Henry Plantagenet, the Count of Anjou. Two years later she was Queen of England.

Within five years of her marriage to Henry, Eleanor had borne him four sons. In Paris, Louis—wed for a second time—still had no male heir. The present and future power of England over France seemed assured. French law forbade a female ruler, and the Capetian dynasty seemed doomed to extinction through the direct line.

It seemed to be, but it was not. A great deal happened in the years between Eleanor's remarriage (1152) and the death of Louis VII (1180). The marriage of Eleanor and Henry, begun in smug indifference to public opinion, deteriorated explicably in the mass of contradictions which had made it so tantalizing at the outset, as the decade-plus age difference between them began to show. Eleanor found that she could not manage Henry the way she had her first husband, and Henry quickly removed her from any means of trying. Even her beauty and feminine charms lost their sway with a husband who bedded every attractive female within his reach. Eleanor's love for Henry soured into bitter invective and she eventually coerced her three oldest sons into rebellion against him.

There was another setback for Henry involving the credibility of his character. The ignominy surrounding the persecution and murder of his one-time best friend, Thomas Becket of Canterbury, tarnished Henry's reputation as a just king and caused a severe rift with Rome. Henry was forced into the humiliating submission of public penance by the Church. After a marginally successful subjugation of Ireland he returned to public prominence.

In the meantime Eleanor had once more imposed her will upon Louis. Together with her ex-husband and her oldest sons she incited open revolution against Henry. Though he managed to quell the rising (and imprison his wife) Henry was forced to turn over more territorial and financial *largess* to his sons than he found comfortable. Tension caused by the rebellion was the onset of a total collapse of loyalty between the king and his sons.

The most shattering defeat to English hopes of future domination over France had come eight years earlier on a steamy summer night in late August when Louis Capet's third wife gave birth to his long-awaited heir. This child—christened *Philippe*—was the "Dieu-Donné" (God-given), the miracle of Louis's old age and answer to his ceaseless prayers. In recognition of this, Paris rejoiced day and night for weeks.

Philippe (later to be called "the Conqueror" and self-styled *Auguste*) took power upon his father's illness in the fall of 1179. He was only fourteen, but unlike any other fourteen-year-old alive. He had long before set his sights upon a plan of conquest surpassing anything conceived of by earlier Capetian kings. His dream was to rebuild the Frankish empire in the model of Charlemagne's great state. But far more precious to Philippe was his secret pledge to visit revenge upon Henry Plantagenet for his mastery over Louis. Henry was aging—time was on Philippe's side. Eagerly he awaited the time when he might undo his father's rival.

Yet Philippe faced one monumental stalemate of a far more immediate nature. His resourceful mother, Adele of Champagne, had four equally ambitious brothers who were all highly placed in the realm. Theobold, Henri, William, and Stephen stood together with their sister as an indomitable wall between young Philippe and his hope of independent rule. There were also the brothers of his father, two of them—Robert of Dreux and Peter of Courtenay—both eager to exert their own prestige and authority over their nephew upon Louis's death. There were hungry male cousins too, both of the Capetian and Champagnois lines—all older than Philippe, all desirous of edging ever closer to the vessel of ultimate power.

This was the tangled set of circumstances which frustrated Philippe Capet. Amongst his relatives—mother, uncles, cousins —he had not one friend. Resentful of their intrusion, the boy devised a plan of his own with the aid of a most unlikely ally.

Philip d'Alsace, Count of Flanders and Vermandois, was the most famous knight in all the world. Handsome, learned, a patron of art and literature, a skilled sportsman, fearless in battle and elegant in manners and dress, he had recently added further glory to his name by fighting the Infidel in the Holy Land. His enormous political importance in the Flemish territories of the north put him in a unique position of power. The county of Flanders was an Imperial fief, but Philip d'Alsace also served as confidant, ally, and occasional arbiter to the monarchs of France and England.

It was much to his misfortune that Flanders was merely a county and not a kingdom, for if any man on earth deserved a king's crown it was he. In all aspects of public and personal accomplishment he was without peer. (There was a bit of gossip about Philip, avidly quoted in his lifetime, which showed the color of his personality: that he spoke French better than the King of France—Geman better than the Emperor—Italian to rival the Pope's—Latin better than a prelate—and even a smattering of rude English, picked up in the brothels of London.)

He became Count of Flanders in 1168, taking over from his father, the redoubtable Thierry of Alsace, who had retired to a monastery to repent his sins. Philip's first act upon his investiture was to marry his youngest sister Margot to Count Baldwin of Hainault, a territory which lay at the southern edge of Flanders. Even at a time when such marital alliances were commonplace throughout civilization, this was a most felicitous arrangement. Together Baldwin and Philip consolidated a cultural, commercial, and industrial renaissance within the Flemish territories, and successfully promoted their own interests. When Philip d'Alsace left for the Holy Land in 1177, placing the business of governing in care of his capable brother-in-law, Hainault and Flanders were the richest territories in Europe.

The Flemish genius for craftsmanship and financial acuity surpassed that of any other European people. Their cities were models of urban industrial organization: clean, commercially efficient, adaptable to future growth and change. Even the newest styles in architecture from France were swiftly recreated by the builders of the north as town halls and churches in Ypres, Lille, Ghent, Mons, and Valenciennes rose in the Gothic image.

A primary source of Flemish wealth and western trade superiority was their corner on the wool and textile industries. Brought from England, the wool was worked in Flemish mills and exported throughout the known world. Cotton, linen, and expensive samite cloth provided a further source of trade revenue. Since these industries were virtually owned by Baldwin and Philip, they profited handily. Also, heavy taxes levied against the merchant classes and the petty nobility allowed the two counts to swell their war treasuries and thus retain their personal power which was tantamount to that of any Christian king on earth.

But Philip d'Alsace wanted more. Having charmed his way into the circle of King Louis of France, he had managed in recent years to supplant the influence of the king's own relatives; of Adele and her kin; even that of Maurice de Sully—the Bishop of Paris—who was Louis's close friend and adviser. When Philippe Capet was coronated in the autumn of 1179 it was Philip of Flanders who carried the golden sword of State in the procession. Now, with Louis's death imminent, Flanders edged himself ever closer to the boy Philippe's side, anticipating the most dramatic powerplay of a lifetime. It was this scheme which brought him to Mons and the chateau of his brother-in-law Baldwin of Hainault in March, the Year of Our Lord 1180....

Part I
March, 1180

$\mathfrak{M}$ARGOT was peevish. She paced back and forth across the rich carpet, the chatelaine at her slender waist glinting like a filament in the sun from the window behind her. The four children had been sent upstairs to bathe and dress for dinner. The table was being laid in the banquet hall. The serving girls were cutting basketsful of fresh flowers from the garden beyond the orchard. But Margot waited, suspense tickling every nerve of her body.

An hour ago her brother had arrived unannounced from Paris, boasting of the "great news" which he would reveal at dinner. And then, without further explanation, he had gone with Baldwin to the smaller reception hall and closed the door, leaving Margot alone with her curiosity.

Engrossed, distracted, she started as Edythe plodded up behind her, balancing a tray. Irritation flooded over her and she glared at the girl. "How many times have I told you not to sneak up behind people that way!" Margot snapped. "Don't carry things to the hall through here. Use the kitchen passage."

Edythe stood awkwardly in the center of the room. She was a mild-faced girl with a crippled foot which caused her to limp. Margot—elegant and vain—hated deformity. Her own children: Isabel, Baldwyn, Sibylla and Henry were as beautiful and perfectly formed as their parents. This girl (who was a few years older than Isabel) was a foundling whom Margot would have sent away years ago but for the fact that Isabel enjoyed her company; and the indulgent Baldwin gave Isabel her way in all things. There was some doubt concerning Edythe's parentage: born of a whore who had slept with half the nobility in Hainault including Baldwin, she was as likely his daughter as anyone else's. That insult, plus Edythe's physical handicap, was loathesome to Margot, who never lost an opportunity to taunt the hapless girl. "Don't stand there like the pitiful cripple you are," she chided. "Take the tray in and then go upstairs and help Isabel dress her hair. My brother will be anxious to see her. She's been out in the field all day with Sibylla and it will take forever to make her presentable."

Edythe nodded and shuffled toward the kitchen leaving Margot to stand, sulky and alone, her pretty mouth drooping. Idly she toyed with the keys that dangled at her waist. Were they going to talk forever? She stared across the room toward the closed door.

While Margot waited, Flanders toasted his brother-in-law with a cavalier hoist of his wine cup. They had exchanged pleasantries and Flanders had detailed events of his journey north. Philip d'Alsace delighted in setting the scene for his triumphs. Knowing this, Baldwin waited patiently.

They were two very different men who had forged a friendship of necessity. Both were aristocrats, equally fitted in statecraft and war; cultured, educated, capable men—patrons of literature, chivalry and the arts; proud Flemings of a noble heritage, intent upon retaining Flemish power within Europe and counterbalancing the social weight of England, France, and the Empire. In these talents and designs they were alike. In character they couldn't have been more dissimilar. Baldwin was complex, sensitive: a soldier with the instincts of a mystic. Flanders was ruthless. Charming in company, he could be the hardest man on earth when opposed.

Baldwin had always played the subordinate role in their relationship. He admired his brother-in-law, but disliked the cunning shrewdness Philip wore like a blazon. Baldwin was always a little distrustful of him, and today he felt uneasy about Philip's sudden appearance to discuss "this most weighty matter."

Flanders refilled his cup and tossed Baldwin a knowing smile. "And now my brother, I have such news as you have never heard...."

Baldwin regarded his guest with trepidation. Philip was a sly one. There was always a trick or two lurking behind his amber eyes, a jest ready at the end of his clever tongue. Baldwin lifted his own henap and drank from it before asking cautiously, "What is this great news?"

Quick as he said it, Flanders replied, "I have betrothed your eldest daughter to young Philippe Capet of France."

Baldwin choked, swallowed, then tried with difficulty to seize up the remnants of his composure. His words tumbled out between unbelieving lips. "You have seen fit to speak in my place for Isabel? *You* have betrothed her? But she is already spoken for! We have all sworn an oath that she marry young Harry of Champagne in four years' time. You know this."

With manly grace Flanders sank into a chair. His fine lips pursed in a sneer, he scoffed, "Oh, Baldwin, you are unbelievably short-sighted. An oath! What is that? It is nothing we cannot break. Who would marry his daughter to a count who could marry her to a king? Expand the boundaries of your imagination, Baldwin. We have something very promising in this. Be willing to take the chance. For yourself—and for me."

Baldwin's shock had paled to uneasiness but he was still regarding Philip with questioning eyes. "Surely my friend this time you have meddled in areas even too dangerous for your lack of discretion. You are, as ever, several leaps ahead of me but I can chart your reasoning. You have undertaken to *manage* Philippe and you feel that by marrying him to Isabel you shall have even greater say in his future."

Flanders retorted with a smile. "There is more, but I think you have pretty much hit the heart of it."

"God's breath," Baldwin exclaimed in honest amazement. Both men drank in silence for a few moments. Finally Baldwin asked, "Have you forgotten that Philippe is not yet king? Old Louis still lives and while he lives he *is* the king. You yourself are pledged to him in friendship..."

"...and as Philippe's political guardian," Flanders reminded. Then with a wave of his hand explained, "Louis' illness has made him incapable of ruling regardless of how long he lives. His time is short. The greatest favor I can do him now is to help the boy."

Baldwin gave Philip a look of scoffing cynicism. "Do not mince words with me. I know you too well to be easily duped. It is not

Louis you wish to help, or the boy—only yourself."

"And *you*, Baldwin."

The Count of Hainault shook his head in dismay. "This is risky business. There is more involved here than you seem to notice. Have you forgotten Queen Adele?"

Flanders laughed derisively. "That bitch! She and her covey of ambitious brothers would be the willing ruin of France if they had their way. Louis himself cautioned me to uphold his son's right to rule against that quintet of Champagnois."

Baldwin supposed that this was true but he had another argument. "Have you then forgotten Henry of England? For many years we Flemings have co-existed with England and France. Now if we pursue the course you suggest, Henry may well look upon us as enemies. Flanders and Hainault together are no match for England."

"Are you speaking of armies?" Flanders asked, "for I do not fear either Henry or his soldiers. I have served him well in the past as you know. As have you. Our economic ties to England are too strong to allow any discord between us."

"And the French barons?" Baldwin asked pointedly, "do you really think that they will sit back passively while a boy king rules through the auspices of a Flemish count? Be sensible! It is not only Adele and her brothers we have to fear but all allies of the Houses of Champagne and Blois." He paced nervously then turned to Philip. "No. You have reached too high this time. Do you wish to plunge both your county and mine into war with England and France?"

Philip rose quietly to his feet and went at once to the table where he poured himself another drink. Facing Baldwin he regarded him steadily for a moment before explaining, "Our natures are dissimilar my friend and our souls sing a different song, it is true. But we are kin through marriage and there is some design in that. I beg you to heed me. You know that I would never allow pride or ambition to shackle my good sense. I am a soldier Baldwin, and I don't act hastily or without reason. I have considered this matter gravely and I believe my plan to be sound. And you must act with me, in full confidence of our joint success."

"I am afraid of the consequences," Baldwin answered simply.

Flanders put an arm about his brother-in-law's neck and chortled in affection, "Baldwin, trust me." Then his face sobered and he looked keenly into Baldwin's eyes. "My dear brother, my dear friend—there is a time in each man's life when his destiny is laid before him clearly and he must seize that moment of opportunity or lose it forever. Our moment has come. If we act now, immediately, with clear heads and confident spirits, we may raise ourselves up as we have never dreamed. Think on *that*."

Baldwin was unswayed. "What fair speech did you make to the boy Philippe to sell him on this madness? He has not so much to gain as we do, save the enmity of England and the Empire, and his own nobles—to say nothing of his family. I would have loved to hear you put *that* proposition to rights!"

Flanders placed his hands on his lean hips as he surveyed Baldwin craftily. "Then hear me. I have promised Philippe, as Isabel's dowry, the areas of Arras, Bapaume, St. Omer—the whole of Artois province. And, upon the death of myself or my wife, the entire county of Vermandois and its annexed portion Valois. This, contingent on the birth of their first son. Is that not tempting enough?"

Now Baldwin's surprise was thoroughly piqued. "You offered all *that*? Sweet Jesus, but you are hungrier for this than I had believed..."

"Plus," Flanders cut in, "since I have no child of my own, no heir of my body—upon my death the territories of Flanders and Hainault will be combined and passed on to you, or to your oldest son if you and my sister are not living at the time."

"You never cease to surprise me," Baldwin admitted, sinking disconsolately into his chair, "but even if that is the bait for Philippe—and I will admit it is considerable—it will still be some time before it materializes. After all, Isabel is so young and Philippe himself is little more than a boy."

"It is some time since you have seen him," Philip reminded, "he will soon be a man. Already he is tall and broad-shouldered, and like his father, hung like a bull as well. And you realize how advanced Isabel is of her years. To look at her one would easily take her for thirteen, even fourteen. She already has more bosom than my wife—though that alone is not too much to boast of. And Isabel is beautiful, Baldwin—truly, in all my years and all my travels I have never seen another female of any age who could compare to her. She has all the finest physical attributes of our two families. Can you imagine what she will look like in a few years? Christ! Once Philippe sees her there is no way he could regret this decision."

After a momentary pause Philip said, "The lineage of our family also intrigues the French boy. The Capets have been waiting for centuries to fuse their blood with the descendents of Charlemagne. More to the point, it was prophesied in the time of Hugh Capet that a child born to that house seven generations hence would bear the blood line of Charlemagne. I admit it is an interesting coincidence, and it serves our cause well; you know how superstitious the French are. So you can see, Baldwin, that aside from her dowry and her beauty, our Isabel has much to offer a French king."

Baldwin sat staring down at his hands, the fingers interlaced, prayer fashion, his fine features set in porcelain coldness. He was as human as his brother-in-law; he itched for the glory that was offered in this proposal. But he had a conscience, and he also had a more personal stake in this matter. He spoke quietly, trying to bridle his emotions. "I wish that you had consulted with me before negotiating away so valuable a piece of my property as my daughter. I can understand your need for haste in this matter, and yet I think..."

Flanders cut in boldly, "The Champagnois hunger for power grows every day, Baldwin. I had to act when I did. I could not have waited."

Baldwin's face was very pale against the darkness of his neatly trimmed beard; his grey-green eyes narrowed in seriousness. "She is *my* daughter, Philip. I love her. She means more to me than anyone on earth. She is my finest, most perfect possession. I knew that someday I must give her up—I did not think it would be so soon."

"I understand your reluctance to release her," Philip answered in quiet knowingness. "She is unspeakably lovely. Would that she were mine, and that I had a father's right to use her in the manner I wished."

Baldwin turned his face away. His voice was solemn. "I love her as any father would."

"Aye, as any father would love such a treasure, and treasure such a love."

Baldwin faced him with resolute calm. "I am concerned for her. She has known the shelter of love and fondness; we are a close family, much together. I loathe the idea of sending her off to live in that wretched heap of stones on the Seine the French kings call a palace."

"She has been *well* loved," Flanders mused.

Baldwin's face was grave. "Take care what you say."

Philip d'Alsace's eyes flamed a deep apricot shade. "There is more at stake here than her feelings, or your own. We are caught within the currents of a destiny and either we swim with it, or we drown...." Then, with less affectation, he said, "Take heed, Baldwin. I am a worldly man. I have seen much in my life; I am not easily shocked. I understand how a man may lust for sweet white flesh, even if that flesh is of his own making. But you cannot play husband to her forever. So rejoice in the fact that I have found a use for her which is beyond anything we could have dreamed."

"I love her too much to use her!" Baldwin insisted.

Philip bent close to Baldwin, his voice pitched low. "We will *both* use her; and use her as benefits us both. I know what I am doing. Philippe Capet has an extraordinary future before him: he has more cunning and ability than seems possible in one so young. With our guidance—the kind of help and tutoring that only men of our qality can offer—he will develop quickly into a formidable power." He straightened up, drawing in a breath of satisfaction. "Isabel is our link to that power. Put that little beauty in the bed of a future king, and I say we shall all be rewarded." His smile was saucy. "And Philippe Capet no less than you or I." A studied pause, then a smile. "Come, let us go in to dinner."

The scent of burning greenwood was pungent in the room and overlaid by the wafting perfume of lavender strewn among the carpet of rushes. The Count of Hainault and his family sat now with Philip of Flanders at the flower-trimmed trestle table in the great hall. They dined pleasantly on capons in vine sauce, pork with a plum dressing, cabbage and almond soup, honeyed red currants, and tansy cake spiced with peppermint cream.

Margot, excluded from the earlier discussion between her husband and her brother, sulked with dignity throughout the meal, waiting for the time when she would be taken into whatever confidences had been exchanged. Her cat-like slanted eyes glinted gold in the candlelight as she looked from Baldwin to Philip and

back to Baldwin, her dangling pendant earrings making little tinkling sounds as she watched....

His verbal petition to Baldwin delivered, his stomach full, his
mind at ease, Philip of Flanders basked enjoyably within this
scene: pomegranate wine before him and Baldwin's family beside
him. He was fond of his sister's family, always doting on the four
children. Flanders and Elizabeth of Vermandois, his wife of
twenty-one years, were childless.

Isabel was his pet, his specially adored favorite. She was a complex child, moody and mature with a way of half-shielding, half
revealing her nature—a subtle coloring of personality lost to
most adults who looked upon children without distinguishing between them.

Between Isabel and her uncle there was a psychic link—a
spark of magic invisible to others but expressed between them in
silent glances and the slightest contact of hands. In a strange and
very real way they understood each other from an emotional
depth which was perplexing even to them.

Philip watched her. She had remained circumspect and unin-
quisitive during the meal—silent, but catching his eye every so
often, teasing him with a half smile, a shaded look. Isabel was an
exotic, beautiful girl with long hair light as flax and blond to the
roots. Her eyes—predominant in her face—were large, grey-
green and infinitely mysterious. *Sea eyes.* Her mouth, the bottom
lip so full and tremulous above her pointed chin, had an incredibly sensual appearance. Flanders knew that she understood her
unusual appeal and deliberately communicated it to him. It was
an easy thing to see how she had so completely captivated Baldwin.

Flanders reached to take her hand now, saying, "Come here
Isabel and sit with me. Your father and I have some astounding
news for you." Without compunction she came to sit upon his
lap, her arms warm about his neck. Looking steadily into her face
he asked, "Darling child, how would you like to be Queen of
France?"

Her lips parted but she did not speak as questions looked out
of the puzzled depths of her eyes. Interpreting the nature of her
wonderment, Philip was quick to explain: "I am of course not
speaking of the current King of France as your husband. Louis is
old and he's dying. I doubt very much that he'll last out the year.

When he dies young Philippe will be king and what a king he will make!" That declaration was tinged with something akin to fatherly pride. "Philippe is a boy of great spirit and ability. He is in fact capable of ruling France alone, even now, despite his youth and without the unwelcome intrusiveness of his mother and uncles. Your father and I are his steadfast allies...." A shade of disapproval passed over Baldwin's expression at those words, but he said nothing as Flanders continued: "In marrying you, Philippe cements the bond between us and shows his uncles and his mother that he is separating himself from them."

Young as she was Isabel understood the value of a powerful political marriage. A young heiress owed her relatives the honor of a good match. One had already been arranged for her: several months ago she had been contractually affianced to one of Philippe Capet's cousins, young Henri of Champagne. But now her talented uncle had managed to find her a king! She knew that she was the pawn in this game, but if the fabulous Philip d'Alsace was confident such a marriage was in the best interests of her family, who was she to disagree? She hesitated for only an instant; gave her father a fleeting, elusive glance; then kissed her uncle fondly on the lips and asked, "When will the marriage take place?"

Philip's white teeth flashed in a ready grin and he embraced her. To his brother-in-law he said, "By God's breath, Baldwin, you and my sister have a magnificent daughter! I swear she will make a fine queen!" Philip rose to his stately height, his strong arms hoisting Isabel high above him. He smiled up at her and she smiled back, as the ends of her long hair tickled against his throat.

Hours later Isabel stood naked in the moonlit silence of her room, winding her hair into plaits and thinking of the news her uncle had brought. Outside a mellow bird cooed in the spring wind and the white willows rustled. Then Isabel lay down upon the bed and waited; after a while she slept. Under her closed lids, her eyes shined.

Baldwin drank heavily that night. He was usually a temperate man but tonight his conscience was on fire with frustration and guilt. Foreboding gnawed at his brain like a maggot.

The fire had gone out hours before and he was alone now with only the darkness in friendless counsel. In a wrath of self-disgust he cursed himself for allowing Flanders to intimidate him. It was nothing new. In the eleven years since his marriage to Margot he had been forced to defer to Flanders in many matters. There had been little friction between them, since Philip's extraordinary arrogance was reasonably tempered with good sense, charm, and much practical determination. Now his boundless ambition had finally discovered a permanent roost; but he needed Baldwin's acquiescence, Baldwin's help, and Baldwin's daughter.

Margot had held her tongue, but not through shyness. Like her brother she was eager and grasping, never sated, always wanting more. The idea of being mother to the Queen of France would feed her greedy appetite for fame and power. It would not matter to her that an oath had been broken to make way for a risky, ambitious and too-soon-settled act of daring. Neither she nor Philip d'Alsace were cautious enough to see that the risks in the matter equalled the promise of gain. Margot was young—only thirteen at Isabel's birth—her youth and Fleming spirit explained her lack of discretion. Philip, scion of the d'Alsace family, was old enough to know better. But his restless, determined spirit could never be satisfied or calmed with anything other than ultimate success.

But distress and silent frustration are pitiable substitutes for resolve, and after a while Baldwin urged himself out of the chair, numb and soul-sick and too weary to contest any longer. The sound of indistinct footsteps escorted him across the hall toward the stairway and up the steps and down the corridor to his wife's room. He paused for a moment outside the door, then turned from it, continuing down the unlit passageway.

Isabel sensed rather than heard his presence just outside her door and when he entered she was sitting up, shimmering in a spill of moonlight. Wordlessly he came to sit beside her on the bed, unwrapping the plaits from her hair while she sat very still, her eyes focusing on his face. "I didn't know what you wanted me to say," she confided.

"There was no time to speak to you alone, though I should have been the one to tell you," Baldwin said soberly. "Philip was so anxious to burble it all at dinner, I didn't have the chance." He took a breath. "Are you angry with me?"

Her gaze was a soft focus of light on his face. "Is it what you want?"

He turned his face from her, his head throbbing from confusion and too much wine. His voice was hoarse. "I don't know."

Gently, as though she were the parent comforting the child, Isabel took his face between her hands, making him look at her. Her voice was soft but very steady. "I want whatever you want. Today. Tomorrow. Always."

Baldwin went readily into her arms, his words tangled in sobs. "I want *you*."

"You have me," she answered, inscrutably calm, "nothing will ever change that." She sank gracefully to the bed cushions, easing him down beside her. "Now hush..."

For a long time he lay weeping in her arms, his head pillowed on her soft young shoulder as she stroked his hair and muttered quiet words of comfort. Her love was pure and perfect and trusting and he received it covetously, drowning in it, until there was nothing else....

Later when he rose to go, she took hold of his hand, bringing it to her lips and kissing it tenderly. "Do whatever you must," she told him, "and don't worry. I understand. It will be all right. I promise you."

His hand slipped away and after a moment she heard the sound of the door closing and she was alone. The bed was still warm where he had lain and Isabel nestled close in it, surrendering herself to the lure of sleep and the unfocused fascination of dreams.

H ARRY PLANTAGENET stirred in his sleep and twisted over to one side. He opened his eyes drowsily, trying to remember where he was. His head ached from a full evening of drinking and a familiar sourness clawed at his innards.

The room was airless and Harry stumbled to his feet and toward the window. He leaned far out, drawing air into his lungs. The exertion caused the vomit to rise in his throat. Retching, he spewed the vile mess at his feet.

Harry felt a little better now but cursed himself for having drunk so much. It was his downfall he knew, and though he was continually promising himself that he would stop, weakness was his greatest weakness—and Harry was too weak to stop.

Drinking was one of the more appealing diversions in young Harry Plantagenet's life. He was twenty-five, the oldest son of King Henry of England, and the designated heir to the throne. Yet he lived a life devoid of purpose, reveling in pleasures which had begun to pall years earlier. His "kingdom" seemed a long way in coming. His father still ruled in England with power and aplomb. There was Marguerite, of course, Harry's French wife— a daughter of Louis VII—but she was no diversion, never had been. And there were problems: his three brothers—younger, shrewder than he, and all ambitious—Richard, Geoffrey, and John. Worse, there was his own indolence every day eroding his natural gifts.

Reclining once again on the bed, Harry smiled approvingly at his most recent pastime. Philippe Capet lay on his stomach, his face turned sideways pressed against the rough *brunette* bedcover, black tangled hair partially covering his face.

Philippe was a strange boy, alternately passionate and cold. Harry knew him better than anyone did, yet really did not know him at all. They had been lovers since Christmas when Harry, seeking a release from boredom, had sought solace in Paris. Harry had known Philippe for many years, of course; they were brothers-in-law, and Harry had participated in the French boy's coronation the previous November. He was so young, not yet fifteen, relatively inexperienced and not really Harry's type. Harry had known many lovers of both sexes but there was something especially appealing to him about this black-eyed youth, so attractive in a sullen, gypsy way.

Harry reached out to stroke Philippe's face and the French boy stirred in his sleep, then cried out. His glazed eyes found Harry and he instantly relaxed. He took hold of Harry's hand and kissed it again and again. "Oh," he breathed, "I was dreaming...."

"You sounded frightened, was it so bad?"

"I don't know," Philippe answered, "I can't exactly remember. Everything was black. I couldn't breathe. Why did you put out the candles? You know I can't stand the dark." He shivered, and then nestled close against Harry's chest. "How fortunate to wake and find you at my side." They held each other silently for a while, Harry stroking the curly black hair. "I wonder if my father ever had another man," Philippe mused quietly. "Did your father?"

In the darkness Harry smiled to himself. "Not your father, surely. And mine? I can't say. Oh, there was a time when old Henry screwed anything that moved. I suppose he's a bit past it now. Of course, he's still got Alais. He's been fucking her since she was a child. It's no wonder Richard doesn't want to marry her. And she loves father, or claims to."

"That's a pretty shoddy way to treat my half-sister," Philippe declared with an undertone of hostility, "Your father is a tyrant! God knows he humiliated my father more times than I care to remember."

Harry loosened his hold on Philippe. "Don't be so dramatic," he teased, "you can't possibly remember that much. All that happened years before you were born."

Philippe struggled to a sitting position. "I have heard stories from Louis. I don't think he was ever the same after Henry took Eleanor from him. He loved her, the bitch!"

"Ah yes, my fabled mother," Harry smiled. "Well I don't think that she and your father were exactly suited to each other from the start. Louis was glad to be rid of her I should think—she hadn't given him a son after all. And we can't exactly complain, can we? Neither of us would be here if Eleanor had stayed faithful to Louis."

"From what I've heard," Philippe protested, "she never was, even before Henry. She scandalized my father in the Holy Land. Sweet Jesus, she slept with her own uncle!"

"I doubt that," Harry laughed. "Mother had always been controversial, so naturally people gossip. I'm sure a lot of the stories were exaggerations."

Surly, Philippe slid down under the covers. "At least the old bitch can't do any damage now that she's locked up. I wish to God Louis had stuck my mother away somewhere long ago."

"You never used to hate your mother," Harry commented. "What makes her suddenly so unbearable?"

Philippe didn't hesitate. "Her whole family is unbearable. God what a menagerie! You could populate the Ile-de-France with her relatives. They're all just settling back waiting for father to die so they can take over. When I was little, mother never had time for me. She was always off somewhere, Champagne or Burgundy, visiting members of her family. But these last months, with Louis so ill, the old stone cunt has been sticking so close to home she wouldn't leave under threat of fire or famine. She's counting the days till father dies and she can take everything for herself and her brothers."

"Don't let it happen," Harry counseled, realizing as he spoke that he would be no match for his own mother in the same situation.

"That's easy to say," Philippe scoffed, "but the whole government is thick with Champagnois. They're in all the positions of power. It's damn depressing too. That's why I've got to look for help elsewhere."

Arrogant and weak-minded, Harry misinterpreted the words. "I don't know what you expect me to be able to do," he said simply.

Philippe rolled over on his back, black eyes staring up at a blackness he could not decipher. "Not you, Harry. I need an ally. How could England and France ever be allies?"

Harry thought about that for a moment in silence, supposing that it was true. He had never considered what his own attitude toward France would be once he was king. He never thought much about anything that he would do when he was king. He just thought about being king. Still, he imagined that Philippe was right and he told him so.

"That's why I'm leaving for Mons tomorrow," Philippe explained. "I am going there to marry the Count of Hainault's daughter."

Harry was slow, but he wasn't stupid. He knew Baldwin of Hainault and he knew immediately what the plan was. He also knew that Philip of Flanders was the power in that part of Europe and that Flanders had no daughters. He pushed himself up on the bed, staring down at Philippe, barely able to distinguish his outline in the darkness. "So," he finally said, "Flanders has put his spell over you. Beware of him, Philippe. He has played many men false. He would do no less with a boy."

Immediately Philippe was contemptuous. "I don't need your permission, and I don't need your advice! Sweet Jesus, I'm not a baby! I'm old enough to make my own decisions. And don't forget, Flanders was my father's choice as a guardian for me."

"But not your mother's, I think," Harry cut in. "Can't you see

Flanders' ambition in this? Once Louis is dead and you are tied to a Flemish alliance, he won't be content with being only your guardian or adviser. He'll be the real ruler and you'll be only a puppet king."

Philippe laughed easily but without pleasure. "Will it be different if I disengage myself from Flanders and, upon my father's death, allow my mother and her brothers to put a paper crown upon my head while they rule instead?" In the dark he reached out for Harry's hand and brought it to his lips. "Please understand that I'm doing what I have to do. I don't have a choice."

Harry drew him into his arms, kissing Philippe's face, and fondling him. "I'm thinking of you," he whispered into the boy's ear. "I love you, I don't want to see you hurt."

"I won't be, just trust me, help me, support me if you are truly my friend...."

"I am, sweet boy," Harry whispered back.

His face buried against Harry's shoulder, Philippe muttered, "I'm all alone Harry, except for you. I'm so afraid, and I can't let anyone know it. You're the only one. I need you so much."

Harry, vulnerable to fears of every kind, clutched him closer. "I need you too," he said.

In the pale sunshine of a Paris morning, Maurice de Sully tended to his garden and waited for his august visitor. She had sent a message the previous night demanding to see him this morning. It was not the first time that Queen Adele had sued for an audience with him, and each time the experience had been unpleasant.

Sully was bishop of Paris, and one of the most accomplished men of his time. The education afforded him in the cloister had raised him above the mediocrity of his humble birth, and his keen wisdom catapulted him into the circle of blossoming intellectual elite within the Paris university coterie. From that point advancement had been easy, and he'd eventually joined the inner orbit of the king's closest advisers. Louis VII, who held good churchmen close to his heart, appreciated Sully's mental gifts and unflinching honesty. Together they had taken upon themselves the arduous and expensive project of razing the old St. Etiénne church on the Ile de la Cité, erecting the foundation of a new Notre Dame de Paris. Since 1163 Sully had been guiding the project personally, much as the fabled abbot Suger had shaped construction of St. Denis basilica, where interior French gothic had its beginnings. It was a personal milestone of achievement for the king's administration, and a fulfillment as well. Louis had a weakness for piety etched in stone.

He also had a weakness for prelates. In his service, Sully had advanced admirably, but he was an honest man who never used his influence to effect gain or personal glory. His strongest tie on earth was his love and respect for the king and the magnitude of the king's high office. Now with Louis dying and young Capet already crowned, Maurice had pledged his loyalty to the heir apparent. Representing no faction, supporting no political cause, Sully's aim was to uphold the right of the young French boy to rule, and to rule without the intrusion of the Champagnois.

For all his wisdom and liberality of mind Sully did have one preconception: he believed it was unnatural for a woman to hold sway over men. For years he had watched, and not without complaint, as Adele of Champagne had coerced and manipulated her husband into a position of subservience to the Houses of Champagne and Blois. Like many prominent men within Louis's circle, Maurice had resented her, and silently awaited her downfall. No advocate of the vain Philip d'Alsace, Sully nonetheless preferred the Flemish warlord to the French Queen. Once Philippe Capet was king, Sully was determined to see to it that he had no allegiance to either the Count of Flanders or to Adele and her greedy, power-grasping relatives.

In a little while the queen came, strolling along the avenue of junipers lining the garden; quite alone, but for two members of her personal bodyguard. She was restless and anxious as ever, vain and haughty but with none of the dignity possessed by Louis's first wife, Eleanor of Aquitaine, who was now queen of the English. Sully had not been part of Louis's *sanctum sanctorum* then; he had never known Eleanor. But he had seen her once, and once was enough to remember her forever. She had been riding through the streets at the head of a caravan with her husband traveling up to St. Denis on a pilgrimage. Lissom figure erect, her head held high, black hair blazing under the sun— Sully would remember that picture forever. She had passed so close to him that the fur-lined edge of her cape trailed across his hand. Then she had turned her head and smiled at him. Sully often thought of her. Of course, she would be old now, no longer beautiful, though in the South men who were young enough to call her mother still sang of her beauty. But young or old, he decided, there was an aura about her that shouted royalty, compelled attention. Only that one glance—that single smile—but it was as close as Sully had ever come to loving a woman.

Adele of Champagne was a different breed of nobility. Her dark Gallic beauty was secondary to her shrill perversity. She was without subtlety, her boundless personal ambition obvious in all she did. Sully had entertained her in many difficult interviews, and they had never disguised their dislike for one another.

Waving aside her bodyguard, Adele strolled over to where Sully bent stripping leaves from his herbs. He waited for her to speak first. With Adele there was never long to wait.

"My Lord Bishop," her shrill voice sliced the air between them, "what is the meaning of this?" She thrust a folded communique at his feet. Quietly Sully bent to retrieve it while Adele looked on, nervously pacing in front of him, biting her bottom lip in her characteristic mannerism of ill-suppressed rage.

If the contents of the letter did not amaze him, its authoritarian tone did. It was an order signed by Philippe Capet and the Lord Chancellor Hughes de Puiseaux, invalidating Adele's claim to her dower lands and revoking her privileges at court. She didn't wait for him to finish reading before she snatched the paper away and began pacing before him again, her nervous hands flicking her trailing braids back and forth. Finally she pivoted around and faced him squarely, shaking the letter with menace. "This is treason!" she breathed, her voice quavering with emotion. "And *you* are behind it! So help me Sully, if it were within my power I would have your head struck from your body here on this very spot!"

"Madam, I assure you..."

She jumped into his sentence. "Don't toy with me! You hate me, you have always hated me...you would like nothing better than to see me stripped of all power!" When he did not attempt to silence her she shouted, "Can you deny it then? Can you deny that you have hated me from the beginning?" Her face was set tightly in distress, her voice was on the edge of tears.

Mildly affected, Sully spoke with gentleness. "Despite our many differences my lady, I do not hate you, nor have I ever hated you. But I will not deny that I would welcome the remove of your influence and that of your brothers from the young king."

"Why?'" she shrieked, her dignity cast aside heedlessly in anger, "why should you wish to see me undone when *I* am queen of this land, and have a right to rule—and when behind my back you uphold Flanders and his intrusion into this matter?"

Meticulously Sully arranged camomile leaves in his sifting basket. To Adele his concentration upon such mundane tasks seemed callous in the face of her distress. Finally he looked at her somewhat pityingly, and tried to explain. "It is not anything to do with Flanders. I am thinking of your son, as you should be."

"My son is a child," she shrieked again. "It is ridiculous to assume that he could rule alone. He needs my help. You have no right to interfere!"

Hysteria in women, particularly one of her rank, was offensive to Sully. Eyeing her shrewdly he protested. "Lady Adele, it was your own husband who sought my help in aiding your son. I am afraid that he too is anxious to remove the influence of your family from the court."

"You lie!" she screamed at him. "My husband would never be a party to such treachery against me and my kin!" She threw the paper at his feet and stalked away. Over her shoulder she called, "You will regret your actions Sully, when I have told my husband of your duplicity."

Deftly he bent to retrieve the fallen document, then carried it over to where Adele stood and put it squarely into her hand. His gaze was unflinching as he eyed her. "You would do well to realize the seriousness of this, madam. You have been evicted—denied access to the palace and stripped of your dower. If you intend to fight this I suggest that you find a more substantial means of doing so than arguing with me. Talk to your son. He leaves today with Flanders for the north. I will meet them at Bapaume. Perhaps you have not heard as yet of his plans to marry?"

Adele's black eyes were riveted to Sully's face, her jaw set indomitably. "Yes, I have heard," she brayed, "and that's one bridal bower that will be put to the torch if I have my way! No one is going to shut me out from my rightful place and take away that which is mine by law—not my son, not Philip d'Alsace, not even you, my lord!" She was shaking, breathless with rage and she prophesied in cold fury, "You have not had done with me, Bishop! When next you see me I shall have an army at my back and you will have tasted the last of your power here!"

"God directs my way madam, not you," he called out sharply as she walked away from him.

"Bastard!" she hissed over her shoulder

They met in the middle of the *Petite Pont* spanning the Seine. Philippe's horse pranced easelessly beneath him and he gripped the reins tightly between his fingers as he glared across the distance at his mother.

"Philippe," Adele called out, "you have denied me access to your person for too long now. . . . I demand an audience."

It was Flanders who answered instead. "Madam," he called out, "you have already been dismissed from the court. Be on your way."

Adele raised herself up in the saddle and flung aside the braids which trailed over her shoulder. With flashing eyes she addressed the count. "And are you now king in this land, my lord? Do you rule in the place of my husband and son; are you the mouthpiece of the crown? My husband's illness has taken away his power of speech, but does my son rule without a tongue as well?"

Young Philippe trotted his horse up to stand beside Adele's mount. Mother and son eyed one another for a silent moment. "Lady," he snapped, "no one speaks for me. You have already had my decision. So take your brothers and leave my realm before I take up arms against you and have you driven from it!"

Her rage made articulation nearly impossible, but she lashed out at him, "Do not forget, my boy, that I have an army as well! My brothers and I will not brook this insult from you. We will use force, and we will appeal to the king on our behalf!"

Philippe's laugh was tinged with ridicule. "The king?" he mocked. "The king is on his deathbed madam!"

"I do not speak of my husband," she shouted back, "for he is powerless against you and this Flemish traitor. I speak of Henry of England to whom my brothers and I will plead our case." She looked past her son at Flanders and called out, "You especially have much to answer for, my lord. You have turned my son against me and my kin! I will have my revenge against you! I am still queen of this land and I will not be tossed aside!"

"By the time your son returns there will be a new queen of this realm," Flanders scoffed, "so enjoy the last days of your reign, lady, and be off with you."

She ignored him, turning her attention to Philippe. He looked very much like her, this tall youth who glowered at her with narrowed, hateful eyes. Adele searched her mind for some words of endearment. She had never been a real mother to him, and at this moment she regretted it. His cold, insolent manner was an affront to her, and painful—but the stab against her rank cut deeper. Speaking to him as a mother would do nothing; the icy midnight of his eyes told her that. She stoked her courage and said, "My brothers and I will do everything in our power to see that this marriage you speak of never takes place." She pointed a sharp-nailed finger at Flanders, "But even if it does, do not anticipate too greatly your power, Philip d'Alsace, for by the time you and my son return with his bride, this city may well rise against you! I still have the power of my office and I will not hesitate to use it!"

"Your office, such as it is, has no power, madam," Philippe reminded her curtly. "Do not threaten me with illusions. I shall marry after my own choice and not allow myself to fall into your hands and be dictated to by you." He drew his horse nearer, as if to pass, with Flanders following closely behind him. "Now get out of my way, lady!"

Tears of rage and humiliation burned in Adele's eyes. "You are a traitor to your own flesh and bone," she shouted. Then she screamed at Flanders, "You are a man of base interests, a false knight! I shall take my case to Henry of England and he shall grind you both into the Flanders bog!" She urged her horse forward with a jerk, pushing through the ranks of Philippe's bodyguard. Flanders raised his arm signaling the men to stop her, but Philippe motioned the hand aside, declaring, "Let her pass."

"She will go to the palace and seek the king's ear," Flanders objected.

"She will seek," Philippe said smugly, "but she will not find. I have given orders that she be turned away."

"But bribery," Flanders reminded him, "she may find a willing enough accomplice."

"No," Philippe answered again, "for her wealth is within my keeping now and whatever baubles or trinkets she has on her person will not be tempting enough. Besides, I have instructed Sully and de Puiseaux to see that my wishes are obeyed. We need have no fear in our absence."

Flanders gazed with hearty admiration at Philippe. How a couple as unlikely as Louis and Adele had managed to bring forth this amazing boy was unimaginable. Years ago, when Philippe was only a child of four, Thomas Becket had written of him, "...truly he is a child of remarkable gifts and strange wisdom...."

Flanders gave Philippe's shoulder a gentle nudge. "What a marvel you are," he exclaimed. "I would to God you were my own son!"

Philippe's lips curved in just the slightest suggestion of a smile. Within the space of a few weeks he had turned his life around completely; made the pact with Flanders, turned his back on mother and uncles, forged both a marriage and a political agreement, and still managed to carve out a promising future territorial gain for his realm. He had even succeeded in astounding the magnificent Philip d'Alsace with his abilities. It was the headiest moment of his young life. "We shall be kin, shortly enough," he commented crisply to his mentor, then urged his horse on across the bridge.

When the time came it was less awkward than Flanders had anticipated. After a few words with Baldwin, Flanders took Philippe and Isabel aside and in the garden, holding them both by the hand, he introduced them for the first time. Radiant and beautiful in ruby-colored silk, Isabel was outwardly serene, and Flanders felt pride in her. There was no giggling, girlish embarrassment in her manner as Philippe Capet took her hand and kissed it gently, symbolically sealing the agreement as he knelt modestly before her.

The wind teased Isabel's hair, trailing it out in strands of tangled golden floss. For a moment Flanders stood as though apart from this tableau and as he watched he sensed a current of wordless fascination pass between Philippe and Isabel. His spirits soared with his ambition. He had been right after all. This would be a remarkable match on all levels.

"God bless you, my dearest darlings," he told the two. Then he kissed them both.

𝕭ALDWIN and his family celebrated Easter at the chateau in Mons with Philippe Capet as their guest. The following morning, under the grey cover of dawn, their caravan began its southwesterly journey toward Bapaume where Philippe and Isabel would be married.

Traveling with them was Gilbert of Mons, Baldwin's young chancellor. Gilbert was precisely the type of subordinate favored by men like Baldwin and Philip d'Alsace: educated, sharp-witted, (with a useful intelligence more creative than academic in nature), assertive, courtly, vigorous, adroit, and good-looking. Gilbert was only twenty-nine yet his career had been an interesting climb to prominence. Brought up in the cloister at Valenciennes, he had trained for the priesthood but had soon left that calling to follow a path of secular advancement (though in deference to Gilbert's religious training, Baldwin had since created him titular provost of St. Germanus in Mons and St Alban in Namur). Facile, with a gift for languages, Gilbert enjoyed considerable freedom in his position: dabbling in law, diplomacy, politics, economics, and arts, and the business of teaching Baldwin's children—it was to his tutelage that Isabel owed a great deal of her elaborate learning. The Count of Hainault treasured Gilbert's advice and respected his judgment: it was the chancellor who had finally reconciled Baldwin to Philip d'Alsace's tempting alliance with the French crown....

From Bapaume the group would continue on to Sens (south of Paris) where Philippe and Isabel would have their coronation together on Whitsunday, the Feast of Pentecôte, June 8th. Such were the provisions which Philippe had made for his prospective bride.

Philip of Flanders, anxious about the delay, impulsively changed the coronation date to May 29th, Holy Thursday—the Feast of the Ascension. He also selected St. Denis for the coronation ceremony; it was only a few miles north of Paris. In

Flanders' reasoning it was urgent that Philippe and Isabel establish their presence in Paris as soon as possible. His concern was not without foundation. Isabel was under the permitted age to marry according to Church Law. It was a technicality only, winked at many times without consequences. But Flanders was afraid that those powerful French barons who resisted a Franco-Flemish alliance would use the six weeks between Isabel's marriage to Philippe and her coronation to take up the matter with the pope and perhaps win him to their side. It would be a simple matter for Rome to sever an unconsummated union between a ten-year-old girl and a fourteen-year-old boy—it was another matter entirely to unseat the girl who had already been consecrated as the future Queen of France. The idea of having Philippe re-coronated had also been Philip d'Alsace's: it would reflect honor upon his niece. For as always, Flanders courted logic and expediency.

The eighty-mile journey from Mons to Bapaume was slowed by intermittent rains and difficult roads. During the week-long procession Baldwin, Flanders, Philippe and Gilbert of Mons were in constant, animated discussion while Isabel suffered the belated pangs of homesickness; keeping to herself, she contemplated her future. She would be lonely at first, she knew. For all of her short life she had basked in the pleasurable shelter of a devoted and loving family, in the approval and pride of her parents and uncle. Now she would be cut off from them (and for who knew how long?) with only the company of Edythe to remind her of home.

Isabel wondered endlessly in silence about Philippe. His manner toward her was stiffly formal, bordering on coldness, but his appearance fascinated her. She had prepared herself not to expect much in the way of his physical appeal, dispiritedly envisioning a gawky, pimple-ridden adolescent, and so her first glimpse of him had been a kind of reward. Philippe Capet was tall, well-built and sullenly beautiful. His skin was dusky and unmarred; the features of his face sharp and strongly set in brooding sensitivity. Extravagant hair, wild and wavy and raven-dark, framed his face. But it was the eyes which riveted Isabel: inviolably black, sloe-shaped and unremittingly severe.

They had spoken only a few times—he was a stranger to her, and an enigma. It was impossible at this point to decide whether or not she liked him. Certainly he seemed self-possessed and much older than his almost-fifteen years. Yet under the careful reserve Isabel sensed another personality: one with the barely restrained anxiousness of a nervous charger. She had the image of an inherent, elemental flame burning at his core. And then she thought: *He's like me. Somewhere down very close to his soul he is like me. And he knows. But only a little.*

ⓄN THE EVENING of the sixth day they reached the cloister at Bapaume, which lay just outside a thickly forested area. The sun had forsaken them throughout the journey. This last day they had been slowed by roads which were nearly impassable.

The ordeal of the trip and a growing shadow of apprehension which had no recognizable form had exhausted Isabel to the fainting point. Stoically she endured the wedding supper which was a brief affair held in the monks' dismal soup kitchen. There had been plans for a flower-decked pastoral celebration but the weather had interceded and Flanders wanted no further delay. Already the poor travel weather had cost them two days. With every passing hour the situation in the south became more tenuous. Flanders did not want the ignominy of seeing his spirited *coup* capped by a rebellion among the French barons. So despite their late arrival, the wedding was hastily scheduled for the following day.

Isabel sat passively with the others in the dingy room, untempted by the food before her. The continuous tedium of the week's travel had afflicted her with a restless boredom. Her eyes burned, her lids were heavy. She swooned in weariness, half-asleep from being stared at. All around her she could feel the eyes watching her, judging her. She longed for sleep though right now there was nothing so sweet as sitting still, so she made meaningless conversation and distracted herself by wishing away the next few weeks.

During the meal Flanders presented her to Maurice de Sully who would preside at the ceremony tomorrow. He had a kind face and a gentle manner—nobleness was evident in his character. But though he spoke to her kindly, Isabel could feel the indulgence in his voice and his eyes, the lofty condescension of a learned man to a child.

When she was finally allowed to go to bed it was very late, but now the dim unfamiliarity of the small, low-ceilinged room kept her wakeful. The storm disrupted any attempt at sleep, but it was better than silence and chased away some of the disconcerting thoughts in her mind. Hainault. Home. Her own room.

She tried to see ahead, to picture her future, but she could not. Weariness swallowed her concentration. Dizzy, dream-soaked, her mind throbbed with images, obscure and unrelated. Formless phantoms, dark galloping mists, wells of blackness. Then falling. Sleep. Dreams...

...she was an uneasy traveler in the land where nightmares begin; trapped in a maze of unyielding dark where flashes of light taunted her in leaping flames of green. All around her were the eyes, emerald and luminous, dragons' eyes fading to a horrible chartreuse. Imprisoned in sleep she fought against green tides swelling up around her. Green. The color of jealousy, suspicion and mayhem. Bile. Gangrene. Corpse color. Great flapping wings enveloped her—choking and stagnant—pulling her down into a morass. Strangling, drowning. She tried to scream before the wash of slime covered her....

Thunder muffled her cry as Isabel jerked to a sitting position on the bed. Shivering she drew the harsh *brunette* coverlet around her. The horror swarmed about the room in choking blackness till a glare of lightning froze the scene into white terror. Trembling with cold and panic she crept down beneath the covers whimpering, the sour taste of vomit rising in her throat.

Terrified and feeling suddenly powerless to avert a predestined calamity, Isabel sobbed in secret, crying for the warmth and safety of her father's arms. She was alone, and feared now that she would always be alone. The dark was evil and she loathed it, but it was her only defense against tomorrow, and morning, and all that threatened her. Still whimpering, and shrouded in anxiety of her ill-omened dream, Isabel trembled into an exhausted sleep, pursued by storms.

Cold morning.
The earth still sodden from the rain smelled lightly of the

grass and flowers but under it all was the deeper, faintly disturbing scent of wet clay.

A cheerless gust of wind buffeted the procession as they made their way across the road from the cloister to where the abbey stood. It was a small group: Philippe and Isabel, her parents and uncle, Gilbert of Mons, and Sully. Philippe wore a samite gown of darkest blue covered with the red cape of State. Isabel, in her thin chainse of grey silk felt cold, gripping her hands together before her as she walked. Involuntarily she shook a bit, her body and spirit weak from sleeplessness. The muscles worked in her throat, fighting to swallow the fear, but that put it in the pit of her stomach which made her feel instantly and irrevocably sick.

Beside her walked Philippe, looking ill-slept and haggard this morning. Isabel supposed that, like her, he was tense, feeling the strain of this day. She had heard rumors of French nobles rebelling in the south protesting this marriage; of King Henry of England marshalling his men on the Normandy border.

Then she no longer had time to think, for they had reached the entrance to the abbey—Sully was pronouncing the pre-marriage blessing. Philippe took her right hand in his and placed a ring on her middle finger. Isabel stared down at it: a huge grey opal in a rich Byzantine setting.

Then they were inside and kneeling piously before the ornate altar, the smoke from the candles smarting her nostrils, bringing tears to her eyes. She heard Philippe repeating his vow in halting, stilted Latin, and though a part of Isabel's mind was totally distracted the rest was clear enough to invoke the use of her tongue and she could hear her own voice, quiet and precise. The blessing: Sully's rich voice rising like incense to the vaulted ceiling. The Sacrament, a final prayer, and they were free to go. Without a word Philippe turned to her, taking hold of her hand. His hand felt cold and unaccustomed to her touch.

Outside it had started to rain. Isabel had to grasp the train of her gown with her free hand to keep it from trailing in the mud. But she nearly slipped as she lurched to keep from stepping on the object which loomed suddenly in her path. Leaning on Philippe's arm she righted herself, side-stepping the wilted mound of feathers. A dead hawk, half-eaten, nestled paltry and brown against the radiant green of the grass. For a moment she regarded it with a sense of revulsion. The half-remembered dream flooded back to her and the ominous night message pressed closer. Then she walked on, shivering under her skin. . . .

Later there was another hurried meal with little talk and even less celebration. Isabel spent her wedding night alone, in the same bed where she had dreamed so uneasily the previous night. Their entourage would spend the next week in this place before traveling south once more, toward the abbey at St. Denis where Isabel would be crowned with her husband.

She knew that she would see very little of him till they came to Paris; it was likely that for the time being she would remain a chaste bride as dictated by her age. But Isabel's chronological age and that of her rapidly maturing body were many years apart. And though Philippe affected an outward show of chilliness there was no doubt in Isabel's mind that he burned with an inner fire as fierce as her own. She was still unhappy at having to part with her family, and especially her father—but the sudden terror of that one night was gone. She would not always be so alone. For if Isabel's instincts told her that Philippe would be indifferent for a time—they also told her it would not be for long

* * *

At the hour when the sun rose over the Hill of the Martyrs—the day being Holy Thursday celebrating the Ascension of Our Lord Christ into His Heaven—Isabel de Hainault, newly taken as wife by Philippe of France—was consecrated Queen of the French beside her husband at the altar of St. Denis and by the hand of Guy of Noyers. In accordance with ritual the girl-queen bared her breast to receive the Oil of Sanctification —the Sacred Chrism—that which Our Lord sent to this earth to Clovis the Frank, first Christian king of this realm. Isabel then prostrated herself before the altar to receive about her neck the pearl cross of her own ancestor Charles the Great, which was given to him by the Pope. At this time she and her husband were summarily crowned, cleansed in spirit with the Sacrament, and given Holy Blessing. After which commencing, a procession was made to the highest point of Montmarte, and while the prelates sang Ascendit Deus in Altum Alleluia, *five thousand birds were released in the air, to symbolize our Christ, who did fly to His heaven in Glory. . . .*

Gilbert of Mons
May, 1180

* * *

Though the description of Isabel's coronation by Baldwin's chancellor was a means of communicating Fleming propaganda, it was essentially a correct representation of events from which several important dictums could be drawn. The fact that she had received her crown at the hand of Guy of Noyers (a close friend of Philip d'Alsace) and at St. Denis, was a direct challenge to the Champagnois. Rheims was the logical coronation site, and its bishop was William, Philippe's Champagnois uncle.

Flanders' idea of having Isabel consecrated as well as coronated was significant in the extreme. Consecration implied a *divine right*, rather than the mere ceremonial ritual of becoming a queen through marriage. The Salic Law prevailed in France— there was no possibility of Isabel achieving any power through her office. Yet the act of consecration gave her an implied and symbolic significance which Philip of Flanders could exploit as an obstacle to further encroachment by the Champagnois, or any outside interference from Rome.

The evocation of Charlemagne's remembered glory was yet one more vindication of the Flemish cause. (Flanders was lucky in this respect: had Isabel's marriage involved an English, rather than a French, heir to the throne, the Count of Flanders could have pulled the name of another convenient ancestor—Alfred the Great—from his bag of tricks.) The life and deeds of Charlemagne had already passed into the perspective of legend, and his beatification in 1166 had established a modern *cultus*. There was little hope of those barons loyal to the Champagnois being receptive to such an obvious lure, but the petty nobility of France would find it hard to ignore the importance of a dynastic link to Charlemagne established through Philippe Capet's marriage with one of the emperor's descendents.

In the seventh generation of the Capet royal line, an heir would be born whose mother bore a blood-tie to Charlemagne. The prophecy had been widely circulated by Flanders ever since the concoction of his bold new initiative. To all but the most cynical, Philippe andIsabel's marriage would seem a mystical and divine inevitability: the fulfillment of a pre-arranged covenant.

Philip of Flanders was brazen but he was no fool. He knew the magnitude of the opposition he faced. Adele and her brothers were not only powerful, they were popular with the French nobles and uncomfortably close to many of the Burgundian barons. Adele had threatened to enlist Henry of England to her cause. Philip had known Henry for many years; they were distantly related by way of the Anjou line. They had been adversaries, they had been friends. So far as this matter was concerned, Philip could not be sure which way the King of England would turn....

In the cold morning as fog moved over the land in gauzy tatters, Baldwin said goodbye to his daughter. She and her husband were traveling on to Paris this morning with Philip of Flanders, and Baldwin did not know when he would see her again.

The lofty towers of St. Denis cast no shadows this day—drizzle cloaked it in an aura of grey. Dwarfed by its magnificence, Baldwin and Isabel walked together toward the little rise which led up to near the chapter house of the cloister, out of the view of the others. Baldwin took hold of her hand and they walked in silence for a bit, aware that the moments were passing swiftly. Isabel gripped his hand more tightly. "We have very little time."

They had reached a bench and sat down wordlessly together, their shoulders touching. A stiff gust of wind had come up and Baldwin pulled his own foxfur mantle close about her shoulders. The hood from her azure velvet cape had blown back and her hair, pulled into a elegant braided coif at the back of her neck, shimmered with highlights, and tiny pearl earrings glittered at her ears.

"Tell me what you are thinking," she said, "don't let us spend our last few moments alone in silence." And when he still said nothing she stroked his cheek lovingly. "Father?"

He gave her a look which she could not read; his voice and words were bitter. "I don't like him. Philip's trust in that boy is ill-placed. He will never be amenable to our will." Baldwin shook his head in discontent. "Flanders has truly allowed himself to be out-distanced this time."

Those misgivings unsettled Isabel. Philippe's formidable sense of self-determination had not escaped her notice, and she had wondered often why her uncle thought him so easily bent to the Flemish will. Still it seemed inconceivable that her brilliant and perceptive kinsman could have misjudged Philippe's character, and so thinking she voiced that to her father.

"In any case it's done now," Baldwin answered, "and I would just as leave I'd never had to meddle in it." His fine features were paled by strain and unhappiness. "I loathe this—sending you off with him, committing us all to the will and whims of that head-strong brat." He sounded so angry, even at her, and Isabel felt hurt that the last few minutes they had left together should be spent in ill-favor. She nestled close to him, trying to buoy his spirits though she couldn't lift her own.

"I know it was not your wish that I marry Philippe, but as you said it is done now and we must face it bravely and with high hopes. Uncle Philip expects great things of us, father, and I shall do my part. I promise I will do everything in my power to prove to the French that this is a good match." She gave him the trembling semblance of a smile. "All shall be well. I promise you that."

Again he ignored her pleading conciliations. "I should curse myself for the coward I am!" he declared. "Why can I never stand against Flanders? Why do I let him dictate to me?"

It was a little late for such second-thoughts and Baldwin's reasoning made Isabel feel uneasy. Then suddenly she brightened. "Why don't you come to Paris with us?" she asked. "Then you can see to it that this new arrangement is commenced in the spirit of good for all concerned."

His terse words dimmed her hopeful little smile. "I cannot. I have business with the Duke of Brabant that will not wait. So I will just have to trust to the instincts of my brother-in-law." He drew out a long, weary breath. "The greatest pain is in losing you. This separation leaves a void in my life which no one else can fill. Above all others in this world I cherish you."

Isabel's voice sounded high and a little off edge. "It is no easier for me, father. It was not my wish to leave you. I will be so lonely...please at least allow me to think that my own sacrifice is worth something to you."

His arms went about her, his lips brushing her cheek. Then he straightened his back, looking down into her face. "You have meant so much to me Isabel, so much."

Her delicate hand stroked his beard, then came to play lightly at his throat. "You have been *everything* to me." She raised her face for his kiss, receiving it first as though it were a sacred thing, a blessing—then pulling him closer she drank in his love hungrily, wanting to prolong every fragment of time no matter how small, when she could rest happily in his arms, knowing that she was loved.

This moment was precious and she froze it into a memory that she might recall in the days to come. Her gaze carried off to the distance. Montmarte, the Hill of the Martyrs, hid the road that wound down into the valley past the convent of St. Geneviève, past the vineyards and farther south into Paris. It was a calm landscape, but Isabel's mind was busy and anxious. She had tried very hard to effect a show of optimism, but beneath her frail composure was an unsettling itch of uncertainty.

Her head made a pillow of his shoulder; her voice was a hush. "He's going to know, Father. Philippe is going to find out about you and me—how can I keep him from knowing?"

Baldwin's fingers cinched her waist, pulling her closer, his senses more intent on her than her words as he answered absently, "He won't necessarily know, Isabel. It is not always possible to tell whether or not a girl is virginal. Just be certain that your manner bespeaks innocence to the point that it satisfies him. In any case, that worry is a long way off."

Her face was pressed to his shoulder so he didn't see how the frown darted between her eyebrows at his words, but she gave the sniffling sound of a laugh and rubbed her cheek to his chest. "You know me well enough to understand that I cannot suddenly feign innocence in these matters."

"If he is anything like his father," Baldwin commented drily, "he'll be too innocent himself to realize that you are not."

She straightened up, shaking her head doubtfully but saying nothing. For a moment Isabel sat very still, just looking at him, feeling her courage draining away, and all at once separation from him was a palpable sorrow she could not endure. Flinging herself against him, her face pressed to the inner folds of his pellison, she gasped, "When will I ever see you again—and how can I live without you?"

She let him comfort her with kisses and soft words and discreet caresses, let him pull her hands closer till they rested beneath his bliaud, and she fondled him with piquant skill. When she had finished, she sank to the ground before him, pressing her face to his knee and forbidding herself to cry. After a little while she saw Edythe making her way slowly up the slope, and then Isabel knew that the caravan was ready and it was time to say goodbye.

Margot was calm as she embraced her daughter; the conflicting emotions showed in her eyes. She loved Isabel but she was jealous too; Baldwin's unreasonable attachment to the girl was a sharp goad to Margot's pride. In Paris, with a husband of her own, Isabel would cease to be a problem. Margot gave her a resolute smile. "God and the saints go with you, my dear," she whispered into her ear and then pressed a small enameled box into her daughter's hand. "Open it when you get to Paris," Margot instructed her.

Isabel kissed and embraced her two little brothers and then Sibylla, taking the weeping girl into her arms. "One day, perhaps soon, father will bring you to Paris," she told Sibylla, smoothing her sister's hair, "and it shall be great fun for all of us, you will see. Now, you must not cry anymore...."

Philippe, impatient to be on his way, was irritated at these protracted farewells. With no love for his own family, he could not understand Isabel's obvious affection for her's. His lips grew tight at the corners, twitching in aggravation. Her duty was to him now, not to her precious family.

"It's time to leave," he said firmly, taking Isabel by the hand. He helped her to mount his horse, then hoisted himself up behind her in the saddle. He signaled the bodyguard, and the cortège turned slowly toward the south. Grasping Philippe's forearm with the fingers of one hand, holding close the enameled box in the other, Isabel turned furtively in the saddle to gaze back at the abbey and at the assembled group of people who stood before it. She waved to them once, twice; then they blurred before her sight as her eyes filled with tears. Isabel looked down at the arm that circled her waist, then to the side at her uncle, riding stately and proud beside them. Forcing herself to stop the tears, Isabel jerked her face to the front, compelling herself to look ahead, down toward the valley and off to the left, where Paris slept in a silvery mist, waiting for her.

The Ile de la Cité lay like a tapered boat in the middle of the river Seine. Paris, her new home. It was beautiful. Isabel closed her eyes and nestled the back of her head against Philippe's chest, breathing in the essence of this moment and feeling somehow comforted.

Philippe's hand brushed her wrist lightly, then he pointed ahead to a forbidding slate-grey fortress which rose like a four-storeyed crypt on the azure horizon. "It was built over seven centuries ago by the early Frankish kings—those called the Merovingians," he explained. "It was erected upon the original Roman structure, a temple dedicated to Neptune."

The Cité Palais, home of the Capetian kings. A vague shimmer of excitement flowed over her. To Philippe she said, "Isn't it spoken that in the days of the Roman occupation in Gaul, Druidic cults worshipped on that very site?"

He looked down at her with a surprised smile. Isabel had never seen him smile before this; it made his face look younger, more pleasant, yet it did not match with his features. Even as she contemplated this, his face grew sober again as he explained, "It is true enough. Sully has told me that when the foundation for Notre Dame de Paris was being dug many pagan relics were unearthed: a stone altar, a sardonyx drinking vessel, even the ring of a Druid priestess. The ring was so unusual, so beautiful, that I kept it." He paused a moment, then continued in a somewhat confidential manner. "The old beliefs persisted here for many years even after Christianity became the established religion of the people. The Druids left no written records of their practices; much of what we know of them is legend except for what Caesar put into his commentaries. But the Druids were a strange people, and they left their stamp upon this land. On cold dark nights the landscape still has the look of the devil about it. . . ."

Isabel hung on his words for a moment, absently caressing his hand and wondering at the quiet thrill that had passed between them as he described the scene. Philippe had felt it too; Isabel knew it by the way his fingers entwined with hers. Pagan rituals having unfolded on land now sanctified by a race of Christian kings: it touched a profound nerve of fascination in her. Then

Philippe was speaking again. "In the north, in England, the Druids worshipped the sun. Here in France—or Gaul as it was then—they worshipped the rain. They held their rituals in the grove of the oaks and apple trees—the grove still stands in the palace courtyard..." He said no more of such things as their cortège approached the city, but Isabel's insatiable curiosity had been teased, and she continued to ponder his words in silence.

The fleeting sense of excitement had ebbed by the time they crossed the *Petit Pont* and reached the filthy road that led to the northern facade of the Cité Palais. From Isabel's hilltop view, Paris had seemed tranquil, almost magical. Now, within its raucous confines she grimaced at the clamor of mingled noises and the evil aggregation of odors that greeted her. The palace, looming so impressively from a distance, was repellingly ugly on closer view. It looked like the ancient sagging ruin that it was: a huge, fantastic hovel rising forlornly above the clotted black mud of the Paris streets. The exterior of the structure was without decoration, its pitted grey facade strung across with dozens of small, irregularly shaped windows.

The interior was dismal—gaping, near-vacant halls reformed by Romanesque arches sunk in sunless gloom—airless, ugly, foul-smelling. In such a room as this they ate a perfunctory meal comprised of alarmingly poor food, and then, leaving the remainder of the party below, Philippe led Isabel up three sets of dim and twisting stairs to the fourth level of the palace where the family apartments were located.

At the mouth of the corridor she halted, repulsed at once by a horrible wafting smell. Involuntarily Isabel pulled the flare of her cape about her nose and mouth to shut out the odor and hide her sudden fit of wretching. Seeing her distress Philippe crooked a dark eyebrow and explained, "I should have warned you of that. The servants' privies are just below, but unfortunately the smell rises and is trapped here. The family uses the ones at the end of this corridor. They are less irritating since the room has a vented glass ceiling. My father's first wife insisted upon it when the smell from the closed-off room nearly drove her mad."

Clinging weakly to his hand Isabel followed him down the corridor, a low-ceilinged, narrow passageway with maze-like turns and twists. She was shivering despite the closeness of the air. Then she realized it was the personality of this place. These walls which shut out sun on even the brightest days had hoarded centuries' worth of tears and transgressions and too many sleepless midnights. The sticky remains of a spider's web brushed against her cheek, and the low sibilant sound of a whisper rustled behind her. God this was an awful place!

Philippe stopped abruptly before a blue-draped doorway, his arm outstretched. "These are your rooms." He parted the curtain, indicating that she should enter first. She hesitated. Her mind was a crazy-quilt of senseless, piecemeal images formed into a single rush of panic. Then just as quickly her reason came spinning back. *There was no menace here.* She was tired, only tired. Isabel stepped boldly into the room. "It is not over-comfortable," Philippe was saying, "but I am sure you will find it sufficient."

She stood beside him, letting her gaze sweep over the room. It was brighter here; an uncovered window splashed pale sunlight across dead grey stones and the edge of a grey patterned carpet. To her left an uncovered archway led to a private chapel; to the right was an even smaller annex—perhaps a dressing *chambrette*.

This bed chamber in no way approached the luxury of the rooms she had occupied at her father's chateaus in Mons, Valenciennes, or Lille. Though she had expected a great show of finery at the royal residence, and was disheartened, she was determined to be agreeable. "It's very fine," she answered. "I appreciate so much that you have seen to these arrangements for me."

He hadn't finished disappointing her. "The girl you brought with you from Hainault will have to sleep below. There are no rooms for servants on this floor."

More isolation. She turned to him. "Is it not perhaps possible to find a room for Edythe here? She is lame—it is hard for her to climb stairs."

He eyed her with a look of cold irritation. "Then perhaps one of the girls who formerly served my mother could wait upon you and Edythe would be spared the trouble."

"Oh, but I want to keep her with me," Isabel responded quickly. "It is only that I would be appreciative if she could be spared too much work. At home my mother used to make her do quite a lot. You see, it is possible that she is also my father's daughter. Because of that my mother hates her, but she has always been a good friend to me."

"It isn't my wish to deprive you of companionship," Philippe answered pointedly, sounding almost hurt. "You may keep her here if you wish." He saw the way in which Isabel scrutinized the room and it aggravated him to know she was comparing it unfavorably with what she had left back in Hainault. "I don't approve of luxurious living," he explained to her silent complaint, "and that is only one way in which I differ from my father and mother. I am pledged to economy in this land. You will find our court very spare. I have disposed of all entertainments here. We keep no musicians, no *jongleurs* or *trouvéres*. We feast no barons or prelates. The money for such fripperies is better spent in giving to the poor."

Isabel didn't care for the way he had said it, his face sobering into dour self-righteousness, but she believed in the spirit of it; in the gesture he was making. If he was truly so prudent, it was nothing he had learned from her uncle. Philip d'Alsace had few enough scruples and none at all concerning spending. Many was the time he had tripled the tax load on his people just to outfit his paladins for a new tournament. He was lavish in all he did.

"You're very wise to have acted as you did," Isabel finally replied when she realized he was waiting for her comment. Then he nodded curtly to accept her approval and launched into a detailed explanation of his reorganization of the court.

Isabel stood limply in the middle of the room, her eyes burning from lack of sleep, unspeakably weary from the accumulated excitement and exertion of the past six weeks. The tiresome plod up three long passages of stairs in this inhospitable, four-tiered dungeon had been the final undermining of her endurance. She looked at the blue damask-hung bed, a singular sphere of color in this cheerless room. It seemed to beckon to her. She longed to stretch her weary body in it and sleep the week away.

She tried to concentrate on what Philippe was saying, shifting on her feet to keep herself alert. Finally, dizzy to the point of fainting, Isabel sank into a chair, covering her face with her hands. "I'm sorry," she interrupted his flow of words, "I suddenly feel ill. . . . I suspect I am over-tired from traveling."

He had been so indifferent, so seemingly unconcerned toward

her since their first meeting, she was surprised when he came to stand beside her, carefully taking one of her hands in his. "You feel flushed," he muttered, "perhaps you need something to refresh yourself." On a nearby table stood a flagon of herbal tisane and two wooden wine cups. Philippe poured one full and brought it to her, offering it gently. It was the first act of personal kindness she had known from him and it touched her. With a faint smile she took the cup, studying him discreetly as she drank. There was something furtive, mysterious about him; even his careless manner of dress enhanced his moody appearance. He was dark and sullen. Like a gypsy, she thought. She remembered her father's words and sighed to herself, wishing she did not have to pretend innocent indifference to this beautiful black-eyed boy.

Isabel drank a little more then handed the cup back to him. "Thank you. I don't mean to try your patience but suddenly I'm quite out of breath. I suppose I may have caught cold on the trip. I catch colds easily."

"You probably need to sleep a while," Philippe suggested, "I will leave you then." Quickly he had turned from her and started to walk away.

Tears moistened her eyes in helpless sadness. All during the journey from Mons she had postponed this moment in her mind: when she would be left alone for the first time in this strange new place. "Please don't go," she called out suddenly, "stay a bit and talk to me." He turned and gave her her a quizzical look as she persisted. "Just a little while."

He came and sat in a chair beside her, feeling awkward and wondering what she wanted and why she looked so sad. Her head was tilted downward, her small pointed chin tremulous as though she meant to cry. If she did he wouldn't know what to do. Doubtless she was feeling homesick but he didn't know what to say to make her feel less so. When she raised her head she looked directly into his eyes. "Philippe, tell me truly, is this place as old as you say?"

Her face was so lovely, her expression so arresting that he found it difficult to concentrate on her words. She had to ask the question again before he answered sharply as if distracted, "Why, yes, of course."

"I think many terrible things must have happened here," she

mused, "There is a strange feeling within these walls—I cannot quite describe it." She averted her eyes. "That corridor is terrifying...."

He nodded. "This place affects everyone that way the first time, Isabel. It is not a very convivial place." He gave a muffled laugh. "If you knew the history of this land and those who have ruled it, you would not have to wonder."

"I do, a little," she answered, so grateful not to be alone, happy even for his distracted presence. "I think that many people have been unhappy here."

She made him unaccountably nervous. It was so hard not to look at her, yet her beauty intimidated him because a child should not look like her or speak like her. She didn't seem like a child at all but a miniature goddess lapped in velvet and peering at him through eyes that held some strange message he could not decipher. Her actions had an inexplicable language all their own. During the ride from St. Denis this morning she had lain so warm and sweet and languid against him, stroking his hand, then pressing her body closer, as though to deliberately arouse him. She was so young. She couldn't possibly be awake to subtle sexual exchanges. And still...

He looked away from her and found his voice. "I told you it was built over seven centuries ago. I'm sure many scenes of unhappiness and cruelty have been played out here."

She thought of the Merovingian king Chilperic and his demon queen Fredegunda; of the pagan Clovis and his passionate Christian wife; of Philippe's own great-grandfather and his bigamous union with Bertrada of Anjou. A hundred years ago another Capetian king, Henry I, had brought an unhappy Russian bride to this place; and lovely Constance of Castile (the mother of Philippe's two half-sisters) had died in childbirth here, perhaps in this very room. A chilly specter of apprehension settled over her and she caught up his hand, clutching it tightly, the nails biting into his palm. "It's going to be so lonely for me here," she whispered, "whatever am I going to do to pass the time?"

There was something threatening in her touch and Philippe eased his hand away. "Sully could arrange for tutors for you," he suggested.

She didn't answer at first, then after a while, her mood suddenly shifting, she smiled teasingly at him. "I have heard it said that you were a most unwilling student."

His look was an amalgam of surprise and anger. "Who told you that?"

"My uncle." She was pulling the gold clips from her hair, easing the strands out long and loose over her back. She turned to him with a small smile on her lips, a suggestive look in her eyes. "He told me that even as a very little boy you preferred to keep your own counsel, to sit by yourself meditating, and communing with your thoughts."

He eyed her steadily for a moment before answering, "And did your uncle also tell you that what I learned from him was worth more than anything I learned from my academic lessons?"

"What did you learn from him?" she asked.

"To be independent—how to get what I want, and how to hold on to it."

She studied his face intently as though memorizing his features. "Is that so important?"

"It's everything."

For a while they sat in silence—she toying with the opal marriage ring on her finger, he sipping absently at the liquid she had left in her cup and watching her, and wondering. "Your name, in the Flemish language, is Elizabeth, is it not?"

"Yes," she answered. "I was given that name at my birth. But we are a combined French and Flemish speaking culture and I have always been called Isabel. It was my mother's own preference, using the French form. She has some Angevin blood, did you know? So as you see I have a little French in me."

"You speak the language very well," he observed. Then draining the last of the tisane from her cup he rose to his feet. "I have to leave you now. I will send up one of the stewards with your things. The girl can help you to get settled in." At the doorway he paused. "Flanders and I will be leaving for Gisors in a few days. I've been summoned there by Henry of England. He thinks I've been too harsh with my mother—throwing her out, and taking away her lands and all that. While I was in the north with your family, she and her brothers went to him for aid and now he has intruded into the matter."

Isabel got up from her chair and came to stand beside him,

peering into his face. She was very small and barely reached his breast. "Philippe," she asked, "was it my uncle's idea that you send your mother away?"

She saw the muscle in his cheek tighten as he looked down at her with black unstinting vision. "It was my decision," he underscored the words, "and you for one, my pretty child, can be glad of it. My mother is no one you would want to meet."

"May I meet your father then? I would like to very much."

He gave her an exasperated look. "Why?"

"Well," she stammered, "because he is my father-in-law."

Philippe shook his head. "He's a dying old man. He's *nothing* anymore. What could be gained from meeting him?"

"But surely," she persisted, tugging lightly at his arm, "I should meet someone from your family. I want to know them."

He felt trapped, anxious. The touch of her fingers tightened the throb in his groin and he jerked his arm away. Her alluring charm rendered him helpless and angry. His voice was sharp. "My dear Isabel, there is no one in my family *fit* to know. As far as I am concerned I have no family. Don't bother yourself with thoughts of them. Just stay in your room and amuse yourself as best you can. Don't go out, don't leave this room. Everything you need will be brought to you."

Incredulous, she stared at him. "You make me sound like a prisoner," she gasped.

He just looked at her for a moment, dizzied by the sea-green of her eyes. "I almost forgot," he said. "I have something for you." He disengaged something from his belt, then unwrapped the cloth pouch and extracted a glimmering item, holding it out to her. "It's Byzantine," he explained, "my father brought it back from Antioch years ago."

The delicate filigree melted in her hand like fine golden lace. The necklace was studded with emeralds, and edged with huge hanging pearls, arranged pendant style. Isabel held the necklace between trembling hands and bit back the tears. It was the most beautiful piece of jewelry she had ever seen. She jerked her head up and stared at him, trying hard to convey her feelings through her eyes, and met a dark enigmatic look. "Oh it's so lovely," she finally said, "thank you, Philippe."

He hesitated for a moment, then bent and placed a chilly kiss on her forehead. "Goodbye. I will look in on you before I leave for Gisors." He made a move toward the exit then halted, turning back to her. "About this place," he muttered, "it is a bit like a prison...." Then he pushed aside the velvet drape and ducked out.

For a long time Isabel stood alone where he had left her, weighted down by weariness and depression and enveloped in the ominous wraith of fear. She tried to relive the singular tinge of excitement she had felt on the slope a few hours ago, looking down at Paris for the first time, but the stone reality around her dashed the memory, and something—some dimly half-remembered dream—flared in her mind as the emeralds glinted up at her. Green fire. Something about drowning...

She fought this mood. *You will become accustomed to it and once you do it will seem like home to you.* But she was lying to herself and she knew that she was. This place would never become a home to her and she would never be happy here.

The thought stunned her even as she considered it. Why not happy? It was her present state of mind that darkened the future and whispered disquiet in her ear. She needed courage. More than anything she needed sleep.

Pulling off her cape and bliaud Isabel stood in the center of the room wearing only her thin silk shift. Her gaze played over each corner of the room. The far wall was dominated by a great tapestry depicting the crowning of Charles the Great by the pope. In the foreground the bed sat upon a high raised dais, decorated with blue hangings and coverlets. A low dressing table with a silver mirror stood near it. Around the floor sat several large chests. It was only then that Isabel noticed the sweet scent of rose water which had been sprinkled over the carpet. She told herself that Philippe must have personally arranged this for her, that she should be grateful to him, yet her feeling of unrest remained.

In front of the mirror she removed the shift and began to comb her hair, carefully fanning the golden strands out loosely over her bare shoulders and arranging the ends which hung below her hips. Then she stepped back, examining her pensive reflection. A ripely budding figure, a face which might have been molded by an artist. Still staring into the mirror she affixed the necklace around her waist like a girdle. The emeralds gleamed against the whiteness of her belly; gold-coddled pearls nestled in the golden fleece below.

Upon the dressing table lay the small enameled box. Isabel picked it up and held it in the palm of her hand. It was oblong-shaped, of wood, and with a green and blue enameled falcon gracing the cover. Carefully she opened it and took out the ring secluded beneath its black velvet covering. She recognized this gift at once—her mother's gold and pearl ring. Isabel had always admired it, and had often heard the story from Margot of how it had been handed down through seven generations of her mother's Frankish forebears. Tears stung Isabel's eyes as she looked down at the ring in her hand. Then she slipped it onto her finger beside the grey Byzantine opal Philippe had put there.

Depression prevailed and her mind fogged over with weariness. Retreating to the bed she closed the curtains around her. Then surrounded by shivering walls of blue, Isabel cuddled naked against the bedclothes and closed her eyes. Bathed in this sleepy warmth, encircled with gold and emeralds, she fell asleep.

The days passed in bland inactivity for Isabel. Sometimes in the evening she walked in the gardens behind the palace but mostly she kept to her room. Lonely and discontented, she slept the days away. At night she sat by the window, wakeful and restless, looking out toward the west where the river widened till it merged with the black of the sky. Unfeeling, unthinking, staring out at an undifferentiated landscape until her eyes burned with the first red rays of the sun, Isabel would drag herself to bed and sleep the hours away till the next night's vigil.

By the end of the first week she was drugged from excessive sleep—her health undermined by nights spent breathing unwholesome air that drifted up from the river—and she caught the cold she had been fighting off since her arrival in Paris. Then, protesting feebly against Edythe's kind ministrations and endless cups of herbal posset, she slept day and night, lost in a dream where ghosts of long-haired kings and their barbarian queens roamed the corridors outside her room—until sleep itself was the enemy.

Ⓞ N A COOL June morning Henry II of England rode out with his small entourage to the spreading elm tree at Gisors on the southern frontier of Normandy—the traditional meeting place between French and English kings.

Some years ago Henry had stood in this very spot, negotiating with Louis of France who had sheltered the rebellious Thomas Becket in his flight from English royal justice. While the two kings had grappled with the controversial matter, a dark-visaged little boy had stood by, apart from his father but watching the proceedings with uncanny interest. It had been Henry's first view of Philippe Capet.

Now after eleven years Henry would meet him again.

Motioning his men to stay at a distance, Henry brought his horse forward till he was at Philippe's side. They dismounted at the same time and stood face-to-face. After only a momentary hesitation, Henry hugged Philippe to his bosom in genuine affection. Wily statesman though he was, and possessed of the ferocious and legendary Angevin temper when incited to rage, Henry was really a fond and loving man. Though sorely reviled by his own four sons he was unreasonably devoted to them. His own John was only slightly younger than this boy. But Johnny could be jovial and responsive to affection, while Philippe seemed devoid of the human juices. There was nothing of Louis in him in looks or manner.

His emotions locked up, his voice betraying nothing, Philippe returned the kiss that Henry bestowed upon him. Henry kept a friendly arm slung about Philippe's shoulder as he examined the youth. "How tall you are," he finally exclaimed, "and you are a fine handsome boy too. But so serious for your age. Can you not spare a smile for your father's old adversary? You see, boy, when you were ill last fall and all France feared you might die, I too offered prayers for your safe recovery. I am glad to see that they were well answered."

Philippe gave him a nervous half smile and answered with only superficial politeness. "My thanks to you, then. It is my hope that you still have my well-being at heart, for I must admit surprise at being summoned here, especially since you have been in conference with my mother and her brothers."

Henry steered Philippe toward a patch of spreading shade offered by the huge limbs of the old tree. Apart, with the French delegation, Philip d'Alsace sat his horse anxiously, watching this pantomime.

"My boy," Henry said with fatherly concern, "you must realize that you have wronged your mother. Now I understand your desire for independence. It is a noble trait in any young ruler, and more to the point, a most necessary one. But you must be fair as well. Your mother has a legal right to her lands and to a draft from the treasury so long as your father lives. Upon his death she has the right to her dower territories and settlement, a provision made upon her marriage to your father. It is due her under the law. If you wish to rule justly, you will not try to set aside her claims...."

Every vague point of debate, every cool argument that Philippe had prepared at Flanders' coaxing came unfastened in his mind and slid from his tongue in pointless rebuttal as Philippe struggled to match Henry's skill with words. Time was against the French boy, and experience. At last he was learning why his father had been beaten down in every negotiation with Henry Plantagenet. Humiliated, anxious to end this ordeal of shame, Philippe assented to every point raised by Henry. At the end of the day they all rode away together to Henry's chateau on the Normandy border where the English king presided personally over a reconciliation between Philippe and all his relatives. Afterwards there was a great banquet and celebrating.

Philippe Capet had failed ignominiously in his first attempt at independent sovereignty.

Isabel was in the garden weaving a wreath of white roses for her hair when Philip d'Alsace arrived. For a moment he stood apart, out of her view, admiring the sight of her—her head bent in earnest concentration, her delicate fingers gingerly removing the thorns and ringing the stems together with soft golden thread.

Sensing a familiar presence, Isabel started slightly and sat up straight, looking at him. Her lips parted in a smile. "Uncle Philip!" she called out, and ran to him. He clasped her in his arms, lifting her off the ground to kiss her on the lips. Under the firm pressure of his thumbs he could feel her budding form and the sensation communicated a tingling that was much too pleasant, so he quickly set her down beside him. Isabel clung fervently to his waist, burying her face against his chest. "Oh Uncle, how wonderful to see you. But so soon! I didn't expect you and Philippe till tomorrow evening at the earliest." She looked up into his face, then peered beyond him. "Is he with you?"

"No," Flanders answered, his voice tight. "I came ahead of the others. I wanted a chance to talk to you before I go back to Ghent."

Isabel's tiny hand rested at his elbow and she led him over to the bench where she had been sitting, urging him down beside her. She cuddled lovingly against him, stroking his arm and rubbing her cheek against his shoulder.

He looked down at her fondly and pulled her closer. "You look pale," he said after a while.

"Only a cold. I'm better now. Mostly I'm starved for company, and news. Tell me, how did it go with King Henry?"

His handsome face turned somber as he studied her in silence. "Your loving husband has dealt us both a foul blow," he finally told her.

For a second the meaning of his words did not register in her mind. Her puzzled eyes tried to read his expression without success. "What are you saying? What happened at Gisors?"

Philip d'Alsace got to his feet and began pacing restlessly in front of her. His rage was tempered with humiliation and his voice with dismay. "You husband has betrayed us!" In answer to her attempt at objection he snapped vehemently, "There is no other word for it!"

Isabel reached out for his hand, urging him toward her. "Here Uncle, please sit down and tell me everything. I cannot believe that Philippe could have done anything so dreadful as you say."

Once again he sat beside her, his arm draped absently about her shoulder. "He succumbed to Henry's doubletalk and went back on every pact we've made. He fully restored Adele's lands to her and her possessions including the promise of the full dower settlement upon Louis's death. Before my own eyes your husband was reconciled with her and his four uncles, whose rights were likewise reinstated." He paused, but before Isabel could say anything he continued, "Adele is also allowed to return to court, remaining close to Louis till his death."

Isabel tugged at his arm, a little shaken, but eager to put them both at ease. "But surely it's no more than Adele deserves. Her lands are her own by right of birth and marriage. It would be unseemly that she be penniless or deprived of her dower. She is, after all, still the queen while her husband lives...."

Flanders would hear no more. His wild gesture of protest sent Isabel's flower crown spinning to the ground as his arm flailed out in exasperation. "Don't you understand? Is it possible that a niece of mine cannot see what is at stake here?" he blustered. "By re-aligning himself with the Champagnois he is in effect removing me and your family from influence in this land!"

Isabel's eyes were downcast as she stared unseeing at the circlet of flowers on the ground. His words echoed in her mind. Could it be true? She couldn't bear to look at him and see the truth of it in his eyes so she kept her gaze distracted. "Has he turned against us then?" she finally asked, her voice thin as glass, "Is the coalition between us forfeit?"

"It could be that serious, yes," he sighed in pain and puzzlement. Then with trepidation he finished, "I can see that I am displaced, that is certain."

"Oh no," she gasped. "Philippe respects you. He relies upon your advice. He needs your help."

"Don't forget, my child, he is also profoundly under the influence of young Harry Plantagenet. I think *he* has a hand in this." He was silent then, his thoughts running deep and dark. He did not really believe that Philippe had been influenced by a third party against the Flemish alliance. Flanders' powers of persuasion were equal to anyone's. The puzzle was young Philippe himself. Had Flanders misjudged him? It seemed that he had. This boy who had shorn himself of outside influences with the help of Flanders had now tossed him off as well! The realization was galling, the prospects disconcerting. Since April Flanders had scarcely ceased to congratulate himself on his wily manipulation of the young Capet. Now he himself had been manipulated, set aside, made to play the fool. He looked at the lovely girl beside him—his bridge to ultimate power. She looked as insecure as he felt at that moment. Her bottom lip trembled slightly. "What does this mean for us?" she asked him. "Has the alliance been broken? What did Philippe say to you? Did you question him on the matter?"

Flanders was almost too humiliated to answer. When he did his voice was low. "He informed me that he had the right to do as he wished, and that he may be better served if I returned to the north for a time."

Isabel shook her head in wonderment. "But you have been here with us since our arrival. You and Philippe were constantly together." Exasperation nearly strangled her. "Oh, I don't understand what this is all about! If only there were something I could do to help you!"

"Yes," Flanders answered forlornly, "if only..." His mind was in a turmoil of pondering. How long would it be before Philippe decided to cast off Isabel, making the Flemish alliance completely void? The thoughts tumbled on in worrisome succession. "I'm tired," he sighed, "I've been riding all morning." He stood up, his hands on his lean hips as he gazed ahead into the warm summer sky. "I'll sleep for a while and see you later in the day."

Isabel started to rise but he motioned her down. "No, don't get up, stay here in the sun. It will help ease that pallor." He brushed a hand against the softness of her cheek and bent to kiss her.

When he was gone Isabel sat for a long time, very still. In her mind hope and fear collided. Danger threatened, presaging downfall. Shivering, she chased the fear to the back of her mind, locking it away. But when she bent to the ground to retrieve the circlet of flowers her hand drew back in horror. It was covered with flies.

The vexing heat of the afternoon dissolved into drizzly chill once the sun slept. Flanders was not soothed. A man of action enraged at his inability to act, he stalked about his room shackled by impotent fury.

Over and over the humiliating scene at Gisors swam in his mind like a sunspot. Philippe Capet, his own creation, fawning and timid before Henry of England, relinquishing every bold step that Flanders had plotted. Reliving it in his mind Philip d'Alsace could almost weep for the frustration he felt.

Wine cooled his scalding sense of shame but with it came gloom and depression. The more he drank the more he hated Philippe. He vowed revenge; first silently, then shouting it to the vaulted ceiling of his room. It was his shouted curses that roused Isabel.

She stood in the doorway to his room. To his blurred, slanted glance she seemed a shadow. Cautiously she came closer, her face at once flooded with glow from the hanging torches, her hair on fire with light. "Uncle Philip?" she asked furtively, "I heard you calling out, are you all right?"

He pushed himself up on the bed—how had he gotten there? —and saw her standing some distance away. "Come here," he beckoned, "sit with me awhile. I am in need of pity."

Without hesitation she crossed the floor until she stood before him, inclining her head slightly to look with concern into his face. "Are you sick?" she asked carefully, "your face is so flushed." She placed the tips of her fingers to his forehead. Her touch was cool and reassuring. "You feel so hot," she said, "can I bring you some water, or some steeped herbs to drink?" Her eyes were wide with concern.

The act of sympathy warmed him. "Just sit with me a bit," he told her. She nestled willingly in his lap, her arms wound round his neck, her cheek against his shoulder. "You're still upset aren't you?" she asked, "and that's why you've been drinking." When he didn't answer she sighed softly, "I'm upset too. I've been thinking all day about what you told me. I'm worried. If Philippe has truly turned against us, what can we do?"

He didn't reply, except to tighten his arms around her, pulling her closer. For a long time they sat silently together while fire-light chased dim shadows across the wall. "How long before you must leave?" she whispered the question into his ear.

Against the brilliance of her scented hair he whispered back, "A few days, perhaps less. I want to see Philippe when he returns. Perhaps..." he let the sentence trail off into silence.

Isabel raised her head to look at him and he could see that her cheeks were wet. "I don't think I can stand it here alone," she told him. "I'll miss you when you leave, I wish I could go with you."

"This is your home now, pet," he answered, only hoping that it would still be true after what had happened at Gisors. "And you will get used to it. You must. It's all still so new to you, of course you feel uncomfortable."

"This is an awful place," she answered in a steady voice even as fresh tears strained her cheeks. "I'm alone, alone all the time. The loneliness is unbearable."

"You have Edythe," he reminded her. "Surely she has taken good care of you."

"She is homesick too. Besides it isn't the same. I miss my family. Little Henry and Baldwyn and Sibylla. I miss my mother. And my father. And I shall miss you." Her voice quavered. "I have no friends here; no one. If this is to be my new life, I would just as soon be dead."

"Now, now," he tried to comfort her, his lips brushing her cheek, her soft hair, her throat, "don't cry, don't cry, my lovely...." His temples throbbed and his dizzy vision was useless so he closed his eyes, his giddy senses drowning in her. They were the same flesh, the same soul. She belonged to him, not to that gloomy boy who had betrayed him.

Against the pressure of his kiss her lips were full and moist. His hands groped lower, pushing up her skirt, caressing the softness of her back. Isabel's lids fluttered at the sensation of his gentle touch, his fingers like music on her skin.

His hold on her grew tighter, she could feel the fierceness firing his blood as he kissed her, his lips on her throat. Easing the fragile web of silk from her shoulders, Philip put his face to her breasts—oh Christ, more rich and ripe and beautiful than even he had imagined! Isabel clutched him all the closer, her arms devouring him, fingernails digging into the flesh of his shoulders and bringing blood. "I love you," she gasped, "I love you so much!"

Even through his clothes she could feel the sudden rush of moisture against her leg; the fresh sweat on his face as he lowered his head to her shoulder. She kissed the top of his head, nuzzling her cheek against the burnished gold of his hair.

Flanders brought her hand up to his lips, kissing her fingers where the blood was. "Sweet, so sweet..." he murmured.

A RECONCILIATION between Philippe and his relatives was formally celebrated at a banquet on Midsummer's Eve. Adele, flaunting her redeemed status, effected a lavish scene. Minstrels and ballad singers were brought from Champagne. Experienced cooks and pastry-makers were selected to create fabulous delicacies, illusion foods and table settings. Once more mistress of the

Cité Palais, she revelled in the snub to Philip d'Alsace and his niece.

Flanders, guarding what was left of his diplomatic sway with the French monarchy had stayed on in Paris, but the outlook was dreary and enemies surrounded him. Always brilliant and talkative, tonight he sat dejectedly by, watching Adele (ever the poseur) as she made spirited conversation and danced with her youngest brother: Stephen, the handsome and brilliant young Count of Sancerre.

Subdued and watching with the same reticence as Flanders, Philippe Capet sat beside his uncle, William the Bishop of Rheims. Depressed at his inability to deal with the English king, Philippe worried further about his rift with Flanders, now that he was more firmly blocked than ever by his mother and her brothers. Demoralized and gloomy, he felt as though his weakness was obvious to all; that everyone was laughing at him.

Near him sat two other men, both in a quandary. Maurice de Sully watched the festivities with shaded interest, with instincts attuned to the essence beneath the gaiety. Like Flanders he resented the re-emergence of the Champagnois and wondered what new method of political in-fighting could succeed in detaching the boy Philippe from them. For himself he was not overly concerned; even the spiteful Adele accredited his worth to the Crown in matters both sacred and secular. He worried seriously though about the damage she and her brothers could bring upon France with their heedless spending and their unwary political adventures before Philippe could assert himself against them.

Hughes de Puiseaux's mood was darker. Restive, he sat at the side of his pallid wife; his slender fingers toyed absently with the food before him. His spirits were steeped in gloom. Upon his appointment as Lord Chancellor to Louis in 1178 Hughes had allied himself closely in friendship with Philip of Flanders, believing that greater security lay in partnership with him than the Champagnois. Now Hughes de Puiseaux's status was unsure, his faith in Philippe Capet waning. The chancellor was only thirty-four, elegantly handsome, and despite the past rancor between himself and Adele he had noticed the sly and covetous looks she cast his way, even tonight. Hughes had charm and a comely appearance—more solid currency than intelligence or ability; if circumstances demanded, he would spend it.

Isabel was late coming down. She was very late. She had very nearly decided not to come at all—for what joy was there in celebrating her rivals' resumption of power? Then she decided that her absence would seem a token of Flemish surrender, so she dressed and then descended to the music and voices below.

Emerald silk chainse long-sleeved and trailing, the Byzantine emeralds from Philippe, unbounded fair hair flowing out shimmering and free to her waist. Isabel stood very still watching, peering past the musicians to the long center table. She saw her uncle at once, near him Philippe and Sully; handsome Hughes de Puiseaux with his less attractive wife. Sitting near them, beside her husband Harry Plantagenet, was Marguerite, Philippe's half-sister. She was dark and sleek like her mother (one of Louis's trio of black-haired wives). From across the length of the room Isabel could hear Marguerite's animated, girlish giggle.

There was another woman swirling in a profusion of persimmon-colored silk, dancing a *tourdion* with a handsome dark-haired man Isabel had not met. Adele was very tall and slender, impressively attractive. Her black hair was plaited into four braids looped at the back of her neck. Her loose silken sleeves skimmed the floor, the knotted girdle at her waist sparkled with pearls.

The air was soft with the sound of flutes, dulcimers and gigues. Isabel crossed to the table, seating herself in the empty chair between Philippe and Sully. The bishop nodded to her with a smile, but Philippe leaned toward her and scowled, "Where have you been? You should have been here an hour ago!"

She reached for the silver porringer which sat on the table between them and poured her cup full with wine. "What is this?" she asked, holding the henap under his nose.

"Raspberry wine," he snapped, careful to keep his voice low, "Don't change the subject! I asked you where you have been for the past hour."

She drank. The wine was thick and sweet with a sour undertaste but it was good and she emptied the cup. At her elbow the *ewerer* offered a dish for her hands. Isabel washed them quickly, then accepted the linen cloth the serving girl held out to her. Philippe dismissed them both with a curt nod then brought his attention back to Isabel. "I was speaking to you."

Her hands sagged in her lap and she turned to him with a curious expression. There was a gulf between them. There was probably nothing she could say to take that disagreeable look off his face, but she tried. "This celebration is for your family and you are welcome to enjoy it. But under the circumstances I'm sure you can see that it is a little unreasonable to expect me to join in." She reached her hand out toward a platter of dried fruit and began to fill her plate but Philippe's strong fingers circled her wrist in restraint. "Just who do you think you are speaking to?" he asked. "And just who do you think *you* are?"

Isabel had never known an unkind touch and the startled look showed in her eyes. But his meanness fueled her presumption and she shot the words back at him, "I think I am the unwilling spectator of my own misfortune, and of your refusal to stand up to your mother and her family!"

His hold grew tighter, crueler—and yet his fingers communicated an odd sensation of pleasure to her. He read the feeling in her face and sent the same look back to her. Just as Isabel thought she would faint from the pain, he released his hold on her. Her hand sped to her lips, her tongue caressing the ugly red bracelet on her wrist. In a voice that was barely audible she said, "Now that you have asserted your power over me, perhaps you might try to prove your manhood with the rest of your family...."

Philippe gave her a long look, his expression unreadable. His coldness hid an unremitting incubus. He wanted to be nice to her, to tell her he was sorry. He ached to reach out his hand and touch that flagrant mane of golden hair, that white throat glistening with emeralds. Her stubborn Flemish pride was a goad to him, infuriating, vaguely threatening. She was not the passive child he had envisioned when Flanders had suggested her as a bride. The French boy had been indifferent to the choice of a marriage partner—Flanders' arrangement had been inspiring: the offer of Artois, the lineage link to Charlemagne had been prize enough. Philippe was too young, too indifferent to women to care what female would eventually bear the next king of

France. His concern was to survive politically in spite of his relatives' designs upon his own power.

Yet here *she* sat, something a world apart from what he had expected. A beautiful child-woman, a subtle, taunting spur to his emerging manhood. She had the aura of provocative sensuality; a beckoning light in her eyes that had disturbed and aroused him since their first meeting. He looked at her now: her sullenly inclined profile, the tremulous lower lip set in pouting, the fine hair shimmering with highlights. The muscles in his abdomen jerked and his throat constricted. He longed to shake her rebellious nature into blind submission, to pummel her with fists and angry kisses—to break her obstinacy with force, and bring her to her knees before him in servile, obedient pleasure.

His thoughts convulsed reason and he beat them back, hating her, hating himself, hating his own isolation most of all. He tried to lay his distemper at the bottom of cup after cup of the wine, ignoring the pale-haired girl beside him—ignoring her though his thoughts were suffused with her. The duller his brain grew the fiercer smoldered his inner pain. He was so tense that when he felt her hand suddenly on his forearm he fairly leapt from his chair. Her touch was agony to his tightly-strung nerves and he yanked his arm away from her. Fighting to catch his breath, Philippe got to his feet and hurried from the hall, without a word to anyone.

Isabel sat staring straight ahead. She seemed to be watching the dancing, but she saw nothing. She felt as though she would cry at any moment. Sully saw her unhappiness and leaned closer, patting her hand affectionately. "You haven't eaten a thing child," he reminded. "Come, let me get you some food. What would you like?"

Isabel surveyed the table in a quick glance. It was a tempting array but she felt too unhappy to eat. "I'm not very hungry," she admitted.

"Now you must have something," he chided amiably, lowering several stuffed figs to the pewter dish before her, and adding an almond cake dusted with marzipan. He was very nice; his kindness eased her a little in this company and she rewarded him with a small smile. "Thank you, perhaps some pork with plum sauce, if there is any. It was always served at our table."

Sully shook his head. "You won't find any pork at this table."

"Don't the French like pork?" she asked, sampling the almond cake.

"Oh, I didn't mean in France. But here at the palace or any-where the Capet family eats. You see, King Louis had an elder brother—the boy who would have been Philippe II—but he was killed when his horse was tripped by a pig in the roadway, just in front of the palace. The young man broke his neck and died soon afterwards." He sighed. "That was more than fifty years ago. Since that time the Capet family does not eat and does not serve pork."

Isabel thought about that for a moment, shaking her head in wonderment. To Sully she said, "You have been close to the king for a long time, haven't you?"

"For a number of years. Over twenty. And of course I have been Philippe's tutor since he was four."

If she was ever to get an honest appraisal from anyone here she knew it would be Sully. "What kind of a child was Philippe?" she asked.

Sully smiled but his blue eyes looked wistful. "He was, and is, very bright, but very lonely. He kept to himself a great deal. I can't say he enjoyed his lessons much...."

"He told me you might oversee my lessons," Isabel responded, remembering when she and Philippe had talked in her room the day of her arrival in Paris. How fretful and nervous he had seemed even then.

"Do you like studying?" Sully asked.

"I like to read. I'd like to see the palace archives. My tutor, Gilbert of Mons, has praised it very highly, as have my uncle and my father."

After a while Philippe returned looking flushed but composed. He said nothing to Isabel though she smiled at him several times. Ignoring her, Philippe spent the remainder of the evening in quiet conversation with William of Rheims, and drinking.

By the time an hour had passed Isabel's head was aching from dizziness, the effects of the music, muted conversation, and the heat of the room. She got shakily to her feet, just about to make her excuses to Sully when she looked up to see Adele standing on the other side of the table, staring at her. "You aren't going?"

Adele asked with mock concern. "Why, we haven't even been introduced...."

Isabel inclined her head slightly, aware that the music had halted and that everyone was watching them. "You are Philippe's mother," she said simply.

Adele's eyes were cold though she wore a bemused smile. "So you are my son's wife." She shot a quick sideways glance at Flanders, then to Isabel she said, "I see that you share your uncle's propensity for greed and theft." Her slender fingers reached out clawlike only an inch from Isabel's throat. "That necklace belongs to me. Where did you get it?"

Isabel could feel herself blushing down to her toes. "It was a gift to me from your son," she finally said, trying to keep the strain out of her voice. "He gave it to me the day of my arrival here in Paris." She turned her head to look at him, expecting some word of support, some statement to validate her claim. Philippe sat in rigid silence, his eyes riveted to the table.

Enjoying the spectacle of her son's submission Adele gave her daughter-in-law a sly smile and kept her hand outstretched. "My necklace, if you please...."

Isabel's hands flew protectively to her throat, caressing the gold-embroidered gems. "This necklace is mine," she declared in a sudden burst of spirit. "I told you that Philippe gave it to me."

The silence was deafening. All conversations had stopped. Even Marguerite's chatter was still. Isabel felt degraded, knowing that everyone was taking in this spectacle and probably loving it.

Finally Sully came to her aid. "Lady Adele," he said quietly "I think you might..."

"Shut your mouth, lord bishop!" she shouted, her voice harsh and vulgar. "This does not concern you. That necklace is mine. It was stolen from me and I want it back." Her black eyes swept over her son's blanched face. "Philippe, I insist you order that child to give it back to me!"

Philippe's hands were shaking so badly that he gripped them together atop the table to stop the trembling. "Mother, please!" But he didn't even dare look at her.

Give her the necklace, give it to her quietly and without an argument. But Isabel's fighting spirit rebelled. *Remember who you are...let Philippe stand up to her.* And why didn't he? Why did he leave the burden of response to her? The silent moments passed as Adele looked on with hateful eyes. *Let her take it from me if she wants.... I won't give it to her willingly....*

Adele's long fingers reached out and snatched the fine piece from Isabel's neck. She heard the clasp break; felt the sharp sting of nails across her throat. "That will teach you to steal my things!" and to Philippe she snapped, "And *you* to give away what is mine." Her voice stroked the words, underscoring the symbolism, enjoying the irony. She gave a haughty swish of her head toward Flanders. "No one who takes what is mine keeps it for very long...."

Isabel stood as still as a waxwork, wishing she could dissolve into the floor. She jerked her head sideways, giving a perfunctory glance to her uncle and her husband but neither of them would meet her accusing look. At this moment she hated them. She was *here* because of them, bearing this mortification because of them. Yet they sat mute; not one word on her behalf. Not even a trifling attempt at taking her part!

Through tear-filling eyes Isabel saw Adele fussing with the necklace, testing the ruined clasp, finally tucking it into her girdle. Isabel shook her hair out long and loose. Loud enough for everyone to hear she spat out the angry words: "Your actions only confirm all that I have heard of you, lady. You would rather break a thing of beauty than leave it intact for someone else...." There was more she wanted to say but instead she turned on her slippered feet and raced blindly out of the hall, past the gasps which followed her as she fled down the long corridor and out the open archway toward the back courtyard. When her feet found the pathway leading to the grove she stopped, her hands covering her face, her body shaking with helpless sobs.

Outside the air was still and the moon shone down in full icy whiteness. Isabel walked with slow steps past the apple trees, toward the massive oaks in the center of the grove. Here it was lonely, but peaceful. Aimless steps carried her toward the oak which stood in the center of the ring of trees. Against the sky its far-spreading limbs contorted into fantastic patterns.

The tree offered dumb support and she leaned submissively against the trunk. *Oh God, God—what has gone wrong and where will it all end?* She had made a small noise against her malediction tonight (too small for the satisfaction of triumph!) but retribution would come. Some force beyond her own small strength was inveighing against her, closing off any hope of truce, blighting hope itself.

Around the base of the tree wound the green leaves of the tangled *viscum album.* Mistletoe. The source of St. John's healing oil. The sacred plant of the Druids. Against the verdant green of the leaves the tiny berries glimmered yellow-white like miniature moons.

She reached out her hand and plucked off a sprig of the plant and buried it against the green of her dress, holding it for a long while. The Druids had worshipped its magical powers and on this night, Midsummer's Eve, all magic was doubly potent. Isabel closed her eyes against the dark and wished.

Her Christian prayers had gone unanswered but the pagan magic was strong, for even as the image of her father's face flooded her mind, she felt his arms taking her tenderly to him, his gentle hands smoothing her hair. He held her so close she could smell his mingled scents of cinnabar and new sweat. But when he spoke her name it was not her father's voice.

Isabel spun around in his arms and stared up into her uncle's face. Startled, she pulled back instinctively, then anger prickled her like a bath of icy water. Her arms flailed out, pushing vainly against him, hating him, hating him more than Philippe—more than anyone because she loved him more than anyone and his betrayal was unbearable.

He pushed her back against the tree, trying to hold her still, pinning her arms down and whispering, "I only want to help you...."

"You had your chance to help me!" she cried, "and you sat by like an impotent old fool, doing nothing, saying nothing!" She tried to wriggle out of his arms, feeling the roughness of the bark scratching her back.

"Stop fighting me," he warned, scooping her up in his arms. She could smell the wine on his breath, feel the hotness of his breath against her face as he held her close to him. The familiarity of his arms lulled her into submission and she laid her face upon the hardness of his shoulder and sobbed.

He carried her to the stone bench near the tree, holding her upon his knee, kissing the top of her head, holding her so close that her body seemed to merge with his. "Forgive me," he whispered, kissing her face, loving her because she was part of him, "my dearest beautiful child...."

"Why don't you care about me?" she sobbed, her sharp nails impaling the flesh of his arms as she clung to him.

Her hair was a golden web smothering him, her girlish arms a trap for his reason. Wine and desire were strong in him, terrifying and inevitable. She was kissing his face, his throat, his chest, despoiling his good intentions in wanton innocence. "Can't you see how much I love you?" she gasped, "how much I want you? I have no one now, no one but you."

His hands were tight against the back of her head, his thumbs caressing her jaw. "Lovely," he whispered, "the loveliest face in the world...." Her features were alight in a wash of moonbeams. She was a silvery thing, a mermaid swept up from the depths of the sea to drown in moonlight. The fragile line of reason was blurred, beyond his reach....

Flanders was fumbling, pushing aside the folds of his bliaud and she, understanding and eager, dropped to her knees before him, her face pressed against his thigh. He clasped her slender neck with impatient fingers, pulling her closer, nearly swooning as her lips closed around him—first hesitantly, then fixing upon him with fervor, her fingers in artful accompaniment.

It was over too quickly, before he could pull away from her and she was choking, the essence of him strong in her mouth. Philip sat quietly for a few minutes, stroking her hair. After a while he pulled her up and she molded once again in his lap, her cheek pressed to his chest.

The moments passed in silence as Isabel snuggled close to him, her arms tight about his waist; dreaming, her eyes wide open. "All those objectionable people," she muttered. "Oh, Uncle Philip, nothing has gone as you planned. What are we going to do?"

He sucked in a low, weary breath. "We just have to wait and see what happens...."

She jerked her head up, her face just inches from his. "But what good will that do? You yourself told me that you had been displaced."

Flanders sighed protestingly. "It may not be so serious as we— I—had first supposed. I was upset when I told you that. I was also drunk."

She sensed his reticence and it irritated her. She had the right to know what kind of a future she faced. She gave him a long searching look. "You thought it was, not so many days ago. Has the situation changed since then? Have you spoken to Philippe? Has he told you differently?'"

He was silent for so long she wondered if he'd heard her at all. Isabel repeated her last words; then he did listen and he looked at her keenly, his amber eyes narrowed. "Yes, I talked to him yesterday."

"Well?" she prodded him.

"He didn't say much—I think he is ashamed of his weakness at Gisors. I suppose it is only natural that Henry would intimidate him; Philippe only restored Adele's lands for that reason. She has won a temporary victory it's true. But if I know anything it is that Philippe hates his mother."

"Yes," Isabel snapped sarcastically. "I could see how much tonight."

Philip tried to convince her. "Each day Louis lives we gain time. Philippe grows more experienced as time passes and when Louis dies Philippe will be ready to take his place."

She was not convinced. "I fail to see how that fact helps us."

She was more inquisitive than Flanders had anticipated and he had to grapple with an explanation. "Philippe is unsure of his power now because he is only acting in his father's place. Once Louis is dead and there is no question of Philippe's singular authority, things will be different. You'll see."

For a moment her blind trust in him wavered. Did he think her gullible, or had he himself been duped? "But I *don't* see," she argued, "even if we do suppose that Philippe will throw off his mother's influence after Louis dies, does that give *you* any assurance that our alliance will be adhered to?"

His fingers were light on her skin, tracing the curve of her throat. "Don't worry about so many things. Let others guide you."

"I have been guided," she replied, "and so far what has come of it? I don't even know if I am to remain here. Adele and her clan seem very much at home tonight."

He gazed with genuine mystification at her. She was an extraordinary child; no child at all. Bright, perceptive, astute, and she wanted answers. "This is a subtle business Isabel," he told her firmly, "it isn't a game of dice where everything is conceded or won in a single throw. Let circumstances develop as they may."

Involuntarily she drew back from him, apprehensive. "But I don't understand you. You treat this all as one great game you've suddenly tired of...."

He caressed the scratch marks at her throat and kissed her there. "Isabel, Isabel..." he muttered, "don't be so eager to decipher events for which you are not prepared in understanding."

She was insistent. "You must speak to Philippe again before you leave. You must make an end of this mystery and find out exactly what his intentions toward us are."

His passion spent, Flanders was once again the politician. He suddenly resented her questions and answered tersely, "You knew that there would be risks involved."

"As if it mattered *what* I knew or *if* I knew...."

His fingers curled tightly around her forearms and his voice carried a warning. "Just mind your place, Isabel."

"But I don't *know* my place, can't you see that!" she cried out in frustration. "I don't know from one day to the next if I'm even to stay here. This is my life you are toying with, not some hypothetical situation scratched out on a piece of paper!"

She fell against the stone bench, hitting her head on the back rest as Flanders leapt to his feet. He was angry now; Isabel knew that, even though his features were shaded in darkness. And it was in his voice and manner. "I have listened with patience to you girl, but I will not be spoken to in such a way. You don't understand the complexities of this situation, Isabel. I know what I am doing. I do not need instructions in diplomacy from you!"

Hastily and without measuring her words she snapped, "No, of course not—so long as your idea of diplomacy is to sit by silently while Philippe's family insults me!"

"I have already apologized for what was allowed to happen to you in there tonight," Flanders shot back at her. "I don't intend to grovel before you, begging further repentence."

Her anger was a bright flame burning in her eyes. "Yes, how much more fitting to have me on my knees before you!"

He bent low, his face close to hers. "What you did was not forced on you!" He clasped her jaw between strong fingers, forcing her to look at him. "And you loved it, didn't you? You're the hungriest little bitch I've ever known. Don't pretend to be innocent. You've had plenty of experience sucking and fucking your father—don't play virgin sacrifice with me!"

That cruelty cut deeper than her anger would protect and she began to cry. "That is a sluttish thing to say! I love my father—I love you!"

"Your love is not the usual affection of a daughter or a niece," he chided her.

"You made no complaint earlier!" she wept. "What I did was out of love for you, because I thought you wanted me to, and because I thought you loved me. Now, for you to say such things..." She was crying openly, not even trying to wipe the tears away. He straightened up, looking down at her, feeling suddenly sorry, but saying nothing. "Go on then," she cried, "leave me, leave me alone to wonder whether or not I will be turned out on the streets, banished, annulled of my station by my enemies and those who may call themselves my betters! I would rather beg in the streets of Paris than be sent home to Hainault in degradation and disgrace because you have failed to make your own plan materialize!"

His voice was hard-edged by cynicism as he answered her. "I am well reprimanded. But I will give you a parting piece of advice, Isabel. If you wish to gain the respect of those 'betters' of whom you speak, you will think seriously before you play another scene like the one at the banquet tonight, or here with me. Your parents and I have always indulged and spoiled you, Isabel. It is true that we have been temporarily disengaged from our goal here, but I assure you, your downfall—and my own—is much more predictable if you continue to criticize Adele and expect Philippe to play your chivalrous protector. He may feel only indifference toward you now, but that well may turn to loathing if you continue to speak your mind on all that displeases you."

Isabel stared up at him. "Philippe is hateful!" she shouted. "If all that you told me about him was true, he would have said something to his mother on my behalf!"

"You think too much of yourself, Isabel, that is your trouble," Flanders answered with firmness. "You are in a new environment. Don't expect to be petted and fussed over as you were at home."

"Why don't you go?" she cried. "Why don't you just go?"

"I am leaving," he assured her coldly. "I'm leaving for the north at first light. I will say goodbye to you now."

"Goodbye, then," she wept into her hands. "Leave me, leave me at the mercy of those who hate me, and don't trouble yourself of what will become of me!"

"You are not without talents child," he answered, his lips twisted in a sneer, "you might try them on your new husband, if you can get his cock away from Harry Plantagenet for long enough."

Isabel covered her ears, not wanting to hear any more, wishing he were dead, wishing that she was, that the earth would suddenly rise up and bury her. She wept until vomit nearly strangled her, then fell upon the ground shivering and whimpering.

When she finally raised her head Flanders was gone. In her mouth she could still taste him, mingled now with the sourness of vomit. He had left her. Left her alone. Left her without even a decent goodbye. Pulling herself up, she dusted the grass and dirt from her clothes. She could no longer hear the music from inside. There was no sound of voices either. Off to the east she could hear dogs barking.

Clouds had formed over the moon. It was dismally dark in the grove now; dark and suddenly chilly. Isabel started toward the path, shivering in the coolness. When she reached the giant oak she stooped, taking the sprig of mistletoe between her fingers, remembering the legend. *The mistletoe must never touch the ground: it was a gift from heaven, sanctified by the gods.* She closed the leaves into the palm of her hand and stood up. All gods were beyond her reach now.

On the path back to the palace she met Sully who had come in search of her. It was a kind act, born of commiseration but she felt too close to tears again to face him or anyone else.

He bent toward her, taking up her hands. "Child you should not be out here alone. I've been searching for you."

She gave him a wavering smile. "You are so kind, but you needn't have worried. I was just walking." And then she added, "Is the banquet over?"

"Yes." He took his own cloak and thrust it around her shoulders. "Adele left shortly after you, as did Philippe. I am sure that the quarrel made everyone uncomfortable."

Isabel hesitated for a moment just beside the row of silver lime trees that bordered the entrance to the grove. The torches that hung above the palace archway quavered light and shadow across his face as she looked up at him. "My lord Bishop, you must understand that it was not my wish to quarrel with Philippe's mother...."

The girl's face was so very pale, her hair was stringy and disheveled. Sully suspected that she had been crying and his heart ached in sympathy for her. Innocent child! She knew so little of the world; it was cruel of her family to sacrifice her to their own interests. Silently he vowed to look after her. Aloud he said, "Dear girl, your uncle must have warned you against the treachery of that lady. The advice should be well taken."

The mention of her uncle brought a sting of moisture to her eyes. "I know very little of these things," Isabel remarked. "I am a stranger here: I fear I shall be a stranger for a very long time." For just an instant she remained by his side, then looking up into his face she said simply, "I thank you for your kindness to me. If you will excuse me now I think I will go to bed." She shook the cloak from her shoulders and passed it over to him. Then in a flurry of green and gold she raced off down the path, getting smaller and smaller, until the corridor swallowed her up completely.

ON THE EIGHTEENTH DAY of September 1180—a fog-strewn afternoon with no hint of sun—Louis of France died, holding tightly to the hand of Maurice de Sully and whispering repentence for his sins. The king was old and sick—ready to die, if slightly fearful—and Sully's presence was a comfort.

There were two others in the room. Alike figures, tall and dark, black-visioned. Philippe and Adele stood together very close (ironically so) and thinking identical thoughts. Between his fingers Philippe clutched Louis's signet ring, taken from the hand still warm.

Sully pronounced Absolution and prayed silently over that prone figure for a few minutes. Then he swept his hands over the king's face, closing his eyes. Silently, his face tear-moist, the bishop rose to his feet. Mother and son looked at one another then at Sully. "Is it over?" they asked in unison.

* * *

Louis Capet had not wished for a splendid funeral, disdaining even the traditional burial at St. Denis, where most Frankish kings since Clovis were entombed. His body was borne south, down the Seine, and delivered up to the white-habited Cistercian monks at Barbeaux in Melun. Philippe, adorned in the purple of mourning, king at last, and dowager Queen Adele in purest white and cloaked with the assured promise of her legal settlement, accompanied Sully as the chief mourners. Isabel of Hainaut, now queen of a land she had scarcely seen save from her window, was left behind at the Cité Palais in the safe-keeping of Lord Chancellor Hughes de Puiseaux.

October came, dressing Paris in a cloak of autumnal fog, by the time Philippe and his mother returned from the south. Isabel had been lonelier than usual. In the afternoons she and Edythe roamed in the garden or played draughts; it passed the time. But Edythe always retired early, leaving Isabel to wander through the passageways alone at night.

Chancellor de Puiseaux had given her permission to study in the dim palace archives library and it was there she spent many of her companionless evenings, reading accounts of the fifth and sixth century Frankish rulers recorded by Gothic historian Jordanes; enthralled by his account of Attila's invasion of Gaul; and the battle of Châlons-sur-Marne with its 300,000 atrocities. Fascinated, Isabel delved even more deeply into time and history: first century Gaul—Julius Sabinus, the patriot who had called himself a new *Caesar*, living with his faithful wife Eponina underground in a crypt for nine years to escape the tyranny of Roman emperor Vespasian. She read of her own great ancestor Charlemagne, and the exploits of his fantastic grandfather Charles Martel.

Isabel, well tutored by her father, uncle, and Gilbert of Mons, combined the skills of her education (she read as well as spoke Flemish, French and Latin) with an incredibly romantic imagination. The tales she read stirred her yearning curiosity, and somehow helped to buffer her isolation.

She was restless, though, and the nights were long and very lonely. She often woke from nightmares or deeply disturbing dreams. Ever since she could remember there had been night terrors; but always there had been her mother and father to sit beside her, smoothing her hair and coaxing the fear away. Now there was no one. The dreams went untold and the uneasiness persisted.

On the evening that the Capetian caravan returned to Paris Isabel waited for hours, hoping that Philippe would come to her room. She wanted to talk to him about the funeral. But when the moon was already high—a milky cyclops eye, white and unblinking—he still had not come. Resolutely she wrapped herself in a grey silk chainse, brushed out her hair, and crept down the corridor to his room.

Isabel had never been in his room, and for a moment her hand trembled against the vivid green drape that covered the archway to his quarters. Hesitating, she drew back, her fingers brushing the soft velvet. Then just as swiftly her mind asserted the action and she pushed past the drape.

The room was surprisingly bright, lit by several hanging torches and the glow of a shimmering fire. Near the far wall was the bed, couched in green hangings, half drawn. Philippe was on the bed—his back to her. He was naked and the light flickering across his body gave a golden cast to his dusky skin. He was hunched over, his body heaving, uttering strangled gasps that sounded like sobs. She knew she was intruding, yet drew nearer, closing the distance between them till she stood at the foot of the bed.

One glance told her that he was not crying. She watched him with fascination. His head was thrown back, his eyes closed. His hands were clasped together at his belly encasing a member of incredible size, his clenched fingers working over the taut flesh in rhythmic strokes. Isabel couldn't take her eyes from him. He was beautiful, transfigured, lost to outer reality. This was the loveliest sight she had ever witnessed, and without realizing it, Isabel spoke his name aloud.

Immediately he jerked to a sitting position on the bed, his eyes staring blindly at her in wordless, furious surprise.

"I'm sorry," she stammered, suddenly embarrassed. "I didn't mean to..." her voice whispered off into silence.

"How dare you come in here like this? This is *my* room! You have no right barging in here to spy on me!"

"I wasn't," she argued feebly. "I only came here because," she looked down at her bare feet, then up at his stricken face, "I wanted to talk to you."

Philippe jerked the coverlet around him and glared at her. "Well, you certainly chose a poor time."

"I wanted to ask you about the funeral."

"What's there to ask? It was a funeral, pure and simple. What is this fascination you have with my father? You didn't even know him."

Her throat constricted in helpless tension. "I'm sorry."

His black eyes glared at her, his lips drawn into a sneer. "You're shocked, aren't you? Perhaps even a little disgusted. In the future perhaps you'll keep out of other people's rooms."

Anger flared her into response. "I'm sorry to disappoint you but I'm not shocked or disgusted. I'm not entirely ignorant of things, Philippe. If you had troubled to know me better you would have learned that by now."

Philippe tossed her a scoffing sneer. "Don't toy with me. You're only a child. You don't know anything."

Instinctively she moved closer to the bed, her hands outstretched, petitioning for his understanding. "Appearances may be deceiving. To many people you are just a *boy*. Does that make it so? I am no more a child than you are. If you were truly the shrewd young genius of whom my uncle speaks, you would have noticed."

"You're very snide," he answered defensively. "How dare you speak to me like this?"

She eased herself onto the bed beside him, her eyes never leaving his face. With every instinct she owned she tried to reach him. "Philippe, we've been married four months and we're strangers. I *could* be your friend if you'd only let me. I want to be. I want to help you if I can...."

"I don't need your help!" he fairly shouted. "What nerve you have!"

"You chose me as your wife. Is it too much to ask that you at least think of me as your friend?"

"I didn't choose you," he snapped, "I didn't even know you were alive till last March. This whole business was your uncle's idea, to bind me to his will just as my mother tried to bind me to her own. Well, I'm king now and I don't need any of you. I'm just as sick of you and your family as I am of my own."

"You married me for my family!" she argued.

"And for all the help they've been I could send you back to Hainault tomorrow without a care. You're as vain as the rest of your brood. Don't flatter yourself. You don't mean anything to me. Not anything at all."

Tears of humiliation threatened in her eyes and voice; she could feel her composure coming apart. "Believe me," she said between clenched teeth, "it's no great joy to be here." She raised her face to the ceiling as though appealing to a Higher Understanding. "God, but the arrogance of men is sickening! If *you* are unhappy with this arrangement, think of my position. No one cared what my feelings were. You and my uncle forged this alliance and now because you can't carry out your respective parts in the bargain you blame and harass me!" She waited for his testy expression to give birth to some cutting remark. When he said nothing she continued: "If this contract with me and my family is so loathsome to you, do something about it. Send me home—dissolve this arrangement between us. Sell yourself to some ambitious French girl. Someone who can give you French prestige with your bigoted French barons—French children, and French hell when you present her with things you've stolen from the French dowager bitch!"

His hand struck out, slapping her viciously across the face. For a second her features seemed to freeze in disbelief, then the tears came, a wild rush of them. Sobbing, she slumped forward on the bed, her hands covering the scalding sting where he had hit her.

Without a thought, Philippe pushed the coverlet aside and leaned over her, his nostrils smarting at the scent of her perfumed hair. Roughly he pulled her close, his arms tight about her and tangled in her hair. She wept against his chest, but her arms encircled him in an instant, her fingernails digging into his back with painful sharpness. With a free hand he swept her tear-matted hair back from her face, forcing her chin up between tight fingers, making her look at him. "I'm sorry, I'm sorry..." he repeated over and over, stroking her cheek, hot from the pressure of his hand. Oh, Jesus, her beautiful, beautiful face!

Anger and passion and love and hate throbbed in him, colliding, mingling crazily. He could taste her tears and her moist hair in his mouth as he kissed her, holding her so close that it hurt. He felt her hands on his skin, her fingers caressing his shoulders, his chest, moving over his belly and below, grasping at him with so much fervor that he was instantly afraid and tried to push her hands away. Still she reached for him, her fingers soft and delicate on his engorged flesh as she whispered, "Let me, I know how...."

Thought, reason, all sensibilities numbed, he reeled back against the cushions. Her hands were sweet on his skin, her lips both soothing and exciting. He closed his eyes, reveling in darkness and the incredible pleasure of her touch; and then in a superb moment he felt his passion erupt inside the warm, safe enclosure of her mouth.

Philippe lay panting, his consciousness flowing out like well-watered wine. After a moment he reached down, pulling her up to him, cradling her head on his shoulder. For a long time they were both silent. He was dazed and dizzy and more at peace than he had ever been. "Your father would kill me," he finally whispered, "and your uncle. They both treasure you so."

Isabel turned her face into his shoulder and her fingers clutched anxiously at his neck. She thought of her uncle's final words, his face set in anger; and of her father, plagued by a guilty love yet sacrificing her to a future he himself could not conscience. The two men who had guided her every breath to this time had now seemingly abandoned Isabel to a future of questionable shadows. All alone and comfortless, she had only Philippe—and suddenly he was everything. Impulsively she wept. "Don't wish you had never seen me!"

He felt her vulnerability and pulled her closer to him. "I don't," he promised, "I don't." Then after a while he whispered, "But Isabel, we mustn't tell anyone about this. They wouldn't understand."

He could feel the flick of her lashes against his skin. "They all hate me," she mused sadly, "you mother, your uncles, your cousins—everyone here at court."

Philippe thought of Midsummer's Eve, of Adele ripping the shimmering emeralds from Isabel's throat, of the shocked silence that had followed. Stroking her arm he soothed, "I never told you how sorry I was for what mother did to you that night."

She struggled to a sitting position beside him, looking down into his face with large somber eyes. "It wasn't so much the necklace, though I did love it.... It was you and my uncle sitting there, watching and listening. You did nothing. You said nothing."

He toyed with a sweeping length of her gilt hair that lay twirled over his midsection. "You put us all to shame, standing up to her the way you did. I hated her so much that night I could have killed her. I wanted to say something—I just..." he paused. "But things will be different now that Louis is dead."

"How?"

He pulled her down next to him. "She's leaving Paris soon, going back to Champagne to settle up her *dotalicium*. Everything's been restored to her, all her lands and titles, her allowance; she has what she wants. She won't be here, not often anyway. It will be easier with her gone. For both of us. You'll see."

"And your uncles?" she asked. "What about them? Can I stand against them? Can you?"

The reminder of reality pinched, but he knew she was right. Drawing her closer, his body half-covering her, Philippe rested his head on her shoulder. "I know, I know," he muttered, "but there's nothing I can do now, not till I'm older, till I can make everyone take me seriously as a king. I need their support and help. I can't rule this country alone—I've had no experience. My father shut me out from everything."

Her fingers were very white against the black disorder of his hair as she stroked his temples. "But what about my uncle?" she argued softly. "And de Puiseaux, and Sully? They are all men of learning and experience. They're on your side. They'll help you against your family."

"My uncle William is one of the most powerful prelates in this country as Bishop of Rheims," he reminded her, "and together my uncles Theobold, Henri and Stephen hold twice as much land as I do. They have formidable armies, and treasuries far larger than anything I have at my own disposal."

"But you are the king, Philippe," she protested, "they are your vassals. Any lands and revenues they hold are under your control."

He shook his head. "No, it isn't as simple as that. I have angered so many people by this marriage, if I so much as try to oppose my uncles, they and the barons they control will rise up in revolt against me and the whole bloody mess will start up all over again." He raised his head from her shoulder and looked at her. "Besides that, I signed a treaty promising to maintain peace with my relatives. My hands are tied. I need time. Time to gain their confidence and my own. To get control of things. I can do it, I know I can, but not all at once. That's what Flanders refused to understand. I didn't betray him at Gisors, I merely did what I had to do. He didn't have to negotiate with Henry, I did. Can you understand, Isabel?"

She nodded weakly, seeing the futility he faced.

"Someday," he muttered, his cheek against her soft hair, "I will rule this land alone and owe myself to no one. In a few years there won't be a man who can stand against me. Then I can turn my attention to the evil that has plagued France since Henry first sat the throne—the Angevin domination over us in all things. Henry is still powerful, but he won't last forever. He's getting old. His sons all hate him. And with them to help me I'll fight him for every inch of land he stole from my father."

Her arms were around him, fond and comforting. "I didn't realize—I didn't know how it was for you. All this time, Philippe, I've been thinking only of myself, of how difficult things were for me, when you carry such great burdens. Forgive me..."

"Oh Isabel," and her name caught in his throat, "I need you so much—help me."

Her kiss was tender, loving, trying to communicate all her feelings of sympathy toward him and her own need of closeness and protection. Gently she urged him back down on the bed, smoothing the pillow under his head, looking down into his face with compassion and concern. "What did you mean about your father shutting you out?" she asked.

He sighed with weariness, remembering, wanting to forget.

"He loved you, surely."

Philippe took hold of her hand. "Isabel, my father prayed all of his adult life for a son, waiting through three marriages and what he called 'a superfluity of daughters' to have one. When I was born it was like a reward from heaven. But soon afterwards he lost interest in me. When I was growing up Sully pled with him often to have me consecrated as the heir apparent, but time after time Louis refused."

Isabel looked at him with questioning eyes. "But why?"

"He was jealous. It sounds foolish, I know. But somehow, realizing that I was the one who would come after him—having to accept that my beginning represented his end—he came to hate me. He shunted me off to the country: I spent most of my early years there, with few advantages, little education, and no schooling at all in the social graces. I was treated no better than a child of petty nobility. My mother was to blame too. Oh she was proud to have been the one to bear Louis his first and only son—but solely for her own prestige. I was never anything more to either of them than a means to an end, a representation of personal triumph."

Isabel had never known anything but love and tenderness from her parents and she winced in actual pain at his words. She understood now—that hot luminous flame burning in his soul; it made him vulnerable, and knowing it, he protected himself with pretended coldness.

She bent over him, her hair nearly covering him, kissing his face and feeling the wetness of silent tears on his cheeks. Her affection touched him, touched him very deeply. He had opened himself to her completely, something painful; something he had never done before, not even to Harry.

He craved her gentleness, the sweetness of her that was mingled with a beauty and passion both exotic and alarming. Holding her he felt desire gnawing at his loins, and this time it was he who guided her hands to the stem of his ardor. She kissed him where he was hers now, utterly and completely, and whispered, "I've never seen anything so glorious, so beautiful, so *auguste*. Now it is mine too. See how it stands beneath my touch, how it loves me?" Then her hands and her mouth were full with him, and in a moment he was dissolving in her warmth.

She rested closer against his abdomen while his hands still clutched tightly about her neck. "You're so beautiful, so beautiful Isabel," he gasped. "I want you so much. Why do you have to be so damn young?"

She kissed the inside of his thigh. "I won't always be. But I want to be something to you now—even if this is the only way. You give yourself to Harry Plantagenet, why not to me?"

He sounded surprised. "How did you know about Harry?"

"My uncle..."

Philippe was quiet for a while. The fire had gone out; he could feel the beads of sweat prickle on his skin and he shivered. "I love Harry," he finally said. "I have for a long time."

"It doesn't matter," she assured him. But she had tasted him now and was greedy for some promise. "Only, tell me that you didn't mean what you said to me before."

"What did I say?" and his voice sounded slow and sleepy. "I don't remember."

"That you wanted to send me away."

"I'd never do that, not after tonight," he murmured, just before he slept.

Philippe awoke to the touch of her hand against his cheek. "I should go back to my room now."

"Wait," he muttered, and raising up, leaning toward the floor where his clothes lay, extracting something from the folds of his surcoat. He straightened up, and slipped a chain about her neck. At the end dangled a silver thing and he held it up for her to see. "This is for you, the ring of the Druid priestess found while excavating at Notre Dame. It's beautiful, and I kept it. Now it is yours."

Isabel brought it to her lips and kissed it. "It's so lovely," she breathed, flooded with feeling. "Is it really mine?"

"Always..."

The deeper meaning had not escaped her. "A pagan relic to symbolize a Christian marriage," she mused. "I should feel shame. Instead I only *feel*...." She reached to kiss him, and he buried his face willingly in the luxuriant tangle of her hair.

END PART I

Part II
Autumn, 1180

THE FIRST HINT of Philip d'Alsace's break from the Capetian fold was his absence from King Louis's funeral. Philippe Capet had not been troubled. He knew Flanders well enough to suspect that his pride was still smarting from their summer dispute, but otherwise he read nothing into Flanders' withdrawal to the north.

Philippe had blocked d'Alsace and the Champagnois as well. Though the royal relatives still bore some attentive watching there was nothing to fear from the Count of Flanders now. So he thought.

Philippe Capet was wrong. Flanders, temporarily diverted by the young king's spurt of independence, was not idle. As always, Philip d'Alsace had a plan, and he didn't hesitate to mobilize his intentions.

At the time of Louis's death, Flanders had made his first move toward realigning the position of his dubious power. From Ghent he made an unannounced journey eighty-five miles east to the city of Aix-la-Chapelle (seat of the Holy Roman Empire). There he arranged a secret meeting with Emperor Frederick I of Hohenstaufen, who was called *Barbarossa*. The county of Flanders was an imperial fiefdom (though not a crucial one in the Emperor's sight). As usual the Count of Flanders had over-estimated his own political magnitude.

The plan which he detailed to Frederick was typically egocentric. *A great alliance of the Flemish fiefs with the Empire, together in*

95

sturdy aggregation against the King of France. Frederick was not an impatient or insensitive man and he was personally friendly with Philip d'Alsace. But he was busy and distracted, outlining yet another proposed expedition into Italy (his sixth since 1152). And Frederick had no quarrel with France. His relations with Louis had been formal and stable; there was no reason for him to cause trouble with the late monarch's son. Philip of Flanders eagerly explained: the boy had betrayed him after promising an allegiance with the Flemish; he had acceded to Henry II's will and reinstated the powers of Champagne and Blois.

Frederick listened. He stroked his red beard and shook his head, politely but firmly refusing Flanders' request. The secret interview ended with an embrace between the two men, but inwardly Flanders was fuming.

What to do now? Back in Ghent, closeted in the highest turret of his tower, Flanders paced the floor in solitude. While icy sleet froze the landscape outside, his brain burned with the intensity of his purpose. There *was* a way. There had to be one! He was not yet forty. Was his life in international politics over? Had his influence seen its last? Would he spend the remainder of his life in the eclipse of Philippe Capet? *Not so long as he breathed!*

On the third night of his solitary vigil the idea came to him. He had seen no one, taken no food, no wine since his return to Ghent. He was weak and tired from the difficult journey to and from Aix-la-Chapelle, faint from lack of nourishment. Yet the emptiness and the solitude and the concentration had licked his senses into a brilliant flame burning brightly at the core of his mind. He would beat Philippe Capet at his own game, outwit him from the inside. And on that very night, he began to plot his deliverance....

Henry of England kept Christmas at Le Mans that year. It was a favorite place for him; his birthplace, the burial ground of his father Geoffrey of Anjou; where he himself had deigned to be entombed when that day came.

It had been a relatively quiet autumn on the continent. Both Poitou and Brittany had been peaceful with no major uprisings. But Henry had been listening to some disturbing rumors. The Count of Flanders seemed to be stirring up trouble again. Henry had heard whispers of a clandestine meeting between the count and the emperor. No fear there. Frederick would never back one of Philip's political brainstorms. Still, if he was looking about for means of expanding his influence, Flanders wouldn't be easily disengaged. Henry meant to signal his opposition to any continental incursion by the Flemish count. Shortly after Christmas, Henry ordered the general *assize of arms*, whereby all feudal tenants would demonstrate their military preparedness: arms, equipment, horses. All landowners of major estates were required to equip their vassals and provide a count thereof.

The word of this was passed to Philip of Flanders late in January of 1181. The significance was clear enough; he promptly gave a similar order to his vassals. In Paris Philippe Capet shook his head in puzzlement, but he marshalled his own men to arms. He could not be sure what game of bluff was going on between Flanders and the English king, he could only guess. At this point, he trusted neither of them.

Somewhere deep in her soul, Isabel had found her salvation. Fear of her own failure was an inherent and intangible motivation, fear of rejection was her most secret and terrible dread. She did not so much fear losing Philippe. Even if she ever came to love him, he could not take the place of her father or uncle. To a Fleming, blood-ties were the strongest bonds on earth—cosmic chains, the Life Force, the very center of the soul. Yet survival rated close behind, and Isabel was struggling to survive.

Her emotions were ambivalent. She would have given the heart from out of her body to be at home in Mons with her family, but she could not, and she knew it; so she could only hold on to what she had now. The only way she could do that was to take charge of her life and keep it. For the time being she had Philippe's unwavering attention, but she was not fooled. That could vanish at any time. Like Isabel, he was lonely, and that fact worked to her advantage. Apart from his nightly (and often daily) visits, she seldom saw him, but during those private times together, the influence Isabel exerted over him was considerable. And yet Isabel was far too realistic, even at her age, to think that such an influence constituted *control* over her young husband.

It was a dangerous game she was playing. Her father had warned her to cultivate a shield of innocence; she had betrayed that almost immediately. It must have been very evident to Philippe that his child-wife was far from innocent, but he said nothing of it to her. Perhaps he was afraid of all that she might be able to tell him.

And so, with Philippe and Philip d'Alsace still very much at odds, the entire security of the Flemish alliance with the French rested upon Isabel's precocious sexual awareness. As for Philippe, he was bedeviled by his young wife. Five months had passed since she had first come to his room that chilly October night. He had never done more than kiss her; never seen her anything but fully clothed. Yet she worked wonders upon him. She frightened him even as she excited his interest. Her sexual talents were incredible: she knew things that he did not know and Philippe did not know how she knew them. She loved exploring his body, and he never demurred. Isabel was an unknown quotient to him and his flesh loved her even though he did not.

Sometimes in company he would watch her when she was not aware of his scrutiny. Distracted by dinner conversation, annoyed by visitors or his family, her sea-colored eyes would take on a dreamy quality, her full bottom lip drooping prettily in boredom. Then, sensing his study of her, she would raise her head and her eyes would focus fully on him for a few seconds. Her moist lips would part slightly and the expression in her eyes would tease him with their secret. Then her lids would droop again, the lashes sweeping her flawless cheeks. Philippe, who knew nothing of feminine charms, was shattered to his very soul. . . .

Isabel was lonely but her unhappiness was a little less acute. In the afternoons she busied herself studying under the firm tutelage of de Puiseaux, and reading Sully's many translations. Her role was limited, there was little society in which she could participate. Yet the sparse court provided her at least with a chance for quiet and reflection she had not known in busy Hainault.

Despite her dismal surroundings, Isabel had all the fine trappings of a queen. She had a marvelous array of clothes: loose-fitting gauze dishabilles and free-flowing chainses of silk in the Flemish style. Since November Philippe had provided her with a liberal monthly allowance, and many gifts of jewelry (this time of his own procuring, not borrowed from the coffers of Adele).

The palace gardens gave Isabel great pleasure. She often kept to the secluded grove of oaks and apples at the northwest side, where she brooded or dozed or sang softly to herself. Then there was the avenue of trees. Sully had pointed out every one of them to her: the junipers whose limbs netted above forming a secluded bower—beyond that the alders, the silver limes and birches, the yews and rowans. There were also the flower gardens whose multitudinous blossoms included such an array of flowers that there was never a time when the palace garden was not in bloom: narcissus, white jasmyn, marigolds, bluebells, acacia, violets, lilies, poppies, and witch hazel. There were roses of every kind: gallica, damask, apothecary, and Christmas roses. To the far end of the flowers and nearly fronting the south side of the Seine was the royal herbarium, little used (except for Sully) since the days when Eleanor of Aquitaine had lived at the Cité Palais. Isabel, who had learned the art of perfume making from her mother, used the herbarium for that chore. Sully had promised to instruct her in the medicinal uses of herbs.

Her life had leveled off to a not unpleasant stretch of days and nights. The reality of her situation fanned her pride a little. For a time, directly after coming to Paris, it had looked as though all was lost, that events were beyond Isabel's ability to control them. But the Franco-Flemish alliance still held, even though her uncle and Philippe were no longer political brothers. For that—and all the rewards it promised—her kinsmen and other interested parties could thank her!

Dowager Queen Adele lay upon her silk-strewn bed watching Hughes de Puiseaux pull on his clothes. He was only partially in her thoughts. She was musing that she had never found a man who could satisfy her.

Vexed by the close heat of the room she flung away the sheet that covered her and breathed a sigh of irritation. Hughes gave a glance toward her recumbent form and smiled. Adele smiled back, indifferent, detached.

She wondered why in all things that mattered men were so incomprehensibly stupid, unable to discern a woman's thoughts or her feelings. Only a few minutes ago he had lain, hot and eager on her breast, taking his pleasure the way a drunk took his wine, with no consideration for her enjoyment.

At first she had appreciated his attentions. He was younger than she, and extraordinarily handsome—an irresistible trap for a vain, prepossessing woman like Adele. A pleasing face and figure had always been the uppermost consideration when she chose a lover. Now she was bored with handsome men. They were self-centered and usually over-confident about their sexual abilities.

Through a veil of memory she saw Louis. In so many respects he had been a good man; she could have married worse. He had been attractive too, though well into his years; at the time of their marriage, nineteen-year-old Adele was half his age. No doubt he'd been a satisfactory lover in his youth, but by the time Adele had come to his bed, urgency to father a son had made him sexually obnoxious and his frequent bouts of impotence hadn't added any charm to the situation.

Adele had endured much: all the tasteless superstitions—the endless prayers that preceded every coupling; the numberless unguents, lotion, elixirs and poultices which Louis had applied with the most heart-rending expectation; the omnipresent priests and other members of the clergy praying over Louis's limp cock with the fervor of Christ raising the dead. By the age of forty-four, Louis had lost all confidence in his manhood.

An ironic smile curved Adele's lips. He'd certainly looked like a man. Shy Louis had been the bearer of the most gigantic male member Adele had ever seen. It was legend throughout Europe that the Capets had the biggest cocks in Christendom. *Poor Louis.* All that massive physical splendor and no son to show for it. *Poor Adele.* After four fruitless years of trying to implant a son within her, Louis no longer tried to pretend affection or desire for his wife. Their bed became a battleground, Adele beseiged by him night after night. Then finally —success, and following an anxiety-ridden eight and one-half months' pregnancy, Adele had given birth to the long-awaited Capet heir on the night of August 25, 1165.

Louis' interest in Adele had waned considerably after that, though a few years later she had conceived with him again—this time a daughter, Agnes, who in the year of her father's death had been sent off to Byzantium, betrothed to the future Emperor.

Following his wife's second and last conception, Louis had

been overtaken by permanent impotence, easing into unmanned old age while Adele discreetly looked for pleasure elsewhere. Louis's court was large and accommodating—there were plenty of appealing men about. Louis had known of her adulteries, but she had been careful not to humiliate him, so he had pretended not to notice. He had been well schooled for tolerance by his first marriage.

In this clammy, uncomfortable heat of the present, Adele lay wondering whether or not she had ever loved Louis. It didn't matter now; but perhaps it did, a little. She tried to recall their first meeting—how handsome he had been, his fair hair (gold touched by silver) shimmering in the sun. He'd been kind too, in the early days before his assaults on her. She supposed that she had loved him, if only a little bit. But she knew that he had never loved her. Louis had loved once—only once—and his love for Eleanor had only died with him.

The truth of it brought tears of resentment to Adele's eyes. *She* had given Louis the precious heir that Eleanor had been unable to provide. *She* had brought her shrewd and useful brothers into the position of steadfast political alliance with Louis, while his own stupid brothers merely fed upon the power of the crown. *She* had brought with her the rich, untroubled resources of Champagne and Blois, while the rewards of his first two marriages had ended in dissolution and death. Certainly those accomplishments should have merited his love.

But it was the same with all men, husband or no. All the men Adele had accumulated in her life, all the handsome lovers she had known during her marriage with Louis, and even since her widowhood (she looked across at Hughes), had only taken from her. They had been flattered at the attentions of a queen—eager to see what bedding a queen could earn them. They had given her nothing in return but momentary escape from frustration and loneliness. Anger at reality—inescapable—quickened into self-pity and depression. None of them had loved her . . . she was alone.

Hughes came to sit beside her, his arm resting lightly across her bare midriff. She curled her fingers tightly about his forearm trying to smooth the wrinkles of fretfulness from her face because she knew they made her look unattractive and betrayed her age. A long and weary sigh dispelled some of her dissatisfaction, but she looked soberly up at her lover. "I'm so unhappy," she confessed.

He bent and placed a kiss on her navel. Adele lay staring at his bowed head, at his fair-colored curling hair. She had always liked blond men. He snuggled his face close against her and absently she brought her hands up to his head, entwining slim fingers in his abundant hair. She laughed to herself, a laugh which only she could hear, but which she suspected any woman could easily appreciate. All men considered themselves to be stupendous lovers. And yet she, who had sampled so many, had never found even one who could halfway fulfill her expectations, or satisfy her own passionate needs.

He sat up. His eyes, so blue, regarded her seriously. Seeing that her mood was real (and surprised in his ignorant masculinity), he gathered her up in his arms and held her close to him. "And should you be unhappy, lovely lady, who has me beside you now?"

She let him hold her but did not respond. "You don't understand. I'll soon be forty. That is very old for a woman."

Her unbound black hair was soft between his fingers as he stroked it. "You are the most beautiful, the most envied woman in France," he told her.

Adele knew that he was trying to soften her unhappiness but she resented his inability to understand. She was grieving the loss of her youth, lamenting a love she had never known. His tenderness was only a momentary salve on a wound which was years old, and fatal.

Hughes felt her tears on his neck and he forced her chin up, looking quizzically into her face, surprised as always to find her harboring a real emotion. "You *are* unhappy," he said, "but look, there is time enough for tears when I leave tomorrow."

Adele's quick mind pushed her depression away, forcing her senses into the light where she could examine them. She pulled back, easing his arms from around her, black eyes intent on his face. "You didn't tell me you were leaving for Paris so soon! Why? My son won't be back from Burgundy for at least ten days."

"I know," Hughes answered, "but there are some things I must accomplish before he returns. I don't serve the king too well in your bed, my love."

Her eyes narrowed in approaching anger, sensing deception. "And do you serve him better in tutoring his child-wife?"

Hughes looked closely at her. Adele's rage was always just under the surface of her calm, a sleeping tiger easily roused. He tried to pacify her. "Why do you hate Isabel so much? She's no threat to you, for pity sake."

"Why do you like her so much?" she snapped. "I do hate her, that little minx. She and that clan of Flemish dissemblers. They are as much descended from Charlemagne as I am! Against my advice my husband became friendly with the Count of Flanders —and much to my disservice now! Flanders has always hated me, and he would do anything to usurp what influence I still have over my son."

It was an argument which had no end; one which they'd had so many times and Hughes did not wish to re-enact it here and now. "Philip d'Alsace is no longer in league with your son against you," he reminded her. "Why are you so outraged? I have heard whispers that Flanders has put honey to the ear of your brother Stephen and that even now the two of them sit in accord together at Sancerre."

"Stephen knows better than to trust that vagabond!" Adele spat angrily, "and Flanders is a fool if he thinks otherwise!"

"Then your fears are groundless," Hughes answered, "there is no longer a Flemish threat. Philippe has denied himself to them."

"As long as that girl is his wife there is a threat!" she insisted. "If Philippe would throw off all Flemish influence, why should he keep Isabel as his wife?"

"She has done no wrong and she is no worry," Hughes was quick to point out. "She is but a child, Adele. Why do you upset yourself so over her?"

"Anyone who looks as she does is never a child!" Adele flared with rage, jabbing at his shoulder with a pointed fingernail. "I hate that girl! And why must *you* spend so much time with her?"

"I don't!" Hughes insisted, "except when she is in my charge. Sully and I prepare her lessons."

Adele wasn't even listening. "She flaunts herself. She even paints her eyes—at her age!"

"You were only now saying that she is no child," Hughes reminded her.

"Shut up!" Adele shouted at him, "you don't understand anything I say! Are you truly so stupid? How did you ever come to be singled out as a chancellor by my late husband? He had a quick enough mind, though God knows no judgment to speak of. My son too has brains, but lacks discretion. His friendship with Flanders, his marriage to Isabel prove that. I am the only one of this family who has the judgment to rule, yet I am nothing!"

He was trying his best to soothe her. "No one is disputing your abilities, your beauty—anything. Why are you so upset? I leave Champagne tomorrow, cannot we have a little time for ourselves in peace and pleasure?" He reached out for her and one hand closed over her breast, his thumb prodding the hardness of the nipple. But Adele was angry and she pushed his hand away. "That little bitch will always find a means of getting her way," she complained. "The money my son spends on her is beyond all reason. And why? He's so cheap with everyone else—but nothing is too good for her!" Her eyes narrowed into slits of suspicious black jade. "You can't tell me that you haven't noticed her."

He had. "She is very beautiful, especially for one so very young," Hughes admitted. "I'd have to be blind not to have noticed that. But for God's sake, she's eleven years old and Philippe's wife. Why should I lust after a child when I have you—the most beautiful woman in Europe?"

Suddenly she despised him and turned her face away. "I do believe she has already seduced my son," she grumbled.

"Your son is almost sixteen," Hughes reminded her with a chuckle. "If he's had her you can be sure it was of his own doing."

With vehemence she slapped him hard across the face. "You are so ignorant!" she shrilled at him. "Thanks be to God for you that He gave you a handsome face, because that is all He gave you! You have the mind of a donkey! Can't you understand me? I'm not talking about sex. I'm talking about seduction! That little slut is exactly like her uncle—shrewd and manipulative instincts under layers of sweet charm." She stopped suddenly, her eyes glinting. "Have you ever slept with her?"

Shocked beyond anger, Hughes leapt to his feet staring down

at her with tenuous forbearance. Shaking his head he answered, "I can't believe what I am hearing."

"Well, you better believe it," she snapped at him, "because I don't believe you!"

He stood looking at her, biting back his anger. He had seen Philippe in this unhinged state many times, and the violent, emotional side of that young man's nature had been inherited from this woman.

But she hadn't finished. "Have you slept with her?"

He hated her for forcing him to such rage. "No!" he shouted into her face. "I have not! Are you insane?"

"Don't hide behind words," she brayed, "have you *had* her? Have you touched her? Has she touched you? Have you wanted her? Have you? HAVE YOU?"

His hands were strong, the fingers digging into her shoulders as he shook her with a violence that surprised both of them. "Does that answer your question?" he rasped. "Does that convince you that I haven't bedded an eleven-year-old girl?"

His violence had shaken her but her arrogance was unbroken. "Yes," she finally answered. "I do believe you but only because I know you don't have the balls for it. Don't tell me she hasn't flirted with you. She's a perfect little whore hiding behind the shield of her youth. Greedy and sneaky like all the rest of her kind. Have you forgotten that she stole my necklace?"

"Are we going to go over that again?" he asked between his clenched teeth. "Lightning from Heaven, I think I'll vomit if I have to hear that tale of woe once more."

Adele felt her anger flickering, fading into sadness and she tried to cling to it, to hold it as her defense against tears. She didn't want to cry; God in heaven she didn't want to cry at this moment. "You don't even try to understand me," she wailed, "you call yourself my lover—yet I am nothing to you!" She twisted around, away from him, covering her face with her hands.

Tenderness and desire for her banished his anger. She was older than he, and not as beautiful as she had once been—and she could be the most venomous bitch alive. But she was lusty and vigorous, with none of the prim bloodlessness of his inhospitable wife. Hughes bent to press his cheek against her back, his arms surrounding her, his hands cupping her breasts. "I'm sorry Adele," he whispered.

He could feel some of the tenseness drain from her as she relaxed against him, her hands pulling his arms tighter around her. "Don't leave tomorrow," she said softly, "stay with me a few more days."

"I will," he promised, "and when I leave for Paris, come with me. Only please let's not fight and harass each other."

Adele twisted around on the bed, smothering her face in his shoulder while her hands pulled at his laces, untying them. She didn't want words and apologies and promises now, she only wanted him. Seeing her eagerness Hughes ripped off his surcoat and thrust it to the floor. Adele tangled her arms about him and pulled him down upon her. "Hurry," she whispered into his ear, "please hurry...."

Cast off by Philippe Capet, reprimanded by Henry Plantagenet, and shunted aside with a condescending smile by Emperor Frederick, Philip d'Alsace rode south in early August of 1181, by-passing the city of Paris. His destination was Sancerre in the Loire Valley, and the chateau of Adele's brother Stephen. He was the youngest of that family; the least important—politically. But Flanders, with canny intuition, had sensed a use for him and planned to accomplish an understanding between them with charm and promises of his own.

Stephen was quite carried away by the demeanor and presence of this handsome, noble lord from Flanders. He arranged a magnificent banquet in Philip's honor, where the Count of Flanders was toasted and watched with shaded interest by several dozen barons and knights in Stephen's service. The following afternoon, Stephen received Philip in private audience.

In a flowing amber bliaud stitched with golden thread, Flanders strode across the rich Saracen carpets of Stephen's audience chamber. There was a small balcony off the room and it was here where Flanders stood, looking out over the fair-shaded expanse of the surrounding gentle slopes; and threading through it the blue-green Loire. All aspects of beauty were welcome to his eyes, and Flanders solaced his restless nature with the view for several minutes. He spoke absently to Stephen who was sitting several feet away. "You do me a great honour to entertain me so lavishly. The banquet last night was a gracious gesture on your part."

"It is you who do me the honor in visiting," Stephen replied with unctuous charm. He was not without questions though, and was still pondering the reason for Flanders' sudden appearance here in the south.

Philip turned from the terrace view and surveyed his host for a quiet moment. Handsome. Dark, like all the Champagnois. An older, more elegant version of Philippe Capet. Canny, but not quite so cunning. Certainly not a threat.

This was going to be easy.

"You are probably wondering at my purpose here," Flanders said at last.

"I must admit to a little surprise when your message was brought," Stephen countered, slender hands resting in his lap. "It has been some time since you and I talked privately. Not since Louis's death, in fact."

"Yes, a very long time," Philip answered a little too quickly. "But it seems to me we have some things worth discussing now."

Circumspect and a little unsure of himself, Stephen regarded Philip with a dark, even stare while the slanting sunlight danced off the amethysts crowning his fingers.

Flanders let his most engaging smile spread across his face, while lifting an eyebrow as though in haughty self-condemnation. "I am not a man of many mistakes, Stephen. I am usually the most careful judge of character. But I made a sad and bitter mistake when I trusted your nephew." He inclined his head slightly and just the proper tinge of cynicism underscored his final words. "He has betrayed me, Stephen."

The Count of Sancerre was shrewder than Philip had measured and he knew that his guest was play-acting. But Stephen, with all his love for drama, sat back quietly in reluctant appreciation of Flanders' talent. "Betrayed you?" he asked coldly, "do you mean in the matter of your niece and his marriage to her?"

Did this elegant young nobleman know something that Philip did not? Flanders was caught off his guard for only a moment. If this was a scare tactic, a bluff, he wasn't about to fall for it.

"No," Philip answered decisively, "I didn't mean that. The marriage itself has not been called into question. Philippe has no wish to dispense with his vow, why should he? My niece is by far the choicest morsel in Europe—though she is still a girl; still, a girl may work wonders as you may know. I am speaking of my own relationship with Philippe. I loved him dearly, thought of him in a special way, like a son." Here his voice nearly broke in honest emotion. "Now he has decided my help and advice are no longer valuable to him." *A pause.*

Stephen caught the irony in Philip's voice. The Count of Flanders was able and decorous, but something must be awry or he would not be here as a suppliant. The silent moments passed.

In a cat-quick gesture Philip turned to Stephen. "I ask you, if Philippe feels this way, what is there for me to do? I have suffered great personal humiliation in this. Although I believe that we shall eventually mend our differences, I cannot allow a boy to undermine my own prestige. I must make him realize his error in pushing me aside. I must teach him a lesson. Can you help me?"

Stephen rose gracefully to his feet and went to stand at the balcony, his gaze taking in the view though he wasn't really seeing it. He was of a pensive disposition, and for a long time he did not speak. Flanders was a cagey individual: one must deal carefully with him; not submit too eagerly, too completely, as a lover might submit to his first swain. Flanders was a man of so many charms. Surrendering to him was an easy thing, and possibly fatal.

So Stephen toyed with the signet ring on his middle finger, turning it over and over as his mind revolved in thought. So the mighty Philip d'Alsace was looking to *him* for some sort of political alliance—but on what security? Stephen's interest was aroused; he was fairly panting with curiosity; but he too was a diplomat, and so he waited.

When the silence had stretched long enough to be embarrassing Philip softened his expression with a quiet, meaningful smile and repeated his last words. "Can you help me?"

Stephen smoothed the folds of his purple velvet surcoat and looked Flanders straight in the face. "It all depends upon what you want from me," he explained. "Quite frankly, Philip, I'm unsure of your motives. And more to the point, we are on opposite sides of this matter. What possible use can we be to one another?" Then he smiled. "You can understand my reluctance, surely."

But the latitude of Flanders' charm was immense. "We *were* on opposite sides, but no longer. I am offering myself to you as a comrade in arms. If the Champagnois seek to have control over Philippe, is it not wise for me to join with you and your family?"

Stephen's dark eyes showed his puzzlement. "I cannot think what you have to offer us. My brothers, my sister and I are now his guardians, and you, quite frankly, have been removed from power within his circle."

Flanders shrugged congenially and rested a hand on Stephen's purple velvet shoulder. "I don't mean to spark discord between us, but surely you must realize that you are the least viable among your family. I know how closely you are held in your sister's heart, but it cannot have escaped your attention that she has since allied herself securely with Hughes de Puiseaux. Theobold, William and Henri your brothers are all more politically important than you are. So when I spoke of an alliance, I meant a joint understanding between *the two of us.*"

Stephen was genuinely confused now. "What kind of understanding?" he asked.

Flanders' tongue was a dagger slicing the words. "A *military* understanding, my friend. Give me four weeks to move a thousand of my men here and place them on your southern border. I will outfit and equip them, but you must lodge them and give me equal right with as many men of yours. Our combined forces will be a signal to the young Capet that he cannot so easily dismiss us, as he betrayed me at Gisors."

"But I have no quarrel with my nephew," Stephen insisted, "What need have I to marshal troops?"

Flanders' laugh was a mixture of amusement and ridicule as he flung the samite mantle from his shoulders and tossed it to the floor. "My dear Stephen, you saw how easily he abandoned me. Why should your family expect more considerate treatment from him? It is quite obvious to me now what his intentions are. He wants to disassociate himself from *all* of us. He feels that he has no need of guardians and soon he will make that clear to your brothers and your sister, even as he did to me. Believe me, Stephen, I know him better than you do, even though he be your own kin. Personally I don't care what happens to Adele or your three brothers. They are self-seekers, interested only in their own well-being, not that of the realm. I am a Fleming, but my niece is now Queen of France; the child she eventually bears

Capet will rule after him. The future of France is important to me. I need a friend, an ally who feels as I do. I believe in your abilities, in your wisdom. You are capable; you belong in the center of things, not buried here in the Loire Valley...."

Stephen's eyes were hard to read but his fine lips parted, the corners twitching in the slightest show of anticipation. When he didn't speak, Flanders sharpened the edge of his proposal. "I will win back Philippe's trust and admiration. I realize now that he needs a far greater rein on his intentions than I had at first believed. You and I shall be the girders which hem him in and keep control of the Ile-de-France. Otherwise he will only end in giving it all up to Henry of England or one of his ambitious sons. What do you say, Stephen? Have we an agreement?"

Stephen stood staring wordlessly out toward the Loire. His right hand found Philip's left hand, clasping it firmly, entwining the fingers. Flanders knew what he was thinking; he knew he had won.

Sprawled lazily in abandon Isabel lay nibbling on grapes and Philippe. It was late morning. The air was heavy, hot in the closeness of her room, while outside all the noises of Paris filled the air.

Philippe lay staring up at a blue taffeta ceiling, drowsy, lost in aromatic fantasies. Little more than a year, and her perfume was everywhere in this room. He had always been acutely aware of scent and the few feminine associations he'd had in his life he grouped aromatically: his mother wafted dark musk and sandalwood; nursemaids smelled of milk and medicinals; whores stank of sweat.

Sweet scents aroused him even more than physical sensation, and Isabel was always suffused with dizzying, heady scent. Even the slightest contact with her transferred her fragrance to him. After lying with her he was left with a strong residue of perfume, making it obvious to all that the young King of France went about smelling of sweet narcissus.

Philippe tried to fight off the drowsy shroud of approaching sleep but it clung to him as seductively as her scent. He reached down for her hand but caught up a clutchful of diaphanous golden silk. His voice was tempered with a sigh. "Isabel, I must leave."

She had been lying with her face pressed to his groin but at his words she rose up. She was wearing a black silk dishabille, open at the throat. Her hair was caught back from her face with a matching silk crispenette, but it reappeared at her shoulders in spectacular disorder. She was feeding grapes into her mouth with one hand, tracing his skin with the other. "Oh, don't leave yet," she persuaded, "not yet..."

"The banquet is only a few hours away," Philippe reminded her, "and I have things to do before."

It was his sixteenth birthday; the event was being celebrated at a banquet that afternoon at which all his relatives would be present, including the sons and daughters of his uncles Henri, Theobold and Robert. Isabel had met them all before at the Christmas and Easter celebrations—and had not liked them. The Champagnois were particularly obnoxious to her personal tastes. Refusing to acknowledge young Isabel as the French queen, they looked instead to their kinswoman Adele.

"I wish I didn't have to be there," Isabel pouted, resting against him, her face pressed to his belly. Then under her breath she added, "I hate your family."

He heard but didn't answer. It was a familiar argument, a useless one. "I've got to get back," he said finally, sitting up, untangling himself from her, reaching toward the floor for his clothes.

Her expression was petulant. "I never see you."

"You'll see me at the banquet."

She laughed. "I *won't* see you. You'll be surrounded by relatives and I'll be off in the corner somewhere hiding my face."

He was standing beside the bed now, holding his clothes and looking down at her. "You're so beautiful—if you would hide that face you must be mad."

She reached for him. "Don't go yet, stay a little longer." She was without inhibition; at times her boldness astounded him. Delicate arms encircling his waist she pulled him closer. "Please, just a while longer?"

He sank to the bed beside her, thrusting his clothes aside, burying his face in her hair. "What is it you really want from me, Isabel?"

"More than I get," she answered, her fingers tickling his midriff, then reaching lower. "How I love to touch you—you are magnificent!" she breathed, sheathing him between gentle hands. "No one else in the world could possibly own anything so *auguste*, so beautiful!"

Philippe sighed with pleasure at the touch of her fingers. She was so sweet, her caresses so exciting. "You are very amorous for one so young," he muttered absently, his fingers clasping soft strands of her hair.

"And you are very abundant for one so young," she whispered. "Lie back...."

Later, after her touch and kisses had taken away his breath once more, Philippe held her close and stroked her hair for a while. Then reluctantly he sat up, pulling her up with him and she leaned to his bare shoulder. "I wish I could have you all to myself," she mused, "and never, never have to share you with anyone, especially your family."

Philippe's expression was somber as he looked down at her. "You are very spoiled, you know? You've always been your family's favorite, and I think they must have given you your way in everything. You don't like it here Isabel because you aren't the center of attention."

She looked sadly at him, the corners of her mouth drooping. "That is a mean thing to say to me, Philippe. I don't like it here because no one likes me. No one is nice to me. Why can't you understand that? You know what it is to be lonely, you told me how unhappy you were as a little boy." Her eyes were filled with so much pleading that it hurt him to look at her and he turned his face away. "Don't you care if I am unhappy?" she asked. "Don't my feelings matter to you at all?"

Philippe stifled a weary sigh. Whenever he lingered too long beside her she would lapse into melancholy and the familiar routine of pleading for consideration would begin. He eased himself out of her arms. "You ask too much of me," he muttered.

She stiffened in anger. "What I *ask* pleased you well enough only a moment ago," she declared. Then, bitterly, "Well—I don't know why I should expect better. You don't love me at all. Not even a little bit."

He gave her a condemning look. "So what? You don't love me either. All you ever talk about is your damn family. I am sick to death of being silently compared to your precious father and uncle, only to be found wanting!"

"That isn't fair!" she shot back at him. "How dare you say that to me! When was the last time I said anything to you about my family? I know how sensitive you are on that subject—and I *don't* compare you to them!" Then she saw how blanched his face had suddenly gone, and feeling sorry for her anger she made her voice an apology. "Is that what you think?" she asked gently. "Is that how it seems to you?"

"That's how it is!" he snapped. "You are always complaining to me about my family—my mother, my uncles, my cousins. How they snub you, ignore you, insult you. Maybe they do, but if it is any consolation they don't treat me any better. At least you know how much I hate them. I don't wave them like a flag in your face!"

"I don't!" she gasped. "I never do that! I miss them, is that a crime? I love them!"

"How well I know...."

"Why are you so angry?" she asked. "Do you really think I care nothing for you?"

"I don't give a damn how you feel about me," he answered haughtily, making a move to rise. But before he could get to his feet Isabel had flung herself into his lap, her arms tight about his hips, her cheek pressed to his belly. "How can you say that?" she wept, "you *do* care, you *must* care! And I could love you, if only you would be nice to me. You are the only person I have in my life now. I think of you constantly, I dream of you, wait for you to come to me.... I want only to make you happy...don't turn away from me, don't abandon me now as all others have...I couldn't bear it, I couldn't...!!"

He clung to her, feeling her tears anointing his flesh and weakening his control. His arms were so tight about her back that he heard her gasp for breath; but she didn't struggle, didn't try to pull away. Philippe closed his eyes, feeling tears of frustration squeeze past his closed lids. He felt her lips sweet and so moist and eager on his flesh; felt himself convulsed with feelings miserable and wonderful, with such want for her that he bit his tongue till it bled.

When she lay limply against him, kissing his chest and his abdomen, Philippe buried his fingers in the golden tangle of her hair and whispered hoarsely, "Can't you understand? They're all jealous of you—my mother, all my cousins. Let them be jealous —why should it trouble us?"

Isabel twisted around on her back and stared up into his face. "I don't care," she said breathlessly, "I only want to make you happy...." One hand rose gracefully to play at the angle of his jaw.

A shade of softness came over his tense features. "Hold me Isabel," he whispered, "hold me, and never let me go..." She didn't let him finish. Her arms captured him, clinging around his neck, pulling him down to kiss her again and again.

When their lips parted Isabel lay looking up into Philippe's face and she reached up to touch her fingertips lightly to his cheek. "Such black eyes," she murmured softly, "such black, black eyes..." She nestled closer, as if to sleep, and with her eyes closed she said, "I think you are beautiful, my Philippe-Auguste...."

"Don't go to sleep love," he whispered back. "I've got to get up."

"No," she answered sleepily, but she was smiling. After a few moments she rose resignedly from his lap. "Philippe, will you make me a promise?"

He breathed in the sweet smell of her and felt faint. "Anything," he answered, "anything."

"When you go to Rennes for Geoffrey Plantagenet's wedding will you take me with you?"

"That isn't until November."

"I know."

"It is a long trip," he warned, "you don't like to ride, and it is a difficult journey."

"You don't like to ride either," she reminded him with a teasing smile, "and you are going. Do you realize that I haven't been farther away from Paris than St. Denis since I came to live here?"

Her charm was an elixir. "If it means so much to you, yes. But I'm wondering why you want to go."

She lowered her gaze. "Firstly, I don't want to be away from you. Secondly, I *do* want to be away from your family. And finally, because I want to meet all those fabulous Plantagenets I have heard so much about. Please take me."

He tousled her hair playfully, feeling strangely giddy now. "Will you be a good little girl if I say yes?"

She giggled, clutching him around the waist. "I *am* a good little girl...." She nibbled little bites at his chest and midriff, then lower until she had made him vulnerable once more. Knowing he could not ignore her gentle assault, Philippe lay back upon the softness of her bed and closed his eyes, perceiving nothing but the incredible comfort of her mouth.

O N A RAINY September evening Isabel sat in her room at dinner. She was not alone. She might have been, for Philippe was away in Burgundy. But Gilbert of Mons had come from Valenciennes that afternoon and now she sat very close to him, talking enjoyably as they shared a meal from a common plate.

"There is a Norman woman here who cooks special things for me when the Capet family is away," Isabel was explaining, indicating the pork. "I can never have it when Philippe or his mother are at the palace."

"I have heard the stories," Gilbert smiled.

In the glimmer of lapping golden light from the fire, Isabel watched him. He was handsome in the best Fleming fashion: blond, with mysterious dark blue eyes, well-molded, noble features. As far back as her memory extended she could remember him—her father's close friend and advisor. Warming herself in his presence she yet allowed herself a momentary interlude of worry and suspicion. Her instinct (uncanny heritage of a canny family) warned that this call, timed when Philippe was gone, was more than a social reunion. Still she chatted merrily on, glad for the use of her Flemish language once more. "What I wouldn't give for Flemish bread and butter again. The food here is shocking bad." She smiled coyly at Gilbert. "Do you know that the French mock our Flemish butter? They laugh and call it *beurriere.*"

The food spread before them was typical of Isabel's tastes: sweet and diverse. They dined on ham with plum and currant sauce; clotted cheese; herbal sallat (a mixture of sweet peas, curly mint, catnip and pennyroyal); baked eggs flavored with dill and oregano; parsley bread with butter; white pastry with quince and pear stuffing; the cheeses of Champagne, Brie and Blois; cherry wine, and almond milk. Isabel found herself eating with great passion and urgency till she was quite sated. At least eating made her feel stronger, somewhat braver. Her thoughts tightened. Gilbert had so deliberately avoided any talk of her most formidable relative. What could be the reason?

He refilled his henap with cherry wine and looked across at her. He drank, felt the dark sweetness of the wine over his tongue, the warmth in his stomach as the liquid settled there. He reached across the table for Isabel's hand. "You seem to have made a place for yourself here. I am proud of you."

"I have," she answered slowly. "Sully has been good to me, and I have come to trust him. He and Lord Chancellor de Puiseaux have guided my studies." She brightened visibly, "I have read Virgil, Horace—the *Chroniques de France;* Phrygius's *History of the Trojan War;* Bishop Isidore's *Origines,*" Isabel gave a slight giggle. "In the midst of all that I read Marcus Aurelius's *Meditations* of my own accord."

He was watching her more closely than she could realize. He patted her hand gently, feeling the life beneath the fine, smooth skin. She had haunted him for a long time. She was not impossibly younger than himself—and he had always wanted her for himself, knowing *that* in itself was impossible. If Baldwin was eternally grateful to his chancellor, his gratitude did not extend to marriage within Baldwin's aristocratic family. Still, Gilbert entertained his vain fantasies....

"How fares your young husband?" he asked, his eyes narrowing at the blush which painted her cheeks.

Isabel looked away. "I don't see him very often. He is unusual, moody, hard to know. We have a certain compatibility ..." her voice trailed off toward the black corners of the room.

Gilbert caught the inference her voice had betrayed and took his cue from that. "In such case perhaps he would not be averse to taking a little advice from you."

Her apprehension quickened into fear. "Shall I look beyond your words?" she asked him, her gaze playing lightly over his face.

Gilbert gave her a look both emphatic and imploring. "Isabel, I know that above all things on this earth you value your allegiance to your family, and I know despite whatever influences you have experienced here you will never forget that you are a Fleming."

She knew what he was about now and pulled her hands away from him. "What has gone wrong now?" she asked, her voice high-pitched and angry, "and in what way am I needed to alleviate it?"

Gilbert shook his head at the bitter undertone of her words. "We all serve as best we can, Isabel."

She shook her head in wonderment. "And to think I believed that you had come here to visit me, to renew a friendship, to bring me news of home." She was very near tears but the itch of her anger prevailed. "What has my uncle planned this time? He and my husband have had no consortium since their original disagreement."

Gilbert of Mons had not risen to prominence for nothing. His subtlety was as seductive as his voice. "Flanders has never forgiven Philippe for the insults he believes he received at your husband's hand. When Philippe allied himself with his uncles and mother, Flanders was humiliated in the sight of all the world," he explained.

Isabel looked down at her hands, clasped together in her lap, the yellow silk of her sleeves flowing over the whiteness of her skin. "If my uncle thinks that and if you and my father also believe it to be true, then you are misinformed," she insisted. "Philippe loathes his family; they have no power here. If my uncle feels that he has been abandoned by the King of France he should know that the Champagnois have been equally unfortunate. Philippe is the ruler here in deed as well as title." She poured herself a little more of the wine and drank it hastily before she looked across at Gilbert. "Tell my uncle this; if he wants a reconciliation with my husband, he should come to Paris and do so. Philippe and he may not be in agreement but I know that my husband both admires and loves him. The very fact that Philippe and I are still married is a sign of that."

Gilbert leaned closer, his eyes bright and adamant. "I don't think you have grasped the meaning of what I have said, Isabel. And I do not think you are correct when you say Philippe has thrown off the influence of his family. William and Theobold particularly are powerful men in France. William is no dissembler; I don't think he would rise against Philippe. But listen, your uncle has already forged an understanding with Theobold and Stephen of Sancerre. I do not know if they plan a full-scale rising or only a series of political hostilities, but your father believes, and I believe, that if your husband intervenes now he can separate Flanders from both Theobold and Stephen."

The room was suddenly overwarm—the air between them stifling and evil. Isabel's mind was swimming. Could it be true? *It was Gisors all over again.* At this moment she could be sure of nothing. For a few moments she sat with her hands covering her face, afraid to move, afraid to think.

Isabel heard him rise, and then he came to stand beside her, draping an arm about her trembling shoulders. She remained resolute and unmoving, as angry at him this moment as she was with her uncle. It had been Gilbert of Mons who had finally convinced Baldwin of the need to forge an alliance with the French. They had *all* agreed then: Baldwin, Gilbert, Flanders and Philippe. There had been no thought of her. Now it was she who was suddenly the only one who could resurrect a solution.

Even as she turned that bitter thought over and over in her mind, Gilbert spoke, standing close behind her, caressing her temples where her hair was silkiest. "You must convince Philippe, Isabel. Tell him what I told you. Tell him to go to d'Alsace and promise to reassert his influence here in Paris. Flanders is a proud man but he is fond of Philippe and can be swayed by him."

She toyed absently with the fluted silk of his raspberry colored sleeve. "If I can sway Philippe," she muttered sadly.

Gilbert bent closer; her senses surrendered to the cinnamon smell of him; his lips brushed her cheek softly. "There is no one you could not sway," he whispered.

Philippe was sour and unapproachable upon his return from Burgundy. He remained sequestered in his bed for the next week with a violent attack of stomach flu, which he in morbid obsession believed to be food poisoning. He would see no one but de Puiseaux, Sully, and the half-dozen physicians who remained in attendance for the duration of his illness.

It was the third week in October before the young king judged himself able to rise from bed. He celebrated his recovery by making a pilgrimage to St. Denis with Sully, and he did not see Isabel before he left. He had made a purposeful decision to stay away from her.

She was the real reason for his visit to St. Denis; the reason he felt the need to cleanse himself with prayer. His illness had been a crucible, plagued by disturbing dreams—the sleeping evidence of his brooding sense of guilt.

He *was* guilty, he felt shame. In the past he had known many instances of remorse for his relationship with Harry but that was nothing in comparison to the tottering extremes of emotion he felt for Isabel, had felt ever since he had first beheld her. Since that moment he had known no peace.

Isabel was uneasy. She sensed this new estrangement between them. She was brave enough to seek out an explanation from Philippe but she had not been allowed a single private moment with him since his return from Burgundy. Her only hope was that Philip d'Alsace would abandon his antagonisms against her husband. But she knew it wasn't likely.

Philippe was pacing fitfully beside the council table as the Bishop of Rheims sat watching the behavior of his willful nephew.

All at once Philippe stopped abruptly and pivoted around to face the serene bishop. "I am sick of you and the rest of your family trying to run my life!" the king shouted. "You've done nothing but lambast and harass me ever since my coronation. I am of age now, I am the king and I don't have to ask your permission for what I do!"

William sighed with exasperation. "Your father was content to have my counsel. The advice I gave you was not in the way of interference but a suggestion. I don't think it is advisable that you absent yourself from Paris at this time. I know that Geoffrey Plantagenet is your friend, but a trip to Rennes at this time seems extravagant to me."

"Let *me* be the one to decide that," Philippe sneered.

William folded his hands before him on the table and looked with stern fixity at Philippe. "You are the one who is forever suspicious that when your back is turned someone will plunge a knife into it."

Philippe pointed his index finger toward William and defiance was in his voice. "When that happens it will be someone from your family who does it!"

"Stop drawing demarcation lines," William snapped. "We are *your* family as well."

Philippe leaned forward, his palms spread flat atop the table. "Yes," he answered, "that is my particular misfortune."

"Your father was content enough with us as kin," William reminded.

Philippe gave a derisive laugh. "He loathed you, and himself for giving you such power. But Louis was a great fool—too much of a fool to defend himself against the likes of my mother's family. But you'll have no such luck with me, Bishop! I'm not your ward, your plaything, your sycophant! I am king of this land and shall do as I wish in all things! I leave for Rennes today!"

William's eyes were a sad reflection of his inner feelings. "I don't know why you see me, your mother and our brothers as your enemies. We are here to aid you, to support you in all things."

Philippe jerked to a stand-still and glared at William with ill-concealed fury. "Only a bishop would dare to tell such an obscene lie as that! You care nothing for me, least of all for my welfare! The day is coming and coming soon when I shall root out all of you and you shall know who is king in this land! Don't think because your authority is pope-given that it is inviolate. Sweet blood of Jesus Christ, I would take on the pope himself if he opposed me!"

William reached out to take hold of his nephew's arm, but Philippe jerked it away. The bishop shook his head in desperation. "You have a great deal to learn about governing. A king is God's mediator on earth, Philippe—His servant of earthly justice. Your concept of kingship is avaricious, cynical—something taught to you by Philip of Flanders."

The young king's black eyes flashed with anger. "Keep his name off your lips, uncle. That business has nothing to do with you!"

William's calm gaze came to rest upon the far wall where a century-old tapestry depicted a damask-woven Christ suffering in Gethsemane. The bishop held his tongue for a moment, then he spoke. "Not even an earthly king can rule alone, Philippe. He must have God at his head and friends at his side. You seem to think that to rule completely means to rule totally, uncontested and without advice. That is not a *just* man's way."

Philippe's handsome features were set in haughty determination. "Not your way, surely. You would expect me to give up my powers to you. Oh, you weave a pretty motif my righteous uncle:

you speak of God, of justice, and of indebtedness to both. But your slyness is evident behind the morality of your words. I don't trust you, I will never trust you!" Philippe began pacing the floor once more, gripping his hands together as though to constrain the full onslaught of his anger.

William's tone hinted at sadness. "What can I say to convince you that I am not your enemy? How can I prove my loyalty? Secure your trust?"

The answer came from the doorway. "Don't grovel before that brat, William." Both Philippe and the bishop turned toward the open archway where Theobold of Chartres stood with Hughes de Puiseaux. The chancellor didn't move, but the count walked briskly toward them and came to stand beside his brother, though his attention was directed at Philippe, whose answer was a dark glower and a sarcastic remark. "Have you come to teach me my will too, Uncle Theobold? I'll have none of your advice! I've had a bellyful of counsel today."

Theobold was the least amiable of Adele's brothers, the least likely to attempt a truce with his young nephew. A few brisk steps carried him to a place directly before Philippe. "My brothers and I have taken all the sauciness from you we intend to take," he declared sourly. "You had better mend your ways, boy."

Philippe's lips twitched angrily. Reaching to the table he snatched up his crown and set it firmly upon his head. "Or you'll do what?" he snapped. Then he stalked toward the archway where de Puiseaux still stood, an eyebrow crooked in puzzlement. "Come with me!" Philippe spit out the words, and jerked Hughes by the sleeve out into the corridor.

Theobold's sharp expression hardened into a deeper intensity as he looked down at his brother. "Did you tell him, William?" he asked.

"No," the bishop admitted. "I am not a party to this, but even so I will not speak against our brother Stephen, or you. Whatever you and he and Flanders have planned has not been confided to me, and I do not wish to hear it," he lifted his gaze to lock with Theobold's, "not even from you, brother."

Theobold was angry, adamant. "That brat has tried my patience for the last time. It is time he learned that putting a crown upon his head does not insure subjugation of all around him, especially us. He needs to be taught a few lessons."

"He is our nephew!" William argued. "Though his attitude is not what it should be, I have no wish to see France involved in civil war merely to satisfy the greedy lusts of a man like Philip d'Alsace. Why do you wish to join with him? It is *because* of him that we have been edged out of our rightful roles. He cares nothing for our family. His only satiation will be at avenging the ills he believes Philippe has done him."

"That is the satisfaction I long for as well," Theobold answered with finality.

"And I still say I want no part of it," William insisted. "I will say nothing to Philippe of Stephen's plans and your own, but neither will I deliver up the Burgundian border to help you."

Theobold's voice was cynical, annoyed. "That is your decision to make, my brother. But I tell you truly from my heart, I would rather look to a man of Flanders' ability, a proven soldier, than to a boy who orders me about like a serf." He touched William's shoulder. "Join us..."

In his private audience chamber Philippe was speaking in frustrated animation to Hughes de Puiseaux, who listened with indulgence. "Oh, the infernal vicissitudes of this office!" Philippe wailed, his forehead pressed to the wall in despair. "Can a day never pass without insults and humiliation piled upon me by those in my service?"

Hughes placed a reassuring hand on Philippe's shoulder, his fingers light on the rumpled moss-colored velvet. "Don't take on like this. Your uncles are noble men. They wish only good things for you."

Philippe jerked his head up and gave Hughes a fixed stare. "Where did you learn that pretty tale?" he asked scornfully. "In my mother's bed?" He pulled free of de Puiseaux's touch. "You are in league with my mother against me! Your loyalty is to her, not to me!"

Hughes managed a smile. "I am not in league with anyone against you. Least of all your mother. It is true that Adele and I are lovers—where is the harm to you in that?" The smile became a cocky grin. "Rather you should be glad of it. How much better for you that Adele be occupied in amorous matters than to be fiddling with the tools of state."

Philippe sucked his cheeks into hollows. "My mother has the sexual appetite of a she-goat, de Puiseaux. Don't flatter yourself that you are the only one who warms her bed. But she is hungry in all matters, and it is those matters which touch me." He turned his face away and muttered, "The day my mother prefers copulation to chicanery you can be sure she's halfway to St. Peter."

"Calm yourself," Hughes replied, "you are not beset by enemies as you seem to think. When you leave Paris today you may do so in full assurance that I will protect your interests while you are gone." He patted Philippe's shoulder once more. "Is Isabel going with you to Rennes? Or shall she be remanded to me—" he caught Philippe's frown and quickly changed the structure of his question, "to my charge?"

"She is going with me. I told you that last week. Are you so lovesick with my mother's caresses that you cannot keep your wits about you?" He was angry; fear and frustration had pushed him to the very limits of his emotional endurance. Worse even than that was the panic: the terrible dread of losing control in front of others. He succumbed to it too often now. Resentment quickened his resolve to be strong. Philippe drew himself up straight and tall, his long slender neck extended royally. "I wish that I were not taking Isabel with me," he declared, "but I did promise her in the past that I would. Should I leave her behind now I would have to listen to her constant complaints when I returned."

"Surely you can command obedience from her," Hughes offered with a bit of a smug smile, "she is your wife. And she is yet young enough to be ruled."

Philippe heaved a dismal sigh. "Females are incomprehensible to me. What God was thinking of when He made them, I'll never know." His eyes had a distant, troubled look, but then in a second his gaze seemed to snap into focus as he looked at Hughes. "See to all matters for me while I am away. You had better hope for your sake and for my mother's that you are truly my relied ally. For if I find you've been up to any mischief with my uncles against me while I'm gone, you will pay. Every one of you will pay, do you understand that?" He waited only for de Puiseaux's assenting nod. Then he turned and walked away.

G͟EOFFREY PLANTAGENET married Constance of Brittany in all proper solemnity at the great cathedral at Rennes on the 13th day of November, 1181. There was little joy for either in this match. Both parties had lost interest in the intervening years since their betrothal. Constance was twenty-one. She had been engaged to Geoffrey for sixteen years.

Hers was a noble pedigree: she was the daughter of the late and formidable Conan IV of Brittany and Margaret of Scotland. By the age of eight Constance had lost both her parents and was thus turned over to the care of her prospective in-laws, to be brought up with the other Plantagenet children. Quiet, intelligent, exceedingly observant, Constance had grown to hate the Plantagenets, all of them, for their pride, their unspeakable arrogance, their terrible greed for power. Much as Marguerite of France and only a little less than the pitiful Alais Capet, Constance was a life-long victim of Plantagenet plunder.

Now she was married to Geoffrey. Physically he was the image of his lovely mother: crystalline green eyes, dark lashes, black curling hair; a wry, wise mouth surmounting a pointed chin. He also had inherited many of Eleanor's gracious ways: a love of music, a sense of poetry, an artistic spirit of incredible clarity. From Henry he had inherited intellect: a mind hard as a diamond and the smooth, able tongue of a diplomat.

Geoffrey was charming, the most charming member of his family. But his affable, captivating manner was infused with all the personal vanity bred of his mother's Provençal background; all the unyielding ambition of his father's Angevin descent.

Eight years earlier Geoffrey (with the support of brothers Harry and Richard) had joined with Philip of Flanders in an all-out rebellion against Henry of England. Flanders had proved quite an influence over Henry's troublesome sons, who were mesmerized by the Flemish lord's brilliant circle of chivalry. Philip, with no sons of his own to impress, made a habit of affecting others'. In the end Henry had beaten down the rebellion and made individual pacts of peace with each of his sons, but the erosion of loyalty between Henry and them had left its scar.

Of all the Plantagenet princes, Geoffrey bore the deepest stain of resentment against his father. It was a living, breathing hatred, born of a child's adherence to his mother's reviled jealousy; fostered through years of domestic deceptions, betrayals, and family crucibles. The battle lines had been drawn within the familial ranks long ago: young Harry on the side of his permissive, adoring father; Richard clinging firmly in devotion to

Eleanor; Geoffrey somewhere in between. Too cynical to be devoted to either of them, too smart and self-seeking to alienate himself completely from either of them, Geoffrey retained a measure of toleration from Henry and Eleanor, while he silently hated them both.

Years ago upon his betrothal to Constance, Geoffrey had been given the promise of his territorial inheritance, Brittany, while his two older brothers claimed the richer possessions of Normandy and Aquitaine. His own purpose in the Great Rebellion of 1173 had been to create a reassessment of that situation and to force his father's hand. Henry, however, remained obdurate: Geoffrey's inheritance was Brittany, and Brittany was all that he could expect.

Geoffrey had other ideas but his perspective had changed. He was finished fencing with his father; it was to no avail. He was through with looking to self-aggrandizing opportunists such as Philip d'Alsace; they had no personal stake in such a matter. He was done taking the proverbial crumbs which fell from his father's royal table; Brittany was a pittance compared with what Geoffrey felt he deserved. He had made an end of trusting his brothers to stand together with him in loyal opposition to Henry's territorial stinginess. When Geoffrey took his vows on the morning of November 13th, he became the Duke of Brittany. It was the springboard to a new, complex and infinitely more creative political experience than he had been allowed before. This time, however, he had deigned to look outside of his regular circle for a fellow conspirator.

It was a curious family gathering assembled at Rennes in superficial harmony for the celebration. There was Harry and Marguerite (temporarily reconciled and seemingly affectionate); Richard, Count of Poitou and Duke of Aquitaine—the envy of his generation; then there was young John who was handsome and witty but ignored by everyone in the family save his father; and there was the king himself, and on his arm the remarkable Eleanor, liberally set free for this occasion from her imprisonment at Salisbury. Isabel met all these splendid Plantagenets, and she was totally enthralled.

Constance was polite to her but aloof. Tall and regal in appearance, she stood several inches in height above her husband. Her looks were cast in an attractive mold of cool blond seriousness. Isabel noticed how she responded without friendliness when they were introduced, but she understood the reason. Geoffrey and the others had cast many fascinated glances at the young French queen and Constance was jealous. Isabel smiled a little to herself.

Richard was marvelous to behold. He was taller than any man Isabel had ever seen, including her uncle, and he looked more like a king than any man in the room. Blond, with glowering blue eyes (one could get lost in them!), he was an elegant, more polished version of his rugged father. Richard's manner of dress was exquisite; no woman could have outshone him. His rich turquoise robe was of cendal, embroidered with gold and overlayed with jewelry that was magnificent and gleaming.

He was superbly built—a flesh-and-blood god—and Isabel found herself blushing as she stared at his huge and muscled arms. She was too preoccupied gazing up into his face, admiring his beauty, to notice black eyes that smoldered with interest at the same sight.

Richard's touch was light, almost delicate, as he took hold of Isabel's hand and bent to kiss it gently. Straightening up he winked across at Philippe, then smiled down at Isabel. "What a beautiful child you are," he mused, and the sound of his voice was tinged with a southern softness. "Philippe, you must have plucked this jewel from the mines of Solomon."

Philippe stood by, awkward and unspeaking as Isabel returned Richard's approving smile. "From the forests of the north my lord," she answered, "which is not so exotic a place." Then soberly she added, "I am honored to meet so famous a man. I have heard great tales of your military exploits from my uncle."

Beside her Philippe pursed his lips in vexation. Flanders. Always Flanders.

Isabel had never before seen the great reception hall at Rennes castle so she did not know that it was usually a dim and dismal place, for today it had been hung withal in glittering, gay festivity. During the feasting which followed the marriage ceremony, Isabel sat at the trestle table beside Henry Plantagenet's youngest son. John was clever and talkative; she found him companionable, despite the fact that his hands kept straying beneath the table to her thigh. Several times she attempted with good humor to discourage him but his pleasant teasing nature kept her from being angry, for he was more playful than rude.

John was only a little younger than Philippe but he seemed far younger than that. John was so high-spirited, so boyish—and Philippe was dour and serious. "I think you are the most beautiful girl I have ever seen." John whispered close to her ear during the meal. "I wish your uncle had found you for *me.*"

She gave him a deferential, smiling nod but her gaze was drifting farther down the table toward Philippe, who had been drinking heavily all evening, sitting in gloomy and unspeaking isolation from the gaiety around him. His moods were a constant puzzle to Isabel and now she wondered silently what had depressed him this time. Idly she wished she could take him aside, probe his ponderous behavior, but he had been drinking so much she doubted he would pay her any attention. So Isabel turned back to John and they chatted with the amiable distraction of fond strangers. Later when she looked again, Philippe's place at the table was empty.

She found herself looking at King Henry and his wife Eleanor who, though long estranged, sat side by side in seeming cordiality. Even as she watched, Isabel saw them exchange a few whispered words. They were a magnificent pair. At sixty, the Queen of England was still slim and graceful. Her dark hair was only partially streaked with strands of silver; it was braided and swept back, fastened with a small diamond clip in the shape of a flower. Eleanor's face, a classic oval, sat prettily upon her slender neck. Beauty at such an age seemed less of an achievement to Isabel than a miracle. She tried to fix her mind forward, envisioning herself at that age, but the distance between this night and those dim, unlived years was too great....

"Your parents are marvelous," Isabel whispered.

Beside her John gave a little laugh, then went back to his eating.

Philippe stood just outside the castle entranceway, leaning against the frozen stones and listening half-heartedly to the music from inside. It was cold here. A sobering wind had come up from the west, smelling of rain.

He was morose, gloom-ridden. Festive gatherings always depressed him. Tonight he was feeling more alone and outside of
events than he could ever remember. Suddenly he was thinking
of his father, missing him unbearably, burdened by a terrible
loneliness and choked by confusion. His feelings were the ultimate paradox: longing for closeness yet disdaining any show of
affection; weeping alone in the dark for love, yet terrified by the
gift or the giving of it; glorying in his high station, while every
day it bore down more heavily upon him. Philippe's life could not
have been more rent with fears and threatening shadows had
Heaven itself deliberately arranged it so. There was no one to
whom he could unburden himself, no one to help. Flanders
would never be his friend again. Harry was no longer interested.
Isabel was more threatening than the reality her teasing charms
dispelled.

All evening Philippe had watched her with envious eyes, observing her shimmering beauty, the way she had of commanding
the notice and attention of everyone in the room. The entire
Plantagenet family had made a great show over her and it infuriated Philippe to see how she welcomed their indulgent approval.
In this she was very like her uncle and the rest of her kin. The
Hainault family vanity and pride was strong in her.

Disturbed, aimless, Philippe turned toward the hall. Just inside
the entranceway he saw Geoffrey, who stood leaning against an
ornamental stanchion as though waiting. He was drinking from a
richly decorated knight-jug and as Philippe passed Geoffrey's
hand reached out to catch him by the sleeve. Philippe's sharp
profile disappeared as he turned his face slowly to look at Geoffrey and asked, "What is it?"

Geoffrey was turned from the light, his features steeped in
shadow but Philippe could see the glint of cat's-eye green. The
young duke held the henap toward Philippe. "Taste this," he
smiled "it is a cure for everything." To Philippe's quizzical look he
explained: "It is essence distilled from seeds of coriander. It is
very powerful."

Philippe took the henap and drank, instantly recoiling from
the bitter taste. "What on earth could this cure?" he asked. "It
has a very bad taste."

"Boredom, for one thing," Geoffrey smiled.

"Boredom?" Philippe put the henap back in Geoffrey's hand.

"That is an odd condition for a new bridegroom on his wedding night."

Geoffrey's smile was sly, sarcastic. "I have known Constance all my life. She loathes my family, dislikes me, and is generally unappreciative about our marriage. It is not exactly the sort of thing that sends one racing to the marriage bed panting with expectation." He took another drink. "The company of women is rather depressing to me," he admitted, "too many of them tend to remind me of my mother."

Philippe laughed sourly. "How odd you should say that. Most of the women I meet remind me of *my* mother, which is justification enough for not liking them."

"And what of little girls?" Geoffrey asked with a grin.

"If you mean *my* little girl," Philippe answered sharply, "she is like the rest of her family—proud, defiant, infuriating."

Geoffrey gave him a perceptive appraisal. "Ah, but she is so beautiful Philippe, so beautiful. There isn't a man here tonight, or boy..." he thought of his brother John, "who wouldn't like to suck the honey from that little flower. She is a blossom from an unknown garden."

"She's but a child," Philippe snapped.

A shrewd laugh purred in Geoffrey's throat. "You don't believe that unless you are blind. I have never seen anyone so fair."

"Yes," Philippe agreed snappishly, "everyone is constantly taking great pains to point that out to me. I do have eyes of my own."

For a moment Geoffrey said nothing. Then cat-like he moved closer, fingers circling Philippe's elbow, closing gently around the softness of a velvet sleeve. His voice was quelled, discreet, nearly a whisper. "Philippe I've got to talk to you, alone...."

Something in his voice, in the touch, in the green flicker of Geoffrey's eyes stirred Philippe's blood to shivering. His gaze searched Geoffrey's face questioningly, then stopped, centering over his right shoulder. "Your mother is coming," Philippe said quietly.

"Geoffrey, my darling..." her words were sweetly spoken yet underlaced with poison. Philippe found himself staring suddenly down into the face of the only woman his father had ever loved. Despite her age she was lovely. Eleanor slipped an arm around Geoffrey's waist and gave his cheek a light brush with her lips.

She gave Philippe a cruel smile but her words were directed to her son. "Constance has been looking for you. Go along now, pet. I want to talk to your friend."

Geoffrey gave Philippe a quick look, then turned toward his mother. For a moment it seemed that he would say something to her but he merely bent to kiss her lightly on the lips. Then he made his way back to the gathering of people in the hall.

Philippe was immediately uncomfortable. He had never met Eleanor before. She surveyed him in silence for a few moments. "So you are Louis Capet's son?"

"Say whatever it is you want to say," Philippe answered "though for the life of me I can't imagine what you could possibly have to say to me." When she didn't answer he gave her a black-eyed look of disdain in answer to her unremitting stare. "Why do you look at me so?"

He could see the gleam of her teeth as her lips parted. "This is the first time I have truly looked on you. It surprises me that you look so little like your dear father."

Philippe's eyes were coals of contempt. "You mock my father even in the tomb! How can you bring yourself to speak his name after the way you treated him?"

She was amused by his anger. "You had little love for him yourself from what I have heard," she chided. Eleanor gave him a close, sneering inspection and shook her head in pretended dismay. "No, you are nothing like him, at least not from what I can see."

He grabbed her forearm and her bracelets clinked in protest. "Jezebel!" he snarled under his breath. "How I loathe you! Louis was a man until you took his self-respect away, humiliating him before the world with your caprices! My only condolence is that you got back from Henry Plantagenet some of the hell you gave Louis!" Philippe's grip tightened around her arm and he smiled at the look of pain that darted between her eyebrows. He pulled her closer, feeling suddenly all-powerful and aroused to nameless fury. "Tell me, lady, what does an old whore like you do when she's locked away from all the hot temptations of the flesh, from the touch of a man?" He was bending so close to Eleanor that she could smell the wine on his breath; he the sandalwood scent of her hair. She felt her slumbering blood stir at the hardness of his grasp, but her nobility rendered her disdainful and she pulled her arm away.

She faced him with dignity. "You may not have your father's face, but I see that you have his prejudices, boy. Young or old I was never a whore and if he told you differently it was to mask his own deficiencies as a man." Her laugh was a silky thing. "Dear old Louis—all cock and no bull." She tilted her chin prettily. "Tell me Philippe, do you have deficiencies as a man, or merely peculiarities?"

Philippe glowered at her. "What are you saying?"

Another laugh. "Your father spilled his passions into his prayers, you spill your's into my son. Did you think I didn't know?"

"I'd think you wouldn't care," Philippe answered bluntly. "What is it to you anyway? Harry has told me a great deal about you, including the fact that Richard is the only one of your sons you care about."

Her eyes were emeralds on fire. "How little you know. I love all of my sons."

Only the realization of her rank and his kept Philippe from spitting into her face. "Bitch!" he growled, "there are still many people in the Ile-de-France who well remember you and *not* with praises, lady. You've never loved anyone but yourself, and never worked toward the good of anyone but yourself. Even your sons, whom you now claim so solemnly to love, you only nurtured so that you could make them despise your husband. Yes, dear lady, I too have heard things. So keep your sanctimonious self-praises, I don't want them." He turned from her but this time her grasp held him back as her fingers clung to his robe.

"I would have thought you would prefer that delicious little girl to my son," she chided him, "though what either of them could find to celebrate in you I can't imagine. Two such pretty people. And you! Your appearance is slovenly, your manners are gauche, and your disposition is colder than marble buried in snow." She lowered her gaze with deliberate indiscretion. "What is it that attracts my son to you? What hidden charms do you possess?"

A murderous, passionate instinct writhed in him at her words and he lunged forward, grabbing her just below the shoulders, pushing her against the wall. "No charms that would be of any use to an aging goddess like you, if your memory reaches back that far. Or would you have me refresh your recollection?" He leaned closer, bending as though to kiss her.

Eleanor wiggled free of his grasp. "Pig! You have only your father's profound sense of frustration, but none of his graces." In the dimness Philippe could see how her slender neck angled into the elegant line of her jaw. Her smile was odd, frightening. "Our fates are strangely linked Philippe. I dashed all your father's hopes, you built them up again. Yet neither of us could find it in our hearts to love him because he was weak, and we hate weakness." She teased him with a knowing look. "You see, I do know you, and better than you think." He said nothing, and after a moment Eleanor walked away into the light, leaving behind a soft rustle of silk, and the faintly disturbing scent of sandalwood.

It was snowing the following morning when Philippe and Isabel left Rennes. Philippe's disposition was chillier than the weather, and although Isabel rode close beside him, she felt the emotional and spiritual distance between them. She still had not been able to steal a private moment with him and the news brought to her in September by Gilbert of Mons had weighed heavily upon her for six weeks. Philippe's purposeful separation from her had built a wall of silence between them.

She had enjoyed the festivities at Rennes despite fretting over Philippe; she had pleasured in the company of the English royal family. But she was wishing now that she and Philippe had stayed in Paris. Nothing was worth this emotional current of antagonism between herself and her husband. Once again he had locked his feelings away. She knew that his mood was dark, it had been obvious to her during their time in Brittany. But she couldn't understand why. He had been so adamant in his insistence to attend—Isabel knew that his uncles had been opposed to it and that William had counseled him against it—but now he seemed to regret his own decision.

Two days from Paris they halted at Chartres, stopping at the Benedictine abbey there. In the chapter house the small Capetian party was housed in comfort. In the chapel of the abbey Philippe and Isabel took the Sacrament, and heard mass. As they knelt together in prayer before the altar, she surveyed him with a sideways glance beneath lowered lashes. Crowned head bowed, eyes closed, his lips moving in soundless piety, Philippe gave the appearance of peaceful and devout submission. But Isabel who knew his face in light or shadow, could see how tightly the skin was drawn over his cheekbones and jaw, how the nervous muscles twitched in his throat.

From under the gilt close-fitting crown his black locks tumbled uncombed about his face. Her prayers forgotten, Isabel studied his profile closely. The patrician nose and chin, the long black eyelashes sweeping his cheeks, the tense and beautiful mouth. How she loved his face; how she loved every part of his physical being! He was beautiful, so beautiful to her eyes, and at that moment she wanted nothing so much as to hold him in her arms and cover his face with kisses.

Her feeling for him surmounted her sense of time and place: a passion born of a thousand intimate caresses in the firelit secrecy of his room or the blue-damask paradise of her own. Without thought of where she was, Isabel leaned toward him, coiling an arm about his neck, fixing her lips upon his.

She was sorry as soon as she had done it, for though he responded instinctively, after a second he pushed her roughly away. Color had risen in his face but his lips were blanched, and he gave her the most hostile look she had ever seen. Then he turned his face once more toward the altar, bowed his head and continued his prayers.

Isabel felt hot tears of humiliation in her eyes, and the sobs that rose in her throat threatened to strangle her. She put her trembling hands together, clasping them, her mind seeking pious words that were not there. She could feel the tears squeezing out between her pinched lids, wetting her eyelashes and trembling down her cheeks.

After a few minutes Philippe rose to his feet, pulling her up roughly beside him. Without a word he half dragged her down the aisle to the door of the chapel, then yanked her outside into the chilly twilight of evening. Even in the dimness she could see the fury written on his face and she cringed before his towering figure.

"I'm sorry," she whimpered, "please don't be angry with me."

His silence was more vivid than words as he glared with a look that said he hated her. When he did speak his voice was ominously quiet, "Get yourself back to the cloister for dinner, and don't you *ever* do anything again like you just did in there," he jerked his thumb toward the chapel.

Isabel looked pleadingly up at him. "Philippe I'm sorry," she repeated weakly, "I didn't mean to make you angry. I only wanted to..."

His right hand flung out and slapped Isabel's face so hard that she fell backwards and collapsed to the ground. "Get away from me!" he rasped. "*Stay* away from me!"

She was too stunned to answer, too stunned even to cry. Philippe was staring at her as she huddled against the cold ground looking so fragile and vulnerable, and for a moment his features softened just a trace. But before he could give in to his gentler impulses he turned abruptly and started off on the road that led away from the cloister. Isabel watched him walking away from her, watched until the surrounding shadows cloaked him. Only then did she begin to cry.

Less than a mile to the south of Chartres Cathedral was a grove of yew trees. The grove and the cathedral were the only interruptions on the landscape. Between them stretched the barren and shaded plain of Beauce.

Philippe stood, leaning pensively against a tree, thinking nothing, feeling much. It was dark now, too dark to see well, but he could just barely decipher the noble contours of the cathedral.

There was peace here, as much peace as he could ever seem to find. The tantrum with Isabel—the way he had treated her—weighed down his spirit, and he had other causes for self-reprobation. In the fourteen months since his accession he had managed to alienate nearly every significant vassal within the perimeters of the Ile-de-France. His uncles were all thoroughly disgusted by his high-handedness. The Count of Flanders and his clan of Flemish nobles (including Isabel's father, no doubt) were all but severed in their transient loyalties to the French king.

And Harry? That was bitter. *How could England and France ever be allies, Harry?* Philippe remembered saying it to him once; it seemed a long time ago. But it was true. More to the point, Harry knew it to be true. Not one word had passed between them at Rennes; not one word when there had once been so much love. That was where the wound bled worse.

Philippe drew in an ardent breath as though to soothe his soul. There was a pungent scent of rain in the air—a storm hanging onto the coatsleeve of evening. This was a strange place, not new to him; he'd been brought here by his father as a child. Even then Philippe had been engulfed by a limitless thrill. The cathedral of Chartres was built on the ruins of the druidic past: in the crypt was the pagan grotto with its ancient *Virgini Pariturae* ("black virgin") carved by Druids in the hollowed trunk of a pear tree. A pagan relic, a Christian sacristy. Like thousands of pilgrims who came to Chartres to "breathe in the Spirit," Philippe sensed a supernatural magnetism here, as if a rude-faced god lived 'neath the ground. It was not holiness one felt here; it was Life.

Beside him he felt the air stir lightly, caught the scent of sweet narcissus, felt the softness of her hair brush across his hand. Philippe turned swiftly around. Isabel was standing beside him.

She had changed her clothes, uncoiled the plaits from her hair. It hung long and loose, stray strands of it caught up by the breeze. The night hid the color of her chainse, but Philippe could see the glint of silver hanging from her ears—delicate silver webs encrusted with stones. Yet it was her eyes which held him, her eyes luminescent in the shadowed splendor of her face.

She was too wise to speak; she felt his mood. In mute and subtle eloquence she brought his right hand to her lips and kissed it, lingering over each finger in tender salutation.

Shame swept over him at her gentleness, and in an instant he had clasped her in his arms, holding her in a close embrace against his chest. Sweetly her arms went around his neck and she rested her head upon his shoulder. Philippe inclined his head to meet her lips, and in the second before his eyes closed he saw the purpling smear surmounting her cheek where he had hit her.

Her lips were moist, delicate. Her kisses proclaimed a fierce forgiveness. When at last he was breathless Philippe raised his head to look down into her face. God how sweet she was! The night-shadows gave her an eerie beauty; the spell she wove about his senses shaded every thought and feeling, and he whispered, "My blood is filled with you, my body, my soul...."

Carefully he lowered her to the ground, then lay down beside her, his arms still encircling her, his lips against her throat. Isabel clung with fervor to him, inciting, tempting. *This was more than a girl he held in his arms; more than a wife or queen.* She was the living embodiment of a legend, descended from a line more royal than his own. She was the stuff of history—and she was young, and sweet, and willing.

It was not the place he would have chosen, yet suddenly he needed more of her than kisses or caresses. This was what he had fought against since his first sight of her. Even then he had wanted her but the fear had held him back. Now the fear was more intense than ever, but passion melted it into merciful oblivion.

Untangling himself from her streaming hair, Philippe took the hem of her chainse between livid fingers and ripped the heavy velvet up beyond her crotch. Too eager now for restraint, too enflamed to be tender, his hands were strong, pulling her tight against him as he invaded her body, lunging forward and taking her with a violence born of lust and love, frustration and fear. Her responses were rich, provocative and as savage as his own. Philippe had expected at least a pretense of shyness from her but there was none as her avid eyes impelled him and her perfume mingled with the sweet scent of her body.

He clung to her like one under sentence of death, blind to everything but the beauty of her face; until even that vision dimmed and he was drowning, flesh and spirit, within her. Then he sagged upon her body in weariness, and then he slept as Isabel held him, stroking his hair and caressing the crown he still wore.

For a long while Isabel lay motionless beside Philippe in this moody shadowed place as the mist settled over her like a shroud, and then at last she slept. In a dream she waded, sodden-haired, through rushing water—buoyed upwards by the current—her body pleasantly appeased by the sensation, until the power of the water overwhelmed her, and covered her, and she floated to the surface, quite drowned.

HUGHES DE PUISEAUX was waiting for them at the mouth of the *Grande Pont* entrance to the Ile de la Cité. Splendidly dressed in bliaud and braies of white velvet hung with golden tassels, astride a cinnamon-colored mount, he made a noble sight against the dreary grey horizon. Yet seeing him Isabel went a little faint inside. This was no formal greeting. Something was wrong. She sensed it in her soul.

Philippe felt it too. His features grew pale with apprehension as he prodded his horse forward to confer with his chancellor. Unable to hear their spoken exchanges, Isabel watched anxiously. At de Puiseaux's words the young king became animated, and thrust out his arms as though in disbelief. Unmoving, too fright-ridden to think, Isabel watched as de Puiseaux produced a folded document and handed it to Philippe, who read it with darting attention. When he had finished, or perhaps before, he threw it to the ground, jerked his horse around and trotted it back toward the royal cortège.

Isabel felt her stomach muscles jerk and her throat go dry as Philippe drew his horse up beside hers. His florid expression told her that something terrible—something terrible involving her— had once again threatened him, and she cringed.

"Your uncle!" he bellowed at her, "your damned uncle has got together with my uncles Theobold and Stephen and the Duke of Burgundy as well to make war on me and invade the eastern borders of the Ile-de-France!"

Anger surmounted her fear of him and she shouted, "Why are you blaming me? You said that *your* uncles are involved as well!"

Philippe leaned forward, his face so close that he might have kissed her but instead he gave her a cruel and accusing look. "You knew of this! Why didn't you tell me?" When she didn't answer he continued, "De Puiseaux told me that Gilbert of Mons came to Paris in September while I was away. You saw him—he must have told you something. You deliberately kept it from me —*why*? Blood of Jesus Christ, I swear you are a worse traitor than your uncle is."

Isabel's hands flew out, grabbing blindly for him but he swatted them away, ignoring her entreaty. Tearfully she persisted. "I didn't tell you because I never had the chance! When you came back from Burgundy I never had a moment alone with you— you ignored me all during the trip to Rennes and while we were there..."

"I would have listened if you had made it known that you had urgent news that would not wait!" he shouted, trying to keep his nervous horse steady beneath him. "You purposefully kept that

information from me to give your uncle a chance to put his conspiracy into action!"

"I would *never* do such a thing!" she cried, "you *know* that I
wouldn't!"

"I *don't* know!" he shouted back, impervious to the scene they
were playing in public. "That adoring uncle of yours has done
everything in his power to frustrate and debase me. Now you
have helped him gain time. What were you doing at Chartres,
trying to soften the blow you knew would be waiting for me upon
our return? What a scheming little bitch you are! Well you'll have
no further chances to use your charms on me because I am finished with you. No matter what happens, I am finished with
you!"

"Philippe!" she screamed, still reaching for him, but he had
already turned away. "Take her back to the palace," he shouted
to Robert of Clermont, then gestured with a wave of his arm to
Hughes de Puiseaux. Isabel felt her horse being urged forward
by the bodyguard and in desperation she turned back. "Philippe!" she screamed, "Philippe!!" A sense of peril seized her
with such force that she shrieked frenzy to the sky till blackness
swam before her and she fell forward. One of Philippe's men was
quick to gather her into his arms before she could fall and be
trampled beneath the hoofs of the horses. At that moment it
would have been the kindest favor heaven could have granted
her.

Less than a week after his marriage to Constance, Geoffrey of
Brittany was called away from Rennes on the order of his father.
The young duke was obliged to ride the ninety-five miles to Le
Mans in a swirling snowstorm. When he arrived at his father's
fortress on the evening of the third day, it was Richard who
greeted him.

"Where is Henry?" Geoffrey asked, stomping the wet snow
from his boots and tossing off his drenched cloak and mantle.
"His message was so urgent I thought for certain you and Harry
had started another rebellion against him."

"Nothing as bad as that," Richard answered, watching Geoffrey cross the expanse of the hall toward the fire. "Harry is here,
in fact, upstairs somewhere sleeping off a hangover. I'm not even
sure what father wants from us, he hasn't told me yet. I think he

wants to talk to the three of us together." He followed Geoffrey, stopping at the long wooden table to pour a henap of wine which he gave to his brother.

Still trembling with the cold, Geoffrey turned from the fire and accepted the drink without a word, eyeing his brother as he drank. Richard was always magnificently dressed, no matter what the occasion. Tonight he was wearing a blue velvet tunic with gold-braided surcoat. Geoffrey smiled to himself. Richard wore blue as often as he did to emphasize the color of his eyes. Geoffrey knew of his older brother's many submissions to vanity, including the fact that Richard used a mixture of lemon and saffron to lighten his hair. Richard was an unflagging egotist, and no one knew that better than his astute younger brother.

"You look like a drowned cat," Richard scoffed in answer to Geoffrey's silent appraisal. Reclining against the back of the wooden chair, Richard propped his feet on the table. "Come sit, my brother—have another drink with me and tell me how you like wedded life."

Geoffrey settled himself across from Richard and poured himself more wine. "I hardly know." Richard pushed the platter of bread and beef across to him but Geoffrey declined with a shake of his head. He reached into the inner folds of his bliaud for the leather-wrapped pouch, extracted it and withdrew a rolled stem of rice paper filled with sage and hashish. Pulling the table candle close, Geoffrey stuck the slender roll between his lips and lit it. Observing Richard's raised eyebrow, he explained, "This is the only way I can face the patriarch. Otherwise I can't even talk to him."

"Well he doesn't approve, I can tell you that," Richard reproved him stoically.

Geoffrey laughed without restraint. "And of course he *does* approve of all the other things we do. Of your drinking and plundering and your pretty French boys; of Harry's debaucheries and his gambling and devotion to his cups; of Johnny's quirky pastimes and adolescent penchant for whores—a few months ago he deliberately set the hair of some dirty little kitchen slut on fire, did you know that?" He leaned back in his chair, resting his aching muscles. He flashed a sarcastic smile at his brother. "Oh, she didn't die, by the way. Yes—father has so much to admire in all of us. Just as we have so much to admire in him. . . ."

Richard's expression was serious as he surveyed his brother's face. "It isn't so very amusing. I've had my belly full of this dissension we've had to endure as our birthright; our inheritance of being part of this accursed family."

Geoffrey gave his brother a mocking smile. "You've said it often enough: *From the devil we came and to the devil we will go.*"

Richard didn't answer. He sat gloomily, his head thrust forward, melancholy chafing at his soul. Geoffrey watched him closely: the set mouth, the stalwart jaw, eyes like cut sapphires that always managed to convey a hard and cynical expression. Despite resembling his father so much, Richard had a very different bearing. Henry's countenance was so energetic he seemed animated even in moments of inactivity. Though Richard was equally vigorous, unmoving his aspect was one of heaviness; phlegmatic and unyielding.

Richard sensed Geoffrey's scrutiny and answered with a dark scowl. "What in hell are you staring at?"

"I'm trying to comprehend your mood," Geoffrey answered lightly. "I will admit I expected a choicer welcome than this: you sunk in gloom, father and Harry nowhere to be seen. I am tired. I've been riding for three days."

"Stop complaining," Richard muttered. "I've already ridden for a fortnight without pausing more than two days in between, and then for battle...."

Geoffrey swooned pleasurably in the influence of forgetfulness, but his wits were still sharp and he laughed aloud at the seriousness of his brother's words. "Richard, you are talking to *me*, not some pretty ballad-singer to impress with tales of bravery and fortitude. I've lived in the shadow of your glory for years. Spare me the chivalrous details tonight."

Richard's mouth curved into a sour expression. "What would you know? Like Harry, you only play at being a soldier."

"Calm down—I'm not in the mood for this," Geoffrey snapped. "I'm tired. I'm going to bed." He made a move to rise.

"Sit down," came the command from across the room. Neither of them had noticed Henry Plantagenet standing at the entryway to the hall. At his words Geoffrey slumped reluctantly back into his chair.

Henry contemplated his sons in silence for a moment, then walked briskly toward them. He patted Richard's shoulder as he passed, then came to stand beside Geoffrey. After only a moment of hesitation he bent and kissed his son on the cheek. Then he flung himself into a chair beside Geoffrey. "I'm glad to see you got here so quickly. Did you have a difficult journey?"

"It snowed all the way," Geoffrey answered, "and I would be interested to know what it is that was important enough to drag me away from Rennes less than a week after my marriage."

"It is regrettable but necessary," Henry answered firmly. "How is Constance?"

"Probably happier than when I left her," Geoffrey chuckled. "Somehow I don't think my presence enthralls her."

"Then you shouldn't mind being dragged away."

Geoffrey narrowed his eyes and set his lips tightly. "Is this a guessing game? I presume what you wanted to say is important, so would you kindly enlighten us? I've been traveling for three days, and since I don't have Richard's remarkable capacity for endurance, I would like to sleep."

Henry poured himself a drink and folded his arms across his chest. "Philippe Capet needs our help. I've learned that the Count of Flanders plans to invade the Ile-de-France with the help of Hugh of Burgundy and two of Philippe's Champagnois uncles. We have got to end this before it goes too far to be stopped."

Geoffrey nodded, saying nothing, but Richard was instantly angry. "Why can't Philippe fight his own battles? I've got enough trouble trying to keep peace in Poitou. Why should I have to involve myself and my men in some family spat between the Capetians and the Champagnois?"

Henry slammed a fist down violently upon the table. "You will do it because I order it!" he shouted. "Damn you, I want peace on the continent! You should be smart enough to know that we all have too much to lose if war breaks out in earnest between those two factions. And as for keeping the peace in Poitou, you could do that easily enough if you weren't constantly pitting one baron against another like dogs in an arena. Jesus, haven't I taught you anything?" After a moment Henry sighed heavily, dispelling some of his anger. When he continued his tone was subdued. "So far I believe Flanders has been bluffing, but we can't be sure. I've been told he tried to drag Frederick of Germany into this business, but he refused, of course."

"I wouldn't trust Frederick," Geoffrey remarked with coolness, "you have had your share of disputes with him in the past. And remember, with Philip d'Alsace there is always room for worry. He is the most persuasive man alive."

Henry gave his son a disparaging look. No matter what he said, Geoffrey would be waiting at the other end of the conversation with an antagonistic, divergent opinion. How like Eleanor he was, even to his all-knowing smile and those mocking, deceptive green eyes. "I think I know Frederick's mind at least as well as you do, Geof," Henry said with finality. "He is a wise man, and knows better than to be taken in by one of Philip's ridiculous attempts at seizing power. By God's teeth I thought Flanders himself had more sense than that."

Harry came into the room just then, trailing sleepily over to the fire. He stood there for some time, gazing vapidly into the flames. "Come over here and sit down," his father ordered. "I *told* you that I wanted to speak to the three of you together. Christ, can't you stay sober long enough to carry on a conversation?"

Harry slumped into a chair beside Richard and gazed passively across at his father and Geoffrey. "I already know what this whole thing is about."

"Why are they fighting anyway?" Richard asked. "And why are you siding with Philippe Capet? Flanders has been your friend for years."

"Give or take a few miscellaneous difficulties," Geoffrey injected with a prodding smile, letting his gaze circle the table before coming to rest firmly on his father's face. He was referring to a forbidden topic of conversaton—the Great Rebellion of 1173 when he, Richard, Harry and Eleanor had banded together with Philip d'Alsace and his brother Matthew of Boulogne against Henry. Flanders had been the real instigator of the plot (which had also had the tacit approval of Louis of France). Only the death of his beloved brother had sent Philip home, besotted with grief and quite suddenly uncaring of what happened between the English king and his sons. That was the Flemish way. No matter how excessive ran their lust for power, their blood ties held as chains.

It was not so within the brooding ranks of the Plantagenet clan with their fierce Norman pride and Angevin maleficence. Henry felt distrust strong in his blood now as he stared across at Geoffrey and his voice bore a warning tone. "That matter is a closed subject," he declared. "I forgave all of you for that. I've told you what I expect from the three of you in this business, and by God you will do it!"

"Philip d'Alsace is a great soldier," Richard mused, "and though unlike them," he indicated his brothers, "I have no personal feelings of friendship toward him, I respect his abilities. Let Philippe Capet stand against him if he can, but why should we involve ourselves?"

Henry's decision was unalterable. "For the same reason I put a stop to the Champagnois plots against him in the past and then tried to reconcile him with his family. Philippe is the rightful king and I will not be a party to any attempts to harass him."

"How very noble of you," Richard sneered. "But I cannot agree. If he is unable to control his family and his barons; if they feel constrained to band together with his former mentor in a covey of dissent against him, then I say he's in more trouble than we can allay." He emptied the rest of his wine into his mouth and set the henap down with a bang of irritation. "Personally, I don't think we should bother ourselves. Besides, he's an impudent snot. And I don't have to remind you, Father, he has no feelings of fondness for you."

"Well he does for me," Harry interrupted, "and I think that Father is right. We should help him. Poor Philippe. He's still only a boy and no match for feckless dissemblers. God knows I warned him against the treachery of Flanders, but he wouldn't listen to me."

Richard's laugh was goading. "That's very interesting coming from you, Harry. There was a time when you couldn't open up your mouth except to say glowing things about Philip d'Alsace. Now you would take an adversary's position against him? What a queer world we are living in."

"My admiration for Flanders has nothing to do with this!" Harry insisted with vehemence. "There are many things about him still to my liking—he is the greatest soldier of our day, the very heart and soul of chivalry."

"The good William Marshal would be ill-at-ease to hear you say that," Geoffrey inserted. "He is your current mentor, is he not?"

Henry slammed his fist down on the table and beside him Geoffrey started. "I've had all the shit from you three I intend to take!" the king shouted. "None of this bantering has anything to do with what I'm talking about! Your opinions of Flanders are of no importance to me. God knows you've all taken your turn at adoring him, admiring him, giving him ten times the respect any of you have ever shown me. Well that's past—and I say he's pestered the French boy once too often. So many of the French barons have joined the revolt against Philippe, he needs our support in the field." After a pause he finished: "He is Louis's boy, and I don't want to see him lose face because of any unsavory plots against him."

Richard was incredulous. "And *that's* your reason for involving us? Because he's Louis's boy? Since when did Louis Capet mean so much to you?"

Henry's grey eyes narrowed as he looked at Richard. "I would never expect you to understand," he finally said, "you're not a father, and you've never been a son."

"So you've said, and often enough," Richard answered under his breath.

"Spare me the rebuke," Henry answered sharply, getting to his feet. Brisk steps carried him toward the archway entrance of the hall where he stood for a moment. Then he turned back to them, his gaze steady and accusing. "There was a time when the combined treachery of you three broke my heart. I've since learned to live with it. I'm not asking for your love, I'm summoning your obedience. As your king I can still command that." He paused. "I'll see all of you in the morning. Goodnight."

Isabel's frenzy had given way to physical collapse and finally pneumonia. For weeks she wavered between this world and the next, as though undecided whether she wished to live or die.

The finest physicians in Paris attended to her but seemed powerless to restore her vitality. Sully, fearful for her life, remained in daily attendance. Edythe never left her side, even sleeping on the floor beside her bed. During Isabel's brief periods of consciousness they forced food into her; more often than not she remained in a stupor that resembled death. Awake or asleep—conscious or insensible—she cried out for Philippe.

On Christmas day Sully gave her Absolution, fearing that she would be dead by nightfall. But by evening she sat up suddenly as though recovered. The physicians charged her to stay in bed till after Epiphany. Isabel was shocked to learn how much time had come and gone during her illness. She remembered it only in vague and shadowy flickers: Edythe's tender ministrations, Sully's kind face above her like a saint beckoning her to heaven.

Days of inactivity intensified her present misery. All news was being kept from her, perhaps deliberately. She had no idea of what had transpired between Philippe and her uncle. She tried to pray. The words came from her lips in practiced religiosity but they were empty of meaning, emptier of hope.

Isabel was terrified, panicked by the secret that she had kept from everyone, most of all herself. She had tried to wall it up in her mind, banish it, destroy it. But truth, though it can be imprisoned, can never be killed.

The evidence of her fear fell in stinging tears to the silken bedcovers. She had endured Philippe's early indifference and enigmatic moods. She had gloried in his body and gorged on it. She had withstood his physical cruelties and even this most recent mortification. All that she had endured. But this last treason was the worse, because it was of her own making. Isabel had surrendered herself finally—fatally—and now she would never be free again. She knew now that she loved him.

Thirty-nine of the most powerful barons in France had joined the revolt against Philippe Capet. Their prime incentive had been his indifference toward them; they had also been swayed by the entrance into the controversy of the charming Stephen of Sancerre—his *largess* to French nobility gave him credence with them. The formidable combination of Philip d'Alsace and Hugh of Burgundy only strengthened the barons' conviction that Louis Capet's son had lost all chance of respect among his subjects and his peers. Although Philippe had retained the loyalty of the noble lords of Paris, that was scarce advantage to the peril he faced now in the field. The young king of France was totally untrained as a soldier.

By the middle of December, d'Alsace and Count Stephen had maneuvered their combined forces some sixty-five miles northwest of Paris at Beauvais on the fringe of the Ile-de-France, while Hugh of Burgundy had moved his troops to Valois, virtually hemming in Philippe's domains on the northern borders. The situation had sent the young monarch, with Hughes de Puiseaux and five hundred loyal knights, fleeing for Chantilly, thirty-five miles directly to the north of Paris. There, only a few days before Christmas, Philippe received word from William Marshal that Henry and his sons were coming to the aid of the French.

King Henry himself did not take the field but his three sons did, with a combined fighting force of over three thousand men. That news, quickly circulated, was enough to detach the Duke of Burgundy from the coalition and by the end of the month he had recalled his men to Auxerre.

Count Theobold of Chartres had also been diverted from his revenge against Philippe. His brother Henri of Champagne had fallen ill at Châlons, and Theobold had abandoned the Flemish-Champagnois coalition to be at his side, leaving only d'Alsace and Stephen to head the rebellion. That combination still represented a considerable threat to the security of the Ile-de-France and would have been enough to give Philippe Capet a sound drubbing in the field.

But on the third of January, a combined force of Norman, Breton, and Poitevan knights under the generalship of Richard Plantagenet swept the rebels from the field at Beauvais, sending Counts Philip, Stephen, and the major portion of their contingent fleeing east toward Compiégne. There, Henry's sons and their men had such a decisive victory that Stephen's forces fled their leader for the safety of the Loire Valley.

Philip d'Alsace's men did not flee. They took up sanctuary with him and the Count of Sancerre at Flanders' fortress at Crepy-en-Valois on the Oise. There they sought to regroup their strength, but before long the Plantagenet forces surrounded the chateau. Within three weeks the Flemish-Champagnois coalition was disbursed, their leaders virtually starved into submission.

Henry negotiated the truce, calling for a future meeting at Gisors in April when a formal treaty would be signed by all parties. Until that time the counts and their men were bound by oath not to breach the peace or congregate in unlawful action against the King of France.

Throughout the entire campaign Philippe Capet had remained submissive to the will of Henry and his sons, while marveling in silent envy at the fighting abilities shown by the three

Plantagenet brothers. While the danger persisted Philippe had been too uneasy to worry over the tremendous loss of prestige which he'd brought upon himself by allowing a covey of outsiders to conduct his war for him. But once the surrender had been assured and then accomplished, he felt totally unmanned by the experience. The victory (the *relief*) was his, but he'd had no part in its making. It was a sobering admission of his own weakness and inexperience. Only his pride kept him from displaying those feelings in the view of his benefactors.

Philip d'Alsace was infuriated by the turn of events. Though he made a public show of great civility, he was furious with Henry for having interfered. He and the English king had been comrades and enemies in turn, but Flanders felt betrayed. He had cause to ponder what bond had been sealed between Henry and Philippe behind his back.

So it was finished, for now. Stephen of Sancerre packed up his injured pride and shattered expectations, returning to the Loire Valley. Flanders went north to Ghent to brood over his latest setback. Young Philippe Capet was becoming an obsession with him. For the past year and a half Flanders had known nothing but frustration and defeat at his hands, and his desire for revenge was strong. It was no longer a case of fighting for the renewal of his own power in France. Flanders wanted Philippe undone. But for that sweet satisfaction, he knew he would have to wait....

IT WAS A COLD evening and the snow was falling outside, but Isabel remained at the window of the palace archives library watching the flicker of a hundred candle flames tracing a path across the *Petit Pont* to the Orléans road on the opposite bank. The pilgrims were Benedictine monks of Saint-Barthelémy and Saint-Magloire from the Ile de la Cité, in procession on their way up to St. Denis.

February the Second—Candlemas. As usual Isabel was alone. She had not seen her husband for over nine weeks. No one had even troubled to bring her information concerning the rebellion against him. Hughes de Puiseaux had left Paris with Philippe and, like his king, had not yet returned. Sully had spent the

weeks following Epiphany at Montmarte; she had not seen or
spoken with him since the end of December. Even William of
Rheims who had spent Christmas in Paris had left shortly there-
after. All the Champagnois family had convened in Châlons to
mourn the death of Henri, the scion of the Champagne-Blois
clan and Philippe's formidable uncle.

Shivering, Isabel stayed at the undraped window, breathing in
the freshness of a solemn winter night. Even noisy Paris was
quiet tonight. It was the snow which brought the hush. It buf-
fered every sound, whitened every dark place.

Isabel pulled the silver fox-fur mantle tighter about her
shoulders and retreated to a chair beside the fire. This room,
lapped in light from torch and fire glow, provided more than the
adequate light to read, but her eyes ached from hours of reading, and her distracted mind repelled any further concentration.

She sat, very small in the enormity of her confusion, feeling
pity for herself. It was a weakness which had become all too common for her since the enforced separation from Philippe, and
especially considering the *way* they had separated. Her illness
had created an added sting to her situation, and aimless time
spent in convalescing had invited bitterness.

*The stewards and serving girls brought her food and drink, banked the
fire, lit the torches when it grew dark. Their servile silence unsettled her,
but the endless questions from Edythe and the physicians irritated her
more. Did she feel better? Was she growing any stronger? Couldn't
they see how unhappy she was, and if so, could they not leave her alone?
Isolation was melancholy, but isolation with constant interruptions and
questions was near to madness. Quietly contemptuous, she retreated to the
silence of her own thoughts. Let them ask their questions. There was still
one thing she had managed to keep secret.*

Isabel had carried that secret in her body for sixty-five days,
until a midnight seizure of abdominal agony had yanked it from
her. That was one week ago this night and still she had told no
one. It was improbable that she ever would. Feelings of ambivalence shamed and subdued her. She wanted no living thing
growing, tumorlike, inside of her. She was too young. Her future
was too murky. Child-bearing—specifically, the birth of a male
heir—was the only security any queen could ever know. Isabel
realized this, yet she recoiled from it in secret dread. She did not
know why. And still it haunted her.

Isabel lingered beside the fire a while longer before wearily ascending three sets of curving stone stairs to the fourth floor. *Exile.* Tonight the narrow corridors beckoned; ghostly and cheerless, airless and cold. A flickering fragment of a shadow preceded her down the passageway. Isabel halted, tense and waiting. A soft, dead echo. A sob. Then silence. The whispering residue of seven centuries. Gloom. Endless and eternal. She paused in brief futility beside the covered archway to Philippe's darkened room, then walked on, dispirited.

It was Baldwin who brought Isabel the news of Philip d'Alsace's surrender the following morning. Isabel was still in bed, reclining in lassitude, her spirits dark as the visages of the nightmare she could not remember.

Baldwin's presence animated her, though the immediate joy at seeing him soon gave way to tears and for a long while she wept in his arms. Finally she raised her head from his shoulder and drew a strand of hair across her face to wipe away the moisture. "I'm sorry, Father," she explained, "but I've been so unhappy, and then to see you, and as the bringer of good news, is a more welcome sight and sound than I have had in many a fortnight." She thrust aside the covers and leapt from the bed. "Let me put on my clothes, then we can take a meal together, and sit here beside the fire and talk. I feel quite suddenly hungry." She turned from her dressing mirror to look at him. "It is because you are here, and I am happy."

Baldwin appraised her silently. She was small, her limbs curved and delicate, but she was richly and beautifully developed for one so young. The sight of her naked breasts stirred him and he looked away.

Isabel pulled a black velvet dishabille over her head and went over toward the fire where she sat combing her hair for a long time. When she looked up, Baldwin was standing before the undraped window. His profile cut sharply against the grey background of baleful clouds. Isabel could sense the malaise, the sudden restlessness. The profile disappeared as he faced her. "I'm deeply troubled by all that has happened. I feel helpless, thwarted at every turn." He drew a breath as though he meant to say more, but the sound as quickly trailed off to silence.

She ran to him, her arms outstretched. Baldwin caught her up, holding her close, his cheek resting on the top of her head. "It isn't your fault," she said quietly, "don't blame yourself."

"I do," he insisted, "I've never stood up to Philip—never, in all the years of our association. I should have fought against your marriage. I should have refused to hand you over as a sacrifice to his ambition."

She should tell him the truth but she couldn't, so she clung weakly to him with a lie on her lips. "I haven't been so unhappy, and everything would be better if Uncle Philip would cease this continual fighting with my husband."

Baldwin set her down with a dour appraisal. "He'll never stop."

"But if King Henry intervened on Philippe's side," Isabel reasoned, "doesn't it compel uncle Philip to keep the peace?"

Baldwin shook his head. "No one can compel Philip d'Alsace against his will. Fighting is his trade, he does it better than anyone. Henry has a country to govern—he can't stand vigil over my brother-in-law forever and don't expect him to come to your husband's defense at every turn, either. No treaty will hold your uncle back when he wants revenge. He'll never forgive Philippe." Baldwin sighed with finality and turned back toward the window. "So far he's left me out of it, but the time will come, Isabel, when he will expect me to join with him against your husband—and then what course can I follow?"

Isabel had never seen him so distressed and it sent her into tremors of panic. "What do you mean?" she asked, though she feared his answer.

He brushed past her and went to stand before the fire, rubbing his palms together to warm them before slumping into a nearby chair. "You know exactly what I mean," he answered after a long silence. "The time will come when Flanders decides to call my loyalties in, expecting me to ally myself with him against Philippe." He toyed idly with the rings on his left hand as he spoke.

Slow, measured steps brought her to his side and her voice trembled a question. "But you would never do that, would you?"

His eyes, sea-green like her own and troubled, gave her a wordless answer. Isabel dropped to her knees before him, her clutching hands imploring his reassurance. "But he has just been put down, surely that is evidence of something!"

He grasped her hands roughly, leaning forward, looking directly into her face. "He fought a combined force of Henry's men and those of his three sons! That is something very different than he would face in fighting me. Flanders has five times the knights in his service than I have; he has a richer treasury, more powerful allies—and he is hard upon my own borders. This is a fear I have lived with ever since he and your husband first quarreled."

She smothered her face against his thigh while his hands stroked her hair gently and she wept. "Oh, Father, what are we going to do? I'm so afraid for all of us."

The hair that he loved shimmered beneath his touch and he skimmed his fingers lightly over it. "It is the fault of the world in which we live. I have always wished to be a man of peace and yet all of my adult years I have been forced into continual fighting. Barely a season has passed that I have not been at the head of an army, fighting to preserve my lands." The tone of his voice was thin and barely audible, as though he were speaking to himself. "Oh, my dearest child, the world is topsy-turvy. How I wish I could bequeath a better one to my children."

She raised a tear-moist face to look at him. "I trust you. I trust you even if I trust no one else."

Baldwin raised her up and pulled her closer till she nestled on his lap, facing him, her head upon his shoulder. "And you are everything to me Isabel. I would give you the soul out of my body."

There was a time when those words, spoken by him, would have been enough. They no longer were. Isolation, sacrifice, and the oppression of anxiety had shaded her character with cynicism. "Why didn't you come to me before this?" she asked suddenly, her fingers playing at his jawline. "Since first I came here to Paris I hoped and prayed that you might visit me, relieve me of some of my loneliness, if only for a few days. But you never did. Why?"

Baldwin grasped her shoulders roughly, shaking her, and his voice was angrier than Isabel had ever heard it. "Don't you understand? You don't belong to me anymore." His expression had gone disturbed and curious, his lips were set tight. "Has he *had* you yet? Has he?"

She turned her face away. "Oh, Father..."

His hands slid from her shoulders, down the length of her

back, exploring her contours, lingering over her. "You were *mine* first, Isabel," he breathed. "You were mine."

It was so cruel of him to remind her of that now, when twelve times twenty miseries had rendered her helpless and despairing. She closed her eyes against the tears, trying to forget that he was the one who had sold her into this unhappy life. The truth fought for expression, and the tears traced her cheeks, falling upon his hands.

Tears of pain.

More like bleeding than crying.

Adele of Champagne had reacted to the in-family conspiracy against her son with characteristic vitriol. She had not been a party to it; and since neither Stephen nor Theobold had confided their intentions to her, she was furious. Now, with the familial ranks of the Champagne/Blois clan split into yet another faction, the dowager queen took decisive control of the situation, and she brought the public discord to an end even more surely than Henry of England had done.

She was angriest at Stephen. She had always known that he was a vain fool, but he was her family favorite so her judgment was tempered by leniency and love. To this point she'd always managed to keep him adherent to her will. Now he'd both disappointed and infuriated her. Upon her return to Paris in mid-February she sent word to him in Sancerre, summoning him to the capital.

He sat before her now, swallowed by the dense shadows of Adele's purple-draped apartments. Intermittent firelight shimmered and faded across his features as he sat, his head slightly inclined, seemingly submissive to his sister's will. She was pacing nervously up and down, up and down the space of floor directly in front of him, tugging at the several long plaits of her hair with distracted and fluttering fingers as she muttered angry, half-audible phrases.

First she had berated him with harsh invective, now she was intimidating him with furious silence. Stephen was accustomed to her moods and generally successful at mitigating them. He tried now, raising his head to meet her angry eyes. "Darling sister, I have told you I am sorry. It was more Flanders' fault than mine, as I explained. He is a convincing, misleading man. And after the way Philippe has behaved toward you and all of us in the past, is it any wonder some of us should seek revenge?"

Adele stood still, standing very straight, her hands resting on her hips as her full bosom heaved in unexpelled anger. "He is *my* son, he is the king of this land. Nothing shall imperil that!"

Stephen came to stand beside her, taking hold of her hand, their shoulders touching. They were nearly the same height. He peered closely into her face. "There was a time when you were willing enough to take up arms against him, Adele. His attitude toward us has not changed, why then has your own?"

Adele's eyes flashed in answer. "How can I make you understand? You owe your power to *me*, Stephen. To me and my ability to produce a male heir. If I had failed as his other wives did, you would be only a petty noble with a handsome face and an aristocratic pedigree." She jerked her hand from his. "How is it that you cannot see that, Stephen? Do I have a count for a brother, or a pigeon-brained imbecile?"

Stephen shrugged off her rebuke with a flippant smile. "I have apologized. You have control of things once again. But I will say this, sweet sister—if I were you I would keep a tighter rein on Philippe, though I think you have already lost him. Flanders or no, without Philippe's compliance we have lost all power in any case."

Adele's hands were busy unbraiding the thick black plaits of hair which fell over her shoulders. "We have *not* lost power!" she shouted into his face; then quieter: "With Flanders safely removed to the north, we can only grow stronger. My son respects my abilities and my intelligence—and he is clever enough to use them to his own advantage. That gives me power. Your power, and Theobold's, and William's—and young Henri's now that our brother is dead—will be indivisible from my own." She clenched a handful of ebony hair in her fist. "But you must trust me, Stephen, and listen only to me." Her expression softened. "If you love me you will promise to be guided by me."

Stephen stood looking at her, as enthralled by the mastery of her mind as the beauty of her form. She had been neatly unlacing the tight bodice of her pellison and as she finished she let the heavy velvet wrap slip to the floor, exposing the thin silk of her chemise. Stephen drew nearer, reaching for her. Adele allowed him to strip the sheer garment from her body. Her eyes downcast, she shivered a little at the feel of his hands, cold on her exposed flesh, but the sensation was pleasant. Gently she brought his hand to her lips, kissing the knuckles. "Will you do as I say? Will you be guided by me and me alone?"

His hand fondled hers. "I have always been guided by you sweet Adele, from the time we were children...."

Her black eyes were languorous. Stephen—how she loved him! Drawing him into her arms, her breasts pressed to the rich embroidery of his bliaud, Adele cooed softly into his ear, "Then come to my bed and make me believe I am still a queen."

He kissed the folds of hair that lapped over her fragrant shoulder; his voice was hushed. "So long as you live there will be only one queen of this land." With his left hand he reached out to quench the candles. The smoky residue rose like vapor, and Adele smiled into the darkness.

Philippe returned to Paris the following morning. A few days later Adele arranged a meeting between them which included also Hughes de Puiseaux, Sully, and her three brothers. Her intuition, as ever, was inviolate, and it told her that her only hope of retaining the power which Louis had so unthinkingly bestowed upon her was to come to some sort of concordance with her son. Within five months he would be seventeen. He was a man now, no longer the fourteen-year-old she had despaired of controlling. She held little love for him and no affection, but he was the son of her body and she did feel a kind of pride that he so closely resembled her in his appearance and personality.

Therefore, to the assembled group she confided her feelings and made several specifications. There would be no more public or private conspiring against her son by members of her family, and there would be no more attempts to bridge differences within the family by allying with outsiders such as Philip d'Alsace and his Flemish lords.

Even Philippe seemed to take renewed vigor from his mother's forceful actions. A treaty of conciliation was drawn up by the assembled group. Then on February 22nd it was read publicly to the people of Paris by Hughes de Puiseaux.

Adele made it a social occasion. A canopy had been set up on the front grounds of the palace. Under it, at a long table, sat Theobold of Chartres, William of Rheims, Stephen of Sancerre,

Lord Constable Robert of Clermont, Adele, Maurice de Sully, Philippe, and Hughes de Puiseaux. After the chancellor had read the declaration of peace between Philippe and his family, Adele stepped briskly forward, a tall vivid figure in yellow velvet and ermine mantle. She spoke engagingly to the crowd.

"Parisians...you have heard the pledge of conciliation read by the lord chancellor concerning the members of my family. Since my marriage to your great king Louis Capet, the families of Blois and Champagne have worked for the strength and welfare of this realm. Since the death of my husband, my son Philippe has benefited from our guidance and advise. Unfortunately, as has been evidenced by recent events, outsiders have tried to intervene, sowing discord among us. But that is at an end this day. Together here before you all, my son is reconciled with my brothers...."

Philippe came forward at those words and stood beside his mother. She, in dignified humility, took Philippe's right hand in hers, kissing his ring as she knelt meekly before him. In mutual accord her three brothers also came forth and followed her example, if reluctantly, while the assembled crowd cheered. Later, Adele further endeared herself to the people by passing among them and distributing liberal amounts of coins from her almoner.

It was Isabel's twelfth birthday. She lay restlessly upon her bed, listening to the thrashing of the storm outside. For the past three days the rain had been swelling the Seine, and black mud ran in rivulets before the palace.

Her disposition matched the bleakness of the weather. Isabel had not been included in the celebration which had followed the reconciliation of Philippe and his family. Though she was glad that at least one faction had ceased to make trouble for Philippe, Isabel understood that his new allegiance to his family made her own position untenable. Except for her presence at court (and that, in a limited sense), the Flemish coalition had completely collapsed. Each day her expectations of remaining Philippe's wife dwindled.

All this hurt her pride, her sense of security, her peace of mind. Yet it cut deeper than that, because now she felt a need to stay with him that surpassed her sense of feudal or family responsibilities. She loved him. She did not want to lose him now. . . .

She was nearly dozing but the muted sound of footsteps in the corridor roused her and she leapt from the bed, racing lightly across the floor toward the archway entrance. Drawing the portiére aside a little she peered out. Philippe was on his way to his own room. Isabel called his name.

He turned toward her, giving her a brief disinterested look. "I'm busy, Isabel," he said curtly, as though anticipating an interruption.

"I want to talk to you," she pleaded, sensing his restraint.

Philippe heaved a sigh of exasperation but started toward her as she ducked back inside the room. He pushed the curtain aside and stood before her. Hands on hips, his shoulders slightly sagging as though in weariness, he surveyed her hastily. His voice was tired. "What do you want?"

She moved quickly to his side and put her arms around his mid-section, her face rubbing his chest. "Only to see you. It has been such a long time. I was frightened that I might never see you again. And since you have returned, you have kept away from me, as though . . ." she looked up into his face, "as though you hated me."

He didn't try to shake himself loose from her embrace but he did not encourage her either. When her petting and stroking began to make him uneasy, he stepped back and pushed her arms away. "I have allowed you to remain here as my wife, isn't that enough?"

She kissed his hands over and over in gratitude. "Then you do realize that I had nothing to do with what happened? That I did not plot with my uncle against you?"

His silence was affirmation and she took small satisfaction in that. *He still wanted her.* He had doubted her, had plagued her with his suspicions, caused her so much pain. But he did still want her. She could feel that, even as he pushed her away from him. "Isabel, I have things to do. Tell me what you want and then I'll see you at dinner."

She retreated to the bed and sat down on it, looking at him intently. Philippe could see how restless she was. There was a half-radiant, half-shaded look in her eyes, a flush on her lips and cheeks. He had nearly forgotten how beautiful she was. Her white muslin dishabille was so sheer as to be nearly transparent. Her hair hung in a tangle of golden floss to below her hips. Philippe felt uneasy, his nerves strained, but he could not take his eyes from her.

"Why have you stayed so long away from me?" she asked.

"I have been busy," he snapped defensively, taking a few steps toward her.

"Today is my birthday."

"I know," he answered. "I have something for you, I intended to give it to you at dinner."

"No I didn't mean that," she gave him a hopeful little smile. "I don't want gifts, Philippe, I want you." That remark did nothing to soften his antagonism. She tried again. "I've been longing to see you, to talk to you, to be alone with you. I was afraid that you had decided to..." She had lived with that fear for well over three months, but she couldn't bear to put it into words. The smile faded with her voice.

"I've been busy," he repeated. "You must understand how much I've had to cope with since coming back to Paris."

"I know," and her eyes implored him to be kind to her, "but it's a cold and rainy afternoon—take a few hours for yourself."

Before he could stop himself he came to where she sat, looking down at her wordlessly, his eyes playing over every inch of her face. "Uncle William is waiting to see me," he offered weakly, the sentence fading out with each word as she reached out her hands toward him, her fingers playing lightly along his hips. All the blood seemed to drain from his face and surge at his midsection. Her fingers were suffused with heat and he felt himself giving way beneath her touch. "Isabel, I..." he began.

Her face was uplifted and she was looking into his eyes as she unfastened the front of his bliaud in one motion, letting her hands glide over his skin. Gently she took one of his hands in hers and pulled it toward her, easing it down inside the front of her dress. Philippe tensed at the fullness under the silk of her skin and nearly pulled away in sudden confusion but her fingers held him. With a quick motion she undid the ribbon of her dishabille and eased the sheer wrap down over her shoulders where it came to fall in limp folds about her waist.

Still looking into his eyes she shook her hair out like a glistening veil about her shoulders. She saw the look that came into his eyes, felt the tenseness as he stared down at her. Isabel had explored every inch of his body, but she was still a mystery to him.

Isabel moved closer to him, pressing herself against his groin. She felt him tense suddenly, aroused to her touch, gasping. But at the contact with her breasts he promptly shuddered, gripped her shoulders fiercely, and spent abruptly against her arm.

His hold on her slackened after a few moments. "I'm sorry," he said quietly, and began pulling his bliaud closed.

But Isabel refused to release him. "No," she whispered, "don't leave now, stay with me...." She fixed her mouth upon the fingers of his right hand, drawing them in, her tongue a warm ally. After a while she stood up, so small beside him, and let the pale, diaphanous garment slip to the floor. Her eyes and voice pleaded with him, her arms sliding upwards, wandering under the material of his bliaud. "Take off your clothes and lie down next to me," she whispered as he bent to kiss her.

Without a reply he allowed her to guide him to a recumbent position on the bed beside her. He was silent, unmoving as she covered his face and throat with kisses. "Hold me," she said softly, drawing him into her arms. The heat of her blood radiated through her skin to his, and a surge of desire for her clenched like a fist inside him. He was terrified.

Isabel sensed the tension that emanated from him and her gentle hands and voice sought to tranquilize him. "Don't be so afraid, Philippe," she told him, "enjoy me, the way I've enjoyed you." When he remained sedately umoving she pulled his hand to her waist, fingering the silver chain that circled there, "the Druid ring," she told him. "I've worn it ever since that very first night when you gave it to me."

His resistance to her had been pure deception and it dissipated totally at the touch of her nipples against his chest. Philippe pulled her closer. Ah, white and rich and creamy, and so lovely!

He let his lips taste her, lingering over her throat and her shoulders, his hands cradling her head, his fingers lost in the billowing sheen of her hair. His tongue found hers, prodding, and pushing deeper into her mouth. Her hair was everywhere, tangled with his caresses, strands of it matted by his sweat and her own, but it was the only gold he wanted, the softness of her skin the only glory he could comprehend. His consciousness flickered, ebbed, and died completely. His hands flew to her waist, grasping her roughly, then flinging her over on her back, his body over her, pinning her down. "Christ," he murmured breathlessly, "I want you, I want you."

Isabel's head was flung back in violent acquiescence, eyes closed. Her moist lips parted as she whispered, "Please, please..."

In the tangle of his thoughts Philippe didn't know if she was pleading with him to stop or begging him to take her; he no longer cared. He leapt forward, embedding himself within her in a single thrust as she clung to him, pulling him deeper, till he was almost numb with fear and craving. "Do you want me? Do you? Do you?" he gasped, but her lips moved soundlessly as her lids fluttered, and her hands flung out to claw the bedcovers.

In a fury of want Philippe fixed his teeth upon her shoulder, feeling the skin break under the pressure, tasting the salty stickiness of sweat overlayed by blood. He felt himself dangling at the edge of frenzy, the blood in his head pounding till the sound of it thundered in his ears like a storm. Her body was the center of a dark universe about to explode into light. Isabel clutched him tighter, more tightly still, crying out because he was hers, hers finally—and in an instant, hers completely and forever.

He lay upon her breast, hearing the thudding sound of her heart even above the rasping of his own breath. Fresh beads of sweat prickled his skin like a thousand tiny stings and he shivered, suddenly aware of how chilly the room had gone in the midst of the storm. Beneath him she lay, barely breathing, hair half hiding her face. Philippe kissed her shoulder where it bled, then she pulled him even closer and whispered into his ear, "Only me Philippe. From now on, only *me*."

END PART II

Part III
March, 1182

WHAT IS THIS morbus aedificandi, *this disease of building? It persists within the Ile-de-France. Everywhere great cathedrals rise to show Man's pride. Two generations ago Bernard of Clairvaux despised the building of those lush Romanesque edifices which he called* Synagogues of Satan. *Today we have the recriminousness of Gothic splendor under the auspices of the Bishop of Paris.*

To build cathedrals as is done at present is to sin against God. Chancels are built higher and higher; architecture substitutes prayers in stone. Christ, who is at our head, is more humble than His church on earth...

The sacristies of all cathedrals of the Ile-de-France have been raided in order to obtain precious relics for display within the newest Gothic masterpiece: Notre Dame de Paris. Even the famed Blue Virgin *of Suger's St. Denis has been brought to Paris. From Our Lady at Chartres King Philippe has taken the fabled pearls of St. Clotilde to grace the sacristy at Notre Dame; they have since been put around the neck of his young queen. Rheims has been looted for its finest relics — these will be blessed by papal legate Henri de Château-Marçay when he consecrates the great altar of Notre Dame on the upcoming Feast of Pentecost.*

For this show of vainglory the money of thieves, prostitutes and other ignobles has been accepted. For this the Jews of Paris were exiled north, abrogated of their debts but for a minimum percentage which has found its way into the personal keeping of the King. All so that Our Lady may

rise as a monument to master builders and master planners.
The Church is God's house, not Man's.

Pierre la Chantre
Summa Ecclesiastica
March, 1182

*   *   *

Elizabeth of Vermandois died at Amiens on April 15th, 1182.
Her passing deprived Philip d'Alsace of the fashionable, brilliant
and celebrated consort to whom he had been married for nearly
twenty-three years. Their relationship had withstood many complications, including Elizabeth's perennial adulteries, and the fact
that she had been unable to bear Philip a child.

The Count of Flanders spent little time in grieving for his wife,
but he was exceedingly distressed in any case. Her death was to
have profound political repercussions, some of which were immediately evident. Vermandois and Valois, her territorial holdings, had been parceled into the marriage package dangled
before the awestruck eyes of Philippe Capet when the anxious
Philip of Flanders had arranged his marriage to Isabel. It had
been folly, as Baldwin had pointed out at the time, but Flanders'
greed at securing a tighter hold upon the young French boy had
been so great that the risk had seemed worthwhile.

Now with Elizabeth pre-deceasing him, Flanders was in the
unenviable situation of having to cede Vermandois and Valois to
the French. It would have been a sustainable loss had the
French-Flemish alliance remained intact. But given the current
hostilities shared between Philip d'Alsace and Philippe Capet, the
former was unwilling to relinquish so prized a share of his land.

Almost at once Flanders decided upon his revenge. This time,
though, he vowed there would be no reprisals from stronger
forces on the continent. On the day following Elizabeth's funeral,
Philip set sail across the Channel for England and an audience
with Henry Plantagenet.

*   *   *

The most epochal of all days in the history of fair France came on the 19th
day of May, the Feast of Pentecost, the year of our Lord 1182 when Paris
raised as one to Heaven in gracious and most profound joy to celebrate Our
Lady—the consecration of the great altar at Notre Dame de Paris.

Henri de Château-Marçay, papal legate and the highest ranking churchman in France, led the procession from Montmarte where hundreds had gathered at sunrise. Our great Bishop, Maurice de Sully, assisted in the ceremony and the blessing of the thousand relics which were brought to grace the sacristy of Our Lady. The King of France and his Queen received the Sacrament and Absolution. Later, before the altar they washed the feet of the poor. . . .

Adam of Perseigne
May, 1182

* * *

Richard Plantagenet had a genius for discord. In the middle of summer the noble barons of Poitou rose against him and King Henry of England had to intervene on the side of his son to insure peace within the duchy. He had sent his son Geoffrey ahead to Limóges (the seat of the rebellion) to pave the way for his own entrance into the city, so that the word might be spread that Henry of England supported Richard's power in the Aquitaine.

Geoffrey, however, saw his mission as a sparkling opportunity to sow further family tribulation. Personally he had little in common with either Harry or Richard, and he was jealous of their power. Geoffrey enjoyed playing them off against one another, then standing back to watch with a bemused smile.

Far more satisfying yet was the chance to circumvent his father's orders. So though he assented to Henry's order to fortify Richard's reputation among the Poitevan nobles, he did exactly the opposite. Seeking out the foremost barons, Geoffrey used his charm and subtle means of persuasion to caution them further against Richard. How much better, he stressed with calm resolution, that they look to the young king—Harry, the eldest brother —who would eventually rule in England and thus make his influence known upon the continent. Richard was warlike and rapacious. Harry was the "heart of chivalry." Geoffrey's gentle propaganda was successful. By the time Henry arrived the barons and even the petty nobles were convulsed in a fervor of spirit on the side of the young king.

Henry was furious, but it was no more than he had come to expect of his sons. Each time he trusted them he was rewarded with betrayal. Time and time again he found himself forgiving them (they were flesh of his flesh, etc.) but it was becoming a bitter cup for him to drink.

When Harry arrived in Limoges it was to the overwhelming cheers of the assembled crowds. Buxom peasant girls threw flowers in his path. Young men serenaded him. Knights avowed his chivalry. Bertran de Born, one of the petty nobles of the south—an aging playboy who had once championed Richard—commemorated the event in one of his charming *sirventes:*

> *Crowned in flowers, ho! Harry Plantagenet,*
> *young king of England, who is his like?*
>
> *Richard fights as a lion*
> *Yet Harry coos as a dove*
> *They bear nothing of each other in their faces*
> *Even love.*
>
> *Forsooth, Richard will be fantastic in his legend;*
> *and Harry will be king—while behind the royal curtain*
> *Younger brother Geoffrey smiles at everything . . .*

Harry was too vain to realize that his surging reception had been the result of Geoffrey's smooth dissemination. He saw only the love that the people had for him, the splendid awe in which they held him, and his "victory" over Richard.

Eventually the shrewd machinations of Henry Plantagenet prevailed and a truce was formed between Richard and his hostile, insurging barons. Those who had captured fortresses and taken up arms against Richard their duke were forced to surrender. At the instigation of King Henry all parties met, were appeased, and went on their way.

The public demonstrations on Harry's behalf had humiliated and infuriated Richard. Henry was also angry, but there was more to trouble him. The young king was now twenty-eight years old, but he was as immature, feckless and undisciplined as a boy of sixteen. Henry's stern reproaches throughout the years had done little to prepare Harry for the position he would eventually occupy. It was as though he wished to spend the rest of his life in meaningless revels.

This latest business had shown the English king that Richard could not stand well against Harry. Henry had always supposed that he could, and the recent evidence to the contrary was worrisome to him. Henry was a logical man: logic told him that Harry, who was so charming and loved by all, was a vain, foolish, capricious, haughty boy with little character and even less reason—considerably less gifted mentally than either Richard or Geoffrey. He would never make even a satisfactory king; Henry knew this and hoped that the combined threat of two ambitious, capable younger brothers would spur his heir to a semblance of duty. But it had not happened.

Before leaving Limóges, Henry took his eldest aside. The king draped an arm warmly about his son's shoulder and nudging him in affection said, "You made quite an impression on the crowds here, my son, but when you are king you will be judged by more than the fine silks you wear or the graciousness of your bearing."

Harry was staring with disinterest out the window, but at those words he turned to give his father a cool lavender-eyed look. He said nothing.

"Harry," the king muttered, "you must have realized that your behavior flew in the face of your brother. It was not good form, it was not good manners..." he stroked his son's shoulder in affection, "and most assuredly it was not good politics. You should not seek to eclipse Richard before his subjects. He resents it."

"What should I care for Richard's opinions?" Harry snapped. "He baffles me with his lack of understanding in how to manage his people. I am sure that I would have no trouble in handling these Poitevans. Richard's personality breeds division and dissent."

The older king was a man of conservative perspective who tended towards orthodoxy. His mind could seize upon facts, balance them, rationalize. It was something he had inherited from his astute mother; his eldest son had none of it. Henry tried now to put his analysis into verbal terms that the indolent Harry could understand and would accept. "My boy I don't want you and Richard at odds, not in public. It instills rebelliousness within the nobles and incites riots and revolts. I don't want the people here in the south thinking that Richard isn't fit to govern."

"Maybe he isn't," Harry replied. "You know what he's like. He gets on the wrong side of people. All he knows is fighting." He gave a winning smile to his father. "Most of what Richard has gotten through his constant wars he could much more easily have won by softer means."

Henry exhaled an audible breath. He knew now that Geoffrey's smooth and clever tongue had been at work again. This would take some careful undoing. "Whatever your brother Geoffrey has said to you," he began, "or to others on your behalf, you must put aside. The Aquitaine belongs to Richard. It is for him to govern, not for you. Don't play-act at being a symbol of these people. If you invite their favor you will invite Richard's disfavor; and difficulties and war will come on the heels of that."

Harry jerked his burgundy-colored surcoat about him angrily. His face was creased in petulance. "How can you say such things to me? I am your favorite, and your heir. Certainly I am your most loyal son." He was silent for a moment before he asked, "And why do you bring up Geoffrey's name?"

Henry was pulling at the cuff of his sleeve with rigid fingers, trying to restrain the anger that was rising quickly within him. "What do you and Geoffrey have working between you?" he asked between tight lips. "Geoffrey isn't inciting revolution in your name for you alone—he isn't that generous. What have you promised him in return?"

Again the petulant expression. "What are you asking me? I've barely seen Geof in these past few months. Why—do you have it in your mind that we've put together some tidy little conspiracy?"

"Would that be so inconceivable?"

Harry slumped into a chair and glared at his father. "I will tell you this much: I *am* tired of Richard. He is a danger to me, Father, a mortal threat. He will never accede to my authority. He will not help me. Have you thought seriously about what might become of me when you are dead?"

Henry was pacing stiff-kneed back and forth in front of his son. "Those are words too much on the lips of all of you," he growled.

Harry ignored him. "Once I am king, Richard will gladly take the field against me, stir up the whole realm against me, and what will I do then? Have you thought how easily, if properly flanked by barons and traitors and possibly Philippe of France,

Richard could wrest the crown from me? Have you thought of that, Father? Have you?"

"There is very little you have thought of that I have not pondered first," Henry answered pointedly. "But why do you mention Philippe of France? What has he to do with this? You two have been closer than decency allows for many years."

Harry shrugged his shoulders. "Perhaps. Perhaps not. You know how quickly the shape of things can change. Richard has as many charms to offer the French king as I have. Today I am in Philippe's favor; tomorrow he may take Richard to his bed. Or Geoffrey. Nothing is certain. Nothing in this world."

The king was regarding his beloved son with an expression close to disgust. "Is that how the world will turn once I'm gone?" he asked, truly shaken. "Is that the diplomacy on which the future of this realm will depend? Whichever of my sons can best fuck the King of France will hold power here? Grace be to God I won't be here to see it!"

Harry laughed till he felt a spasm of coughing rising in his chest. Then gasping, he smirked, "Your outrage makes exceptional theater father, but very little sense. Since when do foul morals make you cringe? Most of the sins I commit I've learned from you, and I could never hope to equal your indiscretions. You've—"

Henry's hand was hard and hot against his son's cheek, and Harry fairly reeled from the blow. Tears of rage and pain leapt to his eyes but his voice was steady. "It has been a long time since you have stooped to that."

"Damn you!" Henry rasped, "you are as heartless as your brothers! Christ Almighty what must I do to garner your love, your respect? I have favored you, adored you, set you above every other person in my life and in my heart. I have accorded you every honor. You rule Anjou and Normandy with me: I give you concordance in Maine and Gascony—you'll get the whole damn kingdom when I'm gone. Isn't that promise enough for your damn greedy selfishness!"

"I rule nothing!" Harry shouted, jumping to his feet. "You have given me titles, Father, but you've never given me any power!"

The words rang in Henry's ears and without thinking he drew back, flinching from his son. Could it be possible that this headstrong, gaudy young man wanted more than the trappings of success? And was there more still? Frustration and bitterness showed in Henry's face. "What else could you want unless it is my death? I cannot conceive of such corruption. Jesus!" He staggered backwards, hands over his face.

Harry stood by impassively, watching his father's formidable fury. He waited, then finally spoke with fitting insensitivity. "You think I only came to Limóges to make a great show of myself and to humiliate Richard. It wasn't only that; there is more. I came because I knew you would be here and I had to talk to you. Are you listening now, Father?" Harry leaned forward, peering into his father's face. "I don't want your death, Henry. That is the truth, if you will believe it. And God knows you are the king, so the power is yours to give or no. But if not the power, Father, then the *means* to do without it..."

Henry's features hardened, tensing into a perceptible likeness of his coin image. "What are you saying?"

"The *money*, Father. The money. That's what I want, what I deserve. I can't live on the pittance you give me or the tiny revenue afforded me in Normandy or Anjou. I can no longer pay the knights in my service. Marguerite is penniless as well, and cannot pay the ladies of her retinue. We cannot maintain any of our former livings or households." He waited for his father to make a comment. "I need your help, Henry. I have the right to ask this of you. I have the *right*."

It was not the first time the young king had come, penniless, to his father, demanding a hand-out. As recently as February Henry had made it clear to all of his sons that he was no longer financially responsible for them. It was at that time he had made his will and told his sons the contents thereof. *They were to expect no more than the territories which had been allotted them years earlier, and minimal drafts from the treasury.* Of course, none of them had been satisfied. Henry had managed to extract a promise of frugality from each, grudgingly given. Now Harry had decided to dance out of that agreement. With measured calm that was very difficult to affect, the king said, "You have run through your inheritance, is that it? What became of the money I advanced to you at Epiphany? Has it gone for your damn fool tournaments?"

Harry's sensitive lips sulked in pouting. "Why are you so

bloody narrow-minded? What is so wrong if I indulge myself with sporting?"

"Tournaments are dangerous events to no purpose," Henry shouted "where young men spar for glory that is meaningless. It is a fool's pastime and that is why I outlawed them in England."

"I don't always take part in them," Harry snapped. "Often I only wager."

"Which is exactly why you are here now, penniless, with your hand outstretched to me!"

Harry stood for some time, examining the meticulous trim of his fingernails. Without looking up at his father he said curtly, "Gambling is in my blood. It is one of the few enjoyable things I have in my life. Would you deny me that?"

Henry soothed his throbbing temples with the light pressure of his fingertips. His voice was sad but stern. "Well, you'll get no money from me, my lad."

"Is that your final word?"

"It is."

Harry turned on his heels. His words, spoken softly, trailed off on the air. "Then I shall go elsewhere."

"To whom?"

Nothing Henry would say could convince Harry that he was wrong. "To Philippe," he answered. "I have credit with him if not with you."

Henry closed the distance between them in a few quick steps. Affection had weakened his resolve. Tenderly he put his arms around his son. "Understand my reasons and try to respect them. At least, let us part as friends."

Harry shrugged free of his father's embrace. His eyes were cold, accusing. "No," he said, "we've never been friends."

* * *

To the noble Count of Flanders Philip d' Alsace from Philippe Capet, by the Grace of God Almighty King of the French, greetings . . .

May it please you to accept condolences of this Most Christian Realm at the death of your much loved wife Elizabeth, of the County of Vermandois.

May it be noted according to the marriage contract between myself and my esteemed wife Isabel of Hainault that under present circum-

stances the county comprising the territories of Valois *and* Vermandois *be ceded immediately in the name of my wife to be held in trust by the undersigned,*

Philippe-Auguste

Written by my Hand; Paris
22nd day of June, Year of Our Lord 1182

* * *

"Where are we going?" Edythe asked, drawing the fine bone-handled comb through Isabel's hair. "You haven't told me yet."

"Chantilly," Isabel answered, "to *Chateau Jolie*. Philippe's father built it for his first wife, Eleanor, because she couldn't stand this place." She surveyed the room with a chilly, observing look. "I can appreciate her misery."

Edythe gathered the golden mane tenderly between deft fingers, rolling the hair into an upswept crown of swirls and adorning it with a circle of pearl-studded hair pins. When she had finished she bent to the dressing table and took up the dangling peridot earrings, and began affixing them to Isabel's ears. "I don't know that you should be traveling at all," she complained. "You should be kept restful and well-covered." Her practiced hand went to the young queen's forehead. "Your fever still has not broken completely."

Isabel turned slightly on the stool, contemplating their reflections in the mirror: her own blond gracefulness; Edythe's sweet, mild face. Still watching the mirror, Isabel said, "I don't happily anticipate the journey but I will be glad to be out of Paris for a while and in the country once again. God in heaven I swear it is these stone walls which have made me ill!"

She had been ill for several weeks. It had been an early, hot summer in Paris—stifling and humid—and Isabel had wilted like a pale spring flower. Since mid-June she had languished in bed, often refusing food. Philippe had finally grown alarmed at her waning health and now he had ordered her to take a few weeks in the country to recover her strength.

Isabel was buffing her fingernails against the pale blue silk of her chainse. "I wish Philippe were coming with us," she mused. "I will miss him."

Edythe had begun collecting Isabel's toiletries from the dressing table surface, cradling the sardonyx, onyx, and amethyst jars in the crook of her arm. Isabel realized that the girl's silence was deliberate. Her voice was curious as she asked, "You don't like him, do you, Edythe? You don't like my husband."

Edythe bent to her task, concealing the vials and bottles within the damask linings of the ashwood traveling chest. When she had finished she strapped the laces and secured the handles and the clasp. "Everything has been packed," she said without a smile.

Isabel took hold of her hand gently, probing the fingers in a questioning touch. "*Why* don't you like him?"

"It is nothing to you, Belle," Edythe leveled her gaze to her mistress's eyes. "I want you to be happy. I don't think you are happy here."

"But that isn't Philippe's fault," Isabel argued gently. "I am homesick. And except for you I have no friends here. If I seem unhappy it is because of that, not because of Philippe."

Edythe's shoulders sagged a little as though in resignation. She had her own feelings, and her reasons for them. But it was futile to argue with Isabel. They were as close as the sisters they undoubtedly were, yet Edythe was and always would be the inferior. It was something she could not allow herself to forget.

Isabel mistook Edythe's mood for submission yet she believed she had sensed a flicker of jealousy. Rising, she affixed the pearl-edged girdle about her waist. "Edythe," she said suddenly, "you are nearly sixteen. Shall I find a husband for you?"

Edythe's expression was indistinct, but a hint of color came upon her cheeks. "Would you have me married? Is that what you wish?"

Isabel tilted her head prettily, her right earring touching her shoulder. "Only if it is what you want."

"Not against my wishes?" Edythe asked.

"Never."

Edythe swung her own light cloak about her shoulders. She wanted very much to be quit of this room. "I have no wish to be a wife," she said bluntly. "And even if I did, who would marry me?"

Affection tempered Isabel's reasoning. "Many men," she said without hesitation, a pure, sweet smile curving her lips. "I don't think you realize it, but you are so pretty, Edythe. Let me find someone for you."

Edythe's nervous hands fiddled with the tassles on her cloak. She looked down at her flat chest, further down at her twisted ankle. "Love makes a liar out of you, Belle," she replied. "I am a cripple."

Isabel's hand brushed softly across Edythe's face, tucking the long brown hair behind an ear. "It isn't right that you should spend your whole life looking after me, Edythe."

Her hand closed around Isabel's. "Let be," she said simply. "I don't want a husband. Understand me, and please abide by what I ask."

The young queen shook her head. "If you should change your mind?"

"I shall not." She glanced around and saw Robert of Clermont peering furtively from beyond the curtained archway. Edythe turned back to Isabel. "The lord constable is waiting. It is time for us to leave."

Clermont entered, took up the chest and started once more toward the door, both young women beside him. Suddenly Isabel came to a stop and looked up at him. "I must see my husband before I leave here."

"Your husband is with the Bishop of Paris, child" he answered reprovingly.

She hesitated. "Nonetheless, I will be away for several weeks and I should like a few moments with Philippe before..."

Clermont's voice was rude, his manner an insult. "The body-guard is prepared and waiting. The weather is questionable. We will doubtless encounter rain. If we do not leave now there is very little chance we will reach Chantilly before tomorrow night. Let us be on our way."

Isabel had stubbornness of her own and it surfaced now. "Lord Constable," she tried to keep the complaining tone from her voice, "is *time* of so much importance in this?"

His lean, craggy face was expressionless but his dark eyes glinted a sense of anger as he surveyed her pale and golden beauty. "I am due back in Paris in three days' time. I will have to ride night and day as it is." Again that look as he defeated her attempt to speak. "Forgive me, but I have more pressing matters on my head than escorting the queen." He hoisted the chest upon his shoulder, gave a small grunt, and motioned to Isabel and Edythe that they should go before him.

Isabel followed them both down the echoing corridors and the stairs and outside into the pearl-grey Paris morning. The sky was fretted with high, humid clouds. It looked like a pot of clotted cream.

"Jailers," she whispered under her breath.

Perhaps it was coincidence, but Philippe Capet was also in conference with the Bishop of Paris on the 27th day of July when Harry Plantagenet came to Paris. On this occasion Sully was immediately dismissed for the day.

"You've changed, do you know?" Harry mused, and after a while he sat up and began pulling on his clothes. Philippe reached his hand across the bed and stroked Harry's shoulder.

"I suppose I have. I'm older." His fingers played gently across the deep bruises which mottled the fair skin of Harry's back and shoulders. "Who have you been sporting with? This looks very bad. Does it hurt?"

Harry shrugged. "Not too much. It isn't what you think. I collected these purple badges at a tournament a few weeks ago. I don't compete as well as I used to."

Philippe let his arms hang limply at his sides and took an audible breath. "Those stupid tournaments! You'll kill yourself someday. And for what? In that at least I wish you would concur with your father."

Their relationship had suffered through absence and events. Harry sensed the separateness. He felt puzzled—tired—sorely dissatisfied. "Leave me alone," he muttered.

Philippe sat up, pushing his tangled black hair away from his face. "What's wrong? You're so peevish."

Harry pulled on his fine linen smock and started to do up the laces, tiny close-woven strips of embroidered damask. "Everything is wrong. I lost miserably in the tournaments at Lille. It wasn't even my money—I had borrowed it from William Marshal. I don't ride or fight well anymore. I don't feel well. I'm not strong." He took a breath. "It must be rather apparent to you that I'm not very good at anything anymore. Kind of you not to mention it."

"Oh, Harry, really," Philippe teased, but he felt uneasy. It wasn't like blithe Harry to be depressed. Philippe reached for his hand, Harry pulled away. He sounded as though he were about to cry. "How could *you* understand? It must be wonderful to be seventeen and able to rise to every occasion." He bit off the words with irony. "Well, that's what being a king does for your confidence."

Philippe thrust aside the covers, got swiftly to his feet and strode to the other side of the bed. He stood for a moment facing Harry, looking down at him, pensive and concerned, then knelt before him, his cheek against Harry's lap.

"Do you want to know the real reason I came here?" Harry asked, absently coiling his fingers in disheveled black curls. "To ask your help." His voice went lower. "To borrow money. I'm not proud of myself, God knows." He sucked in his cheeks and bit his tongue to keep from crying. "But I did miss you, Philippe, you must believe that."

Philippe's arms were around him, strong and sustaining. "It doesn't matter. For whatever reason, I'm glad you came to me."

Later, when daylight had fled from the farthest corners of the room, Harry lay restfully in Philippe's arms. "I remember the first time I ever saw you," he mused. "I had come to Paris with Father, who was here to see Louis about that damned Becket business. You were just a little boy, not even five years old. You were sitting off in the corner watching everything." He rolled over on his stomach and laid his chin upon Philippe's chest. "Becket was very taken with you. He told me once that you were the most amazing child he had ever seen." Harry was full of memory now, taking pleasure in it. He squeezed Philippe's hand lovingly. "Later, when I would come to visit Louis, I remember how you would look at me, your eyes so incredibly big and black. You were so intense, so intelligent. I think I must have loved you even then."

Philippe was remembering too. "I worshipped you. You were glamorous, everyone loved you. That's what impressed me more than anything, why I wanted so much to be like you. Because you were loved, and I wasn't—because you were so happy, and I was unhappy." He clasped Harry's hand tighter, imparting a meaning which surpassed words. "I was a lonely little boy. You were good to me and I idolized you." He was silent for a moment. "Louis never cared for me. That troubles me more than you can know."

Harry left a pattern of kisses on Philippe's chest, then raised his head to look fully into his face. "Henry loves me, or so he says, and God knows I'm none the better for it." He shook his head. "A father is a curse to his children, and sons are nothing but grief to him." Harry left off speaking for a while as he stroked Philippe's arm. "Thanks be to God I've no son. I'd hate to see the loathing in his eyes like that which I feel for my father."

The light had all but gone; there was a cool silence within Philippe's room. He held Harry close, even as he snuggled his face in the softness of the pillow and smelled the sweet residue of narcissus there. Philippe closed his eyes, trying to banish all thought of her, but could not. She had been three weeks in Chantilly and he longed for her even as he felt vague relief at her absence. It was always the same. She both tempted and tormented him. Her beautiful face haunted his dreams. In defense of his fearfulness he pulled Harry closer and whispered in his ear, "You shall have all that you wish, whatever you need."

The remnants of Harry's pride wilted a little at that. "On what security? I must tell you truthfully Philippe that if you loan money to me there is little guarantee that I will be able to repay it."

Philippe's fingers entwined with Harry's. "It is no loan."

"A gift then? Charity?"

"Not charity. Repayment for friendship and kindness. For the love which you showed to a lonely little boy." There was a stab of feeling in his voice. "Harry, I'm lonely still...."

A soft, sweet kiss banished a tiny portion of the memory; the mild sound of Harry's voice dispelled the rest. "Never lonely, not so long as I am with you, love."

As they slept a light breeze came up off the river, filling the room with scent of night-blooming flowers. Faint patches of stars glistened in the heavens, and torchlight rippled upon the smooth surface of the Seine. The people of Paris slept, unknowing that their king lay in the arms of an English prince, while a balmy redolence of narcissus hung over him and seeped into his dreams.

Isabel's return to Paris, which had been planned to coincide with the celebration of her husband's seventeenth birthday, was delayed when she suffered her second miscarriage of the year on the 19th of August. In answer to Edythe's frantic missives, Philippe sent four of the finest physicians in Paris to care for her at the *Chateau Jolie* in Chantilly.

They could do little for her. She needed Philippe and the assurance of his love for her; his attention and concern. She did not realize that Philippe was deeply involved in his own worries which, though not caused by Isabel in any way, were attributable to her, and compromised her position.

Robert of Clermont had been scheduled to serve as emissary for his king at a meeting with Philip of Flanders at Amiens on the 15th of August, the Feast of the Assumption. It was to be a conventional occasion at which time the Count of Flanders was to formally concede his hold upon the territories of Vermandois and Valois, giving them over to the custody of Philippe Capet.

But when Robert arrived at Amiens he was met instead by one Tristan de Brandeis, the local burgher and Philip's vassal. The Count of Flanders had conveniently absented himself to Valenciennes but the message he had left behind with Tristan was emphatic: *No Vermandois.*

Humiliated and subdued, Robert returned to Paris with that message where he stoically bore the shouted rage of his king. *A contract had been signed—Flanders had promised those territories upon the death of Elizabeth!* Flanders had to capitulate because the law decreed it so! Hughes de Puiseaux was sent scurrying to the archives library to dig out the copy of the marriage contract.

Philippe held the document between unsteady hands and read the fateful passage: "*. . . in the event of the death of Elizabeth, the true Countess of Vermandois and Valois, these lands and their said appointed revenues shall be ceded in their entirety to Philippe of France, as a portion of the dowry achieved by his wife, Isabel of Hainault, in the situation that: the Count of Flanders has no heir of his body; and the matter of transfer is agreeable to both the Kingdom of France and the County of Flanders at such time as is dictated by events herein described above. . . .*"

Philip d'Alsace's elegant smugness laughed out at him from the ink-scored parchment. A legal trap. A clever double-meaning. A sharp two-edged argument. This was reprehensible and the King of France would not be the unwitting victim of such mockery!

At once he authored a stentorian reply to the Count of Flanders, demanding the surrender of Vermandois and Valois, threatening the use of an outside arbitrator to decide the matter. Then, with righteous forbearance, Philippe put his hand to an urgent message directed to Henry of England, expressing outrage over this new interference by Flanders and requesting the

English king's help in open mediation between the three parties. That accomplished, he wrote yet one more communique: to Emperor Frederick, d'Alsace's overlord, announcing the count's decision in the matter of Valois and Vermandois, and petitioning intercession by the Holy Roman Empire.

These messages, bearing Philippe's signet stamp and royal seal, were dispatched at once by special courier. The swift and decisive action somewhat abated his anger. It was obvious that since Flanders was bound by his word not to encroach upon the French king's power, he was attempting intimidation by means of threats. But Philippe was hopeful. Perhaps the vital passage in the contract did not read so precisely as he would have preferred, but the outside parties called to mediate the situation would at once discern Flanders' miscreancy and discredit him. It was only a matter of waiting.

Assured of a judgment in his favor, Philippe turned his energies toward the business of his realm, never considering that he had misread Flanders' capabilities and wit once again.

* * *

...there is a chamber at the king's residence in Winchester most beautifully decorated with many-colored pictures of various forms. By King Henry's order a blank space had been left, where he afterwards caused to be depicted an eagle with four eaglets perched upon it, one on each wing, the third on its back tearing at the parent with talons and beak, whilst the fourth—no smaller than the others—sat upon its neck and waited to tear out the eagle's eyes....

When some of his friends asked Henry what the picture was depicting in its meaning, Henry said: "They are my four sons, who will not cease persecuting me until my death. And the last-born, whom I now embrace with qualmless love, will inflict upon me the greatest peril of all..."

> *Gerald of Wales*
> August, 1182

* * *

Oh, my soul, wherefore art thou troubled, and why am I sorely vexed? Henry of England woke with the words on his lips. It was several moments before he traced the sentence to the works of Marcus

Aurelius he had been reading the night before, though he could not connect them to the dream which had awakened him.

The room congealed in darkness but for the sputtering remains of a fire in the grate. Morning would be late today. Through the uncurtained window he could scent the approach of a rain-sodden dawn. The imminent moisture radiated an ache all through his body. With care for his pain Henry settled into a sitting position on the bed and threw back the *serge* bedsheets. Beside him a warm female body moved, twisted over, and muttered his name sleepily.

His mind was usually clear upon waking yet now for a moment he could not remember where he was or who lay beside him. Then in a flash of clarity he knew suddenly: he was at Argentan fortress in Normandy, and this girl beside him was a nameless trollop. In the pensive mood which he now entertained he would have welcomed the quiet, worshipful company of Alais Capet, but he had left her behind in London with John.

Again the dream images reflected in his mind as tiny pieces of shattered glass giving back the light. A dim, dense forest suddenly pierced by a stream of fog-shrouded sunlight. Soft words. The image leapt in his mind. *Eleanor.* Ruby-lipped and shining, glossy raven hair tossed sassily in the wind. *Eleanor.* Radiantly beautiful, as he had first seen her, those many years ago. *Eleanor.* Green-eyed and glorious, trembling in his arms—sweet alabaster skin gleaming beneath his touch. *Eleanor.* In the years before ambition, jealousy and revenge had made her his enemy.

He had not loved her for many years, yet the memory of her persisted in painful dichotomy: too much loveliness to be forgotten, too much wretchedness to be remembered. Stone poetry, blossoms spattered with blood. A thousand contradictions, a thousand consequences of their lives together. Now only memory remained.

Memory, and a legacy of hate. The hate of his sons for him. Eleanor had wrought that; he had wrought hers. When had it all begun? They had loved each other once, he and Eleanor. It had been a marriage of convenience designed for gain and prosperity, yes—but oh, it had been so much more than that!

Rosamunde. She too lingered in the veiled corridors of his memory. Sweet, unspoiled girl with none of Eleanor's pride or villainy. Henry had loved her, basked happily in her quiet company. She had been dead for six years now, but a hundred troubadors' songs remained to praise her. Legend had transfigured his Welsh mistress. Rosamunde had not been so beautiful as Eleanor, or as passionate. But her gentle sweetness had consoled him against his wife's infuriating, demanding personality. Poor Rosamunde. All the years she had been his mistress she had waited with the patience of a child to become his wife. He had never actually spoken of marriage, but he had given her tacit reason to hope. She had given him children: two sons and a daughter. But finally—her fragile spirit weighted down with remorse for her sins—she had shut herself away in the chapter house of a nunnery, and there she had died. Since that time Henry had taken many women to his bed, but he had loved none of them.

Unless he loved Alais. She too had borne him children, and she had been his most constant female companion since the death of Rosamunde. That she loved him was evident in her fierce refusals to marry Richard, though she had been promised to him for many years. Richard cared nothing for her: his tastes ran to fair-haired, pretty soldiers and poet-knights like Bertran de Born. Alais belonged exclusively to Henry (and to John, for the king was most generous to his youngest son) but he was weary of her. She was sweet and her adoration was a balm on his uneasy spirit. But she was meek and a mild, dutiful lover—and Henry was bored with her.

He was nearing fifty but he had lost none of his virility and his appetite had increased. There was no shortage of willing girls who gladly spread their legs for the King of England, but Henry's diverse tastes had found satisfaction only in Eleanor. They had not lived as man and wife for fifteen years, but he could not forget how she had felt in his arms. Even after he had ceased to love her, even after they had come to hate each other, Eleanor had offered him infinite sexual delights. Since her there had been hundreds, but none like her, none to excite him as only she had....

Restlessly Henry tossed in his bed as his mind turned to yet one more lost love—perhaps the greatest love of all—certainly his most tragic loss. Becket, his dearest friend, partner, and brother in the soul. Twelve years since that ghastly night in cold Canterbury Cathedral.... Henry closed his eyes against the awful remembrance which came too often now on dismal mornings before the sun was fully up. *Becket.* His tonsured head bloodied, his cantel shredded from sword blows. *Becket!* Henry thought of his own sons, all gone the way of corruption so prevalent today. They would never understand the purity of a chaste male love. *Becket!* The tears which came too easily now, came once again. . . .

Ⓣ︎HE KING OF FRANCE could heal. Everyone believed that.

On holy days the poor who suffered from scrofula would press close to his bodyguard as he passed on his way into the cathedral to hear mass. According to the tradition of his office, Philippe-Auguste would give a fleeting touch of his hands to the unfortunate ones, or he would allow the fringe layer of spectators to touch the trailing folds of his cape. Many an ailing man proclaimed himself cured that night, for having observed the king, and partaken of his majesty.

Whether or not they actually were cured is impossible to say. Yet no other prince on earth, not even the pope, could claim to heal and be believed. That power belonged only to the anointed of God. The King of the Franks—whoever he might be, saint or reprobate—*was* God's anointed.

It was October 1182, nearly three years since Philippe-Auguste had assumed the power of the crown, and what an amazingly full three years it had been and how much change had taken place! Philippe—who was logical and intrepid and wise beyond comprehension—had made his share of early mistakes, but he had also learned from them.

He had learned to strike a balance: He was neither too approachable, nor too humble. Of course, the royal dignity had to be protected, but Philippe managed to keep his rank unassailable and his person accessible at the same time.

At seventeen his youth was still a drawback, but he gave himself the semblance of experience by using every bit of knowledge and instinct he owned. Philippe had a tidy, logical mind. He never forgot a fact which he could use to his advantage in debate or counsel. Yet the year just past had been full of revelations that he could not rule by intelligence alone. A royal *demesne* was only as secure as the ability of its king to preserve it. (Groups of knights were not *armies* in the sense that the term would later apply. They were aristocratic adventurers pledged to an individual code of honor. They responded to a monarch at their head, but only if he could lead them in the field.) Realizing his deficiencies as a horseman and soldier, Philippe had begun to submerse himself in the arts of war. Each morning he trained in the dusty jousting field behind the palace, riding lap after lap around the lists in full corselet, practicing dexterity with axe and sword.

In administrative aspects of kingship he was in his element. Philippe was a more visible monarch than Louis had ever been, because he understood the value of keeping close watch over every inch of territory, and being known to do so. Within three years of his accession Philippe had already traveled the whole of France and her crown-associated territories. Since the Ile-de-France was hemmed in on all sides by potentially hostile neighbors (with the exception of crown-annexed Champagne), it was necessary for the king to pay frequent visits to his fortresses on the frontiers.

Paris was his chief interest, however, and he doted over his capital with the fond concern of a lover. By 1182 the city had a population close to one hundred thousand inhabitants, and there was a constant influx of transients. Parisians were a diverse group: merchants and peasants, students and priests, vendors and builders, artisans and soldiers, craftsmen and shopkeepers, hawkers and laundresses, aristocrats and prostitutes. They made a vivid, pulsing city, the most heterogeneous population in Europe, and their fortunes and futures rested upon the broad shoulders of their young king.

Philippe had done much to improve the appearance and the commerce of Paris. The road which ran from the palace to the other end of the Ile de la Cité had been widened, to improve travel conditions, and recently Philippe had ordered it to be paved with stone. Hawkers and vendors now sold beneath a wooden awning which Philippe had caused to be built for them, so that all street merchants might traffic their wares in any weather. The slum area where the impoverished Jews had lived prior to their forced exile had been cleared, the houses taken down and replaced with a *hotel dieu* (hospital). Alongside it a row of wooden housing had been constructed to serve as lodgings for the students who flocked eagerly to the city. (These students were a questionable asset to the populace. Many of them were ill-bred and boisterous disturbers of the peace, who boldly stole fruit and vegetables from vendors, or called out obscene praises to any passing housemaid.)

The cost of the city's face-lifting was not to be had for nothing, but a fund for just this had been established, aided partly by a token toll deposited by any individual crossing the Seine to the Ile de la Cité from either bank by way of the *Petit Pont* or *Grande Pont*. Philippe had instituted this measure almost immediately upon his coronation. At first the thrifty Parisians had grumbled loudly. But since no one, even the king himself, was spared the cost of two *deniers* for each passage, they soon bore it stoutly enough.

Rich or poor, the citizens of Paris were united by the example of their king. It was obvious to all that the business of kingship was no mere array of ritual to Philippe Capet. He worked at the job. Three times a week he held audience in his presence chamber, meeting with common people as often as he entertained nobles. Unlike Louis, who had taken advice from the most ill-advisable sources, Philippe listened to everyone. He may have implemented few outside suggestions, but he extracted opinions from all. Philippe *knew* Paris in all its significators: commerce, philosophy, education, religion—they were the pulse of this great city which he had made his own. His shrewd intellect, his vision; the humility edged with a good deal of plain Frankish stubbornness and common sense—all this made him unquestionably the first truly *French* king.

Philippe's single remaining problem lay in satisfying the nobles and most especially his own family, but he had set upon a plan to remedy that. At first he had believed he could by-pass their goodwill. He had since learned otherwise and it had been a costly and embarrassing lesson. Therefore, he had recently reorganized his *curia regis*, balancing it with selections of nobles and family members, both Capetian and Champagnois.

This was no token honor. It had to be earned. No one served the king in high office merely because of family ties. Philippe had seen too well how Louis had failed by sharing out his sovereign rights among ambitious courtiers who claimed blood relationship as their sole qualification for service.

There were very few of his family that Philippe cared to entrust with any real power. He'd found that by giving them carefully measured duties he could restrict their power while yet ensuring their loyalty. Adele had been helpful in dealing with his Champagnois uncles. Stephen and Theobold had remained distant from Paris, concentrating their energies upon their domains in the Loire Valley at their sister's firm request. Adele's pact of peace had humbled them considerably. William still sat at Rheims as bishop, but his relationship with Philippe had recently undergone a positive regeneration, and the king had come to see him as a friend rather than an adversary.

Robert of Dreux and Peter of Courtenay, the two surviving Capet uncles, were aging and remained close to their own holdings. Two of Robert's three sons had been consecrated bishops during Louis's reign: Henry at Orléans and Philip at Beauvais. Their titles provided them with liberal authority in their districts, but Philippe closely monitored their power. The Count of Dreux's remaining son, Robert II, was a typically sound-headed Capet whom the king found useful in matters of cost accounting and computation of tax revenues.

The last-named Capetian cousin was Peter's son Pierre, the young Count of Nevers (a territory he had inherited through a providential marriage). Pierre was only a few years older than Philippe and the king considered him callow and irresponsible. Pierre spent much of his time competing in tournaments, but his royal cousin did see fit to use him from time to time as a diplomatic messenger, since Pierre had a pleasing appearance and the tongue of a flatterer.

Of the Champagnois uncles, only Theobold and the late Henri had heirs. Philippe thoroughly disliked Theobold's sons, and he engaged them in only minor duties.

There was one additional Champagnois cousin employed by the Crown. Though the death of his father had made young Henri of Champagne count of that domain and saddled him with enough responsibilities to warrant his attention, he was happy to remain at Paris, in the relatively mediocre position as keeper of the king's personal accounts. Henri was the only Champagnois of his generation who personally liked the king, and he did not disdain the tiny token renumeration he was paid for his services. (It was true that no one grew rich in Philippe's service. It could be said that in this he resembled his ancestor Hugh Capet, whose frugal administrative traits had seemed parsimonious in the wake of centuries of Merovingian and Carolingian splendor.)

Henri of Champagne's willingness to leave behind his wife and son and rich estates to subsist in Paris in a thankless and relatively minor position had little to do with either loyalty or humility. It had everything to do with Isabel.

Three years ago Henri's family, and hers, had instituted a betrothal between the two of them. At twenty, Henri had been reluctant at the thought. Isabel had been only nine at the time and the marriage would not take place for several years. He had even come to Valenciennes in December, 1179, to convince Baldwin that the match was impractical. But one look at Isabel had been enough to change Henri's mind.

She had smiled knowingly at his tongue-tied fascination, peering at him through eyes which promised every delight a man could conceive. Henri had gone happily back to Champagne, secure in the belief that this prodigious beauty would soon be his for the taking. Five months later, Isabel had become the bride of Philippe Capet.

Henri had no end of fantasies about Isabel. Since all his work was done at the palace, he had the opportunity to watch her continuously: in corridors, at table, and in the archives library where she spent so much of her time. Somehow, such close proximity to Isabel satisfied a certain amount of Henri's unfulfilled desire.

Isabel liked him. He was pleasant and educated, and she could talk to him in ways she could never talk to Philippe, who cared little for conversation in any case. Many mornings Isabel came to the archives room to read, yet lingered to talk to Henri of philosophy and the arts.

He was her ceaseless admirer, but he was the only one. After two and a half years in the capital, Isabel still lived in virtual self-imposed exile within the palace. The people of Paris hated her. When Isabel did appear in public the announcement of her name was always met with jeers and rude shouts. The Parisians hated her for her nationality alone; it was all they knew of her. Those who knew more ignored the fact that she knew Frankish history, literature, and spoke the language better than most French, including her husband.

A recent source of antagonism against the French queen had been the highly-publicized gift to her of St. Clotilde's pearls. Pierre la Chantre's widely-circulated diatribe had galvanized angry opinion among many of the French bishops regarding Philippe's all-too-cavalier act of adorning his wife with sacred relics. Unfortunately the greatest amount of their rancor was directed at Isabel rather than their king. The consensus of opinion was that if a son of the devout Louis Capet had committed such a sacrilege, it was the fault of the female who had inspired it. No one who looked like Isabel could be blameless.

The stream of propaganda against her was endless. No one cared to know her, but everyone wanted to know *about* her. What the palace serving sluts didn't babble freely in the marketplace each morning, Adele's relatives gloatingly served up as dinner gossip to their aristocratic friends. Anything and everything Isabel did or said was fair game for malicious exaggeration or deliberate misinterpretation. Habits of the most unoffending caste became caprices. Casual remarks, reworded, became slanders. All of Paris seemed to know that she received a monthly allotment of 2,000 *sous* from her father; that she bathed daily in milk of almonds and crushed seed pearls; that she wore the finest silks, samites, furs and jewels. All *that*, they said, for a child—a foreigner! Didn't it prove that she was greedy, extravagant, superficial, and thoroughly Flemish? Why didn't she give to the poor? Have a French girl to wait upon her rather than a Flemish one? Visit hospitals? (She *did* give to the poor, but because it reflected favorably upon her it was never talked about. She kept only Edythe to wait on her because she trusted no one else. And if Isabel didn't visit hospitals, it was not for lack of pity but because whenever she left the safety of the palace she was subjected to cat-calls, or worse—some of the bolder Parisians had been known to throw garbage at her.)

The hateful judgment of the populace had made Isabel a prisoner of her room, yet she could not withdraw completely enough to escape from ridicule. Even the king's own bodyguard made sniggering wagers among themselves each day, guessing at the number of visits Philippe would make to his wife's room before nightfall.

Because her physical relationship with Philippe was the only real pleasure in her life, Isabel thought of little else. There was no lack of passion or excitement between them. With all her worldly, inventive skills, Isabel always had some new erotic sport for them, and Philippe, so smitten by the mere lure of her, needed little encouragement.

Still, Philippe's libidinous preoccupation with his wife did not blind him to the liability of her public persona, although her sexual talents tempered what might otherwise have been a harsher judgment of her worth. Faced with a constant barrage of resentment and protest against his wife, and fearing that in time it might contaminate his own public favor, Philippe had set about to popularize her image.

He began by giving her a place of honor in his audience chamber where she sat beside him during meetings of the *curia regis* and public hearings. At first she enjoyed this new preroga- tive accorded to her, but after a short while Isabel grew dissatis- fied with the honor. The proceedings were seldom interesting to her. Isabel would sit passively, exquisitely adorned and bored. After a few weeks she simply stopped coming.

In November of 1182 Parisians celebrated the third anniver- sary of their young king's coronation. Philippe, in accordance with his campaign to laud his wife, combined the celebration with a public veneration of Isabel's own ancestor, Charlemagne. It was the sixteenth anniversary of the beatification of the emperor, and Philippe further commemorated the event by presenting to the sacristy of Notre Dame a signet ring which had once belonged to the great Frankish hero. It was a configuration of gold and rare amethysts, believed to have healing powers. To Isabel, Philippe presented (in public ceremony) an amulet interfaced with braided locks of hair from the emperor's head; and a pewter bracelet set with rubies, which he placed upon Isabel's left arm as a public reminder that their queen—like her famous ancestor— was left-handed.

The first week in November was designated for a celebration of the Capet/Carolingian union. There was public feasting for three days on the *esplanade* fronting the palace. *The Sword of Ro- land* was given a dramatic reading by Arnaut de Mareuil, a famous Provençal troubador who had spent much time at the court of Baldwin of Hainault.

Philippe's efforts were poorly rewarded. The Parisians were

happy to partake of the free food, but they paid their deference to Adele rather than Isabel. The barons and the petty nobility were pleased enough to sit at the ribbon-festooned tables of honor near their king, but they ignored Isabel's name when they toasted with their wine cups. The Champagnois sat in stiff communal acceptance of the queen, but they were resentful of Philippe's purposeful exaltation of her background and, save for Henri of Champagne, they regarded her with rude neglect.

On the final day of celebration, a spectacular *tableau vivant* depicted the life and deeds of Charlemagne. Philippe had personally selected a group of *trouvères* from Nantes to perform the drama. He had even arranged for the cloth-makers of Paris to concoct splendid original costumes for them and he had borrowed some of the artisans from Sully's staff to paint the scenery backdrops.

As it happened the *tableau vivant* was performed beneath a dismal canopy in a chill drizzle. Miserable and shivering, Isabel sat beside her husband and watched the colors drip dolefully from the canvas backdrops and the players stumble through their speeches, shaking with cold.

The day's festivities ended with a drenched meal and the suspension of all activities. The king vomited wine which had gone sour and the queen, swooning from weariness and the cold, fainted from her chair onto the muddied grass below.

T̸HE GIRL had been kneeling for over three hours on the canvas-covered floor, tensing only at the intermittent sound of the vespers bell from St. Geneviève up the hill beyond the vineyards. Torchglow gave highlights to her rich brown hair, and sparkle to her serene expression. The artist, watchful, narrowed his eyes and gripped his charcoal stick tighter—scratching it across the surface of his parchment roll. His strokes were studied and distinct, endeavoring to capture the purity of her face.

Her name was Roselyn Hereward. She was the daughter of an English baronial family and well known as a doer of goodly works for the poor and the sick. The French called her *Le Donne Rose*. She was a pure-faced young woman whose image had been reproduced in stained glass as a madonna figure at Noyers and

Chartres. Now the artist was taking her likeness for the windows at Notre Dame.

With hundreds of others, Roselyn was a participant in the making of this great cathedral which had become the virtual focal point of Paris. The building site constituted a city in miniature. It was a spectator attraction as well. So many people crowded into the square each day that had the Ile de la Cité truly been the boat it resembled, it would have tipped at its stern and sunk out of sight into the Seine.

People, everywhere. Peering from the windows of cookshops, crowding about cluttered winestalls, gaping from the open doors of wooden dwellings or merchant houses, or stopping for a while at the edge of the square to linger with their wares and baskets upon their shoulders, all of them eager to catch a glimpse of the activity.

It was a colorful spectacle: stout quarrymen, hoisters, and scaffold-setters in their heavy wool tunics and tight leather braies; the artisans—who might be part of several groups of planmasters, designers, sketch artists, sculptors, glass devisors, goldsmiths and color advisers—all in the loose white smocks and leather aprons of their trade. The vigor of their collective enterprise gave the men an aura of virility, and many a Paris maiden stood in the shadows of the cathedral watching, and giggled behind her hands.

And so the crowds came, eager to absorb the flair and creative atmosphere of a hundred skilled craftsmen at their work. Nothing had so unified Paris since the days of Clovis, when a delicate virgin named Genevieve had convened the populace in the streets to pray for deliverance from the Huns.

It was in the midst of such activity that Philippe stood on the afternoon of a ruthlessly cold December day, and waited for Maurice de Sully.

Philippe waited with impatience, warming his hands within the miniver folds of his pellison. Beside him in rows the canvas tents flapped against the poles which tethered them, their stained, sagging roofs bearing evidence of rain and exposure to all weather. The gutted cellar remains of St. Etiénne were hardly visible, filled with sand, and topped by piles of grey stone blocks, awaiting use by the ropes, hooks, and pulleys which would place them. The fragmented sounds of chisel, spar, and hammer were everywhere on the air.

Sully came into view, ringed by a dozen followers. His head was bare, white hair blowing in the wind. He called out a few departing instructions, then came briskly forward, taking up Philippe's outstretched hand and kissing the ring. "My apologies for delaying you," he professed, and swept open the tent flap for the king to enter. "The Master of Works had some figure changes that had to be dealt with at once." Sully followed Philippe into the tent and over to the long table in the center of the enclosure. Atop the table surface was a clay *molle* in the image of the cathedral design.

A half dozen artisans left their work to kneel submissively before their king, till Philippe fluttered an impatient hand to indicate they might rise. "Wait outside," he told them.

"I have some window designs to show you," Sully said when they were alone. Pushing aside bottles of dye and oxides, he cleared a space, then brought out a shaft of parchment rolls from a deep drawer beneath the table.

Philippe stripped the fur from his shoulders and slung it carelessly to the bench beside him. "I see little of you these days, Sully." His gaze flitted aimlessly about the room. "It used to be we had much time for one another. Now I see my barber more often than I see you."

Sully unrolled the crackling parchment scroll and smoothed the sheets out upon the table surface. He peered over his shoulder at Philippe. "You are kept occupied in your duties, and I have much work of my own, as you can see. My very household is turned into an annex of this project. I have a half-dozen of my artist-designers living with me at the Episcopal palace. There is a constant noise of people coming and going, so that even my sleep is muddled." His voice had the high, excited quality of someone who is continuously besieged by activity, and adores every minute of it.

He passed a drawing to Philippe. "It is unfortunate that I have had to decline your last several invitations, but many is the time I have taken my meals here at this table so that I might continue my work without interruption."

Philippe's voice hinted at complaint. "Yet you have the time to attend the lord provost at the Episcopal palace."

Sully bent to his work. "How have I displeased you?"

Philippe dropped himself onto the bench and stretched his long legs out before him, the ankles crossed. "I sent a message to you last week to dine with me at the palace, and you declined. Yet that very night you hosted a banquet for some of my own barons." He narrowed his eyes. "Did you really think I would not know what goes on beneath my nose?"

Sully's expression crinkled into little lines of irony on both sides of his mouth. "When your mother leaves Paris and returns to the Loire Valley I shall be glad once again to honor your invitations."

Philippe looked down at the paper he held in his hand. It was a charcoal sketch with the ink coloring half filled in, depicting Bernard of Clairvaux. The face was unoffending and even cherubic, little like the man whom Louis had called "the greatest maker of sermons on earth since Christ." Philippe put the paper in his lap and looked up at Sully. "After all these years I would have thought you and Adele could find a means of bridging your differences."

Sully had brought out several pages of figures and he was studying them now. "She is a headstrong woman," he muttered. "I wonder that you can endure her as well as you do."

The bishop's dislike for Adele was something Philippe had learned to take for granted years ago, and he understood it well enough. Yet mother and son had entered into a period of relatively civil relations recently so Philippe could afford to be lenient in his judgment. "She is no trouble to me now that she has at long last assented to my authority."

Sully pondered his thoughts, wondering if he should speak. Warily he said, "I only speculate if you have not exchanged the influence of one female for another."

Philippe pressed the tips of his fingers together beneath his chin. "What do you mean?"

"Your wife is greatly criticized."

"By many people," Philippe agreed, "but I did not think you were one of them."

"She is not what I had expected."

"Nor I."

Sully held up his hand in a gesture of truce. "Hear me. When first Isabel was brought to Paris, I felt deeply for her circumstances. I wanted to help her. Yet now it is evident to me that she exerts an unwholesome influence over you, and by means which are indecent, considering her age."

Philippe's breath faltered a little in his chest. Now he understood this sense of impending argument which had strained his relationship with Sully the past few months. Philippe had withstood no end of criticism about the much-despised Isabel from all other quarters, but this source was new. "Look here, Sully," he said defiantly, "I've no doubt you gave ready advice to Louis on private matters, but *my* life is my own."

Sully took up the parchment from Philippe's lap and put it on the table with the others. "Your father was a saintly man. Carnality had no place in his nature."

"He was a pious fool!" Philippe declared. "And I would not be like him for all I own!"

"I don't think there is much chance of that," Sully mumbled.

Philippe dug the heel of his boot into the dirt. "My father had *three* wives, yet he pleased you well enough."

"What he did was not for his own pleasure but for the sake of getting an heir, as you well know."

Contentious, Philippe shot back, "And aren't I allowed the same rights with my wife?"

Sully's voice was stiff. "Her age should answer that question."

"Oh, this is useless!" Philippe's voice flared into anger. "I came here to discuss matters concerning the cathedral, and nothing else. If you wish only to make a sermon at my expense, I shall wait upon you some other time."

Sully's hand was a gentle restraint upon Philippe's shoulder. "After so many years and all that has passed between us, do you have so little love for me that you would make an end of my company rather than take my counsel?"

Philippe's lips twisted in petulance. "I do not like to be questioned on private matters."

The bishop rested a hand tenderly upon Philippe's head. This was the boy he had baptized and taught to pray; the youth whose coronation and marriage ceremonies the old bishop had solemnized. So much turmoil had gone into the making of this young man, and it was part of his nature. Sully put a balm of kindness into his voice. "I am not blaming you my son. Women are dark, and darker still are girls who ripen before their time. Who connive to make men sin in their minds."

Philippe sounded more hurt than angry. "It is not Isabel's fault that she is beautiful."

"No," Sully conceded, "but she flaunts her beauty in ways which are willful. Her clothes, perfumes, and jewels are indiscreet and invite wanton attentions. It cannot have escaped your notice that half the men in your service are smitten by her. They look at her with lust and whisper vulgar insinuations behind their hands. It detracts from her dignity, and from your own."

Philippe brushed Sully's hand away. The truth of the bishop's words galled him. Philippe had said the same thing to Isabel many times. But for an outsider, even Sully, to voice such a criticism was another matter. Vainly he sought to defend his wife. "It is the nature of women to behave that way. Especially beautiful women. My mother, as you know, has always been much the same. Jewels, perfumes, pretty things—they are all a woman has to amuse herself."

"And a girl? A *child?*"

"She is my wife," Philippe answered sharply, "and she is the queen, despite whatever ill-will you or anyone else may feel toward her. I am sick of hearing criticism against her. Let any man who wishes to dispute her station say it to my face!"

"I am not disputing the legitimacy of her station," Sully replied, "you know that. I am warning you of her influence over you. You are too *aware* of her. She has her will of you."

Philippe thrust out his hands, questioning. "What are you saying? That she influences my decisions? That she thinks for me? Rules for me?"

Sully didn't flinch. "She doesn't need to rule for you. She rules *you.*"

"That's enough!" Philippe shouted, jumping to his feet at last. "I refuse to listen to any more of your slander. You priests are all alike when it comes to women. You bully and malign them, especially if they are young and beautiful, because you resent them as the one thing which is denied you!"

Sully's vivid blue eyes gave youth to his face. "You are wrong Philippe, but you can't see it. Young men think sex is the primary motivation for all emotions. Someday if you live long enough, you will learn that there are deeper passions than the hot impulses of youth." He paused, and his expression went sad. "I am an old man now, thank God, and well past the itch of the flesh. I speak to you out of the concern of my love for you, not because I envy your place in Isabel's bed."

The deserving reproof embarrassed Philippe, but not enough to subdue him completely. After a moment he snatched up his discarded pellison and tossed the fur recklessly about his shoulders. He fitted his fingers into soft chamois gloves and cleared his throat. "I see that we have nothing to talk about. You have made your comments. Now hear mine. Think whatever you wish of Isabel, but she is my wife. It is for me to mitigate her behavior and discipline her as I see fit. But I never wish to hear you criticize her to my face again." Indignant, he pushed past Sully and at the edge of the tent stood for a moment, his hand poised on the rough canvas of the tent flap. Philippe's expression was hard. "Build my cathedral, bishop," he hissed over his shoulder. "Leave the domestic matters to me!"

The fire was burning low, fed by intermittent drafts when the wind howled through the chimneys, stirring up the flames. Shadows played on the wall like silent, scampering ghosts when the light wavered and the wind blew.

Philippe and Adele sat alone at the long table in the great hall, lingering over wine in dispassionate silence. The serving girls had taken away the food long ago and tossed the bones to the dogs who snarled over them in the dark recesses of the room.

Isabel had gone upstairs an hour ago. Adele's bickering and Philippe's glum silence had been too much for her. Philippe was in a particularly bad temper tonight. The argument with Sully that afternoon had upset him, but it was not of that he was thinking now.

He was mentally re-reading the message he had received this morning from the Count of Flanders. It had been a repetition of their earlier communications: *No Vermandois*. Since the mid-August refusal to relinquish the territories, Philippe had sent several messages north and the response was always the same.

The emperor and Henry of England had remained outside of it all, saying nothing. It was obvious that they were not going to be any help to France. Yet Philippe could not be sure if they had been in contact with Flanders or not. While it was unlikely that Henry would ally with Flanders in anything more than tacit support, Emperor Frederick's position was a little more difficult to discern. Philippe wanted Vermandois enough to fight a war against Flanders for it, but not if it included fighting the Empire.

Late in September Philippe had written to Baldwin of Hainault, demanding his father-in-law's support. No answer had come as yet and Philippe knew why. Baldwin did not wish to invite the wrath of Flanders. He wished to remain neutral, but that was fast becoming impossible. Sooner or later Baldwin—like all of them —would have to choose.

"You're very solemn tonight."

Adele's words disturbed his fitful musings. When he didn't answer she persisted: "You have scarcely moved for the past hour and you've said nothing. I have been waiting since morning to speak to you. Do I have your ear now?"

No peace. Philippe drew a hand across his face. He felt cold and the taste of the wine had gone sour in his mouth. He was tired, yet more willing to slump on this hard wooden bench than trudge up three levels of stairs to his bed. He would almost have preferred to lie down on the straw beside the dogs and pass the night in this room.

Adele's voice was shrill with exasperation. "Didn't de Puiseaux or Clermont give you my message?"

His hands were covering his face and Philippe's voice came out muffled and indistinct. "They may have. I don't remember. I've had a busy day."

Her nagging was pitiless. "Why do you purposely avoid me?"

Philippe propped his elbows on the table top with a bang and stared past Adele at the smoke rising eerily from the fire grate in the wall. "What do you want, Mother?" he asked resignedly, and waited.

Now that he had given her leave to speak, Adele seemed reticent. She fussed with the tassels of her mantle, her pearl-draped wrists making anxious little movements. She was nervous and wary; a dark, sleek cat cautiously circling an intended prey. All at once she looked up. "Have you seen the dispatches sent back from the East?"

He shook his head. "They were brought in this afternoon just before I went to speak with Sully. I haven't read them yet. I haven't had the time. With you and Sully and de Puiseaux and Isabel and everyone nagging at me from every side it's a wonder I get anything accomplished."

She reached across the table for the flagon, lifting it to add a little water to her wine. "You don't take nagging from any of us. You've been especially unpleasant tonight. You had Isabel near tears a half dozen times during dinner. You've taken such pains recently to ensure that the rest of us treat her well. You might apply that rule to your own behavior."

"I've fought with everyone today, including Sully," he spat, "so don't you start in on me. And since when do you give a damn how I treat Isabel?"

"Your father had a much more even temper than you," Adele complained. Then under her breath she muttered, "Louis was a good man."

Philippe struck the table with his fist. "Goddamn you, woman! I'm tired. I'm in no mood for your wailings. Say what it is you want to say, and be done with it!"

Once again she distracted herself with her bracelets, then cast her eyes down timidly, a faint and thoroughly female smile curving her lips. He knew this approach. She wanted something from him, and all her overtures to that end were tempered with sex. He bit back his cynicism and said nothing.

"Philippe," she began, her voice sweet as honey, "I have had messages of my own. And since you say you have not read the dispatches from the East, I will tell you some news which is of interest to us. Alexius Comnenus is dead."

Weariness and distraction had dimmed his concentration. "Who?" he asked.

"The young emperor," she answered, a note of rancor creeping into her voice. "Your sister's fiancé."

He dismissed the news with a shrug. "So?"

"He is dead. Murdered by his uncle, the infamous Andronicus, who has seized the crown."

Philippe took up her cup and drank from it. "So what do the Byzantines want?" he asked, then immediately answered his own question. "I suppose to negotiate some new marriage treaty. Who is offered for Agnes now?"

Adele came to sit beside him, pressing close, her fingers curled tightly about his wrist commanding his attention. "The news is worse than you can guess," she confided. "Andronicus has already declared that he will marry Agnes!"

Philippe's expression didn't change. "I suppose he'll demand some new dower settlement," he complained. "Damn greedy foreigners. No doubt whatever Louis provided has long since been used up."

Adele's eyes were bright with frustration. "Don't you understand? The money isn't important. He wants Agnes!"

Philippe eased out of her grip. "What difference does it make? She was promised to an emperor—it seems she shall marry one after all."

"That man is over seventy!" she cried.

Philippe drummed his fingers thoughtfully on the table top, ignoring Adele's distress. "I remember Louis talking about Andronicus. They met when father was in Antioch." He cast a sideways look at his mother. "This prospective husband of my sister's is reputed to be a great lover. Many women, including his own niece, have openly declared their love for him. He sounds very glamorous."

"He is old!" Adele shouted. "He is a satyr! I would rather see my daughter dead than the plaything to such a man!"

His laugh sounded harsh and obscene in the somber room and he jostled her with his elbow. "When did you become so prim? You have bedded enough men to have lost your dainty discretion."

Her eyes were black and gleaming. "I've never pretended to be virtuous, though you've no right to criticize me. In matters of the flesh we are much the same."

He twisted around to face her, confronted by the sultry scent of her perfume. "That's right," he conceded, fingering the pearl above her breasts, "I am the son of your body..."

She pulled away from him, misgiving of his attitude because he was drunk, and in a sour mood to begin with. Her expression appealed for his understanding. "Don't compromise the sanctity of your sister, Philippe. Think of her situation, and have Christian pity for her!"

Philippe finished the wine in his mother's cup and poured more. "Don't be so naïve," he told her. "She's been living at that debauched court among depraved Easterners for nearly three years. She's sure to have learned something of the ways of the world. Twelve-year-olds ripen early these days, or hadn't you heard?"

Anger hardened her features. "She is an innocent child."

Philippe bared his teeth. "Innocent? Not if she's anything like you."

With a howl of fury Adele slapped his face, her rings leaving a jagged cut above his mouth. For a second he seemed bewildered, as though she had slapped his wits to the winds. It had been a long time since Philippe had been slapped, and never by his mother. His tongue licked away the trickle of blood at the corner of his mouth. He continued to stare at her. "Don't ever do that again," he warned.

"You would do anything, anything, wouldn't you, just to hurt me!" she cried. "Even abandon your own sister! How you must hate me to be so cruel!"

"There's nothing I can do about it!" he shouted into her face. "It's out of my hands."

Furious at his obstinance, Adele flailed out with her left hand, sending the glass porringer shattering to the floor. "You could send word to the pope!" she screamed at him. "He would intervene in this even if you would not. There is not one Christian king in Europe who would not send armies to recapture my daughter rather than deliver her up to this pagan sacrilege!" Her face was contorted. "She is my daughter! *Do something!*"

Philippe lunged to his feet, nearly knocking the bench out from under her. "Your daughter!" he taunted. "You were about as loving to Agnes as you were to me. You are a travesty as a mother."

He had broken her at last, dissolved her anger into tears. Her chin trembled as she looked up at him. "How can you speak such ignoble words? Being a son is easy. Motherhood is a curse!"

"Motherhood?" he cried, his expression curdling as he spat upon the floor. "The very word makes my stomach churn. The brothels of Paris are filled with women more fitting as mothers than you ever were." When she raised her hand to slap him again he caught her wrist in mid-air and twisted it brutally. "You never loved me, you were never a mother to me. Christ Jesus, half the men at court fed at your breasts, but never your son!"

The lampblack at her eyes had smeared into dark patches upon her cheeks, but Adele, who so loved her beauty, was too

despairing to care. "What do you know of motherhood?" she
wailed. "I went through hell just to conceive you!"

He let go of her arm at last, laughing at her pain. "Hell for
you? For Father more likely. Spreading your legs is what you do
best."

She grabbed blindly at him, her bracelets catching in the embroidery of his surcoat. In an instant Philippe pinned her wrists
together with a swipe of his hand and held her back. He leaned
close, his expression wolf-like. "How many have there been,
mother? How many men have tracked their filth through your
bed? And when I was a child, how many nights did you spend on
your knees before one of father's soldiers, while I cried myself to
sleep, afraid of the dark, with no mother's arms to comfort me?"
With a grunt he shoved her back against the table, pronouncing
his words like a curse. "Go peddle your grief somewhere else.
I've had enough of you for one night."

Adele flung herself at his feet. "I gave you life! You owe me
something for that!"

He looked down at her disheveled, submissive form with pitiless austerity. "So you did. Thank you. But you live under the
grace of my protection now. Remember that. I bowed to your
rank once because I was too young to assert myself. But never
again. *I* am the law."

Pride was gone, even anger. All that remained was a tiny flame
of loyalty. She sprawled at his feet like a beggar. "Please," she
wept, "don't abandon your sister! Don't shame our family!"

He pushed her grasping hands away with a kick of his boot.
"Forget it. Agnes is nothing to me. I don't give a devil's damn
whom she marries. And don't get any clever ideas about getting
Henry of England involved in this. I've had the last of outsiders
interfering in French concerns."

"I will go to him!" she vowed amidst her sobs. "I will!"

Philippe laughed. "It won't do you any good, though, because
he won't be interested in helping you this time. You see, there's
nothing in it for him. And I don't think your charms would be of
any use. He already has all the whores he needs."

She felt the rush of cold air as he brushed past her, his boots
crunching shards of glass into dust on the stone floor. At the
entrance to the hall he turned back once more, his voice echoing
through the drafty room. "There is one way in which you may

prove useful. Ply your womanly wiles upon the Count of Flanders and get my territories. He might be interested, since you're about the only bitch he hasn't bedded."

Adele ripped the pearl broach from her shoulder and flung it viciously in his direction. "Go fuck yourself!" she screamed.

"You first, mother," he called over his shoulder, and disappeared into the shadows.

She sank forward, making a pillow of her arms as she wept into the darkness, still hearing the diminishing echo of his footfalls on the stairs above her. "Satan take your contemptible soul!" she whimpered, but only she heard.

𝕴N THE WHOLE of an elegant, gamboling Christmas court, Richard Plantagenet felt uncomfortable and remote. He was at a distance from the festivities and from the family members who gathered at Caen, in Normandy, to celebrate Christmas.

Almost all the family were there: Harry and Marguerite, Geoffrey and Constance, Richard's sister Matilda and her husband Henry of Saxony, with their children. John too, although he was nearly as glum as Richard. King Henry had recently secured a betrothal for his youngest son. John, called "Lackland" because he had no inherited territories, was dissatisfied with the heiress his father had secured for him. Not only was Hadwisa of Gloucester unsightly, she was a full seven years older than her prospective bridegroom.

Richard had deeper concerns than marital alliances. Since the past summer he had noted with alarm the cordiality which had sprouted between his brothers Harry and Geoffrey. Richard had no proof that Geoffrey had "arranged" the humiliating events in Limoges, but he had suspicions. In September and November Geoffrey had made trips to visit Harry in Normandy while Richard, far away in Poitiers, had trembled with the thought of what those two dissemblers were planning together.

Here at Caen this Christmas they were in each other's company constantly. It seemed that everywhere Richard looked he could see Geoffrey and Harry huddled close in quiet conversation that ceased whenever he approached. They hovered together in the dark spill of shadowed corridors; rode off together in the chilly fog of fierce Norman dawns; retired whispering each night to the same room.

Bertran de Born, the troubador-knight, had come to Caen as Harry's guest, and his presence provoked further malice in Richard. Bertran was a logical suspect of any trouble-rousing. Overlord of a small estate in the Hâuteville region of the Aquitaine, Bertran had spent his past twenty years in a limp imitation of Philip d'Alsace's chivalry, easing himself close to the outer edges of the high nobility with his charm, skill at arms, and as a writer of pithy, sardonic verse. He had great illusions of his own importance, and that made him dangerous. Richard had trifled with him, more piqued by de Born's skills as a poet than a lover, and the dissolution of their former relationship presaged trouble now. De Born, turned enemy, could prove villainous. His power in the Aquitaine meant little, for many men ranked above him. But his famous *sirventes* were read and praised throughout the provinces of the continent, and his opinions carried surprising public and political weight. Now he was Harry's friend, and Geoffrey's. What did it all mean?

Richard was sick of the deception. He was not afraid to fight any man face-to-face but he had no stomach for duplicity and faithless friends. Or relatives. That was another sobering realization. It had been many years since Richard had been forced to endure a stretch of seclusion with his family, and he had nearly forgotten how unpleasant they all were.

There was only one person at Caen that Christmas season with whom he shared any sense of comradeship. He was a Welshman in Richard's service named Aaron ap Rhys, who in an attempt to disguise the social ignominy of a Jewish mother, had changed his first name to Trevyn. Stocky, blunt-speaking, carelessly dressed, he didn't fit the mold of Richard's usual companions. Trevyn had no predilection for chivalry, romantic ballads, or young men. But he was a good friend and jolly, with the typical Welsh exuberance and a nimble way with a tale.

Everyone kept busy at Caen that season, occupying themselves with the frantic little pastimes of people who are unhappy and not very comfortable with one another. Constance and Marguerite fussed over Matilda's children. Matilda doted over her depressed husband, who had so recently been evicted of his holdings in Saxony by Emperor Frederick. John amused himself with a laundress on a bed of straw behind the stove. Harry and Geoffrey and Bertran de Born conversed with hushed tones in secret places. Richard and Trevyn sat together in the common hall drinking wine and coriander, exchanging bawdy stories for hours at a time, till the drink vanquished them and the tales played themselves out as mute images in their befuddled dreams.

Henry Plantagenet had little time for court gaieties this season, though it was he who had brought this gathering of his family together. He sat at the council table in his audience chamber, looking out past shaded grey glass at the barren landscape and the scampering snow that covered it.

Earlier in the month he had met with Philip of Flanders who, eager to keep Vermandois out of French hands, had requested the English king's help in finding a new bride. Vermandois would be her wedding gift: the final, ignoble signal to France that the Count of Flanders bowed beneath the hand of no man.

The King of Portugal had a nubile daughter, and Henry was engaged in making terms for the marriage between her and Philip. Having disappointed d'Alsace in the past, Henry would redeem himself with this act. It was flagrantly obvious that Flanders' feud with the King of France would be a major item of discord on the political agenda for years to come, and Henry saw the necessity of keeping a careful balance. Should he lean too obligingly toward either one, he might upset the delicate equalization of power that existed.

Henry splattered a thickness of hot wax upon the folded edge of the letter and plunged his signet ring into it. That single act would cause Isabel of Hainault a thousand tears. But Henry didn't know, and he didn't care.

By the end of January Richard was back in Poitiers and there he heard the first faint rumblings of what he had only suspected in Caen. He had been right to mistrust his brothers, he could see that now, and terribly, terribly wrong to put himself at such a distance from them.

Clever Geoffrey was at the center of this new conspiracy. He had succeeded in puffing up Harry's pride to the point that Harry actually believed that he (with Geoffrey's help) could wrest Normandy from Henry and the Aquitaine from Richard. Now *there* was a plan to topple the balance of power! For without the rich resources of the continent, the power of England would be but a little thing.

If Richard was attacked by his brothers, the King of England would come to his aid. That was Geoffrey's reasoning, and his grandiose plan would ensnare them both. In defeating their brother, he and Harry would defeat their father as well. Normandy, Brittany, Aquitaine, Gascony and Maine would belong to Harry and Geoffrey. They had already secured the promised help of Count Raymond of Toulouse and Hugh of Burgundy. That, combined with Geoffrey's three thousand Brabantine mercenaries, fifteen hundred men-at-arms from Brittany, and Harry's own two thousand Norman knights, would make a respectable army. And that did not even count the barons in the Aquitaine who would gladly join *any* rebellion against Richard.

Geoffrey had worked out the details of the rising with the exactness of a torture master. There were to be two seats of the rebellion: Tours and Limoges. Harry would bring his men south from Rouen to Tours; Geoffrey's would come east from Rennes. At the same time, Burgundy and Toulouse would march their men to Limoges where they would meet up with Geoffrey's hired mercenaries. Cut off from his father's forces in Normandy, Richard would be trapped. Before Henry could send for his reinforcements from England, it would all be over.

It was mid-February before the news of impending revolution reached Henry's ears in Normandy. He was not surprised. There was always some trouble brewing in the south, and he felt certain that if war did come, Richard would put an end to it. He turned his attention to other concerns.

By March Limoges was in tumult and Harry was holding the city against its own barons. Alarmed, Henry gathered up two thousand soldiers and came to Limoges, hoping to reconcile his sons to some peaceful settlement. But when the king reached the outskirts of the city he was met by insurgent troops and he barely escaped injury from a shower of arrows.

He made his stand outside the city, and for the next several weeks messengers shuttled back and forth between his camp and that of his sons, bearing the fluttering white banners of uneasy truce. With Richard cut off in Poitiers, where his armies were fighting Geoffrey's mercenaries, the English king was determined to achieve a settlement with his two perfidious sons.

Yet he seemed unwilling to see the seriousness of this affair. It had happened so many times before. He had brought his sons to heel for their transgressions in the past, and he would do it again. Henry refused to see that this was no longer a matter of youthful caprice on the part of his sons; that they were not merely rebellious boys under the troubling influence of some outside antagonist. *They were the dangerous purveyors of malice and treason, and they wanted Henry's blood.* Some of the king's closest advisers had warned him of this many times, but he would never listen.

Shortly before Easter Richard successfully disbursed the Brabantines and marched his men south to Limoges. Panicked by this turn of events, Harry presented himself suddenly in Henry's camp, terrified and servile and begging for mercy. At last seeing an end to this miserable affair, Henry kissed the boy and pardoned him in the presence of all those assembled. A general truce was called for the observance of Easter, and the king made plans to return to Normandy the following week.

Once again he had misjudged the ability of his sons to hurt him. After Easter Harry retreated to the rival camp and there, upon a bitter scolding from Geoffrey, he fell back into his role as rebel and traitor.

The news of Richard's southwest progress induced Harry to send Marguerite north under guard to Paris, with a message for her half-brother. So far Philippe Capet had remained discreetly outside of the tumultuous events taking place on the fringe of his *demesne*. The rebels sensed that he had no wish to become personally involved. Yet his antagonism toward the English king was well known, and it was upon this fact that Harry was depending. Philippe didn't disappoint. He gave sanctuary to the distressed Marguerite, and immediately dispatched 400 men-at-arms to Harry's aid.

It was too late. The fantastically concocted conspiracy was coming apart. In Brittany, Constance refused to answer Geoffrey's demands for more money. The Brabantines, beaten back by Richard's men and unpaid for many weeks, had retreated to Angoulême. Cheated of payment, they would withdraw from the revolt, or worse, turn on the rebels themselves. The revolt would never succeed without them. They would *have* to be paid.

While Geoffrey stayed at Limoges to hold off Richard's army, Harry traveled south in search of booty. Town after town went over to the side of the rebels: Aixe on May 23rd, Uzerche three days later. The crowds went wild at the sight of young Harry, splendid in his violet silks, his golden hair kissed by the light of a summer sun. The barons, weary of Richard's ruthlessness, willingly swore a new allegiance to Henry Plantagenet's first-born son.

At Rocamadour Harry and his band of brigands looted the rich shrine of St. Amadour, stealing the jeweled reliquaries, the gold crosses, and all else of value. With his own hands Harry took the sword of Roland from the sacristy to pawn as payment for his troops.

It was his last act of sacrilege. On June 3rd, feverish and puking and barely able to sit his horse, Harry started north once more. Illness had made him urgent to reach Limoges, but he only got so far as the vineyards outside Martel when, shaking with dysentery, Harry collapsed from his horse onto the dusty road.

They carried him by litter to a farmhouse and somebody sent for a priest. A bishop came with two pious nuns to pray for the young king, but everyone knew he was dying. At long last, fearful for the state of his soul, Harry asked that he be clothed in his crusader's cloak and set upon a bed of ashes to signal his repentance.

William Marshal held his young lord's hand and wept without shame. Only he knew that the messenger dispatched to the English king at Limoges had been rebuffed. Henry had finally stopped deluding himself that his sons could be faithful. Surely this latest news of Harry's illness was yet one more trap to deceive him.

It was June 11th, the jewel-bright morning of a summer's day, when Harry Plantagenet, who was not yet thirty, gazed wanly out the open window up into the last sky he would ever see, and whispered his father's name.

In a woodcutter's shack at the edge of the forest outside Limoges they found the king of England sprawled over a plump redhead upon a bed of straw.

Five Norman knights jostled their way inside, nearly filling the tiny room. Henry sat up, roused by the noise, and got to his feet, knotting a dirty blanket at his waist to cover himself.

William Marshal pushed in past the others and stood for a moment looking at the king. From beneath his arm he withdrew a folded garment and put it into Henry's hands.

The king stared down at the fine white linen cloak with its emblazoned red cross visible by but a single bar of scarlet. Wailing, he threw his body to the ground, concealing his face in the dirt, rending the earth with his fingers. Hell would hold no surprises for him. Powerless, the king of England raged into the dust.

* * *

"Now every grief and woe and bitterness,
    The sum of tears that this sad century's shed
Seem light against the death of the young king
    And prowess mourns, and youth stands sorrowful.
No man rejoices in these bitter times.

"All pride in battle, skill in song and rhyme
    Must yield to sorrow's humble threnody.
For cruel death, that mortal warrior,
    Has harshly taken from us king of knights;
Beside him charity itself was mean,
    And in him every noble virtue shone.

"So pray we all that God in His sweet grace
    May grant His pardon to the young English king,
Who yesterday was valiant knight;
    Now he is fallen to the great lord Death
And leaves us naught but sadness and despair..."

Bertran de Born
June, 1183

* * *

The messenger accomplished his business quickly and rode away soon after so that the queen might shed her tears in private. But Eleanor did not weep. She sat for a long while in the close confinement of her little garden at Salisbury, absently drawing the woollen wrap closer about her shoulders, because it was so cold for June.

Anger sat close upon her sorrow. *Henry was to blame for this!* All her troubles had begun with him. There had been years of frustration and boredom during her first marriage, but all the pain had come later, with Henry. Louis had been a bauble, something to trifle with and toss laughingly away. His adoration had offended her because she could never return it, and she had despised his willingness to accept her abuse.

She thought of him often these days, preferring to recall a life before Henry. She had known little satisfaction as Louis's wife, but she'd been younger then, and life had been more pleasing. Poor foolish Louis. His love had engulfed her like a stifling perfume. It had been easy, even tempting, to hurt him. Yet there had been some moments of pleasure between them. . . .

She reached up, brushing her fingers against a low-hanging branch of her peach tree, remembering a time over thirty years ago and far away in the East. Louis had not wanted to take her on crusade but her charms had bought his favor. Eleanor had envisioned a heroic adventure in romantic settings but from the beginning the great endeavor had been a series of misfortunes. . . .

Eleanor had come to hate the crusade, their marriage, him. All seemed bogged down in fraud and failure. Then had come the surprise attack at Mt. Cadmos, and for a few hours Eleanor had waited in terror at the camp with the other women, fearing that Louis was dead. All her indifference toward him had paled beside that fear. On her knees she implored God to spare his life.

Dawn had pronounced a safe return: Louis, wretched and bloodied and soaked with sweat, leading his pitiful band of scavenger knights back from Mt. Cadmos. God had chosen to give Eleanor another chance.

She had bathed the blood from her husband's body with her own hands, bandaged his wounds, and massaged his flesh with oil of herbs. Then beneath the pink blossoms of another peach tree Louis the warrior-king had made love to her savagely, and for the last time. What a man he could be when he forgot that he was king, and God's anointed!

For a few days Eleanor had loved him with her whole soul. Then the demands of life and circumstance had overtaken her once more, and the love had died forever. Shortly after that they had separated: Louis going on to Syria, she returning to France. When Louis returned to Paris, the remnants of a failed crusade behind him, they had talked seriously of divorce for the first time. Then had come her meeting with young Henry of Anjou, and after that nothing Louis could have said or done would have kept her interest or her heart....

At last the tears came, making little splashing patterns on her folded hands. Even near the end of their marriage Louis had been amenable to her advice, knowing she was cleverer than he. But Henry—so greedy for every crumb of power— had never consulted her in matters political or personal. The first years of their marriage she had borne him sons with dutiful regularity while he was busy making a pet of his chancellor Thomas Becket, and sporting openly with any woman who took his fancy.

Wasted and abused, her offering of love to Henry had decayed into malice. Deceptions had grown into confrontations. Arguments had escalated into wars. All her energies were bent toward destroying the only man she had ever loved.

It was not enough for her alone to hate Henry. Gleefully she had weaned her sons away from him, cosseting them in the cultured surroundings of her palace in Bordeaux. There she had sung them songs and taught them poetry, but between the music and the laughter she had whispered tales to them of their father's treachery, until she saw her own bitterness mirrored in their eyes.

The hate had grown in her till it was all she knew. It had cost Eleanor her marriage, her peace of mind, her freedom, and now even her son. She looked down at her tear-splattered hands. *Henry had done all of this.*

It was all lost to her now. She had nothing to show for the efforts of her grand, gay youth: only the trinkets of petty affections and one horrendous love, spent, and all in vain. It was past—the reckless flirtations, the wide-eyed idealism, the secret glint of pleasure winking back from within the silver circlet of a teasing mirror. She would never again command a man's favor or bargain for it by using the loveliness of her face or her body. Only her wily intelligence remained to serve her now.

For all that she had been forced to endure, Eleanor would

have her revenge. Someday, perhaps soon, Henry would be dead. Richard, her best-beloved child, would sit upon the throne of England. That would be her reward for grim years of waiting. She lifted her face and stared ahead into the setting sun.

* * *

A group of heretics live in France. They have named themselves Ca-puciati, the "white-caped Friends of Peace." They preach the brotherhood of Man and clothe themselves in humble raiment, but they are heretics all the same.

These apostates are led by a simple carpenter who names himself Dur-and Dujardin. It has been said of him that he preaches according to Christ's own words, yet he sins against that same Christ by denying the power of the Church which Christ Himself did ordain during His time on earth.

Why a man does evil may be difficult for all but God to know. Dujar-din may wish only to make his name a famous thing, or he may be a misguided visionary. Yet, already, hungry and power-seeking Flemish mercenaries have clustered about him and his Capuciati, eager to enforce this "brotherhood" with their swords. For the security of the church on earth, politics and heretics make an uneasy brew.

In Paris the king of France has spoken out against all enemies of the Church, most especially the Albigenses. Yet his queen, who is a Fleming, has sent a pearl and ruby ring to the Durand Dujardin, as if to denote her favor to his cause. What say the king of France to this treason?

Godfrey of Lincoln
August, 1183

* * *

Philippe's temporary accommodation of Marguerite was exhibiting all the signs of becoming a long-term arrangement. After months of wrangling he had been unable to re-negotiate her dower settlement with King Henry. Harry's death had now voided the prior contract, and restored the Vexin to France. Henry was unwilling to part with it and had thrown up a number of legal and administrative roadblocks in Philippe's way. Until such time as that matter was resolved, Marguerite would remain a ward of the French crown.

Her tenure at the Cité palace worked no hardship upon Philippe, who had grown to like her. Accustomed to the complainings of his wife and mother, he found his half-sister's uncritical disposition a gratifying change. Marguerite had no intellectual pretensions, and she was an eager, solicitous listener to his every word. Knowing well where her own best interests lay, she had cultivated Philippe's confidence, and agreed with each opinion he expressed.

Isabel was thoroughly provoked by Marguerite's presence at court and resentful of Philippe's indulgence of her. She had borne the insult in grudging silence for a while, but by the end of August she had lost all patience with the situation. It was as if Philippe was deliberately baiting her. Whenever they fought now, and it was often, Marguerite's name was never far away.

"When is she going back to England?" Isabel asked one night when he came to her room. It was late. Once again he had lingered too long downstairs over wine and conversation with Marguerite. Once again Isabel had chosen to spend the evening alone in her room.

It was not the sort of greeting Philippe appreciated, especially since he was still smarting from his wife's unwise involvement with the *Capuciati*. Godfrey of Lincoln's words had been circulated throughout the city, doubtless at the prompting of Isabel's enemies among the nobility. The episode had caused Philippe considerable embarrassment and he had not yet forgiven his wife. Isabel knew his feelings and yet she refused to let the matter rest. Only someone with her colossal nerve would dare to anger him further.

"It's hot in here," he said and crossed abruptly to the window, thrusting aside the heavy tapestry which covered it. He stood there for a while, looking out over the slender, curving line of the river. Tiny boats floated on its even surface like decorations made of paper. Stray sounds mingled, hanging on the thickness of the night air. Barking dogs. A child crying. At the far end of the bridge a lolling soldier laughed with his companions and threw pebbles into the water.

Philippe turned from the window and began pulling off his clothes. "Why didn't you come down to dinner tonight?" he asked.

She rested limply back on the bed and closed her eyes. "You know the reason. I'm sick of her. When is she going back where she belongs?"

He tossed his boots to the floor and came to sit beside her. His voice was tempered with restraint. "I don't know. But until Henry agrees to furnish some means of subsistence, it is my duty to provide for her. And there is still the matter of the Vexin. Now it belongs to France again, I must do all I can to keep it. Henry wishes it to be settled on Alais as a part of her dower yet he delays her marriage to Richard for reasons of his own. He will learn he cannot have his way in both matters." Philippe looked down into her placid face, interpreting her silence as indifference. "I am boring you with talk of politics," he observed.

Her wrist lay lightly across her breast where it rose and fell with her breathing. A bracelet shone there, its rubies rare and blushing. "Politics doesn't bore me," she snapped, "for it is mother's milk to my family." At last she opened her eyes. "Philippe, I know the Vexin is important, but you'll never keep it if Henry truly wants it back, so why all this useless delay involving Marguerite? The sooner you settle it all, the happier I will be."

"You could be kinder to her," he protested, "she is, after all, a widow, bereft of home and station. In her place you would wish for the same courtesy."

Those heedless words brought Isabel to a stiff sitting position. "You dare to reproach me, when for years I have lived here friendless as a beggar? What great pains have been taken to assure *my* ease of spirit? Who has shown *me* courtesy?"

He was trying to control his temper. "I was not making comparisons, only suggesting that you make her feel as welcome as my mother and her family should have made you feel."

Isabel stripped the bracelet from her wrist and flung it in his face. "Why should I? How *dare* you concern yourself with her comfort when you ignore mine! It is your indifference more than your family's slanders which has made me a stranger here!"

"Enough, Isabel..." he warned her.

With all the arrogance of her Flemish heritage she glared at him. Haughty and contemptuous, she slid the sheet up over her shoulder, taunting him with her beauty. "Get out of my room," she hissed, "and don't come near me again until you've sent that bitch back to England."

He sprang at her, twisting her arm brutally. "No one talks that way to me, by God!"

She shrieked for him to let her go, and when he tried to cover her mouth to silence her she sank her teeth into the palm of his hand.

For a moment Philippe sat staring at the wound, then angrily he pushed his hand into her face, smearing her cheek with blood as he shouted, "Do that again and you'll be the one tossed out, not Marguerite!"

Isabel twisted away from him, holding the tassled velvet cushion against her breasts as if to protect herself. "Demands, threats!" she cried, "But for Marguerite soft words and smiles and all the time you can never find for me!"

He needed calm and quiet. She was turmoil. Exhausted by his own anger Philippe slumped forward, hands covering his face as he mumbled, "I don't think I realized until just now how much like my mother you are. Neither of you can bear to have another female of rank around you."

"Another *woman*," she corrected him sassily.

Philippe took up her discarded bracelet and passed it back and forth from one hand to the other as though trying to determine its weight. "Marguerite is my sister. I enjoy her company. I don't see how even you could be jealous of something as innocent as that."

She snatched the bracelet from him. "Can't you? You've passed more time with her these last few months than you have with me in all the time I've lived here."

"That's ridiculous."

"It's true!"

"Perhaps if you were as pleasant as she is I would seek you out more often," he answered quietly. "You and everyone else make impossible demands upon me with never a kind word or action. Marguerite is the only one who offers me solace and friendship instead of criticism and contradictions."

"Friendship?" Jealousy ate at her like acid. "You ridicule my every effort to be a friend to you. And even if she is pleasant, what right has she to be so? She is a widow. She should be in a convent grieving the loss of her husband, not living here at the expense of your purse and my patience!"

"She is kind," Philippe insisted, "and kindness is no crime."

"She is a vain, silly woman," Isabel answered bitterly, "and I am sick to death of her. Tell me, what forged this great understanding between you and her—the fact that you bedded the same man? Does that work some excitement on your senses which I cannot offer?"

His clenched fists tightened. "You have a filthy mind and a cruel tongue. I should beat you for those words."

"Do so," she spat, "at least it would prove you are a man, instead of simpering, sentimental—"

That was as far as she got before Philippe silenced her with a vicious slap. As she wept into her hands he sat, distraught and wordless. He wanted to feel sorry for her but could not; she was too pitiless herself to warrant pity from him.

"You have pushed Marguerite at me by your behavior," he finally said. "You sit alone and sulk, you hide yourself away here or in that damnable library, you do anything to avoid seeing people. It is no wonder Marguerite has become so popular with everyone. She makes friends among the nobles, visits houses of charity, and patronizes the good sisters of St. Geneviève. She performs the duties of your office while you shun the court, yet you complain to me of her presence here. Make up your mind, Isabel. Either stop complaining and accept Marguerite, or handle the social life of the court yourself. In any case, remember the dignity of your office and behave like a queen."

She sat up, rubbing her eyes. "Being Queen of France is nothing! And you *know* how I am treated! If I hide it is to escape humiliation at the hands of your subjects! What about me? Don't you care about *me?*"

"I have tried to make things easier for you," he shouted back, "and my efforts were resisted by everyone, including you. For pity sake Isabel, I am tired of being in the middle of your damned domestic tragedies."

A ruby earring shimmered a warning from beneath the folds of her hair. "Why don't you simply say what is on your mind. It isn't my attitude toward Marguerite that is bothering you, it's that business with the *Capuciati*, the things Godfrey of Lincoln wrote against me at the prompting of your pious churchmen!"

Philippe grabbed her by the shoulders, shaking her roughly. "Listen, I have suffered great humiliation from your entanglement with that group of heretics."

She twisted out of his grip, her words poised and ready to fly at him even before he had finished. "How do you *know* they are heretics? What do you know of them? Is the Bishop of Lincoln suddenly your eyes and ears?"

Philippe's hands were shaking and he braided the fingers together. "Religious and political matters are none of your concern."

Her lips pursed in a sneer. "Godfrey of Lincoln is a fool! And he has a grudge against my family. He once lost a small fortune wagering against my uncle in a tournament and since that day he has hated me and my kind." Isabel gave a disparaging little laugh. "Were he not the king of England's bastard son, he would have risen no higher than a clerk in a counting house. Yet despite all that, you still take his word over mine!"

"You admitted that you sent the ring to Dujardin," Philippe reminded her.

Her eyes flashed in contempt. "It was an act of charity, no more. How many times do I have to tell you that?"

"Such charity breeds ugly rumors."

Her full bottom lip quivered in defiance. "Are you going to allow a bishop—a bishop of Lincoln, the last place God made!—to influence you against your own wife?"

"Shut up Isabel," he threatened, jamming a fist beneath her chin. "I've had enough criticism from you for one night."

"And what of me and my feelings?" she wailed. "Nothing I do pleases you or anyone else. I am criticized no matter what I do!"

"For good reason."

"For *any* reason!"

Overcome by weariness, Philippe let his hands sag in his lap, palms up. The one was bruised and swollen, beaded with blood stains where she had bitten him. He studied the wound for a moment, then wordlessly held it out for her to see.

Penitently she entwined her fingers with his, resting her cheek upon his hand and cleansing it with her tears. Philippe gathered the weeping girl in his arms, wrapping his body around hers. She tried to speak but his kisses silenced her, his arms dispelling the clutching apology of her hands.

His kisses strayed over her beautiful, upturned face, his
tongue darting out to lick away the blood from her cheek. She
was a compulsion he could not resist and for a moment their lust
transcendedall that had gone before.

Some hours later Isabel awoke, peering from out of sleep-
glazed eyes at the burning candles. She felt pinioned to the spot,
then realized her hair was caught tight beneath the weight of
Philippe's shoulder. Smiling just a trace she reached out and
barely touched her fingertips to his forehead.

Once again they had left everything unreconciled, discarded
like trash around them, and somewhere outside this bed all the
same problems remained. She had a sense of urgency, of time
running out; of an immediate need to get up and wash her face,
but she didn't pursue it. It was cooler now. A breeze had come up
from the river. On such a night sleep came easily.

She settled her head close on Philippe's shoulder, and yawned
into her outstretched hand.

*   *   *

*To Richard, Duke of Aquitaine, Count of Poitou— from his father
Henry of England—greetings and affection. My son, in the wake of your
brother's much lamented death, it is my duty to prepare you for the role
you must now occupy in his place.*

*Though I pray Jesus my own death be far removed, I must in consid-
eration of the vast territories held under the crown of England, see to the
best behalf of my affairs and beseech your aid in attaining a unity of
purpose amongst the family of which you are now the eldest surviving
son.*

*Therefore I entreat that you now give up all claims, all titles, posses-
sions and accouterments as regards your past tenure as Duke of Aquitaine, and surrender the aforesaid duchy to the control of your brother
John.*

*Acknowledging that such a transfer will require a considerable tolera-
tion on your part, I have prepared to pass to you the responsibilities which
were the former property of your deceased brother, in preparation that you
succeed me as king upon my death.*

*It would be an indication of your desire to heed my will that you come
at once to Argentan in Normandy that we might debate these new pro-*

posals with membes of my council, and in a spirit of renewed friendship and understanding.

Written this day, being Michaelmas, September 29th, 1183, by my own hand and witnessed by Ralph of Newstead in my service, I commend me to yourself in true affection and respect.

Henry Rex

* * *

It was waiting for her somewhere behind a shivering veil of expectation and Margot lunged toward it, her body heaving and slick with sweat. Behind her crouching form she could hear Baldwin's husky panting, yet she was alone now, alone in a universe of her own making. Pleasure caused her eyelids to droop, yet she kept her dizzied vision focused on the mirror before her.

Margot lived in that mirror now, only in the mirror. Golden hair, luxuriant breasts crowned with copper nipples, lustrous amber eyes giddy with sensuality—the image fascinated her. Baldwin's hands were deft and subtle on her hips and abdomen where it swelled into her six-month pregnancy, but she barely noticed him. Alone she rode a whirlwind of lust to a frenzied counterpart within the mirror.

Exhausted, Margot slumped forward, burying her face in the fur, scenting the squander of old sweat and passion there. Cold now, she drew her hair about her shoulders and pressed her hands to her breasts for warmth. Baldwin leaned forward to kiss her, then swept up his velvet pellison and covered her.

Margot lay quietly watching him pull on his clothes. "Are you going down?" she asked, "it is very late."

He drew a hand across his beard, extracting a golden strand of her hair, then bent to do up his braies. "I have a few things to put in order before Flanders arrives. He should be here at first light."

A slim hand crept from beneath the velvet and she stroked his knee. "Stay, I haven't done with wanting you."

He nuzzled her hand and kissed it. "I'll be back later. But I need some time alone now, to think. Once your brother is here there will be no time for me to resurrect objections."

Margot rolled over on her back and looked sleepily up at him. "What are you going to tell Philip?"

Baldwin gripped his hands together between his knees. "There is little I can say that he will accept just now."

"Is it true he has married again?"

He nodded gravely. "And without any opinion from me. It seems nothing will persuade him against the course he has charted."

Margot's eyes had the gleam of a leopardess. "Does it mean war, my darling?"

He came to lie beside her, his head cushioned by her arm. "Flanders has determined to give Vermandois to his new bride; actually he has already done it. When Capet hears of this..." Baldwin let the sentence die on his lips. "I cannot see how our son-in-law, so keen to keep what has been promised to him, can submit to this. So inevitably war must come. Unless I can convince Philip otherwise."

"Can you?"

He turned to look at her. "We both know the answer to that."

She knew where his thoughts were. "And Isabel? What does this mean for her?"

"I cannot say. I am afraid to consider it. Perhaps, if Philippe truly loves her..." but it was too much to hope for.

Margot's laugh was sour. "Love? Does that young bull love anything but his own power? He is a stranger to love. He turned his own mother out in the beginning, remember?" She pursed her lips in doleful memory. "How fortunate and promising things looked for us in France then."

Baldwin stripped the cloak from her shoulders and warmed his face at her breasts. Margot felt her flesh respond to his touch but her mind was elsewhere. Teasing his neck with her fingernails she asked, "And if you dare to resist my brother, what then?"

He raised his head to look at her and his eyes communicated a sense of defeat. "If I resist, he will insist. If I stand on my resistance, then war will come." Even as he spoke the words, the reality made him shiver. War with Flanders! It could mean the end of all Baldwin held dear.

Panic heated his desire and he pulled her hands to his belly, helping her to unloose the half-drawn laces. Willingly he bloomed once more within the clutch of her eager fingers as he murmured, "It seems then that to keep my own lands safe, I must make war upon my daughter and her husband."

Margot eased her body over his, shuddering with pleasure at her ability to excite him after so many years of marriage. Isabel and her plight seemed very far away. Margot's words drifted down to him like perfume. "Then you must do it," she whispered.

N EAR THE MIDDLE of the third century A.D. a young apostle named Dionysius came to Paris to preach Christianity to the Gauls. He became the first bishop of Paris and was later beheaded at the order of the Roman governor, but the influence of his preaching changed Gaul forever. In 636 the Merovingian king Dagobert established an abbey on the place of the bishop's martyrdom and called it *St. Denis,* from which time this spot became the sepulcher of Frankish kings.

The feast of St. Denis—bishop, martyr, and patron saint of France—was commemorated on October 9th, and for the whole week which encompassed that date church bells rang throughout the Ile-de-France and the people of Paris celebrated.

A few miles to the north of the city, thousands of pilgrims pitched their tents in the field beside the Orléans road and near the abbey which Abbot Suger had built in homage to St. Denis and named for him. These pilgrims came, many from far away, to receive the blessing of bishop Sully as he passed among them, and to hear the sermons he delivered twice daily during the festival week.

In Paris a livelier pageant took place as noble and peasant, servant and scholar, priest and prostitute mingled joyously in the spirit of celebration. Thrifty Parisians opened their money pouches to buy souvenirs, wine, and food from the stalls set up along the bridge. Minstrels capered in the streets, masked and costumed, dancing to the music of flutes and drums, throwing kisses to the pretty girls who ringed the square to watch and listen. Even the workmen at Notre Dame ceased their labors to toast one another with wooden cups of free wine which the merchants of Paris had provided in great copper vats at each street corner, and ill-humored professors from the cloister school topped their sober black mantles with garlands of autumnal flowers.

Isabel could hear the music in the palace garden where she sat alone, a tiny prayer book sagging in her lap. She had designed it herself with characteristic skill and delicacy—a project to occupy her time during one of Philippe's absences from Paris. She turned the pages aimlessly, her eyes glancing over the words and drawings, but they were only gilded images upon a page, nothing more.

Isabel had been taught to believe that God lived in the words, in the drawings of martyrs and saints, but she could never find Him there. He dwelt in secret—in the mysterious recesses of the sacristy, in the high arch of cathedral spires, in the words of men like Sully. The realization of what He was eluded her. Sometimes kneeling at mass, clutching a rosary in ardent prayer, Isabel experienced faint stirrings of spiritual ecstasy, but the feeling was vague and distant, something she could not touch or understand.

She sat now, fingering a drawing of the crucified Christ, trying to feel something of His love and sacrifice, closing her eyes to fix the image in her mind—but it was Philippe's face she saw instead. Between physical and divine love there was a great disparity: she cared too much for one to comprehend the other. God existed; that she knew. But He was very far away.

Her mind buzzed with distractions and she put the book aside. Philippe had left her bed before the sun was up to ride away on some urgent business, not saying where he was going or how long he would be gone. She resented these absences which were the cause of so much discord between them. On nights he was away Isabel would toss restlessly in her bed, consumed by the jealousy of her suspicions. Who slept beside Philippe when she was not with him? By the time he returned Isabel was usually so angry and frustrated that she managed to spoil the reunion with complaints which ended in arguments. What a tangle it all was.

It was her own fault. How much less complicated her life would be if she did not love him. Love made her jealous, and jealousy made her vindictive and resentful. He didn't love her as he should—and all the passion in the world wouldn't change that. There was little enough tenderness in Philippe's nature and what he had was meted out to Marguerite. Isabel seethed at the thought. She wanted *all* that he had to give.

Isabel could hear the laughter beyond the garden wall. It depressed her further to know all of Paris was celebrating while she sat alone. Edythe had gone to the fair with some of the palace serving girls, but perhaps she had returned by now. Isabel decided to go indoors. She and Edythe could take a meal together, and then read or play draughts before bedtime. The anticipation of companionship urged Isabel to her feet.

As she started back to the palace through the grove she met Henri of Champagne on the path. "I missed you in the library today," he called out.

Their outstretched hands met and he kissed hers, taking care not to brush her fingers with the roughness of his beard. "I have been out here most of the day," she answered. "I was going in now to find Edythe. Have you seen her? She went with some of the others to look at the fair."

He still held her hand. "I thought you might have gone."

Isabel looked up at him. He was so tall, like the rest of Philippe's family. "I didn't feel like going," she answered, shifting on her feet. "Philippe's away. Besides, it would only give the people of Paris another chance to hoot and sneer at me." She began walking again, Henri following close beside her, but after a few steps her feet stopped on the path. "I left my prayer book in the garden," she said, making a little nervous half-turn, and then, "...no matter. I'll send one of the stewards for it later." She sat down on the edge of a bench beneath one of the huge oak trees. "Sit with me Henri." She patted the place beside her. "I need your company today."

They talked for a while of unimportant things, and as they did Isabel lifted her chin to scan the tops of the trees. They were nearly barren yet some sparrows played at being leaves on the topmost limbs. "Those birds see more of Paris than I do," she observed.

Henri's dark eyes mirrored a true feeling of sympathy, and Isabel looked closely at him. He had a good face. Handsome, if one didn't look too closely or too long. There was a certain softness to his expression, an almost feminine curve to his lips that contrasted with Philippe's bold, sullen features. Like all the

Champagnois he dressed well, though the rich dark colors he chose made his skin look as white as a girl's.

"There are finer places than Paris to see," he was saying, and Isabel knew by the note of pride in his voice he was referring to his native Champagne, where he ranked above all other men. "Troyes is an exciting city, Isabel, much like Mons—you would like it I think. Nearby, my chateau sits on the Seine tributary and overlooks the plain. Champagne is like nowhere else. The air is warm and dry and sweet to the senses. It is beautiful. I would love to show it to you."

Isabel tucked a loose strand of hair behind her ear and silently scoffed at his pretensions. Aloud she said, "And would your *wife* make me welcome?"

He drew nearer. "*I* would." His hand found hers. "No, don't look away Isabel. I must speak my heart. To see you each day, to be in your company, having only your friendship and knowing I can never have more, is torment to me. I love you so much..."

She pulled her hand away. "I am the king's wife."

"You should have been mine."

Why couldn't he simply be her friend and leave it at that? Isabel sighed in vexation. "You married shortly after I did. If you were so sick with love for me, why were you so anxious to take another bride?"

Henri winced as though her words had hurt him. "I married to secure my inheritance. It was my father's wish. Blanche was his choice, not mine. She means nothing to me."

Isabel gave him a queer smile, both sad and amused. "I wager there are many men who feel as you do."

A tiny spark of cruelty flashed in his eyes. "And is your husband one of them?"

So this was where he had been leading her. The composed expression of her face soured into petulance. "I know this: he is not sitting in a garden with another man's wife proclaiming his love for her." She glared at him from behind the barricade of her sentence.

Henri's words came close on the edge of hers as though he had known what she would say. "That is because my cousin the king loves no one. He has no emotions. It is his nature."

Isabel could be angry, yet laugh at the irony of his words. "You don't know him as I do, that much is obvious," she scoffed.

That intimation made it easier for him to want to hurt her. "And do you *know* how he feels about you?"

He had no right to question her, provoke her, whatever his motives. "These are private matters," she declared and gave him a sideways, warning glance that proclaimed queenly authority.

Henri grasped her hands firmly. "These are matters which touch me too deeply to be ignored. You were promised to *me*, Isabel! It was only through your uncle's manipulations that my marriage contract to you was put aside and Philippe was allowed to take you for himself. There was nothing legal or ethical about it, yet men who knew better and had the power to avert it, like your father, stood by and did nothing, for the sake of their own gain."

Exasperated she cried out, "Why are you reminding me of all this? I had no say in any of it!"

Henri looked down at the hem of his surcoat which had fallen over her skirt, blue against blue like a small lake. "You could have loved me as your husband, Isabel," he said sadly. "You could love me still."

She thrust his hands away, anger shining in her eyes. "It is not your disappointed love that makes you speak so, it is resentment at being cheated of what was *yours*—a signed contract, a piece of paper—how dare you call that love? You are no different from my uncle or my father. None of you care anything for my feelings."

His arm flailed out in protest, nearly hitting her. "I am the *only* one who cares! Don't you understand what is happening? While we sit here arguing, Baldwin and your uncle are planning a military seizure of Vermandois and your husband is this far away from annulling his marriage to you in retaliation." Henri leaned close, his voice pitched low and earnest. "I could have let you find out later, from your family or your husband, but I came here today, determined to save you whatever heartbreak I could."

Flustered and unbelieving, Isabel leapt apart from him, and color infused her cheeks. "I don't know what you are talking about or what you *think* you know. There have been bad feelings between Philippe and my family in the past, and the matter of

Vermandois is still unsettled—but this talk of war and divorce is new to me. Where did you hear such a thing, and from whom?"

Henri folded his hands across his knee and explained. "I was in the corridor this morning when the king was talking to Hughes de Puiseaux. A communique had just arrived from Philip of Flanders. The count has married again and taken back Vermandois for his bride. Hearing this, your husband was furious and swore that if Baldwin of Hainault would not aid him in forcing Flanders to cede Vermandois to France, he would cast you off to spite them both. Those were his exact words."

There was too much plausibility in what Henri had said for Isabel to feign disbelief any longer. So that was the reason Philippe had left Paris so suddenly this morning; the reason her recent letters to Baldwin and her mother had gone unanswered, and Flanders had disregarded his niece's many written pleas for unification. Damn them all! She felt dizzy, unable to take it all in. "I don't understand," she muttered. "Why didn't Philippe say anything to me? How could he . . . " she took a breath, "how could *they* do this to me? How could they be so cruel?" She covered her face with a fluttering hand.

Henri held on to her free hand for an instant, then let his fingers slip away. He could only guess at what she must be feeling. He stood up, looking down at her bowed head and the hair that lay like golden streamers over her sagging shoulders. "Come inside," he offered gently, "rest. Warm yourself by the fire. Have some food, some wine. You'll feel better."

Isabel looked up at him, her eyes dry and defiant. "I'm not cold and I'm not hungry. I just want to be left alone."

Henri stood awkwardly by, hunching his shoulders and looking at her with pity. Isabel waved him away. When he reached out his hand she turned from him. Her voice was as cold as she could make it. "Why don't you go and have your dinner? You've accomplished what you came here to do."

"I never meant to hurt you," he muttered, and walked away as Isabel stared after him, saying nothing.

That night it rained, and by morning Isabel's abandoned prayer book was only a little lump of mush, its ruined pages stained by faded colors which dripped into the ground and were lost forever.

LANDERS welcomed Philippe Capet to Amiens. He had already achieved the greatest part of his victory: Philippe had come to him. So when they met in private ceremony at Flanders' chateau outside the city, the count was bold and assured. There was something more, however, that Philippe, even in his disordered state of nerves, could sense. Philip d'Alsace was aglow with the resurgence of youth.

Beside him was a slim, dark-haired girl, richly dressed. She had a bearing of shy dignity and kept her eyes level to the floor. Flanders introduced her as Beatrice of Portugal, the new Countess of Vermandois—his wife. She greeted the king in a few faltering words of French, then retired to the far side of the table to take her meal in silence while her husband and Philippe exchanged words she could not understand. When the meal was finished Philippe dismissed her and she went obediently to her room, having played her ceremonial part for the evening.

They were alone now. Flanders smiled and stirred melted honey into his wine. "You've grown to manhood well," he nodded to Philippe. "And I? I am young again. Soon I shall have the son I have prayed God for all these many years. You cannot know the joy I feel."

Philippe could manage little more than a sour smile. "Soon? Not so by the look of your wife's flat belly."

Flanders shrugged congenially. "We have been married only a short while. If she is not yet pregnant she shall be, soon enough."

The king ignored the boast. "I did not come here to talk of that," he said sharply, then reminded Flanders of his purpose. "Vermandois was promised to me and I intend to have it."

Arrogance rang in Flanders' voice. "You have not met the conditions of the contract. You have no son. Also, at the time of your marriage I had no idea I would yet have a chance of an heir for myself. That changes everything."

Philippe sat tense and straight, taking his wine in little sips. "Amiens itself was part of the dowry settlement," he reminisced, "and though you may occupy the city, the bishopric belongs to the crown of France under a law of vassalage concluded during my grandfather's reign."

Framed by the fire, Flanders sat with wings of flame upon his shoulders, and laughed. "History and logic in one lesson," he taunted. "Do you really think I'll be put off by a sixty-year-old point of law? Take your case to the Bishop of Amiens if you like; you are free to do so." He leaned back, propping his booted feet at the edge of the table. "Take it to the pope. But by the time all the legal entreaties have been accomplished I will have my son, and every part of Isabel's dowry will rightfully revert to me. That *too* is the law."

For a while neither of them spoke. Flanders sat back, a bemused and leisurely smile on his face, and filled his belly with wine while Philippe stared dismally down into his own cup. He was a fool to have come here, and despised the impulse which had made him do it. His memory strayed back over the past four years to the promising beginning they had made. There had been so much to bind them together then. Now they were less than strangers. Yet there was no time to pity present circumstances. Both were locked into their stubborn positions, but more than a piece of land was at stake. Vermandois was a symbol of power, a final proof of who was stronger.

To plead with Flanders was useless and demoralizing. Only one way remained. Philippe squared his shoulders and folded his arms across his chest. "I won't be cheated," he declared. "If you persist in withholding my wife's inheritance I will fight you every way I can. I'll send an army against you if I must." He saw a flicker of amusement dance in Flanders' eyes, remembering that it had taken the King of England and three of his sons to thwart an earlier Flemish uprising, and Philippe tried to erase the memory with his next words. "Don't think I cannot do it. Much has changed since you knew me last."

"I wouldn't doubt it," Flanders tossed the words back at him, "but all this threatening is useless to both of us. There is an easier way." He drank deeply, watching Philippe over the rim of his cup, purposely delaying, making the king fidget in his chair. Finally Flanders set down the empty henap and pushed it aside. "Say what you like, my boy, you will never defeat me in the field. No one ever has. And despite what allies might rally to your cause, you will never get your father-in-law to help you." He grinned, full of satisfaction. "Baldwin has already pledged himself to me."

Philippe had supposed that the vacillating Baldwin had been bullied into supporting the Flemish position, but the count's next words undercut any illusions he may have had about changing Baldwin's mind. "Don't think that a threat to divorce his daughter will work to your advantage. Baldwin owes too much to me. Ours is an old tradition, an old family. Isabel's situation, though unfortunate, means little beside that."

So it had all been arranged! Philippe could envision them, plotting together in a tight little circle of conspiracy while defrauding him of his rights and laughing as they did so! But before he could speak, Flanders had waved a hand, petitioning silence. "Let me put my solution." He spoke the words as if he had memorized them. "Vermandois and its annexed portions are mine. They shall remain mine, whatever you do. Still, in view of our past friendship, and to save you embarrassment, I would like to suggest an amicable settlement." He paused, affecting drama. *"If you agree to divorce Isabel* you will release us both from our original obligation. Divorce would void your promised inheritance, but in a way which reflects no weakness on your part. I will have my lands back and you will not have been shamed by it. To make amends for your loss I shall make you restitution of 6,000 *sous.*" He cocked an eyebrow in emphasis. "I am not ungenerous. You will be free to make yourself another, more providential marriage, and the whole business will be ended without bloodshed or disgrace."

Philippe stared back, uncomprehending. Flanders, who had worked so diligently for the Franco-Flemish alliance, was now petitioning for its dissolution. And divorce! Philippe had threatened it often enough, usually as a means of determining Isabel's loyalty, but never in earnest. Flustered, the king nearly upended his wine cup. Then, steadying it between his hands, he replied stiffly, "You have misread me. I don't want to divorce Isabel."

Flanders' eyes glittered as cut stones, cold and brilliant, empty of feeling. "Are you quite sure?" Then he laughed. "I know that look. You're itching for her even now, aren't you?"

Philippe's cheeks flushed hotly. "So what if it's true?" he snapped.

Flanders repaid with a malicious look. "She's exquisite isn't she? All that gold silk and fair white flesh and eyes that promise everything." He stared off toward the shadows, biting ruthlessly at his thumbnail. "Christ, what man wouldn't think twice before throwing all that away?" The sweat dribbled from his upper lip onto his chin. "Ask Baldwin. Ask *me*."

He hadn't meant to go that far. He'd wanted only to taunt Philippe into accepting the divorce. But suddenly the need to tell was a torrent inside him, rushing to his brain and spilling heedlessly from his lips till all of Isabel's secrets had been betrayed.

When he had heard all that he could suffer, Philippe bolted from the room, chalk-white and puking. As soon as he reached the edge of the corridor he stopped and slumped against the wall. Above the sound of his own sobs, Philippe could still hear Flanders laughing.

Isabel sat with hands in her lap while Philippe repeated Flanders' cruel disclosures, not bothering to ask if they were true because her silence answered that. Her composure in the face of his accusations was astounding. When Philippe left her room he was closer to tears than she was.

Isabel followed him out into the corridor, however, catching hold of his sleeve, forcing him to look at her. "Are you going to send me back to Hainault? Divorce me? What?" she demanded.

"I don't know," he answered grimly. Then after a moment he said, "I wish that I had never met you."

She could not see his face, it was swathed in shadow, but his voice was full of scorn and Isabel drew back. "I would have told you the truth if you had ever asked me," she replied, and then, sounding almost haughty, "I can't believe you never guessed it."

"Christ!" he muttered under his breath, and walked away.

The rains came in November, heavy, lasting for days.

Adele's entourage made slow progress north through dripping woods and dismal countryside. She had been absent from Paris for many months. The dispute with Philippe over Agnes's safety had kept Adele away and news of Marguerite's residence at the palace had provided still further incentive. She had even less tolerance for Marguerite than Isabel did.

Adele was restless and unhappy. Age had made her desperate. She was now forty-two and her beauty was fading. Though she pampered herself it was impossible to forestall the inevitable. She brooded endlessly. Since there was not enough to keep busy with in the administration of her lands, she diverted herself with new lovers.

Once discreet, she had now grown careless about her paramours, no longer choosing solely from the ranks of the nobility. How boring such men could be! They were too involved with their own power. Adele needed the stimulation and novelty of a different kind of man.

One in particular had recently caught her eye. He was a handsome blond musician newly brought to court to "cheer" her. His name was Michel and though fairly commonplace among handsome blond musicians he did have the distinction of being exactly four months younger than her own son. Adele fawned over him in the disquieting fashion of a mother/lover.

It didn't matter to the dowager queen that the liaison exposed her to gossip. No one dared criticize her openly except the clergy, and most of the bishops tactfully ignored the indiscretions of the woman who gave so generously of her wealth to the church. Sully was one of the few clerics honest enough to disapprove her behavior regardless of favors, but he was too honorable to spread calumnies, even when they were deserved. Gratified by her long absence from Paris, he could afford to be charitable.

But now Adele was coming home to the Cité Palais with her new lover and some changes would be made. Invoking the authority that Isabel had been unable to assert, Adele had arranged for the despised Marguerite to be removed from the palace and housed outside the city at the convent of St. Geneviève. This she had secured through the influence of de Puiseaux, who had managed to convince Philippe of the idea shortly before his departure to Amiens. Isabel was enough of a rival. Adele wanted no others.

There was no festivity of celebration to greet Adele upon her arrival in Paris, however. No bodyguard of the king met her party at the *Grande Pont* to escort her through the muddy streets of the city. No gay banners hung in welcome at the palace entryway. Rain ran miserably down the grey stones of the fortress walls, while off to the side beneath a wooden awning near the *esplanade* a small group of serving stewards hunched closely about their charcoal burners, warming themselves against the chill.

The interior of the palace was equally cheerless. Adele dismissed her retinue and followed the dim corridor to the great hall. A lean hound snatched at her skirt as she passed and she kicked him away with her boot. He snarled but retreated to the corner and Adele continued on her way toward the hall, silently cursing her son. Each time she returned from the richness of her palace in Champagne she was shocked anew by the shabbiness of this place. How different it had looked when she and Louis had reigned here, filling it with laughter and music and the constant gaiety of parties.

The great hall was empty and silent. Adele stood for a while in the center of the vacant room. It was cold. No fire had been laid so early in the afternoon, and the air was stale from last night's meat. Upon the far wall, imprisoned in their iron racks, a few torches smoldered in mute offering to her presence.

Adele knew nothing of what had so recently transpired between her son and his wife, yet a sense of melancholy and disorder sulked in the shadows as though waiting to make itself known to her. Adele shivered and turned away.

The feast of St. Andrew marked the beginning of Advent, the four-week period preceding Christmas. Isabel joined Philippe and his two Capet uncles in the seven-mile pilgrimage to St. Denis. It was their first public occasion together since the "breach," but it was strictly ceremonial. She spent the night in the adjacent chapter house while Philippe maintained vigil inside the church with Sully and several monks of his order.

Philippe had said nothing about a divorce, yet the hope of reconciliation seemed an indulgent fantasy to Isabel. Why he had not immediately arranged for her dismissal from the court was a question which baffled even her quick mind. He had not forgiven her, that was certain. Each time their eyes met she saw the evidence of injury and betrayal which she had put there. Even Sully looked at her with ill-concealed scorn as if Philippe had told him. That thought brought a satiric smile to her lips. More likely the wise bishop had known all along. . . .

Isabel's sense of guilt had receded into a bitterness that was nurtured by Philippe's cold silence. She had accepted his indiscretions with Harry and other young men as a part of her husband's nature which she could not change. Why couldn't he do likewise for her sake?

There was nothing for her to do but wait for Philippe's decision, yet Isabel determined to make one final effort on her own behalf. As they made the silent journey back to Paris, she stared pensively at the faded landscape and formed the words in her mind.

* * *

... as my father you owe me more than you have given me of late. The silence to which you cling has done me insufferable injury. When I write to you, you do not answer. If you have ever loved me, if you love me still, you will prove it now by using your power to bring to an end this long contest between our family and the crown of France.

It was for the good of us all that my marriage was contracted; it will be to the detriment of us all if it is ended. You alone have the power to convince my uncle that it is to all our interests if he mends the breach between Flemish and Frankish participants in our joint coalition.

There is little time. My marriage has been imperiled because of threats and calumnies to my character by Philip d'Alsace, and by his determination to deprive my husband of the legal inheritance to Vermandois and Valois. Philippe and Flanders remain impervious in their opinions. I can do nothing. It is up to you.

I shall not petition your help again. I shall instead make options of my own.

Isabel de Hainault
December 2, 1183

* * *

It seemed as though all the options had run out on the night of December 21st when Philippe came to her room for the first time in over two months.

"I have made a decision," he announced, standing at the foot of her bed.

Isabel lay swaddled beneath layers of miniver, her back supported by cushions of pale blue velvet powdered with fleur-de-lis stitched in golden thread. She had been dozing when he came in and now she rubbed her eyes to wakefulness and smoothed the

hair back from her face. "What do you want?" she asked him
tonelessly.

He had begun to grow a beard and it made his face look older,
even less pleasant than usual. "I want you to listen to me," he
answered immediately. "I am leaving for Senlis tomorrow. There
I shall convene a council to seek the means of dissolving our
marriage." He paused, waiting for her cry of sorrow or outrage,
but there was nothing. Her face reflected none of the despair he
had envisioned. It was as though she had not heard him. His
voice became strident. "Divorce is the only answer, Isabel. Obviously you cannot continue as my wife now that I have learned
what I have learned." He shifted on his feet, uncomfortable in
her presence, eager for the meeting to be at an end. He took a
deep breath. "I have no choice!"

Her expression hardened and the faint specks of green came
to life in her eyes. "What a liar you are!" she gasped. "If Vermandois was served up to you tomorrow my *past* would be mirac-
ulously forgiven!"

Color flooded into his face and all the composure was gone
from his voice. "You dare to call *me* a liar when you deceived me
since I first knew you?"

"My father and my uncle deceived you," she shouted back at
him, "not I!"

"You did," he answered, "you lied with every breath, with
every kiss." His voice faltered a little and he turned his face to
the side, trying to compose himself. "I loved you so much! Yet
even from the beginning I felt guilty for wanting you. *I* felt
guilty! And all the while..." It was very hard for him to keep
from crying as he said the words, for they were his true feelings.
Then in an instant he had squared his shoulders and his voice
was firm again. "There is nothing more to say, Isabel. I am leaving for Senlis tomorrow as I told you. From there I go to Brittany to meet with Geoffrey Plantagenet. I won't be back in Paris
till early February." He paused, still not letting himself look at
her. "Of course, it will take many weeks to settle the matter of
our divorce, perhaps longer. Until such time as that, and a
proper escort can be secured to take you back to your family in
Hainault, you are welcome to stay here." Philippe looked down at
the floor, not willing to face her with his final comment. "You

may keep all I have given you in the past as a token of my esteem."

"Wait!" she cried out as he turned to leave, her arm outstretched, the fingers pointing at him. When he spun around to face her she relaxed a little and her arm fell limply to the bed once more. "All you have given me..." she repeated. "Is that your farewell speech to me? How could you have lain so close upon my heart so often, and then walk away from me forever with such words as those on your lips? You remember *nothing!*" She twisted the Byzantine opal from her finger and threw it in his direction. It bounced off his chest and skidded away somewhere into a corner of the room, lost in darkness.

He stood perfectly still for a moment. "Goodbye, Isabel," he finally muttered, and then he left her.

The blue velvet drape fluttered a little at his exit and then fell still. She continued to stare at it; at the vacant doorway, at the table beside it where the candles burned. Then her tears obscured it all.

*   *   *

To Henri, Count of Champagne, from Henry Plantagenet, King of the English, greetings.

Please advise the Queen of France that I shall be keeping court at Gisors until the third week in February and that I will be pleased to grant her an audience at any time before that time, as requested in your recent communication.

I enclose a ring bearing my signet seal. You will tell the queen to bear it on her person so that she might identify herself and her purpose here when she passes through my guards in crossing the frontier to Normandy.

Henry, Rex Anglorum
January 10, 1184

*   *   *

The mixture of gems sparkled up like a jeweled salad as they caught the wavering glow from the fire. Pearls, emeralds, rubies, pink topaz, sapphires, opal and jade—set into a profusion of gold and silver chains, ring bands and delicately wrought earrings. Isabel looked down at the heap of jewels with impassivity, then slapped the crocheted-gold cover of the box over them and latched the coffer before handing it over to Edythe with these words: "This will be the last thing you have to do. Tomorrow morning take this to the herbarium and conceal it among the discarded leaves. Lock the door when you leave and keep the key on your person at all times." Isabel produced a small silver key hanging on a chain from within the deep folds of her black velvet pellison. She pressed the object firmly into Edythe's open hand. "Under no circumstances let anyone know where they are, or even that they have been hidden. Let it be thought I have taken them with me."

Edythe curled her fingers around the key, then looked at Isabel quizzically. "Why are you taking all these precautions?" she asked. "And where are you going? You must tell me. You act as though you will be gone for a long time. Surely if you were returning to Mons you would not leave me behind!"

Isabel took back the coffer of jewels while Edythe slipped the chain over her own head and slid the key down beneath the brown neckline of her wool chainse. Then once again the casket of jewels was thrust back into her perplexed care.

The queen looked hastily around, her gaze darting to each corner of the room, then with a satisfied grimace she nodded. Everything was prepared. Bringing her attention back to Edythe she assured her, "I am not going back to Mons. I have already told you that. But where I am going you cannot come. It is enough to have to account for my own safety. I cannot be burdened with looking after yours." Then in a gentler tone Isabel added, "Do not worry over me, my dear. I shall be sufficient to myself, and in any case I am not traveling alone. Perhaps I shall be back in a fortnight. At most no more than three weeks. But whatever happens, I shall return here. Then, if needs be, we shall return together to Hainault."

Edythe knew little of the circumstances at work behind this event, only that a divorce was in the air. But she had noticed a change in Isabel's behavior, a change that went very deep. It had been evident for some weeks, but more obvious since Henri of Champagne had brought her a sealed letter three days ago. Since then Isabel had been active with her packing and the storing of precious items. Now as the hour grew close on midnight she was dressed in black velvet from boots to hooded cape, preparing to travel—where?

She indicated the chapel annex with a sweep of her hand. "For tonight hide the casket in there. Put it in the reliquary. But tomorrow morning take it to the herbarium as I instructed."

Edythe shuffled into the chapel room to accomplish the chore. When she returned Isabel was pulling on her velvet gloves, as black as the rest of what she wore. Then she bent toward the remaining bottles on her dressing table and dabbed herself quickly with perfume. She gave a last glance into the mirror, speaking as she looked. "Do not be troubled for your own safety, Edythe. While I am away Henri of Champagne will be in residency here at the palace; he has promised to look after you."

Her boots made soft footfalls across the floor. At the archway Isabel took up the two heavy satchels she had packed. They were made of chamois leather and had woven handles which met and tied in the center. Edythe, dragging her lame leg, hustled to Isabel's side. "If anyone remarks upon my absence," the queen was saying, "say only that I have gone to pray at St. Denis for a few days." She halted, and her lips turned up in a sarcastic smile. "It is possible no one will notice I am gone. But if they do, say as I have instructed you." Isabel dotted Edythe's face with several kisses. "Goodbye. May all be well with you." She turned toward the doorway.

"But if the king should return?" Edythe called out suddenly.

Isabel wrestled the strap of one satchel up over her shoulder, the other one she took in her hand. "He will not return before I do," she explained. "He is in Brittany and will no doubt halt at Chartres for Candlemas. Do not fear. I shall be back before then." She gave one further kiss to Edythe's face, then swept past the drape into the musty corridor. "Pray for me," she called back over her shoulder.

A circular moon rode high above the clouds and Isabel was blacker than the night she passed through on her way down the path to the herbarium.

The satchels were heavy but she carried them easily, making urgent progress past the shadowed outlines of trees and flowering bushes, all bare now but for the Christmas roses which bloomed at the edge of the path.

Amid the indecipherable tangle of dead vines the herbarium was crypt-like, and Isabel shivered with excitement and cold as she approached it. Just then she saw a tall figure step out from the darkness. Isabel halted, then regained her breath with a gasp of recognition. It was Henri. He was there, waiting for her, as he had promised.

She had gone to him two weeks ago with a semblance of her plan: a meeting with Henry of England, to seek his aid on her behalf in the matter of the impending divorce. That much of it had been Isabel's idea, but the Count of Champagne had made it possible by securing an invitation from the king, and arranging an escort to take her to Gisors.

"Thank God," Henri said breathlessly, taking the burdensome satchels from her and placing them on the ground. "I was ready to come upstairs after you. The monks will be ready to leave after their midnight prayers."

The monks he spoke of were a group of Cistercians, on pilgrimage to the abbey at Rouen. Their presence would assure the queen's safe conduct to Gisors fortress. For her return to Paris she would have to seek the protection of a bodyguard provided by the English king.

"So you are still determined to do this thing." It was not a question; Henri knew well enough how stubborn her purpose was. He glanced down at her clothes with a frown. "Are you dressed warmly enough?"

She spread her arms, indicating the thick folds of black velvet: chainse, pellison and cloak. He nodded his approval. "Your horse is saddled and I will ride with you to the monastery. The horse is at the side of the palace, just over there," he pointed a short distance away, "out of view of the palace bodyguard, as you requested. We had better start."

Isabel had been too preoccupied these past few days to appreciate his help in bringing her plan into being, but quite suddenly the realization took hold of her with incredible force. She wrapped her arms about his waist, snuggling her cheek at his chest. "You've helped me so much," she breathed the words softly, then offered a kiss with her upturned face.

He held her rather timidly and answered, "It is next to nothing."

"To you perhaps. To me it is salvation."

He cringed a little at her exorbitant optimism. "Don't hope too grandly in all this, Isabel," he warned. "The King of England may not wish to interfere in your husband's business. And even if he does, Philippe may take no notice of it."

In the past she might have wilted at such words, but nothing could undercut her confidence now. She was fueled with some strange sense of power, invulnerable to doubt. Smiling up at him she said, "You have already done your part. Don't worry after the rest. It is my concern."

Henri hesitated for a moment, then bent to kiss her, pressing her lips gently with his own. Isabel sighed and held him tighter. Her embrace was freely given and hinted at more, but he fought against the sense of rising excitement. "We must leave," he whispered into her ear, "the monks are waiting."

Isabel pulled at his sleeve, urging him toward the herbarium. "They know I am coming. They will wait." She tugged at the latch, freeing it. The door swayed open, creaking softly.

Henri followed her inside. The room had a domed glass roof that sliced the sky into pieces like a pie. It was cold in here and the air smelled of damp earth, old oils, dead flowers. She led him to a bench in the center of the room and sat him down. Standing, she was only a little taller than he was sitting. She pressed close, her hands busy at his neck and shoulders, her teeth nibbling at his beard. Her voice was the loveliest sound he had ever heard. "Do you want me?" she asked. But before he could answer she silenced his lips with kisses.

Even through the camouflage of her heavy velvets he could feel the rich curves and elegant lines of her body, and the heat of her—a fire in the blood that seemed to come right through her skin. Then in the midst of their embrace she pulled away and stepped back, quickly stripping off her cape and pellison, pulling off her boots and the braies she had worn for riding. One by one she tossed each piece of clothing to the ground beside her.

Gracefully Isabel sank to her knees in front of him, her fingers untangling the laces of his braies. Smiling she drew his penis out, unmistakably small and slender but sweetly scented with oil of summer roses in the way that fashionable gentlemen perfumed themselves. She kissed it over and over, wetting her lips each time, teasing the tip with her tongue as she carefully pulled back the skin with her fingers. The sensation was so intense it took away his breath, and all he could do was speak her name over and over again.

The promise of her naked breasts wavered before his closed eyes and he pulled her onto his lap, parting her chainse in one swift movement, wetting her skin with his tongue. The taste of her was sweeter even than her scent, and nothing in all of reality could have been so miraculous to him at that moment as the act of loving her. He could not hold her closely enough, could not fill her deeply enough. He was above himself, riding a wind of insufferable beauty as Isabel clung to his neck with coiled arms, murmuring wanton incentives into his ear.

Whether he whispered her name or screamed it he could not remember, only that in an instant she took him beyond anywhere he had ever been. Then shivering with her own satisfaction she spoke his name and grew limp against him, her head coming to rest upon his shoulder like a slumbering child.

It was a while before he could think or even move. Isabel covered his lips with her warm, moist mouth, and stroked his hair. Her languorous kisses stirred him again and this time, driven by lust rather than love, he pushed her down upon the bench and sprawled over her, taking her with a force that sent his own head pounding.

His energy had dislodged the last neat swirls of her hair and when he had finished Isabel lay silently breathing through her open mouth, her face framed by sweaty curls. She let him hold her for a little while, then gently eased out of his embrace to rise and dress herself once more, without a word. He sat watching her, then stooped to retrieve her discarded gloves, curling his fingers around them. They were still imprinted with the warmth of her hands. "Don't go to Gisors," he said suddenly, his voice sounding too loud and urgent. "You must know how doubtful it is that King Henry will do anything to help you."

She had nearly finished dressing, but paused to cast a vaguely disapproving look in his direction. "You arranged this for me. Why do you suddenly change your mind?"

"Because it's foolish. If Philippe truly wishes to divorce you he will do it. You cannot stop him. Accept that. Come back to Troyes or Châlons with me and I will make you my wife."

Isabel took the gloves from him and fitted them carefully over her hands. "You have a wife already."

"I would divorce her tomorrow if I could marry you."

Isabel's deft hands fluttered over her disheveled hair, capturing bits of it into place with pearl-edged pins, then she covered it all with her cape and hood. "And you have a son," she reminded him. "No Henri, don't try to dissuade me. I know what I must do." She felt at her earlobes, the dainty fingers securing hanging pearls the size of moonstones. Then with a sigh she finished, "If Philippe succeeds in his plan to divorce me, I shall consider your offer of marriage. If not," she drew back a little into the shadows, and the darkness swallowed all but her eyes, "then we shall have other meetings, I promise you." There was a hushed rustle of velvet as she moved to the door, holding out her hand for him to follow. "Come now," she whispered, "we must go."

On the evening of the following day the band of travelers halted at Nantes for a meal and a night's rest. But while the monks ate, Isabel sat in the library of the chapter house, looking out the window at yet another cathedral going up across the road, and wrote her ultimatum.

Inspired, her wits sharpened by purpose and lack of sleep, she wrote the document through without an error or a change. Then she read it, made her copies, and went to bed.

* * *

In the event that my marriage to Philippe-Auguste, true King of France, is dissolved, I—who am called Isabel de Hainault—declare myself deserted and abandoned by him, my rightful husband in the sight of God; and by my family equally forsaken, for they have refused to substantiate my lawful inheritance, the counties of Vermandois and Valois; and it is this which has caused my husband to estrange himself from me.

Since my first-betrothed partner, Henri Count of Champagne, has since married and made himself an heir on the body of his wife, I have no "husband presumptive." Being that is true; and I am two months less four days short of the fourteenth anniversary of my birth, I declare myself as ward of Henry, King of England; by right of prior contract (which read) he is my own guardian and I am in his care till such time as my husband reinstates me as his wife and queen; or, in case of the divorce being fact, the King of England selects for me another husband.

If Count Baldwin of Hainault and Count Philip d'Alsace of Flanders —who are my kin in the flesh—will not sustain my rights and inheri-

tance; if my husband—who has known me in the sense of a wife—will not shelter me nor give me succor, then by my will be it known: That They Have, by right of LAW, foresworn their claims to me; and I shall obey as the will of good King Henry dictates, or his pleasure is known. I put this down in my own hand and by no false will am swayed; but say that having taken refuge in prayer and the Sacrament and acknowledging the blood sacrifice of my Maker—as I pray for His grace,
    Signed, my hand and seal,

> Isabel, *lately called Queen of the French*
> Mantes, Abbey of St. Gabrielle
> *January 16, 1184*

* * *

Ralph of Newstead, burly and ill-mannered, directed Isabel to a small audience chamber where she could wait until the king would see her. For a while she occupied herself with a view from the window, but soon it grew too dark to see beyond the shaded glass.

Worn by the past three days and nights of little rest, Isabel pulled a chair close to the fire and sat down, rubbing her palms together. Her fingers felt stiff from clutching the reins and her back ached for a soft bed. Having reached her destination, she felt almost too tired now to accomplish her purpose. Depression stooped her shoulders. Perhaps this had not been such a clever idea after all.

She was dozing, her head tilted toward her shoulder, a stray lock of hair brushing her cheek, when Henry burst into the room. "My child," he called out, striding up to her, "welcome to Gisors."

She was on her feet in an instant, bending her body in a show of courtesy, but when she nearly toppled over in weariness Henry took up her hand in a firm grip. "Spare yourself, girl. Protocol between royalty is something I dispensed with years ago." Giving her a closer look, he said, "You have grown even more beautiful since our first meeting, if that is possible. And I have grown older. Now how may I help you?"

During the long ride from Paris she had prepared a greeting

but now her tongue felt thick and awkward in her mouth. "My lord," she stammered, unable to say more.

He put an arm about her shoulders, steadying her. "Come child," he said, "share a meal with me and rest yourself. There is time enough to talk when you feel stronger."

Smiling gratefully through her daze of weariness, Isabel let him lead her from the room.

An hour later she felt stronger, sustained by good beef and raisin wine. There was no mention of politics as they ate, only talk of small matters, and before long she felt relaxed in his company, studying him over the rim of her cup.

He looked much the same as she remembered him from Rennes although she supposed the dimly-lit surroundings concealed the traces of age on his face. He was not handsome, and yet his total appearance was very pleasing. His hair and beard were an exact match of reddish-brown hues, but with a fair cast, thick and full. Neither tall nor short, his body was ably made and marked by a rugged dignity. His eyes were the finest feature in his face. They were storm-grey, and even in the dimness, bloodshot, full of disappointments.

After he had eaten very little, Henry pushed his plate aside with as much vigor as some men might fill it up again. He watered his wine liberally and then sat back to drink it, his chin tilted toward the ceiling. "Your husband wishes to divorce you," he began, "and you want me to change his mind. Is that it?"

"Has Philippe been in contact with you?" she asked warily, dabbing at her lips with a cloth.

"No, but news of that sort travels fast."

"My uncle, then?" The sound of her own voice gave Isabel confidence. "Has he enlisted you in his wicked plot to discredit me?"

His voice was sharp and direct. "Flanders is my friend, but that's no concern of yours. It should be enough that I am willing to hear your part of the story. Don't badger me, just state your purpose."

Only a few minutes ago she had felt as though she liked him. He had seemed reachable and pleasant. Now he was talking like a politician. The change angered her. Making a slight move to rise, she said, "If, as your attitude dictates, your sympathy rests with my uncle's point of view, there is little need for me to say anything. It seems to me you have already made up your mind not to help me."

The sound of his heavy fist against the table silenced her. "Sit down!" he barked, "and stay sitting until I have given you leave to go!" When Isabel had obeyed, paled by fright at his anger, he pointed a finger at her. "I have had more than my share of trouble these past few years, and much of it has come from your family. Not your fault, I realize, but all the same the problems between Philippe and your uncle have taken my attention away from my own concerns far too often. Your husband writes to me, insisting that I put an end to Flanders' threats of war. Flanders implores me to take his side against Philippe. I've had my belly filled to puking with this situation. They both want my help, and yet behind my back the two of them connive to sustain the rebellion of my own sons against me."

The show of anger had subdued her, but a touch of spite still rang in Isabel's voice. "Then why do you have to do with any of them? I should think that it would be easier for you to close your ears to all entreaties, rather than have to pick and choose between them."

The somber lines of his face creased in an ironic smile. "It is not easy for a king to do anything. You see child, power is not only a tool, it is a weapon. A weapon which can just as easily be used against me as to my good. Because I have power, others often seek to engage me in disputes which have no benefit to me, but which can cause difficulties. Therefore it is sometimes advantageous for me to withhold help when it is asked."

She answered him without flinching. "Then why don't you simply say *no* to Philippe and my uncle? You seem to be saying *no* to me!"

Her arrogance tickled his anger and yet it excited him because it hinted at a precocity and wildness even more tantalizing than her beauty. Had this girl-queen come here with a plan to seduce him to her will, to bargain for his favor with her body? That thought was pleasant. She was young, but he'd known virgins younger than her, and as he studied the rich curves of her body with discreet awareness he realized happily that this girl was no virgin. Even two years ago at Rennes he had contemplated her full breasts and wide-spread hips with voluptuous satisfaction. No girl developed as well as that and as young without having been fucked well and often. Even as he considered that, Henry cleared his throat and spoke pragmatically, as though her body was the farthest thing from his thoughts. "Don't be pert with me, Isabel. You will hear my opinion when I am prepared to give it." He folded his arms across his chest. "Now tell me, where is this letter you mentioned to me earlier?"

From within the travel-worn folds of her black velvets, Isabel withdrew the rolled sheets, offering the top one to him. Henry took the paper and held it close, squinting at the fine, small script. Then with a grunt he got to his feet and walked to the fire grate in the wall. Leaning close to the light he read the document once, and then again. When he had finished he turned his back to Isabel and stood facing the fire.

She waited for his response. Finally, spurred on by anxiousness, she explained, "I mean to send one to Philippe, one to my father, and one to my uncle." She rushed to the end of the sentence, then stopped abruptly. "...with your approval, of course."

Henry came back to the table and placed the letter in front of her. He dropped himself onto the bench, his back to the table, regarding her with a pensive scrutiny for what seemed a very long time. Unsure if her spirited essay had displeased him, Isabel fussed with a loose coil of her hair, ringing it about her finger in an effort to ease her nervousness. "That's quite an epistle," he finally said, and she looked up. "You certainly have your uncle's talent with words."

"I can reword it if you think it is too bold," she offered, trying to sound meek.

He chuckled. "Bold it is, most definitely. A bold and empassioned letter written by a bold and impassioned young woman." His hand hovered over hers for an instant, then he patted her fingers and laughed as he did so. "That letter is sure to put the fear of God into those three peacocks. Very clever of you to use me as a threat. None of them is likely to miss the point of that."

Her cheeks colored and she turned her face away, but Henry took her chin between his fingers and turned her to look at him. "No, don't blush because you think you ought. You were right to speak as you did. An invalidation of the marriage contract would cause you to belong to me..." His eyes read her face as though he had divined some hidden truth betrayed by her expression before he finished, "...in the purely technical sense of the word, of course." After a pause he took his hand away and got stiffly to his feet. "Tomorrow I will see to it that your messages are dispatched, one to each. Then we shall talk more." He reached down for her arm and helped her to her feet. "Now I will show you to your room."

Isabel gathered up her papers and put them into Henry's outstretched hand. As they walked together toward the stairs she looked up at him, a tiny smile on her lips. "Would it be inconvenient for me to have a bath?" she asked hopefully. "I would sleep so much better if I could."

"Of course," he responded. "I'll instruct one of the girls to help you."

He led her to a room on the second floor where her baggage had already been deposited. He fussed with the lock, then the heavy oak door swung open. "If memory serves me, you should be more comfortable here than at the Cité Palais," he observed. "Here at least it is possible to keep out the winter drafts." Isabel paused halfway inside the room. "I'll get Therésa to haul in a tub for you," he promised. Then he started off down the corridor.

"Henry," she called out and he stopped, looking back over his shoulder. Her eyes were enigmatic, hard to read. "Thank you for your help. I cannot tell you how much I appreciate it...."

"We'll talk tomorrow," he said and winked at her. "Enjoy your bath."

NIGHT WAS COMING on like a triumphant army, its shadows sweeping over the land. Beyond the promontory the sea stretched away into blackness, the darkening sky nibbling at its edges.

The cold was intolerable and Philippe quaked with it, his hands thrust deeply into the furrows of his sable pellison. The wind shrieked in his ears and he had to lean forward in the saddle to hear what Geoffrey was saying before the wind could blow the words away.

"...Brittany tests a man," Geoffrey repeated, his voice piping and shrill. "There is no better place on earth to train an army."

He touched Philippe's shoulder. "Have you thought a little of what we discussed at dinner last night?"

Philippe nodded, his frigid fingers gripping the reins tighter, restraining the restless dance of his horse. "Good," Geoffrey remarked, "let's go back and talk more on it." He indicated the clouds above which rode the sky like phantom sailing ships. "It will be raining soon. We'll have to ride hard to get back without being drenched." He jabbed a booted heel into his horse's side and they started off in a run, the pair of them, horse and rider, fleeing across the sand like a drunkard chasing the moon. With difficulty Philippe turned his mount into the wind and, flinching, followed far behind.

They sat cross-legged, close as lovers, on the fur mat before the open fire, drinking mulberry wine from the same cup, their knuckles still white with cold. "But I don't understand," Philippe protested, "what difference it should make to you if I divorce Isabel."

Geoffrey rubbed a hand across his chin, wiping away the droplets of wine that glistened on the hairs of his beard. "A divorce is silly," he explained. "You give away too much and yet gain nothing."

"What else can I do?"

"Look," Geoffrey reasoned, his hand resting lightly upon Philippe's knee, "forget trying to get the better of Flanders. You never will. You'll never get Vermandois either, at least not without a long fight, perhaps not even then. So you will have severed your marriage for no purpose. Where is the sense in all that?"

Philippe's dark eyes mirrored a sense of hurt. "And what about the rest of it?" he asked, "How can I keep a wife who has been the willing concubine of her father and uncle?"

"That is not so strange," Geoffrey replied, tucking a bit of bread into his mouth and washing it down with wine. "My own father was sleeping with both Marguerite and Constance for years before marrying them off to Harry and to me. It happens all the time." He grinned. "That is a king's prerogative."

Philippe looked instantly insulted. "Only for men like your father."

Geoffrey shrugged. "That was what I meant, of course. Old

Henry must possess every girl who incites his interest. It might be that d'Alsace and Baldwin are the same. But Isabel belongs to you now. Why give her up merely because they had her first? Forget divorce. Forget Vermandois. You would do better occupying yourself in holding the Vexin against my father. It is worth ten times more than a Frizian swamp."

Philippe bristled. "I don't need you to tell me which lands are vital!"

Geoffrey tempered his voice with softness. "I was only suggesting you look elsewhere."

"But Vermandois is mine!" Philippe insisted, his tidy mind locked into the logic of his proposition.

"Listen," Geoffrey exhorted, nearly upsetting the wine in his eagerness, "what would you say if I offered Brittany to you instead?"

Philippe laughed politely. "You can't be serious."

"But I am."

"Why? To affront your father?"

Handsome Geoffrey conceded the point with an impish smile. "If I said not, you would know me for a liar. But that is only one part of my plan. Surely you can't have missed the implication of my gift."

Philippe turned over on his back, arms pillowing his head. Every conversation with Geoffrey seemed to entail a guessing game. "I suppose I have," he said, sounding bored.

"Then I will say two words to you," Geoffrey offered and leaned closer. "A navy."

Philippe stared up, unsure. "What?"

"My friend, only the great lords of the north, men like Flanders and the emperor, have great navies. Even England has little sea power to boast of. With a port and a navy to fill it, the Ile-de-France would be an unrivaled power in the west. Think of it, Philippe—the vast trade possibilities with eastern ports! Italy, England, even the Empire, would be nothing alongside France."

That possibility had never occurred to Philippe but in a single moment he weighed its worth and could not dispute it. He had only one question. "And why would you be willing to help me gain all this?"

The smile on Geoffrey's lips was insolent and he let his head droop to Philippe's shoulder. "Need you ask me that after last night?"

Philippe pulled away. "Passion and politics are ill-fitted companions. It is not wise to interchange them."

The young duke straightened up. "Perhaps. But do you doubt that in both matters we are very much alike?"

Their pleasurable exchange of conversation at dinner last night and all that had followed it converged in Philippe's mind. Geoffrey had much more to offer than Harry ever had, but could he be trusted? Philippe brushed his fingers over Geoffrey's cheek. "I loved your brother greatly, but I knew better than to be cajoled into supporting his wars." He leaned back on his elbows, looking at Geoffrey with narrowed eyes. "I have vast ambitions, some of which I divulged to you last night. But I am practical enough to appreciate my limitations at this point. I am not yet prepared to take on the power of England."

"I said nothing of England," Geoffrey replied, looking unspeakably innocent.

"Be sensible," Philippe scoffed, "what do you think old Henry will be doing while you declare Brittany annexed to France? In two days time every man-at-arms in Normandy will be breaking down your door at Rennes, and Henry's troops in the Loire Valley will be flooding the Ile de la Cité." A doubting frown creased his forehead. "It just isn't possible, Geoffrey. Your father isn't a dullard, you know. At any sign that you and I were becoming friendly, he'd be sure to get suspicious and that would mean trouble for us."

"There won't be any signs," Geoffrey argued, stripping off his fur mantle and tossing it aside, "at least none that he will see. Our progress to these ends will be slow and subtle." He fussed at the laces of his smock, untying them carefully, then stopped to look over at Philippe. "Don't you see my reasoning? We are young. Time is on our side."

Philippe stood up and stretched with the litheness of a cat. With deliberate slowness he began pulling off his clothes. "You speak as though Henry has one foot in the grave. But he isn't dead yet. Look how easily he swept aside your rebellion last summer. He is still a power to be reckoned with."

The delicate lines alongside Geoffrey's mouth settled into a pout. "That was the fault of your precious Harry. He was no soldier. I would have been better off to lead the revolt myself, without his help."

Philippe tossed his boots and braies to the floor atop Geoffrey's discarded clothes and stood for a moment, his naked body bronzed and beautiful in the firelight. Then kneeling beside Geoffrey he took up the porringer and emptied it swiftly. Wine glistened on his lips as he spoke. "If we are to do as you suggest, we must court caution. I want no possibility of war with England now or at any time in the future. Since this last rebellion your father and Richard have been uncomfortably close. That worries me much."

A teasing smile played over Geoffrey's lips. "You need not fear. Henry's best days are well behind him."

"Perhaps," Philippe agreed stoically, "but we cannot simply *wish* your brother Richard away. When Henry is gone he will be king, no doubt. The thought of facing him at the head of the combined armies of England, Normandy and the Aquitaine is not a pleasing one."

Geoffrey's arms coiled about Philippe's shoulders and their lips met, hot and seeking. Philippe lowered his head to Geoffrey's chest, his teeth making sharp little bites over the flesh. Holding him close, Geoffrey sighed with pleasure and smiled at his own genius. "Don't worry about Richard, Philippe my love. He is much less of a threat than you might think."

"How do you mean?" Philippe asked, letting his fingers toy with the soft dark hair on Geoffrey's chest.

They kissed. Geoffrey nibbled at Philippe's ear, then prodded it with his tongue before he whispered, "Just this: my father has already determined to take the Aquitaine away from Richard. He has promised the succession in return, but that is a bluff. He is so afraid of Richard that he wishes to see all power passed to John at his own death. Thus, John is to have the Aquitaine *and* the crown if my dear father has his way."

Philippe's head jerked up and he stared at Geoffrey, not sure for a moment if it was a joke. Then a smile crossed his face. The smile became a grin and then a laugh, and before long Geoffrey was laughing too. They laughed and laughed, locked in each other's arms until exhausted at last they tumbled together in a heap upon the fur. Dizzy with pleasure and power, Philippe yielded to Geoffrey's eager lips and closed his eyes. "John!" he muttered to himself, and laughed once more.

Isabel was still asleep the following evening when Henry brought dinner to her room. Yawning, she pulled the sheet up around her shoulders. "I can't believe I have slept so long," she exclaimed. "Why didn't you send someone to wake me?"

He settled a large tray at the edge of the bed, "You were tired from traveling," he replied, "you needed to rest."

She slipped easily from the bed, wrapped in a fur coverlet, and pulled a pale green chainse from her satchel before disappearing into the adjoining annex room. "It was kind of you to bring me a meal," she called out to him.

Henry poked at the fire, then tossed another log into the midst of the flames. "You left a lot on your plate last night," he answered, looking up as she came back into the room. "You must be hungry by now."

They sat facing each other on the bed, eating from the same tray. It was an act of intimacy she had never known with Philippe, who ate only at table, and then with as little talk as possible.

"Your letters were dispatched this morning," Henry told her after he had mumbled a blessing over the food. "They were sent to your husband in Paris, to Flanders in Ghent, and to Baldwin in Mons. What do you plan to do with yourself until they are delivered?"

"It is Philippe who most concerns me," Isabel replied, nibbling at a piece of fruit, "but it may be as long as three weeks before he returns to Paris." She stripped a bit of fat from a slice of pork, then wrapped the meat with bread. Holding it close to her mouth she asked, "Could I remain here until then? I have nowhere else I can go."

Henry thought about that and then nodded. "I will be here till the middle of February. So long as that, you may remain as well."

Isabel smiled her thanks, then peered beneath the covered dishes and plates, searching for something sweet. "Philippe should be back in Paris shortly after Candlemas. After Senlis he went on to St. Nazaire in Brittany to see your son."

Henry choked on his wine. After a fit of coughing he croaked out the words, "He is with Geoffrey?"

"Yes," she replied, not understanding his alarm. Henry

grasped the henap roughly at its base and flung it across the
room. Stunned by his outburst, Isabel explained quietly, "They
are friends."

"They are conspirators!" he bellowed, shaking a fist in the air.
"Good Christ, will the time never come when I am safe from the
evil intentions of my sons and their cohorts?"

Her hand trembled lightly upon his forearm and her voice was
cautious. "Why does that upset you? It seems innocent enough to
me."

"What do you know of it?" he grumbled, tossing his meat back
onto the plate.

She spoke more boldly. "I know of the trouble between you
and your sons and the wars that came from it, but since the death
of Harry I have heard it said that Geoffrey has done homage to
you and begged forgiveness. If that is so, how can you think he
would stir up more dissent?"

"An oath of fealty means nothing to Geoffrey," Henry responded dismally, slapping a fist into his palm, "and with your
husband to help him, he could aspire to even greater treasons."

"It's not what you think, I'm sure," she tried to persuade him.
"Perhaps I cannot speak for your son, but I know Philippe well
enough to make a judgment. He is already facing the threat of
war with my family. Why would he wish to invite a confrontation
with you? Especially when he hopes, as I know he does, that you
will eventually intercede on his behalf?"

He pondered that for a while, staring glumly at the floor.
"Then why are they together?"

She had wondered too. Philippe had given no reason for going
to Brittany. There was only one answer Isabel could think of.
"You must understand," she began, "Philippe has certain habits.
You doubtless know of the relationship he shared with Harry. It
is possible Geoffrey appeals to him in much the same way." She
looked placidly into his stern face. Taking up her own cup she
poured it full with wine and handed it to him. It was no good if
he got side-tracked on other matters when she wanted him fully
committed to her own concerns. "Don't worry. I know the ways
of the world, the ways of men, and I tell you this: whatever
Geoffrey and Philippe have between them, it has nothing to do
with you." Her sweet smile was designed to convince him further.

Henry took her offering and drank till the cup was empty,

then sat back to watch as she ate. The fire lapped light and shadow over her humid beauty. He stroked his beard thoughtfully. What was wrong with Philippe Capet that he preferred the company of men to this honeyed girl? His careful glance measured the fullness of the curves beneath her clothes. She was a smug little bitch in her way, sensing the tug of interest between them and enjoying it, but pretending not to notice the eager flush of passion on his face. Such sensual precocity was wasted on a boy! Before he could choose his words more carefully he had told her so.

Isabel had gone back to her food and answered him without looking up. "Oh I don't know. He's much less of a *boy* than you might imagine."

Henry laughed. Such conversation came easily from her lips. "I've heard the stories."

"From Eleanor?"

"Yes," he admitted, "though it seems, despite his size, good Louis had little to offer as a lover."

Isabel pushed the tray to the foot of the bed and licked the wine from her lips. "Philippe is different."

He was beginning to understand her and the realization brought a lustful smile to his lips. "It would appear that there are aspects of this marriage which you hold much dearer than your crown."

Isabel looked at him, not sure if he was merely teasing, or trying to make her angry. He was a hard man to read, though certain sides of his nature were already very clear to her. Henry was vigorous: she'd heard the stories of his many mistresses as nearly everyone had, and yet Isabel had the feeling he had not been satisfied for many years. Something in his eyes told her that. Or was it only vanity after all: both of them thinking they held a special fascination irresistible to the other?

Her fingers skipped lightly over the coverlet. "It is true I don't care about the crown," she said, "but all of this is very private and hard to explain. I'm not sure you would understand."

How typically female she was, how shamelessly young! Henry grabbed her wrist and held it. "I understand this: I don't care if your precious husband boots you out or not. What is it to me, after all?"

She bowed her head, golden streamers of hair nearly covering her face as she did so. "Nothing, I suppose."

He let go of her but leaned closer. "Young or old, you women are all alike! It isn't enough to have a good man in your bed, you must *own* him, clutch him to your breast, like gold. Why does every woman put her stock in romance? This need for cherishing and being cherished, it's nonsense, all of it. . . ."

She looked at him with a minglement of pity and surprise. "You don't really believe that. You couldn't."

Henry's voice was hoarse, bitter with remembrance. "What do you know? Child, I've been old longer than you've been alive. Love is a cheat and you are a fool my little beauty if you believe in it too dearly."

He was even more complicated than she had guessed, and jaded. She felt sorry for him, and vaguely motherly. "What do you believe in then?" she asked.

"This," he said and took her in his arms. "Only this."

An instant, only an instant to evaluate her feelings; a moment to decide if she wanted him or not. And then the moment passed, and wanting or not wanting didn't matter because he was kissing her and she did not resist nor did she wish to.

Eagerly and with her help Henry stripped off his clothes and flung them to the floor. For just a moment Isabel was disappointed. He was not beautiful like Philippe. His flesh was firm enough, but blotched with many scars and signs of age. Most of the hair upon his chest was grey. But below his chest—ah, that was nice. She closed her eyes and reached for him.

Henry's grunted promises were all obscenities: he would do *this* to her and after *that,* then *this* again. His peasant vulgarity excited Isabel, but there was more. How sweet the touch of a man who'd known so many women in his life. She sighed with contentment. *Legend. He was a legend.*

It was dawn before either of them slept.

Henry snored comfortably that afternoon while Isabel took a bath and washed her hair. When she returned to her room he was awake and sitting up in bed, eating a slice of bread from last night's dinner tray.

"That is no way for a king to feed his appetite," Isabel teased and took the bread from his hand. "I was just downstairs and ordered a meal to be laid for us."

"Come here," he pulled her into his arms, "and let me feed myself on you."

Two hours later they went downstairs to dinner.

"I'm so happy," Isabel told him as she cut into her meat. "I haven't felt this good in months. You're wonderful to be with, Henry. You truly are."

Henry stirred the potage in his bowl and tasted it. The broth was hot and spicy, laced with vegetables and herbs. He wiped his lips and looked across the table at her. She made a delicious sight, engrossed in eating. "And you make an old man feel young again." The words were spoken lightly, but his eyes proved them to be true.

As they ate they talked of many things. Isabel was alive with curiosity and Henry found himself recounting stories that he hadn't told in years. Childhood memories of his mother's wars against King Stephen. Himself a king at twenty-one with Eleanor as his bride. The struggle with Becket and its ghastly consequences. The years of turmoil which had followed, as Eleanor incited Harry, Richard and Geoffrey to treason against their own father.

Isabel watched Henry closely as he spoke of Eleanor. His voice was full of enmity as though he'd never loved her, or if having done so, had forgotten it long ago. As for his sons, he had praise for only one of them.

"Johnny is a good boy," he said and pushed his plate away. "He's a little irresponsible now but he'll grow out of that in time. He loves me, that's what counts in a son. He's the only boy Eleanor gave me who does. There's Godfrey, though. Godfrey loves me."

Godfrey of Lincoln. Isabel wasn't likely to forget him and what he'd written about her. She wondered if Henry knew of that but decided not to bring it up. "Yes, Godfrey," she mused, "is he your son by the famous Rosamunde?"

He hesitated, looking down into the bottom of his empty cup. "No, I met her years after he was born. She gave me several children too, but they all died as infants."

"And now you never speak of her?"

"Not often." He filled the cup and drank till it was empty once again. Rosamunde. That memory was a pressed flower closed between the pages of a book he seldom opened now. And yet the fragrance lingered. . . .

Isabel realized she had crossed the boundary into a private place. She didn't want to risk his anger but the subject of his legendary romance interested her. *Ask a hard question softly and you'll get an answer* Baldwin had told her once, so she kept her voice discreet and sympathetic. "Was Rosamunde as lovely as the poets say?"

Was she? The years had dimmed the memory of her face and all the other things about her. The feel of her, sweet and submissive in his arms. Her gentle voice that only spoke to praise him. How good she had been, how kind—and how greatly Henry had betrayed her. A single tear escaped his eye and rushed down into his beard. *Forgive me, Rosamunde, forgive me all the lies!*

"Forgive me," Isabel said. "Is the memory so painful for you?"

"All memories are," he said and wiped a hand across his face.

"Then you must banish them by concentrating on the future."

He patted her hand affectionately and thought how sweet she was. "At my age, Isabel, the future holds as many terrors as the past. You wouldn't understand that. You're too young to know what terror is."

Her laugh was rich with irony. "If that were true, Henry, I wouldn't have come here." Her face held him in thrall as he watched the subtle change that came into her eyes. "Think back upon your life at my age. What you were telling me before. You knew what sadness was, and trouble. So do I. Bad memories haunt us only if we let them, and so far as the future is concerned, is yours any less secure than mine is?"

She was so lovely it was hard to believe she was equally as wise. "You're right," he said, "it doesn't bear repeating." He took hold of her hand and, without releasing it, rounded the table to stand behind her.

Her face bloomed like a flower as she tilted her chin to look up at him. "Take me upstairs," she whispered, "and I will teach you to forget the past."

She had made him feel young again. Not wanting to diminish that, she let him carry her upstairs.

Outside the town of Chartres, a mile beyond the cathedral, Philippe stood in a little grove of yew trees and looked out toward the white-washed sky where the snow was falling.

It was cold and the world seemed empty but for him. When the wind rattled a branch behind him he jumped at the sound. After a moment he relaxed but turned his head a little, anticipating a presence that was not there.

Philippe pushed at the snow with booted feet as the pale sky deepened to vague shades of grey. Then when the light was gone he straddled his horse and rode away.

The king of England was keeping to his bed late on these long winter mornings.

The entourage who had come to Gisors with him lounged in idleness. They could not attend to business, nor even satisfy themselves with hunting because the king shunned their company and kept them posted to the common hall. There they amused themselves with drink and dicing, while upstairs Henry concentrated his attentions upon the girl who had been his bed-mate for two weeks.

Isabel was happy here. She loved doing things for him, little tasks like those she had done for her father. Mending the lining of his clothes. Polishing his boots and stitching them where they were ragged. She served him food and stirred the honey in his wine.

And he could talk to her; that surprised him. Isabel had as much capacity for making conversation as she had for making love. "How beautiful you are," he told her one evening as she sat at his feet before the fire. "I think if you were my wife I would lock you up away from all the world and visit you each night in secret." He patted the top of her head with a burly hand.

She looked up over the border of her sewing and gave him a wan smile. "I may as well have been locked up for the past four years. Philippe never lets me see anyone. I'm like a prisoner in that awful place."

"He's jealous," Henry winked at her, "and I don't blame him."

Her hands went limp over the material. "It isn't only that, Henry. He simply doesn't want to see me happy. When first I came to Paris, Sully and the chancellor de Puiseaux helped me with my lessons. They were about the only people that I saw. Philippe even resented that! Then later de Puiseaux was too busy to spend time with me, at my husband's instigation I am sure.

And Sully stopped liking me a long time ago. He thinks I am a bad influence on Philippe."

Henry found that amusing. "No doubt any priest on earth would agree with him. They are a suspicious lot." Then as an afterthought he asked, "What about your husband's family? Have they been unpleasant to you?"

"Unpleasant?" she sniffed contemptuously. "They've been despicable. All of them, except Philippe's cousin, Henri. He's been very kind to me. As you know he was the one who made it possible for me to come here." When Henry made no reply Isabel returned to the business of her mending, assiduously engrossed in making little stitches in the cloak he wore for riding.

Henry watched her as she sat, her head thrust forward in concentration, her hair tousled about her shoulders like a sunburst in the firelight. "You're so sweet," he mused. "I don't think you have any idea of how sweet you are. Your husband must be hard-hearted not to love you."

Her fingers stopped abruptly, the needle glinting between folds of woollen cloth. "He loves me. It's only that he hates my family so much, for what my uncle has done to him, and now, my father."

"And that is what you hope to remedy by coming here?"

She put the cloth aside and went to him, wrapping her arms about his neck. "Don't make fun of me. I didn't know what else to do."

He pulled her onto his knee and held her close against his chest, rocking her gently. She was so warm and yielding, resting in his arms like a sleeping child. The firelight dappled glowing shades of orange and gold across her flawless face. The sight of her was so lovely it made his heart ache. "Don't expect too much from me, Isabel," he said, trying not to sound unkind. "I have done all I intend to do. If Philippe is persuaded by your ultimatum not to divorce you, so much the better for you. But if it does not work, there is nothing more that I can do."

She raised her head and looked at him with sea-colored eyes that saw deeper than he knew. "You could, Henry. You could if you wanted to. You've settled difficulties between my family and the French before. You could do it again. You could do it for *me*."

Isabel slipped gently from his lap as he stood up, looking down at her, his eyes the color of an approaching storm. "I told you my feelings about this the first night you were here, and a half dozen times since then I have repeated it. There is not enough charm in all the world or even you to change my mind once I have made it up. Remember that, and this last week will be as pleasant for us as all that has gone before."

By the examples she had seen, Isabel should have realized that all men were the same, and kings moreso than the rest. Philippe was always unmoved by her pleas, why should this man be any different? Henry was older, seasoned, with more reasons in his past to make him cynical.

"Would you say, then, that without your interference, he is likely to divorce me?" she asked, with little hope.

It was not a conversation that Henry wanted to pursue. He gathered up the papers he'd been reading earlier and tucked them away inside the folds of a heavy leather satchel which he tossed to the floor. Then he sighed and straightened up. "Isabel, you know the answer better than I do. Can't we just leave it there?"

There was no point in belaboring the subject any further, but she had one question left to ask. "If you were my husband what would you do?"

He walked to the bed and sat down heavily on it. "You ask too many questions, questions which I cannot answer." He held out his arms to her. "Let's be done with all the words and go to bed."

She went into his embrace and put a kiss upon his cheek but she would not be so easily put off by his indifference. "This divorce may be a little thing to you, Henry," she reminded him, "but to me it is worse than anything else."

He saw the threat of tears in her eyes and felt uneasy. *Poor child.* Her vulnerability stabbed a little at his conscience. "Divorce is not so terrible," he told her, "and no matter how you feel you must learn to live with whatever happens."

"But I love him! I will die without him!" The words seemed incongruous in the circle of his arms.

Henry's voice was spiked with irritation. "You won't die. Believe me girl, to die is not so easy."

Isabel knew she had no right to expect sympathy from him but she wanted it all the same. It was her own fault, needing him to understand her when there was no reason why he should. At least he hadn't lied to her. From the first night Henry had been indifferent to the divorce and had said so. *Leave it be* she told herself and blinked away the tears. "Henry," she asked as he stripped the cloth from her shoulders, "why did you never divorce Eleanor?"

"Bad politics," he muttered, distracted.

"Bad marriage."

"Only at the close," he answered, his rough hands fondling her silken skin. "There was a time when Eleanor and I were happy. She always said that Becket came between us, and Rosamunde, and other women; I'll hold she thinks it to this day. But there were a thousand better reasons."

She kissed him, holding his face between her hands. "When I saw the two of you together at Geoffrey's wedding, I thought I had never seen a couple so fitted for one another."

His bawdy laugh boomed in her face. "Oh we *fitted* alright, it was the rest that didn't work." When Isabel tried to respond he grabbed her in a rough embrace and blotted out her breath with kisses. "Now to bed with you my little golden wench and let us be well fitted." Henry hoisted her to the bed and pushed her back on it, his hands tight on her naked hips. "What a body you have," he exclaimed, "you are magnificent!"

The firm pressure of his hands had driven away her doubts and Isabel smiled up at him. "I thought that men preferred girls with slim hips and long elegant legs."

Henry slapped her rump with an open palm. "They have their place, but there's nothing nearly as important as what is between them." Lowering his face to her belly Henry buried his beard in a triangle of plush blond curls. "So sweet the taste of a golden cunt," he murmured.

"Henry, you're so vulgar," Isabel giggled and settled herself more comfortably. "I don't doubt Eleanor minded such nasty talk."

Henry got to his feet, hands fumbling at his clothes. His teeth flashed in a grin. "After fifteen years with Louis?" he laughed. "By God girl, she loved it!" Freeing himself he pushed forward, settling himself between her slim white thighs, his hands busy at her breasts. "And so do you."

A sigh escaped her lips as he filled her, and the last of her guilt dissolved. He was right. She did.

* * *

There were four of them. Tall, broad-shouldered knights of the king, the Lions of England grinning on their shields. They approached in unison, footfalls oddly muffled. There was a sudden sound of unsheathed steel. Screams. Shouts. Then the blood ran everywhere.

Henry nearly tumbled from the bed as he tried to stop them. "No more!" he cried, but everything was black and silent. Sweet Jesus, it was only memory. He'd had the dream again.

Alarmed, Isabel sat up and reached for him. "What, Henry, what?" She leaned to the candle and lit it.

Henry was slumped forward, arms extended, leaning on his knees. His breath came in deep heaving sounds. "Thomas," he sobbed. "Oh, Thomas..."

The fire was nearly out and it took Isabel several minutes to coax it into flames again. That done she poured a cup of wine and brought it to the bed. "Here," she offered, and when he took it in his own hands she pulled the woollen coverlet up around his shoulders.

The trembling had stopped now, and the tears. He was himself once more and ashamed for having let her see him this way. She looked so concerned, so lovely, her hair in pale swirls like an aureole about her face. "What is it, Henry?" she asked when he had drunk the wine and set the cup aside. "What did you dream that troubled you so much?"

The memory was fading, receding into the darkness where all nightmares live when dreamers are awake. Henry leaned back against the pillow and drew a deep breath. "Don't fuss over me," he grumbled, but his tone was self-reproving. "I'm too old to be frightened of a dream."

She climbed into bed beside him, curling up within the folds of the blanket, her head resting on his chest. "It was about Thomas Becket, wasn't it?" she asked.

Across the room a log splintered in the grate as flames consumed it greedily. "Yes, Becket," he answered, staring at the fire.

She slid her arms about his naked waist and held him to her tightly. "Tell me about it."

"It doesn't matter," Henry answered, stroking her hair, "go to sleep."

For a long time Henry sat holding Isabel as she dozed in his arms. He yearned to sleep but a fragment of the dream kept him wakeful. Something about it had been different this time. Over and over again he replayed the images in his mind until the realization came in a livid flash. Tonight the murdered man had not been Becket. Tonight the face beneath the mitre had been his own.

"**I** KNEW NOTHING of this," Hughes de Puiseaux insisted, his glance darting above the page. "I didn't even realize Isabel had left Paris."

Philippe's face was strained by weariness. He had only just returned to the palace—tired, ready to sleep—now he was faced with this. He pulled the paper from de Puiseaux's hands and tossed it to the floor. "Clermont tells me it was delivered ten days ago, put into his hands by a messenger from Henry of England."

De Puiseaux looked puzzled. "I don't understand. Henry is at Gisors. Is that where Isabel has gone?"

The king's answer was a wordless glare. Hughes sank his hands into the velvet folds of his pellison and started to pace the length of the council chamber. Neither of them spoke for several minutes. Finally de Puiseaux stopped abruptly, looking over his shoulder at Philippe. "She couldn't have gotten to Gisors alone," he declared, "someone must have helped her, but I can't imagine who."

The toe of Philippe's boot scuffed the floor as he kicked it. "I can," he answered.

Within the hour Henri of Champagne had been summoned to the council chamber and confronted with Isabel's written ultimatum. He submitted quietly and patiently to Philippe's questions. At the end he said, "My lord, I didn't think much of the queen's plan but she insisted that I was the only person she could trust to help her." Henri raised his head and stole a glance at Philippe who was looking off toward the far wall, his handsome profile sharp against the background of cold grey stones. Henri cleared his throat. "She was distraught, terrified that you truly meant to divorce her. Taking pity on her situation, I did all I could. Surely that is not so wrong, given the circumstances."

"The circumstances are none of your concern!" Philippe shouted, pointing a finger close to Henri's nose.

De Puiseaux's hand was a firm restraint upon Philippe's shoulder. "This is getting us nowhere," he told both of them. Then addressing Philippe, "Shall I go to Gisors myself and fetch back the queen?"

"Yes," Philippe replied immediately, "and you can leave at once." De Puiseaux bowed and quietly left the room. Philippe picked up the queen's letter and read it over once again in silence, glaring at the arrogant, slanted script. There was no end to her defiance. Did she really believe that he would bow to her dictates, tremble at her elusive threats? He flung the letter from him in disgust.

To Henri he said, "In the interests of kinship I will be lenient with you. I could take your lands away as punishment for what you've done but in my heart I know that friendship for the queen blinded you. You have served me well in the past. On the strength of that, cousin, you may keep all honors and titles which are yours. But you may not remain in Paris. I cannot take the chance that you might decide at some other time to meddle in my business. Go back to Troyes and see to your own affairs. If at some later date I wish to bring you back to court I shall do so. Until that time I prefer that you stay away." He waved his hand in a gesture of dismissal.

Just then Robert de Clermont came in, several members of the king's household bodyguard following in his tread. "Your mother is only recently returned from Chantilly," he announced, "and says that she knows nothing of the queen's departure." He gave a glance as Henri left the room without a word, then turned his attention back to Philippe. "Do you want me to question the queen's attendant, that crippled girl?"

Philippe got to his feet. "Don't bother, Clermont. I've learned everything I need to know. But be prepared to leave for Rheims with me tomorrow morning. Before I make a final decision concerning this divorce, I want to confer with my uncle." He started toward the door. "I won't need you any more today. I'm going to my room. Tell the guards to make certain no one disturbs me."

Clermont followed him out into the corridor and through the

great hall. "Would you like some food brought to you?"

Philippe was already on the stairs. "No," he called back, "I want to sleep."

Upstairs Philippe paid a hasty visit to his private chapel. Then without undressing he fell into his bed. Beside him on the other pillow lay the Druid ring, where Isabel had put it on the night she left. Philippe seized it in his hand and the silver chain spilled out between his fingers. How cold it felt without her flesh to warm it.

He tossed the ring away. Then he lay down and went to sleep.

Isabel left Gisors on February tenth. Henry had arranged for her to travel with a group of forty Cluniac monks who were on their way from Rouen south to Paris.

It was a grey morning, and chilly. The sky was piled high with clouds that promised snow later in the day. Their progress would be slow. Isabel gripped the reins and turned her horse to fall in step with the others. Her black hood ruffled in the wind and obscured her face for an instant before she pushed it into place.

She twisted in the saddle and looked back. From high above her Henry leaned from a window, watching. Even from that distance she could see his smile. Touching a black-gloved hand to her lips, Isabel blew him a discreet kiss and mouthed the word *goodbye*.

Ahead the landscape swam in a blur of early morning fog and tears. What troubles waited for her at the end of this road? Dismally Isabel raised her hand and waved without looking back.

Edythe greeted her mistress with a fond embrace. "I was so worried," she explained as the two young women huddled together by the fire in the queen's bedroom. "Everyone has been asking questions and the king has discovered where you were. He left two days ago. I don't know where he went."

"I know," Isabel replied, drawing closer to the warmth. "I have already spoken to de Clermont. He told me Philippe went to Rheims to see his uncle. He wouldn't say if it had anything to do with me." She looked up suddenly. "Are my jewels safe?"

Edythe fussed with a dinner tray, slicing bread, cutting cheese. "I checked them only yesterday," she answered, "no one has disturbed them. And I have kept the key with me always." She drew out the chain with the key dangling at the end of it.

"Good," Isabel mumbled, rubbing her hands together to get them warm, "You have done your job. Now I must do mine, or at least complete what I have started."

Edythe looked up from her chore with uneasy eyes. "What are you going to do?"

The queen chewed nervously at a broken thumbnail. "I'm not sure. But I'm still determined to make Philippe change his mind about divorcing me." She pulled off her boots and set them by the fire to dry, then began removing her soiled traveling clothes. Edythe handed her a thick slice of bread topped by cheese and Isabel ate it greedily, brushing aside the crumbs that spilled on her lap.

"Let me get you some fresh clothes," Edythe suggested and began sorting through an open trunk.

Isabel waved her away. "First have someone bring me up a tub and heat some water," she instructed. "I want to take a bath and wash my hair."

Bathed and wrapped in a woollen shift, Isabel sat on a fur rug near the fire, wincing as Edythe pulled a comb through her wet hair. It was only early evening, yet Isabel felt tired enough to sleep. Too bad that her mind was so alive with problems, of which the divorce was only one.

In a few days, perhaps sooner, Philippe would return to Paris and she would have to face him. She had no way of knowing if her letter had changed his mind or if it had reconciled him with her father and uncle. It was doubtful either had taken place. She would have to explain the trip to Gisors, admit to having involved Henri of Champagne, and then, most difficult of all, feign innocence about her three-week stay with the English king. And even if she managed to achieve all that, there was yet another problem, one which grew more serious with each passing hour.

She watched as Edythe turned down the bedcovers, then made her decision. "I don't think I will sleep right now. Go down to the kitchen and find the Norman woman Richilde. Tell her I wish to see her alone in my audience chamber in an hour. Then come back here and help me to dress."

Puzzled but unquestioning, Edythe left the room.

* * *

"I need you to help me," Isabel explained. Her voice was low and she waited until Edythe had closed the door to say any more.

Now they were alone. The old woman shuffled forward, her hands clasped beneath sagging breasts. Her face bore traces of forgotten prettiness, the features coarsened by old age and fat. But the eyes were dark and clever. "You are the queen," she said, "I am only an old woman. How I help you?"

Isabel drew the fur close about her shoulders. There had been no time to lay a fire in the grate and the room was cold. She wavered for a moment, undecided. This was risky and it was not wise, but she could not afford to wait much longer. She regarded the servant with expectant, cautious eyes. "I have heard that you are good with potions."

The dark eyes lit with a twinkle of realization. "I make brews to cure all ailments. What is yours?"

A moment of hesitation, then the truth. "My flux is late and I need something to bring it. Can you make me up a brew that will help?"

Richilde's lips stretched over a half-vacant mouth. "You think you make a baby that is not your husband's?"

From an embroidered almoner Isabel withdrew two golden florins and held them out to her. "This should be enough to buy your assistance and your silence."

The coins gleamed like golden eyes from the center of Isabel's outstretched palm. Richilde moved closer but did not take the money. She smoothed the folds of grey wool over her hips and looked closely at the queen, nodding her head in grim agreement. "Tomorrow morning see that you take no food. I will bring you a mixture made of mistletoe and other herbs to drink. Drink all of it, while it is hot. Eat nothing. Then if you do as I say, whatever you have in your belly now will be gone by nightfall."

Isabel felt the coins slip from her hand into her lap. Could it be so easy? "And you will promise to tell no one?"

Richilde hobbled over to a bench and sat down awkwardly. "You will excuse me my lady but I have been all day at the ovens and I need to sit."

"Of course," Isabel mumbled absently, and waited. Then, "Can I trust you to be silent?"

Richilde's laugh was crude but filled with friendliness. "I understand better than you think. I was not always old and fat." She smiled wistfully, remembering. "Sometimes a husband is not enough for a woman who burns inside."

Isabel looked away. "I don't even know if I am pregnant. I just want to make certain that I'm not. . . ."

The servant shrugged her shoulders in indifference. "No need to fear. You are not the first royal woman to come to me with a baby made in a stranger's bed." She smiled when Isabel looked up. "Aye, Lady Adele had need of my mixtures many times in years gone by."

The queen leaned over and pushed the coins into Richilde's hand. "Tomorrow morning then."

Once more the money was refused with a laugh. "What good is that to me? People would only say I stole it."

"Please take it," Isabel insisted. "I owe you something, certainly."

A gnarled hand patted Isabel's wrist. "I have all that I need. A warm bed of straw behind the ovens. All the food I wish. A new dress every summer. A cloak in wintertime. I am content." She belched under her breath. "Sometimes when the brothels are full I even have young men who come to me, too full of wine and lust to care that I am a fat old woman. Life is good. Save your money for the pretty things a young queen needs. It is no use to me."

"Very well," Isabel agreed and put the coins back inside her almoner, "but don't forget what you have promised." She hesitated for a moment, then bent and put a kiss on the old woman's cheek. "Bless you for helping me, Richilde."

"Don't worry, child," the woman said and patted the young queen's abdomen, "by tomorrow evening you will be rid of this."

Isabel pressed her hands together mockingly. "Please God," she said.

For three days Isabel lay bleeding in her bed, too weak to utter the smallest sound. Edythe stayed near, changing the blankets beneath her body, offering cool cloths for her skin and cups of rain water to drink.

There was so much pain and too much fever for her thoughts to come coherently, but one remained: if Philippe returned to Paris now and found her in this condition he would soon divine the circumstances, and *all* her efforts would have been in vain.

Shadows grew up around her, flapping tongues of indefinite grey flame. She was falling, falling into the hole of the world, trying to hold on but hurled into a deeper darkness with the universe shoveled in on top of her. Only a speck of consciousness lingered—a tiny light to tell her where she was. In her mind's eye Isabel could see herself. She was dead. She was in hell.

But it was not so two days later when she awoke to find herself recovered. The bleeding had stopped. The fever had gone. Isabel was weak as a kitten but she was alive, well and no longer pregnant. That was reason enough to bring her from her bed, and with Edythe's help she washed herself and dressed.

Philippe had still not returned. Anxious for some news, Isabel sought Sully's counsel at the Episcopal palace late that morning. So far as the bishop knew (or would tell her) the king had already initiated the divorce. She listened unhappily to his words, then went back to the Cité palace and told Edythe all she had heard.

"Then that is it," Edythe answered gloomily. "We are going to be sent home to Mons."

"No!" Isabel insisted and stamped her feet. "I will not be pushed into accepting a divorce that I do not want!"

Edythe regarded the queen with pitying eyes. "But what can you do to stop it?"

For a long time Isabel stood at the window, looking out at the city below. "Something," she muttered too low for anyone to hear. "I can do something."

Two men stood whispering outside the king's own council chambers, Constable de Clermont and the pale-faced Bishop of Rheims. Philippe bore the distraction for a little while, frowning, bent close to the table. He was involved in his papers and trying to concentrate but the voices kept disturbing him. Finally he raised his head and looked disapprovingly in their direction. "What is it?" he asked, annoyed.

Clermont came briskly forward, his gaunt face dark and solemn. "My lord," he said, "it is about the queen."

Philippe's eyes stopped over Clermont's face. "What about her?"

"She has been found at last."

"Where?" Philippe asked with the splendid arch of an eyebrow. "I saw de Puiseaux upon our return this morning and he told me she had left Gisors a week ago."

"She is in Paris."

"Here? At the palace?"

"Not now. Sully says she spent last night praying at the cathedral."

"But why? Where is she now?" His voice was sharp with exasperation.

Clermont glanced to his left where William had come to stand beside him, then turned back to the king. "I'm not sure how to say it."

"Say what?" Philippe bellowed.

The lord constable cleared his throat. "She is out in the street, speaking to the people."

Philippe's temper had almost reached its limit. "What people?"

"The *people*," William answered silkily. "She is dressed like a beggar maid and distributing your wealth among the poor folk. It is, I take it, her way of winning them to her side, hoping that they will force you to reinstate her as your wife and queen." He seemed slightly bemused and more than a little impressed by Isabel's methods. "You will remember Philippe that I told you she has some most ennobling characteristics."

Philippe was out of his chair in an instant. "I don't believe it!" he stammered, "what kind of nonsense is she up to now?"

William raised a graceful hand and beckoned toward the eastern window. "See for yourself."

After a night of public prayer in the cathedral Isabel had put on the rags of a servant and spent the morning walking through the streets of the Ile de la Cité, giving out silver coins to everyone she passed. The Bishop of Rheims was only half correct in saying she was distributing the king's money. Some of it was her own. The rest, because she did not have enough, had been borrowed from the king's personal and most private treasury, a collection of many thousand coins he kept hidden beneath the false bottom of his bed.

In her left hand Isabel carried the symbol of a suppliant: a lighted candle taken from the altar of Notre Dame. As she walked through the muddy, rutted streets she chanted psalms in a sweet, clear voice. Even in her rags she was the most lovely sight the people of Paris had ever seen.

At last, after circling the island and pausing to speak to the people in each street, Isabel made her way back to Notre Dame where she stood upon a pile of stone blocks before the cathedral and delivered her appeal to the populace. First she held up the long leather satchel where the coins had been, turning it upside down to show that it was empty. "My friends," she cried out in a voice that carried to the farthest fringe of the crowd, "now I am as poor as all of you!"

There were a few cheers, some indifferent babbling among the curious, and several shouted insults which the queen ignored. Instead she stretched her arms out wide as if wishing to embrace them all. Her voice echoed with clarity and defiance. "Good people of Paris, we have enemies! My husband, your beloved king, has enemies!"

"You are the enemy," a harsh female voice called back but the woman was quickly silenced by the grumbles of others in the crowd who exhorted the queen to speak.

It didn't matter that the rain was soaking through her clothes to the skin, that her hair was wet and tangled, and her bare feet were cold and bruised from walking over stones and frozen ditches. She felt invulnerable, buoyed up by waves of encouragement from the crowd she faced. "Hear me!" she cried. "It has long been my only wish to make peace between the people of my race and you. Between my family and my husband's family. For this act of goodness and Christian charity the king's own enemies —and the enemies of all France—have sought to discredit me in the past. Now, not satisfied merely to oppose me, they seek to force my husband to abandon me as his wife." She paused to draw breath, feeling her blood surge with excitement as she continued, "But I am more than just the king's wife! I am your anointed queen! That right has been given into my care by God and I say to you now *by God* no man has the right to take it from me!"

The rain streamed like tears down her beautiful uplifted face as she raised her arms toward heaven in the manner of a pleading saint. "My husband has been deceived! His soul is in jeopardy! Good people, pray with me that he might throw off the evil will of his enemies, and do God's will by keeping me as his wife."

With the power of a mystic Isabel held the crowd in silence for a moment. Then came the final, unforgettable thrust at the people's collective emotions as she struck her abdomen with a closed fist and shouted, "It is God's will that your next king come from my belly! Such was it prophesied in the lifetime of Hugh Capet. If my husband deserts me now his actions will justly call the wrath of God upon all the people of this land!" She swayed and seemed near to fainting as she screamed out the final words, "Sweet Christ, succor me!" Sobbing, she flung herself to her knees and bowed her head toward the ground.

There was a moment of absolute, shocked silence as every eye in the crowd focused upon her. Isabel stared into darkness behind her closed eyes and waited. Then, as if a signal had been given from heaven, the crowd began to roar with cheering.

They followed her through the winding, narrow streets to the palace, chanting her name like a song. Philippe was watching from the window as the multitude approached. They had the look and fervor of a victorious army, and they were led by one small, rain-soaked girl.

"God keep our queen!" they shouted, and, "Long live Isabel of France!" It was spectacular the way they cheered her, as if in her, a foreigner, they had found a symbol of French unity. Philippe stood unspeaking by the side of his uncle, who was smiling discreetly into his beard. It had been William's defense of the queen this past week which had finally persuaded Philippe to dismiss the Council of Senlis and abandon the plans for divorce. This final act of bravado—mobilizing the people of Paris in the streets—had proved the truth of William's claim. *She was a queen if any girl deserved the title.*

The crowd continued to convulse in shouts of support for Isabel, petitioning their king with raised fists and waving arms to keep her as his wife. The Bishop of Rheims leaned close to his nephew. "They are calling for you," he said, but Philippe scarcely heard him. He was watching Isabel. Even from this distance he could read the message blazing in her eyes. *Come down and face me if you dare.*

He met her challenge with a cold, dispassionate stare although his heart was beating very fast. William's voice came again, close to his ear. "Don't you think you ought to tell her what has been decided?"

From the muddy *esplanade* below, Isabel watched, her anxiousness giving way to panic within her breast. What was he going to do? Would he simply walk away, ignoring her and the shouting of the crowd? Had he already gone too far in instigating the divorce to have his mind changed by a howling mob and her brave acts of defiance? The seconds passed as she waited, hardly daring to draw breath. Then at last Philippe left his place by the window and Isabel felt her knees grow weaker. A prayer, muddled and inarticulate, raced in her thoughts. *Oh God, please God help me now if You are ever going to help me....*

A few minutes later Philippe appeared before them on the steps of the palace and at the sight of their king the crowd grew hysterical with cheering. He accepted their ovation with silent dignity, his tall figure arrogant and erect. Isabel could not take her eyes from him. How handsome he was! Dressed all in black, he looked thinner than she remembered him from several months ago. His trim black beard accentuated the beautiful contour of his jaw. *Please God, give him back to me, dear God, and I will never let another man touch me again so long as I live.*

Philippe raised his hand to petition quiet from the people and immediately the noise died to a flutter of excited whispers. With an air of formality he descended the steps and made his way toward the front of the mob where Isabel stood. She tried very hard to smile at him as he approached, but her lips trembled in a sudden sob of emotion as he stopped in front of her and opened his arms in greeting.

For the remainder of her life Isabel would recall that moment. She stumbled forward, faltered, then collapsed at his feet. If he spoke at all she did not hear him, because the people had gone wild with cheering.

It had happened at last. His strength and will had finally absorbed every part of her and she did not care. Clutching at the dirt with ringless fingers, Isabel hid her face against the soft leather of his boots and sobbed.

Later she did not remember how she had gotten to her room or who had taken her there, only that she had slept for several hours and when she awoke it was dim evening and Philippe was beside her.

Her eyelids felt so heavy, it was impossible to lift them and her lips moved soundlessly for a moment before she was able to make the words come. "Is everything all right now?" Her fingers grasped the velvet front of his bliaud. When he tried to quiet her she persisted in a louder voice, "Philippe, I have to know!"

He sprawled over her, kissing her with such a force that after a while she began to fight him because she could not breathe. Only then did he release her, his breath still hot upon her cheek and he whispered, "Nothing will ever separate us again, I swear it!"

There was something hanging from around his neck. A chain. At the end of the chain, a ring. Isabel closed her hand around it and brought it to her lips, kissing the fretted silver as if it were a part of him.

Before very long amid gasps and whimpers and disheveled clothing she had all of him though she could not have enough of him and in the morning when she woke in the circle of his arms it was as if nothing had gone between their last time together and last night. It would never be better; she would never be happier. Isabel lay back upon his chest and went to sleep.

END PART III

Part IV
November, 1184

SMALL BOATS trimmed with ribbons and autumn roses encircled the graceful banks of the Ile de la Cité like a lover's knot. Torches burned brightly outside each house and shop in Paris. There was singing at the end of every street. Everyone was celebrating on this mild mid-November night because that afternoon Isabel of Hainault had given birth to a healthy child.

The King of France had a baby daughter.

He had prayed earnestly for a son, but from the moment little Jacqueline-Marie was put into his arms, Philippe adored her. She was a black-eyed beauty, the image of her father's Champagnois ancestors, and so tiny it was hard to believe she wouldn't break apart in his embrace.

He smiled down at Isabel who lay pale and half-sleeping in the bed. She was too weary to return his smile but her eyes lighted with contentment and relief. Two days ago when the first of her pains had started Isabel had been afraid she wouldn't live to see her first-born child draw breath. Now the pain was over and although she was exhausted by the ordeal, she felt no worse for having suffered the experience. The child was perfectly formed and she was well; and in time Isabel would get well too and regain all her strength. There was one regret. If only this child had been a boy.

It seemed almost a waste of nine long, difficult months and the agony of childbirth to produce a girl, knowing she would have to do it all again, at least until she bore a son. Isabel thought of her own mother, giving birth year after year, and the image of it soured in her mind. Nine births in the space of fifteen years! Already Isabel had three brothers and a sister she had never seen. Was that the future that awaited her? The very thought depressed her to the point of tears.

Weakly she reached up and fondled Philippe's arm. "I'm so sorry I wasn't able to give you a son."

She sounded genuinely apologetic and a ripple of tenderness for her spread over him. He took her hand and kissed it, his lips warm on her cool skin. "Don't be sorry. I've never been so happy in all my life. You've given me a precious gift." He smiled down into the face of his sleeping daughter. "There's plenty of time for us to have a son."

Isabel rested back against the pillow and closed her eyes. "Yes," she sighed, "plenty of time."

Philippe's enthusiasm for his infant daughter did not wane as the weeks passed. Each day he could be found in the nursery, watching as his darling child was bathed and dressed by her nursemaids. The king's counselors smiled indulgently as he reported to them daily of her progress: what a good child she was (she seldom cried), and wasn't it amazing that she already recognized her father!

Immediately upon his daughter's birth, Philippe had decided that Isabel would nurse the child herself. The descendant of the proud Capet and Carolingian lines would not be suckled at the breasts of a common woman. To Isabel this process was a barely-tolerated interruption in her day, but Philippe saw it as something of a mystic rite. Whenever possible he arranged his own schedule so that he could be present, for what sight could be more beautiful than his adorable daughter feeding at Isabel's flawless breasts? The business of kingship seemed infinitely tedious in comparison.

The birth of the little princess had also caused a change in Philippe's mother. Although Adele had anticipated her role of grandmother with displeasure, one look at the child had dissolved her apprehensions. Her own daughter was lost to her—vanished somewhere amid the splendors of the Byzantine court—and now Adele heaped love and attention upon Jacqueline-Marie with almost savage retaliation. The nursery had been arranged to the exact specifications laid down by the fastidious dowager queen, and this included directions that the room be decorated with the same tapestries and hangings that had clothed Philippe's nursery.

In the midst of all the fuss paid to the newborn hild, Isabel felt somewhat ignored. She was more contented than she had been a year ago but that emotion was quickly ebbing into boredom. She wanted to love her baby the way Philippe did, but the feeling simply wouldn't come. There were too many complications. Motherhood was drab and too demanding, and even her strongest perfume could not disguise the smell of milk that leaked from her nipples and spoiled her clothes.

She ached for Philippe but he seemed preoccupied and more interested in his daughter than his wife. And when he did return to Isabel's bed, what then—another pregnancy? By God she would prevent *that* as long as she could! Nursing a baby was said to keep a woman from conceiving, or so she had heard. At least that was in her favor. And if it didn't work, there were other methods.

Isabel stared out the window at a steel-colored January sky and decided it might be time to arrange another meeting with Richilde.

Early in 1185 Geoffrey Plantagenet came to Paris.

His purpose was both social and political. Many letters had passed between him and Philippe in the eleven months since their meeting at St. Nazaire. Together they had plotted fortifications of certain border castles, discussed a future movement of their combined troops near Normandy, and the possibility of recruiting mercenaries from the north. These were only plans. It was too soon for either man to commit himself to any public action, and too dangerous. If Henry of England suspected that his son and Philippe Capet had any dealings between them, there would be hell to pay.

Actually circumstances had been very favorable for the conspirators in the past year. Henry was too preoccupied with his plan to get the Aquitaine away from Richard to waste time on worrying about a friendship between Philippe and Geoffrey. Although he had been upset last year when Isabel had mentioned such a thing, he had since forgotten it in the course of other problems.

Henry was no longer master of his situation. His decision to take Richard's lands was rash, unfair and, worst of all, foolish. He was determined to set his beloved son John against Richard, and he would stop at nothing to accomplish this.

Richard was puzzled: what had he done wrong? He was serving his father's interests loyally in Poitou and Aquitaine. His reward for this was suspicion, betrayal, and the steady resistance of his father to name him as heir to the throne, even though young Harry had been dead for more than a year.

Matters grew more ticklish when in the summer of 1184 Henry had ordered John to take an army into Richard's domains and fight him for them, though he gave his youngest son neither money nor the means to accomplish this. It had been an empty threat, the kind that Henry made too often these days.

In June of that year Henry had returned to England, leaving John behind in Normandy. Geoffrey, who had thus far stayed clear of the controversy between his brothers, saw his chance at last. He convinced John that war against Richard was in both their best interests and before very long the two of them had raised an army and invaded Poitou.

It had not been a very long or very serious war. Richard had moved quickly, striking back with a ferocity that had earned for him the epithet of "Lionheart." By November of 1184 a meagre peace had been struck between the brothers. John, who was always bored by war because it entailed too much hard work, was glad to call an end to it. Richard, too, for other reasons. During his involvement with the fighting, new troubles had broken out between the barons of the Aquitaine and his presence was needed there once again to settle the strife.

Geoffrey's losses had been heaviest: many shrines, castles, and churches in Brittany had been sacked by Richard's forces. But he was happy in a way. Skillfully, and with wicked determination, he was clearing a path for himself. With Richard and their father at cross purposes, he could see his own star rising. John was still too young and inexperienced to be counted on. Henry knew it, though he denied it—and that left only Geoffrey. He was on the very brink of snatching the succession for himself.

Fortified by this knowledge he made his way to Paris and the company of his newest friend and ally.

* * *

"She's adorable," Geoffrey told Philippe as he rocked the baby in his arms, "though I must admit I am partial to girls. My own little Eleanor is nearly Jacquie's age. You must come to Brittany some time soon and see her." He looked over at his friend and smiled knowingly. "I do believe that fatherhood has worked some magic on you. You seem much happier than when I saw you last."

With a care that approached delicacy, Philippe took the child from Geoffrey and laid her in the cradle. A grey-haired nurse-maid hustled to his side, covering the sleeping baby with a quilt. The king stood by, smiling down at his daughter and gently fingering her fine, black hair. "Yes," he sighed contentedly, "things are much better for me now in many ways. Baldwin of Hainault has joined me in my struggle against Philip d'Alsace and I have had assurance of an army from the emperor as well. When spring comes we will face Flanders in the field and put his braggart oaths to the test of battle. Then, if we defeat him, as I know we shall, I will finally get possession of those territories which should have been given over to my care two years ago." He looked up. "And of course the messages from you have been most encouraging."

Geoffrey put an arm about Philippe's shoulder. "I bring you news which may be more encouraging still."

"Good," Philippe answered "and we shall talk of it, but not here. Later, when we are alone...but first we must go down to dinner with my wife. Come."

Together they walked toward the door but Philippe turned back for one more look at his daughter. His face lighted with a quiet expression of joy. "She is the finest thing that has happened to me in this past year, or any other."

"I can see that," Geoffrey smiled. He and Philippe left the room together.

Isabel was laughing.

The wine shimmered in her cup, reflecting a pale glow of pearls and peridots. She was dressed in light green silk, her hair woven into a braided coil atop her head. She was relaxed and looking lovelier than Philippe had ever seen her look before. And she was laughing.

It was Geoffrey who had made the difference. All through

dinner he had charmed her with his ribald riddles and witty conversation. He had the means to charm anyone with his handsome looks and elegant manners and his subtle show of flattery. His brother Harry had been the same; so too was Richard if the tales of him were true.

So enchanting, these sons of the English king. Poets and warriors both. Philippe picked at the food upon his plate and wondered how a man could learn to speak the words which softened the expression of a woman's face. Isabel laughed and Philippe looked at her. She knew what he was thinking. He could read the answer in her eyes.

That evening as the winter light faded into darkness, Philippe and Geoffrey rode away to the forest of Vincennes outside of Paris, where they spent the night alone in a woodsman's hut.

"You're a lucky man," Geoffrey mused as they reclined on the floor in front of a seething fire. "Isabel is exquisite, more beautiful than I remember her." Squinting into the fire Geoffrey asked, "How do you tear yourself away from her?"

"If memory serves me, your wife is not unattractive," Philippe observed, tracing the line of Geoffrey's beard with his finger.

"That's true," he answered, nuzzling Philippe's hand, "but Constance is a proud woman."

"Proud!" Philippe laughed. "Womanhood has never known such pride as Isabel possesses."

Geoffrey turned over on his stomach, propping his chin beneath a fist. "In Constance pride has turned her flesh to ice. I can't believe the same is true of Isabel."

A thousand images wavered in his mind. Then Philippe sat up abruptly, knotting his hands between his knees. "No," he admitted, "Isabel is different."

Heated by wine and fire and each other's arms, the two men slept till dawn. When Philippe awoke the two-room hut was empty. He threw a foxfur mantle around his body and pulled on his boots and braies. Then he went outdoors and stood off to the side, pissing into the snow. He had just finished and was pulling his laces closed when he looked up and saw Geoffrey coming toward him, his arms filled with logs for firewood.

They went inside together. "I've been chopping wood," Geoffrey said proudly as he tossed the logs into the fire.

"Hardly the work of a king's son," Philippe answered, trying to sound disparaging, but he was only teasing. It was always very hard for him to be light-hearted, even in such intimate circumstances as these.

They tore bits from a loaf of bread and Geoffrey sliced the cheese with his dagger. By the time they sat down to eat their food and wash it down with goatsmilk, the wood was burning rapidly, though it hissed in places where the snow had left it wet.

They talked of the summer wars and what had come of them, of a future plan for capturing Normandy when all the preparations had been made. All the signs looked good for them, as Geoffrey hastened to explain. "I can't believe my own luck. Richard is digging a grave for himself and John grows more worthless every day."

Philippe stuck a piece of twig between his teeth and gnawed at it thoughtfully. "But he is still Henry's favorite?"

"Oh, yes," Geoffrey answered quickly, and pulled the shell from a boiled egg, "but even Henry knows that John is just a child."

"Hardly a child," Philippe disagreed. "He is very near my own age."

"In years," Geoffrey laughed, "but in years only. John is the laziest person on earth. He wishes only to eat, drink, and chew on little girls. It's about the only thing he and my father have in common."

"*Common* is right," Philippe said sounding self-righteous and disgusted. "But what about Richard? Why does Henry refuse to name him as the heir?"

Geoffrey's eyes were downcast but an insolent, knowing smile played across his lips. "It might well be that father is seriously looking elsewhere for a successor to the crown."

"John? But you said . . ."

The smile grew into a self-satisfied grin. "Last November at West Minster palace, in front of both my brothers, Henry named me *custos* of Normandy in his absence." His eyes gleamed, green and exaltant.

A thrill surged in Philippe's groin. "I can't believe it," he said, nearly breathless at his friend's good fortune, and his own. "That sounds as if . . ."

"As if the whole inheritance were about to be settled upon me?"

Geoffrey asked with an uplifted eyebrow. "That's it, I'm sure."

"Henry's announcement must have made the Christmas court very interesting," Philippe observed.

Geoffrey laughed. "You should have seen what it was like. Mother was there, and my sister Matilda, both of them trying to look younger than they are. John came to celebrate his birthday, Christmas Eve, and ended by getting drunk and puking on the table. And throughout the whole time Richard and Henry watched each other like two hungry jackals over the Christmas pudding."

"And you?" Philippe asked, "what did you do to pass the time?"

Geoffrey's moist lips brushed against Philippe's cheek in a kiss. He whispered something close to Philippe's ear and Philippe laughed, his mouth wetting at the image. "We're very close to having everything we want," he said, and their lips met.

They made love till the middle of the morning then lounged by the fire till noon while outside the wind was stirring up the snow.

"As long as I hold Normandy in my father's name I shall have a lot of money in my keeping," Geoffrey was saying to his friend. "Just think of the army I can raise! This is only the beginning for us."

Philippe rummaged in the satchel where the food was kept until he drew out something that sparkled in the light. "Here," he said and slipped the ring on Geoffrey's left hand middle finger. "This is to celebrate our friendship."

It was a silver ring edged with emeralds and its cnter bore the king's device in miniature. Geoffrey looked up with questions in his eyes. "This is your seal."

Philippe nodded. "I am creating you Seneschal of France. If I am going to keep your counsel you should occupy such a position."

A quick frown darted across Geoffrey's brow. "But what about the members of the *curia regis,* and your barons? Won't they wonder what is going on? And Henry—might this not hint to him that we have plans?"

"Not if we tell no one of it for the time being," Philippe answered. "It will be our secret until we are too strong to worry about anyone interfering with our aims." He caressed Geoffrey's cheek with the tips of his fingers. "We will have all that we want, in time. But we must be careful. In any case, I have to settle my quarrel with Philip d'Alsace before I can give attention to our matter. Then when Flanders has been shown I can't be trifled with, you and I will take back all of England's lands on the continent for ourselves."

The picture of such a triumph pleased Geoffrey well and delight glowed in his eyes. "There is nothing we cannot do together," he vowed, and threw his arms around Philippe's neck.

Philippe laughed and hugged him back. "Amen to that," he said.

P RINCE JOHN was growing restless.

He had recently turned eighteen, yet he had virtually nothing but the clothes on his back and a single horse to call his own. Henry had made a great boast about dividing up Richard's inheritance and giving some of it to John, but as usual that had come to nothing. Just as the wars of the previous summer had come to nothing. That was fine for Geoffrey. He could afford to play at war. He had all the resources of Brittany at his disposal and for the time being he had Normandy as well.

John had nothing, and it was so unfair. Since boyhood he had been the landless youngest son. He had been Henry's favorite too, but what good was that if it brought no gifts or blessings with it? This business of a betrothal to Hadwisa of Gloucester was another problem. John had no wish to marry her. She was ugly, and too old for him. It was true she would bring a large dowry, but the thought of spending his life on some obscure country estate, cut off from the center of society and power, depressed him. What kind of future did that offer for the son of a king?

Henry knew his son was dissatisfied and seized upon a means of pacifying him. Years ago John had been given the title "Lord of Ireland." It was Henry's way of threatening the rebellious Irish with his power. He had never expected John's appointment to come to anything, but now he saw a chance. There had been figting among the three great kings of Ireland this past year, and disunity among the Norman colonists. Hugh de Lacy had been Henry's procurator in Ireland for ten years and the king had suspicions that de Lacy was more anxious to serve his own interests than those of England. What better excuse than to send young Johnny there to oversee this matter? Once Henry had set his mind to do this not one of his counselors could sway him from it, though many of them tried.

When that had been settled Henry was free to turn his attention to other business. Every day some new problem rose to confront him. He had been asked to mediate the tiresome and long-running quarrel between his son-in-law the Duke of Saxony and the emperor. Philippe Capet was writing to Henry weekly, demanding payment of Marguerite's dowry and expenses. There were tax riots in the north. Empty bishoprics in the south. All this demanded Henry's time and his talent as a statesman. Then in March of 1185 another crisis materialized.

The Patriarch of Jerusalem came to England with a message from his king. Baldwin IV was dying and he had no heirs. He was Henry's cousin, descended from the same Angevin bloodline, and he was offering the crown of Jerusalem to the English king upon his death in return for a new crusade. Matters were very unsettled in the Holy Land. Saladin the Infidel held both Syria and Egypt in his control and the Norman settlements there were fearful of being overrun completely. The Patriarch repeated the words of his king with gravity: *Take the crown, oh my brother, and protect my lands from the armies of the devil....*

Henry was not interested in fulfilling that request. He had too many problems of his own to solve and had no intention of giving up his crown to accept another. What happened in the Holy Land was of no concern to him, and the prospect of leaving his rich lands at the mercy of his sons while he went off to administer a paltry desert kingdom at the age of fifty-two was too absurd to contemplate. He told the Patriarch that the matter required much consideration and sent him away disappointed.

Immediately Henry began making preparations for his son's expedition into Ireland. At Windsor, during the final week of March, John was knighted by his father's hand. The evening before the ceremony John had left his vigil in the chapel and had sneaked downstairs into the kitchen for a taste of beef and red wine. All candidates for knighthood were expected to fast and pray for a period of twenty-four hours preceding their investiture. But Johnny laughed at all such rules and thought they were beneath him.

Henry accompanied his son to Milford Haven where a fleet of sixty ships was launched. Three hundred soldiers and twice as many knights were making the voyage with him, along with several luminaries of the English court. One such individual was Gerald of Wales, a sharp-tongued, pompous churchman who had become famous for his many writings. Gerald was making the trip in order to compile a history of Ireland, but he was much more interested in chronicling what he was sure would be young John's blunders. It was one of Gerald's most enjoyable endeavors: he loved to document the failings of Henry's sons, as if to say, "These who could have been the best have given themselves up to folly."

He was right. This venture was damned to defeat from the start, as Henry should have realized it would be. John had nothing to commend him to his troops and he cared nothing for diplomacy. He and his circle of knights (who were little more than his youthful drinking and whoring companions) dishonored themselves daily. They laughed at the Irish nobility and pulled their beards in jest. They raped the Irish women, and stole from the Irish churches.

Corruption was a red stripe on the back of their disgrace. Money given into John's care to pay the English foot soldiers went into the coffers of his friends instead. Titles were purchased and sold. Church property was expropriated and sold for huge profits which John divided among his favorites. Precious stones were gouged from chalices and icons, the gold melted into coins.

War came, inevitably. What was left of John's army (for many of the soldiers had deserted for lack of pay) was defeated in battle by the king of Limerick and had to take refuge at a fortress near the coast. Dismayed by the barbarity of his own countrymen, Hugh de Lacy fled to the countryside and refused to answer John's written pleas for help.

A scant nine months after setting out upon his great adventure, John was recalled to England by his father. Gerald of Wales had sent detailed letters of events in Ireland, and reading them Henry nearly tore out his hair with fury for what John had done.

John returned to London in disgrace. Before very long, however, he was able to cajole himself back into his father's favor by blaming all his calamities upon the procurator. Hugh de Lacy was a traitor, John insisted, and had sought to undermine the English expedition from the first day. John had meant only to make himself agreeable to the people, and de Lacy had spoiled it all!

Henry knew better, or at least he should have, but the great love he bore John wrestled his good sense into submission. Of course de Lacy was at fault. The more he thought on it the more convinced he became. Henry considered replacing his procurator but the Council fought it so he dropped the idea for a while. In the meantime Henry made up his mind that as soon as peace could be restored in Ireland he would send John back, and this time in a role where his authority could not be questioned. Immediately the king sat down and wrote a letter to Pope Urban II requesting permission to name John Plantagenet as king of Ireland.

Several months later a response arrived, granting Henry's request. Pope Urban, in a show of courtesy that bordered on the ironical, sent Prince John a symbolic gift. It was a crown made out of peacock feathers.

* * *

Days of evil are upon us as God visits His wrath on the unworthy. On April fifteenth of this year a violent earthquake shook the center of England, scattering much which was good, including the cathedral of Lincoln. What can we say when God seeks to demolish His own house? Surely it is a sign to us that our ways are sinful and God seeks retribution for our evil.

We frolic in wickedness, yet ignore the duty which we owe to God. In the East the Infidel grows stronger, yet no army from Europe rides forth to oppose them. Where are Christ's own warriors, and the kings who would lead them? Where are the priests to preach a new crusade to the people of our land? God calls, yet Christendom is silent. God listens, and yet Christendom is still. Let the broken stones of Lincoln be a symbol of our crumbled moral state. Hear us oh Lord! Give us fire in our bellies and strength in our loins. Teach us. Transfigure us. Pity us...

Peter of Blois
De Acceleranda
June, 1185

* * *

All along the border between Hainault and Flanders the villages were burning. People screamed in the streets and animals ran wild as the soldiers of Philip d'Alsace scattered everything before them. What had once been a solid bond of friendship and trust between the two counties had collapsed like a sand castle when Baldwin of Hainault had declared himself aligned with the king of France against the Count of Flanders.

War had begun in April and now it was July. Just south of Amiens the armies of Philippe Capet and Baldwin were approaching: six thousand knights on horseback and fifteen thousand men at arms. Soon they would confront the Count of Flanders in the field.

Baldwin was heartsick at the attack upon his lands and yet he had expected it. Flanders was fanatical when it came to loyalty and now he believed both Baldwin and Philippe had connived to betray him. He had retaliated by burning Lille and Valenciennes and damn near everything that stretched between. Only Mons had escaped the pillage of his men. But after Philip d'Alsace had done everything to Hainault that he intended, he was forced to turn south and face the armies of the king of France.

Flanders was no fool. He was outnumbered five to one. There were a few brief skirmishes but no great battle, for when Flanders saw how large an army he was faced with, he gave an order that his troops stand down. Considering all the complications which had gone before it, the settlement was accomplished with surprising ease.

No formal agreement of surrender was concluded at this time, although Philippe Capet was quick to make his demands known. Henry of England had been watching the situation from London, where messengers had kept him up to date on all matters regarding France. One day in early August a communique arrived from Amiens, stating that the Count of Flanders had surrendered to Philippe and Baldwin, and requesting Henry's help in mediating terms.

The king of England sent back this proviso. *Vermandois would be divided.* France would gain control of Amiens, Montdidier and various small fiefs in the western region of the county. Philip d'Alsace would retain Peronne, St. Quentin and Ham; *all* territories (including Arras and Artois) to pass unconditionally to the king of France upon the Count of Flanders' death. Baldwin would be paid in coin by Flanders for all the damages his lands had suffered, and by Philippe Capet for the military expenses it cost him for supporting France. The other terms, including lists of castles taken from the Count of Flanders and now given into the care of France, would be drawn up more specifically at a later date, again with Henry Plantagenet acting as the mediator.

Capet had never been more jubilant. This was the first great victory of his life. Flanders took defeat with uncommon grace, and pledged that he would cause no further problems for the king of France. He made a similar promise to Baldwin, but with less enthusiasm. Philippe's betrayal could be understood. He was a Frenchman. Baldwin was Flemish; and for one Fleming to betray another, especially when kinship was involved, meant inflicting wounds which could not be healed. Because of this there was bad blood between them for the remainder of their lives.

Despite elixirs, potions, and the fact that she had continued to breast feed her baby, Isabel was once more brought to childbed at the end of August.

It was too soon. She was not scheduled to deliver until late October, but the news of her uncle's surrender to Philippe and Baldwin had overwhelmed her with emotion, and brought about a siege of early labor.

The pain was so severe she nearly died. Between waves of unconsciousness on the evening of the second day, she finally gave birth to twins. Edythe was beside her, wiping away the sweat with a linen cloth, and somewhere in the background stood the tall, slender figure of Adele. Sully was in the room, but Isabel couldn't see him though she heard his voice, rich and unmistakable, murmuring psalms above the jingle of his prayer beads.

Light dimmed before her eyes although Isabel strained to keep them open. Her lips moved soundlessly. *Bring me my babies.* But she could not say it. She was too weary and her throat was dry. The canopy above her head seemed like a blue tranquil sky and Isabel yearned to float up to it, all her fatigue dissolving in its serenity.

Murky dawn awoke her with vague shafts of light across her face and it was then they told her what had happened. Dull-eyed and unbelieving, Isabel listened as Adele explained in a consoling voice. There had been two of them, a boy and girl, blond like their mother, and both of them born dead.

* * *

A week later when she was feeling strong enough to walk unsupported, Isabel visited their tiny tombs. The dead infants had been shut up within the vault of Notre Dame, the first inhabitants of that cold, dark place. Amid Latin inscriptions of religiosity on their tombs she read the words *Baldwin & Margot,* for Isabel had not wished for them to go into their graves unnamed.

Their effigies had been cut from stone by some of Sully's craftsmen. Isabel stood before the tombs, two yellow roses clutched in her hands. It was not so much grief as bitterness that squeezed her heart. *God had done this to her.* He had done it out of spite because she was a sinner. Even now He was probably watching and rejoicing in her misery.

God knew the things that she had done. He knew the appetites of her body and the obstinance of her mind. It was for this that she was being punished, and it was unfair, because God Himself had given her a nature that was hungry and perverse. Why then did He torment her and refuse to hear her prayers?

Prayers. The very thought filled her with contempt, and she was done with them. They had never helped her in the past and were likely to be just as worthless in the future. Scornfully Isabel scattered the petals of her roses on the floor, then turned and walked away into the shadows.

September's end brought long afternoons of hazy sunshine as Paris shed her summer colors and dressed her trees in shades of autumn gold.

In the garden of the palace Isabel fingered the heavy damask fabric which lay across her knees and smiled in secret embarrassment. It wasn't very good. Needlework had never been one of her accomplishments, even when she tried slavishly to reproduce the delicate stitches Margot had taught her as a little girl. This piece was a battle standard, meant to be a late birthday gift for Philippe, though it would probably take another week of work till it was finished.

The pattern was pretty, though, even if her technique was wanting. White re-embroidered damask, powdered by a hundred fleur-de-lis stitched in pale blue thread and bordered with a fringe of gold twine. She had been working on it since the early

days of April and throughout the summer when her confinement had given her little else to do.

The pregnancy and its woeful outcome made a painful memory, so Isabel chased it away and thought of more promising
things. A month had passed and she was feeling better. Philippe
would be back in Paris any day. That was a cause for joy, and how
she welcomed it! These past four weeks had seen too many sor-
rows.

Edythe had taken a bad fall on the stairs several days ago. She
was limping worse than ever and it was unlikely she would ever
walk without a crutch. Two weeks ago, after many days of
wretchedness, Hughes de Puiseaux had died of a summer fever.
All through his illness Adele had nursed her lover at the palace.
His death had been hard for her; she hadn't left her room since
then.

Philippe would be hard-hit by the news. De Puiseaux had been
more than the king's chancellor, he had been his friend. Isabel
tugged at her sewing and thought of the unhappy surprises that
awaited her husband upon his victorious return.

She was just finishing her dinner that evening when one of the
serving girls appeared beside her with a message. Geoffrey Plantagenet had come ahead of Philippe's entourage, and he was
waiting just outside the room.

"Show him in," Isabel told the girl, "and have one of the others
bring him food and wine." When the servant hesitated the queen
clapped her hands in irritation. These damned *pucelles* moved
with all the grace and quickness of a wounded cow. "Go now," she
snapped, "and hurry."

Geoffrey was charming, just as she remembered. No wonder
Philippe was so beguiled by him. He was unique among men,
even the cultivated ranks of the nobility. Never awkward; never
at a loss for the right word, the perfect gesture. He was all the
more pleasing because he seemed so sincere, and perhaps he
was, or at least more often than he was believed to be. When
Isabel told him of her recent misfortune, his jovial attitude vanished at once and tears came to his eyes.

"How sad that Philippe wasn't here to comfort you at such a
time," he exclaimed, stroking her hand. Then, after a dutiful

pause, he asked, "But how is your little Jacquie? She was so lovely when I saw her last...."

It was easy to talk to him and so she could relax and tell stories of her little girl, who was well, growing swiftly (as Adele never tired of pointing out, Jacquie was likely to be tall, in the manner of her father's family). But the child was also a chattering magpie. "Which proves," she told Geoffrey laughingly "that in some ways at least she resembles her mother."

"Good for her," he smiled.

"But you have not come here to listen to tales of my daughter's nursery," Isabel said, slicing off a piece of white pastry and putting it before him. "So tell me," she looked up from behind the thick flourish of her lashes, "what is your purpose?"

He nibbled at the pastry, gingerly dusting the crumbs from his sleeve. "Philippe is still in Amiens," he said after a while, "but he will be leaving soon. I was there, with his army, when your uncle surrendered. It was my job to act in my father's absence, helping to set down terms of peace. After the interim documents were drawn I left, to come here and arrange for Philippe's return. I want a great show of public celebration to greet him when he rides into the city." Geoffrey took up her hand and kissed it tenderly. "If you are feeling strong enough, I would be pleased to have your help."

Isabel wasn't sure what that might entail but she told him that she was willing. They spent the remainder of the evening planning what they would do. It was happy being in his company. It was nice to have a friend.

Under the banner of the French king, a mixed army of soldiers made their way toward Paris.

Baldwin had allowed his men to follow after the triumphant French contingent if they wished, but he returned to Mons. He had been forced into this; now it was over and he spurred his horse toward home.

But Flanders was different. He rode brazenly beside Philippe Capet, heroic in defeat. He held himself erect and his gold hair glistened in the sun. No one who saw him would have guessed that he had just surrendered almost half his landmass to the man who rode at his side.

All along their progress Flanders' jaunty good humor never wavered. Outside the gates of each city he threw silver coins to the poor. He did everything with style. The graciousness with which he took defeat made him seem even more splendid. As they rode toward Paris, Philippe almost envied him.

"I can see them!"

Geoffrey was standing at the very edge of the palace roof, leaning a little over the stone barrier, his eyes fixed on the farthest point of the Orléans road.

Isabel joined him, looking out toward the north where the fields and vineyards lay. Just beyond that, hidden by the gentle slopes, was St. Denis. Geoffrey and Isabel watched together as the multitude of men on horseback drew nearer, flooding down into the valley, choking the road with their numbers.

It was a bright autumn day and Isabel had to shield her eyes against the spectacle. In the distance the soldiers gleamed like little silver toys, their shields transformed into tiny mirrors by the sun. Above them fluttered a hundred banners in colorful array. Side by side flew the standards of France and Flanders: the golden fleur-de-lis, backed by vivid blue; a crouching yellow leopard sitting upright with his paw outstretched on a square of scarlet. Behind these were raised a host of other pennons in heraldic design and brilliant colors.

"There's Philippe!" Geoffrey exclaimed, enthusiastic as a boy, "and there's your uncle right beside him." Isabel saw them too, and nodded.

"It's exciting, isn't it?" he asked, then turned back to the view before she could make an answer.

She moved closer to him, shielding herself against the wind. "I wonder what he's thinking," she said beneath her breath.

"No doubt he's thinking it is wonderful to be back home again," Geoffrey said, taking one of her cold hands in his.

Isabel looked up at him, then out at the horizon. "I didn't mean Philippe," she told him, "I meant my uncle."

It was evening when the caravan marched into Paris.

There were fewer of them now, only Philippe and Flanders and a hundred or so of their men. The majority of them remained outside the city in the fields beside the Orléans road.

Isabel and Geoffrey had ordered pavilions of blue and scarlet to be erected for the men, and had sent stewards from the palace to distribute sweetmeats, cakes, and wine. Each French knight received a token seven *deniers* for his service to the king, while each man-at-arms was given two. From her own monies Isabel had provided each Flemish soldier with five *deniers*.

Also in consideration of the soldiers' comfort, eight hundred prostitutes from the city had been transported to the camp. This action had a logical ancillary: it would keep thousands of roistering, drunken men out of the Paris streets, where they would otherwise have come in search of female company.

The king's contingent celebrated in more modest fashion. An evening mass was said at Notre Dame, then there was a parade of minstrels through the torchlit streets. Afterwards the royal party moved indoors to the great hall of the palace where a lavish banquet had been laid in honor of the king's return.

Philippe pretended to enjoy himself, but he was scarcely in a mood for celebration after the unhappy news Isabel had told him, and he left the table early. By contrast, Flanders was having a fine time. He leaned back in his chair and listened to music, soft as incense, that drifted from the gallery above. It was good to be among his friends again; good to taste the fruits of peace.

He tossed bones to the barking hounds and sneered at the watchful barons. These were the same men who had resented his closeness to Louis Capet a dozen years ago. They preferred Flanders as an adversary to the French crown rather than a friend; he was less a danger to them that way. They had mistrusted him in the beginning, and they still did. Hah!—he and Philippe were friends again, and these fat, odious barons could eat shit cinders for all he cared. Flanders was once more a powerful ally to the King of France, and there wasn't one damn thing that they could do about it.

Look at them. Wondering how he could take his defeat so elegantly. *Let them wonder.* They were stupid. They didn't know that in a way he had won after all. It was better to renew his friendship with the king than dispute over a little strip of land. He had learned that, though it had been a hard lesson. Whatever he had lost in giving up half of Vermandois, he had more than recompensed himself by building promises on the ashes of old hates. It was worth the temporary sacrifice of his pride, and he had no regrets.

Flanders lifted his cup and toasted the future.

Geoffrey leaned close, smelling of almond oils and cinnamon. "Having a good time, my lord of Ghent?" he asked with a saucy smile.

"Enraptured," Flanders mocked and popped a candied cherry into his mouth. He looked to the center of the table, and seeing that Philippe's place was empty asked, "And what about the king?"

Geoffrey's slim hand hovered over a pink crystal serving dish that was formed like a sea shell. He recognized it as just one of the pretty things brought back from Amiens. He gathered up a handful of candied cherries and rolled them in his palm, smirking at Flanders as he did so. "The king is upstairs with his wife," he said at last, "and having a better time than we, I'm sure...."

Flanders realized that Geoffrey's closeness to Philippe and his presence here at court signaled him as a new power to be reckoned with, but he had no trouble with that. He'd known Geoffrey for many years, and always seen him as the most promising of all Henry's engaging sons. What a future this young man had before him now with Philippe as an ally! He smiled at the thought.

"You seem very pleased with yourself," Geoffrey said, and there was a trace of peevishness in his voice.

Flanders clapped him on the back. "I am," he replied, "as indeed you must be also. We are all friends again."

Geoffrey's gaze carried to the edge of the great hall, but he was seeing more. "Yes," he said, "it's a good time to be alive."

At the end of October Phillipe went south with an army. Hugh of Burgundy was taking too much power for himself. Since summer he had been turning out his nobles from their castles, and claiming both their lands and possessions for himself. The impoverished barons had petitioned help from the French king. Philippe, ever mindful of encroachment on his own power, was glad to stand with the Burgundian nobles in their struggle. So at the end of October Philippe went south with an army.

Flanders went with him.

Geoffrey remained behind, and for good reason. Philippe had

publicly named him Seneschal of France the week before, so he stayed in Paris to assume his duties. Those duties were a matter of much controversy. The office of seneschal had an implied significance but little power; would this be an exception? There were already mutterings of discontent among members of the *curia regis* who felt this was the king's way of giving inordinate power to his "favorite."

Philippe had refused to name a successor to de Puiseaux. France would have no more chancellors, he said. It was meant to shed a glow of honor on the fallen statesman, but that was not how it was received. Had the decorative role of seneschal and the policy-making duties of chancellor been combined to suit the fancy of the king's brash young friend? There was not a man among the French nobility who did not know of Geoffrey's reputation as a schemer and betrayer of his friends. What did he want from Philippe Capet?

And what did Philippe want from him?

Isabel no longer trusted her uncle, and she meditated on the subject more than she let be known. It was such a puzzle. Why, after two years of refusing to give up his claim to Vermandois, had he suddenly agreed to surrender it to Philippe, even allowing an outsider—Henry—to dictate terms? Why was Philippe so eager to believe in the loyalty of a man he had denounced time and time again? It was very odd, all of it.

The breach between the two great lords of Hainault and Flanders seemed irreparable and the fact that Baldwin hadn't come to Paris presaged bad political relations for the future. Philippe and Flanders on one side, Baldwin on the other. It was a dangerous situation, and all the danger weighed against her father.

The fears turned over in her mind, like the tumblers of a lock. Was there some pact, some secret coalition in the works between Flanders and Philippe? Had *that* been Flanders' price for the surrender of Vermandois—France's promise to uphold his hostilities against the Count of Hainault in the future? Were Philippe and her uncle plotting actions to these ends even now?

The more she considered it the more convinced Isabel became that her father had two very powerful enemies in Flanders and Philippe. If he had only come with them to Paris, she could have warned him. She wanted to stamp her feet in fury. Why didn't he realize it was in his own best interests to restore a sense of trust among the three of them? How could he have misread the situation so completely? The danger of it was becoming clearer to her with every passing minute.

There was something Isabel could do; just *what* she wasn't sure. A plan, imperfect and unfinished, leapt into her mind. She needed power of her own in order to achieve it. That would take time and effort and a great deal of money. The money she could get from Philippe. The rest she would have to manage for herself.

For the time being she could feel secure. Philippe and her uncle would be away in Burgundy for many weeks, and much too busy to stir up any trouble for her father. By the time they returned to Paris in December, she would have already put her own plan into motion.

Every day the people of Paris lined the edges of the street, waiting for Geoffrey Plantagenet to pass by them, magnificently dressed and riding on a white horse.

He seemed like a figure come to life from some splendid tapestry. In his cap he wore a sprig of *planta gesta,* a saucy reminder of his grandfather, Count Geoffrey of Anjou. It was he who had taken that emblem as his own device and made it his surname; and with his wife Matilda, daughter of the English king, he had made a race of princely warriors from his loins.

Young Geoffrey of Brittany wore his heritage well.

It was whispered among the French that he had become a close friend and adviser to their king. That may have troubled the nobility, but the common people harbored no such suspicions. He was generous to the poor, and that was all they could see. In the past weeks Geoffrey had made many gifts of money to the local houses of charity, and every day he threw handfuls of silver coins to the tradesmen in the streets. He had further shown evidence of his *largess* by giving a gift of seven oil lamps to Notre Dame. They would burn perpetually, in memory of his late brother.

Harry had been well-loved by the French who saw him as the epitome of chivalry and grace. Now Geoffrey had become the people's newest idol. They applauded him in the street, bowing low as he rode by. Young girls cast their eyes down shyly and threw flowers at him as he passed.

They cheered the queen too, for she was much in evidence these days. She appeared in public often, riding through the streets with the Bishop of Rheims at her side and her adorable little daughter on her knee. The people still remembered Isabel's spirited display when she had pleaded with them to prevail upon the king to keep her, but the birth of Jacquie-Marie had done even more to make her popular. Everyone, including Sully and the rest of the clergy in Paris, had seemed to warm to Isabel now that she was a mother.

In appreciation for the new affection shown to her, Isabel had commemorated the fifth anniversary of her husband's coronation by feasting the people of the city, rich and poor, on All Saints Day. She had arranged for canopies to be set up along the river bank, and all who came were given wine and fish and little cakes of marzipan in exchange for a single *denier*. Then, in a public ceremony, Isabel donated that money to the building fund at Notre Dame.

This new-found popularity worked to Isabel's advantage. As queen she had no power of her own, but the goodwill of the people had given her a subtle means of influence. The nobles cast a wary eye: she was no longer someone they could ridicule or ignore. The Bishop of Rheims was her friend: that made her acceptable. Because of that all the other Champagnois were forced to accept her too.

Isabel savored her popularity, but not from spite. It was useful. She could hold it up to Philippe's peevish scrutiny and prove she had some political stature of her own. In his absence she had feasted the poor in the Paris streets and entertained the rich at her table. With Geoffrey's help she had recently welcomed an ambassador from the court of Sicily to the palace and staged an opulent banquet in his honor. She had been very busy in these past six weeks—all her acts directed toward a single purpose.

It was possible that Philippe would be outraged when he learned of all the money she had spent in her campaign to win favor, but she didn't think so. Her extravagance, meted out carefully and where it could be most beneficial to the reputation of the crown, had done a lot to polish Philippe's social image—an aspect of his kingship he had never understood. If only he could be made to realize that! Sexually she had been able to manage him from the beginning. Now she had found one more method of persuasion.

He had become so powerful. If she didn't take something for herself, and soon, she would fade into insignificance beside him. Up till now, Isabel's only means of influence had been achieved by pleasing Philippe in his bed. But she would need *all* her talents if she was to put her plan into effect, and at the same time convince Philippe that she was right.

By the last week in November Philippe and his army had brought the Duke of Burgundy to account and returned his landless nobles to their castles. Flushed with this victory he went north again, but not to Paris. There were still several incidentals regarding the partition of Vermandois which needed to be settled, and so Philippe went directly to the fortress of Belvoir in Normandy where he met with the English king.

Henry received him from a sickbed where a violent attack of stomach flu had kept him for the past ten days. The illness had left him feeling lonely and bad-tempered, and it cheered him to have a visitor. Philippe was friendly—victory had improved his disposition—and he seemed genuinely concerned for Henry's health.

Philippe lingered at Belvoir for several days and when Henry was feeling better they transacted business. The final documents were drawn and signed and both men said how glad they were that the hostilities between France and Flanders had been ended. Yet even as they made good-humored conversation and took their meals together, Henry was uneasy in his mind. The news from Ireland had been devastating. He said nothing of this to Philippe, but regarding Geoffrey there were questions which needed answering if Henry was to rest peaceably in his bed at night. Why was his son still in Paris when he should have been at Rennes, seeing to the business of his duchy? What role did Geoffrey envision for himself in the politics of France, and why had Philippe named him seneschal?

Henry asked subtle questions to these ends, but Philippe's answers were ambiguous. "Geoffrey is my friend," he replied each time Henry's prodding grew too obvious. And that was all that he would say.

* * *

Cruel news comes from the East.

Good Baldwin IV the "Leper" king of Jerusalem has died of his wretched illness without an heir and his crown passes to his sister's son who is but a child of five. Raymond III, the Count of Tripoli, will act as regent for the boy and this is good—for the child's step-father Guy de Lusignan hungers for a crown as well.

Some men have told that Henry of England should accept the offer to rule Jerusalem, for it was suggested last year he should do it. Why has he refused? For what good is it that there be strong princes in the West when the Holy City is well besieged by threats from Saladin and the Infidels? Mayhap Henry cares more to hold Normandy against his treacherous sons than to protect the citadel of Our Lord from the very knights of Satan.

But where on God's earth is righteousness served, when everywhere He is mocked and the hands of His children stink with blood? In Constantinople the mob have overthrown their emperor Andronicus Comnenus and put him to cruel death by torture in the arena of the Hippodrome. Andronicus himself was not blameless: it was he who took the child Agnes Capet as his wife and ordered the murder of her intended husband who was his nephew. Yet even the death of such a man as he should not be made a sport for the howling mob.

Let the soldiers of Christ be strong in will and thus go forth to protect the Holy places. But in God's name, let us now scour out the bastions of Christianity too, for well they need it....

Robert de Auxerre
Chronicon
December, 1185

* * *

There was an empty field behind the Cité Palais where the cooks dumped garbage from the royal kitchens. Once this place had been the king's own tournament field. Eleanor of Aquitaine had reigned as *Queen of Love and Beauty* there on many summer afternoons. Tall knights in shining coats of mail had ridden to victory in the lists with her silken favor tucked into their helms. It had been the scene of so much pageantry and color; so filled with cheering voices and brave deeds.

Now it was ugly and deserted. Weeds grew among the kitchen

slop and the wooden viewing stands were sagged and rotting. Philippe Capet hated tournaments and he had banned them early in his reign. Ironically, the last public jousting event in Paris had taken place at the time of his coronation when Philip d'Alsace had organized a costly tournament in Philippe's honor. The nervous boy had watched the spectacle for only half an hour, then at the first sight of bloodshed he had pitched forward in a faint. Once revived, he had spent the remainder of the afternoon vomiting behind the stands.

The mature Philippe Capet was made of stronger stuff and it was unlikely he would react so violently to the sport as he had five years before. Yet his edict against tournaments was still in force. None were allowed in Paris or for fifty miles in any direction of his city. He had spoken of restoring the field, but only for the sake of cleanliness because it stank in summer and attracted flies. Philippe had enforced strict laws against dumping garbage in the Seine: by royal edict a man could lose his hand for such an act. But what good was it to keep the river clean when his own palace was steeped in smells of filth from the dumping grounds behind it? Before leaving Paris in October, Philippe had asked Geoffrey to arrange to have the field plowed under, and all future garbage taken to another spot five miles south of the city.

Geoffrey did this, and more. One day early in December, when Philippe was still away in Normandy, he brought Isabel to inspect the work that had been done. He led her along the path through the garden and beyond, keeping his hand over her eyes to preserve his surprise as long as possible.

At last they stood still and Geoffrey took his hand away. Isabel stared out over the expanse of the field, unable to believe the transformation. All the debris had been removed and the ground was smooth with fresh turned earth. The old stands had been replaced by strong new ones. A wooden fence surrounded the entire area like a Saxon stockade.

Isabel shivered in the wind and took hold of Geoffrey's hand for warmth. "Why have you done all this?" she asked. "I don't understand."

"As a surprise for Philippe."

It was clear to her now, what he intended, and her doubt grew. "This is hardly the sort of surprise that Philippe will appreciate."

Geoffrey gazed proudly at his achievement. "He asked me to restore it and that is what I have done."

Flakes of snow tickled her face and Isabel brushed them away with a gloved hand. "Yes, but you've prepared the field for tournaments again, and you know Philippe's edict against them." She shook her head doubtfully. "He won't like this, I can promise you."

"The law restricts tournaments as regular events," he reminded her, "but this is something special. Between the two of us I'm sure we could convince Philippe to allow a single tournament in honor of his birthday this summer. It was for that very reason I had all this work done." He smiled engagingly at her, a small boy begging for a second candied apple. "He will be twenty-one in August. I want to give him a spectacular show to honor the occasion. Don't you think he would agree to that?"

Her tone was skeptical. "It would take a great deal of convincing."

He put his thumb beneath her chin and raised her face toward his. "That is your job, Isabel. With a little delicate pressure applied in the right places..." Then he laughed. "My dear you could convince the devil to take a bath in holy water. Please, won't you use your charms to help me accomplish this?"

He was such a good friend to both her and Philippe. In the weeks since Philippe had gone away to Burgundy she had been in his company every day. In the evenings he played music for her and sang lovely songs that he had written. He was cheerful and so good to be with. Little Jacquie-Marie adored him. Perhaps one little talk with Philippe wouldn't hurt....

Isabel smiled and gave him her answer. "Very well, I shall speak to him about it. But remember Geoffrey, I cannot promise that he will agree. Also, you must let me choose the proper time."

"It is in your hands," he said and kissed her gloved palms in mock subservience.

Isabel laughed, then pointed to the middle of the field where some shapeless object lay atop the clods of dirt. "What is that?" she asked.

Geoffrey leaned slightly forward, squinting. "I don't know." He started walking toward it, and when he had nearly reached the middle of the field, stopped and bent toward the ground. His

hand paused above a heap of twisted entrails protruding from
the belly of a mangled dog. The animal's tan hide was soaked in
scarlet, and without thinking Geoffrey dipped his fingers in it.
Then as if he had been bitten he pulled his hand away.

"What is it?" Isabel called out to him, her words blown by the
wind.

Geoffrey wiped his fingers on the lining of his pellison and
stood up. *Why was he trembling?* "Blood," he called back.

𝔍OR THE FIRST TIME in more than twelve years, Eleanor of
Aquitaine was coming home to France.

Henry had summoned her to Normandy and she had no illusions about his reason. He had kept her cruelly imprisoned for
all these years, separated her from her sons, humiliated her with
his mistresses. He wouldn't have granted her this sudden benison
unless it had some profit to himself.

At Bayeux, when Eleanor arrived there from her frigid crossing, Henry met her and explained his purpose. He wanted her to
take back the Aquitaine from Richard, and reassert her rights as
duchess there. It would make the barons easier to deal with, he
pointed out, because they resented Richard and his constant involvement in other wars.

Eleanor was not fooled. She knew Henry's intentions. By forcing her to take back Richard's territories, her husband meant to
curb their son's growing power. John's ridiculous attempts at seizing Richard's domains had resulted in ignominious failure, so
now Henry had decided to extort the territory by legal means.
What a ruthless hypocrite he was, and how she loathed him!

At the table they sat across from one another, separated by
many years of bitterness. Henry put his terms to her and she
listened, unmoved by the protestations of sincerity. In the end
Eleanor agreed to what he wanted, because there was very little
else that she could do. Everything she had or hoped to have
depended on his favor. Her imprisonment at Salisbury was not
pleasant, but Henry could make her circumstances far worse if
she defied him. So finally she signed the paper that he rudely
thrust at her, but what she signed and what she promised in her
heart were two different things.

Richard arrived in Bayeux two days later and graciously accepted Henry's edict. Grim-faced and silent he stood before his parents and their assembled witnesses, and put his hand to the document which released the Aquitaine to Eleanor. It helped him to know the spirit in which she had agreed to this. He knew she would never sell him out, not for all the threats that Henry could make. She would hold the Aquitaine, but she would hold it for him, and when it became possible for her to do so, she would return it. Nothing could ever make him doubt her.

But still it was shameful to stand before all these people and play at giving up his rights merely to satisfy Henry's greed and stubbornness. Richard held himself erect and kept his chin high while the ceremony lasted. Later, when he was all alone, he drank too much and cried himself to sleep.

Yellow gold. The light of a thousand torches. Music, dancing. Much that was good to eat. Laughter and light conversation. Wine that was red and lips that were even redder. Rich scents of cinnamon and lavender and orange peel. Silver platters filled with a dozen kinds of roasted game and fruits that dripped with honey. Silks of many shades. Jewels that burned with light against the whiteness of a woman's skin.

There was Christmas feasting at the Cité palace.

It was the most fabulous celebration Paris had seen in fifty years. The Christmas court was a glittering congregation of poets, clerics, chroniclers and nobles from all over France, come to revel in the hospitality of their young king and his splendid Flemish wife.

Isabel had arranged this festivity with Geoffrey's help. Philippe, who knew next to nothing of the social arts, was amazed at how the great hall had been transformed to lavishness and glitter. Even Adele, who was praised for her abilities as a hostess, was grudgingly impressed by Isabel's magnificent array of guests.

What a lot of famous people had been assembled here!

Robert de Torigni, the abbot of Mont St. Michel, sat at the king's table beside his long-time friend the Bishop of Paris. Like Sully, he was a builder; a man of intense vision. He had made many improvements upon the *Mont*, that glorious abbey put up by the Benedictines two hundred years before. The edifice was a legend among the French, and Torigni loved it with the kind of intimacy and passion only true men of the spirit can understand.

Yet on the *parvis* this morning, standing in the snow in front of Notre Dame, the old abbot had looked upon Sully's unfinished masterpiece and wept. Later he had told the king, "When it is completed no cathedral this side of the Alps will compare to it."

Another guest at this festivity was poetess Marie de France. She was a distant cousin to Geoffrey Plantagenet, related through the Angevin bloodline. She was partly English but the French liked her for her eccentricities and talent. Marie was wealthy, pretty and indifferent to conventional behavior, as artists often are. She had traveled extensively in Europe and the East, where she had met and married a penniless Norman knight, and all for love. The French adored the tragic and romantic poetry she wrote, and Isabel, who so loved the arts, admired her very much.

So did Marguerite Capet, Marie's close friend, who sat nearby. Marguerite had been surprised at the queen's invitation to come back to court for this occasion. Isabel did not like her; that had never been a secret. Yet in these last few days she had received Marguerite with courtesy and friendliness and had even given her a fine white velvet chainse decorated with pearls as a gift. After Twelfth Night Marguerite would once more be returned to the convent outside of Paris, but for now it was pleasing to feel young again, and to dance with handsome men.

Isabel was a vivid flash of color in scarlet silk and new rubies which Philippe had brought back from Burgundy for her. She was poised and laughing and exquisite, and if any of these people in the room had doubted that a girl so young could make a suitable queen for France, they did not doubt it now. They watched her, some with satisfaction, some with envy, and there was one among the company who watched her more closely than the rest.

From over the shoulder of his uncle Theobold, Count Henri of Champagne followed Isabel's every movement with his eyes. It had been more than a year since he had seen her last, and in that time a day had never passed when he had not thought of her. The memory of that single night in the herbarium burned in his mind like a brand. He had known the deepest and most secret beauty of her body. Now here she sat, close enough for him to touch, ripe and forbidden.

Henri watched. She left her place beside the king and came

farther down the table to greet Alain de Lille. He was a scholar-poet and a theologian, a virtual hermit who had lived in Paris during the early reign of Philippe's father, but who had long since removed himself to Cîteaux. There he lived simply, mingling with students, working at his writing. He spent little time in the great world these days, yet at the bidding of the queen he had come back to Paris for this celebration. Alain had known her only from her letters; she had flattered him with her knowledge of his writing. Then when he was introduced to her in person he had been so overwhelmed by her beauty he had composed a poem for her on the spot.

Henri watched, envying the old man her company, and Geoffrey watched too, thinking he had never seen a fairer face in all the world. Philippe looked on in fascination. She was so completely *his* now; he could ignore the other eyes that praised her. Yet he felt a prick of jealousy all the same. Beauty, charm, grace, and intelligence. She radiated them effortlessly, like Geoffrey did, and Philippe felt awkward in comparison. *Isabel and Geoffrey.* They were rare and shimmering things and they belonged to him. He loved each of them all the more because he had the other, they were two separate aspects of a single passion. They gave him everything he needed, and they promised more. Isabel had already given him a daughter and soon, perhaps next year, she would bear him a son. Geoffrey had pledged Brittany to him, and soon the two of them would take Normandy for themselves.

Philippe listened to the sounds around him, voices and music, and basked in all the surfeit that success can bring. He felt his power growing every day. How far he had come in just these last twelve months; how much more would be accomplished by the following Christmas? With Isabel and Geoffrey to inspire him, there was no limit to what he could do. Philippe drank his wine and watched his two lovers with a greedy and secret joy.

The year 1185 was waning.

The year 1186 awaited like a flaming dawn.

Having successfully waged war against Flanders and the Duke of Burgundy, Philippe Capet turned his attentions to yet another conquest.

The viscounty of Berry had been disputed for many years, claimed by the kingdoms of both France and England. Its first association with France had come in 1100, when fat and sensual Philippe I had purchased it with his own wealth in order that he could legally seduce its heiress. Because his passion, like his appetite, was never sated, the king had soon tired of his toy and he had cast her aside without ever bothering to annex Berry to the crown.

When Henry of Anjou had become King of England he had brazenly taken Berry as his own, since it touched conveniently upon the borders of his domains in Anjou and the Aquitaine. King Louis had sent troops to recapture it, but that was only a half-hearted gesture, since he had known Henry would continue to frustrate his claims of ownership. Finally a settlement had been concluded which satisfied them both. Louis had pledged his young daughter Alais to Henry's son Richard in a marriage bargain, then had tossed in the promise of Berry as her dowry. A pact to this end had been signed by the two kings in 1177.

Now, nine years later, that marriage was still only a promise written in faded ink on dusty parchment tucked away within the archives of the Cité Palais. Yet on the strength of that betrothal, Henry still claimed Berry as his own. Tired of the delay, Philippe decided to dispute the hypocrisy of that position. He sent a communique to Henry. *If Richard did not marry Alais within the month, France would take Berry back.* He waited for an answer but received none, then wrote again. Once more his demands were ignored.

That was all it took for Philippe to make his decision. He began preparing an expedition into Berry. By the time spring came, he would be ready to seize it for himself.

While Philippe trained his men for war, Isabel was busy hatching her own plans. Before Christmas she had sent a letter to Gilbert of Mons, warning the chancellor to cast a cautious eye upon Philip d'Alsace. She also had a suggestion for bringing Hainault closer into France's bosom. Her brother Baldwyn and her sister Sibylla were now fourteen and twelve and it was time that marriages be arranged for them. Without consulting Philippe, but in the hope that he would agree to her choices, Isabel offered the following names as spouses for them. Baldwyn would marry Marie, the youngest sister of the king's own cousin, Henri of Champagne. Sibylla would be given to William de Beaujolais, a young seignoir from the Burgundian line of Philippe's family.

There must be no time wasted in deliberation. Isabel urged an immediate reply, and signed her name.

* * *

Fair is she, Isabel the queen,
Of lovesome form and eyes aglow.
No one can see her but his tongue
Turns golden in her praise.
No sun can look upon her but turns pale
With envy at such beauty.

She springs from legend, might runs in her
blood;
From lineage ancient and austere,
Invoking dreams of battles won
By Carolingian steel;
Of triumphs slumbering in her past,
Of glory living in her eyes.

All Paris knows her for their loved queen
And praise her for her radiant smiles.
Yet behind a dove-like gaze her eyes conceal
An aspect of refined and infinite mystery.
She is a mythic queen, from pages old,
The like of beauty never seen before
By this old world . . .

Geoffrey Plantagenet
Lais and Ballads
March, 1186

* * *

Philippe had agreed without too much coaxing. He took little interest in the marriages of his cousins, and in any case no one could claim that Isabel's family was unworthy of such connections with his own. Baldwyn and Sibylla could marry whichever of his kin Isabel selected. It was really quite inconsequential to him. He didn't know that Isabel had contracted this arrangement to protect her father against Flanders and himself. If he thought on it at all, Philippe supposed that she was merely exercising one of her few prerogatives as queen. He should have known better, but then he really didn't know her very well.

Baldwin was worried about money.

It was Easter and he had gathered his barons and retainers at his home in Mons. The news he had to give them was not pleasant. He was deeply in debt. Flanders had still not paid the reparations owed him, and since then there had been another war against the Duke of Brabant. The deficit had risen to over forty thousand Valenciennes *livres*—an extraordinary amount. Regretfully Baldwin announced that he would have to impose huge tax increases on his subjects in order to raise the money that he needed. There was grumbling among the men assembled, but just a little. Baldwin was well loved by his people, and they were willing to sacrifice for his greater good.

After everyone had left he sat pensively before the fire in his room, plagued by the thought of his debts, and worried about the upcoming marriages of his children. Yet another tie to Philippe Capet. Was it worth the political entanglement?

Margot read his silence as misgiving, and came to sit on the arm of his chair to cheer him. Her fingers tickled playfully at his beard as she leaned close to him. "What is wrong?" she asked, cooing in his ear.

Baldwin reached up and took hold of her hand. "I need your counsel," he sighed. "I can't be sure of my decisions anymore. Did I do right in sanctioning these marriages? Will they work to our advantage, or will this be just one more thing I will regret in time?"

It was easy for Margot to become impatient with her husband whenever he behaved this way. *She* was never weak or indecisive. But her love had always found excuses for him in the past, and it always would. She leaned closer, winding her arms about his neck. Her breath was sweet in his face, her voice was mellow. "This is a wonderful chance for us to forge a better relationship with France. God knows we need it, Baldwin, now that my brother has deserted us. We can consider ourselves very fortunate that Isabel looks after our interests so well. It is a cause for rejoicing my darling, not for worry."

A shaft of sun coming through the window caught the sheen of her unbound hair, turning it into ribbons of light. She was such a lovely, golden thing! How many thousands of times had he lain on Margot, lived in her?—then later, holding her in his arms, listened enrapt to her soft words of advice on matters of state and war, too complex even for most men to understand. How strange it was: she had come to him as a child—now, in experience, she had grown older than he.

They kissed, their arms entangled, strands of golden and brunet hair mingling. He nestled against her breast, drawing comfort from the warmth of her body. "I need you Margot," he whispered. "I need you for so many things."

She kissed the creases of worry from his forehead. "You must continue to need me my darling, and trust me too, for I would never give you bad advice."

"I know that," he answered. She had cheered him slightly and he could smile. "Then advise me on this, my love. How am I to pay Sibylla's dowry, when already I am faced with more debts than I can manage?"

She had an answer, as she nearly always did. There were not enough problems in all the world to outwit Margot when she was thinking clearly. She tucked her fingers into the bend of his elbow. "I have a plan," she confided. "Isabel writes that Henri of Champagne will pay a sizable dowry, ten thousand *livres* and gold plate, for his sister to marry our Baldwyn. It will be dispensed within the week. We can use that money to pay Sibylla's *dot*." Her lips brushed his forehead lightly. "So you see, it will cost us nothing. Actually, the Champagnois will be paying their own dowry!"

Baldwin's arms encircled her waist and he pulled her close. "Ah, Margot," he sighed, "I thank God every day for giving you to me."

What happiness!

Whitsunday, the 18th of May, had been chosen as the date when young Baldwyn and Sibylla would be married to Philippe's cousins. And at Chateau Thierry, in the great hall of the royal residence, Isabel was reunited with her family once again.

Her parents had changed very little. Margot, newly burdened by yet another pregnancy, looked youthful and still as lovely as Isabel remembered her from six years ago. Baldwin was thinner and his beard had gone a little grey but otherwise he was much the same.

But young Baldwyn and little Sibylla—how different they were! Her brother was nearly fifteen. He had grown up tall and husky and blond as a sun god. Flanders must have looked quite like him at the same age. Sibylla was only twelve, though she looked older. She was taller than Isabel and very slender, but a few months of marriage would be likely to enhance her subtle curves. She was wearing a modest yellow dishabille, and there were daisies braided into her long dark hair.

Later that afternoon William of Rheims feasted the royal party at an outdoor celebration. The mild spring air was filled with music and the fragrant scent of food and flowers. Amid the babble of festivity, Baldwyn and Sibylla were introduced to the two young people they would marry on the following day. Pretty, dark-haired Marie of Champagne was on the arm of her brother Count Henri. She was a charming girl with lively eyes and a sweet smile. Baldwyn seemed to take an interest in her at once.

And Sibylla? She looked happy dancing with her future husband. William de Beaujolais was good-looking: slender and fair-haired, and he had exquisite manners. Isabel watched the two of them and smiled at the delicate way in which William held her sister by the hand. He was twenty, she only twelve, and yet they seemed perfectly matched; there was an obvious attraction between them already.

Isabel picked daintily at her food and sighed with mild contentment. She was well pleased with her accomplishments, with the choices she had made. Her brother and sister had engaging, attractive marriage partners, and the ties between Hainault and France would be all the stronger now for her efforts. She had done well. She mused on that and watched the door, waiting for Philippe.

He arrived at dawn, dusty and out of breath after riding all night. Isabel found him later in the morning, in the room next to hers. He was bathing in a big copper tub, rubbing his hair with a towel when she came in. Philippe looked up as she entered, but he didn't speak.

She stood some distance away from him. Her voice was small and obstinate. "I waited for you all evening and half the night. The guests were asking after you; I didn't know what to tell them."

Philippe pressed a thick sponge to his chest and watched as the tiny rivulets ran down his belly and back into the water. "You might have told them that a king has work to do," he grumbled. "Also, you should know it pleases me not at all to sit drinking with members of your family. It is your duty to entertain them."

Isabel bowed her head and said nothing.

He knew her mood. She was disappointed, angry that after so many weeks of separation he could find no time for her. She wanted his love and acceptance. It would have been very easy to pull her into his arms now and suspend all their antagonism with passion. But that was not what Philippe wanted. Her beauty and the promise of her sweet body were less tantalizing than the plan that was whirling in his mind.

Geoffrey was waiting for him at Gonesse.

Philippe had arranged to meet him there; he was leaving as soon as the wedding ceremonies were over. (He would have preferred to miss them altogether, but dreaded Isabel's fault-finding if he did.) At Gonesse he and Geoffrey would stroke their cherished plan into perfection. *The conquest of Normandy.* Until this point it had been too much to hope for, but now it was in their grasp.

"Philippe..." The sound of her voice cut into his concentration, the words hard-edged by complaint. "I had hoped to have some time alone with you."

"I'm afraid that isn't possible." Philippe drew himself up and wrapped a linen towel around his body. Isabel came closer then, her arms outstretched as she reached to dry him, but he turned away. His mouth was set in a cynical expression. Her every move was so deliberately *female* and suggestive, bent on seducing him to her will. Today, more than usual, he resented that. In his most distant and unemotional voice he explained, "I simply don't have time for you today. I came only to see my cousins married to your kin. Then I must leave." Unmoved by her disappointed silence he turned to face her and finished, "Geoffrey and I have important business to accomplish."

She looked at him with heartbreak in her eyes. "I've missed you so much, I've waited so long. How can you just dismiss me like a servant—without even a kiss?"

He fidgeted, vaguely guilt-ridden. It would have taken so little effort on his part to be kind to her, but at this moment he cared nothing for her state of mind. Let her feel hurt, neglected. With all that Philippe had on his mind today, there was no time for him to sympathize with Isabel's imagined sufferings.

His voice was curt, discharging her. "I shall be back in Paris by the end of next week. We can be together then."

Isabel stood for a long while without answering, staring at him as if he had done something cruel which she could not forgive. Finally she left; Philippe let her go in silence. Then he began pulling on his clothes.

The king stayed only long enough to enjoy a cup of spiced wine with the bridal party and make a toast, then he took himself away to Gonesse. Isabel made an attempt at merriment during the wedding feast which followed, but before long she retired to her room upstairs.

Late that night, very late—perhaps even the newlyweds had gone to sleep—Henri of Champagne awoke, startled, as a delicate shadow passed across his face. It was a moment before he recognized her.

"Isabel?" His arms went out to her.

She leaned over him and covered his face with kisses.

It was a hateful dream.

She was lying in a fabulous bed made of stone and precious jewels and Geoffrey Plantagenet was at her side. Above them was a ceiling all of glass. There was a sense of shame—of fear that she and Geoffrey might be discovered. From far off came the sounds of singing. A choir. Mass was being chanted. Then Sully appeared above them, pouring out red wine into a funery urn, and splashing it over the glass slab, making little drops of red, like blood.

All at once terror took her in its teeth and she screamed, beating against the glass to get out. There was panic and madness. She cried out for Geoffrey to help her break the glass. But when she looked at him he had turned to stone. . . .

The sound of her own voice screaming Geoffrey's name over and over again catapulted Isabel into wakefulness. Immediately Henri's arms went around her and she sobbed on his chest, repulsed by the phantasm of her dream.

The words tumbled from her lips as she told the dream to him. He listened patiently and when she had finished, kissed her throat and shoulders, whispering an assurance in her ear that dreams had no meaning.

Her eyes haunted him from out of the dark. "But it was so horrible, like a vision of my own death." She began to shudder. "I'm afraid..."

He kissed the fine hair at her temples where it was damp with sweat. "You are with me, you are safe."

Finally she relaxed enough to lie back on the bed as he lay over her, his body hard and reassuring. She clenched her legs about his back to draw him deeper. But even as he bloomed inside of her a primal desperation, thick as passion, struck at her—and suddenly all the efforts of her future promised only ugly retribution and death. Isabel gripped him tighter and cried out, "Henri, I'm so afraid of dying and going to hell for my sins."

Hunger had pushed the power of reason from his mind. Hell and dying had no meaning as he rode her harder, his face lost in the warm valley of her breasts. "No sins," he gasped, his words halting and meaningless, "no sins..."

Isabel left Chateau Thierry on the following day.

"I had hoped you would stay longer," Sibylla complained as the two of them took breakfast together early in the morning. "It has been so many years since I have seen you. I expected we would be together for longer than two days."

The dream, and lack of sleep, had left Isabel feeling cross and nervous. Her hand shook as she splashed a little rain water into her wine and spread her bread with butter. "I'm sorry Sibylla but it can't be helped. I have things to do in Paris, and yet I must be slow in getting back. Jacquie-Marie shouldn't be made to travel too many miles at a time. Philippe is always worrying that something will happen to her."

"She is such a beautiful child," Sibylla mused.

Isabel bit into the bread and chewed it, then looked up, a question in her eyes. "Did you learn anything of married life last night?"

Sibylla's hazel eyes glowed with secret happiness. "I learned that I still have much to learn."

"And where is your husband this morning? I'd have thought the two of you would still be lingering in bed."

Sibylla shrugged. "William went hunting with the other men.

He told me to be up and dressed when he returned. He says he doesn't want his wife to be a slug-a-bed."

Isabel dabbed at her lips with a linen cloth. "When are you and William leaving for Beaujeu?"

"Next week. We'll be here till then."

"And Baldwyn and Marie," Isabel asked, "what about them?"

"They're going back to Hainault with mother and father the day after tomorrow." Sibylla took hold of Isabel's hand and with a hopeful smile she persisted, "Can't you please stay a little longer? It would be so wonderful if you did."

"I'm sorry, no." Isabel swallowed the last of her wine. "I have to leave today." Then she flashed a sudden smile. "Don't fret. Your new husband will keep you far too occupied to think of me or anyone else. Tell me, is he a good teacher?"

Sibylla giggled, tints of pink rushing to her cheeks. "I believe so," she admitted. Then she leaned closer, her voice pitched low and confidential. "The duties of a wife are more pleasant than I had suspected."

Isabel smiled indulgently into her sister's innocent eyes.

At Gonesse the candles burned low that evening as Philippe and Geoffrey planned their assault on Normandy.

"I have already secured the promise of ten thousand mercenaries from Brabant and Germany," Geoffrey was saying, "and they will be ready to move by the end of summer."

Philippe rubbed a hand across his brow. "But can you be sure that Henry will remain in England for that long?"

A triumphant laugh lolled in Geoffrey's throat. "Yes. He's planned to spend the rest of the year there. If you and I descend upon Normandy by mid-September we will find it open to us, save for my father's troops. Still, what good are soldiers with no one to lead them, aye? Richard will be far away in Aquitaine, no remedy to my father's troubles. Then, with all of Normandy, Brittany, and France united as one, we will deal with my brother Richard at some other time and place."

"It all looks very good," Philippe agreed conditionally, "but we must take care. Not one word, one inkling of our intentions must reach Henry's ears."

"Of course."

The king gathered up several sheets of parchment where their aims had been drawn and tossed them into the fire. He stood there, looking down at his boots for several moments, before he turned back to Geoffrey. "There is something you should know," he began. "I have agreed to give the Vexin back to your father."

Leaning his elbows on the table Geoffrey stared at his friend in an expression of genuine surprise. "You gave it back to Henry? But why?"

Philippe raised his hand like a bishop giving benediction. "Be patient and hear my method. Last week I stopped at Gisors to see him and we talked of many things; the Vexin was only one of them."

Geoffrey puckered his lips in a petulant expression. "It is news to me."

"Trust me," Philippe urged. "I know what I am doing." He crossed the floor and sat down beside Geoffrey. "First of all, the matter of Marguerite has at long last been settled. Henry has now sworn to pay all the monies owed to me for her support since Harry's death. He has also secured a proposal of marriage for her from the King of Hungary."

Geoffrey rolled his eyes in perturbation. "Who cares about such things? We have more important matters to consider than whether or not my sister-in-law marries again."

"It is *all* important, love," Philippe argued. "Hear me out. The ambassadors from King Bela's court will visit Marguerite next month. It is likely a match will be made. If it is, I cannot stall any longer in holding the Vexin, especially since Henry now wants it settled on Alais as her dowry, in exchange for Berry."

Without a word Geoffrey got to his feet and began to pace back and forth between the table and the window. It was a hot night, the *portière* was drawn back to expose a black square of sky filled with little lights that winked like shining pinpoints from the village on the other side of the river.

Finally Geoffrey spun around, his expression animated by disapproval. "But I don't understand! Only a month ago you took an army into Berry and scattered the English. It was nearly yours and with another expedition it *could* be yours, without any negotiation!" His voice was high-pitched in exasperation. "And how can you give up the corridor into Normandy as though it were just another piece of land?"

Calmly Philippe folded his hands on the table and looked up at

Geoffrey. "In a few months our combined armies will have captured Normandy. With that accomplished the Vexin scarcely
matters." He smiled then, an action which meant much because
he so rarely did it. "Geoffrey, it is better this way. We must be
careful. All the world knows us to be friends, and many may
have guessed at our intentions. If your father hears any gossip
about our foray into Normandy it could ruin us now." He extended his hand to Geoffrey, who took it, and their fingers
braided in a tight grip of brotherhood. "Don't you see? What
could more clearly prove my good faith to your father than the
act of giving back the Vexin? *Now* he believes that I'm afraid of
him, that I'm backing down. He could barely restrain his joy
when we signed the agreement. It was like feeding fresh meat to
a starving hound."

Geoffrey threw his head back to laugh heartily and he hugged
Philippe to him in a loving embrace. It was marvelous the way
Philippe's mind worked, even more precise and devious than
Geoffrey's own. All the doubts had been assuaged now and they
kissed, their tongues hot and wet, their blood stirring with excite-
ment for each other's mind and body.

"I love you," Philippe said suddenly. "I love you for more reasons than I can count."

Arms around one another they stood at the window for a long
time, looking out at the night, a perfect peace between them. A
breeze came off the river, touching their faces as softly as a silken
banner. Beyond their vision, far to the west, the clouds were
gathering.

Sad news in the form of a folded communique was brought to
London in July. Hugh de Lacy had been murdered by a band of
Irish rebels. Henry's hands trembled as his eyes scanned the terrible sentences. He knew why this had happened, and yet even in
the privacy of his room would not admit the truth of it to himself.

All the same, Truth shouted back at him from between the
scribbled lines. There had been no peace in Ireland for a year;
none since the English troops had driven it away. Now Hugh de
Lacy was dead, sacrificed to John's iniquities and Henry's foolishness in putting love before honor.

When the matter was put before them, Henry's counselors

were firm: John must never again be allowed the chance to botch so important a project. Let the king send a seasoned diplomat to settle affairs between the Irish and their Norman colonists! But despite the uniformity of their decision, Henry was resolute. It was John whom he had chosen to rule Ireland in the future, and John it would be. As soon as passage could be arranged and a hand-picked army of knights assembled, he would sail for Ireland again.

This newest enterprise was scheduled for the middle of September. But by the end of August another communique bearing unhappy news, this time from Paris, changed Henry's plans—and more than that—forever.

RENNES was a pale, prosaic substitute for Paris but Geoffrey knew he had already stayed away too long. So much had to be accomplished in Brittany before he returned to France in August.

There was a matter of taxes. Geoffrey needed money badly, both for personal and military purposes. To achieve his aims he would have to reassert his power in the duchy and force revenues from the coffers of the greedy barons who hated him.

The political climate was relatively peaceful; there had been minor uprisings in the past six months but nothing serious. Constance had ruled well in her husband's absence. Unfortunately for him she had ruled fairly, and that meant the treasury was empty.

Geoffrey was determined to remedy that in a hurry. The nobles had money and they would pay. But he had returned for still another reason. Geoffrey was on the brink of triumph, and now he wanted a son.

The sweat dripped from his beard onto her breasts.

Geoffrey was pushing, filling his wife with the promise of an heir. It was all he needed to excite him and that was good, because she brought nothing to the experience. Constance lay beneath him, still as a dead woman, taking her breath in tiny gasps. But they were gasps of exertion, not pleasure.

Because she hated it, and tried to close her ears to the sounds. Passion made every man ridiculous. The halting breath, the leaping buttocks, the stupid words that meant nothing. He was her husband and she loved him—yet at times like this she loathed him because what *he* was doing to her had no relation to love.

Too often at night the memory came back.

Geoffrey's father, the old king, smelling of sweat and things that were worse than sweat, pushing himself between her legs. He had told her she would be grateful to him someday for all he had taught her, but Constance had only learned to hate him for it. She hated Henry and the memory of those times to this day.

With a groan Geoffrey rolled off of her and lay on his back, arms covering his face. Sneering, he acknowledged her muffled sigh of relief—so glad that the ordeal was over and she could go to sleep. *Cold-blooded bitch.* Did she think it was a joy for him to spend himself inside so spiritless a woman; did she think her cunt was made of gold? Well, she could relax. As soon as he planted the seed of his child within her belly, she could have her chastity and her empty bed. It would be no sacrifice for Geoffrey. He didn't care much for women anyway. At least not women like his wife.

But there were *other* women. Women who burned with the kind of passions only men were supposed to know. Eleanor, his mother, she was one of these, at least she had been when she was young; and Philippe's mother too. Adele was middle to her forties, yet she still burned; her cunt was hot. Geoffrey knew that from experience. More than once when everything was dark and secret she had slipped into his room at the palace and kept him panting through the night. Geoffrey smiled to himself. Some women never lost their appetites.

And there was Isabel. She had never been in his bed, but he had wished her there. So had she; Geoffrey had sensed her desire. He had even thought of going to her, thought about it often. But always something had held him back. *What?* Love of Philippe? Fear of Philippe?

Geoffrey looked over at his wife. He could barely see her face in the darkness, but he knew that she was sleeping. Her chest rose and fell in a rhythm of shallow breathing. The flesh between her legs must still be sticky with his love, but Constance was asleep.

*   *   *

Constance wanted a son as much as Geoffrey did. She knew the importance of an heir in order to secure her own position. Though she was Duchess of Brittany by right, she only reigned because Geoffrey was her husband: Geoffrey was an English prince, and Brittany belong to England.

A son would protect her power and her future. There was very little else for her to care about. So she was joyful to find that she was pregnant by the first week in August. When she told Geoffrey, he said he knew she was carrying a son.

Immediately they left Rennes for Paris, arriving on the sixteenth of August, just in time for Geoffrey to organize the tournament which he had planned for the French king's twenty-first birthday celebration. Isabel had sent a letter to Rennes at the end of June, saying that Philippe had been persuaded to allow it.

Later when she thought about that awful day, or dreamed of it, Isabel could not remember the events in any logical succession. The images leapt in her mind, distorted fragments of reality: cheers, grinning faces, hot sun burning on her shoulders, and the dreadful stink of blood.

It had all begun so happily. A thousand nobles dressed in bright, brave colors; a hundred banners fluttering overhead. Strange how the colors fixed themselves in her memory, as though they mattered. Herself in a pale pink chainse sheer as a spider web, sitting close beside Philippe. Marguerite Capet, dressed all in purple, flushed with excitement because in two days' time she would leave her dreary widow's life behind in Paris and go to Hungary to marry King Bela. And Constance, her icy blond beauty set off by a bliaud of frost-blue samite, raising her cup to toast the champion knights as they rode by.

Geoffrey, in green trimmings, had smiled beneath his visor. He trotted his horse to the railing, lifting his lance in honor of the king, then led his group of knights to the center of the field. It was only meant to be a mock battle; just a display of skill with weapons. Finesse in handling pole-axe, lance, and sword. No blood. That was against the code of such events; outside the law of chivalry.

How had it happened, what had started it? Just a little thing;

no one remembered. There were insults, shouts of protest exchanged between the knights. Most of the spectators thought it was a part of the performance. Somehow a French knight's *hauberk* was sheeted, pierced. Horses clashed; there was a cry of vengeance. Geoffrey was unhorsed and thrown to the ground. The French knights scattered his comrades, pressed forward; near. "Give way!" they shouted. But he would not conform to custom by laying down his sword beside him in the dirt.

Instead he threw his helmet to the ground, and sweat shined on his face. He cursed the French knights, called them cowards, spat on them. Horses charged. Of their own accord? Because they were driven forward? No one knew.

Geoffrey was down, hidden from view of the spectators by churning hooves. Philippe screamed. The guards reached out and grabbed the king or he would have thrown himself into the arena. Constance sobbed and clung to Marguerite, who sat beside her, numbed by shock. Isabel watched the scene helplessly, and in silence. Then puffs of tan dust obscured it all.

A distraught band of people huddled in the great hall that night, waiting for news. Constance slept sitting up in a chair, two of her attendants nodding at her feet. Isabel paced the room in tireless repetition. Whenever she paused or sat down even for a moment, her anxiousness soon propelled her to her feet once more.

Hours passed and others joined the dismal circle. Wine was brought and drunk. No one spoke. Henri of Champagne followed Isabel's every movement with his eyes but she didn't seem to notice. Marguerite sobbed relentlessly, hour after hour. This tragedy was a keen reminder of her husband's death. William of Rheims kept a quiet vigil with his rosary beads. Beyond the hall, near the palace doors, were members of the king's own personal bodyguard. They stood shoulder to shoulder and their swords were drawn in an attempt to keep out the curious mob that pressed closer from outside.

In an anteroom across the corridor from the great hall, Geoffrey lay unconscious on a bed of straw, surrounded by a dozen surgeons. They bound his wounds tightly and gave him belladonna to drink, but there was little they could do to stop the bleeding and nothing they could do to stop the pain.

Sully was there to perform the sacrament of Absolution, and the king was there to hold his lover's hand. The surgeons would have preferred that Philippe wait with the others, but he would not be moved. He bent close, leaning upon the body of his friend, staining his own clothes with Geoffrey's blood.

Dawn, opaque and humid, came at last. Geoffrey groaned and mumbled Philippe's name. The surgeons leaned closer; one of them pressed a cup to Geoffrey's lips. He coughed and spit the liquid out; he shivered. Then with a long sigh he lay back upon the bed, unmoving.

Sully muttered words in Latin; his right hand made the airy sign of a cross. The surgeons put their instruments away. The Duke of Brittany was dead, they told the king. There was nothing more that could be done for him. Philippe stared back at them, smiling queerly, as though he hadn't heard.

For over an hour he sat there, still holding Geoffrey's hand. Finally Sully bent down and whispered something in the king's ear. Philippe looked up, dull-eyed, uncomprehending, then stumbled to his feet.

Geoffrey's grip held fast. Philippe began to tremble, then to weep. One of the surgeons rushed forward to pull the hands apart. He could not do it. They had to break the dead man's fingers before Philippe could be free.

A decision had to be made.

Church law was adamant on this point: all those who died in tournament play died in a state of mortal sin. Such men as these were denied church burial and all other blessings which any other man, however sinful, was allowed. When the bishops Sully and William reminded the king of this he grew hysterical, screaming curses at the Church, at the pope, and at God Almighty. He vowed that his friend would not be treated like an excommunicant, laid low in unhallowed ground. He would take his own life rather than consent to such a thing! Before their startled eyes Philippe pulled forth a dagger and flayed the skin of his left forearm to prove he was in earnest.

Sully called the guards and ordered that the king be taken to his room and watched closely. Then he and William of Rheims retired to the council room to seek a solution. Neither of the men could ignore the way in which Geoffrey had died, but their concern for the king's well-being overwhelmed all other considerations.

After hours of deliberation William snatched up a fragment of discarded hope. Nine years earlier, when Geoffrey had been knighted by his father's hand, he had made a pledge to fight in the Holy Land. He had taken the Crusader's cross as proof of his intentions. Though the vow had never been fulfilled, the promise was enough, according to Church edict. *All those sworn to defend Christendom were entitled to everlasting life in God's kingdom.*

The two bishops agreed that Geoffrey's covenant assured his salvation. To dispute any controversy they decided to announce that the duke had died, not of his wounds, but of a fever. It was not for the sake of Geoffrey's soul or reputation that these two men of God had agreed upon the lie, but for Philippe. He would surely go mad if some way was not found to assure the soul of his beloved a place in heaven. When Sully told him of the decision, the king fell sobbing to his knees. Sully held him to his bosom, and stayed with him throughout the night.

In her own room Isabel listened to the sounds of weeping. Philippe. Constance. Marguerite. The whole of the Cité Palais was lamenting. The cries echoed up and down the corridor, and seemed to bleed into the walls. Isabel pulled the coverlet up around her face and willed herself to sleep. Anything was better than living through these hours. Anything. Even nightmares.

Philippe would not see her; why, she didn't know. On the morning of Geoffrey's funeral Isabel went to her husband's room and was turned back by the guards, at his command. He was busy. He could not see her. That is all that they would say.

From his place at a table in the room, Philippe listened as Isabel argued with the men, insisting they allow her to come in. Her voice, pitched high like that, usually annoyed him, but today it was something he could ignore. There was so much else to distract him. He stared for a time at the sheaf of blank parchment in front of him. Then he pressed a trembling hand to the paper, and wrote the news of Geoffrey's death. He affixed his seal and signed it, then thrust it into the hands of a waiting messenger. The letter was for Henry Plantagenet, in London.

* * *

It was noon and raining as the funeral cortège made its way from the palace down the twisting, narrow road to the other end of the island where the unfinished cathedral sat, the Seine lapping just beyond it.

Geoffrey would spend eternity at Notre Dame. It was the king's wish. Philippe wanted Geoffrey there, as close to him as he could be. Some, like Sully, thought it a wish born of morbid fascination, but Philippe was in no state to be disputed.

Like the central figure in an epic tragedy, he rode slowly behind the funeral cart, his eyes fixed straight ahead. He was flanked on either side by Isabel and Constance, both dressed in somber shades of grey, their blond hair completely covered by circlet and veil. Behind the royal trio walked a gathering of nobles, followed by Carthusian monks and white-robed Cistercians. At the rear of the parade was a contingent of knights from the king's household guard.

Before the great altar Sully spoke his mass. Then to the accompaniment of a final prayer, all that was mortal of Geoffrey Plantagenet was lowered into the tomb within the vault below. There was a sudden rush of incense as funeral vases, filled with smoldering scents of herbs and oils, were lowered into the darkness to be sealed up inside the tomb.

It was all too much for Philippe. He gave a great cry and rushed forward, as if to throw himself into the vault. The guards pulled him back and wrestled him to the floor. He sobbed throughout the remainder of the ceremony, and Isabel wept too at the sight of her husband, restrained by soldiers and yelping like a dog gone mad.

When the service was over the king was removed to the palace and put to bed like a child. Guards were placed outside his room, for Sully feared what he might do if left alone. At last Philippe fell asleep, his senses dimmed by exhaustion and wine that was laced with herbs.

Isabel remained sleepless for many hours, her mind locked into replaying every detail of the past three days. There seemed to be no end to sorrow in this unhappy place; she'd known so much of it in the last six years. Isabel shivered beneath her skin, remembering her first impression of the Cité Palais: forbidding, grim, uninhabitable. In all this time she'd never learned to feel at home within its dim corridors and grey stone walls.

No happiness; none. She closed her eyes against the images of death, and things worse than death, but they mingled in her mind with half-forgotten dreams and fears as yet unrealized. There was a sense of uncompleted doom in all of this, as if Geoffrey's death was the precursor of yet more misfortune in the time to come.

Sleep made Isabel the prisoner of disordered dreams, in which Geoffrey joined the myriad of restless spirits who roamed the corridors outside her room. Sometime before dawn he came and stood beside her bed, his face bone white and ghastly. He whimpered piteously, then opened wide his bloodless arms and called her name.

Henry received the news of Geoffrey's death with little emotion. He loved his children, all of them, but had always regarded Geoffrey with suspicion. This clever son of his had gone to Paris and thrown himself upon the bosom of the French king. Now he was dead and all it meant to Henry was that the clever son had ceased to be a threat.

Reports from France declared that young Capet was prostrate in his sorrow, his body sickened and his mind unhinged by constant grieving. *Let Philippe Capet shed all the tears that needed weeping.* The King of England had better things to do. It surprised Henry that his son should have invoked such loyalty. He had been cold and heartless beneath the exterior of his charm, always needing to buy the goodwill of others which his nature could not earn. But not so with Philippe. That was a puzzle. Of course those two had shared more than friendship. Henry's lips twisted in an ironic sneer. Whatever that corrupt alliance had betokened, it was over now.

But there were complications resulting from Geoffrey's death, and they pricked at Henry's mind. Grief-stricken though he was, the King of France had been keen-witted enough to send a list of exorbitant demands to Henry. Capet claimed wardship of Geoffrey's daughter, and the child Constance carried in her womb. He also petitioned custody of Brittany now that Geoffrey no longer lived.

Furious, Henry had dispensed of these demands by tearing the letter into pieces with his teeth. The promises his son had made to the French king had no meaning now, and Philippe Capet could be damned if he believed Henry would honor whatever treason they had worked between them.

Problems, problems, everywhere he looked! With Geoffrey's death Richard became the logical successor to the crown and that meant admitting something Henry was unready to accept. Richard was certainly the best choice, possibly the *only* choice, but Henry rebelled against the idea. He didn't like Richard or his way of life. He didn't wish to hand over the promise of his crown to a man who wore more jewels on his person than any woman; a man who took smooth-faced boys to his bed.

What galled Henry most was the fact that Richard was so infuriatingly capable: as a soldier, as a leader—it was even possible he had the makings of a statesman. While Richard was not easily loved by people as Harry had been, he was respected, and he was feared.

Henry feared him too. He feared his abilities, the growing power that threatened to eclipse his own. If he was to name Richard as the successor now it might prove troublesome. Indeed, it *would* prove troublesome. Assured of the crown, Richard might decide to hurry things along, assert his reputation in other areas besides Poitou and the Aquitaine—Normandy, for instance. The thought of that sent Henry's blood pounding.

John. He wanted John to succeed him, but Henry knew he couldn't make his wishes known as yet, though many people, and that probably included Richard, might have already guessed that was his intention. Yet it was important for Henry to keep his sons guessing. Any public word on the matter and Richard would take it as a challenge; the reprisals could be disastrous. As for John, he was not ready to shoulder such responsibility. He was still too immature; he had a lot to learn. But if Henry had to give up his power to anyone—and someday he would have to, though he loathed to think on it—at least it was going to be to the son he loved best, and trusted.

There was still another son he cared for—a bastard by a woman whose name Henry had never known. Godfrey of Lincoln had been the king's chancellor for several years. He was a good worker, and loyal, too, with a singularly unimaginative but useful intelligence. Godfrey was thirty-five; he had been in the king's service since the age of seventeen.

Thirteen years ago, in a fit of fatherly affection, Henry had named Godfrey as Bishop of Lincoln. Though he had retained the title, Godfrey had never allowed himself to be consecrated because he believed himself unfit for such a holy office. Blunt and simply spoken, he was at heart a soldier, and had spent most of his adult life in the field. Recently he had decided to step down as bishop in order to devote his time to soldiering and the business of being chancellor. Those offices, plus the honor of being at his father's side, were reward enough for him. As for any other pretentions Godfrey may have had, he dispensed them through his writings, which could be suffocatingly self-righteous, as Isabel of Hainault had discovered when he attacked her innocent involvement with the *Capuciati* movement.

So with Godfrey removed from Lincoln, Henry had to find a replacement, and for this he selected a most remarkable man. Hugh of Avalon was unique among churchmen. He had no interest in ecclesiastical advancement. He was a monk at heart. A member of the Carthusians—a humble, contemplative order— Hugh would have preferred to labor in his work unnoticed by the world, but Henry had changed all that a decade earlier.

He had first met the Burgundian monk at the *Grande Chartreuse* in France. Perhaps something in the personality of this slight and quiet man recalled in Henry the memory of Thomas Becket, for immediately the king had decided to take him into royal service. In Hugh's honor Henry had founded Witham Abbey in the county of Somerset, planning to raise him higher at some later date. When Godfrey saw fit to resign from Lincoln, the perfect opportunity revealed itself. That was Henry's view. Hugh had another.

There were many months of negotiations. Hugh simply did not want the job, but Henry would have no other in his place. Try as he might, and he tried mightily, Hugh could not sway the king from his adamant intention, so in September of 1186 he was named Bishop of Lincoln. Ironically, Hugh was not the only one to raise objections. Half the English clergy were outraged that the king should have chosen him. The See of Lincoln was most desirable to any man who wished to make a place for himself in the world.

That was not the only comic element adrift in this touchy situation. Since Lincoln Cathedral lay in ruins from the earthquake, Hugh's new domain was little more than a gigantic heap of stones standing high above the city! For this reason it was decided that he be invested of his duties at London. A great procession was arranged to travel from the priory at Clerkenwell, southward through the city to the king's residence at West Minster.

Tales of Hugh's goodness and charity had preceded him and so the poorfolk of the city thronged the streets to see him as he passed by, riding his spotted palfrey, with a small bundle of all his earthly goods strapped to its saddle. Hugh was dressed simply in coarse wool and sheepskin, while all other men in the procession —soldiers and members of the clergy—wore fine silks and many jewels.

The contingent of the bishop's escort blushed deeply with embarrassment: why would a man who had been raised up so high in the great world dress like a beggar? The king's soldiers found it comical and they sniggered behind their hands. A few of them even drew close behind the bishop's mount, using their swords to try and unloose the ropes which held his pack, so that the sight of him, riding with his belongings tied to his own horse, would not shame them in front of the king.

But Henry, who was equally unpretentious, was gladdened by Hugh's modesty and welcomed his new bishop with a warm embrace. Together they stood on the steps of the royal residence, waving to the cheering crowd and tossing handfuls of silver pennies into their midst. Hugh, in all his humility, blushed at the ovation.

Slack-jawed and bored, young Johnny stood off to the side a little, smiling a crooked, hypocritical smile. All of this silly fuss annoyed him, made him tired. He had no part in it; just an onlooker, never more. He drew in his breath and winked at a pretty girl who stood on the edge of the crowd. Henry was putting the mitre upon Hugh's head. Ho hum, more bother. John wished that this ceremony would end, so he could go indoors and have his supper.

* * *

Geoffrey's death had done terrible things to Philippe.

Four weeks had passed since that awful day in August and in that time he had refused to leave his room, to eat, to bathe. Grief had made a ghost of him. It was as though he had ceased to live at all.

Isabel had deliberately stayed away from him the first two weeks or so, knowing he needed to be alone. Now every day for the past ten days she had brought a tray of food to him but he would only take a little bread sopped in wine. It was barely enough nourishment to keep him alive and each day he grew thinner.

When she talked to Philippe he never answered, except to curse her and order her from the room. She tried her best to cheer him, bending close to mouth mild words of comfort in his ear, but he only turned his back on her and said he wanted to be left alone. Nothing she or anyone else could do or say would restore his rationality.

For some reason that Isabel could not understand, Philippe had chosen to blame her for Geoffrey's death. *You are to blame.* He had never actually said the words, but they were in his eyes each time he looked at her. There was a deeper message, one she hardly dared to comprehend, because it was worse than anything that had ever passed between them, spoken or unspoken. *I wish it had been you,* it said; *I wish that you had died instead of him.*

It did no good to tempt him back to reality with his little daughter, because Philippe wouldn't see her. He would not go to the nursery, nor would he allow Isabel to bring the child to his room. He didn't care about her now; any more than he cared about Isabel or his mother or the men who worked for him. Geoffrey was dead, *Geoffrey,* his only friend. Nothing else mattered, no one.

Isabel feared for his reason more than his health. He had lost the will to live, the ability to function. Day after day he sat on the floor of his room, his shoulders covered with one of Geoffrey's cloaks, staring wordlessly into the ashes of the fire grate. Was he going to grieve forever?

"I've brought you some food" Isabel said, setting a tray on the floor in front of him, just as she did every morning. She stood for a moment looking down at his crouched form, her heart aching in pity for him. He looked terrible! His eyes were ringed with shadows, and his neat beard had become a thick black stubble which accentuated the thinness of his face. "Please eat something," she begged, "you can't go on starving yourself."

He looked at her with dead eyes, then turned his face away. "I don't want anything from you," he answered. "Just take the food and go."

She knelt beside him, her hand a gentle pressure on his knee. "Philippe," she said quietly, "you have to stop this, you must! If you don't wash yourself, and get some rest, and eat, *you* are going to die!" She tried to kiss his hand but he pulled it away. A single tear faltered on her cheek. "Treat me however you like, but have a care for yourself for God's sake!"

His voice was hollow, emotionless, and he looked at her as though she were a stranger. "Why do you come here every day when you know I can't stand the sight of you? I've told you that I wish to be left alone. I have nothing to say to you. I don't want to see you. Go away."

Isabel got to her feet, smoothing her hands over her hips. "Will you at least talk to Sully?"

"Why?" he asked, twisting the word, making it sound ugly.

She swallowed. "Because he can help you."

"No one can help me," Philippe answered. "No one."

Tension had thinned her voice to a high-pitched, tiny sound. "Jacquie-Marie?"

"I don't want to see her either."

For a moment Isabel wavered between tears and anger, then just as suddenly she was furious with him, and stamped her foot hard upon the floor. "Then are you going to sit here forever, until you die of filth and starvation? Look at you! The poorest wretch in the street looks more a king than you do! Scour off the dirt and see if somewhere beneath it you can still find yourself!"

Even her anger could not move him and he spoke without looking up. "If the smell offends you, go and douse yourself with perfume."

"It is your behavior that offends me, Philippe," she said in a quieter voice. "It offends everyone, and it offends God."

Now he did look at her, staring incredulously into her face. "God," he repeated slowly. "How can you dare to mention God to me? I had God's favor once, but you drove Him away with your wickedness."

That was too much to take from him and Isabel began to cry. "I'm not wicked, I'm not! How can you say that to me when all I want to do is love you and help you."

"You can't help me!" he shouted.

"Why?" she shouted back, "Tell me the reason!"

"*YOU!*" he screamed, "you are the reason! God is punishing me because of you, can't you see that?"

So he had said it at last; still she couldn't believe it. Isabel folded her arms across her breasts and gave him a pitiless look. "Because of me? What have I done to call God's judgment on you? I'm your wife. I *love* you! How can that be wrong?"

The outburst had unsettled his frazzled nerves and now Philippe began to tremble. He gripped his hands together in his lap to steady them and spoke to the fire grate instead of her. "Sully was right about you. You *are* dark. You put ideas into my head I never had before. You enslaved me with your body, with your beauty. *That's* what you did, and that's why God is punishing me now."

She could have laughed at the absurdity of his words but they were too hurtful, and her only recourse was to hurt him back. "And what about your love for Geoffrey?" she asked, her voice sharp with a bitterness she had never felt until this moment. "Was that such a pure, unsullied thing compared to what you feel for me? Is your reason so clouded you can honestly believe that God would punish you for loving your wife, and bless you for loving another man?"

Philippe waited a long time to answer. He was laughing, laughing wildly, his head thrown back like a jackal screaming at the moon. Isabel moved a few steps away from him, afraid, a tight feeling of sickness growing in her stomach. Then at last he sobered, and faced her with glowing, fevered eyes. "Don't confuse my love for Geoffrey with what I feel for you. He was my friend, and the only person on earth who ever truly loved me. You're just the painted strumpet your uncle picked for me to marry. Do you really think God credits lust and fornication between people just because they are man and wife? That's all it has ever been for us, and it makes me sick to realize it at last. I don't love you. I never have."

It took a moment for the barbarity of his words to take hold of her, then she merely bowed her head and muttered, "Oh."

"*Oh!*" he mimicked cruelly, then under his breath mumbled, "Stupid bitch." He buried his face in the folds of Geoffrey's cloak. "Go away, Isabel. Don't come back tomorrow, or the next day, or the next. I don't want to see you."

She had heard enough and turned away, taking slow steps toward the door. Then she paused, her back still to him, and said, "I am going away, tomorrow. I'm going to Beaujeu to see my sister. Edythe is staying behind to look after Jacquie-Marie."

He didn't answer.

Isabel turned around and looked at him. He was staring straight ahead. She waited for him to say something but when he didn't she said, "Constance is leaving too, did you know that? She is leaving for Brittany tomorrow morning." Another pause. "Philippe, did you hear me?"

"I heard."

Her voice and her attitude begged for his attention. It was degrading, but she couldn't help it. "Won't you at least say goodbye to me, Philippe?" Isabel made a little sniffing sound that was meant to be a laugh. "Well, I know one thing. If you had been the one to die, instead of Geoffrey, he wouldn't be sitting here like this, sunk in despair, wasting himself!" But it was no use; she was only provoking him. Her voice went lower. "I love you Philippe, if that means anything at all."

He wasn't listening; it was impossible to reach him now. He had withdrawn into his own secret world of brooding and Isabel had no door to follow him. She fingered the grey silk skirt of her chainse, then turned away. "Goodbye," she said and pushed the velvet drape aside.

His voice made her hand stop, white and still upon the green of the material. "And how long will you be away, Isabel?" he asked.

It was only a tiny piece of hope but she clutched at it. "I don't know, a month. Maybe longer." She tried to make her voice sound sweet.

Philippe turned his face; he grinned at what he was about to say. "Good. Make it as long as you like. In fact you can't stay away long enough to please me."

"Oh God..." she muttered in pain, as though he'd hit her.

After a second she ran crying from the room. Philippe listened to her fleeing footsteps, laughing till they dulled to a faint echo. Then he began to cry.

With Isabel away from Paris, Philippe was truly alone.

Hardly anyone came to his room now, only a kitchen steward once a day to bring him food, though he seldom ate it. Weakness made him shiver; he felt close to death. Wine was the only thing that gave him strength now, and he emptied the porringer at his elbow.

It was early October, and cold. A fire was laid in the grate of his room and Philippe sat staring at the flames as the hours of each dark night passed. His behavior, all he was doing, was wrong, he knew that—but it didn't help him to know. Without Geoffrey, without the promise of Normandy and all that they had planned together, Philippe was lost.

The flames kept him company and Philippe stared back at them, trying to make sense of it all. Nothing could ever bring Geoffrey back. Not all the love and need in the world could do that. Philippe needed someone else to take his place, another ally, someone he could trust. Maybe someone he could love.

Where could he find such a man?

The silent answer came to him from the darkened corners of the room. *Henry Plantagenet had yet another discontented son.*

That night, for the first time in nearly five weeks, Philippe ate a full meal, then climbed between the covers of his bed to sleep. When he dreamed, it was not of Geoffrey.

Isabel had taken a small contingent with her: twenty soldiers of the household guard, ten mounted knights, a half dozen pack horses, and a traveling companion—Henri of Champagne.

In the royal residence at Melun, one day out from Paris, Isabel waited till all the household was asleep, then slipped unnoticed into Henri's room. They made love beneath the same bed hangings that had covered Abelard and seven Capetian kings. When Isabel fell asleep at last in Henri's arms and dreamed, it was not of Geoffrey.

Clear weather and a swift horse brought Isabel and her party to Beaujeu early in October, where she was happily reunited with her sister.

Four months of marriage had transformed Sibylla into a radiant young woman who laughed easily and flushed with pride at the mention of her husband's name.

"...and he's so good to me," she told Isabel one morning as they sat amid the dying colors of the garden, "I have only to request a particular wine or a certain kind of food and it is put before me. I have dancing and entertainments and fine clothes to wear. And best of all I have a good and loving husband." As she talked Sibylla dangled a length of yarn above her kitten's head. "I'd always thought you were the lucky one Isabel, to have our uncle arrange such a worthy marriage for you. But now you have done the same for me. William may not be a king but I could not wish for a finer man, and I have you to thank for giving him to me."

Puzzlement and a little bit of envy. That's what Isabel felt; instinct. Poor Sibylla. So happy. She was as fragile and unknowing as the pretty yellow butterfly that hovered in the space between them. Isabel reached out to touch it, but it leapt from her outstretched fingers and rose high above their heads.

Sibylla folded her hands across her abdomen and smiled a timid, secret smile. "Darling sister, I have another reason to be happy. I am carrying William's child, due to be born in the spring, at Eastertide." She patted the blessed area of her body. "God has been so good to me. Thank Him, Isabel. We are both so lucky."

Tears—for whatever unnamed reason—dimmed her eyes. "Sibylla," she said, and that was all Isabel could say. She opened her arms wide.

While Isabel remained at Beaujeu, Henri went ahead to Troyes to wait for her. *Maybe* she would come to him there. *She would come.* Henri believed that with all his heart, and it was all he thought of. He sent his wife to Châlons with most of their household. He ached for the time when he could take Isabel in the bed which should have been hers as a bride. Sweet blood of Christ, he *ached* for her.

Isabel left Beaujeu after two weeks.

"When the child is born, come stay with us in Paris for a while," she told her sister as they said goodbye. Sibylla promised, then she and William stood close together in the pearl grey dawn, and waved to Isabel as she rode away.

* * *

There was such joy in her body, such joy as he held her close.

"I love it this way," Isabel told him, stretching her legs farther apart to span his hips as she sat upon his knees.

"I love it any way with you," Henri answered, painting the skin between her breasts with his tongue. "I've never wanted it so much with anyone; never enjoyed it with any other woman as I have with you."

She teased his beard with her teeth. "Because you love me."

"Yes, because of that, and other things." Henri took one of her breasts between his hands, sucking at it like a fruit.

Isabel unloosed her hair and draped it about his shoulders, dressing him in it. "And what about your wife? Does she give you all you want?"

They kissed rapturously, one breath upon the other, then Henri whispered in her ear, "Blanche does it as a duty, nothing more. I don't believe she ever feels anything."

"Then she's such a fool," Isabel said, and her words were etched with meaning, "and worse, she's a fraud. A woman who cannot make her lover happy is no woman at all."

He nibbled at the opal stones that graced her ears, then flicked at them with his thumb. "You don't need any gems to make you beautiful," he said, sounding almost angry. "You don't need anything to do that. The less you wear the more perfect you are."

Henri was sweet, gentle, and he worshipped her; it would have been so easy for Isabel to love him were it not for Philippe. She felt guilty taking Henri's love and giving him only pleasure in return, but it was all she could ever give him, and at this moment it was enough for both of them. Her hands roamed lower, teasing, stroking. "I like gems," she cooed in his ear, "and some more than others. Have you a gem for me, my love?"

He laughed and drew closer, all his senses stung.

"And is it harder than a diamond?" she prodded him further, "Redder than a ruby?"

The sound of her voice was enough to make him drunk.

Later Isabel lay beside him while he slept, though she was troubled by wakefulness. Without his arms around her or his weight upon her body she felt lonely and miserable with shame.

Complications had made her life unbearable, and she was sorry, intensely sorry for so many things.

Isabel lay on her back looking up into emptiness for a long while. She thought about Paris and wondered if Philippe was wakeful too, staring into the night, hating her.

I CE CAME to Paris in November and diminished the number of small boats upon the river. Fewer torches burned along the river banks and in the streets. Fewer bonfires gleamed at distant points outside the city. Fuel was scarce at this time of the year. People drank their wine unmixed, for sake of warmth, and went to bed at sunset. The rich and poor alike bundled themselves as best they could, snuffed out their candles early, and took their pleasures in the dark.

There was one part of the city where the lights burned through till morning. It was ugly here, on the avenue *Chaussée St.-Lazare*. Stone huts of Merovingian design dotted the road; low-ceilinged, pocked with age. The Cemetery of the Innocents lay just beyond; it had been a burial ground since Roman times and on rainy nights the dusty smell of death hung on the air. But the stone huts? They were full of life and laughter.

Soldiers and students and a few priests came here and spent their money on wine, hashish, and whores. The brothels always did their best business in the wintertime. *Keep cunts and cups against the cold, and you'll stay young until you're old,* a bawdy rhyme proclaimed. The men who came here agreed.

Most every night these past few weeks the king had come to the old stone hut at the very end of the road where Fabiana lived with twenty other women of her kind. These women had come to Paris from other places, mostly Toulouse and Languedoc, where religious fanaticism among the people had driven sinners out. Here they were welcomed eagerly into the population. A city the size of Paris could never have too many prostitutes.

Fabiana was only twenty, and prettier than most of the other women. Her face was smooth and free of pock scars (rare among the poor), her teeth were good, and her breasts were firm and big. The king satisfied himself with many women of this house, but every night he chose Fabiana, and every night he took her first.

Perhaps it was vanity, but she liked to think that the king found her more pleasing than the others. She found him pleasing. He was the most handsome man that she had ever seen; so much more handsome than any of the other men who came here. Sometimes after he left, Fabiana would kiss the bruises on her skin that he had put there, and wonder if she dared to love him.

The king was generous.

The thought ran through Fabiana's mind like a chant and she braced herself against the pain. He always left behind a goodly sum of silver *deniers,* always more than the fee called for. Sometimes he brought her woollen cloaks, and once even a sheepskin pellison. To Fabiana that had been the best gift of all. She slept in it, when, by early morning, her work was done and she was allowed to go to sleep. It was the only warm piece of clothing that she owned.

Yes, he was generous, this young king Philippe-Auguste; handsome and generous. Too bad Fabiana so seldom saw his face. The light was dim in here—her room was furnished with only a straw pallet, basin, and a few flickering candles—and anyway he usually took her from behind. She clenched her teeth, barely able to keep her balance as he shoved against her. The pain was hot, exciting. There was always so much pain with him, even in the usual way. When he wanted it like this it was so intense she sometimes thought she would faint before he finished with her. But please God, not before...

Fabiana arched her back and thrust a hand frantically between her legs. It didn't matter what she felt with the others; usually she felt nothing, not even pain. But with him she always wanted it to be different, to feel everything she could. *This was an honor most women would never know.* She must not forget that. Her breath came in gasps, grunts. Fabiana crammed a corner of the blanket deep within her mouth, crammed it tight inside as he was crammed inside of her; she tried to keep her cries from coming so they would not offend his ears. *Honor.* She must make herself remember that when the pain was bad. Honor. Remember. *Remember.*

His hands were rough, tight against her body, and he seized

her hips with a brutal cry. He rammed against her once, twice; he cried out louder. After a moment he pulled himself from her, then got shakily to his feet. He went immediately to the basin where he washed himself thoroughly, then dried his hands and penis upon his bliaud before he put it on.

Fabiana felt the sticky liquid ooze between her legs and down her thigh as she slumped gratefully to the floor. Her face was hot and prickled with sweat, although the room was cold. Fabiana felt an awful weariness mixed with relaxation as she closed her eyes and listened to the sounds of washing; to the soft sounds of the king pulling on his clothes.

She was nearly dozing and his voice startled her: "Here," he said and sprinkled several coins on the floor at her elbow. He pulled a coarse-woven brown cloak from beneath his arm and tossed it at her; Fabiana lunged forward to kiss his boots in appreciation. Philippe looked down at her, saying nothing, then moved to the door.

"Cover yourself," he said before he left.

Adele stood in front of Geoffrey's black basalt tomb in Notre Dame and whispered a tiny prayer that only God could hear. Poor splendid Geoffrey. The news of his death had not reached her ears in Sens, where she had been staying since July. It was late November now, and Adele had returned to Paris to find many things gone wrong.

Sully had told her the stories of Philippe's violent grief and self-imposed isolation; then the sudden change to an attitude of sloth and promiscuity. He drank too much and rode away each night, returning at dawn, sleeping till noon. When he attended meetings of the *curia regis* he was either rude or inattentive. Grief was one thing; Sully felt for the king in that. But this behavior ... something had to be done. Philippe had lost touch with all the instincts which had once marked him so specially.

"Where has Isabel gone?" Adele asked Sully on the following afternoon as she paced the empty council chamber. "I believe she could restore Philippe to himself if she were here. She has a power over him the rest of us don't have." Adele stopped and jerked around to face the bishop, her eyes fierce and determined. "For God's sake Sully, bring her back!"

He raised a slender hand to quiet her; the shrill sound of her voice was hard to bear. "My lady, you must understand it was Philippe who sent her away. At least he condoned her going. Since the death of his friend he has changed toward his wife. He refused to be alone with her, nor would he even sit beside her at his meals." His fine voice went lower. "With my own ears I have heard him say he hates her now."

Adele planted her hands firmly on her hips and regarded Sully with a doubtful look. "That is very strange. From what I could see the two of them have been happy together since the birth of Jacquie-Marie." She began pacing again. "What could Geoffrey's death have done to change that?"

Sully's blue eyes crinkled at the corners; he didn't have the answer. "It is a complicated matter. There are many things involved which I do not understand. But I know this: Philippe himself has changed—how much you can guess from what I have told you. He has turned his back on all of us who care for him. He has even lost interest in his little daughter." He caught Adele's sharp, dark frown and nodded. "Yes, it is most unusual and I am powerless to do anything. All of us are powerless. I have prayed..."

Adele half turned, her lips parted to make an answer when they heard a halting step in the corridor. All at once the door flew open and Philippe stood there. He looked at the two of them, then hobbled in, rubbing his knee with a gloved hand.

"My horse threw me," he explained and dropped himself to the bench beside the fire. He motioned to the porringer which stood on the table several feet away. "Bring me some wine," he told his mother, and when she brought it he snatched the henap from her hand. He drank, then smirked at them, lifting a saucy eyebrow. "You two make a fine pair of tale-bearers. Tell me, what brings two such dissimilar souls together? I seem to have caught you in the midst of gossiping."

Adele's nervous fingers tapped out a rhythm on the table top. "You look terrible. What has happened to you, Philippe?"

His laugh was dry as dust. "Do you really have to ask? I'm sure our friend the bishop has told you all there is to know."

"Yes," she answered, trying to keep the strain out of her voice, "but you could tell me more. This isn't like you, Philippe. I know you, or at least I thought I did. I can't believe that you would allow the death of one man..." she floundered for a moment, unsure of what to say, "...to ruin you, your life, your reputation."

Flippancy turned to spite in an instant and Philippe half rose before the pain in his leg forced him down again. Furious, he shouted, "The death of one man? Hold your tongue, Mother! You know nothing of what Geoffrey meant to me!"

Adele struck the table with a closed fist and shouted back, "I know what your family should mean to you! Your wife, your daughter, me! Yet you shame us all. Why did you send Isabel away? Where is she? Why has she been gone so long?"

Philippe shook his head in mock dismay. "Can I be hearing this from you? Why do you suddenly care so much about Isabel? You never liked her." He shot a quick, cruel glance at Sully. "Nor did you, bishop. Both of you did your best to make things difficult for her. Why all this sudden concern? I would think you'd both be pleased if she never came back to Paris."

"You were the one she ran away from!" Adele accused, her index finger pointing menacingly in his direction. "Why did you send her away? So that you could squander your manhood in the brothels?"

Philippe gulped the rest of his wine, then wiped a hand across his chin and set the cup aside. To Sully he said, "Shall I make a pact with my mother, bishop? Shall I promise to give up whoring if she does the same?"

Sully's lips twitched and his voice was stern. "She is your mother, Philippe, whatever she has done. Because of that she deserves your respect."

Adele spun around, blustering. "Whatever *I* have done? Now you accuse me? I am not the one in question here! I'm not the one who has turned my back on our family!"

Before Sully could respond Philippe snapped at her, "You turned your back on me the day that I was born! All you could ever think about was yourself, and how many pretty boys your wiles could attract!"

"A fair assessment of yourself, I'd say!"

"Enough of this!" It was Sully, finally provoked to anger by their exchange. "Please," he said, his voice pitched at its normal level once more, "there is no need for recriminations."

"There *is* a need," Adele kicked at the table leg with a slippered foot. "I have the right to know why my son is throwing his life away."

"*My* life?" Philippe sneered, "What about yours? You've always done exactly as you wished, lived as you pleased—you've no right to point a finger at me."

Adele came closer, nearly tripping over the hem of her skirt. "Listen to me," she said, and her voice trembled with emotion. "I've made my share of mistakes, but I've also had my share of troubles. I buried my husband, my best-beloved brother, and my lover. I have lost my daughter to a place as far away as death. I have withstood your abuses, the wars against my family, the threats to take away my lands. But through it all I never let myself fall into the state you are in. At least I can say that for myself!"

Philippe raised his arm as if to strike her, but he heard Sully's gasp, and let his hand fall limply into his lap. "Leave me alone, Mother," he growled, "leave me alone, both of you. I've had enough of your smug disapproval for one day. Get out."

"I'll get out," Adele answered, "but first let me say this: the bishop may be concerned for the state of your soul, but my interest is more practical. There are at least a hundred sealed dispatches upstairs in the library, awaiting your attention. I've seen them myself! Your counselors are turned away every day; the whole business of government is falling apart, while you waste yourself with drink and prostitutes. For God's sake, Philippe, if you care nothing for your own responsibilities, at least give them over to the care of someone who does!"

"Get out of here!" Philippe snarled and threw his henap in her direction. It struck the heavy pennon of her sleeve and rolled spinning at her feet. Adele kicked it to the corner of the room and then strode to the door. To Sully she said, "I knew he wouldn't listen. He's never in all his life listened to anything I've had to say. Let him do as he pleases." She gave a last glance toward her son. "Do as you like. Drink! Whore! Crawl home each morning! I'm finished with you." She flung the door open, then slammed it at her back.

Sully covered his eyes with a wrinkled hand and Philippe felt ashamed. They meant well, his mother and the bishop, and he did owe something to them; at least he owed them an explanation. But it was useless because they would never understand. Philippe closed his eyes and saw a pool of blood upon the sand, and he saw Geoffrey: all his brilliance, wit and promise trampled into ruin.

Philippe stretched his injured leg and tested it with a little weight. It flared in pain and he quickly relaxed it. To Sully he said, "Have you finished with me, too, or is there more that you would say to me?"

The bishop raised his head. "And would you listen? I think, Philippe, though you may not credit it, that you need my counsel now as you never have before."

Anger and argument had become a reflex with him. "Counsel is not necessarily criticism."

"Have it your own way," the bishop answered, sounding weary. He rose with some difficulty and shuffled toward the door. Philippe watched him go. This seemingly ageless man would be seventy in a few years. Today he looked old, his shoulders stooped beneath the loose linen *dalmatic*. Pausing at the door he looked back at Philippe and there was sadness in his voice when he spoke. "In the past you have argued with me, but you have listened, too. I fear it is no longer so."

Philippe's voice trembled on the edge of an apology. "A little kindness would go a long way."

"Yes, for all of us," Sully answered with a pale smile. Then he closed the door quietly behind him.

Having driven away all company with his rudeness, Philippe was left alone to bear the pain of his wounded leg in silence. He sat without moving for a long time, wondering how he could ever find his way back to the life he'd known before. Geoffrey's death had changed so many things. It seemed impossible now to trust, feel tenderness, or love. If there was an answer, some way to dissolve the bitterness, Philippe did not know what it was or where it could be found.

He scarcely heard the timid knock on the door, the opening of it, the sound of uneven footsteps coming closer, so he was surprised when he looked up and saw Edythe standing a few feet away. She carried a wooden bowl beneath her arm, and her hands were full of linen cloths.

"What do you want?" he asked, mildly annoyed.

She was not bold enough to look him full in the face; instead she stared down at the tips of her shoes. "I heard the lord constable say you had injured your leg and not attended to it. I have brought something to soothe the pain."

Kindness instead of criticism. He beckoned her to come closer. "Very well. Let's see what you can do. Have you any talent with the healing arts?"

Edythe was blushing furiously though she struggled to remain calm. "Some, sire," she told him and knelt down beside the bench where he sat. The bowl and the cloths were placed on the floor, then she looked up at him with a shy smile. "Have you something I can use to cut?"

He drew his sword and handed it to her. Edythe laid it across her lap then began methodically to unwind his leather wrappings. When she had finished that she slit the left leg of his woollen braies from his thigh to below the knee. Even the slightest pressure of her hand caused him to wince and mutter a quiet oath. Edythe's eyes widened in alarm and she removed her hand.

Philippe relaxed a bit and managed a grin. "It hurts," he admitted.

"It is badly swollen," she responded, bending closer to examine the bruises, "but there is no tear in the skin. It requires a dressing of camphor and burdock root. Then I will bind it, but not too tightly." She extracted a handful of ointment from the bowl and carefully applied it to his knee. Her touch was gentle but practiced. Philippe thought her hand trembled a little.

"Is there something wrong?" he asked.

"Sire?" her brown eyes looked out from a thin, pale face.

"Are you afraid of me?"

"No, sire."

"Then why do you tremble?"

With her free hand Edythe tucked a long strand of brown hair behind her ear. "I only fear to cause you greater pain than you already suffer." She took up one of the cloths and laid it across the application, then with a longer piece of the linen made a bandage about the knee. "Is this too tight?" He shook his head. Skillfully she wound the wrappings about his leg, then secured it firmly with a knot. "There," she said and took her hands away, "that will reduce the swelling and help to ease the pain. Still, you should take care. Try not to walk on it for several hours."

"I'm not a cripple!" he snapped at her. As soon as he had said the words Philippe remembered her affliction and felt truly sorry. "Forgive me," he said, and laid a hand upon her shoulder, "I didn't mean to say that. You've been kind and I should be grateful. I'm afraid I haven't been myself for quite some time."

Once again her cheeks colored. "It is not my place to question you, my lord," she answered, gathering the unused cloths and bowl.

"Thank you for your help," he said. She nodded, smiled, and got awkwardly to her feet. She was already half way across the room when his voice turned her around. "What do you hear from your mistress?"

Edythe shook her head. "Nothing. But I am surprised she has stayed away so long."

"So am I," he answered.

She hesitated, feeling uneasy. "The dressing should be changed twice daily. Please send someone to fetch me when you wish it done."

"I shall." Then, as an afterthought, "Is my daughter well?"

"Very well," Edythe answered. "I take good care of her."

Out in the corridor Edythe leaned against the wall. She took a deep breath and closed her eyes. Beads of sweat shined on her forehead and she could not stop shaking. Six years at the palace, and today for the first time she had been alone with him, spoken to him with no one listening. The thrill overran her with so much force she felt close to fainting. For the next few hours Edythe was happier than she had ever been.

It was the third letter scribbled off in as many weeks, dispatched to London in the care of a special courier. In Caen Richard fretted, waiting for his father's answer. It was imperative that he and Henry meet face-to-face in Normandy. There was trouble.

Yet even if his terse messages spurred the English king to heed this new danger, it was doubtful he could make a successful crossing now. Since mid-November the coast of Normandy had been assailed by storms and God alone knew what conditions were at Dover.

Richard paced the floor of his room and waited, but he was worried. Perhaps the storms had kept his messages from even getting to England! Perhaps Henry had not yet heard that the

King of France was building a fortress on the fringe of the Normandy frontier which was close enough to attack Gisors in half a days' slow march! There had been news from Brittany, too: unwelcome news of rebellions as the Bretons declared all English law invalid in their land, and sang the praises of the King of France. Each day Constance's belly grew bigger, and when her child was born, and if it was a boy, Philippe's claim of wardship could presage trouble for the English. Henry had made it known that he thought Philippe's demand was unrealistic, and he would not give over custody of Geoffrey's posthumus child. But what if Philippe forced the issue? Constance trusted him; she hated the Plantagenets. It was just one more cause for worry.

Each day Richard paced the empty council room in apprehension, pouncing upon each dispatch as it was set before him. When Christmas came there was still no word from Henry.

Philippe spent the first week of December praying at St. Denis. He had ceased his debauchery as suddenly as he had begun it, and soon he would be ready to assume the old responsibilities of his life once more.

He fasted, took Absolution, prayed. He roamed among the tombs of his ancestors, and felt the wounds on his spirit slowly heal. This was all atonement of a sort, a way to purge himself of all the sins he had accumulated these past many weeks.

When Philippe returned to the city, Isabel was there. They made no personal reconciliation, though they greeted one another with public courtesy. That night Isabel went alone to her bed; Philippe went alone to his.

The following morning Philippe and Isabel and a small group of clerics made the customary pilgrimage to the abbey church of St. Germain-des-Prés, a mile from the palace, where the king and queen washed the feet of one thousand poorfolk.

Isabel was feeling weak that morning. Her skin was hot, yet her body shook with chills. Breath came with difficulty because her lungs ached. She had caught cold coming back from Champagne, and last night she had not slept well.

The ceremony lasted the entire day. The royal couple took turns kneeling before the lines of men and women, washing their scabby feet with linen cloths and dabbing them dry with lambswool. As a further show of charity after that was done, all the mendicants were given bread that had been sopped in warm goatsmilk.

During the ritual Philippe watched his wife with grudging admiration. She looked so beautiful and fragile in her black velvet bliaud, her pale hair shaped into a braided coil at the back of her neck. It was only now, looking at her, that he realized just how much he had missed her. How could he have sent her away? Blamed her? *Hated* her?

She was so tiny, like a child, and Philippe felt all his anger give way to sudden tenderness. He longed to hold her in his arms, to kiss away their four-month-old estrangement. If Isabel would only forgive him, he would never be unkind to her again!

It was early evening as they prepared to leave the abbey, and Philippe took hold of her hand. Isabel looked up at him, her face white and strained. He was about to say something when she gripped his hand fiercely and gasped, "Philippe, I think I'm going to faint...." She had barely finished speaking when she swayed, then fell limply into his arms.

At the palace Isabel was put into her own bed and covered with fur quilts. Giles de Jocelin, the king's physician, was called to attend her.

"She's very ill," he told Philippe. Edythe, who hovered nervously at the king's elbow, listened too. "It was foolish for her to go out into the cold today with such hot skin. It may be she has inflamed her lungs."

"She only returned to Paris yesterday," Philippe offered. "I didn't know she was sick. She said nothing to me."

Giles held up an onyx vial, then put it into Edythe's hand. "Give her to drink of this whenever she wakes. Remember that she must be kept well-bundled against the cold, otherwise the ague may set in. Tomorrow morning give her fruit juices piled with ice to cool her blood."

Edythe nodded gravely.

Philippe felt a rush of panic in his throat. "Is she going to die?" he asked.

The physician glanced toward the bed where Isabel lay tossing in delirium; he spoke in a hushed voice. "The queen is a very tiny person, and has a nervous disposition. For such women, illness saps strength very quickly. She has a propensity for fevers; you will recall I have treated her before. In the past she has always recovered her full vigor. But this time I do not know. I will see that she has all she needs, that is all I can do." He turned to Edythe. "You will administer to her when I am not here?"

"Of course."

Philippe touched Giles's sleeve. "You will stay at the palace to-night, and for as long as the queen needs you," he commanded, leaning toward the door and beckoning to Robert de Clermont, who stood in the corridor. "The lord constable will prepare a room for you. Should Isabel have need of your healing methods during the night, I want you close at hand."

The physician inclined his head in obedience. "I shall do exactly as you say."

When de Jocelin and Clermont had gone out Philippe turned to Edythe. "Oh God, I'm so afraid she's going to die," he said.

Edythe wanted to fling herself into his arms and comfort him. She had loved him since the first day she and Isabel had come to live in Paris. That love had grown greater with the passage of time, till now it was a desperate, secret joy within her breast. She would have done *anything* for him.

So now she tried to ease his worry over Isabel with gentle words and a soothing voice. "My lord, we will do all we can for her, and God shall do His part." She paused, herself uncertain. "I cannot believe that He would take her from us."

But he wasn't really listening to Edythe; he heard another voice, his own—the hateful accusations of the past ringing in his ears. How many times since Geoffrey's death hadn't he wished that Isabel had been the one to die instead? Now God was punishing Philippe's wickedness by threatening to take her after all! It was too horrible to bear.

Fear for Isabel led to concern for his daughter, and close to panic he instructed Edythe, "See to Jacquie-Marie. Isabel was with her for a while this morning and may have passed the illness on to her."

Edythe set the vial de Jocelin had given her on the queen's dressing table. "Be sure to administer the medicine if she wakes," she reminded him as she left the room.

When he could no longer hear Edythe's footsteps in the corridor, Philippe threw off his pellison and climbed into bed beside his wife. Cautiously he slipped his hands beneath the furs. Isabel's skin, always so soft, was hot and dry. Oh God she WAS dying!

Her lips moved soundlessly. *Stay with me, stay with me.*

He slept holding her, and dreamed. Her skin was hot, so was his; they were both burning, cast down into hell for their desires. High above them Geoffrey stood, pouring oil into the flames— and he was laughing.

The peacock feathers arrived in London after Christmas.

With them came Pope Urban's sanction for young Johnny's coronation as the King of Ireland. Henry was radiant with joy. At last he could hand his beloved, landless son a gift of some magnitude. With it would come a means to curb any assumptions Richard had of gaining the crown without a fight. A king of Ireland could become the King of England easily enough. Henry hoped that Richard would understand that, and remember.

There was a great procession in the abbey of West Minster on the first day of the year 1187. John's crown was laid upon the altar and blessed by the Bishop of London. The following week John was scheduled to be crowned, then sent off to Ireland to rule. All the arrangements were made, and John was gloating over his good fortune. Then something happened to disrupt it all.

Trouble in Normandy. Richard's frantic missives reached Henry's hands at last. The English king had been tucked away in London far too long and Philippe Capet had seen an opportunity in that absence. Henry was confused. Philippe had given back the Vexin without so much as an argument, now he was trying to forge a pathway into Normandy! What did it mean, or did he dare to ask?

It was possible the situation had been exaggerated; yes, there was always that chance. Richard was such an alarmist. But all the same *he could be right* and Henry didn't dare ignore the threat. He had to go back to France immediately.

John's coronation was quickly written off as Henry made plans to return to Normandy whenever safe passage could be arranged At Dover castle, high upon a hill above the water, the king and his entourage waited a week for the coastal storms to clear. Johnny sulked about the loss of his crown, until he found a

pretty laundress to comfort him. Henry sat by the fire in the
chilly council room and conferred with his advisers.

He had brought along his most useful counselors: three men
who had always helped him in the past. Godfrey was one; Godfrey the chancellor and bastard son. Henry was very fond of him,
liked to have him close at hand. Godfrey gave good advice and
he was one of the most loyal men in Henry's service. The Archbishop of Rouen, Walter of Coutances, was a wise old man, and
the Norman barons bowed easily beneath the power of his persuasion. It was possible Henry would have need of his subtle
rhetoric. William de Mandeville, the Earl of Essex, was one of the
king's closest friends. He had a crafty intelligence and was clever
at details.

These men were the brains of the English monarchy. Together
with them, with Richard, and the barons, Henry would dispense
with Capet's threat to pece along the Normandy border, if indeed there was a threat. For himself, Henry had doubts. Philippe
Capet was quite unlike his amiable father, it was true, but Henry
did not think him dangerous. He was just a boy! Henry Plantagenet did not tremble at the actions of a boy.

On the morning of the seventh day at Dover, following a
meagre breakfast and a hasty mass, Henry and his entourage set
sail for Aumâle.

No joyous Christmas feasting at the Cité palace. No festivities
of any kind as the year 1186 ended. Isabel was recovering, but it
would be weeks till she was strong enough to leave her bed. She
slept the days and nights away, oblivious to the gay sounds of
holiday merrymaking in the streets outside the palace.

Philippe celebrated a Christmas mass at St. Denis but it was the
only observance he made. He was kept busy with matters of administration; too busy to lament the lack of a Christmas court.

His months of idleness had produced a huge backlog of work.
There were charters to be written and signed. Plans for the pav-
ing of more city streets once warm weather came. Deeds of sale
for property—confiscated by the crown in lieu of taxes paid—to
be drawn and witnessed. And there was the constant matter of
raising money.

The Notre Dame building fund was waning as costs rose steadily for the project. Labor, materials, and the cost of importing

both were proving a terrific drain on the allocated budget. Philippe had settled upon a method of resolving that. He was bringing the Jews back to Paris. Jews were primarily merchants, and merchants meant money. Philippe required each returning Jew to pay a steep repatriation fee. The money was then transferred to the building fund. The king didn't care if his cathedral was built in part by contributions from unbelievers, so long as it *was* built.

But even as Philippe kept busy, administrating the needs and commerce of his city, he was concentrating on a far wider landscape. Things were happening out there in the great world. Henry Plantagenet had come back to Normandy, alarmed at the presence of French troops on his border. Philippe had anticipated that; invited it even. It was time to let the king of England know just how matters stood between them; how things were now and would be in the future.

Henry was losing control, Philippe could sense it, and he smiled with satisfaction at the thought. It wouldn't be long now —not long before the son of Louis Capet could recapture every inch of land that had been stolen by the English and still more after that. It was inevitable. It was justice. It was all Philippe could think of.

There was only one thing on earth he wanted more.

She was only dozing and woke suddenly when the darkness of his shadow covered her. "Philippe?" she asked sleepily and reached up to take his hand.

It was impossible to see his face, but the sound of his voice was pleasant to her ears. "Are you feeling stronger?" he asked. "I've been so busy in these past few weeks I haven't had the chance to look in on you, but Edythe tells me you are much improved."

"Yes," she answered, "I am better now, but for a time I believed that I was going to die." Isabel scooed over on the bed as if to make room for him, but her eyes still kept him at a distance. She could have banished the memory of the past few months by merely opening her arms to him but Isabel didn't want to. *He should be made to understand what he had done to her.* All the bitterness and doubt and separation that had gone on between them since Geoffrey's death had left ugly scars, and scars, if touched, still hurt.

He knew what she was feeling. "I was worried," he said, and Isabel looked back at him, confused, sad, slow to forgive. They had played this scene so many times, both of them stubborn and resisting, but in the end there was always an unspoken truce of passion. Feeling it now, Philippe grabbed her by the shoulders and pulled her close, their lips touching. "I want you, Isabel," he gasped, "I want you."

Her pride rebelled in a sudden gush of anger and Isabel struggled out of his arms. "But you didn't want me last September! Then you would have *liked* for me to die. And like the fool I am, I would have gladly given up my life to make you happy. But no more, Philippe. No more..."

Philippe's hands were tight on her shoulders, cruel and caressing. "I don't care about what happened then. It all seems very long ago. You want me. Why won't you admit it?"

She looked up at him with self-pitying eyes. "As you once said to me: I'm here, isn't that good enough?"

"No," he answered and slid his hands around her throat. He could feel her heavy pulse beneath the pressure of his thumbs.

Isabel didn't move. She was afraid of his strength and yet excited by it. Her voice was as small and meek as she could make it. "You're hurting me."

He did not take his hands away. "Where were you all the time you were away from Paris?"

There was something ominous in his voice, something subtle that she could not miss. "I was in Beaujeu with my sister," she answered quietly. "I told you that."

"And where else?"

Isabel tried to pry his fingers from her throat. He *did* know! Someone had told him or he had guessed. "I went to Champagne, to Troyes, for the Autumn fair," she admitted.

Philippe relaxed his grip a little, but his voice still threatened her. "You were with my cousin, weren't you?"

"Henri?" The name caught guiltily in her throat.

"*Were* you with him?"

She shook her head violently. "Not *with* him, not the way you mean it. I stayed at his chateau in Troyes, a family courtesy, that's all."

"I don't believe you," he said and took his hands away.

"It's true!" The conviction in her voice rang so strongly she nearly believed the lie herself.

Philippe moistened his thumb and slid it back and forth across her bottom lip. "I know you, I know your ways."

She drew back a little but her eyes were bold. "I did nothing. Nothing wrong." Isabel's fingers stroked the angry marks at her throat. "And if the stories your mother tells of your behavior while I was away are true, that is more than *you* can say!"

She cringed too late and he slapped her, flinging her back on the bed. "Whore, whore," he taunted, standing over her.

They had suffered through many times of crisis in the past, but Isabel had never known him to be as cruel as this. She peered up at him through a veil of disordered hair, tears shining in her eyes. "How can you treat me this way? How can you act as if *I* am the one to blame for all the trouble between us? I have done everything I could to make you happy. But now, like so often in the past, you turn your back on me when I need you most!"

The tone of her voice was so honest, so utterly lacking in affectation, it was impossible to pull a cynical face or hide the impulse which told him now to take her in his arms. Isabel was sweetness itself! Why was it always so difficult to be kind to her?

Wretchedness only served to intensify her beauty, and when she looked at him the sense of betrayal was too strong to face. *Oh, Isabel!* He fell into her arms weeping—speaking her name over and over like a plea.

Whatever they had done to hurt one another in these last months while they were apart no longer mattered; *all* that had gone before was meaningless. What love could not make right again, at least passion could erase.

Their tears and sweat mingled, giving strong scent to the perfume on her skin. Lips, arms, legs—Isabel clung to him with every part of her. She knew nothing, felt everything, wanted more.

His strength and her desire were overwhelming, and the power of it threatened to damn her or kill her, or both. Each gasp that came from Isabel's lips seemed to be a living thing, her own life spewing out as if he was taking more than just her body. Her love, her mind, her soul—everything was his.

"Give me a son, Isabel," Philippe cried out as her sharp nails flayed his skin. "Give me a son!"

All the promises of heaven and salvation paled beside the human thrill of flesh on flesh. She cried out with her own fulfillment, and an instant later Philippe bathed her body in his warmth. Their forgiveness was complete.

"I never want to be apart from you again," she sighed, and raised her face to lick the beads of sweat from his beard.

Twice more that night he took her, and it was dawn before he left the room. Isabel was asleep by then, a death-like sleep of bliss and exhaustion and no dreams. As she slept the bruises darkened on her skin.

𝒮CRAPS OF FOOD littered the council table. Empty plates and half-filled henaps glinted in the light of a dying fire. Voices which had earlier been pitched in tones of reason were now raspy and argumentative, giving evidence of weary men who had been closeted together for too many hours.

They had been convened since early morning and now it was evening. The winter sun had set unceremoniously an hour ago. At the far end of the table sat Henry Plantagenet, hunched over a stack of unrolled maps and other papers. He looked rumpled and ill-slept. Clustered about him were Archbishop Walter of Coutances, Earl of Essex William de Mandeville, and two of the king's sons, John and Godfrey.

Across the room from the others stood a third son, handsome Richard Plantagenet, the remaining member of the assembly. He stood sullenly before the fire, the bright color of his hair rivaling the thick gold chains about his neck. His broad back was turned toward the others, and his purpose was greater than a need to warm his hands and face. As long as Richard didn't look at them, it was easier for him to ignore what they were saying. Not that it mattered.

Talk, talk, talk! What good was this endless wrangling? They had been at Aumâle for two weeks and nothing of any importance had been decided yet. Squabbling was the business of clerks and clerics, not soldiers! Richard's nature rebelled against the inactivity more and more as each day passed. It was mid-February and the snow pressed close against the fortress. Hunting, even riding for pleasure, was impossible in this weather. Richard felt as though he'd been sealed into a tomb. Here they sat, locked in stubborn arbitration over minor points, while the danger of an invasion from the south grew every day.

Henry slammed his fist on the table and Richard started at the sound. "I don't understand it!" the king blustered and jabbed a thick finger against the map which lay before him. "Our last reports say Philippe Capet had one thousand of his men no closer to the Normandy border than Chantilly. Now we hear rumors that he has moved them and two thousand more as far south as Blois. How could he do that in so short a time? Is it Normandy he wants, or Anjou?" Henry spit upon the floor to show his rage.

The archbishop shifted in his chair and cleared his throat. "Whichever one he wants my lord, an invasion at this time and in this weather would be inconceivable."

Godfrey bent low over Henry's shoulder, squinting at the map for a moment. Then he straightened up, snapping his fingers at John who lolled in disinterest at the other end of the table. "Bring us another candle, boy," Godfrey ordered.

Richard turned his head in time to catch the knowing look John passed him. Neither of them had any love for their half-brother. Richard merely thought Godfrey a fool, but John was deadly jealous of him. He despised all rivals for Henry's affection, and Godfrey was the greatest rival of all. Pouting, John set another candle down before them, lingering at his father's elbow for a word of thanks. When none came he went back to his place at the other end of the table and slouched in his chair, barely listening to what was being said.

"Perhaps these aren't the same troops," Godfrey pointed to the curving line that divided Blois from Tours. "Perhaps these," his finger moved northward, stopping at the inked inscription *Vexin*, "are the men your son Geoffrey raised prior to his unfortunate end." He allowed himself a secret little smile. Godfrey never tired of reminding Henry that his legitimate sons were treacherous.

His attitude was so transparent it made Richard want to vomit. From across the room he bellowed, "For Christ's sake Godfrey is your brain between your horse's ass? The men that my brother Geoffrey raised were mercenaries, men who fight for pay and pay alone. They don't stand their post for six months out of loyalty." He stamped a spitting ember into blackness with his boot.

The archbishop tapped at the map with his knuckles. "I think perhaps they *have* been paid. It's not unlikely Philippe Capet would seek to keep them in his service, especially if he is planning an invasion."

"He's planning something," Henry mumbled. "What are we going to do about it?"

William of Essex clasped his hands behind his head and leaned back in the chair. "There isn't much we can do in this weather. Actually, Henry, I wouldn't worry, not till spring comes. Capet's no general, not on his own. His best adviser is the Count of Flanders, and we know he is in Soissons now. As long as those two are kept apart there's no great danger to us."

John dangled a bit of beef between his fingers and tucked it into his mouth. All this talk of invasions and moving troops was boring, but de Mandeville's comment had given him an idea. John smiled engagingly and directed his words to Henry. "Maybe we should send soldiers to Soissons to capture the Count of Flanders. That would keep him out of Capet's reach."

He had thought it was a brilliant plan, but the others appraised him with collective annoyance. "This is serious, my boy," the archbishop muttered, "we aren't playing games here." To the king he said, "How many men does Capet have, do we know?"

"It's hard to say," Henry answered, and propped his feet upon the table. "What matters most is how quickly he can move them."

"What matters most," Richard corrected him, "is *where* they are. This new information about troops near Tours is a puzzle. I think we may have misread the situation, and it is Tours, not Normandy, which is in danger. For myself—"

"For *myself*," Henry interrupted him, "I am here because of you. You brought me here with your constant belly-aching and your urgent letters. You tell me Normandy is in trouble, and I come running. Now you reverse yourself. What help is that to me?"

In defense of himself Richard shouted back, "I'll tell you if you give me the chance to explain." He expelled a long breath and wiped the moisture from his brow. "When I wrote to you I did not know about the troops at Blois and Chartres. I was certain

Capet was after Normandy. I still believe he is. But I think he plans to make his first move in the south and that means Tours, perhaps even Anjou. God knows his ambition could embrace them both, and Normandy."

Henry considered that for a moment, then dismissed it. "No," he replied, "I don't think so. Philippe is much like his father— always envying me my most prized domain. It's Normandy he's after. I know how that boy thinks."

Insensitive bastard. Richard tossed aside his empty henap in disgust. "You *don't* know how he thinks! You don't know anything about him! Face facts; this isn't your precious Louis we are dealing with. He can't be trusted—I've been telling you that for years. He's a threat to you, can't you see that?"

"Threat..." Henry waved the word away.

"Yes!" Richard barked. "Philippe would piss in the Sacred Chrism if it would buy him one single town in our domains!"

Henry's face went livid. "And just what do you know about him, about his methods? He's no friend of yours."

"That's right," Richard countered, "and he's no friend to you either. I don't claim to know him well but I've watched him since he came to the throne six years ago. He alienated all his family, everyone! He doesn't care who he uses as a foil against his enemies. I've never liked him, never trusted him. Believe me, Father, I know what I say. I have a soldier's instinct about these things."

Before Henry could respond to that, Godfrey stepped forward. "I think you should remember who you are talking to," he mouthed the words priggishly and stole a glance at Henry to see what his reaction was. The king looked up; a tight smile of appreciation for Godfrey, a warning expression in his eyes for Richard.

John yawned noisily into his fist. "Are we finished?" he asked. "If I don't get some fresh air I'm going to pass out."

"Go ahead," Richard muttered, "we won't miss you."

"Shut up!" Henry yelled, and shoved the porringer to the floor. "I'm sick of this continual bickering. We have important work to accomplish."

"Well we've been here all day, *every* day, for two weeks and nothing's been decided yet," John sulked, but nobody was listening.

John was a petulant, spoiled young man but he was sensitive, too, and Henry's attitude bruised his feelings. It was always this way when there were other people around, and most especially Godfrey. Whenever *he* was there John found himself displaced in his father's affections, and that was unbearable because he reveled in Henry's love and favoritism. How much nicer it had been in England when he and Henry had spent so many hours together, sharing the same plate, the same wine, the same women. That was the way John liked his father best and in later years he would remember him that way.

He nodded, nearly dozing, and de Mandeville cleared his throat. "If Prince John is tired, I'm sure we would have no objection to his leaving...."

"Prince John is *not* tired," Henry snapped, "and he is not leaving. No one is, until we settle this."

Richard came to the table and sat down, poking his fingers amid the discarded bits of beef. His body ached for want of exercise, and his eyes were tired. "I don't see what there is to settle, Henry," he said, then stuck a piece of meat between his teeth and chewed it. "When this weather clears we should mobilize our forces and move south to protect Tours and Anjou. It is not a problem of troops. It is a problem with Philippe himself. As soon as possible you should meet with him in person. Let him know that England will not tolerate his interference. Stand up to him."

"I don't need you to tell me how to deal with a king!" Henry shouted, "I was leading my mother's troops against King Stephen ten years before I made you in your mother's womb!"

"A slight exaggeration," Richard muttered, tight-lipped.

"If I might speak," Godfrey interceded, "I think the king knows best how to approach this problem. Whatever judgment he makes is good enough for me."

Richard glared at his half-brother and hated him. "No one asked you," he said.

A dull pain had settled on either side of Henry's forehead and he tried to soothe it away with the gentle pressure of his fingertips, making tiny circular patterns at his temples. Rage was costly and he felt the effects of it more keenly each year. In two weeks he would be fifty-four, and that was old. He looked Richard fully in the face. "William is right," he said, trying to sound reasonable. "Capet can't do anything in this weather. Let's make our plans, then when the weather has cleared..."

"There is more at stake here than the weather," Richard cut into the middle of Henry's sentence. "Our biggest problem is Philippe. You must not appear to be afraid of him."

"Afraid?" The utterance was somewhere between a laugh and a snarl. "Why should I be afraid of him? He's just a boy."

The force of Richard's fist against the table sent some of the maps skittering to the floor. "He's not a boy! Blood of Christ, Henry, he's not fifteen years old any more! He's a treacherous, devious man. He'll do anything he can to bring you down."

Stubbornly Henry defended his position. "What makes you the authority on his character? I've had more dealings with him in the past than you have. He's headstrong, I'll admit, and ambitious. But he's reasonable. I've helped him in the past, many times. He'll remember that."

Richard wanted to scream his frustration, but he only clenched his fists together in his lap. "Was he remembering your kindness while he and Geoffrey plotted the overthrow of Normandy? You've seen the proofs from our men in Brittany; you know what Philippe and Geoffrey were up to. If Geoffrey hadn't got himself killed in Paris they may have been able to pull it off. Do you think Philippe is going to forget those ambitions just because you pat him on the back and give him a little fatherly advice?"

Henry stroked his beard in silence. "It was Geoffrey who instigated that," he said at last. "He was trying to get at me by encouraging Philippe's ambitions." He folded his arms across his chest. "Geoffrey was always a troublemaker."

It was all so sad and funny and so typical of his father. Richard's strong mouth twisted in an ironical smile. "That's right, blame it on Geoffrey. It makes it so much easier, now that he's dead and can't defend himself."

Henry's voice was hard. "You know what he was like. He would have done anything to hurt me."

"Yes," Richard agreed. "I should know. He dumped enough shit on me."

The pain in Henry's head was like a burning rock behind his eyes. He rested his elbows on the table and leaned forward, squinting at his son. "We both know what Geoffrey was. And I say that without his influence Philippe would never have concocted such a plan."

The thousand perfidities of Geoffrey's nature replayed themselves in Richard's mind. "Yes," he said sadly, "Geoffrey was the
devil's handmaiden and the world is better off without him. But
you are blind to the truth. You always have been. So long as you
can blame your sons for all the evils done to you, there's no need
to look elsewhere. Don't you see what traps you lay for yourself?
Blame your sons, blame your wife! Blame everyone except those
who are most guilty! You see conspiracy in every act of every
person where it least exists, but when it is right before your face
you ignore it and call it friendship. Jesus, Henry, open your
eyes!"

William de Mandeville covered his face and the archbishop
turned his head away. *This bitterness between Henry and his sons
would destroy them all some day.* How many wasted hours had they
endured in silence, while King Henry and his sons exhumed
every dread act of the past?

They were like two stags locked together by the horns: Henry
and Richard staring at one another, alone in their anger. "You
have no right to speak to me that way," Henry blustered, spewing
his beard with spit. "You've been party to a few rebellions against
me yourself!"

John sipped nervously at his wine, wishing that the two of
them would stop. He didn't like to hear the fighting. It recalled
bad memories of dark rooms at night and tears; shouts and accusations and whispered plots of betrayal; of wars and scheming
older brothers, and a mother taken away in chains when he was
hardly old enough to say her name. He wished the ugly pictures
in his mind would go away, but only drink did that, or the soft
feel of a woman's skin.

Richard's voice shook with emotion and self-pity. "I've paid for
every blow I struck against you, Henry. I've apologized and knelt
before you asking pardon, but you'll never let me forget! The
past is all that counts with you. You drag it out at every opportunity, reading out the list of your misfortunes like God's book of
judgment." He got to his feet, kicking the chair aside. He was
disgusted with the situation, with himself for allowing Henry's
words to hurt him. "I'm sick to puking with all of this," he mumbled. "Let's just forget it."

"No, let's *not* forget it!" Henry shot back. "You brought it up.
You finish it!"

"Finish what?" Richard bellowed. "You don't want to hear anything I have to say. I tell you, Philippe Capet is an enemy, but all you can see is what your sons have done wrong."

"With good cause."

"Jesus!" Richard shouted. "Henry, have you forgotten why we are here? The King of France is planning to invade some part of our domain: south, north—it makes no difference. The most important thing is that we crush him and his ambitions before it is too late!"

They were startled by the sound of another voice: both Henry and Richard had almost forgotten there were other people in the room. Archbishop Walter coughed into his hand and then he said, "You make it sound like doomsday, Richard."

"It may well be," Richard answered, rubbing the sweat from his beard. He made a gallant attempt to control himself. "Look, all of us have the same idea or we wouldn't be here in the first place. Philippe Capet is about to start a war against us! That much is obvious. He's no fool; he clearly feels that he is ready. That should tell us something."

It was all too much: the worry, the fighting, the incessant recriminations. Once Henry had been a match for anything but now it seemed so futile. But he couldn't weaken; not in front of Richard because that's what Richard wanted. With a grunt Henry took up his henap and slaked his thirst. To Richard he said, "I'm no fool either. I'm not afraid of Philippe, and for good reason. This act of his, pushing his troops about the map, is just his way of challenging me. It's a bluff, no more. As soon as we make a show of strength he'll gather up his men and run back to Paris."

Richard fingered the gold medallion at his chest. "I don't think so."

"At least we can be glad he no longer has an ally in Prince Geoffrey," de Mandeville said, sounding proud of his logic.

"It doesn't make any difference," Richard answered. "If Geoffrey *did* plan the overthrow of Normandy himself, who do you think was beside him all the while, whispering words of encouragement into his ear?"

"You're a soldier," Henry taunted, "but you talk like a girl! Maybe you don't have the balls to go against Capet, but I do. I handled Louis and I can handle him. If you weren't so damned anxious to prove you're right about Philippe, you'd know that."

It all had such a familiar sound. Anger had faded to a sick feeling of discouragement and suddenly Richard felt very close to tears. "I am right," he answered, "but by the time you come to understand that it may be too late—perhaps for all of us." He held up his hands as if to dismiss himself from the entire situation. "Do what you wish. Sit here and debate with these men who are afraid to call you wrong. Bully them with your office. Talk all night. Talk all week. But remember this, Henry, it won't change anything. You are cosseting your own destruction. You don't need my help." He turned and began walking toward the door.

"Sit down!" Henry barked, "I haven't finished with you."

Richard halted abruptly and his spine went rigid, but he didn't turn around. "I have. I won't stare straight ahead as you walk blindly into the trap Philippe Capet has set for you. Settle it yourselves. I want no part of it. Goodnight."

"Richard!" Henry shouted, and then louder, "RICHARD!!"

The word echoed back upon the closing of the door. The king lunged forward, striking the table over and over with his fist. Godfrey stood at Henry's elbow, looking down at him with pitying eyes. Walter and de Mandeville said nothing.

John bowed his head and fiddled with his signet ring in silence. The memories were alive inside of him; boiling, and they tasted like vomit in his mouth. He laid his head upon his folded arms and closed his eyes.

From the chapel below her bedroom, Constance could hear the sounds of Easter mass being celebrated by the household as she held her newborn son to her breast. A sense of calm settled over her mind and body. The pain was over now; forgotten, and weariness was sweet as she suckled her baby boy. This was her hope, her future. Someday he would inherit all that was hers. Nothing, no one, could take that promise from her.

The midwives bustled about the room, oddly quiet in their tasks, but Constance was aware of only one other person in the room. At the foot of the bed stood William Desroches, her chancellor. Constance smiled at him and offered her right hand as he came closer. He squeezed it in a firm grip of admiration. "You are a brave woman, Constance," he told her. "All of Brittany salutes you for your courage."

Faint tears of appreciation stung her eyes. Throughout these past few months William had been her constant friend, her bulwark. It had not been easy for her to carry the child of a dead man beneath her breast. Grief at her husband's death had been further complicated by the interference of Henry Plantagenet. He had sent a never-ending set of written directives to her, insisting she forswear her allegiance to Philippe Capet once her child was born, and promising war if she did not.

The King of France was not particularly to her liking: Constance wondered at his motives, as she wondered at the motives of all men. But he had been her husband's friend, and because of that she trusted him. For the time being her son would be safer in the legal care of France than England. But someday this tiny child would hold Brittany, and hopefully when that day came he would owe himself to neither sovereign. She felt she could not wait till that day came. It would be her own liberation from a lifetime of political indebtedness.

In his communiques Henry had made it known that if her child was born a boy he should be named for him. Yet another Henry! Constance had thrown each letter into the fire and watched it burn. Let Henry Plantagenet burn as well, cast into hell where he belonged! Her child would not be named for him. Her child would bear a name that marked him as one of his own people.

Smiling weakly she looked up at William, then down at her child. Already she loved him with such a fierceness it made her heart ache. "Arthur," she murmured sweetly, "I shall call him Arthur."

"Welcome to Paris, my lord of Mons."

Isabel smiled up at Gilbert as he took the hand she held out to him. He kissed the fingers, lingering over the delicate skin he'd come to love so long ago. Then he released her hand and stepped back to admire the changes in her.

Isabel was more radiant than he remembered.

This was no longer the nymph who had enthralled and tempted him. Isabel was truly a woman now; seventeen, and at the zenith of her beauty. She'd grown taller, though not by much, and her splendid figure was displayed in a tight-fitting azure chainse with clinging neckline and low-hanging girdle. She was voluptuous, but with delicate bones that marked her as an aristo-crat. The essence of her sensuality, which he so well remem-bered, had been enhanced by marriage and motherhood.

He had never wished so much that she belonged to him.

It was early May. Two weeks ago at Mons, Gilbert had received a letter from Isabel. She was carrying her husband's child once more and this one would be a son. She knew it with all the in-stincts of a woman. Further assurance had come to her in the nature of a dream, wherein angels had drawn a boy child from her womb and wrapped it in a cloth of gold.

Obsessed by the knowledge that she carried Philippe's heir be-neath her breast, Isabel had decided the time for repentance was at hand. She needed to cleanse herself with God's forgiveness in order to be ready for the great honor awaiting her in October when she bore Philippe's son.

There was a problem though, for Isabel could not trust one priest or other member of the clergy in all of France with her secret transgressions. The admissions of the confessional were private, yes—but she was too shrewd to think that the informa-tion might not, in some way, be used against her. Philippe knew some of it but he did not know all, and that was the way she wished to keep it. A few pieces of silver to line the almoner of an untrustworthy priest—that was all it would take to bring her down completely.

But Gilbert would keep her secrets. Whatever she revealed to him would be for their ears alone, and God's. Isabel could have her forgiveness and her privacy too, and Philippe need never know. She explained all this to Gilbert as she led him by the arm to the private chapel in her room.

He told her he would do exactly as she asked.

She prayed silently for a quarter of an hour while Gilbert donned his *chasuble* and set out the holy tools of his work. When the time for confession came, Isabel knelt before him and told all there was to know.

When she had finished, Gilbert absolved her with Christ's blood and body and administered a blessing on her cheek with holy water. She hugged her prayer beads to her heart, kissed the hem of Gilbert's *gonne,* and knew that she was saved.

* * *

Henry gathered up one thousand of his Norman knights and took them south. Since the early days of May, King Philippe's men had swept through Berry like a fire gone wild. Now they lined the borders of Maine and Tours, all the way south to the city of Chateauroux, in preparation to march on Aquitaine.

The King of England had tried to forestall events with all weapons of diplomacy which had been so useful to him in the past. In April the two kings had met at Gué St. Remy where Philippe had made deliberately excessive demands. He claimed legal custody of Brittany and the infant Arthur; the right to re-take the Vexin, the complete removal of all English troops within fifty miles of any border of the royal French *demesne,* or any fiefs held in trust by the Crown. There was yet another condition: Richard would marry Alais Capet immediately, or all her dowry —lands and money—would be returned at once.

Philippe could afford to make the dictates: everything was in his favor. He had assembled a tremendous army, and there was a promise of more men from the Imperial forces in Lombardy. All of Europe was watching: waiting, cautious, unwilling to cross the French king lest they regret it later.

In mid-May the Count of Flanders deserted to King Henry's camp. He had his reasons, and in any case it was but a small annoyance to Philippe. Flanders would be back, once he found Henry had nothing worthwhile to offer him. Meanwhile the threat of open war was growing. The French were in position to attack a half-dozen English strongholds on the continent, and it was doubtful that Henry would be able to hold them back.

Richard had been right all along.

The boy was a man now, and he would not be stopped.

Henry flung Philippe's most recent message to the ground. "I don't understand how this happened!" he wailed. "I should have stayed in England and got clear of this mess."

Richard slumped into a camp chair beside his father. "I hardly think that would have been possible. Wherever you had chosen to be, 'this mess' as you call it, would still be upon us." He glanced uneasily at Henry. "I did try to warn you."

Yes he had. But it made no difference now. Two days ago King

Henry's forces (led by de Mandeville, Richard, Godfrey and John) had flooded into the city of Chateauroux, and driven back Philippe's men a few miles to the south—a meagre victory. Now both armies were encamped on either side of the Indre River. The knights and other fighting men waited upon the word of their commanders, while the commanders sent terse messages back and forth across the lines, and schemed in secret behind the cover of their tents.

"Philippe's demands are preposterous!" Henry grumbled. "How can he dare to claim Brittany—and my grandson—for himself?"

"If the reports from Brittany can be believed, the barons are more than willing to name Philippe as *custos* for the duchy," Richard answered. "If that will keep him at bay it might bear our consideration."

"No!" Henry shouted, leaping to his feet. "I will not give up what is mine to him without a fight! If you tell me to do otherwise you are no help to me." He threw a woollen cloak about his shoulders and went to the edge of the tent. He stood there for a long time, his gloved hand holding the canvas flap aside, letting a little of the spattering rain fall at his feet. He was staring across the black line of the river at a landscape he could not see, wondering when everything had begun to go so wrong, and why he was powerless to stop it.

Behind him he heard Richard smoothing out the discarded piece of paper; then, just as Henry had done, he threw it aside. The two of them were silent for a long while. There was very little left for them to say that had not already been spoken.

Henry cleared his throat. "Perhaps we could fulfill one of Capet's conditions." He turned abruptly, facing Richard. "If you were to marry Alais..."

That was as far as he got. "No," Richard shouted back, "I will not marry Alais and you know the reason why I will not. Do you really think I would shame myself with such a union? Do you take me for a fool?"

"She *is* your fiancée," Henry reminded him.

"She is *your* mistress! John's too, no doubt; the two of you share everything."

Even in the dimness Henry's eyes looked tired and bloodshot. "Don't be such a prig. What do you care if the girl's no virgin?

You don't like women anyway. You don't even have to bed with her if you're too dainty for the task. Just do your duty as a prince and marry her."

"No!" Richard shouted, "forget it. You'll have to make some other bargain with Philippe."

"Very well," said Henry, hostility in his voice. "I'll find another way."

Long after Richard had gone to his own tent, Henry lay wakeful, trying to ignore the pains that ran like scars up and down his legs. Oh, for the softness of his bed at Chinon and the comfort of a woman's arms! He was too old to bear the rugged indignities of a soldier's life.

Yet here he was, and it was too late to leave. That would give Philippe his victory no matter what happened on the field. Everyone would say, *Henry is afraid.* And they would be right.

But perhaps there was still time to avert the unhappy conclusion he had so often visualized these past few weeks. It was possible there would be no battle...but that would mean bowing to Capet's ridiculous demands. Was there another way? Henry was tired, too tired to rationalize his situation. If only there was some solution. Perhaps. *Perhaps.*

Sleep was coming, stealing into his mind like a guilty friend returning. Henry rolled over on his side and pulled a wool coverlet close about his ears. He was shivering; even wearing his sheepskin bliaud and covered with the blanket he was shivering.

It was so cold for May.

Richard was with his father the following afternoon when Godfrey came to announce two visitors from the French camp.

"Show them in," Henry answered brusquely, then when Godfrey had gone out he turned to Richard. "Stay here and observe my method. I was awake most of the night trying to come up with a solution to our situation—"

His words were interrupted as Godfrey ducked back into the tent and held the flap aside for two tall, well-dressed men. Richard recognized them both: William of Rheims and Theobold of Chartres.

Henry greeted them with a solemn nod of his head, though he did not rise. To Godfrey he said, "Bring chairs for the Count of Chartres and his Grace of Rheims..."

Richard stood with his back turned, symbolically distancing himself from the situation. The men seated themselves with dignity. Theobold spoke first.

"We come as envoys from our royal nephew as you requested. It is Philippe's understanding that you have a proposal for us."

Henry bowed his head and swallowed the lump of emotion in his throat. "I have only this to say, and ask you to carry back my words to your king: For many years I have been a sinner, but now it is my will to repent of all my wrongs and reconcile myself with God. In order to achieve this I wish to travel to the Holy Land to fight against the pagans who assail our faith. I cannot do this unless the king of France will grant me a truce in order that I might fulfill my pious obligation without fear of sieges by his armies while I am away. Tell this to your king also: that if he will not grant me two years' grace in which to accomplish this, it is *he* who must answer for the state of my soul before God." Having said this speech, Henry leaned back in his chair and covered his face with quivering hands.

William and Theobold looked at one another, passing unuttered thoughts between them. They had not been swayed by Henry's words: this was obviously a bluff and it was difficult for either of them to pretend belief. William coughed to gain the king's attention. "I shall tell Philippe what you have said. But I cannot guarantee his answer, nor will my brother or I try to influence his mind." He rose, and Theobold with him. "In any case my lord, the state of your soul is your responsibility."

With gracious bows to Henry and his sons, the two men left the tent. Richard and Godfrey stood by in silence, neither of them able to meet the king's unhappy eyes. He seemed diminished, a waning candle in the wind. He had humiliated himself, thrown himself on the pity of Philippe Capet and his uncles, and now there was nothing more to say.

Henry sat for a while, hands covering his face. All at once he began to shake, then sob, his body heaving till the cloak he wore fell from his shoulders onto the muddied ground.

Philippe had just finished his bath and was dressing when William and Theobold returned. He sat upon the camp bed, stretching out his long legs as he fitted fine *chamois* boots on his feet while his uncles told him what the English king had said.

"Don't tell me you believed him," Philippe laughed when they had finished. "That tale has grown as grey as he has, and well it might. He used it often enough to extract promises of a truce from poor old Louis."

William waved an artistic hand to intercede. "The point should be well taken nonetheless. Henry is within his legal rights—"

"Don't speak to me of his rights," Philippe snapped as he pulled his bliaud on. "He is getting only a little of what he deserves in return for all the things he did to hurt my father. You both know that; you've said it often enough in the past. Don't turn weak-bellied on me now and expect that I should make things easy for him." He tossed the mantle about his shoulders and stood before them, scowling darkly.

"What you say is right," Theobold agreed, "but my counsel to you is this: wait and see if he fulfills his promise. If he does not, then challenge him in the field. If he does keep his word, then you have bought us all some time."

Philippe sat down before the table which had been laid for him and indicated they should do the same. "I'm not the one who needs time," he told his uncle. "That is Henry's worry. Let him meet *my* terms."

William mumbled a hurried blessing over the food before turning the conversation back to politics. "He will in time my boy. But there's no need to hurry things along." He broke off a piece of bread and handed it to Philippe. "Be patient."

The king dipped his bread into a bowl of honey and tasted it before he spoke. "Are you saying that I should withdraw our troops?"

William and Theobold exchanged glances. "Yes," the bishop said at last, "for the time being."

Philippe eyed them wordlessly, then drew the dagger from his waist and began to cut his meat with it. "Why?" he asked.

"For one thing it will save a great many lives," William explained.

Philippe choked a little on his food as he gave a small laugh. "Is that reason enough?"

William nodded gravely. "I think so."

"Philippe," Theobold said as he wiped his fingers on a linen cloth, "there are other reasons, more practical reasons. Your purpose as I understand it, is to humiliate Henry. This is the best

way to do it! Make him sign an agreement to fight the Infidel. If
he fulfills his promise, you have won. If he does not, then you
have proved him to be a liar, and you have also won."

For a moment the king appraised them both with a look of
misgiving, then slowly a broad smile stretched itself across his
face. "Perhaps you are right," he decided, and stripped a bit of
fat from his meat, tossing it aside. "Yes: the King of England
shall have his truce. Write it all down William, and make it binding. See that Henry puts both his seal and signature to it, and
have it witnessed by one of his priests." He grinned at the prospect, holding his greasy knife aloft, his fingers tracing the edge.
"And if in three months time Henry shows no indication of making good his promise, then I myself shall bring him to account
with this!" He savored the expression of alarm on their faces,
then laughed to show that he was joking. "Don't worry," he said
and went back to eating, "I'll be sure to clean it first."

Flanders was waiting for Richard outside his tent, kicking the
mud from his boots. He seized Richard's sleeve. "A word with
you," he muttered.

They went inside together. "Have you eaten?" Richard asked,
and Flanders nodded. "Then take some wine with me." Richard
motioned to a pair of chairs close to the *brese* where the fire was,
then crossed to the table where a flagon sat beside two pewter
henaps.

Flanders doffed his fawn-colored pellison and sat down, admiring the surroundings. Even in the field Richard kept himself
in luxury. Fine Saracen carpets covered the ground, and heavily
embroidered damask hangings decorated the canvas walls of the
tent. Fine things always lifted Flanders' spirits. He took the cup
that Richard held out to him and sniffed at the wine: a deep,
sweet vintage from the south.

They toasted one another, then Richard sat down with a grunt.
"Say what you came to say and I will listen, though I confess I've
had a belly full of talk today."

There was a brief pause. "My words will put you at your ease."

Richard stretched his legs out, warming his feet by the fire.
"What do you want, d'Alsace?"

Flanders chuckled. "What do *you* want, that's more to the
point, isn't it?"

The wine felt rich and dark on his tongue and Richard savored it before swallowing. "Are you asking me?"

"I know you are at odds with Henry."

Now Richard laughed. "Is that supposed to be a secret?"

"It's no secret to Philippe Capet. You should talk to him, Richard; just the two of you, without Henry. In the future you will be forced to deal with him more and more. You need to know what kind of man he is."

"I *know* what kind of man he is," Richard said, biting off the words, "And so must you, to have left his side for ours."

Flanders heaved a sigh. "You aren't listening to me. I think that you should meet with him. At least give him the chance to find out what kind of man *you* are."

Richard emptied his cup and set it at his feet. "I have no authority to make a separate peace with him against my father's will, if that is what you mean. Henry would call that treason, and he would be right."

"Henry needn't know." Flanders leaned close to Richard, and there was a serious set to his face as he spoke. "Don't make the same mistakes with Philippe that your father has; use your experience and be guided by it." He wiped the droplets of wine from his mouth. "Henry's a beaten man, Richard. He's lost his touch. I've seen it just in these few days I've been here, and I'm getting out." He raised his cup as though to toast the idea.

"Back to the French king?" Richard seemed amused. "You are like a faithless woman, d'Alsace. I think Capet must be tired of you treading back and forth between the lines by now. Will he have you back?"

Flanders drank, then wiped his lips again. "He will understand. Ever since our reconciliation he has felt kindly toward me."

"Then why did you desert him for my father's cause?"

Flanders smiled, unoffended. "I have been remiss in my relations with your father for some time. I depend upon the good will of the French king it's true, but I depend upon your father's favor as well. I was testing his benevolence, that's all. Philippe will understand that."

A frown creased the noble rise of Richard's forehead. "You still care very much about Philippe, don't you?"

The Count of Flanders finished his wine and stood up. "I have no son of my own, Richard; no child at all, and I never shall. Philippe is the closest thing I've known to a son." He reached for his pellison. "I'm going now. I think you should come with me." He smiled at Richard's grave expression. "Just to talk..."

Undecided, Richard hesitated. "I don't know what purpose it will serve."

There was an unsettling gleam in Flanders' eye. "I do," he said.

Philippe was busy at his maps when the Count of Flanders brought Richard to him. The king's black eyes flashed a wordless greeting, but he did not rise. "Join me," he said, and swept aside the dinner leavings with his free hand. Then he smiled slyly at Flanders. "I see you have returned. Can I depend upon you to remain this time, or shall the sunrise find you under yet another banner?" It was said without much guile, just as d'Alsace had predicted.

Flanders' tanned face crinkled in a self-deprecating grin as he and Richard seated themselves. "As always I am your servant."

"Indeed," Philippe answered, playing for a while at being serious. Then he laughed at Richard's sober expression. "Relax, my lord of Poitou, you are among friends." Then suddenly his expression darkened. "Why did you come, Richard?"

Richard stared down at the sapphire on his middle finger, distracting himself with the light that danced atop it. "I felt the need to talk to you, to explain that whatever happens between you and my father, I bear no personal grudge toward you."

"That's kind," Philippe said, lightly mocking.

Richard's tone grew harder. "It's true." He raised his head and looked directly into Philippe's face. "Both sides have been imprudent, my father excessively so. But you have no right to the Aquitaine and you know it. Take your troops away and there will be no recriminations in the future from my armies there. I promise you that."

"Do you?" Philippe brushed a tangle of black curls back from his forehead as he laughed. "*How* can you promise such a thing? To begin with, the Aquitaine is no longer yours; it was, I believe, given over to your mother's care sometime ago. Which is another way of saying that it now belongs to Henry once again, just as it did when he first stole it from Louis, together with his wife."

It was hard to meet those cold black eyes and speak one's mind while doing it. Richard shifted uneasily in his chair, he cleared his throat. "What has been done in the past by my father or yours, cannot be undone. It is the future we should concern ourselves with."

"It is *only* the future which interests me," Philippe replied instantly, "you might convey that to your father."

Richard looked down at his folded hands and wished that he had not come here. Capet was too intimidating and Richard felt unequal to him in this setting. "Look," he said, "I just think you should understand my feelings about all this. I support my father's cause, though not his methods. I don't strike bargains in his name, and certainly not behind his back. Politics is his game; yours too I suspect. But it has nothing to do with me."

The blunt honesty of those words seemed to soften Philippe's haughty expression and he smiled. Richard thought that he looked very handsome when he smiled. "I appreciate your honesty," the French king said, "Perhaps I can give you something in return to put your mind at ease. I have agreed to give your father the two years of truce he requested so that he might seek his repentance in the Holy Land." He raised an eyebrow at Richard's show of interest. "That pleases you? I hope this settlement shall please us all in time. You see, I am not personally vindictive. I only seek to maintain what is mine."

Fine words, but Richard wondered if they were true.

He stood up and thrust his hand out toward Philippe. "I am glad this business is at an end. I confess to little love for politics."

Philippe grasped Richard's hand and held it with curious tenderness. "We'll talk again," he said.

Richard rode slowly back to camp, puzzling over his meeting with Philippe. He felt unsettled; something was tugging at his mind. *Talk to him* Flanders had said. *Know him better.* Yet after their brief exchange, Richard felt he knew even less than before.

There was something though, something he could not deny. An element of fascination was closely entwined with Richard's dislike of Philippe. Richard had known many men but never one who so combined the essence of both coldness and passion in his nature. Something in his attitude was vaguely reminiscent of Geoffrey. No wonder those two had appealed to one another.

But Richard did not want to think of that; did not want to think of Geoffrey and Philippe together. At the mouth of the camp he dismounted, then walked the distance to his tent. God it would be good when all this bothersome business was ended and he could return to Poitiers once more! Far away from his father.

Far away from Philippe Capet.

He'd slept only a little while when he was jostled awake by the rough hand of a soldier. Richard squinted up at the intruder, his senses swimming to the surface. He pushed himself to a sitting position. "What is it?" he grumbled.

"Your father is calling for you," the soldier explained. "He asks that you come to his tent at once."

There was more grumbling as Richard pulled on his boots and braies and threw a sable mantle about his shoulders. Then grabbing a torch he pushed his way past the soldier and went out into the dark.

Henry sat at a wooden table, his shoulders hunched and shapeless under the cover of a heavy woollen cloak. He bent close to a stack of papers, studying them intently.

Richard strode up to him, looking grim and tired. "I wish your summons could have waited," he said, "you took me from my bed."

"A pity," Henry snapped, "but this is more important than sleep." He nearly upset the table as he lunged forward, his finger pointing to a single paper which bore Philippe Capet's signature. "See this? The King of France has agreed to my demands at last!"

"Agreed?" Richard asked incredulous, "*Your* demands? What do you mean?"

"He has agreed to the truce."

"I know," Richard answered, and to his father's questioning look he added, "it was whispered about the camp. But I don't see it as a cause for celebration. I know you well enough to know you don't invite a trip to the Holy Land at this point in your life."

"Richard, Richard . . . of course I don't intend to go. But this is something else; I have a plan."

"No more plans," Richard objected, "this thing is over."

Henry snatched up the paper and waved it in Richard's face. "That's what you think. I have him now. By Christ, I have him!"

Exasperation and interrupted sleep had made Richard cross. "What are you talking about?"

Henry leapt to his feet in triumph, a hectic flush of joy coloring his face. "Now that Philippe believes all has been settled, I shall give him a surprise he never expected. I want you to give orders that our men attack the French camp at dawn."

It took a few moments for the impact of his words to penetrate Richard's understanding. "You want *what*? An attack? And after signing the truce with Philippe?"

"Don't be such a fool," Henry shouted. "Who cares about the truce? It doesn't mean a thing."

"You humiliated yourself to get it, it meant *that* much to you," Richard shouted back.

"I did not humiliate myself," the king answered in a low, hard voice. "I only salvaged what I could from this fiasco, without your help. That is *survival*, boy, not surrender."

"I will not do it!" Richard screamed in frustration, "I want no part of it!"

The son and the father regarded one another for a moment. The air between them was charged with enmity and perturbation. "Why do you oppose this?" Henry asked at last, for he was truly puzzled. "*You* are the soldier, the one who favored battle in the first place. You should be pleased."

Richard grabbed up the torch. "If you think that, then you don't know me very well."

Henry watched his son move toward the entrance to the tent. "You will do as I say," he promised, "or you will regret your obstinacy at a later time."

"Don't threaten me," Richard warned and pushed his way outside. He walked swiftly toward his tent, looking up at the sky as he went. The stars had gone, and the air was piquant with the scent of smoke. It was just beginning to rain.

News of the "surprise" attack filtered through the lines and across the river before the night was over. It may have been that Philippe Capet had spies within the English camp; or perhaps he merely had long ears. Whatever the case, he alerted his men as soon as he knew Henry's plan. The French were up before the sun; dressed, ready to attack.

Godfrey brought news of this to Henry, who was at once overtaken by terror at the consequences of his own rash plan. A surprise attack upon the French camp would have worked in his favor; a defense of their own lines would not. Henry had made things ten times worse than they had been before! He cursed himself and called loudly upon God to help him.

God was not enough. Richard was sent for.

"Tell me what to do!" Henry implored.

There were no words to describe what Richard was feeling as he stood before his father. The older man was white-faced, sobbing; he looked pitiful, and Richard felt ashamed to be his son. All the delays, the lies, the blunders—all the times Henry had closed his ears to any advice—it had come back to trap him now; him and all the rest of them.

Richard looked away, fighting a rising sickness in his stomach. "This is a disgrace," he muttered, "and you are to blame."

"I know that!" Henry wailed, "don't waste my time in repeating it." He brushed a hand across his face, erasing the tears. "Help me."

There was a note of despair in Richard's voice. "What do you want me to do?"

Henry drew a breath of relief and clasped Richard by the hand. "Go back to Philippe. Arrange another truce. Tell him anything you like. But get him to call off his attack!"

"I can't do that!" Richard insisted. "How can you ask me such a thing?"

Henry seized Richard by the shoulders, holding him fast. "Because it is the only way."

"No! If you want another truce, YOU go to Philippe and beg for it! I've had enough of this theater of deceit."

The king was beyond caring that his dignity was shattered. He would beg, threaten, do anything he had to in order to secure Richard's help. "If you desert me now," Henry promised, "I will see to it that you never get the Aquitaine back again! I'll have your mother sign it over to John at the point of a sword if I must, unless you swear to help me!"

Richard threw off his father's hands and turned away with a grunt of disgust. He wanted to feel anger: instead he felt only humiliation and pity for his father. Henry had finally grown too old to outrun his own lies. He had failed: and not grandly as he had so many times in the past, but foolishly, a victim of crude miscalculation. There wasn't even enough manhood left in him for Richard to hate. "I'll go," he agreed in a disheartened whisper. "It is my duty as your son. But this time I will make peace with him on my own terms."

"Thank you," Henry croaked as tears ran down his wrinkled cheeks. Then he followed Richard outside and watched him mount his horse.

It was a dull morning. The sun was a pale gold orb on a pillow of clouds. There was a hint of rain in the air, and the scent of moisture still lingered from last night. The camp was buzzing with activity as men girded themselves for war. Henry had given the order when he learned what Philippe planned to do, hoping even then that a battle would not be necessary.

Philippe was dressed for battle, strapping on his sword when Richard entered, out of breath and anxious.

The French king looked up. "I wish I could say once again that I welcome you, but unfortunately that sentiment has been made invalid by your father's treachery." His eyes scanned Richard's face for an answer. "Why have you come?"

Three witnesses—the king's two Champagnois uncles, and the Count of Flanders—watched as Richard threw himself at Philippe's feet in a symbolic show of homage. His voice was tight, the words spurred on by urgency. "I have come to ask you for yet another truce, my father's action notwithstanding. I shall submit myself to any punishment you deem appropriate; should you wish to keep me as a hostage to my father's word I shall accept it humbly." He unloosed his sword and flung it to the ground. "I ask you to take this as proof of our intentions. One word from you that the truce is secure and my father's army will withdraw."

Philippe glanced up at Theobold and William, then d'Alsace. They all knew Richard better than he did, and their expressions told him that this was no trick. Gently he put his right hand on Richard's head. *A show of pardon.* "Stand up," he said.

Richard's fine clothes were rumpled, as though he'd slept in them. That amused Philippe. It made Richard seem less lordly and more human. "Don't look so solemn," the king admonished him, "as I told you yesterday, you are among friends." He motioned for the others to withdraw and as they went he instructed them, "Go to the English king and tell him I accept the terms as he offered them before, but warn him also that I shall hold him to them. There shall be no battle if his troops are moved and out of here before the sun goes down. Tell him also that Richard, by his own will, remains behind with us until these measures are accomplished."

He left Richard's side and followed the three men to the mouth of the tent. There they stood speaking for several minutes, mumbling in tones which Richard could scarcely hear. At last, with a subtle gesture of his hand, Philippe dismissed the others.

Now the two of them were alone.

After his humbling display, Richard felt uneasy. Philippe knew that and tried to dispel his anxiety with a smile. "Sit down," he said, but even though it was meant to sound friendly, he couldn't keep the sharp note of authority from his voice. "Have you taken breakfast?"

"I'm not hungry," Richard muttered, then at Philippe's bidding he seated himself.

"Some wine, then?" Philippe paused, the porringer uplifted in his hand.

"Indeed."

As he waited, Richard scanned the tent, disinterested. Everywhere he looked the emblazoned symbol of the golden fleur-de-lis met his eyes.

A cup was thrust into his hand. "You will recognize this, I am sure. Cherry wine. From Bordeaux, a region you know very well," Philippe explained. "It is my wife's favorite."

Richard nodded. "You treat me with exceeding courtesy," he said.

Philippe laughed. "I have more reason to rejoice than you can know." He took a sip and the wine glistened on his lips as he spoke. "Yesterday a message reached me from Isabel in Paris. Once again she has my child in her. She says that all the signs substantiate her belief it is a boy." He hoisted his cup. "So when I drink this now it is in her honor, not yours."

"Of course," Richard flushed a little, and he raised his cup to meet with Philippe's. "To your son."

Pleased, confident, Philippe settled back in his chair and immediately turned the conversation to political, not personal concerns. "I respect your act of coming to me, Richard," he said simply. "Be assured I do. I know your father to be a liar and a dissembler; but I trust you. Truly."

"I am glad of that."

Philippe was enjoying this. His lips curved into a smile. "Do you trust your father?"

Devious. God he was devious. Clever. And cruel, too; he knew where to twist the knife. Richard finished his wine in silence, then pushed the cup aside and looked across at Philippe. "Why do you want to know? Why do you care?"

"I *care.*"

Richard was a man who spoke his feelings, always. He did not make a sport of juggling words. Because of that honesty he loathed Philippe's obscure manner of extracting information, as if merely to satisfy his curiosity. "What is it you really want with me?" he asked. "I think you had better say, because your method is too subtle for me."

A tolerant smile stretched Philippe's lips. "Very well, since you prefer the direct approach. I would like to have your help. In return, I would give you mine. That should be worth more than anything your father has to offer you."

A moment of consideration, as though Richard wasn't sure. "Are you asking me to change sides? To leave my father's cause for yours?"

"Cause," Philippe grimaced at the word, "Richard, there is no *cause.* There is only land, and the men who own it."

"And those who try to take it."

Philippe laughed. "If it pleases you to say so."

There were beads of moisture on Richard's forehead and he wiped them away. "I cannot believe that even you could be so cynical."

"I speak the truth."

"You speak treason," Richard corrected him.

For a while they said nothing and the only sound was the heavy splashing of rain against the canvas roof. The scent of wetness was everywhere: strong and sweetly rustic as it mingled with the smell of earth and horses' dung.

Philippe reached over and touched Richard's sleeve. "Before you judge me too harshly let me make my reasoning clear to you. To begin with, I know the trouble that exists within your family."

"Exaggerated," Richard scoffed.

Philippe raised a hand to silence him. "You forget that Harry and Geoffrey were my friends. They told me all there is to know.

From childhood I knew what kind of man your father is. Louis told me much as well. Can you deny that Henry has set you aside time and time again?"

"Is that what Geoffrey told you?" Richard asked, and his voice was bitter. "Because he schemed to make it come true."

"Geoffrey did what he had to, but at least he didn't deceive himself about your father's motives," Philippe argued. "Henry has made it clear just how much he values your advice and your abilities." He snapped his fingers in front of Richard's face. "Not *that* much! Why do you stay with him? You owe him nothing."

Richard's eyes, blue as ice in twilight, narrowed as he studied Philippe's face. "I told you once before that I am not my brother Geoffrey, and I will not make myself a traitor as he did, just for the sake of getting even. What strife has passed between my father and myself is none of your concern, Philippe. Do you know what loyalty is? I owe him that. I serve him so long as he lives and wears the crown. That is my duty as his son."

"Well, good for you," Philippe answered, mocking and sarcastic, and he got to his feet, pushing the chair aside. He leaned his palms flat against the table and looked straight at Richard. "Why are you so hostile to me? I have tried to be understanding of your problems, I have offered you my help."

"Your help doesn't come cheap, I'm sure," Richard answered grudgingly.

"Is my meaning so obscure?" Philippe's heavily lashed eyes were unrelenting.

"No, it's very clear."

"You think I want to turn you against your father?"

"Of course," Richard laughed, "or at least you want to use me as a cudgel to beat Henry with. That *is* what you intend, is it not?"

"Perhaps I have other reasons."

Richard stood up and folded his arms across his chest. "I am a soldier," he proclaimed, "you must speak to me as a soldier."

"A soldier, yes," Philippe answered, making the words sound silky, "but a poet too. Such things cannot be misinterpreted by poets, surely."

Richard rounded the table. The two men stood looking at each other for several moments. The air between them was alive with curiosity and doubt. "Just what is it that you *want?*" Richard asked curtly.

The time for truth had come. Philippe laid his hand on Richard's shoulder. "I want us to be friends."

"Friends," Richard scowled and shook off Philippe's touch.

The king's expression was unreadable. "Richard, your reputation precedes you by more years than I can count. Why are you making this so difficult for me?"

Richard looked away. "So this is your way of repaying my father for his treachery?"

Philippe laughed. "Richard, Richard—don't be so grim about this. I'm offering something to you, not demanding. And if the truth be told, I've been fascinated by your looks and your legend for a long time." He reached out and placed his fingertips beneath Richard's chin. "Look at me and tell me, if you can, that you don't feel the same."

Richard stared into the blackest eyes he had ever seen; the most handsome face. Slowly his hand came up, the fingers curling around Philippe's wrist, but it was a grasp of unity, not a restraint. "Philippe," he said, "I don't know you very well, but what I do know makes me hesitant to trust you."

Philippe pulled Richard's hand to his lips and kissed it. "You will learn to trust me, as your brothers did." He looked deep into Richard's eyes. "They loved me very much, both Harry and Geoffrey did, and I loved them. They learned to trust me, because I gave them reason to. You can trust me, Richard, I promise that."

So many questions, so much doubt. But all of that seemed very small compared to the sudden rush of passion Richard felt as Philippe put his arms about his shoulders and pulled him close. They kissed many times, the gold and black hair of their beards mingling.

At last Richard pulled away, but his breath was still hot upon Philippe's face. "Don't think that you can use me as a weapon against Henry. I want you, but I won't be made a pawn so you can satisfy your hatred for my father. Before we go any further I want you to understand that."

Philippe brushed Richard's lips with another kiss; his hands caressed Richard's shoulders. "This has nothing to do with vengeance. I am not thinking of your father now. Only of us: of the friendship we can build together."

There was an inkling of a smile on Richard's lips. "You *did* say I was your hostage...."

Philippe laughed again: that rich and beautiful laugh that made Richard's senses tingle when he heard it. "I meant that in the mere technical sense, my friend." He fingered a lock of Richard's golden hair. "You see, I already think of you as my friend. In time you will feel the same, I swear it."

Whatever else was said that morning neither man remembered. The rain came down. Outside the tent a guard stood by so the king and his guest would not be disturbed. The soldiers were told to take off their battle gear. Everyone was going back to Paris. Inside the tent, on the pale blue cushions of the king's bed where the fleur-de-lis was emblazoned in gold; amid groping hands and hot kisses and flesh that demanded to be satisfied, a new alliance between Philippe Capet and yet another of Henry's sons was being forged.

Later they lay together, almost sleeping, covered by an ermine rug, and lulled by the sound of rain coming down outside.

"I should be leaving," Richard mumbled against Philippe's chest. "It must be afternoon by now."

Philippe bit softly into Richard's shoulder. "Don't ever go. Come back to Paris with me. Give yourself a chance to know me better."

Relaxed and giddy, Richard laughed and rumpled Philippe's hair. "I think in these last few hours I've learned everything there is to know of you."

Their tongues met, teasing. "There is so much more," the king assured him. "We are ideal as lovers, but I want to show you the kind of friend I can be. Prove me..." He kissed his lover's throat, then let his tongue go lower, licking the sweat from Richard's brawny chest.

"We *are* ideal," Richard agreed. "I've never known such joy in love."

"Then come to Paris. Be with me, stay with me. Let your father be taught a lesson for neglecting your advice, for ignoring your abilities."

"Yes," Richard breathed, "you *are* right! What loyalty has he shown me? Why should I care for his feelings?"

"I care," Philippe sighed, "and I *feel.*"

It was evening before they left his bed.

Across the river, Henry waited.

The Count of Chartres had brought the news of Philippe's acquiescence to Henry's terms. That had been this morning. All
day the English king had waited for Richard to return, but when
the sun went down he still did not come back.

"Where is he?" Henry grumbled. "What is he doing?"

Godfrey had keen instincts; he was very sure of what had happened. Still, out of care for his father's state of mind he tried to
calm him. "I don't think you should concern yourself. No doubt
he will soon return."

Henry slapped a fist into his open palm. "Perhaps I was wrong
to send him. Maybe I should have sent someone else."

"You did well to send him," Godfrey answered patiently. "After
all, he did secure the truce, just as you asked. Don't worry after
it. Go to bed and rest yourself. No doubt by the morning Richard
will have returned."

By morning the French camp had dispersed. The tents were
gone; the soldiers, the king—and with them, Henry's son.

END PART IV

Part V

Summer, 1187

T HESE WERE quiet months. There were no wars, no important parlays. No envoys made their way between the powers of England and France.

But that was only the look of it. The summer of 1187 was alive with change and subtle hostilities.

In June, Constance of Brittany was forced to marry against her will. It was Henry's doing, his way of out-foxing Philippe Capet and keeping the duchy as an English possession. Prodded by threats that her son and daughter would be taken from her if she resisted, Constance married the Earl of Chester, although she loathed the look of him. He was ugly, and so small that he scarcely reached her breast.

June also saw Richard Plantagenet in Paris, living at the Cité Palais as his brothers had done in earlier years. It took very little time for this news to travel back to Chinon, where Henry was told that Richard and the French king were inseparable ("Eating from the same dish at mealtimes, sleeping in the same bed at night..."). Henry worried about what this new closeness presaged, and sent many urgent letters to his son, which were ignored.

In July Sibylla came to visit Isabel in Paris, bringing along her baby daughter Gabrielle, and intending to remain till the queen's child was delivered in October. Isabel was pleased to have her sister's company, partly from affection, partly because she saw so little of her husband these days. He was too busy spending his

time with Richard. Isabel's disposition grew sour as she thought
of it. Nearly every day the two men hunted together in the forest
of Vincennes close outside Paris; at night there were other
sports. Always so much time for Richard. Never enough time for
her.

Isabel didn't like Richard, although he treated her with utmost
courtesy. His chivalric manner could not hide the fact that he
knew nothing of women. Gossip said that he shunned them except for dancing! Isabel could believe that. Sometimes, as she sat
with him and Philippe at dinner, she would study Richard's face
and attitude. *You are a fraud,* she would think. *For all your strength
and brave deeds, you are a fraud.*

He was humorless, too, compared to Geoffrey, which did nothing to improve the dourness of Philippe's personality, the way
Geoffrey's perverse wit had. *Boring.* That is how Philippe and
Richard seemed to her and each night as Isabel passed dinner in
their company she would stare at them and think, *You are boring.*

Sibylla was equally tiresome, because she only wished to talk of
having babies and how wonderful her husband William was. The
two young women would sit together in the garden, sewing, and
Sibylla would talk of such things, while Isabel smiled and nodded, pretending to listen. But her mind was really very far away,
as it nearly always was these days, because no matter what she
seemed to be doing, Isabel was thinking of the dreams.

They had begun the end of May, shortly before Philippe returned from Chateauroux. Now they came nightly: dim dreams
in which she floundered through thick fog toward a voice that
called out her name. More disturbing than that: it had become
difficult for Isabel to separate the dreams from wakefulness because now, awake, she had a sense of always being watched, of
being listened to. It was unsettling and frayed her nerves to the
point where she wondered at her own ability to reason.

She was withdrawing more and more from the world and she
could not help it. She had an image in her mind of a circle that
was growing tighter, and in some way it was all related to Geoffrey, though she didn't understand how that could be. It was as if
some essence of his personality still lived on in the halls of the
Cité Palais where he had died, and what remained of it called out
to her.

Isabel brooded on this subject endlessly, unable to speak of it to anyone because no one would understand. She had always been so imaginative; from childhood she had suffered dreams so true she could barely tell them from reality. But this was more frightening than anything she had ever experienced in the past. Isabel had a sense of being pulled against her will into a situation she could not escape.

August came with its pall of dust and heat, kindling small fires on the outskirts of the city. It was too hot to spend the time hunting now, so Philippe turned his attention back to more tedious matters in the council chamber.

Richard gave no indication that he planned to leave Paris, but he was vague about his commitment to Philippe. The French king had tried very hard to be patient, sure that his closeness with Richard would eventually produce an unswerving alliance between the two of them.

So far it had not happened—not out of bed, that is. It was exciting to make love with Richard; exciting in a way that Philippe had never known before with any other man, even his beloved Geoffrey. That seemed to be sufficient for Richard, who had little taste for politics, but it was not enough for Philippe. This relationship meant little to him if something more significant than sex could not be managed.

Every week the letters came from Henry, and every week Richard threw them away. Philippe pondered the actions of his friend. Was Richard considering a permanent break with Henry? He would touch lightly on the subject, trying to extract some type of promise, but Richard would only laugh and say he did not wish to speak of it. He had come to Paris for love he said, and not political dealings. Philippe would answer with a sour smile that pretended appreciation, but all the while he was itching to move against King Henry's lands, and for that he needed Richard.

There was another vexation, a smaller one.

Isabel was in a strange mood these days. At first when he had come back to Paris at the end of May, she had been in such fine spirits, and they had celebrated the conception of the child she *knew* would be his heir. But recently she seemed so moody and withdrawn. It was odd to see the listlessness in her manner, the vacant look in her eyes as though she were living in a world he could not reach.

What could it be? Well, women were strange creatures, and Isabel had always been a particular mystery to him. No doubt her pregnancy was a further cause of her behavior. Wasn't it always said that women weren't quite themselves when they were carrying a child? Didn't they have strange moods, cravings for unusual things to eat? He'd heard that somewhere. Yes, that was probably it.

Jealousy, too; he sensed that Isabel was very jealous of his relationship with Richard. *Odd.* She hadn't seemed to mind Geoffrey. She probably resented the fact that Richard was immune to female charms. That was always certain to get a woman's back up.

Oh, well; perhaps the later stages of her pregnancy had depressed her. Maybe he should give her something, a token to let her know that her swelling belly had in no way defaced her beauty. Women needed to know those things. *A new necklace, or a pair of combs.* Yes, she might like that.

He would see to it at once.

In the middle of the first night in September, Isabel woke from another of her dreams. A sense of curiosity, sharper than fear, drove her from bed and led her toward the window.

The scent of the river was very strong tonight; it seemed to penetrate every corner of the room. Isabel leaned far out of the window and the smell grew even stronger. She could see it too, coming off the river in a mist.

Below, the garden was swathed in shadows; only the white flowers of the night were visible. The branches of the yews and white willows made soft noises in the breeze but as Isabel listened she could hear another sound. A wail that was faintly musical, like a song. Isabel. *Isabel.*

She tensed. Someone was walking in the garden below, but it was too dark to see. After a moment the moon came out from behind the cover of a cloud and then Isabel could see him fully. His eyes rested on her face for just an instant.

It was Geoffrey.

In the morning Edythe found her on the floor, unconscious.

Louis-Philippe Capet was born four days later, premature by one month.

Isabel had been in the garden with her sister; they were talking, sewing. Sibylla left for only a few minutes. When she returned Isabel was gone. Shortly after there were shouts and screams coming from the river bank, and Sibylla rushed to the edge of the garden to see what had happened.

Isabel had waded into the water, and had disappeared; she was drowning! Two soldiers leapt into the river from their place on the bridge and managed to reach her. Sibylla would never forget the sight of Isabel, her hair matted like seaweed, as they pulled her from the water. By the time she was taken to her own room, Isabel was already in labor....

Despite the early birth and Isabel's difficult delivery, tiny Louis was healthy and strong. Philippe held his newborn son close in his arms, lightly stroking the infant's soft blond hair. But there was little joy in the act as Philippe looked beyond his son to the bed where Isabel lay. She was so weak! The midwives had done their best, but Philippe had sent for his physician, Giles de Jocelin. His opinion? Isabel would be fortunate to live through the night.

Philippe should have stayed with her that night. But panic at seeing the life drain out of her was too horrible to face, so he went to his bed and lay there, wakeful all the night, mumbling frightened prayers.

In the morning he went directly to Isabel's room and was relieved to find that she was still alive. Edythe was asleep on the floor beside the bed, but Sibylla was sitting up in a chair, holding little Louis to her naked breast, nursing him.

She looked up when Philippe came in. "How is she?" he asked.

Sibylla looked as though she had been crying most of the night. "A little better, I think," she answered, "but still bad. I'm so worried about her."

Philippe went over to the bed and stood for a while looking down at his wife. Her face was very pale and dotted with tiny beads of moisture. Her hair was a tangled mass of golden floss about her head. *Please, Christ, keep her safe!* She was sleeping fitfully and Philippe reached out his hand to touch her cheek. That seemed to unsettle her even more; she groaned and he took his hand away.

"Where is de Jocelin?" he asked, turning to face Sibylla.

She smiled wanly down at her nephew, then unsmiling faced Philippe. "He was in earlier and left some medicine, but we can not give it to her till she wakes."

He shook his head sadly, almost in desperation. "Why did she do it, Sibylla? *What* was she doing?"

"I don't know." A sob caught deep in her throat. "I just can't help feeling that if I had stayed with her, if I hadn't left when I did..."

"No," he said, and the word managed to sound generous the way he said it. "I don't think that would have made a difference. She's been acting so strange lately. I don't know what's wrong with her. These past few weeks I've felt as though I couldn't even reach her."

Have you tried?

But Sibylla forced herself to hold back the words. It was not her place to say such things, not right to judge her brother-in-law, especially since he was the king. So instead she lifted Louis to shoulder level and held him out toward Philippe. "Would you like to hold your son for a while?" she asked.

He came and took the baby from her arms. Sibylla had neglected to close the neckline of her dress, and suddenly Philippe found himself staring down at her beautiful young breasts. How sweet and wonderful, the change that marriage and childbearing could make in the body of a girl. She saw his scrutiny; moved quickly to cover herself, her cheeks flushing with embarrassment.

"No don't," Philippe said, and reached out to stroke her left breast, his thumb nudging at the milk-sopped nipple. "You look so much like Isabel," he muttered. His words made Sibylla blush deeper.

At last he took his hand away and she fastened the front of her chainse. She didn't know what to say, and in any case if she spoke now her voice would tremble.

"It's all right," Philippe said in a voice that sounded as though he were laughing at her, "I'm not going to hurt you." He handed the child back to her then, and left the room without another word.

Sibylla held the baby close and shivered beneath her skin. *No one had ever touched her in that way.* Certainly not William. Even in his show of love he was respectful to her. But Philippe had touched her as if she were a whore. It shamed her to realize that the feeling had excited her.

Tears hurried down her cheeks and fell on little Louis's up-turned face. Her lips began to move in silent prayer.

Within a week Isabel had recovered sufficiently to take regular meals and spend some time each day nursing her child. She was delighted with her beautiful new son, and scarcely remembered the agony she had experienced in giving birth to him.

She would have preferred to forget the incident just prior to having him, but no one would allow her to forget. Philippe. Sibylla. Sully. They all came in their turn to question her. *Why had she gone into the river?* It was all they could seem to think about.

Philippe brought her a grey opal ring and necklace and spoke to her of duty. Sully lectured gently on mortal sin. Sibylla wept and said she didn't understand why anyone so loved and beautiful should want to kill herself. *Suicide.* That is what they all believed she had tried to accomplish, and because of that they were ashamed of her.

There was no way to make any of them understand. If she told them why she had gone into the river and what she had seen, they would think her mad. *Was she?* Isabel was afraid to ask herself the question.

Illusion. Madness. Dreams. They mingled in her mind till she could hardly separate them. Even with her eyes closed Isabel could see the memory and she shivered at it. *Geoffrey, beckoning to her from the middle of the water, holding out his arms and begging her to come to him.*

Richard prepared to leave Paris at the beginning of October.

Philippe seemed mildly offended when Richard told him. "Why are you going now?" he asked. "You said that you might spend Christmas here."

"I intended to," Richard answered, "but look at this." He thrust a folded letter across the table at Philippe. "Henry is back in Normandy at last. That leaves Chinon free. I'm going there to take my part of all the treasure Henry's hoarded away within its walls, and use it to fortify some of my castles in Poitou."

"You might throw a little of it my way," Philippe sulked, "My expenses at your father's hands last summer were very heavy, and I was never indemnified for them."

There was a slightly contentious look in Richard's eyes. "What expenses? The whole campaign was your doing, don't forget." He gave a chuckle. "You are very much like Henry in that way, if no other. You cling to every piece of silver..."

Philippe held the letter in his hand for a moment, then tossed it back to Richard. "Wait till you have a kingdom of your own to manage, you'll see. It takes money."

"I *do* know something of such things," Richard answered. "I did more than wield a sword in Aquitaine, you know."

"Wielding a sword is your best talent," Philippe replied. "Managing money is mine."

"Perhaps. Though it seems to me you spend more money than you ought in buying jewelry for your wife."

Philippe's black eyes flashed a warning. "That is none of your affair."

"No," Richard snapped, "but it is my opinion anyway."

Philippe crooked an eyebrow. "Wait till you have a wife of your own, you'll see. It takes a lot of money." They looked at one another for a moment, then both of them began to laugh.

"She is very beautiful, it's true," Richard conceded.

"She is that. And it is the least I can do for her after giving me my son," Philippe explained. He held out his hand toward Richard. "Come back soon," he said.

IN THE EAST the fabric of Christendom was unraveling.

It had begun in the summer of 1187 when a marauding band of Christian knights waylaid a group of Moslem pilgrims who were on their way to Egypt. Almost overnight the word went out to all the followers of Mohammed: destroy the Christian armies of the West.

Guy de Lusignan had muscled his way to power in Jerusalem following the death of King Baldwin, so the burden of defending Christendom in the East fell on him. He was a brave man, but a foolish one, and his overconfidence resulted in his armies being defeated by the forces of Saladin in July. Guy was captured, and with him, the most sacred relic of all: the True Cross of Christ.

At Saladin's orders all Templar knights and Hospitallers captured at the Battle of Hattin were executed, but de Lusignan was set free. He had promised never to raise a sword against a Moslem again, but he broke that pledge soon enough and came back with another army.

The Moslems were fighting from strength, and their capacity for revenge was brutal. One by one the coastal cities fell to their numbers: Acre, Haifa, Sidon, Beyrout, and Gaza. Finally, in October, after three months of fighting, Jerusalem was taken.

Jerusalem the Holy, citadel of the Christian faith!

The news sounded through Europe like the drum of Judgment Day. Pope Urban died shortly after the news was brought to him, and men everywhere spoke of seeing evil omens in the sky. It was as if the world were about to end.

Richard was in Tours early that November when he heard what had happened, and suddenly the business of spending his father's wealth on building up his fortresses meant nothing. Richard's religiosity had always been very strong, but this new challenge was like a second baptism.

Immediately he made a pledge to fight the captors of the Holy City. The newly chosen pope, Gregory III, had called upon the knights and princes of Europe to mount a new crusade. Richard made his promise a public thing when he took the cross from the hands of Archbishop Bartholomew of Tours. He was among the first to do so.

It was the most meaningful act of his life.

In Caen, Henry took the news in more pragmatic fashion.

Jesus, what a time for this to happen!

He had committed himself to make a pilgrimage to the Holy Land by signing that stupid truce with Philippe Capet. Now this! Henry would be hard-put to delay fulfilling that vow of service, with all of Christendom up in arms over the fall of Jerusalem and the other Latin strongholds. Henry's anger was tinged with the shades of irony. *My luck is made of shit.*

When he was told that Richard had already taken the cross, Henry was furious. How typical of his son to rush into this without first weighing the consequences, and those consequences could prove damaging to Henry.

Richard was fanatical (Henry found him so) but he was no fool. He would never leave for the Holy Land before certain

matters had been settled, things like the succession, for example.
There were other concerns, too: the final disposition of Henry's
empire at his death—Richard would want assurance of what
lands would be his if he was going to be away for several years.
There was also the situation of his betrothal to Alais; *that* needed
fixing. Richard would want answers, and he would want them
very soon.

Disconsolate, quite alone except for John and the most loyal of
his retainers, Henry spent a dismal Christmas Day at the fortress
in Caen. He was thinking seriously of going back to England at
the beginning of the new year. That would be one way to escape
responsibility for these decisions. He had all but decided to do so.
Then Richard arrived at Caen, three days after Christmas.

He was full of enthusiasm and plans, and though he may have
given some consideration to the concerns Henry had envisioned,
Richard was far more interested in borrowing money from him.
It would cost far more to equip himself for an expedition to the
East than he could manage from his income as Count of Poitou.

For three days after his son arrived, Henry would not see him;
for still another two he would not speak to him. Then at last, on
the final day of the old year, Henry took his son aside and told
him these words which had been well rehearsed:

"Because you are my son you are very precious to me, and it
would grieve me deeply to be so abruptly parted from your company. For this reason I have decided we shall travel together to
the Holy places: I, to fulfill my commitment of the truce, and
you because you have so recently taken the cross. Side by side we
shall fight to preserve the honor of our faith."

Richard was nothing short of astonished. He had begun to
think his father would never speak to him again. Now these fine
words! Was Henry being honest with him, and if he was, how
soon would this joint pilgrimage commence? Richard had hoped
to resolve all his business quickly and be on his way by June, but
he doubted very much that his father had planned so early a
departure.

He put these questions to Henry.

"My son," Henry said, turning his backside to the fire, "we
have many matters to settle before such a trip can be made, not
least of which is our policy towards the King of France. With

Philippe's profound ambitions no longer a mystery to us we can hardly go off, the both of us, and leave our lands to his mercy."

Richard knew what Henry was implying. "What do you suggest?" he asked.

The king rubbed his palms together, then hid them within the folds of his mantle. "Do you promise me, here and now, that you will stand with me against him? Will you give up your pretended allegiance to him?"

Richard bowed his head. "I owe no allegiance to him, Father. Only friendship."

Henry's voice grew sharper. "Will you submit yourself to my authority as you ought?"

"I know that I have disappointed you in the past," Richard admitted, "but there was no treachery in my actions, nor is there now. You must believe that."

"You stole my treasure from Chinon."

Cool but respectful, Richard answered, "I took that part of it which was mine." He spread his arms in a gesture of exasperation. "Henry, for years you handed out money to Harry as if the world was his, but very often you have been unfair to me in that regard, and for less reason. I don't waste wealth on gambling the way he did, and I don't steal from my people either, as Geoffrey did."

Henry waved a hand to show he wasn't interested in such comparisons. "Just give me your promise," he said. His face was set in a grave expression. "Promise that you will enter into no agreement, political or otherwise with Philippe that will undermine my power."

Those were strong words and Richard couldn't miss their implication. Henry seldom made any mention of his power diminishing in any way, simply because he refused to believe that it was possible. If he could speak that way, then he was truly intimidated by Philippe Capet, and moreso than Richard had ever supposed.

"Do you promise?"

"My relationship with the king of France is personal," Richard explained. "I was his guest in Paris, not his fellow conspirator." His voice went lower. "Although I do believe he would have liked for me to be."

"His *friend*," Henry commented sharply. "Last winter you were the one who warned me of his treachery and malice. And now you consider him a friend."

Richard looked away; his voice was quiet. "You know what kind of a friend I mean."

"I do," Henry grumbled, "and that in itself is a political affrontry to me. *Three* of my sons, all in their turn, running off to Philippe Capet whenever he snaps his fingers or shakes his penis!"

"It is my own business, Father."

"My *business* is ruling!" Henry raged, "and I will not permit a son of mine to set up against me with my enemies! I've tolerated too much from all my sons in the past, I realize that, but I am not willing to allow it any more!"

Richard touched Henry's arm lightly. "Philippe is my lover, Henry, nothing else."

"Lover!" Henry scoffed. "Christ Jesus, that's disgusting. Why does he constantly seek to seduce my sons, with that delicious little cat he's married to?"

"How do *you* know her?" Richard asked, frowning.

The king's face lighted with the pleasant memory of Isabel. "She came to me once," Henry said and cleared his throat. "I did her a favor." He smiled at Richard's doubting look. "I saved her marriage."

"Whatever," Richard said, and waved the words away. "In any case, Father, my lovers are my own business. God knows I've never concerned myself with yours."

"All right," Henry agreed, "I shall say no more on that. But this much I will say. Swear your fealty to me anew, and before all the witnesses of my court, and you shall have all you need to subsidize your venture, I promise you." He paused, and then reached out to clasp Richard's hand. "Do this for me, Richard, and I shall forgive your many months of absence, and your neglect to answer my many letters." The hand squeezed tighter. "As you once pointed out to me, it would be in both our interest to forget the past."

Richard nodded. *Henry was right.* It was time to resolve the differences between them. This new endeavor, upon which he had so greatly set his heart, required forgiveness. Also, his rejuvenated sense of religious zeal had caused Richard to question the worthiness of his relationship with Philippe. If he was going forth as a soldier of the cross, he wanted to cleanse himself of all past and present sins.

He smiled tight-lipped at his father, and then impulsively the two men embraced. "We shall go together," Henry whispered in his ear.

The year 1187 was only three days gone when Sibylla and her little daughter left Paris to go back to Beaujeu. William had come to join them at the palace for Christmas, but there had been little festivity at the court this year. As she crossed over the *Grande Pont,* traveling south once more with her child and husband, Sibylla scarcely paused to look back.

She knew that she was going to miss her sister, though Isabel was moody company these days. Perhaps it was the dreary environs of the Cité Palais which had drained away all the light-heartedness of her spirit that Sibylla remembered so well from when they were children. She could understand it though; the palace was loathsome! Sibylla had come to hate it in her few months stay there. Poor Isabel. Banished to such a place in the midst of the grey and dirty city, while Sibylla lived on open land beneath a swell of green hills, surrounded by fresh air and miles of beautiful scenery. In comparison, Isabel was a prisoner.

It was Philippe's fault, too; Sibylla believed that.

Choleric and rude-mannered, *he* had made Isabel unhappy. A few times Sibylla had said as much (or tried to) but not too often, because Isabel could turn instantly waspish and unpleasant when anyone spoke against her husband.

How could she love such a brutish man? Barely a month after Louis's birth Sibylla had noticed ugly bruises on Isabel's arms and throat. The images they conjured were even uglier, and Sibylla shuddered just to think of it.

What fortune for her that William was so kind!

January, and still no word from Richard.

Philippe was privately humiliated at his lover's silence. Richard had taken the cross; Philippe knew that, of course. All the world knew by now how Jerusalem had fallen, and it had not taken long for word to circulate that Prince Richard had been among the first to answer Pope Gregory's call for a new crusade.

Like Henry, Philippe cast a chary eye upon this Holy War. It was fine to talk boldly of recapturing the Christian citadels, to dream of dipping a sword in Moslem blood. But such chivalric glory built no empires in the West, and that's where Philippe's concerns were centered.

If this crusade fever went on for too much longer, Philippe was afraid that he would be pressed into taking the cross himself, and right now that was the last thing he was prepared to do. He was much more interested in acquiring Normandy. *Normandy!* It was what Philippe dreamed of; the return of Normandy to the royal *demesne* after nearly three hundred years of self-rule and association with England. There was far more glory to him in that than in scaling the highest tower walls of Acre!

Still, pragmatic as he was, Philippe knew there was a possibility that he would have to go to the Holy Land, or at least promise to do so. He had been careful not to make any mention of that to Isabel. Philippe didn't need to have the divinatory powers of a mystic to know how she would react to that. She was resentful if he left her for a month or more. But a year? Perhaps two? It didn't bear thinking about, at least not now.

Of course Philippe had *no intention* of going, not if he could help it. He had too much important and unfinished business in France. Philippe was a builder; for nine years he had labored to build an intricate mosaic of power. Carefully he had cultivated the French ties to crown-annexed Champagne while keeping its nobility (his relatives) from taking too much power for themselves. He had relaxed the tensions between France and Toulouse; beat back threats from Burgundy, and established his rights as suzerain in the territories given him by way of Isabel's dowry.

A tremendous pattern of success in nine years' time.

Now the ultimate challenge: to strip Henry Plantagenet of his power, and take away his continental domains. Philippe felt that he had already made substantial progress to these ends; he was unwilling to let his efforts be subverted by events taking place two thousand miles away.

Philippe had always been ambitious. Now, with a son to plan for, he was even more anxious and determined to succeed in all his aims. His father had frittered away his power, involving himself in useless causes and rebellions which had brought him little more than a questionable measure of authority, and the ill-will of Henry Plantagenet.

But Philippe was different. He wanted to secure each piece of land he could, incorporate every border fief into the whole of the royal *demesne,* so that when he died he could hand his son an empire even bigger than the one Charlemagne had ruled over.

Thes were illustrious dreams, but Philippe was confident he could make them come true. He had every potential to do so. Fortune had been good to him, but much of Philippe's success was due to his own determination to succeed.

He had already considered betrothing Jacquie-Marie to the infant Arthur. That would give France a foothold in Brittany once more, now that Henry had seized it back by forcing Constance into marriage with one of his most undesirable lackeys, the Earl of Chester. There was a personal motive behind the idea of the betrothal too: a marriage between Philippe's adored daughter and Geoffrey's son would help to keep alive the memory of his sweet friend, and all they had meant to one another.

It was yet too soon to arrange a marriage alliance for little Louis. Philippe didn't wish to commit his heir to a promise that would likely be broken (given the political uncertainties of the time), long before the boy came of age to marry. But one thing was sure: Louis was going to have a different kind of life than Philippe had known. He would not be pushed aside, ignored, his schooling left to happenstance and the whims of ineffectual priests. Louis was going to have the finest tutors, the most comprehensive training in statecraft and war, and all the love and attention Philippe had been denied.

These plans kept him occupied, but he could not keep his mind off Richard, and it was that concern which made Philippe so irritable as he sat at dinner with his wife and mother one cold evening in mid-January. *One more day.* He had decided to give Richard one more day to contact him in Paris; when that day was over Philippe would gather up his army and march on Normandy. *That* was sure to light a fire beneath both Richard and Henry and show them that Philippe Capet meant to take all he wanted.

"More cream?" Adele held out a porringer to him.

Philippe took it and poured a little of the cream on his pastry. Isabel and Adele exchanged a subtle glance, wondering who would be the first to say it. Philippe had been surly and unspeaking through the meal.

"You aren't feeling very friendly tonight, are you?" Adele asked her son. "You've hardly had a word to say to either of us."

He stirred his potage, then tasted it. "You and Isabel have been doing enough talking for ten people."

"Don't be so nasty," Isabel told him, and although she didn't really want to say it she couldn't help adding, "you always seemed to have enough to say at table when Richard was here with us."

He gave her a disdainful glare but said nothing.

"Ah yes, Richard," Adele said, laughing lightly. "He's an odd sort."

"He has nice manners," Isabel muttered, but her voice was edgy and sarcastic.

"Nice manners, yes," Adele agreed, "but so formidable." She sneaked a quick look at Philippe then turned back to Isabel. "I think what he needs is a woman's legs around his back."

Caught by surprise at Adele's humor, Isabel nearly choked on her food as she laughed enjoyably. "Be quiet, Mother," Philippe snapped. He looked at Isabel. "You too."

"It's true," Adele replied, "it's unmanly the way he shuns female company." She allowed herself a secret little smile. "He is nothing like his brother Geoffrey."

"Richard is my friend," the king protested, "and I won't have you saying filthy things about him."

Adele ignored him and looked at Isabel. "I do believe that Richard is very naïve about women. I'm sure he thinks our breasts are just for holding up our dresses."

Both women laughed until Philippe silenced them by throwing his henap to the floor. "I told you to shut up!" he shouted. "My God, you talk like a pair of courtesans, both of you!"

Isabel sobered in the face of her husband's anger, but Adele still had her taunting face on. "Don't be such a prig, my boy. I have a right to my own opinions."

"If you keep them quiet," Philippe grumbled.

Adele laughed gaily and went about cutting her meat. "Each time I come back to Paris," she observed, "it seems to me your disposition has grown more sour."

Philippe wiped his mouth with a cloth. "I wonder you come back at all, Mother. You find so much to criticize here, and

Champagne is so much nicer, you always say."

"It is," Adele said, chewing her meat daintily, "but the men are better looking here in Paris."

Isabel gave her an indulgent smile, but Philippe seemed offended. "At your age I'd think such things would cease to be important considerations."

She pointed her knife at him. "The older you become the *more* important it is; for men *and* women. Just wait and see."

They all ate in silence for a while, then Philippe looked in Adele's direction. "It would please me greatly if you managed to keep your liaisons private. I find it very humiliating to hear my mother's illicit deeds talked about in the streets of the city, like some common slut."

Adele was about to reply but Isabel spoke first. "Philippe, you know very well how people like to gossip. It's none of their business, or ours, what your mother does."

He was accustomed to Isabel's objections but it infuriated him when she called him to account in front of anyone, particularly his mother. "I should have realized you'd take her part," he fumed. "Women like you and mother tend to stick together."

"Explain that!" Adele said, nearly upsetting her wine as she lunged forward toward her son. "I won't be slandered by you or any other man!"

"You're a slut, Mother, admit it."

"Philippe!" Isabel gasped.

He pointed his finger at Adele. "You know very well what I am talking about. It was bad enough in the past when you consorted openly with men of high station, de Puiseaux and the rest, but you cannot expect me to condone Justin de Foix!"

It was no surprise to her that he should say that. They'd had this argument several times in the last few weeks, since he had discovered that his mother's most recent lover was a brawny young stone cutter half her age. Justin de Foix was handsome and arrogant, an itinerant artisan offering his services to many of the cathedral sites. Presently he was working at Notre Dame and that was where the dowager-queen had met him during one of her periodic inspections of the work.

Usually their assignations took place at Adele's chateau on the fringes of the city, but several times she had brought her lover to the palace and that made Philippe furious. He had never learned toleration for his mother's habits, and the older she became the more problems her promiscuity created for him.

"Justin de Foix is none of your concern," she sniffed at Philippe. "I can take whatever man I wish to my bed and nothing you say can stop me!" She flung her henap to the floor and stood up, glaring at her son. "Mend your own ways before you talk that way to me again!"

They could hear her jewelry clinking as she hastened from the room.

Philippe watched as she went, then with a grunt he turned back to his wine.

Isabel's gaze was a soft light on his face, her voice almost a whisper. "Why did you have to say those things to her?"

Yet another complaining female voice. Philippe turned to glower at his wife, but did not answer.

He set out for Normandy on the following morning with a substantial army at his side, but they got no farther than the border when they were stopped. Henry's troops were strewn across the entire frontier. Rather than engage with them, the French king gathered up his men and proceeded on to Gisors where Henry Plantagenet was waiting for him.

The two kings greeted one another with a show of courtesy, and then the familiar squabbling began. For three days they did nothing but argue over the betrothal contract between Richard and Alais, and whether or not the Vexin would be returned to the custody of France.

In the midst of all this petty quarreling there suddenly appeared a man of peace. The Archbishop of Tyre had come to impress upon all the kings of Europe the dreadful plight of their Christian brethren in the East, and to ask for help. When he found Henry and Philippe involved in their peevish concerns, he preached them a pious sermon which so moved the two monarchs that they blushed with shame at their selfishness.

There was no escaping the inevitable. They bowed before the archbishop, kissed his ring, and together made their pledge to go forth in battle for the holy cause of Christ. Following their example, the Count of Flanders did likewise. Then a thousand knights came forward to take the same vow.

It was a glorious spectacle: each man robing himself in a crusaders cloak adorned with a cross—white for England, red for France, and green for the Flemings. They sang brave songs of heroes' deeds, and raised their vivid banners toward the sky. By nightfall there was not one man in this assembly who had not declared himself for Christ and the crusade.

Each man was caught up in the fervor of the moment, but for at least two of them it did not take long to secretly repent of the decision. Henry and Philippe had made their commitment in a mingled spirit of moral responsibility and political good sense, it's true, but they had also been manipulated by the archbishop to serve as an example for all of Christendom. The two men understood each other's mind well enough to know that neither of them welcomed this crusade. Therefore they pledged to embark upon the expedition at Eastertide of the following year, both hoping for some intervening circumstance to postpone it.

Henry sailed for England at the end of January.

It was a relief to leave so many problems behind in France, though he quickly acquired new ones. At once he called his earls and barons together at Geddington, and with the assistance of Archbishop Baldwin of Canterbury, opened discussion on the matter of the crusade.

The problems began when Henry announced exaction of the "Saladin tithe." *Each man would be taxed one-tenth of all his income and movable goods.* The money would be turned over to the crown in order to help finance the crusade. A similar tax would be levied in France and all other domains in Europe. It was the pope's way of assuring ample financial support for the crusade in the event that public enthusiasm died out before the venture was commenced.

Henry had called for many taxes during his reign but none so controversial as this. There was grumbling and dissent in every county where the king sent his men to collect the tax and it was not accomplished without violence. It was the same in France when Philippe announced the Saladin tithe in early February. This was the first time ever that men from all stations in life had been asked to pay so great an amount at one time, and for one cause. It was hardship, not lack of devotion, that made the subject controversial. Eventually both monarchs had to amend the tax, then abandon it altogether.

In the midst of this trouble there were other complications. Hugh of Lincoln had involved himself in some dangerous politics while Henry was away. This was the case: the king's chief Forest Justiciar had been persecuting certain members of the clergy for "having taken the king's own game" from the royal woodlands. The charges were unprovable, but the Justiciar, Geoffrey FitzPeter, continued to prevail upon the suspected men. Bishop Hugh looked into the evidence himself, found it wanting, and then promptly excommunicated the Justiciar.

It is easy to imagine Henry's reaction. His own edict, a remnant from his struggle with Thomas Becket, forbade that any of his officials be excommunicated without his knowledge. Geoffrey FitzPeter was the king's close friend. Whatever he had done, no action—temporal or spiritual—should have been taken before Henry had been notified! Hugh of Lincoln had not only violated the Constitutions of Clarendon, he had very possibly made a new and serious enemy: the king himself.

Hugh was summoned to Woodstock immediately.

He came upon Henry in the forest where the king was resting with his companions after a day of hunting. As usual he disdained ceremony, and sat upon the ground stitching a bandage for his hand. When Hugh approached the king looked up and saw him standing there, but went on with his sewing, pretending not to see.

Hugh bore the king's rudeness for a while, then sat himself down in the midst of the company. "How like your cousins of Falaise you are," Hugh observed.

Though the others present may not have understood his meaning, Henry knew well enough what he meant. The bishop was referring to some of the king's ancestors: low-born leather workers of Falaise who had been related to William the Conqueror.

Henry paused a moment to look down at the menial task he was engaged in, then, no longer able to pretend anger or indifference, he fell forward on his face, convulsed with laughter at the bishop's gentle mocking.

Later they talked more seriously of the matter that had brought Hugh there, and the bishop defended his actions against FitzPeter. When all the reasons had been told, Henry could see that Hugh had been honest in his judgment. The king made his own wishes known: Geoffrey FitzPeter was ordered to do penance. Since he was basically a good man, the Justiciar submitted willingly. He was then forgiven for his misdeeds and the scourge of excommunication was lifted.

Henry was relieved when that matter was settled. He did not want a breach between Hugh and himself because he truly loved the man. The fatal break with the archbishop Becket was still a scar on Henry's conscience, a painful one. He wanted no more quarrels with churchmen who were close to his heart. Henry was more sentimental than most men knew.

He was also more cunning.

When spring came, Henry was ready with a new conspiracy.

The man who had been out-witted by the French king had set his mind upon a plot against his own son. Although Henry had promised to aid Richard in every way he could, he was secretly complicating his son's efforts to prepare for the crusade. He had already sent a great deal of money south into the keeping of Richard's enemies, men like Aymar of Angoulême and Geoffrey of Rancogne. The purpose was to buy their cooperation in an insurrection against Richard. Raymond of Toulouse, another long-time rival of Richard's, had been similarly bribed.

Henry was taking no chances. The longer Richard could be kept in the south, the longer his commitment to the crusade could be postponed—and with it, Henry's own.

By the middle of April Isabel had once again discovered she was pregnant. She cursed her carelessness and even hoped in secret that she would miscarry. Four pregnancies in three and a half years! That was enough.

She said nothing of this to Philippe. He was leaving soon with his army and would probably be away all summer. Meanwhile she began to make preparations of her own. With Philippe gone there would be no reason to remain in Paris through the summer. Isabel had decided to spend the hot months at *Chateau Jolie* in Chantilly.

She would have liked to leave her children behind at the palace but knew she didn't dare. If anything happened to them while she was away, Philippe would never forgive her. So she would

have to take them; Edythe too, and a few of the palace serving
girls as well, since the chateau had no permanent household in
residence.

There was one thing more: Isabel had written a letter to Henri
of Champagne and sent it on to Troyes. Her message was deliberately vague, in the event it fell into other hands. *I am spending
the summer at Chantilly,* it said. He could decipher the hidden
meaning for himself.

Bad luck.

Richard had suffered nothing but bad luck since coming south
from Normandy three months ago. In February he had sent off
a letter to William of Sicily, asking for a loan of money and supplies for the crusade. King William was a close friend; he was also
Richard's brother-in-law, the husband of Joanna Plantagenet,
Richard's favorite sister. It was May now, and still no answer to
his request! Richard waited anxiously for it to come. He had
hoped to be on his way to the Holy Land by June.

That seemed unlikely now because there were other circumstances to frustrate his plans. A new rebellion had suddenly broken out in Poitou, instigated by Richard's old enemies Aymar of
Angoulême, Geoffrey of Rancogne, and Geoffrey of Lusignan
(who was older brother to the King of Jerusalem). Settling this
was going to take time. They had captured a few of Richard's
castles and now he would have to assemble a band of his Brabantine mercenaries to recapture those holdings.

Richard had many faults, but dishonesty was not one of them.
It would never occur to him that this rising had been deliberately
planned and financed by his father in order to keep him busy on
the continent. He didn't realize Henry was that desperate.

In England, Henry spent his days in desperation.

There was ugly news from France. In Normandy John reported that once again Philippe Capet was busily engaged in
building a fortress close to the frontier. *The bastard!* Just who did
he think he was dealing with? If Capet's actions went unchecked
for too much longer, the whole future of England's might, and
Henry's, would be at stake.

At fifty-five Henry Plantagenet was still more vigorous and active than most men who were years younger than himself. But he was tired. He had spent his whole life fighting: first to secure his possessions, then to hold on to them. Now, when he should have been enjoying the result of his perseverance, he was being forced to fight again.

He left London and went to Woodstock. Alais Capet was there, and Henry wanted a few days alone with her before leaving England. Whenever he needed rest and quiet, he went to her. She was many things to him: an understanding friend, a gentle lover, a patient companion. He hadn't always been good to her, but she was very dear to him. Sometimes he felt that in all the world there was no one who truly loved him—loved him completely and with gentleness—except for Alais.

She lived on the fringes of his life, yet she never complained. She had loved him for too many years to resent what he had done to her: ruined her chances of marriage, caused her name to be dishonored in all the courts of Europe. It was unlikely that she even blamed him for that.

To be the mistress of a king was lonely. Alais had no friends, no family to cheer her. All she had was Henry, and she had reconciled herself to that many years ago. She *clung* to it. It was all she had.

They had eaten and made love.

Henry lay in Alais' arms, wondering what her astute half-brother was doing in Normandy. He didn't want to think of things like that, at this moment all he wanted was to enjoy the feel of her fingers as she stroked his hair, and listen to the soothing way she spoke his name.

"Sleeping?" She bent close to whisper in his ear.

Henry shook his head. "Just relaxing, just enjoying you." He tightened his arm around her waist and kissed the dark folds of her hair that brushed his arm.

"You were so quiet at dinner."

His answer was a deep sigh as he snuggled closer, hiding his face between her breasts. God what comfort in the flesh of a woman! Passion, and then peace. That's what a woman's love had always meant to him. He felt his loins stir at the touch of her. There was such wisdom in flesh; the only wisdom.

Her voice was soft, but he could feel the resonance of the words as she spoke them with his face against her breast. "How long can you stay with me this time?"

Henry raised his head and looked at her, then brought his hand up to caress her cheek. He had an almost fatherly affection for Alais, and why not? She had come into his care as a child, and in his mind—no matter how many years she had been in his bed—she was a child still.

"My sweet little girl," he mused, "how I will miss you when I return to France."

She looked at him hopefully, her dark eyes forming a question. "Couldn't I go with you?"

"No," he said immediately, "I want to keep you safe, far out of the reach of Richard and your brother." His head sank to her breast again. He loved her breasts. They were big, the way he liked them, with dark, heavy nipples that tasted sweet when he sucked them. "Hold me," he whispered, flicking his tongue over her skin.

Alais held his head between her hands and kissed his shaggy hair. "My brother..." the word sounded strange in her mouth. "It seems so odd to say it. I've never even met him."

"That's no great loss to you," Henry grumbled, "he isn't worth the knowing. It's hard to believe the two of you shared the same father in sweet Louis. Philippe is nothing like him."

"I've heard it said his wife is very beautiful."

She wasn't baiting him. She knew better than to do that. But she was insecure. Alais was little more than plain-faced, and her lonely life discouraged any trappings of glamour in her dress. That didn't matter to Henry. He chose his women for their willingness and not their beauty. Alais didn't have much passion in her nature, but she *was* willing, always ready to submit herself to all the sexual whims of the king. Henry liked variety in his bed, and Alais did her best to make him happy.

"She is beautiful," Henry answered and raised his head to look into Alais's calm face. "She's very sweet too, much too sweet for that cold-blooded bastard. He nearly divorced her once. How much better it would have been for her if he had done so."

The images wavered in his mind: Isabel's lush beauty, plundered by her husband's cruel hands; her darling golden cunt, so wet and hot, stuffed with the famous Capet treasure. How Henry would have liked to keep her for his own. A girl like that could make a man stay young forever!

Alais read his expression and she felt a little sad, but as always her concern was for him. "Is there trouble in France?" she asked. "Is that why you have to go back?"

"It's nothing I care to talk about now," he told her. "I just want to enjoy being with you."

She tried once more to convince him. "I wouldn't cause you any trouble if you took me with you, Henry." Her eyes begged him to agree, and she hugged him closer. "It hurts me so much whenever you go away."

He pulled her down beside him on the bed. "I'll come back to you the first chance I get."

They kissed, and for a long time they held one another without speaking. Alais was feeling cold and afraid, and she did not know why. She could not count the number of times she had said goodbye to him, but she'd never felt so threatened as she did tonight. Kissing the creases on his brow she murmured, "I'm going to miss you, my love."

"And I shall miss you."

His voice had the sound of tenderness and it put tears in her eyes. "Henry," she whispered to him, "I wish at least one of our children had lived. Then I would always have some part of you with me."

Henry twisted over on his back and peered up at her. "It is possible we will be lucky yet," he said, and a glimmer of lust shined in his grey eyes. "I'm still man enough to make a child."

"I know that you are," Alais responded, and passed her fingers lightly over his beard. He needed to be assured often of his virility these past few years. His goat-like abilities had been legend since his teens; he feared to lose his manhood. The flesh was everything to him.

For herself, Alais didn't care. Her love for Henry was not a sensual thing. He was her symbol of strength, and her protector; the only man she had ever cared for. Alais bent to kiss his lips. "You are a wonderful lover," she murmured.

Her words and her kiss relaxed him and he reached to coil a lock of her hair around his finger. Then suddenly the smile faded and his expression grew sober. "Have you been happy with me, Alais? Tell me honestly, have you?"

How could he wonder? Her voice trembled with emotion as she answered. "My life would have been nothing without you."

"Oh Alais..." His big hands engulfed her frail shoulders. "Do you remember the first time I took you? You were twelve, just a child."

She remembered. "I loved you even then," she mused, but her lips tightened. "And you loved Rosamunde."

Yes, Rosamunde. The essence of her gentle spirit seemed to linger in this house Henry had built for her at Woodstock and this bed where he had made love to her a thousand times. Alais had been too young to be jealous of Rosamunde then, but in the year that followed, the memory had flayed her, he could tell.

"Don't speak of Rosamunde," he said. "She doesn't exist, except in memory. You're the only woman in my life now, and the only one I love."

Alais wanted, *needed* to believe him. "I know that," she answered. "And I want you to know this: no other woman has ever loved you as I do. Not Rosamunde. Not Eleanor. Not anyone."

Gratitude touched him like a sweet kiss, and Henry's eyes filled with tears. "My darling girl," he said, enveloping her in his arms, "you mean more to me than all the rest put together, and I will never let you go."

Her breath stirred like a light breeze on his face as she spoke. "I have no wish to go anywhere, except to follow you."

His smile was kindly and appreciative, it smoothed the lines of care from his face, making him look handsome and years younger, the way Alais first remembered him. "Neither of us are going anywhere right now," he said. "We're going to stay here in this bed." He rolled her over on her back and rested his chin between her breasts. "I'm going to fuck you till the sun comes up."

Alais tried to free her mind from all thought as he kissed her and ran his hands along her hips, but one matter tickled at her consciousness, keeping her distracted. "You didn't bring Johnny with you this time, did you?" she asked. She hoped he hadn't.

Henry raised his head from her breasts. "I know you don't like him, Alais, but he's a good boy in his own way, and he's very fond of you."

Alais smiled a sad, ironic smile. Because of that "fondness" of which Henry spoke, she had been forced to take John to her bed many times. Henry had wished her to do it, had instructed her. He was obsessed with giving Johnny everything he wanted. It flattered Henry's vanity and made him feel as if he was a loving father. He didn't seem to care how Alais felt about it. Nor did John.

At first Alais had been unwilling to be mistress to her lover's son, but she'd soon learned to tolerate the situation. And she felt a little sorry for John. He was a misfit. Often when she held him in her arms she had the feeling it was really a mother's love he needed.

Alais could sympathize with that.

Her own mother had died giving birth to her, and less than two weeks later Louis had wed Adele of Champagne. Alais, the unwanted infant princess, had been sent away to live with the Capet relatives in Dreux. Then, at the age of seven, she'd been given over to the care of the Plantagenets, for she had already been betrothed to their son.

In her whole life Alais had seen her father fewer than a dozen times. Often, when she was just a girl, she had lain in Henry's arms and dreamed of the fair-haired man so far away in Paris, whose face she could barely recall.

Henry's voice brought her back to the present.

"Johnny's in Normandy," he explained. "That means there's only me for you to entertain, my love."

She ran her fingers through his hair. "Johnny's just like the rest of us," she mused. "He only needs to feel that he is loved."

He nestled his beard against the soft white flesh of her belly. "Oh, Alais, Alais, Alais," he moaned, "I love you so very much..."

Later she lay contentedly beneath the weight of his heavy body as he thumped against her and sought to prove he was just as much a man as he had ever been. "Is it good? Is it good?" Henry grunted in her ear, as Alais held him close and whispered yes, trying to forget that soon—so very soon—he would be gone from her again.

It was good. When it was over Henry pulled the coverlet up around her sweaty shoulder, and kissed her with the fondness of a loving father. "Sleep, sweet girl," he said, and closed his eyes.

* * *

Richard had known frustration in his life, but never anything
as bad as this! Since April he had been engaged in a series of
wars with the rebellious barons of Poitou. No sooner had he defeated them—driven their numbers back to Taillebourg, taken
the fortress and secured it, scattered his enemies—then he was
faced with yet another crisis.

Count Raymond of Toulouse, Richard discovered, had been
sending money and troops to the aid of the rebels. The count
was an old rival and Richard's blood grew hot with rage when he
heard of his treachery.

Richard took an army and ravaged the border of Toulouse. He
even captured Raymond's lover, Peter Seilun, who was also a
high-ranking magistrate of the county. When Raymond found
out that his "favorite" was being held a prisoner under barbarous
conditions, he retaliated with an army of his own. As a result
there were some border skirmishes where many men died, but
Richard would not release his celebrated prisoner for any
amount of money or any amount of threats.

Now it was Raymond who took hasty action. He ordered the
capture of several members of King Henry's household who
were traveling through Toulouse and had them imprisoned. It
was considered a most savage deed. Travelers from any royal
court were supposed to be assured their safety. Raymond had
broken the code of Chivalry, and Richard was going to make him
pay for it!

Complications. Recriminations.

Richard had involved himself in a ruinous turn of events.
What money he had been able to raise for his venture to the
Holy Land had been spent to pay his mercenary troops. Wasted
money. Wasted time! And for all of it, Richard was still no closer
to leaving on his grand crusade.

At this point Philippe Capet entered the situation when he
came to negotiate between the two men at Toulouse in early
June. Because their counties were a part of the continental domain, both Richard and Raymond were the vassals of the king of
France. Philippe intended to use his authority to bring about a
settlement of the hostilities. War among his vassals meant plundered villages, burned crops, ruined herds. *It meant a loss of revenue to the crown.*

He tried to mediate between the two men, but his efforts were in vain. Neither Richard nor Raymond were willing to compromise. Both complained to Philippe of injuries done them; both demanded restitution for their trouble. For three days Philippe heard their disputations, and found little satisfaction in his role as peacemaker.

He was especially disgusted with Richard whose decision to take the cross had changed everything. When they met at Toulouse Richard's attitude was cool, dispassionate. The love relationship which Philippe had hoped would grow into a solid political alliance had deteriorated badly during months of separation.

Frustrated and disappointed, Philippe withdrew, leaving the quarrelsome rulers to resolve their own differences. For if Richard would not be a lover or a friend, then he could damn well be an enemy for all Philippe cared! He left Toulouse and set about his own plans.

Philippe went back to Chateauroux.

He occupied the town with mercenaries, and dreamed of even greater things. There was a plan for the full-scale invasion of the Aquitaine. Who could stop him? Henry was still in England, and his troops in Normandy were under John's command (*that* said enough right there). Richard was far too involved with his little wars to notice an advance by Philippe's troops. He would be sorry. They would *all* be sorry.

But Philippe took one last diplomatic precaution. He sent a message to Henry in England. *Is it not possible for you to keep your son from ravaging the lands of Raymond of Toulouse? The dispute between them has worked hardship upon me....*

Henry sent back a terse reply.

I knew not of it.

Manage it yourself.

ℐSABEL'S MILK tasted like sweet cream.

Henri of Champagne lay on her breast. He drank from her and held her in his arms and loved her with all the passion he had repressed since their last meeting.

It was late June in Chantilly.

Isabel clung to him in desperation, as if all the ordinary acts of love could not satisfy her, and when it was over she lay silently in his arms. Sweat kept their skin close, yet even as Henri held her tight upon his heart, Isabel seemed distant from him. He could almost feel her thoughts vibrating, troubled and silent, in the darkness.

She was meditating upon the confusion of her life and all the actions which seemed to lead her back to the same shadowed place, twisting round and round again like stone stairs in a tower. The logic of her experience was hopelessly beyond her, all the mistakes of the past scattered at her feet like unstrung pearls.

Why had she brought Henri here?

Isabel knew the reason.

This friendship had become as addictive as love. It was unsettling. Just one more complication in a state of circumstances she could not control. Henri had become necessary to her now, almost as necessary as Philippe, because he pulled in the outer edges of her life that her husband had never thought to touch.

It was because of the dreams too—dreams which plagued her, making her afraid, making her need Henri—that Isabel had brought him here. She could not share the nightmares with Philippe, because they dealt with Geoffrey. But Henri heard them with patience; made her feel less threatened. Because of that she loved him in a way which had meaning only to herself....

She knew he was not asleep, that his thoughts were wandering with hers. After a while his voice came out of the darkness, floating close upon her ear. "Isabel," he asked quietly, "what do you feel for me?"

She groped for his hand and found it. "You've asked me that before and I have told you. I love you for your kindness. Your friendship." Isabel snuggled closer. "And I enjoy having you in my bed."

Friendship. She made the word sound beautiful. Full of meaning. Full of passion. But for all that it was just a word, after all. Henri slipped his hand beneath the sheet and fondled her swollen abdomen. "There is no place on earth I would rather be than in your bed. Still, I don't like to see you *this* way."

"Do I seem ugly to you now?"

He traced her throat with a necklace of kisses. "Of course not. If anything you are more beautiful than before." His hand crept upwards, balancing the weight of her left breast upon his palm.

"Though I would not have thought these could be richer, fuller..." Then suddenly his voice turned slightly petulant. "Seeing you like this reminds me too keenly that you belong to Philippe."

She pressed her face to the silky black hair of his chest. "Right now I belong to you."

He wanted it to be true. God knew she felt as if she belonged in his arms! He kissed away the sweat from her forehead while Isabel nibbled at his beard. "But do you *want* me?" Henri whispered, "do you truly want me?"

Her one hand disappeared beneath the sheet, then at last she stripped away the covering altogether. She bent her face to his belly, her tongue darting out in gentle licking kisses. His skin was so white there, and delicate as a girl's. It made her want to cry. There was such vulnerability and sweetness in the flesh. Such sadness and joy!

She raised her head to look at him. "You see? I *do* want you...."

Later that night they sat together by the uncovered window, trying to draw in breath from out of the humid night. The air smelled sweet and heavy.

"I came here to escape the heat," she said, fanning herself with a fluttering hand, "yet we've been sweltering since we got here, same as in Paris." She entwined the fingers of her left hand with his. "Still it is better for the children here. The city air and its ill-humors are bad for them."

He squeezed her hand. "I heard of the birth of your son. You must be very proud."

"Louis is a fine child," Isabel answered. Though her face was turned from him, Henri knew that she was smiling.

He touched her belly lightly with the tips of his fingers. "When is this one due?"

"In the fall." She looked down at her burden and patted Henri's hand that covered it. "October. I'm so big already, I think it might be twins again."

Henri studied her face, retracing the features he had memorized years ago. The moonlight had turned her skin to silver and accentuated the deep shadows beneath her eyes. She looked ghost-like, beautiful and strange. He felt suddenly afraid for her.

"What's wrong?" Isabel asked, seeing the change in his expression.

"I worry about you. Childbirth is hard. My own wife nearly died bearing our daughter last spring, and she is far stronger than you."

Isabel kissed his knuckles, praising him for his concern. "The women in my family are small, but fertile. My own mother has borne ten children and will doubtless have more, yet she was well enough when I saw her last." The words faded into silence then as she tightened her grip on his hand. "But Henri, my love, I *do* worry. Each time I have given birth I've felt myself come close to death." Her voice faltered and she looked up into his face. "I'm very afraid of dying, Henri."

Love for her overwhelmed him, and Henri gathered her into his arms. "Don't speak of dying! I would give my own life to keep you safe from harm."

They kissed, and as they did Isabel felt his tears wetting her face. *How sweet he was.* Already she had grown too dependent upon him and that must end, for both their sakes. Into his ear she whispered, "Stay with me all the night my dearest, but promise to be gone in the morning. We cannot risk that anyone should discover we are here together."

He answered between gasps and kisses. "I shall do whatever you say."

Isabel felt as though she were deceiving both Henri and Philippe; wishing she loved one and not the other. But wishing was useless and nothing would ever change, because it was Philippe she loved, and it would always be Philippe. Henri's passion provoked her to tears and she wept, "It would be better for us both if you did not love me."

His kisses fell lightly on her upturned face. "Forbid me, then! Forbid me to love you."

She knew what it was to love and be denied. "I cannot," she answered. "I cannot."

John was urging Henry to return to Normandy.

Since May he had been sending frantic letters to his father in England, describing events which were taking place on the continent. When Chateauroux fell to the French on June 16th, matters took a more serious turn. By invading Berry, Philippe Capet had broken the truce in which Henry had put so much faith. It seemed that if the French king was willing to risk all that such a breach implied, he was likely to have more definite plans in mind for the future. Dangerous plans.

John suggested his father send an army to Chateauroux to challenge Philippe's hold on the city but Henry was not prepared to do that. He was a conservative man at heart. He never fought unless forced to do so; unless he could not find another way.

At this point he still preferred to negotiate.

So, near the end of June he sent Baldwin, Archbishop of Canterbury and bishop Hugh of Lincoln to meet with the French king. They came not just as envoys of England but of the Church as well. Henry hoped their pious presence and learned conversation in the art of debate would influence Philippe against further encroachment upon English domains.

Henry should have known better, he should have learned his lesson by this time. Philippe was not one to be swayed. He received Baldwin and Hugh with a show of graciousness and courtesy, then promptly disagreed with everything they said.

It was simple, he explained. *He* had not broken the truce. It was Henry's fault for allowing Richard to ravage the territory of a French vassal, Raymond of Toulouse. That was an act of war and by lending tacit support to such destruction, Henry was the offending party. France was merely retaliating as her king saw fit and right. After four tedious days of talks, Baldwin and Hugh went away, dissatisfied.

Philippe smiled as he watched them go.

In England Henry did not smile as he listened to what his two emissaries told him, and he made a swift decision to cross over to the continent at once. Perhaps if he and Richard were to combine their armies along the borders of Touraine and Berry they could force Philippe to withdraw his troops from Chateauroux. That would keep Aquitaine safe for the time being, and forestall any hopes Philippe might have of going north to capture Normandy.

After riding all night from London, Henry arrived at Dover as the sun was rising on yet another humid summer day. At the fortress high above the sea he conferred briefly with the Earl of Essex and other of his advisers. Then he went down the hill to the harbor where a ship was waiting for him, flying the banner of England. There was yet another standard shivering in the dull morning breeze: the grinning leopard of Plantagenet significance, imprisoned on a square of violet silk.

Henry's blood was racing as he bounded up the wooden gangplank, his retinue trailing far behind. In a small way he was glad Philippe had broken the truce, for even if it did not relieve Henry of his lately-made crusader's vow, it did leave him free to strike back at the Capet with everything he had.

He stood at the bow looking over the side of the ship where tiny waves lapped up to meet it. The water was calm, almost flat, and it stretched out before him like an azure carpet. Beyond it was Normandy, land of Henry's ancestors, *crux* of the Anglo-Norman nation he had built. He was determined to protect it at all cost, and against any foul devices of the king of France.

Behind him was England, its familiar chalky coast receding into dimness as Henry sailed away from it. He looked back for just a moment, experiencing a twinge of melancholy he could not explain. It was much like the feeling he'd known two weeks ago at Woodstock when he kissed Alais goodbye. He pondered it, then just as quickly shrugged off the feeling and stared defiantly into the distance.

He had seen England for the last time.

All over France the cattle and the crops were dying. It had been a barren summer, and the rivers that criss-crossed the land ebbed low at their banks. For too many weeks there had been no rain. Drought had turned the lush green hills to faded tufts of grey. Children cried from hunger in their sleep. The wells were emptying.

It was late July; hotter than almost any man remembered.

Sign of a bitter winter yet to come, the poorfolk said, for it was well known among those who worked the land that a hot and arid summer presaged early frost and lingering cold weather a few months hence. Food was scarce now and would be scarcer once the chill set in. The people worried, and grumbled as they went about their work.

For they could see the hand of God in this misfortune—a

wrath visited upon them because the Holy cities of the East had fallen to the Infidel, with yet no prince of Europe set to go against the enemies of Christendom. Rumors of wars among French vassals in the south caused fresh resentments. Was not God punishing the poor for the sins of noblemen who raided villages and plundered sacred shrines?

The common people didn't understand these grudges and blood battles of the rich. They only knew that when one lord fought another it was the poor who suffered most. They prayed to God that very soon their young king would redeem them all by going far across the sea and winning back Jerusalem. Then God would smile, and once again the rain would come.

Isabel had not intended to stay the entire summer at *Chateau Jolie*, but as it happened, she did. One hot July night her pains began, and by the morning Edythe had helped deliver her of two boy babies, born more than two months prior to their time and thus, born dead.

Isabel went nearly mad with grieving.

Within the week an escort of the household bodyguard conveyed the tiny hand-made coffins back to Paris for burial at Notre Dame. But it was impossible for Isabel to leave Chantilly at that time, though she would have liked to go; it was weeks before she could even leave her bed. When she did it was only to take a little air in the garden. There she would sit among late blooming flowers, staring at a fading landscape, seeing summer at its ebb.

It was God's design. *There could be no end of dying.*

* * *

. . . our good king Henry is still a soldier.

August has been a time of tribulation but our good lord leads us, and we, his soldiers, follow. We have joined with the armies of Prince Richard, and together forced the king of France out of Berry, where he has no right to be, though he claims it as his own by means of conquest and descent. It is the ignoble Phillipe-Auguste *who prevents my lords Henry and Richard from fulfilling their pledge to fight in the east. . . .*

Now he has sent the bishop of Beauvais, his cousin, to spread tumult in

Normandy. Aumale has been invaded, its fortress burned to the ground. But King Henry says we shall retake Mantes by September. The king of France has retreated back to Paris...

William the Marshal
Letter fragment
August 25, 1188

* * *

Summer was ended.

Isabel returned to Paris early in September. She had lost weight, and looked very pale—but physically she was recovered enough to ride a horse all the way from Chantilly to the Ile de la Cité.

Emotionally she was in turmoil.

Guilt for her liaison with Henri, and the sense of being persecuted because of it, assailed her in equal measure. She felt that God was punishing her for sins which were her nature to commit. She brooded over this. She felt afraid.

In the crypt at Notre Dame there were two new stone boxes; nearby were the others, little Baldwin and Margot, and just beyond them a splendid basalt tomb, black with emerald edging.

Geoffrey, you were my friend!

A candle seemed too small an offering. Instead she gripped the roses in her hand till the thorns pierced her, then smeared a finger kiss in blood beside his name.

Sibylla was back in Paris.

William de Beaujolais had been appointed to the *curia regis* and brought his wife and little daughter to live at the Cité Palais at the king's request. It was Philippe's way of being kind. He was worried about Isabel's state of mind. She had taken her recent misfortune badly, even though he had assured her that as soon as she was strong again there would be another pregnancy. In any case, the company of her young sister was sure to cheer her.

Sibylla? She was carefree as a song. At just past fifteen she saw herself the luckiest young woman in the world. She had the husband she had always dreamed of, and a beautiful daughter. In January there would be another child, hopefully a son. She could not have been more happy with her life had she herself been queen.

Paris seemed less of a dismal place to her now. Hot autumn

sun shined on the slate roofs and dull grey stones of the city. The rushing Seine seemed undiminished by the summer drought. It was as blue as the sky which covered it. Birds filled the trees.

I will be happy here, Sibylla thought.

On September 18th there was a banquet in the great hall to celebrate the eight years that Philippe had worn the crown. William and Sibylla led the dancing while the king and queen looked on, Philippe in rare high spirits. Sibylla looked past the whirling colored shapes of silk and jeweled damask, and saw him laughing, his profile raised against a wall of flames.

Isabel, subdued and pale, sat close beside him. There were stains on her sheer pink chainse, the greasy print of Philippe's fingers near her left breast. He pulled his wife into his arms and fed her a little wine from his own cup. When a drop of it rolled down her chin he kissed it away with his tongue.

The room was hot and filled with people. Sibylla poured a little water on her neck to make her cool; she gripped William's hand beneath the table. Just at that moment she needed more than anything for her husband to know she loved him above all men on earth. Yet her gaze carried beyond his face, toward the center of the table where the king sat. *Isabel is bewitched by him,* she thought. *She would give up her soul rather than lose him.*

Before the meal was halfway done, Philippe had pulled Isabel to her feet and led her from the room.

It was late September in Gisors, and hot.

After three days of talks nothing had been decided. Henry and Philippe had come to this familiar meeting place to discuss an end to the latest series of hostilities, but before very long the two men were locked in stubborn confrontation once again, this time at the conference table. The petty tone of their bickering was not to be believed.

They were fighting over a tree.

Henry and his men had arrived first, claiming shade under the famous old elm tree, while the late-coming French sweltered in the hot sun, unprotected. Philippe interpreted this action as a deliberate breach of courtesy, and refused to recognize the authority of the English king to dictate any terms of settlement so long as he and his men were denied an equal place of shade beneath the tree.

When Philippe came out of his tent on the morning of the fourth day, Henry crossed over to meet him. He extended his hand to Philippe, but the French king spurned it, and turned away.

Henry squinted against the sun. "We must come to some agreement, lad. Neither of us can afford to pay mercenaries who sit idle while we parlay. Not in these hard times."

There was a sprinkling of laughter from the English contingent but Philippe ignored it. "So you say. What you do with your mercenaries is your affair. What I do with mine is my own. I wouldn't waste my breath if I were you."

Henry took a step forward. "We are wasting time Philippe, and in the heat at that. We simply have to come to some kind of settlement."

"Do we?" Philippe's sharp words rang in the air. "My men are at Chateauroux, that's all I know..."

"Your troops were swept clean out of Berry, in case you don't remember," Henry answered, mopping the sweat from his forehead with his sleeve. "And with Bourges in my control, Chateauroux scarcely matters."

"If it does not matter you would not wish to have it back," Philippe argued cunningly. "In any case, my mercenaries can hold it against your men, and Richard's, at any cost."

"Your mercenaries; yes, perhaps," Henry laughed, "if they have not already disbanded for lack of pay. Regardless, they must go. You have no right to Chateauroux or any part of Berry, and you know it."

Philippe was perturbed for many reasons, including the fact that Richard had purposely stayed away from this meeting, just to avoid seeing him. How false his lover had proved to be! Philippe looked dourly at Henry. "You want me out of Chateauroux," he grumbled "and yet you offer me nothing in return. Where is the benefit to me? What do *I* gain?"

Henry was tired of this. The two of them had been shouting at one another for three days and nothing had been solved. They were bluffing, both of them. Philippe's mercenaries may or may not be sufficient to hold Chateauroux, but he was almost certainly unable to pay them. Henry had the same difficulty with the Welsh bowmen he had brought to France. He could not remain on alert for a prolonged period of time, watchful over Capet's every action and the movement of his troops. They needed a binding concordance, a settlement written down on paper.

Wearily, Henry put the terms once more. *If Philippe would return Chateauroux and the fortresses he had taken, he would not be forced to pay reparations for the damages of war. Likewise, Henry promised that Richard would withdraw from Toulouse, and do an act of homage to Philippe for his continental domain.*

Philippe spat upon the ground. This was all too reminiscent of the first time he and Henry had met at Gisors, and the memory of that humiliating day soured in the French king's mind. "Fuck you, old man," he sneered, and walked away.

Scorn and futility. Henry proposed another meeting for October, then gathered up his men and rode away toward the Loire Valley. That very night Philippe ordered the destruction of the Gisors elm. It took half the night for two strong men to cut it down.

Traveling south toward Chatillon-sur-Indre, Philippe Capet brooded over the ill luck which had overtaken him. For the first time in his association with the Plantagenets, he was facing the combined strength of Henry and Richard. It was a formidable task.

Something *had* to be done to separate Richard from his father.

Last year it had seemed possible. Love had made Richard and Philippe so close. Then had come the evil news from Jerusalem, and Richard had chosen spirit over flesh.

But he would come to regret the day he had disappointed Philippe. By God, he *would*.

No change.

The week of meetings at Chatillon-sur-Indre was a repeat of what had transpired between the two kings earlier at Gisors. Henry offered the same terms. Philippe gave the same answer.

Then suddenly he had a change of heart. He *would* give up the fortresses he had captured in Berry, he declared, but only if Henry would cede to him the castle of Pacy. It was a strategically important fortress on the Norman border between Evreux and Mantes, and Philippe demanded its possession as a "pledge of good faith" by the English king.

It was unthinkable, and Henry refused to give it up. Once again the conference was suspended and everyone went home. There was no longer any question about keeping the mercenaries employed: both monarchs issued orders to disband them, despite the fact that none of the men had been paid in months.

Philippe went north toward Paris by way of Bourges, taking his Brabantines with him. He had promised them full payment as soon as they crossed over into the royal *demesne*. The men had been grumbling for weeks, threatening retaliation for their impoverished state, but the promise of money soon quelled their resentment.

Once they reached Sancerre, however, Philippe went back on his word. Protected by two thousand of his own French knights, he did not have to fear what the disgruntled mercenaries would do and so he turned them out, unpaid. To assure his own safety he had his soldiers strip them of their weapons and horses and even their outer clothing, leaving them naked but for their braies!

The Brabantines screamed curses at the French king, but he laughed at them and shouted back, "This will teach you Flemish pigs to threaten me! You did nothing in my service but sit by idly and eat the food which I provided. I owe you nothing more in return."

He pushed his horse into the midst of his double rank of bodyguards, then spurred it north, without even looking back.

At Orléans the king consulted with his advisers.

Flanders was there, and Philippe's Champagnois uncles, all looking on with doubting frowns, distressed by the king's continued stubborness and his refusal to make a truce with Henry Plantagenet. What had begun as a worthwhile gamble to take control of Aquitaine had deteriorated into a foolish, petty quarrel which the nobles on either side could no longer conscience. Count Theobold of Chartres and his brother, the Bishop of Rheims, had discussed their feelings with Philip d'Alsace and elected him their spokesman.

"We have come to a decision," Flanders told the king. "For myself, at least, I can no longer be a party to this continual antagonism of the English king."

The words had barely gotten past his tongue when Philippe flew at him. "Listen, d'Alsace, if you have once more chosen to follow Henry instead of me, I swear to God I will not take you back into my service the next time you wish to return!"

Flanders raised his arm, chest level, as if to pledge his sincerity. "That is not what I am saying. My loyalty is to you and only you; no other. But this lamentable situation with the English has gone on far too long. I have sworn that I shall not lift my sword against another Christian till I have fulfilled my vow to fight for our Lord in the Holy Land."

Philippe's eyes narrowed. "What?"

"It is so," Flanders told him, lowering his voice, trying to sound meek. "Therefore I urge you to seek a peaceful settlement with Henry and his son, and as soon as possible. If you like, I shall arrange another meeting between the two of you."

Philippe looked past d'Alsace, his gaze smoldering over the faces of Theobold and William. "And do you feel likewise?" he asked his uncles.

They nodded with one accord.

"Shit," Philippe muttered.

In Paris the windows of the king's council chamber had been newly fitted with colored glass, the first in the palace to be so treated. One of the windows faced the river, with a southern view of the city. For a day and a night Philippe sat looking out of it, pondering what he would do next.

He had disbanded his mercenaries; now the nobles refused to fight! Henry would hear about that, certainly. When he did, Philippe would be in even less of a position to bargain than he had before. It was damned inconvenient. It was humiliating.

Philippe considered the situation for a long while, then quite suddenly made his decision. That night, as a full moon rose high above the city, and nearly everyone else slept, he sat down to write a cryptic letter to the king of England. Finished, he read it over, and smiled with secret glee.

Carefully Philippe signed his name, affixed his signet seal and then went across the corridor to the common room. With an unceremonious kick he roused two of his bodyguard from sleep and ordered them to rise at once and dress.

Muttering quiet oaths beneath their breath, the men pulled on their clothes and boots, and strapped their swords into place. The king instructed them in their duty: the letter was to be put into the hands of Henry Plantagenet, and no other. Then he bid them go.

Mounted on swift horses, the two men clattered over the bridge and onto the road beyond, galloping past shadowed vineyards and fields of dying wheat. They rode without stopping, because the king's business was urgent.

They were at Gisors before the sun was fully up.

Mid-October in Paris and still no rain. No rain at all.

These last two days thick clouds had choked the sky, but they only hung there, sagging like paper decorations at a ball. The air was heavy, alive with a sense of waiting.

Philippe was waiting, waiting to hear from Henry. Then at last the answer came. *The matter raised in Philippe's letter would be discussed more fully at a meeting near Bonsmoulins the middle of November.* When Philippe read that he could barely restrain his joy. Now he had only to wait a little longer—and everything he had worked to achieve would follow.

On a humid night just hours before the storm came, Philippe pulled Isabel from her bed and carried her to the palace garden. They made love in the druid grove among the oaks and apple trees, just as they had done so often in the past when things had been happier between them.

"I feel as though we were young lovers once again," he told her, holding her close upon his chest. "There was a time, when first we were together... before all the trouble started with your family, when everything was so good between us—do you remember?"

Her arms circled his waist covetously. "Don't say that, my love. It has always been wonderful between us, even during the bad times."

"I know," he agreed, fondling her bare shoulders. "I can't even imagine how it would have been if we had never married."

She licked his throat, then let her tongue wander to the thick hair of his beard. "I never wanted anyone but you," Isabel whispered, and at that moment it was not a lie. He was the only one. *The only one.*

Her hair lay in golden streamers across his chest. Philippe gathered a handful and pulled it to his lips. Soft. Smelling of flowers. So sweet! A sudden tenderness for her jerked inside of him. Isabel sensed his reaction and couldn't help trying to take advantage of it. Her heart was beating faster; it frightened her just to say the words. "Philippe," she pleaded, "please promise me you will not go to the Holy Land. Promise that you will not leave me!"

Since late last spring when first she had heard that he'd taken the cross, Isabel had used a dozen different arguments to make him change his mind. So far Philippe had shown little evidence that he truly wished to go, but that could change easily enough if he and Richard came to an understanding once again, and Isabel dreaded that more than anything. Richard, bull-strong and beckoning, drawing Philippe into his world of manly adventure: it chilled her just to think of it.

Philippe knew her objections, the arguments she feigned which could all be expressed in three words: *don't leave me.* He didn't want to leave her, didn't give a damn for the crusade, and had told her so many times. Yet Isabel persisted in bringing it up: always at moments like this, and always with desperation in her voice. *Women are ruled by their emotions.* Philippe knew that. But emotions seldom made good politics, and in the future politics might determine whether or not he fulfilled his crusader's vow.

She felt delicate in his arms; fragile. But Philippe knew her strength of will. Isabel would fight with every bit of charm and wit she owned to keep him with her, and at this moment it was what he wanted too. "Let's not speak of such things now," he said and rolled her over on her back. "We have far better means to pass the night...."

His hands, his lips, the very sound of his voice excited her. Isabel reached for him, her hands encircling his taut flesh, stroking him into readiness for her. "It's so beautiful," she murmured. "Oh, my darling Philippe, it is the most beautiful thing in all the world! I want it all to myself; I want it to be mine and no one else's!"

He pushed her head between his knees and held it there as Isabel satisfied herself on the flesh she loved so well. No one could make him feel as she did. *Oh Christ, he wanted it to last forever.* "Drink all you want," he gasped, and shuddered as she licked up every drop of passion.

They slept in the hulking shadow of the huge old oak tree, where mistletoe twisted round the craggy trunk like a green primeval wreath. It was still dark when they awoke to the gentle sting of rain upon their skin. Philippe tossed Isabel's torn and

ruined dress aside and covered her with his cloak, then gathered
her into his arms and carried her inside. Upstairs in her damask
bed they made love till dawn stretched its grey shade across their
faces, and the scent of wetness seeped into the room.

Then they slept again.

Flanders' decision to force a peace agreement between Henry
and Philippe was a matter of conscience. He was sincere in his
espousal to raise no sword against a Christian till he had helped
to free Jerusalem. He was a fervent man, strong in his faith,
despite his many human faults.

He was getting old and death was often on his mind. Philip
needed to repent the wickedness of his life, to sanctify his sinful
flesh by shedding heathen blood. And he was tired of playing
stupid, petty politics with the kings of Europe. A settlement of
the hostilities couldn't come soon enough to please him.

In that spirit he accompanied Philippe to Bonsmoulins.

This time the Plantagenets turned out in force. Henry had
brought Richard and John with him, also Godfrey. The King of
England spoke with Philippe privately before the conference was
begun. Together they decided upon the course of action which
they would take; all that Philippe had written in his letter. Then
they concocted a different story for the others.

Philippe held the precious piece of paper in his hand and
gloated silently. This had been less complicated to arrange than
he had guessed. To Henry he said, "You will sign this tomorrow
in my tent, before all the assembled witnesses of both our courts.
Until then we are bound by our secret oath to one another."

"Yes," Henry agreed with a jerk of his head, "if you will swear
to me that all we have said will remain secret till this document is
signed."

"But of course," Philippe answered, clasping Henry's hand.

It was the most delicious lie he'd ever told.

It was Richard's custom to take the Sacrament and make his
confession every morning, whether or not he was encamped with
his army or engaged in war. A man who lived in the palm of
danger as Richard did, felt his own mortality with keen awareness. It was wise to remain in a constant state of grace, rather
than to risk damnation merely for the sake of sloth.

On a chilly morning in mid-November as a dawn mist blew off the surface of the river, Richard rose from his devotions and made his way back to the tent for a hurried breakfast with his younger brother.

"Why do you wake me so early?" John wailed as Richard shook him by the shoulders. "I never rise before the sun."

Chuckling, Richard doused his brother's face with wine. "The sun rose a full hour ago. The sky is dark because a storm is near. Get up, Johnny, take a meal with me. This is no time for idling like a recreant. This is a most important day."

John sat up glumly and gazed through sleepy eyes at Richard's vacant bed alongside his own. The cushions were arranged in neat order and the coverlet was folded. John smiled. His brother was a man of fastidious habits who never stayed in bed beyond the dawn unless some illness plagued him. Or unless some handsome favorite tempted him to stay.

John shook his shaggy hair in place and wiped away the droplets of wine with his hand. He looked across at Richard, who was dipping bread into a pot of honey and eating with the dainty manners of a high-born maiden. What contradiction there was between Richard's brawny, muscled form and delicate habits. John slumped back against the cushions and yawned into his fist. "What makes this day more important than any other?"

Often Richard wore a grave expression regardless of his mood, but this morning he was smiling. "This is the day our father makes his peace with Philippe!" he declared. "When that is done and all the terms are settled, nothing shall bar my way to the East." He lifted his henap in a symbolic toast. "That, my brother, is a cause for celebration."

John slipped back beneath the covers and turned his face into the softness of the cushions. "Only *that?*" he muttered, and closed his eyes.

The spirit of affection chided Richard's disapproval for his brother's attitude. Despite his laziness and folly, Johnny was a good boy. "Go back to sleep," he answered, and sloshed a little water in his wine.

Two hours later all the principles were assembled in King Philippe's tent. Even John was there. Henry described the situation in perfunctory terms. *Both sides had agreed to give back all their gains*

since the two kings had taken the cross in January of that same year.
Philippe would relinquish Chateauroux and all parts of Berry and in
return Henry would not extract payment for the mischief done in Nor-
mandy by the French king's cousin in his raids on Mantes and Aumâle.
Richard would release the county of Quercy into the custody of Raymond
of Toulouse, and take the city of Chateauroux for his own.

Philippe scarcely dared to breathe as the document was read.
He had staked his luck on the certainty that Richard would reject
those terms and he was not to be disappointed. Immediately
Richard's face turned red with choler. How dare his father agree
to such an uneven settlement behind his back! The gains he had
made in the south against Toulouse were worth far more in revenue than Chateauroux and its few crumbling fortresses could
offer.

He turned to Henry and before all the witnesses proclaimed,
"I will submit my person to the Count of Toulouse and stand trial
by his will for the crime of ravaging his lands. But I shall *not* give
up what I have gained by lawful conquest." His eyes moved from
Henry's face to Philippe's. "And I will fight any man who says I
must."

Henry shuffled his feet nervously and cleared his throat. This
was not what he had expected. Philippe had assured him that
Richard wanted Chateauroux! Unsteadied by his son's outburst,
he kept his eyes level with the floor, saying nothing.

Philippe had an answer, one which he had rehearsed a dozen
times since the possibility of this brilliant plot had struck him. He
extracted a second document from his sleeve and waved it under
Richard's nose. His voice was hard-bitten in revenge. "Perhaps
my lord Richard would prefer these terms." Philippe bent his
head to the paper as if to read, but he had already memorized
the words. He quoted them aloud with relish. "*In exchange for*
receiving the overlordship of Aquitaine, Anjou and Maine; as well as the
hand of Alais Capet who is his promised bride, my son Richard shall be
denied the crown of England at my death, which, with its attendant por-
tion Normandy, shall be settled upon my best beloved child and heir—
Prince John . . ."

Philippe's head jerked up and he glowered at Richard, who
stared back at him, stunned to stupefaction. Philippe smiled a
hideous, hateful smile. "Congratulate yourself. You have the

Aquitaine back in your keeping once again, with all its pretty singing boys and good French wines."

Flanders and the king's Champagnois uncles knew nothing of this secret alliance between Philippe and Henry. Like Richard, they stared glassy-eyed at one another. Then with one accord all attention shifted to Henry. His face had gone a dour grey and he was trembling violently.

Philippe's smiling face bleared before his eyes. Henry lunged forward, grabbing the forbidden document, but Philippe snatched the paper from his reach and thrust it at Richard's chest. "Read it," he demanded.

"There is no signature!" Henry shouted, spit dribbling on his beard, "I signed nothing, do you hear? This is a foul trick..." He pointed vehemently at Philippe and croaked out the words, "He did this! *He did this!*"

Philippe laughed wickedly. "You did it to yourself, old man! You thought you could appease my appetite with *this,*" he threw the original agreement with its stated terms of settlement into the air and it came to land at Henry's feet. "But instead you only showed everyone what a liar and a fool you really are!" He turned to Richard who still held the traitorous document in his hands. "Is that written in your father's hand?" he asked.

Richard nodded ruefully, too distressed to speak.

"Then you know that what I told you more than a year ago is true. Your father means to invalidate your claim to the succession. In return he promises to give you what is already yours by right!" Philippe's lips twitched sourly but his black eyes shined with a glow of triumph. "Can you look at that paper and deny what I have said?"

Again Richard nodded. There were tears on his face.

The onlookers were silent. A sense of collective embarrassment hung in the air. Henry was flailing his arms, shouting wild curses at Philippe. Godfrey came forward to restrain him. John looked on, befuddled, not quite able to assess the situation. His brow wrinkled but there was a smile of gratitude on his face, for he had understood one thing which had been uttered here this morning and it was enough. *Henry had named him to wear the crown.*

All at once there was a sound of muttering among the company who seemed to be caught midway between dismay and awe at Philippe's brazen tactics. Richard, having calmed himself, came forward and faced his father with a look of unrelenting hatred. His voice was as hard as he could make it. "So at last I see what kind of man you truly are! By the blood of our Savior, I swear to you I would just as soon be dead as learn what I have learned before these witnesses today..."

"It was all his doing!" Henry screamed, fighting Godfrey's hold on him. "Don't you understand what he is doing? In separating our loyalties he has beaten *both* of us! Can't you see that? Are you a fool?"

"Yes, I am a fool," Richard declared wretchedly. "I am the biggest fool in all the world, but only because I believed the oaths you swore to me!" New anger seized him and he drew back his hand as if to hit his father. Then, just as readily, Richard let the arm fall limply to his side. "You aren't even worth the effort," he declared, and turned his back to Henry's piteous cries.

Richard went to Philippe, and threw himself at the king's feet. "I pledge myself to your service, and before these people here assembled, do homage to you for the English territories in France." He reached up to clasp Philippe by the hand. "And I do beg you to forgive my father's ignominy, and not judge me by his acts of treachery." He kissed the signet ring on Philippe's hand.

Philippe stooped, drawing Richard to his feet, and the two men embraced like brothers. The French king bestowed the kiss of peace. Then he whispered something into Richard's ear.

Henry's mouth was frozen in a speechless gape. Suddenly he saw it all, in a flash of recognition more real than any he had ever known. Philippe had planned this; he had never intended to negotiate a settlement of peace! One by one he had stolen Henry's sons away, bribing them to his will with shrewd promises and a treacherous, indecent love. *Lies, all lies.*

Pushing his courtiers aside, Henry stumbled from the tent. Outside he fell upon the ground and lay there until Godfrey came to lift him up, mumbling words of comfort. It was the dutiful offering of a son to his despairing father, but Henry was too miserable to care. He wept into the rough wool of Godfrey's pellison, and for the first time in his life Henry knew it was too late.

Philippe Capet had beaten him.

The game was almost over.

* * *

By evening the clouds had broken, spilling rain. It flooded the river at its banks and turned the ground to slippery, yellow mud. The French wrapped themselves against the cold and huddled in their tents close beside smoking charcoal brners, while rain soaked through the shivering canvas walls.

The English had gone that afternoon, all but Richard. He'd remained to ponder his decision and the changes it would mean in his life. There was no going back now; he knew that. Henry's betrayal—offering the crown to John in a written proof of his deception—had been the final one.

Richard had made the best choice, the only choice.

Outside, the sky was very dark. The wind had blown the moon away. Richard followed a ceremonial row of torches to Philippe's tent. He entered, bringing a little of the rain and wind with him. With a jerk he pulled the flap shut and secured it.

The gold-trimmed hangings and painted fleur-de-lis shimmered in the light of a low-banked fire. Philippe was sitting up in the bed, covered with a silver foxfur, looking pleased. He extended his hand toward Richard. "I've been waiting for you."

For just an instant Richard hesitated, then he rushed forward and dropped to his knees beside the bed. Philippe tossed the fur aside and reached for him.

"My love," he said.

WRAPPED in a cover of grim November fog, Henry and a diminished group of followers went south to Anjou. John and Godfrey were with him; also Marshal and other members of the king's circle of close friends and advisers. But there were many men who stayed away, and Henry read a rueful message in their absence. They were waiting to cast their lot with the victor when the wars began in spring.

For the present, bad weather and the approach of Christmas had put an end to this season of tribulations and Henry was glad of it. There was no escaping from what awaited him in the coming months, but for now it was good to rest at the fortress in Saumur and spend his days in quiet brooding.

It was obvious that he was ailing, though Henry tried to hide the symptoms of his pain. As each day passed he grew more determined to avenge his son's disloyalty. Philippe scarcely mattered now. It was Richard whom Henry wanted to bring down.

The days grew colder, winter deepened. Henry watched from his window as the landscape paled and ice slowed the rushing current of the Loire. He prayed, and waited for the spring.

And dreaded it.

In the dim bedroom there was the sound of gentle breathing. On the wall a slender shadow rose and fell, and a girl's voice whispered, "Do I please you well, my lord king?"

Henry was lying on his back, the girl over him. He reached to stroke her moving hips. Soft flesh. Strong bones. *Christ, the marvel of a young girl's body.* "Ah, that's it, that's it, my precious! How young you make me feel. How kind you are."

Their hands met in mid-air, fingers braided. "It is you who are kind," she answered. "I've eaten good food for the first time in many months since coming here. And since you took me to yourself, I've had a warm dress and a new cloak as well...."

Breath rumbled in his chest. "A fair exchange."

For a while there were no words between them, only sounds of love. Later, when the last murmur had died away to the dark corners of the room, she lay above him, nearly dozing, while Henry ran his fingers through her long black hair. "Say your name, my child," he prodded.

She laughed. It was a low and husky sound, a woman's sound. "You know it well as me, I've told it to you before."

"Tell me again."

"My name is Eleanor," she said. Then teased, "Eleanor, the king's young whore."

He gave a little laugh, then sobered, trying to remember: how the name had sounded on his lips a thousand times, how it had felt to say it. But too much time and too much pain had gone between. He held the other Eleanor close upon his breast and asked, "How do you come to have a noblewoman's name?"

Her kisses fell upon his face, light and eager. "I may be a whore; my mother too. But my father was cousin to the king of Arles. Because I had his blood in me, my mother named me so."

"She named you well," he said, then clasped her in a powerful embrace.

Afterwards she gathered up her clothes and prepared to go.

Henry was half asleep, but at the sound of the door creaking open he stirred and sat up on the bed. "Don't go," he muttered, his hand outstretched.

She came toward him, clothed in shadow. "Have you not done with me?"

Their hands met and he kissed hers, smiling into his beard. "At my age, child, one never knows, but I'll say this. I'm far too old to waste a night by passing it alone." He could smell the leavings of his passion on her, and it roused him to lust again.

She giggled as his eager hands tugged roughly at the opening of her chainse. "Careful, lord, you will ruin it."

He ripped the cloth down below her waist and pushed his face between her breasts. "You shall have another one," he swore.

Henry forced her to the floor and sprawled over her. "Do you promise?" she whispered in his ear.

"Yes," he answered, unable to say more.

The king, and a new dress. Contented, Eleanor sighed, then smiled into the dark.

Sibylla was sitting by the window with her sewing.

"You are really much more talented than I," Isabel observed, looking down at her own ragged stitching. "Somehow I always manage to spoil the pattern."

Sibylla compared their efforts discreetly and nodded.

The two women laughed.

Close by, sitting on the rug in front of the fire, the children halted briefly in their playing, curious to see what the adult merriment was made of, then they went back to their game. Jacquie-Marie was amusing little Louis and Gabrielle by building towers out of wooden blocks.

The two sisters returned to their sewing, silent for a while. Outside the comfort of Isabel's warm room the rain was coming down, sounding like a rushing river from the sky. It had rained every day since the beginning of December, and Christmas was little more than a week away.

Sibylla was very near her time of delivery and she grew more excited as each day passed. She yearned to present her darling William with a namesake and heir. Her prayers were ceaseless and fervid petitions to that end. Secure in her faith, she knew God would not fail her.

Isabel was pregnant once again and she too hoped for a son, but more than that she prayed for a healthy, living child. She could not help but think the many miscarriages and still-births had hurt her chances for giving birth in the future. *Just one more son,* she prayed. *Another heir.* Then the succession would be safe should anything unforeseen befall little Louis, and she would have done her duty as Philippe's queen.

There was little doubting that Sibylla saw pregnancy as an unequalled blessing. Like their mother Margot, it seemed to enhance her well-being. Certainly marriage and motherhood had transformed Sibylla from a pretty girl into a vibrant woman. *And she was so happy.* Contentment glowed in her eyes and she was always smiling.

Isabel envied her; pitied her too. It was unreasonable for anyone to be as innocent and trusting as Sibylla was. Isabel, who had lived for so long on the edge of anxiousness and desperation, felt a mingling of awe and irritation for her sister's attitude of calm.

Isabel looked past her at the children. Gabrielle was the very image of Sibylla as a child, with her brown hair and hazel eyes. Louis resembled Isabel more each day, while Jacquie-Marie was Champagnois dark, with her father's stubborn jaw. It was odd to see a parent's features reflected so clearly in a child's face. It blurred the line between generations, and seemed to make time stand still.

Not so many years ago she and Sibylla had sat together on the floor, playing games full of childish imagination. Those had been such carefree days, at home in Mons, secure in the closeness of a loving family. Isabel had not known anything so comforting as that since then. Children were lucky to be children. She had grown up far too young.

Louis scurried over to her and was pulling at her skirt with chubby fingers. Isabel lifted him to her lap and held him close against her shoulder, murmuring a Flemish melody that Margot had sung to her when she was little. Louis snuggled his face at the neckline of her chainse and Isabel unloosed the front, offering him one of her white breasts. He took the nipple in his mouth and sighed with childish satisfaction.

He was such a sweet and sensitive child, quite different in temperament from Jacquie, who was headstrong and defiant like her father. Louis was timid and gentle, and though he seldom cried, he coveted attention. Philippe adored him, and so did Edythe, who was virtually the child's nursemaid. But Louis was happiest when he was cradled in his mother's arms.

"You're so lucky, Isabel," Sibylla smiled, and a wistful look lighted in her eyes. "If I can have a son for William I will never ask God for another blessing."

Isabel reached out to take her sister's hand and squeezed it lovingly. "My prayer is that He will keep you safe during your childbed, for that is the most important thing of all. You are very young Sibylla, and you have many years to give birth to sons for William."

"I know," she answered, and her gaze carried to the little girls on the floor. Gabrielle had fallen asleep with her head in her cousin's lap, and Jacquie, in an imitation of her mother, was singing softly to the child. It was all so lovely and sad; so temporary. Sibylla bit her lip and said again, "I know..."

Smoke came from the chimney of the woodcutter's hut.

Philippe and Richard had come to the forest of Vincennes for hunting, but the rain had banished them indoors. There were other sports. For ten days they had scarcely left their bed.

Philippe turned over on his stomach and rested his cheek on Richard's hip. He yawned with pleasure. "I fear I could become very satisfied with a life like this." Then he laughed. "You are a wicked influence on my usually prudent habits."

Now Richard laughed, and reached down to lose his fingers in Philippe's thick black hair. "There is nothing prudent about you, my love, in bed or any other place. At Bonsmoulins you vanquished Henry and proved him for the liar he truly is." Richard paused, and then his voice grew stern, self-blaming. "You saw it all along Philippe—you saw his deception—while I, his son, was blinded to the truth for years. The bastard. The damned double-dealing bastard!"

"Calm yourself," Philippe said, climbing over Richard to lie at his side. Their chins were almost touching. "Henry isn't a problem to either of us, not anymore. Come spring, we'll drive him out of France, and take all his territories this side of the Channel for ourselves." His strong teeth gleamed as he stretched his lips into a sneer. "It will be *so easy.* By the time we take the field in spring, two thirds of all his army outside of Normandy and Eng-

land will have come over to our side. Think of it Richard! *All*
shall be ours! And when Henry sees what we can do to him and
he realizes at last the threat we are to him, he will be forced to
accept you as his heir."

Their tongues met in a slippery kiss, then Philippe lowered his
face, biting the gold chains that decorated Richard's neck, unfastening them with his teeth. Richard's thick arms closed tight
about Philippe's waist, holding him in a brutal grip.

But something was tugging at Richard's mind, taking him away
from Philippe, even in the circle of his arms. He could not keep
it to himself, he had to say it. "Is that the same arrangement you
made with my brother Geoffrey? Was he to gain the crown in
return for giving you everything you want in France?" The last
was spoken bitterly.

Philippe sat up abruptly, staring down into Richard's blue, accusing eyes. "We have no secrets, you and I. God knows we have
become as close as flesh can be. Why should it bother you to
know that Geoffrey and I once loved each other?"

"It's not the love that troubles me," Richard grumbled, "it's
knowing that the two of you made plans together."

Philippe's fingers brushed lightly over Richard's knee. "I can't
believe that after all that has gone between us this past month
and these last few days you could be having second thoughts
about casting in your lot with me."

He would not be misled. "You didn't answer my question."

Philippe crossed his arms over his naked chest and glowered
arrogantly down at Richard. "It was hardly the same situation,
my friend! Your father was in a more powerful position at that
time. I could hardly have hoped to bring him to his knees three
years ago! And besides, Geoffrey didn't care about the crown. He
only wished to make me happy, to give me anything I wanted."

The words did nothing to soften Richard's conviction that he
was lying. "Geoffrey was greedier than any man alive, including
you. If he could have had the crown without a fight from me, he
would have slit Henry's throat to get it."

The black eyes that looked back at him were cold. "You didn't
know him the way I did." A sigh. "Geoffrey had the most brilliant and original mind of any man I ever met. It was power he
wanted, not the crown, though he *could* have had both eventually

if he had set his mind to it. If he'd lived long enough. He could have had anything. He was so clever."

"Devious," Richard corrected, and then his voice went lower: "It's only that I have to know that I mean more to you than just a way of getting what you want from Henry."

Insulted, Philippe jerked his head in a gesture of disapproval. "What an unkind thing for you to say! I can't believe you could really mean it."

Richard folded his hands across his belly. "It had crossed my mind."

Their eyes met in a wordless exchange and kindled something secret. "I might say the same of you, you know," Philippe argued. "You could be using me to help you fight your father."

Richard leaned on his elbow and looked up at Philippe. There was meaning in his eyes. "Yes, I could be. But I'm not."

"And I believe you."

Richard reached out to fondle Philippe's hand. "I don't want to doubt you, but I'm sure you can understand how it might be possible."

Without answering Philippe got up and threw a cloak around his shoulders. Richard watched. "Where are you going?" he asked.

Philippe pulled the door open. "I've got to piss."

When he came back inside, Richard was sitting up in the bed, looking sullen. Philippe crossed to the table to pour some wine for them and Richard's voice followed him. "We should be getting back to Paris. Let's be prepared to leave at dawn tomorrow."

Philippe looked back over his shoulder. "Not in this rain."

"Then on the following day."

Philippe brought the wine to Richard and sat down beside him. They both drank in silence. Then Philippe said, "You seem suddenly quite anxious to leave. I thought you liked it here. I thought you were enjoying my company."

Richard's head was thrust forward. He was looking disconsolately down into his wine. "I need to believe in you, Philippe," he mumbled.

The feel of Philippe's arms around his shoulders caused the gloomy Richard to relax a little. "Believe in this then: I love you." Philippe's voice was firm but hushed. "Do you understand me

Richard? *I love you!*" He wrestled Richard around to face him
and they kissed, each tasting wine in the other's mouth.

Richard tossed his henap aside, then pulled Philippe down on
the bed with him, their arms tangled, their bellies pressed tight
together. "I love you too," he declared, "and to hell with all the
rest."

Later they ate a meal of cheese and bread.

"You may have been right about us leaving after all," Philippe
said, stretching his long legs out, warming his feet closer to the
fire. "We are very nearly out of food."

"There are still a few things in my saddle bag," Richard replied, pointing to the corner where the leather satchel lay.

Philippe unwrapped a cloth pouch and tossed a bit of beef to
Richard. "I'm suddenly very hungry," Philippe said and winked
at his friend.

Richard's gaze carried far off to the corner, where the low-
hung ceiling slanted into shadow. He could hear rain dripping
through the ill-patched roof onto the floor somewhere in the
room. It was a lonely, melancholy sound.

His shoulders sagged in depression. "I'll be glad when this
whole thing is over," he declared suddenly. "I'm not looking forward to going up against my father, not with the stakes so high as
they are. He's going to fight back with everything he has." The
corners of his mouth drooped. "It could drag on indefinitely."

"Does that matter?" Philippe asked, raising a dark eyebrow.

Richard leaned his elbows on his knees. "Yes, it does. I'm tired
of these constant delays, I just want things to be settled. I want
the crown, the Aquitaine, and the assurance that Henry will not
go back on his word once he promises them to me. Then I can go
to the East with an easy mind and a peaceful heart."

In a rare spirit of sympathy, Philippe drew close to Richard
and gave him a tender kiss on the forehead. "My sweet friend, I
want the same thing. But first we must bring Henry to his
knees." He saw the quick frown. "We *must*. There is no other way.
And then, when all has been secured, we shall go together to the
East." He kissed the knuckles of Richard's hand. "And together
we shall drive the pagans from the Holy places."

Richard gnawed at his thumbnail and was silent for a while.

Then he said, "I find it difficult to believe you are as eager for this adventure as I am."

"Do you doubt my religiosity?"

"No," Richard answered immediately, "but I doubt your ability to leave your wife behind."

It was not the first time he had made a veiled slur against Isabel. He was jealous of her; Philippe knew that and accepted it. Women were all mothers and sisters to Richard, or dainty ornaments leaning on his arm for dancing. *He knew nothing of them.*

"Of course I won't enjoy a separation from Isabel," Philippe answered tartly, "but there's nothing I can do to remedy that."

"She can," Richard said, pronouncing the words like a prophet, "and I wouldn't be surprised if she succeeds."

The muscles of Philippe's face tensed, anticipating anger. "I don't know what you mean."

"I mean that she'll do *anything* to keep you with her."

Philippe gulped down most of his wine, and then belched under his breath. "There's nothing she can do. If I decide to go, I'll go." He smiled teasingly. "Isabel is just a tiny little thing. She can't keep me here against my will."

Richard was not smiling; he was in earnest. "She *is* your will."

Philippe kicked at the stone hearth with the toe of his boot. "Nonsense," he grumbled.

"Isabel is like a fever to you," Richard protested. "I've seen it many times. She walks into the room and suddenly you forget you are a king."

Philippe was more amused than he was angry. "Christ Jesus, Richard, open your eyes! Is it odd for a man to want to fuck his wife! Especially if she looks like Isabel? Don't tell me that you haven't had a few thoughts in the same direction. Yes, even you. Every man who has ever seen her looks at me and wishes he were in my place, and not just to wear the crown." He sighed. "Of course I don't blame any man for wanting her. There is no other woman on earth like Isabel. One look at her is enough to raise a dead man's penis."

"I wonder you aren't jealous," Richard said.

"Sometimes I am, though no other man would dare to touch her. Still, the gentlemen of my household amuse themselves with staring at her, wondering what it would be like to bury themselves in her."

Richard stroked his beard thoughtfully. "I've had women, but I have never lusted for them. Actually I feel pity that they must submit to men. Women are so delicate. Each time I've lain with a woman, I've been afraid of hurting her." He said the words earnestly, truly meaning them. "With men, it's so much more equal." He paused a moment. "Love between two men is better, because both of them want it. With a woman you can't help feel like an intruder."

Philippe spit his wine into the fire and it flared up, red and hissing. "Christ Almighty where have you been looking, in a convent? I've never known a woman yet who didn't prefer a good fuck to a love song."

There was a tiny flush on Richard's cheek. "Whores perhaps. Women of high birth are different."

"The hell they are!" Philippe proclaimed, stretching himself out next to Richard on the floor. "I've been screwing whores since I was thirteen, but I have never found one who could compare to Isabel. She has an appetite that makes any man look feeble."

Richard's strong mouth sulked. "I think that is very unusual for a woman."

Philippe shrugged. "Perhaps it is. But I wouldn't have her any other way. Her blood is so hot, her breasts so sweet. Her body is like a part of my own." He looked at Richard and fumbled for the right words. "If you could know how it feels to be inside of her! When I take her I *know* her pleasure, just as surely as she knows mine. I've never felt that with any other woman, and I know I never will."

"Or any man?" Richard asked.

Philippe smiled nicely and his face looked almost kind. "As you said, it is different between men. You and I are many things to one another: lovers, friends, brothers..." He moved closer and slid an arm around Richard's stalwart back. "We have a fine and promising future together."

Richard searched for truth in Philippe's eyes. "Does that include our journey to the East?"

"Yes," Philippe answered, his whisper floating close upon Richard's ear, "after all has been secured for us in France." He rolled over on his back and spread his arms to his lover. "There is nothing that we cannot do . . . together."

Richard kissed him with a wet and open mouth. "God help us."

Philippe gave a throaty laugh. "God help Henry."

There were no festivities, not even snow. John had never known such a dismal Christmas. Henry had been in bed for several days and this time it was not a woman who kept him there. He was suffering with hemorrhoids, and his pain was extreme.

The physicians treated him with applications of salves and ointments and a special potion made of crushed seed pearls mixed with oils of balm and belladonna. They prescribed boiled fish to eat and liberal doses of water in his wine. The faithful Godfrey saw that all these measures were accomplished, and he kept a vigil at the king's side each night.

John strayed in and out, standing by the bed to exchange a few words with his father. He never lingered very long; he was too depressed for that. *What was happening to Henry?* John had never known him to be vanquished by an illness. It was even more frightening to consider what his brother and Philippe were planning back in Paris. How would Henry ever be able to put down the threat of their rebellion when he was too weak to stand, or even rise from his bed?

What would John do when spring came if Henry was still too sick to lead a defense against them? There was Godfrey of course. He was a fine soldier. And de Mandeville, and William Marshal. But if the king of England was too ill to sit his horse, he was too ill for battle. In which case the logical successor was his son and heir. *And that was John.*

He loved Henry, that was the worst part. John loved him more than he loved anyone else in the whole world, and it was a terrible feeling because he was so afraid that Henry was going to die. *Please God, don't let it happen!* John hadn't said a sincere prayer in a long time, but he was praying now.

At night, across the corridor in his own room, he would hide his face among the cushions and sob without restraint. Sometimes Eleanor, the king's young mistress, would come and slide into bed beside him. They would hold one another and make love from a sense of need, and weep together over the king's condition before they slept.

In his mind John had the image of a circle growing smaller.
He had never felt so alone.

Richard was not alone. He had Philippe. For the time being
that was all he wanted. When the two men returned to Paris they
were full of plans. They were in each other's company every day,
and when Christmas came they celebrated with a morning mass
and a full night of drinking.

Isabel spent all of Christmas day sitting at her sister's bedside.
Sibylla's delivery was difficult and lasted many hours, but it was
worth almost any price because, finally, a little before midnight,
she gave birth to a husky, squalling son.

The tight-lipped midwife clothed him in a woollen wrapping
and set him at his mother's breast. "He's so beautiful," Isabel
muttered, leaning close to inspect her tiny nephew. "Oh, Sibylla,
I'm so very happy for you!"

The young mother smiled weakly and reached to take hold of
Isabel's hand. "Thank you for staying with me. I think I would
have been quite afraid without you. There was so much more
pain this time." Her voice faded to a whisper and Isabel had to
bend close to hear the words. "The pain doesn't matter now. I
have my son. I'm going to call him William Tristan." Sibylla
looked so weary, but there was a radiance in her eyes. "Oh Isabel,
God has been so good to me...."

She was still smiling as she fell asleep.

In January 1189 the feeble truce of Bonsmoulins expired.

In February Henry agreed to meet with Philippe and Richard,
so that a binding treaty might be struck between them. But before the scheduled date arrived, Henry sent another message
saying he would not be able to attend. He was still in too much
pain to ride a horse.

Philippe laughed and crumbled the paper in his hands.

The month of March was full of turbulence and sadness.

Henry turned fifty-six on the fourth day of the month. It was a
grey day of little celebration. Rain fell steadily and as afternoon
deepened into evening it turned to silvery sleet. A cold wind blew
off the troubled surface of the Loire and scurried round the
thick stone walls of Saumur fortress.

Henry lay alone in his bed with Godfrey sitting at his feet.

There was very little talking. The sounds of wind and rain and a fire in the grate held sway within the dreary room. Henry rolled over on his side and grumbled, restless in a dull half-sleep, then flung the covers off. Gently, Godfrey smoothed them back over his shoulders once again, and stroked his cheek till the older man slept more peacefully.

John looked in, standing at the doorway for a moment, unobserved. He wanted to go to Henry, put his arms around him, beg him to be well again. Instead he turned away and tip-toed down the corridor, where pretty Eleanor waited outside his room.

On the same night, far away in Paris, William de Beaujolais was thrown from his horse when it stumbled on the rain-slippery stones near the palace *esplanade*. Two soldiers of the guard who were standing watch beside the bridge found him and carried him inside. The king was told; he summoned his physician.

But William was already dead.

Sibylla's grief was a heavy, silent thing.

She would not talk and she could not cry. She sat for hours staring out of the window, hardly noticing if it was night or day. She nursed her infant son, held Gabrielle on her knee; but these were empty actions born of habit.

William's body was taken back to Beaujolais where it would be entombed beneath the high altar of Avenas, among the monuments of his family. Sibylla had wanted to accompany the funeral caravan, but Isabel discouraged her from doing so. The physical and emotional consequences of such a journey were too exhausting, she explained.

Isabel did what she could to comfort her sister, but there were no words or actions, however kind, to assuage the grief of a fifteen-year-old widow. *If only she could cry, perhaps some of the grief would go.* But Sibylla floundered, comfortless and unspeaking in an isolation she had built against reality. It was almost as if she did not believe William was dead. Each night she sat at her window, as though waiting for him to return from an afternoon of hunting.

It was not an easy situation for Isabel. By the time a week had passed her nerves were fragmented. She had lost so much sleep and weight caring for Sibylla, and pregnancy added the physical discomforts of nausea and swollen ankles.

Because of all this anxiety, the sleepless nights and troubled days, Isabel was brought to childbed early, on the eve of her nineteenth birthday. It was far too soon; she was not due to deliver until middle June. The hours of painful labor produced yet another still-born baby, this one a girl.

The dead little princess was hastily named Genevieve-Therése. Sully performed a token baptism, and then the child was taken out of Isabel's arms, to be put away forever in the darkness of the crypt at Notre Dame. Isabel sobbed forlornly in her husband's arms. *So much suffering, and only death as a reward.*

Philippe did his best to soothe her. "There will be other children," he said, trying to make the words sound meaningful.

She could not tell him what she already knew.

It was too late.

𝕿HE LOIRE VALLEY was beautiful in the spring.

Henry Plantagenet was filled with a sense of renewal. He felt it in his blood, in his soul. Recovering from his illness had made him feel vigorous again, giving him an illusion of being young. He gathered up his entire entourage and moved them a few miles south to Chinon, then sent a message to the King of France.

They met for a series of conferences near the Anjou-Maine border at the end of April. The meetings dragged on through the middle of the following month, but nothing was decided. It was an impasse from the beginning. Philippe was obdurate in his terms for a settlement; Henry was inflexible in his refusals.

There was no pretense of friendliness or courtesy on either side. Henry hated Philippe now, and feared him too, above any other man on earth. And as for Philippe, he scented Henry's ruin and was hungry for it, like a jackal lusting for a fresh kill.

Richard stood beside him all the while, cloaking his betrayal in an attitude of righteousness, nodding in fervent agreement to everything Philippe said. He seemed to have few opinions of his own, Henry thought contemptuously. Licking the French king's balls had made him subservient and stupid.

The conference adjourned at the end of May, though the two monarchs arranged to meet again in a week. Henry was glad for the delay. He needed to buy time. It was his only weapon against Philippe Capet now.

There was one hope left to him, and Henry seized upon it with cunning determination. *Pope Clement was angry.* He had grown disgusted with the failure of Christendom's kings to make good their promise of leading a new crusade to the Holy Land. He had written strong letters to both Henry and Philippe, threatening reprisals by the Church if they did not soon settle their domestic quarrel and set forth as they had promised to do more than a year ago.

To this same purpose Clement had dispatched a papal legate in his name, Cardinal John of Anagni, whom he hoped would be able to persuade the kings to their sacred duty. The cardinal had sent word ahead of his arrival, offering to meet with them near Le Mans in early June.

The kings, with their assembled bishops, nobles, advisers, and courtiers came together at La Ferté-Bernard, a tiny market town on the river Huisne surrounded by vineyards. The cardinal joined them on the following day. He lectured the two kings on their responsibility as leaders of a holy cause; he spoke to them of love and brotherhood.

As he listened, Henry could feel his luck changing with each word. Suddenly he was full of confidence for the first time since Richard had defected to the French camp. A little time alone with the cardinal, that was all he needed! Philippe Capet might be a wily politician, but Henry was master of that game. He swore to win the cardinal to his side. If the public misfortune of a traitorous son did not weight the scales in Henry's favor, then perhaps good Angevin gold would do the trick.

He would win. By God he would extricate himself from this!

And so it went. Henry had his secret little parlay with the cardinal, but the public councils with Philippe were less to his liking. The French king would not alter his terms: *Richard would get the crown of England. He would get the Aquitaine. He would marry Alais.* And there was even one new demand: Philippe and Henry would go on crusade, and John would accompany them. This, because as Henry's favorite son, he was suspect.

Henry would not agree to any of it and repeated his original terms. *John would get England, Normandy, and the crown. Richard would be reinstated as the Duke of Aquitaine.* And Henry had a new condition too: since the advent of Richard's treason, the King of England had decided to invalidate the long-standing betrothal between Richard and Alais, and she would be given to John instead.

Richard did not *want* Alais, he had never wanted her. He was not keen to marry any woman, certainly not his father's strumpet. But he wanted his rights, and Philippe (who was anxious to secure the marriage to his own gain) had convinced him to fight for her.

Each day Philippe put his same terms to Henry.

And each day Henry refused them.

After four days of constant haggling between the kings, the cardinal stepped forth once more to have his say. It was obvious that he was mouthing Henry's words as he blamed Philippe for the hostilities and threatened to pronounce excommunication upon him and lay all of his domain under an *interdict* if he did not accept Henry's terms immediately.

Philippe was far too astute to be fooled by the cardinal's brash intimidations. He spat upon the ground to show his contempt. "Liar!" he declared, "Pander!"

It was said before a hundred gaping witnesses from the two sides, including the famous chronicler from Henry's court, Gerald of Wales, who sat upon the ground, recording all that was taking place at this assembly.

The day was over-warm for June, and bleached with sunlight. Emotions were skittish; tempers quick to kindle. There was little doubt that before the afternoon was over, the breach between the hostile participants of the conference would be even wider than it had been before.

Henry's face turned a furious purple, but he said nothing.

The cardinal stammered, the heavy flesh around his face shivering as he spoke. "Mind your words, Capet. I am the pope's own messenger, and God's!"

Philippe shaded his eyes against the brilliance of the sky and shouted back, "You are no better than a whore, selling yourself for gold! The King of England may have bought your favor but he will not buy my obedience, nor will you!" He turned to Gerald and pointed vigorously at the roll of parchment in his lap. "See that you write this down, cleric: I am a king of my realm, and the leader of my bishops. We recognize no cardinals in France, and I will not allow an unclean cardinal to dictate my responsibilities. My great-grandfather defied the will of Rome when it meddled too closely in his affairs. I shall do likewise." He jerked around to face the legate. "Pronounce as you like, good Cardinal. I will see you in hell before I give up my rights to the pope or to any other man!"

The cardinal turned away and would not answer.

Some of Henry's men shifted on their feet, embarrassed. If the French king's accusation was correct, if Henry had slandered his own cause with a cheap bribe, then he had ruined a chance to salvage his position by an honest appeal to Rome. The men who served him saw the sense of desperation in his actions, and they understood what it meant.

Henry was a beaten man.

There was nothing that could save him now.

Henry sped to Le Mans in hope of sanctuary, while the French troops captured La Ferté-Bernard and its surrounding fortresses. Henry's army had dwindled to a mere handful of loyal knights and retainers, including William Marshal and Godfrey. John, who had not attended the meetings at La Ferté-Bernard, had stayed behind at the fortress of Saumur.

Le Mans was Henry's city. He had always loved it more than any other. Here he had been born, so too would he be buried, as his father Geoffrey of Anjou, had been buried nearly forty years ago. Henry refused to believe that Philippe would attempt to take Le Mans against its sturdy city walls, or that God would allow him to take it even if he tried.

Le Mans was *his.* He would not abandon its people, he would not forsake the city, leaving it to fall into Capet's greedy palm like an over-ripe fruit.

But Godfrey and Marshal doubted the good sense of such a plan. "You must escape into Normandy," Marshal told him, "and then get word to England for reinforcements. As it now stands, Philippe and Richard will be upon us in two days, no more."

Godfrey nodded in grave agreement.

Henry would not listen. "Here I am and here I shall stay for now," he said. His tanned face lighted with a weary smile. "It is not such a bad place to be, aye? Don't fear, my friends. I have an idea which will discourage the French from coming in."

With a party of his knights Henry rode to the edge of the city where the Huisne River lay. They destroyed the single bridge which spanned it, then returned once more to Le Mans. That was scarcely enough to deter an army on the march, only slow it down a little. But it was all Henry could hope for.

That, and a miracle.

At the head of his army and with Richard at his side, Philippe marched unopposed through the woodlands of Maine on his way to Le Mans. He was hot with purpose now, his blood burning with excitement at the prospect of taking all that lay before him for his own.

On the night of June 11th, Philippe's army camped outside the city. He lay in his tent, comfortable in Richard's arms, awake, and dreaming of the following day. Richard snored pleasantly in sleep, but Philippe was taut and anxious. Waiting. Waiting for tomorrow.

He was out there somewhere, that Old Legend. In the citadel perhaps; somewhere safe behind the city walls, and waiting too. Across the few miles which separated them, their thoughts seemed to meet and mingle in the dark. Philippe could almost feel their souls touching.

He closed his eyes and the sensation deepened.

The sky was lighted early on the following morning, colored by shades of orange and red before the sun was up. The outskirts of Le Mans were burning furiously, and shooting tall flames into the sky.

Philippe cursed aloud when he saw what had happened. This was Henry's doing! He'd given orders to burn the fringes of the city, hoping the fire would spread to the French camp and drive them back. The cunning old bastard was keen-witted as a fox, refusing to be drawn into the net.

Philippe cursed until he saw which way the wind was blowing. It shifted just at dawn, turning the flames around till they had gobbled a path into the midst of the city. The defenses at the gate were left unprotected, and Philippe's army poured into the breach.

Alarmed, Henry took what he could salvage of his army (only

some seven hundred knights) and fled the burning city with Marshal, de Mandeville, and Godfrey at his side. Other members of the king's entourage took flight and followed at his heels: the clerks, bishops, laundresses, and the writer Gerald of Wales, all of them terrified at being caught up in the melée of flames and destruction.

The King of England was in abject retreat.

That afternoon, his eyes bleared from smoke and too little sleep, Henry paused a while on the northern slope above Le Mans to look down into the ruins of his flaming city. Ragged clouds of smoke rose high above the scorched and crumbled buildings. But at the tallest point of the citadel Henry could see a fluttering banner: Philippe's flag set with fleur-de-lis. It was the final, mocking symbol of defeat.

It cut him to his soul to watch but Henry couldn't turn away. His whole life was smoldering into dust and ashes down there among the ruins of his birthplace. His father's bones lay encased by chilly marble in the cathedral crypt. Now Henry felt just as dead.

Marshal brought his horse close and reached over to grip the king's shoulder in a comforting squeeze. "We must push on to the Normandy frontier, my lord Henry, where we can strengthen our numbers and make a stand against these devils."

Tears fell from his eyes as Henry stared down into the valley. "What great wrong have I done to deserve this?" he asked, his voice cracking with despair. "Why does God punish me with infamy and disgrace?"

Marshal shook his head, muttering in a low tone, "No man can know these things Henry, for they are mysteries. Let us save what it is possible to save, and leave the rest to Him."

"No!" Henry roared, shaking off Marshal's hand. "I have suffered enough!" He raised a menacing fist at the sky, screaming aloft to an invisible deity. "You have taken everything from me, everything I hold dear to my heart. You have flayed my poor flesh with injuries, turned my seed to poison. Now you steal the city of my birth and give it to a vile usurper! You are a God of shit and misery, and I shall not bow beneath your hand. I curse you! *I curse you!*"

His words boomed like thunder above their heads.

The kings' men trembled at his blasphemy, their faces pale and stricken. Godfrey leapt from his horse and rushed to Henry's side, but he kicked him away and refused to be silenced. "You punish me like Job," he bellowed at the sky, "but you will not have that part of me which is most precious to you. You will not have my soul! I pledge it to the devil, that is MY revenge!"

Henry was shaking violently and he would have pitched from his horse, but Marshal caught him, set him upright in the saddle, and thrust the reins into his hands. "My lord, take care," he cautioned.

"Oh Marshal," the king wept, "I am finished, I am undone...."

In the heat of middle afternoon the party rode without stop toward the border, picking their way through woodlands, hurtling over patches of dry riverbed. It was a furious flight to sanctuary and some fell along the way, perishing from exhaustion or from thirst. There was no time to stop for rest or water.

Henry rode hard, and never once looked back.

A white star rose in the evening sky and pulled the moon up with it. A wind moved off the surface of the Sarthe. A dozen miles ahead lay the invisible line separating Maine from Normandy. Tomorrow Henry's men would cross over to the border town of Alençon.

Tonight they would sleep here at Fresnay. The fortress was very small and there was only room and food enough for Henry and a few of his close companions. The other men sought refuge in the streets and taverns.

The plump *castellan* ordered meat and bread hustled from the kitchen and set before his celebrated guests. They had not fed themselves since sundown on the previous day, and all were hungry. The men stuffed themselves with food and called for wine, though most of them were near to dozing by the time the meal was through. A dark-eyed girl with rounded hips moved slowly among the group, filling wooden cups with wine as the men talked.

"We must be up and out of here before the sun comes up," de Mandeville told Henry. "I shall rise earlier and gather up our troops. Just a short ride into Normandy and we are safe."

Godfrey belched into his fist and grumbled, "I only hope we are safe tonight." He looked across the table at his father. "I think it might be wise to keep a watch on the edge of town, lest some of Philippe's men have followed us this far."

The king shook his head and mumbled a refusal. He looked ill and tired, his grey eyes bloodshot from hours of riding in the sun, unshaded. Lines of care and weariness cut deep patterns in his face, and the firelight showed up the grey in his beard.

"You must sleep, Father," Godfrey told him.

Henry was taken to a room on the second floor. With a grunt he fell into his bed without undressing. He was asleep before Godfrey could finish pulling off his boots or drape a cloak over his body.

The girl who had served them wine appeared suddenly in the doorway, half in shadow. "I've come to make the king feel more comfortable," she said.

Godfrey glanced over his shoulder, frowning. "The king is sleeping," he snapped, "and is as comfortable as he needs be."

She came toward him, ringing a coil of dark hair around her finger. "I've never seen a king before, though long ago my mother bedded one." She traced the outline of Henry's leg beneath the linen cloak. "Is this him? Is this the great Henry of England? It was he my mother laid with. She said he was a handsome man in his youth." The girl's voice was tremulous and filled with awe.

Godfrey knocked her hand away. "All sluts tell tales of bedding with a king," he growled.

She gazed at Henry on the bed, and then smiled slyly up at Godfrey. "Your face is much like his."

"He is my father."

The girl was standing very close to him, her full breasts rising and falling with each breath she took. Godfrey recoiled from the stink of her: sweat and garlic and other smells the origins of which were best left unimagined. Yet all at once he reached out and pulled her to him, bending her arms behind her back as he kissed her.

He was not normally a man of spontaneous passion. There were several women in his keeping back in England, courtesans enjoyed discreetly, as fitted a former bishop and a man of Godfrey's stern morality. But tonight, hard-pressed by failure and wearied by defeat, this girl seemed to him the most desirable piece of flesh in all the world.

Godfrey shoved her into a darkened corner of the room, and

stripped the soiled garment from her body as she giggled softly.
Her breasts leapt out as if to greet him. The nipples were hard
and rouged over with vermilion.

"Such pretty teats," he said.

She writhed against him. "Are you truly the king's son?"

"Yes," he answered. He was beyond caring who he was.

She lay back on the floor and drew her knees up level with her
shoulders as he knelt beside her. "I've heard great stories of the
king's son, a warrior called Richard Lionheart by all and feared
by many. Are you he?"

"No," he admitted with a laugh as he unloosed his laces and let
his manhood spring free.

She reached up to fondle it and smiled. "It's so nice and fat,
like a summer sausage." She wetted him with her mouth for a
while, then guided him inside her. As he began to rock against
her she asked, "What is your name if it is not Richard?"

The breath was already thick and rapid in his chest. "What is
yours?"

Her fingers slid beneath their bellies, squeezing his heavy sac.
"It doesn't matter."

"Neither does mine," he answered, pushing harder.

*　*　*

*...all here is doubt and confusion. Men ask questions, but there is no
one fit to answer, save the king, and he is gone!*

*Yesterday we came forward here to Alençon, where he was to meet with
his Norman barons and secure a horde of knights, so he might rescue his
French lands from the grip of Philippe-Auguste, yet suddenly King
Henry had a violent change of heart.*

*Though all who serve him begged that he might send word to England
for an army, he refused. He then ordered Godfrey, who is his chancellor
and natural son, to make what army he can out of the Norman knights
who wish to follow (though many are reticent, fearing the great numbers
of the enemy, which I have seen with my own eyes).*

*Saying thus King Henry took himself from the safety of this place,
determined to return to his fortress of Chinon on the Vienne. We who
have followed him for so long and know him well, do not understand why
he has done this thing.*

*Though Godfrey raise a thousand knights, it would still be folly for
Henry to put himself within the French king's reach. Worse than all this*

he is ailing and sweats with pain and fever. I would not be surprised to hear he has died during his flight.

Gerald of Wales
Letter fragment
June 14, 1189

* * *

From boyhood he had been a hunter. Now, himself the quarry, Henry fled south toward Anjou once again. Let others say what they would, he no longer cared. An instinct deeper than reason was leading him back to the cradle of his race.

He had seen his own death the day Le Mans was burned, felt it during the mad rush north to Alençon. It would be a waste of time to spend his last days gathering an army in Normandy, or in waiting there for troops to come from England. All the possibilities of stopping Philippe's march had been exhausted. Another war would only squander time.

Henry wanted to die at Chinon.

He wanted to end his life surrounded by a few loyal friends and the only sons who had ever loved and honored him. They would be there. Godfrey had promised to come south in a few days, and Johnny was already waiting at Saumur.

Marshal would come, and de Mandeville; perhaps a few others. They were all that Henry needed now. In the end it didn't matter how a man numbered his friends, only how much their faithfulness and love was worth.

As Henry and a few remaining members of his bodyguard picked their way south through small and untraveled roads, Henry's turbulent thoughts fixed upon Richard. With all the energy left to him he cursed his son. What a weak and treacherous fool Richard was, eagerly selling himself to Philippe Capet from a sense of bitterness; trying to steal from Henry what he had never tried to earn!

But there would be a reckoning. Henry knew he could not die in serenity until he looked Richard in the face again. There was too much left unsaid between them, too much hate unsettled. He longed to pray that God would keep him whole until he reached the Loire Valley. But now he hated God as much as Richard.

Johnny, my beloved son. There was love in that thought and it pulsed in his mind with promise. The miles between them diminished with each hour that passed. Johnny, in all his foolishness and sloth, knew more of love than Richard would ever understand. Johnny was faithful, and there was comfort for Henry in that.

The king and his men swung wide to the west as they made further progress south. At this point the roads were planted thick with French patrols. Many times in those futile, waning days the king was forced to hide himself in the underbrush or behind the covering of trees in order to avoid capture by Philippe's troops.

Henry was beyond any sense of humiliation now. Hungry and ragged, his clothes stained with sweat and smeared with dirt, he pushed himself beyond the limits of his strength. There was only one respite left to him.

To die in peace at Chinon, and in Johnny's arms.

𝕴T HAD BEEN many years since Europe had seen such an army. French troops under the scarlet banner of the *oriflamme* and the pale blue blazon powdered by golden fleur-de-lis. Knights of the Champagnois, clothed in vivid blue and gold. Richard's bold Poitevans dressed all in red. Breton soldiers from the ghost of Geoffrey's army. Proud Flemish troops decorated with the insignia of the golden leopard. And an ever-swelling band of deserters from the English camp.

Philippe and Richard had overrun nearly all of Maine. Now as the days of June decreased they led their multitudes south, toward the city of Tours. All along their progress, towns and fortresses fell to them with little or no fighting. It was a march of triumph.

The victory would be but half realized until Tours was taken. Philippe did not doubt that the city would be his, though he wished Henry would surrender it without a fight. It was too fine a place to ruin with fire or the other untidy leavings of a siege.

Word had filtered through the lines that Henry had come south again. That rumor, be it true, pleased both Philippe and

Richard. Soon Henry would relinquish all he owned in France to them. When he did, their power—in partnership and separately —would be a wondrous thing.

Richard had never been so happy in his life.

The crown was all but his, and now he had a lover who was both friend and ally. They would accomplish fine and noble things together. They would make peace between France and England. They would go to the Holy Land and rescue the sacred places. Nothing could spoil the love and admiration they held for one another.

That was the kind of dreamer Richard was.

At Amboise on the Loire, little more than a day's slow march from Tours, the army halted to make camp. Philippe and Richard ate a meal together in their tent, then the king left for a while to confer with Flanders and his Champagnois uncles.

In his absence Richard bathed, then perfumed his beard and trimmed it. He set out a fresh wardrobe for the next day: ice blue samite garments set with precious stones, and an array of finger rings. He wanted to look his best when they drew up beside the defenses at the gates of Tours. It was unlikely there would be much fighting. Perhaps already Henry had given word that the city surrender without opposition.

Philippe returned shortly after dark. Richard was sitting up in bed covered only by a sheet, and drinking heated wine. He was naked to the waist, his magnificent chest gleaming with scented oils.

Philippe sat down beside him on the bed. "I have a surprise for you. A visitor."

Richard shrugged his shoulders, unaffected. "A messenger from my father? Someone newly converted to our cause? Whatever his purpose, bring him in quickly so that we may dismiss him all the sooner. There is only one man I wish to see tonight and that is you."

Philippe held up his hand as if to give an oath, and smiled enigmatically. "Wait and see, my love..."

Just then the tent flap parted and a man came in. He was shrouded in a heavy cloak, his face in shadow. But the voice was recognizable in an instant. "Hello, Richard," he said, and tossed the cloak aside.

For a moment Richard didn't understand; and then he did.
It was Johnny.

For two days Henry lay at Chinon suffering the effects of his
illness. The wild flight south had awakened half a dozen old injuries to his body, and so now it was pain, not only failing health,
that enfeebled him.

Godfrey came, as he had promised, but there was still no word
of John. Against Godfrey's protestations Henry insisted on making the short journey to Saumur, for the king was certain John
must still be there. When Henry's pleas became too pitiful to
ignore, Godfrey tempered his objections and went with him.

They didn't find John there, which was no surprise to Godfrey.
He didn't doubt the silly little coward had already taken safety
behind the stone fortresses of Normandy; it was just as likely he
had sailed away to England. But although that was Godfrey's bitter appraisal, he said nothing of this to his father.

Henry was still at Saumur the following day when two agents
of the French king came to him. They had not come at Philippe's
will, but at the urging of their own conscience.

"What do they want?" Henry groaned, tossing restlessly upon
his bed.

"Just to see you, Father," Godfrey told him.

Henry's voice took on the strength of defiance. "If Capet
wishes to make terms with me, let him come himself. Unless he is
too occupied fucking my son."

Godfrey came closer. "It is his grace of Rheims, and the Count
of Flanders. Old friends, my lord."

Henry nodded. "Yes. Help me to sit up Godfrey. Then bring
them in."

It was an awkward meeting since neither of the visitors could
keep the look of pity from their eyes as they faced the king. The
Count of Flanders did most of the talking. He explained that the
French king and Richard had planned to take Tours on the following day.

"Make your peace with Philippe," he urged. "End this war."
When Henry shook his head in disapproval, d'Alsace nearly
shouted, "You are dying from it!"

Henry waved away the objection with a trembling hand. "I am

dying anyway. No matter what I choose to do; no matter what cities of mine Capet takes for his own. It makes no difference now."

"Philippe will want to see you," the Bishop of Rheims said, squinting past pitying tears. "Will you agree to whatever place and time he names?"

The old fierce look came back into Henry's keen grey eyes. "Let him take Tours before he dictates anything to me!" The sweat ran down his cheeks like tears. He looked at Flanders, tiny lines of irony creasing at the edges of his mouth. "You chose the right side after all, my friend," he said.

Then he lay back upon the bed and closed his eyes.

Godfrey hustled over to plump the cushions beneath Henry's head. "He'll sleep now," he muttered, turning back to the others. "He tires easily when the pain is very bad. Tomorrow, if he is feeling strong enough, we shall return to Chinon. Tell the French king *that*."

They nodded and went quietly from the room.

Outside in the courtyard Flanders leaned upon his hand and wept. "For thirty years he was the greatest power on earth! Why has God left him to die in misery and disgrace?"

The bishop gazed up into a cloudless summer sky. "All flesh is grass," he answered.

Tours fell to the French on July 3, 1189.

Immediately Philippe sent word to Chinon that Henry meet him on the following day at Colombières. Godfrey showed the letter to William Marshal. "Good Marshal, please go with him," he wept. "I cannot bear to see my father humbled by those villains."

With Marshal and a few other loyal knights beside him, Henry managed to ride several miles before he was overtaken with the pain of his injuries. Because of this he was forced to seek rest at a lodging of the Knights Templars where he was given an herbal posset to drink and put to bed. Henry pleaded with Marshal to go forward to the meeting place, and tell Capet of his illness, explaining the delay.

Meanwhile Philippe and Richard waited anxiously at Colombières.

"He is lying!" Richard fumed when Marshal told them what

the king had bid him say. "This is merely a ruse he has concocted in order to escape his rightful judgment."

Marshal looked deep into the cold eyes of the man who once had been his friend. "By God, you are a devil," he growled, "for no one else could speak so harshly of the flesh who made him!" He turned to Philippe with his hands outstretched, petitioning. "Is it beneath your dignity to come in person to the bedside of a dying man? Is your heart as black as that?"

Philippe sneered back, his strong jaw set and unrelenting. "The victor does not pay calls upon the vanquished. Bring your king here, as I have instructed you to do."

They were both devils. Marshal spat contemptuously on the ground, then leapt upon his horse and rode away.

Slowly Henry's tiny caravan made its way to Colombières

The day was sultry, hot. Veins of lightning illumined low clouds on the horizon. Thunder grunted beyond the western slopes and the still air smelled of rain.

Philippe squinted into the hazy sunlight and stretched from the waist as Henry's pitiful little band approached. He gave a sideways glance to Richard, then spurred his horse ahead.

The two kings halted a few feet apart.

Philippe muttered a terse, unfriendly greeting. Henry stared back at his youthful enemy. He was so handsome and arrogant, without a trace of kindness in his eyes. Henry's clouded senses called up the memory of lovely, golden Isabel. How could anyone so sweet and tender find anything to love in this cold, uncaring man?

Philippe frowned at the wretched man before him. *God, the old bastard really did look sick.* As a concession he jerked the scarlet cloak from his own shoulders and tossed it to the ground. "You may sit on this if it will ease your discomfort," he said.

A flickering of scorn lighted Henry's eyes. "Do you think I came here to sit for hours in the hot sun and pass the time with you? Just tell me what you want and let me go."

Philippe shrugged his shoulders. "As you prefer. I don't expect this will take very long." He pulled a roll of parchment from within the folds of his pellison. "These terms are fixed," he snapped, "and NOT subject to negotiation."

He was just about to read when a spear of lightning struck the ground between them, flashing sparks and smoke. Their horses reared in fright and both men nearly fell. Marshal rushed to the side of his king and righted him, propping him upright in the saddle with his own strong hands.

By now Henry was shaking violently, weak with illness and alarm. He listened without response as Philippe read the cruel terms of surrender, a long list of demands which the dying man could barely comprehend. *Henry would do public homage to Philippe. He would relinquish Alais into the care of guardians appointed by the French king. He would give up all his Angevin domains, and recognize Richard as the suzerain, and heir to the crown of England. He would agree to join Philippe and Richard on a sojourn to the Holy Land. He would surrender claims to Auvergne. And lastly, he would administer the kiss of peace to Richard as a symbol of contrition.*

Philippe explained each point in pitiless detail.

When he had finished Richard brought his horse alongside of Henry's and the two men looked at one another. Neither felt any sense of recognition in the other, only a hatred that reached forward into the grave. Richard's voice was shrill and brazen. "So you have finally been brought to account for all your vices."

"Vices?" Henry's voice cracked in a hoarse laugh, "there is no greater vice than a betrayal of a father by his son!"

"I didn't betray you," Richard countered fiercely. "I merely gave you back what you deserve!"

The old king's reddened eyes clouded with tears. "I loved you, Richard! Why have you done this to me?"

Richard's anger caught in his throat. "Don't think you can make me feel sorry for you now, you damned self-pitying bastard! Your love has been a lie for as long as I remember. You don't know how to love! You begged me to trust you, then stirred up discord behind my back. Thank God Philippe has finally shown me how false you really are!"

The old man's hands shook helplessly as he clasped them at his breast. "God pity you if you put your trust in *him*," his eyes strayed over Philippe's face. "In time he will do the same to you, Richard, as he has done to me."

"Words," Richard scoffed. "I've heard too many words from you and all of them are lies. Do the deed, and let's have it over." He leaned forward in the saddle, positioning for Henry's kiss.

Henry reached out, taking Richard's head between his hands,

kissing his brow. This was his own flesh! His and Eleanor's. They had made him in some hot moment of passion long before their love became a lie. *How could a seed of rapture turn to poison?*

The gesture done, Richard tried to pull away, but Henry held him still. Their faces were nearly touching as he whispered close to Richard's ear, "I pray God grant I will not die till I have had my revenge on you!" Then his hands slipped away and he sagged forward, nearly falling from the horse.

Marshal scrambled up behind him, steadying the ruined king in his arms. He took up the slackened reins and jerked the horse to a full turn. "May God send you both to burning hell for this!" he screamed over his shoulder. Then he spurred the horse into a trot.

Richard watched until they disappeared beneath the dip in the road. There was a pain in his heart he had never known before, a seizure of regret for the misery of the situation. It was not of his making; he had never wished it so! But something deep within him was suffering all the same. Silently he cursed his father. They would never meet again, not in this world. Perhaps only in the hell which Marshal had predicted....

Philippe motioned to de Clermont. "See that the list of deserters from King Henry's ranks is sent to him when it is ready." Then with a sly expression he added, "but bring it to me before it is dispatched. I want to be certain all has been done according to my plan." He winked at Richard, and reached out to take hold of his hand. "It's over now," he said.

Long before he reached Chinon, Henry had to be transferred to a litter. It was a long and arduous journey. He lay helpless upon a makeshift pallet, the sky passing above his head in deepening shades of blue as evening stalked the golden heels of daylight. If they did not reach Chinon soon he would die out here on the dusty, vacant road.

Henry seemed to sleep. Yet he was conscious, his thoughts locked into stupefied awareness. All his life he had fed his appetites—hungry for power, for wealth, for the hot flesh of a woman's body. Now at the end he longed only for a soft bed and a cool drink of water.

They carried him to the end of the winding road and through the cobbled courtyard. As he passed under the massive arch of the entryway he turned his head to glimpse the final rays of the disappearing sun and knew he was seeing it for the last time. He had come home to die in the land that gave him birth.

Godfrey tended him all that evening, washing his fevered body with clean cloths, replacing the soiled clothes with fresh braies and an embroidered bliaud of his own. *Sleep was coming now, sweet and beckoning.* But first a cup of cherished water was put to his lips. Henry drank it with gratitude, and felt a deep peace settle over him.

Perhaps it was not so bad to die. He was comfortable now, and he was not alone. Godfrey was sitting close beside him and soon John would come. Two faithful and loving sons. What more did a man require?

Henry's dreams were vivid particles of the past shot through with sensations of remembered heroism. A boy, fighting at his father's side. A young man leading an army under his mother's keen, approving eye. There was a beautiful queen beside him then, taunting him from behind the cover of an innocent smile while her husband watched, unknowing; pulling him into the recesses of the doorway to wet his mouth with hungry kisses. And then once more the brutal picture of a bloodied altar, the image of a love cut down by antagonism and jealousy in a grim cathedral on a winters' night.

Becket. But the face beneath the mitre was his own.

He felt a little stronger in the morning, enough to eat the food which Godfrey brought. "You look as if you didn't sleep at all," Henry said, and squeezed his son's hand in affection, "but I suppose you passed the entire night here with me."

"It seemed to make you rest easier to know that I was with you," Godfrey answered with a hint of pride in his voice.

Marshal came into the room just then. He looked rumpled and ill-slept. Godfrey looked closer and could see that there was more. Marshal's face was set very tight, and there were grim lines beside his mouth. In his hand he held a rolled paper with a hanging seal suspended at the end of it. *Philippe's seal.*

Even Henry's dulled eyes read the signs of distress on his friend's face and he pushed himself upright on the bed. "What is wrong?" he asked.

Marshal came to the edge of the bed and thrust the paper into

Henry's hands. "It is worse than you can imagine. This is the list of traitors who left you to follow after the French king and your son." His hand shook as he ran a finger along the column of names from the bottom to the topmost portion of the page. It was a moment before he could bring himself to speak the words. "Here, at the beginning—at the very head of the list—is the name of your youngest son, Prince John."

The signature, scrawled in John's own untidy hand, swam before Henry's eyes. *It was not possible.* Despite all the other cruelties he had been forced to suffer in these past weeks, Henry could not believe that this was possible. It was some foul trick devised by Richard and Philippe Capet, another arrow aimed at his bleeding heart.

John would never...

The paper slipped from his hand onto the floor.

It was true. In an instant the reality overwhelmed him. *It was true.* He groaned aloud, a cry so filled with pain that any man who heard it might think he had been run through by a sword. "Oh John," he sobbed, "it was for you I incurred all this misery, for you that I threw my life away! Can you desert me now as all your brothers did? Oh John, my darling child, my *heart!*"

Godfrey reached out to comfort him, but the broken king was past all means of comfort. He turned his face to the wall and would not be moved. "Let all things go as they will," he muttered tonelessly, "I no longer care for myself or all the world...."

Those were his last clear moments. After that he slept in fitful snatches; woke, moaned, clung to Godfrey, sometimes recognizing him, sometimes not. Late in the afternoon he managed to pull the sapphire ring from off his finger and push it into Godfrey's hand. "This is yours," he whispered, "for you have always been a true son to me. Truer than any seed sown in the body of my wife. If God grants that I may live, I will set you higher than any man in my realm. But if I do not, then may God himself reward you for your goodness."

Godfrey wept. *A father's love was reward enough!*

Henry's eyes seemed placid in his haggard face. "How I wish I could recall your mother! She must have been an angel to give birth to such a loving child."

"Not an angel," was Godfrey's choked reply, "a camp follower, a common whore..."

Henry shook his head and tried to smile. "They are the only honest women on God's earth."

Then he slept again.

That evening they carried Henry to the chapel and laid him on the floor beside the altar. He had refused the Sacrament for these many days, but now he mumbled a confession and took the Host to cleanse himself of sin, to preserve the soul which he had promised to the devil on the day Le Mans was burned.

God or the devil. It made no difference to him now.

Once more he was put into his bed, knowing this time that he would never leave it. Godfrey held him, brushing away the flies that settled on his face. Only Godfrey, and no other, beside him now to share his desolation.

Henry was too weak to say a single word, but even the fever could not burn from his mind the ugly images of regret. Silently he lay lamenting for the wasted efforts of his life; the silly toil which in the end had come to nothing.

To know in death that life itself is futile: that is Man's greatest punishment of all. Henry grieved for his life; not for the ending of it, but for the love misspent and the hope misplaced and all the other fond and precious feelings which had brought him here, to this.

Despair and bitterness merged with truth as his senses faded.

He was just a fool, and he was old, and he was dying.

And there was nothing else.

Henry died in Godfrey's embrace at sunset on the following day. The bastard son who had remained faithful while all the other sons proved false, gazed out the uncovered window at an early evening sky set with pink clouds too beautiful to be endured, and sobbed for the pity of his loss.

Later that evening he and Marshal rode the short distance to Fontévrault Abbey where they made provisions for the king's burial and dispatched a message to Richard telling of Henry's death. By the time they returned to Chinon, most of the remaining household had fled, carrying away everything of value. Even the king's body had been stripped, left naked on the bed without so much as a piece of linen to cover his shriveled member.

Shame on a conquered king!

Godfrey dressed his father in borrowed clothes, but there was not a single article of royalty with which to decorate his person. Marshal searched the ransacked chests and found a ragged piece of gold embroidery to fashion as a tawdry crown, and a wood staff which they put into his hands to serve as a makeshift scepter.

In this travesty of royal state Henry's body was borne down the hill early the next morning, supported on the shoulders of a few devoted knights. Godfrey and Marshal walked behind, joined at the last by Stephen, the Seneschal of Anjou, who, having taken dinner with the King of France only a few days ago, had now come to pledge belated honor to his fallen lord.

As the cortège drew closer to the town they were besieged by a crowd of poorfolk seeking alms. It was the custom at the death of so great a statesman that a goodly amount of coins be given out to all in need. Their almoners empty, the mourners turned to the seneschal for he was richly dressed and wore rings on every finger.

"Give these good people something," Marshal ordered him.

Stephen's heavy face flushed in surprise. "Why I have nothing to give them," he insisted, "for the king's wars with his son and Philippe of France have left me a poor and hungry man."

Marshal's dark eyes flashed, warning of anger. "You look fat enough to me!" he declared, jabbing his fist into Stephen's belly. "And if you have no wealth of your own you surely have some which is the king's, for you grew rich in his service these many years, and profited by his bounty, to say nothing of what you undoubtedly stole from him!" He reached out and jerked several of the golden chains from Stephen's neck, and tossed them boldly into the midst of the crowd.

Men and women, with their vacant, gaping mouths, pressed forward, their dirty hands outstretched, fighting one another for the unexpected prize. It was a mocking conclusion to the tragic episode of Henry's death.

At Fontévrault some of the vanished dignity was restored to the king's estate. A group of solemn nuns came out to meet the caravan, chanting psalms in voices that were high and sweet. It was a curious irony that of all the women who had known Henry's love and held his scarred and husky body in their arms, there were only nuns to mourn him at his death.

That evening, as a choir sang somewhere in the church, Richard came to stand a while near the high altar where his father's body lay. None who stood close by, like William Marshal, could tell if the son's passive expression denoted sorrow or relief.

Richard stared down into his father's face and felt nothing.

He murmured a brief prayer, and as he did so a line of blood began to flow from the king's nose, curving down into his beard. Richard knew this for an omen and stepped back, amazed.

The blood was an accusation.

Murderer, it said.

Philippe was halfway to Paris when he heard of Henry's death. *Richard was King of England now.*

That meant their relationship would have to change. From this point on, their goals were bound to be in opposition to each other's. Philippe took a few moments to brood over the situation. And then, impatient, he spurred his horse toward home.

He was famished for Isabel.

They had been apart for nearly three months, and suddenly he could think of nothing but sinking his flesh inside her. He'd been able to push her from his mind while he was in the field, spending his passion in Richard's bed and the pursuit of Henry's ruin. Now that was over and the lure of Isabel called him back to Paris. He didn't even stop at Chartres to pray.

He had never ridden so hard in all his life.

Open-mouthed and panting, Isabel gazed up at the grey silk canopy and embroidered silver birds above her head. All of her feelings seemed captive to this moment, fused like those splendid birds upon the silk.

She lay unmoving as Philippe pushed his face between her legs where she was already sodden. His tongue was an expert instrument, brutal and hard. Isabel could hardly summon the strength to respond to him, but she crossed her ankles behind his head and pulled him closer.

If he did not fill her soon she would go mad.

But when he did she felt she would go mad as well. God, he was even more a man than she remembered! Why couldn't he live in her forever? Why couldn't she take his strength with her to the grave?

Philippe's hands cinched at Isabel's waist and heaved her bottom up higher. This was worth a hundred victories over Henry; a thousand castles or a million crowns. He closed his eyes and pumped furiously against her.

She held the Druid ring between her breasts and said his name.

END PART V

Part VI
Summer, 1189

$\mathfrak{R}$ICHARD wasted no time putting his affairs in order.
There was much work needed to be accomplished in France before he could think of crossing over to England for his coronation. He spent the remainder of July traveling through Anjou, Touraine, and Maine, laying down his dictates to the magistrates and barons, suppressing any hint of lawlessness which might have grown out of the recent wars.

Richard was a harsh man and some of his doings seemed unfair. He promptly confiscated all the lands of all the men who had deserted King Henry, and yet he sought to reward those who had kept faith with his father to the end. It may have been an act of warning to *all* traitors, or perhaps he was really feeling guilty after all, knowing he'd aided Philippe in hounding Henry to his death.

But there was one conspirator who was lovingly received into Richard's circle. John—whose motives for abandoning his father had been unclear even to the cunning Philippe—was treated with a show of graciousness and ceremony when he met with Richard at Rouen in early August.

The reconciliation between the two brothers was a puzzle only to those who did not know them well. Richard loved John with much the same measure of indulgence Henry had, for despite his flawed nature John was a lovable fellow. It was equally typical of Richard that he suddenly wished to reunite his family, after he'd spent so much time and effort supplanting it the past two years.

There were other relationships which needed mending.

Immediately after Henry's death, Richard had begged William Marshal to remain in royal service. He *needed* Marshal, trusted him. The famous knight was a soldier and administrator and more than anything he was a friend to the Plantagenets. In the years since young Harry had first brought him into the royal circle, he had become almost a member of the family.

"Will you stay, Marshal?" Richard asked. "I beg you to."

In the end the faithful William agreed, for he had come to care too deeply for the fate of England and its king to give any other answer.

Richard was well pleased.

Immediately Marshal was directed to return to England, where he would carry out a special mandate for the king, his first. It was written out in a proclamation by the king's own hand. William read the document and smiled, for he was glad.

From this day, Queen Eleanor was free.

It had been so many years since she had truly been a wife, it was difficult for her to feel a widow. Eleanor took the news of Henry's death with calm ambivalence and a trace of incredulity. She had never quite believed it was possible for him to die.

Henry Plantagenet. The greatest power on earth since Charlemagne. Eleanor had never known a king so kingly, a man who was so very much a man. She had hated her love for him, then later she had grown to love the hate. There had been everything between them but indifference.

She wept a little, but her tears were for herself and not for Henry. All the happiness she'd ever known had been because of him, and all the misery. The two emotions grew together in her mind, inseparable. She had learned to live with both of them, because even that was better than forgetting.

Oh Henry, if you'd kept faith with me you'd be alive today!

But it was over. Eleanor shed her tears in private, then closed the last of her regrets away. For the first time in many years she had a future. It didn't matter that she had lived for nearly seven decades. She felt young again, excited. With Richard's inheritance assured, Eleanor had come into her own.

She dismissed her jailers on the day the news of Henry's death was brought to her, but remained at Salisbury for Richard's messenger to come. When Marshal put the document of freedom in her hand she nearly wept again, this time from joy.

Instead, she smiled—a sweet, completely female smile which brought out the dimples in her cheeks. William kissed her hand and marveled at the loveliness in her face which age had not yet stolen. After all that had happened to her and all she had been forced to suffer, Eleanor was still beautiful.

He toasted her with wine and told her that.

Richard had named his mother Regent until he could return to England. Thrilled with her new responsibilities and the prospect of a reunion with her cherished son, Eleanor set out for London with a splendid retinue. Everywhere she halted people rushed to greet her, throwing bouquets of flowers at her feet. They remembered her as the legendary beauty of thirty years ago, the queen presiding at her *courts of love* where knights and troubadours sang songs of praise to her. She seemed so little changed now, riding by on her chestnut palfrey, whose straps were decorated by a hundred jingling bells.

To the people, Eleanor looked as lovely as she ever had.

But her progress toward London was not merely an opportunity to show herself so that others might render homage. Now she was at liberty once more, Eleanor was intent on restoring that right to every prisoner in the land.

Capriciously, perhaps unwisely, she ordered each jail or place of forced detention opened, its inhabitants set free. While the wary Marshal doubted the good sense of this, he did all according to her will, for she was Regent now.

In late August John was wedded to Hadwisa of Gloucester, who, though unattractive, provided him with considerable estates upon their marriage. Richard had also increased his younger brother's wealth by endowing him with several counties, plus the Duchy of Cornwall.

At last John was a rich and happy man.

There was no more exciting place on earth than London that late summer of 1189, as all was made ready for Richard's coronation in September. He was anxious to begin his reign officially, more anxious still to have all ceremonious occasions at his back, so he could prepare for the crusade. It was all he thought about, even as his day of days approached.

Before leaving Normandy he had sent a letter to Philippe in Paris, urging him to be present at the coronation. Richard had spent enough time at the French court and now he wished to return the courtesy with a show of English hospitality to his friend.

By the time he had reached Southampton there was a reply waiting for him, decorated with the familiar hanging seal. The letter, beautifully scripted in the hand of Henri of Champagne, conveyed a lusty greeting to the English king.

But at the end was a rude message.

Philippe was busy, and he would not attend.

The creative talents of Richard and his mother had never been put to better use. Together they supervised each glittering detail of the coronation, so when the day arrived all was perfection. It was the most splendid show the good people of London had ever seen and they pressed forward in multitudes, dumb with awe, to witness their new king—a handsome man of regal elegance— take himself to West Minster Abbey at the head of a parade of nobles, all dressed in rich and sparkling array.

That was the good news. Later, there was trouble.

During the feasting which followed the solemn ceremony, groups of Jews presented themselves in front of West Minster palace, eager to salute their king with gifts. Turned away by ill-mannered courtiers, they began a riot in the streets. This brief scuffle quickly grew into general lawlessness as Christian by-standers attacked some of the Jews and killed them. These same citizens then went forth to wreck every synagogue within the city, and set fire to houses in the Jewish sector.

Many families were burned to death inside their homes before a group of nobles, dispatched by the king himself, could set upon the troublemakers. But by this time the rioting was so far advanced that no amount of armed soldiers could restrain it.

As though a signal had been given, disorder spread throughout the country. Nearly every other city followed London's example in the days to come. There was one particularly violent uprising in York, which had a large Jewish population. But everywhere there was burning and bloodshed.

Some men said the king himself had decreed the riots, for he was known to hate Jews and was resentful they had lived so contentedly under his father's reign. It was true that Henry had been a friend to them. So long as they obeyed the laws of England, they were protected under those same laws. But that was Henry's way.

Richard was a different man entirely.

To be fair, he had not incited the riots nor did he conscience them, and quickly saw to it that the evil-doers were fined and put to punishment. His motive was not justice, but anger. He deplored these riots which had spoiled the feast of his coronation, and so he vowed they would not occur again. But something of his magic had been damaged.

It was not a favorable beginning, to be sure.

Richard was selling everything.

Buildings, bishoprics, royal appointments—all were for sale.

In one burst of fury Richard even declared that he would sell London itself if a buyer could be found. It was not just an idle comment. His mind was firmly fixed upon a single purpose. He *had* to raise the money to finance his expedition to the East.

Like his brothers, Richard had no money sense. That was one of the many traits which the sharp-minded Henry had been unable to pass on to any of his sons. Furthermore, Richard was cursed with an unending need for personal luxury. Because of this, and all the fighting he'd been party to in the past two years, his own private wealth was greatly diminished at this time.

The royal treasury, kept at Winchester, was a vast sum, but it was not enough to equip Richard's new enterprise, and a cache of other expenses were piling up as well. The monies spent on the coronation had been considerable, and Richard had been forced to borrow against his estates in Poitou to pay most of them. He was swamped by a rising tide of indebtedness on all sides, the threat of which only strengthened his resolve, even if it did infringe on his enthusiasm.

Thus the favors were meted out and paid for.

There were some important vacancies in key positions of both Church and State, and Richard promptly filled them—not with those who necessarily merited the honor, but with men who could afford to pay the most. William Longchamp, a detested and unsightly dwarf who had served as Richard's chancellor in Aquitaine (some men were heard to whisper he had served in Richard's bed as well), was made Chief Justiciar in England and also nominated Bishop of Ely. For this privilege Longchamp paid four thousand pounds into the coffers of the realm, which Richard happily set aside for the crusade.

All the offices of English government, great or small, were up for sale. In every county the sheriffs were made to pay if they wished to keep their positions. They were only reinstated if not outbid by other men. Those who resisted Richard's cruel edict (and there were many) were imprisoned, their property made forfeit to the crown.

Richard managed to make one generous appointment.

In the time preceding the estrangement from his father, he'd often known Henry to speak of Godfrey as a possible candidate for the see of York. Therefore, Richard fulfilled his father's wish in naming Godfrey archbishop, and at the same time soothed his own conscience, for now he could claim to have made peace with Henry's restless soul.

But Godfrey was still required to pay a token sum.

In large and small amounts, the money was pouring in.

Having consummated his marriage, John went forth to Wales at Richard's bidding. The Welsh barons and princes, who had been kept so firmly under Henry's restraining hand, had broken into fresh rebellion when they learned that he was dead.

The trouble was not significant enough to warrant much attention, but Richard wanted all such actions stopped before they could flourish into a full-scale war. Considering John's poor record as a diplomat and soldier in Ireland a few years back, it was somewhat ironic that Richard should choose him for such a task.

Whether or not John would have bungled matters once again was never to be known, since most of the rebels had laid down their arms by the time he arrived. The chief conspirator was Prince Rhys ap Gryffud of South Wales, and once he learned his barons had not elected to support him, he was forced to surrender as well.

John required Gryffud to return with him to Oxford and

render an act of homage to the king. The two men became friends along the way, and toasted one another during many a long night of drinking and reveling in local brothels. It may not have been diplomacy in the truest form, but one thing at least could be said for John: he could appease the most resentful enemy in the world with a few ribald stories and a goodly supply of wine.

The fellowship ended abruptly when they reached Oxford.

Richard was too busy raising money to grant the Welsh prince an audience. Instead he sent a servant to deliver a brief treaty of accord which he himself had already signed. Furious at this breach of courtesy, Gryffud put his name to the paper, then left Oxford within the hour.

John said nothing but he winced at Richard's haughtiness.

He had never learned the importance of making friends.

* * *

In shaded sleep, when thoughts are true
And memories full of nights of bliss,
When time dispels all broken dreams
And paints past agonies with gold,
I yet uncover heartfelt hopes, of love
Which even now are real.

From thousand moons and thousand stars
And million kisses in between
Which fed my soul, so long denied,
I cannot separate my tears
From all the lovely liquids spilled
Or flames of love, from hell.

My heart, so touched by melodies
Of joy and promise long ago,
I let it fly, as now I must.
But in the dark when dreams come back
To haunt me of a lover lost,
I weep for what is gone.

Eleanor of Aquitaine
Fragment of a lost poem
October, 1189

* * *

PHILIPPE had never been so hungry for his wife.

Since his return to Paris in July, he'd spent each night and nearly every afternoon with her. It was almost the way it had been for them at the beginning. No memory, just passion. And a sense that time was an enemy they could not fight.

Isabel lay with Philippe's cheek against her breast and listened to the rain falling on the stones outside her window. It was late afternoon, but dim as evening. The sun had not been seen for many days. Isabel loved when the wind blew just that way and rain turned everything to shadow. The sounds and images stirred up remembrances of Mons.

Nearly half her life had been spent in Paris, and yet Hainault would always be the place she thought of when she thought of home. Isabel doubted she would ever visit it again.

Philippe's voice sounded close beside her, almost as if it came from her own body. "Are you asleep?" He raised on his elbow to look into her face.

Isabel smiled back at him, weary and at peace. "I never sleep when I'm with you. It's such a waste of time."

He ringed the nipple of her breast with kisses.

Later she was dozing, but roused to the sound of him pulling on his clothes. "You aren't going?" she asked.

He gave a glance toward the bed. "I promised to meet Sully for an hour or so. He has some new designs he needs to show me, or so he says."

Isabel reached out for his hand. "It sounds more like a conspiracy to take you away from me."

He sat down on the edge of the bed, leaning to light another candle. The flame leapt up, illuminating her face in quavering shades of gold. Philippe studied her face for a moment, intent on its loveliness. She never looked more beautiful than she did after they had just made love—yards of tangled hair around her face and shoulders, her pale skin rouged with a blush of exertion.

"Sully is more understanding than he used to be," Philippe

explained, "or at least he knows better than to make complaints about the time I spend with you. I've warned him of it enough."

"Spend time with me now," she smiled and opened her arms to him.

Sully could wait.

Isabel loved his strong, broad shoulders and the feel of his body moving over hers. But after a moment she cautioned him, her lips to his ear, "You must not deal too roughly with me now, my darling. I don't want to lose this child as I did the others who were early born."

Philippe slid his hand along her belly, caressing the fine, soft skin which separated him from his unborn child. "We needn't fear for this one, love. It was made after my triumph over Henry, the greatest victory of my life. God will keep it safe as a special blessing to us." He stroked the inside of her thighs with his heavy penis, then bent to kiss the tiny drops of moisture that glistened on her plush triangle of gold curls. "This is the sight I love best in all the world," he muttered, "for there is nothing finer..." With those words still on his lips Philippe pushed inside with a grunt of pleasure. Then he rode her till both of them cried out with exhaustion and joy.

He rolled over on his back and pulled her on top of him so that their flesh would not be separated even now, after all had been enjoyed. "My angel," he whispered, his lips so close to hers, "I never want to be farther from you than this."

He meant it. Isabel knew he did. There had never been so much love between them as in these past four months. All of their passion had combined with feelings of tenderness in equal measure, and now they felt so close.

But circumstance threatened to ruin it all.

Philippe was committed to the crusade. With Henry dead and Richard on the throne, there was no longer any excuse for a delay in going to the East. Richard was planning his departure for July of the following year and he expected Philippe to accompany him. A year and a half had passed since the fall of Jerusalem, and still no western kings had come to fight! The trouvères had begun to sing mocking songs about the tardy monarchs.

Philippe's vow of taking the cross had been only half sincere at the time. Now he did not wish to go at all. He saw no hope that Jerusalem could be retaken, and any other reason for going seemed insufficient and hardly worth the sacrifice of leaving his domains behind for two years—to say nothing of his wife.

Isabel was full of panic that he might go.

To live without him for so long would not be possible. Her appetite for him was too prodigious to be so long denied. Philippe knew that. They seldom spoke of it, but it was always there. Even now.

"If you go away I don't know what I'll do," Isabel muttered against his chest.

Philippe tightened his arms around her, but did not answer.

"It makes so little sense for you to go," she argued, but her voice was sweet and uncomplaining. "Think of what you could accomplish here while Richard was away! You could have Normandy, Anjou, the Aquitaine for yourself, while he's off fighting Moslems in the East."

Philippe smiled at the sincerity of her words. "You talk as if conquest were an easy thing. A prize like Normandy doesn't fall into your hand like a ripe apple."

Isabel sat up and looked down at him with a sulky expression on her face. "Don't treat me as if I were a numbskull! I've been hearing tales of conquest since I was at my mother's breast."

He had not forgotten her rich and able heritage, but she was a woman, with a woman's view of things. She did not understand that to conquer did not mean simply to put an army in the field and lead them! He reached to take a handful of her hair then stroked his face with it and kissed it lovingly. "To take even Anjou would need all the resources of my realm. Normandy would require still more than that," he explained.

Her hands moved over his chest, the nails sharp and tickling. "You took Le Mans and Tours in the space of just two weeks last summer! Why should it be more difficult a second time? At least you would have something to show for all your efforts." Between kisses and little sucking nips at him she finished, "You deserved a piece of Maine and Anjou after all you did to secure it. I still wonder that you didn't demand a settlement with Richard after Henry died."

Philippe had never listened much to anything Isabel had to say but occasionally she surprised him with her well-informed appraisals. She was so beautiful and tempting, it was always hard for him to remember she had wisdom and ambition too.

He squeezed her shoulders, enjoying the feel of her delicate bones beneath the flesh. God, there was no one like her! "I wish it were so simple," he said in answer to her mild accusation, "but fighting with Richard and fighting against him are two different things."

She raised her head. "Not if he isn't here. Why do you think I suggested it?"

A sigh passed his lips. "I really don't want to talk about this now."

A familiar look of obstinacy flashed in her grey-green eyes. "We *have* to talk about it! In three weeks you go to Normandy to meet with Richard, presumably about the crusade. We have to make some kind of decision now!"

"*I* have to make a decision," he corrected her. "You know better than to tell me my will, Isabel."

She lowered her head slightly in contrition. "I'm sorry. I spoke from excitement. I know the decision is yours. But I have a stake in this too, Philippe."

His hands strayed to her breasts, to the fine hard nipples that were shaped so perfectly and tinted with a deep shade of rosy pink. He squeezed the sweet white globes that filled his hands. What pleasure they had given him in the past. What pleasure now!

He loved her so much. He wanted her more every day.

How could he leave all this beauty and passion behind for the sake of a desert crucible of blood and flies?

Isabel's hands clasped his in a loving covenant. "I am being selfish I know, Philippe, but only a little, which is not so terrible. You see, I'm no longer the twelve-year-old girl who sulked whenever you went away. I understand this business more than you can know. But I want what is best for both of us, my love. I want you to have all that your greatness and power deserve. You could make great gains for France in Richard's absence. You may have needed him to help you bring Henry down but you don't need him any more."

Philippe pushed her over on her back and rolled on top of her. Every part of her excited him, even the sweet, high sound of her voice. He nestled his chin between her breasts. "I don't wish to leave you any more than you wish for me to go," he said. "But I have made a vow to Christ, and even if He will release me from it, I fear the Church will not."

Isabel held him to her in a vicious grip of love. "There are ways."

"Richard will press me as hard as he knows how. I tell you, my love, to change this course will not be easy."

Her breath was close upon his face. "You'll find a way, you *must* find a way."

He pushed her legs apart and entered her in an instant. What glory! What was an earthly crown compared to this?

"Your body is the sweetest thing God ever made," he moaned.

Isabel gasped in giddy pain as his teeth made bites upon her neck. "I'll never let you go," she whimpered, "you are mine until the grave makes ghosts of both of us."

Philippe closed his eyes and pushed deeper.

Outside it seemed as if the rain would never stop.

For the first time John and Godfrey had a common purpose. *They were both outraged at Richard.*

He had been generous to both of them, but now he was exacting a hard price. He had drawn up a charter conferring his brothers' separate powers of ownership; the ranks and honors which he had bestowed upon them were implicit in the wording. Then in an ending paragraph he promptly stated that concurrent with his own departure for the Holy Land, both John and Godfrey would be required to leave England, and stay away for a period of three years.

Clearly, he did not trust them.

Richard had aimed yet another insult, this one of consequence only to John. The king had made his will, naming Geoffrey's son Arthur as his heir. Though this was in accordance with tradition (the child's father having been next in line to succeed Richard), John despised the action all the same. His objection was rooted not just in selfishness, but good sense. *How could Richard embark with any peace of mind upon his hazardous and lengthy sojourn—from which he might not return—having settled the succession on a child who was still wetting his blankets in the cradle?*

On one point at least Eleanor intervened on John's behalf.

He should not be banished to Normandy, she told Richard, for there he could cause more problems than he could ever bring about in England. Eleanor also explained the implausibility of putting John in close proximity to supporters of the French king, lest they gain his ear. Because Richard valued his mother's advice, he soon relented and lifted the ban on his brother's presence in England during his absence, but he did so with reservations. It was not until much later, with Richard far away in the Holy Land, that John permitted Godfrey to return as well.

But at this moment Richard was still in England, and he had a lot on his mind. Besieged by details on all sides, he was anxious to put everything right so he could begin his long-awaited journey to the East. There was a hasty conference with King William of Scotland and a peace treaty was signed, assuring Richard that his northern borders would be safe from attack while he was gone. He accomplished a similar concordance with the Welsh. These were not merely diplomatic ploys. Wales and Scotland, by way of Richard's carefully worded agreement, had furnished considerable monies to the royal war chest.

Despite all the measures taken to increase Richard's crusade fund, there was still a problem with outgoing expenses. He as yet owed his friend Philippe Capet nearly 24,000 marks for the wars against King Henry, since Philippe had borne most of the expense. That would have to be paid off in the next few months. There were also the spiraling costs of government to contend with. Even in his fervor to secure all he could for the crusade, Richard could not assign all incoming money to that purpose. He was trying his best to meet all his financial obligations to the degree possible, but since he knew little how to economize his extravagant tastes, this was not easy.

Originally it had been Richard's wish to depart England immediately after Easter, 1190. Now that date was beginning to look unrealistic, so Richard had substituted middle June instead. The question was whether or not Philippe would be ready by that time. The two kings agreed by letter to meet at Normandy after Christmas in order to fully discuss their plans for the coming crusade.

Richard was beside himself with anticipation.

Philippe was contemplating a way out.

*S*HE COULD SEE the flames from her window, and smell them too. The stink of burning, borne upwards on thick layers of black smoke, filled every corner of the room. It was an ugly incense: sharp, pungent with the smell of grease, like fat pigs roasting.

In the courtyard below they were burning Englishmen.

Constance turned from her window. *Let them burn.*

These were the last of the men who had come to Brittany two and a half years ago. They had come with the Earl of Chester, the odious man whose bed she had been forced to share. But he was gone now, fled back to England in the midst of the Breton uprising, and all those cohorts of his who had not gone with him were now cooking in the flames.

She was glad.

He was not out there, her detested husband, burning with the others—but she wished he was. *How she wished.* Of all men on earth, Constance hated Randulf de Blondeville, Earl of Chester. Of all the wretched things Henry Plantagenet had done to her, forcing her into marriage with Randulf had been the worst.

With Henry's death the Bretons had thrown off all English influence, and that included Randulf. Constance had no doubt that she was rid of him for good. He would not come back to Brittany now for fear of being killed by the angry populace who hated him, but he had left a memory behind.

Constance was pregnant with his child.

She had conceived with him in May, and now it was the middle of December. She hated the life which grew inside her belly. It had been made from Randulf's lust and her own abhorrence. Sometimes she prayed that it would die.

Constance wanted no reminder of this loathsome marriage; she wanted a divorce. Already she'd petitioned King Richard for consent. He would "take it under consideration" he had said. There was small security in Richard's promises; he was a liar like his father had been. But the new king had done one thing to please her: he had named Arthur as his heir.

Her lips curved in a smile as she considered it. Richard was likely to be away for years; he might never return to England. And if he did not, her son would inherit *all.* Arthur was not yet three; it would be many years before he reached his majority. But in the meantime Constance was as able as any man to serve as regent. Until the time came there was Brittany to govern, and another childbed to endure.

Constance wandered over to the window once again. The smell was lighter now, there were only ashes left on the cobbled square. *Arthur would rule over England someday.* She must remember that as this unloved child grew inside her, reminding her of things best left forgotten.

The wind caught up the ashes and scattered them amid the snow.

Too much rain.

It had rained nearly every day since the beginning of December and the Seine was flooding at its banks once more. The dampness seeped into the grey stones of the palace, and kept everyone close beside their fires.

Isabel had never felt so isolated. Philippe was away in Normandy seeing Richard, and he would not return till after Christmas. Besides Edythe, who was always busy caring for the queen's children, there was only Sibylla for company and her mood was as gloomy as the weather.

Isabel was anxious, fretful.

She worried that Philippe would be seduced to Richard's will and agree to follow him to the East. That anxiety was a physical strain which burdened her with sleepless nights and endless bouts of nausea. Her child was not due to be born till middle April and already Isabel feared greatly for her own health in the intervening months. Her strength was wearing thin, eaten up each day by frustration and worry, aggravated by hours of forced idleness.

Louis had developed a heavy cough and Isabel spent many hours at his bedside. The fear that illness might carry him off was very real to her. She had felt God's retribution too many times in her life to doubt its power. God was always taking things away from her, Isabel mused bitterly. If He took Louis now, she would turn her back on Him forever.

All she could do was pace the floor and worry.

She needed to share the burdens of her life but there was no one she could turn to. Certainly Sibylla was no help. She scarcely seemed to live at all; even her children had ceased to hold her interest. Isabel decided that this attitude of sloth must be stopped.

"You need to marry again," she told Sibylla one afternoon close to Christmas, "you have been too long without a husband."

The passive expression fell from Sibylla's face and she looked startled, even angry. "How can you suggest such a thing? I shall never give myself to another man so long as I might live. William is dead, and I grieve for him."

"You grieve too greatly," Isabel replied, sounding matter of fact. "It is not good for a girl of sixteen to retire from life."

Sibylla fed a little soup into her mouth, then swallowed it. "I do not choose to love another man."

Isabel stirred honey into her wine with brisk strokes and eyed her sister. "You did not choose to love William in the first place. I found him for you, remember? I can just as easily find another man to please you if you'll give me leave to try."

Her voice went low. "It has not even been a year since my husband's death. My grief is deep. What sacrilege it would be to take another man into my bed!"

Isabel spilled a little wine on the front of her chainse as she drank. "To make such high-sounding promises of faithfulness to a dead man is the same as throwing your life away. You are too young to go into your bed alone each night."

Sibylla stared past her sister's face into the flames of the fire grate. "I don't care for such things any more."

Isabel flung her spoon aside in irritation. She had heard enough. "What nonsense you are talking! Stop being such a child and you will realize what I say is right." She looked closer at her sister. "If it is your income you are worried for, you need not fear. I have talked to Philippe about this, and he has said you may retain your rank as Lady of Beaujeu even if you marry."

Sibylla threw her napkin to the floor. "Money is no inducement to me," she insisted, her cheeks coloring. "William's lands and inheritance are entrusted to me as the guardian of our son. I need no assurance from the king or anyone of my rights!"

Isabel's mouth, full and red as a summer poppy, twisted into a petulant expression. "This is more complicated than you know. Without a lord to reign in Beaujolais the revenues will be greatly diminished. Philippe will have to put a *seignior* in William's place until your son comes of age. You will have very little influence over what monies are accorded you. But look, with a new husband by your side you could hold in trust all that has been promised to your son, and still be assured of a new title and station."

These were practical opinions but Sibylla would have none of them. "You speak of lands and titles," she complained, "but I care nothing for such things now my husband is dead." She swept a length of brown hair back from her face. "Can we speak no more of this? I have listened long enough."

"Very well," Isabel answered tightly and drank the last of her wine. "But when you crawl into your bed alone each night, remember what I have said."

Sibylla looked up, her hazel eyes alive with puzzlement and innocence. "You talk as if there was nothing worse."

Isabel stared down at her folded hands and said not a word.

It was late December in Normandy, and very cold.

Philippe had come to Nonancourt on the frontier to meet with Richard, but the reunion between the two men was not as pleasant as either might have wished.

Richard was a different man now that he was king. His blunt soldier's manner had been replaced by an attitude of haughtiness, and the subject of money was ever on his mind. He was plagued by details; edgy, tight with his words.

Philippe had come to pose his objections to the crusade but Richard's enthusiasm for the venture made it difficult. The two kings fenced with words and made agreements of a general nature, but before very long Richard had divined his friend's reluctance to go.

Finally Philippe confessed his unwillingness.

Postpone for yet another year? Richard was infuriated at the suggestion, insulted that this great adventure meant less to Philippe than it did to him (though he had long guessed as much). What was this new objection?

He knew in an instant. *It was Isabel.*

Philippe relented at the last.

The lure of Isabel, of her sweet sexual favors, diminished in his mind when he was not with her, and the eloquence of Richard's fervent pleas had moved him deeply. Thus the two kings made their pledge to one another and signed a compact: they would set out for the East together in late June.

That night while Richard slept, Philippe lay wakeful at his side, wondering what he would tell Isabel when he returned to Paris in a few days. She would never forgive him for this deception.

He wondered if he would ever forgive himself.

Richard lingered in Normandy only a few days after Philippe had gone. He took himself to Brittany to meet with Constance. He wanted to assure her of the inheritance he had promised Arthur and discuss the divorce she had requested from de Blondeville.

There was yet another reason. Richard had come to ask his former sister-in-law if she would marry him. Since she wished to divorce her present husband, and since her son was already the acknowledged heir, it seemed logical to him that they should marry.

It was not a question of *loving* Constance. He did not love her. He did not love *any* woman. He certainly did not wish to be a husband, and yet in the past few months his mother had made more than a few intimations that it was time he took a wife. Richard was beginning to believe that she was right. He was a king now and was expected to make an heir.

With Constance as his wife and Arthur as his recognized heir, Richard would not have to concern himself with begetting a child of his own body. Of course there would be some problems. A marriage between a man and his brother's widow was only lawful in the eyes of the Church if the pope pronounced a special dispensation to permit it. But Richard was well regarded in Rome, and he anticipated no trouble in securing one.

But there was a problem with Constance.

At first she refused to see him, and Richard was told she was recovering from childbed and the stillbirth of her infant daughter. He waited at the court for a full two weeks before the duchess of Brittany received him at last.

He was unfailingly cordial to her, kissing the pale hand she held out. They passed a few moments in polite talk of trivial matters, but immediately Richard put his suggestion she rebuffed him, indignant that he would even consider her for his bride. The idea that she would tie herself to the Plantagenets again was absurd; surely he must realize how Constance hated all of her late husband's family.

How great a fool could the man be?

But Richard made his courteous proposal all the same, and Constance listened, hating every word he said. She struck an attitude of indifference and insensitivity, then sent Richard away unsatisfied. He did not appreciate her high-handed behavior and would not forget it in the future.

Geoffrey had been right about her, Richard brooded.

She was an ice-cold bitch after all.

January was an even, uneventful month.

Philippe returned to the Cité Palais following Twelfth Night, full of false explanations for his wife. His participation in the crusade had been indefinitely postponed, he told her. Because she loved him and because she wanted to, Isabel *believed.* In the end he would have to tell her. Why he delayed it now he did not know. *But he could not bear to see the pain in her eyes when she learned the truth.*

He hated himself, but there was nothing he could do.

Philippe told all of this to his mother, but made her promise she would disclose none of it to Isabel. *He would do it in his own good time* he insisted, and secretly hoped for some great crisis to keep him in France before the end of June.

But there was so very little time.

February was a month of blessings and long winter days.

Louis's cold had gone completely; Sibylla seemed less sulky than before. At the middle of the month Isabel gave a banquet to honor the acclaimed poet, Chrétien de Troyes, for he was very near completion of the epic *Perceval Le Galois,* the story of a knight who searches for the holy chalice of the Last Supper. Chrétien had enjoyed the rich patronage of Isabel's family for many years, and also that of the Champagnois. The inspiration for *Perceval* had come from a book of legends, given to him as a gift by the erudite Philip d'Alsace.

"I wish you could have been there," Isabel said, speaking to her husband of the banquet later that night as they lay in her bed. "Chrétien is going to dedicate the finished work to you."

Philippe turned on his back and pulled Isabel into his arms. "Then I am afraid it is wasted. I wouldn't know a poem from a peregrine."

Isabel left a sweet pattern of kisses on his shoulders and chest. "What does it matter? Such instincts are for lesser men. *You* are a poem, my love."

There was no woman like her in all the world.

"No," he said, "but you are..."

She felt impermanent in his arms. But her words were strong and carved with meaning, like epitaphs in a slab of stone. "Of a hundred thousand times I've said the words *I love you,* it is a thousand times that much and many more I feel it in my heart..." Isabel clasped his hand and drew it to her breast. "Can you feel it, my darling? Can you feel the love which lives inside me?"

Philippe fell over her, smothering her breath with kisses. What need for poetry? What use for words? So long as he was hot and hard inside of her, Isabel cared for nothing else.

A log popped in the fire grate, shooting out embers which smoldered for a little while, then blackened and fell apart like rotting cherries on the cold stone floor.

ISABEL turned twenty on the twelfth of March.

Twenty! Surely it had only been a year or two ago that she'd been ten, and married, and newly crowned a queen; only yesterday she had looked on Philippe for the first time. But it was half a lifetime ago.

So the queen was turning twenty. The people, who had come to love her, celebrated in the streets. Adele arranged a banquet and all the nobles of Paris were in attendance to wait upon the pleasure of the queen. Isabel dressed herself in St. Clotilde's pearls, a chainse of pale grey silk, and ermine mantle. She sat close beside her husband on a raised dais in the great hall, nodding her head as each man raised his henap in a toast to her.

They all drank wine until the late hours of the night. When it was near to midnight Philippe, who was quite drunk by that time, gathered up his wife and carried her from the room amid the ribald cheers of all who watched. Upstairs he stripped her naked but for the pearls she wore, and left so many kisses on her body that she trembled and begged for him to take her.

They made love till morning came. Then sleep was sweet.

* * *

Philippe left for Pontoise on the following day, and sometime that evening while he was gone Isabel went to the palace archives library to read a while. It was too dim there, so instead she went to the king's council chamber which was spacious and kept lit with torches all the night.

Strangely she felt like an intruder here. The room was silent and unattended, filled with a sense of anxiousness and doubt. Firelight trembled eerie patches of shadow on the far wall. Alone on the long and narrow table lay a document, neatly placed, as though waiting just for her.

Isabel went toward it, hand outstretched. It was in Philippe's writing, she recognized that at once. She picked it up and read, from a sense of curiosity at first. But it took very little time for her to comprehend the meaning of this single piece of paper.

The wording was concise, cruel.

It was an edict, written within the framework of a will. *On my departure for the Holy Land in June, this year of 1190*, it began, *I do place the administration of my realm in the hands of my wife, Isabel; of my mother Adele of Champagne, and Maurice de Sully, who is bishop of Paris—that they might serve as Regents in my absence, and see to the workings of justice and good government while I am gone...*

There was more, but she did not read it.

What was the use? Despite all the promises—all the lying *I love yous*—Philippe had done exactly as he had wished, aligned himself with Richard after all. A betrayal in ink, written down on paper, surely that was worse than any other kind.

The hateful page slipped from her fingers and disappeared beneath the table. For a moment Isabel could not think; when she did she prayed that she was dead or dreaming; that she was anywhere or anyone save where she was and who.

Isabel's breath came in small and shallow heaves. If she even moved so much as a finger now she would faint or vomit. The room began to waver a little before her eyes and a sudden pain leapt in her belly. Sweet Christ! She was alone and Philippe did not love her and the pain of childbirth was upon her now and it was much too soon.

She screamed and reached out for a hand that was not there.

* * *

Adele was leaning over, her face pinched in a serious expression. She wore a dishabille and her hair was loose, as if she had been called from sleep. "Hush child," she soothed.

Isabel squinted up into her face. "Where am I?"

"Your room." Adele's voice was tight. "The household guards summoned me when they found you on the floor downstairs. But now you must lie still and not upset yourself or the pains will return."

The awful memory came flooding back. "Philippe..." she said.

"He isn't here," Adele answered, smoothing Isabel's hair, "he left for Pontoise yesterday, remember? But I can send word to him if you like."

Isabel turned sideways on the bed. "He's gone, he's gone!" she wept.

"Only to Pontoise."

Isabel shook her head woefully. "The paper..."

Adele had seen the paper on the floor and understood. She squeezed her daughter-in-law's hand. "I knew Philippe's plan but he wouldn't let me tell you."

Isabel began to sob. "He lied to me! He swore he had changed his mind about going to the East. He told me that two months ago when he returned from Normandy. He even repeated his argument with Richard to me, word for word! He let me believe that he would stay with me, yet all the while he was making plans to leave. How could I have meant so little to him for so long, and never realized the truth?"

"That is not the truth," Adele insisted. "It is because my son loves you that he lied. He did not wish to hurt you."

"He has *betrayed* me!"

Adele turned away to hide her own tears of frustration. "If you do not believe me, I will fetch the king back to Paris and you can hear it from his lips."

She was about to rise when Isabel pulled her back and gasped, "Don't leave me now! The child is coming..."

She was in too much pain to care where Philippe was.

Heavy rain splashed against the grey walls of the Cité Palais.

It was evening. Isabel had labored for a dozen hours but the child would not be born. The midwives prodded her mercilessly with their rough, untidy hands till she felt they would tear her apart. She had screamed so often her voice was nearly gone, and now she could only whimper.

Adele had stayed close beside her all the day. Edythe too; and Sibylla paced the room, anxious and fearful. Giles de Jocelin, the king's physician, had come in the afternoon to give Isabel an herbal potion to relieve the pain, but it only made her vomit. He took Adele aside. "Bring Bishop Sully here," he instructed, "for if the child does not come by nightfall, the queen will die."

Adele nodded grimly and sent for Sully. She also dispatched Philippe's young chaplain, William le Breton, to Pontoise with a letter describing Isabel's condition, and urging the king to return at once to Paris. On her way back to Isabel's room Adele met her nephew Henri of Champagne in the corridor. He was wild-eyed, and his face was very pale.

He grabbed Adele's arm. "I just saw de Clermont in the street. He told me you have sent for Sully to perform Unction on the queen. What has happened?"

"It's the child," Adele explained, wiping a weary hand across her face, "I fear it is already dead and that is why it cannot be born."

"And the queen?"

Adele pulled away from him. "She is dying, Henri."

He stared at her for a moment, then fell to his knees and began to sob. "Oh Christ no, *no!*"

Adele looked down at him with pitying eyes. She understood. Her nephew's affair with Isabel was no secret to her. "Calm yourself," she said and stroked his hair. "I've sent for Philippe, and when he returns he must not see you in this state."

"I must see Isabel!"

Adele bent down and helped to pull him to his feet. "Later," she said, "when I can get the others from the room." She looked at him for a moment, then kissed his mouth. "Till then just wait outside."

She was gone before Henri could say another word.

Sully gathered up his instruments of Absolution and hustled to the palace, remembering a Christmas night eight years ago when he'd waited at the bedside of the child-queen Isabel, expecting that she would not live. She had seemed innocent and helpless then. Later he had learned what subtle sorcery she could work on a man's mind; how her beauty and body could enslave a king.

How willfully she flaunted her female magic!

Often, when she caught the bishop's eye, she would smile her teasing, half-seductive smile as if to say, *You cannot fight me.* He had said more prayers on her behalf than he could count. He had feared for her salvation. But surely now Isabel would be different. She had seen death's intimidating face.

As Sully came into her room the midwives were just wrapping the second of two dead infants in a woollen coverlet. Isabel was propped in a sitting position on the bed. Her head was thrown back and she was sobbing—from exhaustion, from pain, from grief. When the women made a move to take away the bodies of her dead sons, she screamed and had to be restrained.

It was Adele who managed to subdue her, ordering the midwives to leave the room. Then with her own hands she placed the two tiny bundles at the queen's feet. "No one will take them from you," she soothed Isabel. Then she beckoned to Sully.

He came to stand beside the bed and Isabel looked up at him. Her voice was hoarse and faint. "If you have come to baptize my sons you are too late, bishop."

He took hold of her hand. "I have come to pray with you."

A bead of blood slipped from the crack in her bottom lip. "To pray over my corpse, more likely. Tell me Sully, *am* I going to die?"

She was haggard from hours of suffering, and yet she was so lovely! Even Sully's dispassionate eye was struck by the unearthly beauty of her face. He tried to give her an encouraging smile. "We are all going to die, my lady."

Her eyes were luminous, all-seeing. "If you cannot spare my life, don't trouble to spare my feelings, Sully. I know now that I am going to die." Her hand slipped from his hand to the bed.

Isabel watched as he performed a useless baptism on the two infants. When he was finished she asked, "Have you a wafer and a bit of wine for me? Take it away if you do, for I do not want it."

Sibylla rushed to her sister's side. "Please Isabel, do as the good bishop directs. He can help you."

Isabel pushed her away. "No one can help me," she hissed, "him least of all. Go away, all of you, and let me die in peace."

Sully bent close, pressing a cross of holy water to Isabel's forehead. "You must consider the state of your soul."

"I don't care about my soul!" she screamed at him. "Let God take it, or the devil, it makes no difference to me."

Sibylla began to weep, and Sully's hands were trembling. He felt a keen responsibility for this girl's salvation. He could not let her die in the heat of her sins. "Pray with me," he said and clasped her hands firmly, "it will ease your mind."

She tried to pull away from him. "I don't want to pray! I want the taste of Philippe in my mouth, not your sacred wine of Absolution." She shook off Sully's hold and turned her face away and wept. "Leave me to my misery and pronounce your prayers when I am dead. I have nothing more to say."

Adele came forward and spoke to Sully in hushed tones. "Go downstairs and wait a while. She is too distraught to heed your words now, but later she will have need of you."

He nodded grimly, then left the room.

Adele came to the edge of the bed. She smoothed the blanket over Isabel's legs and asked, "Do you want me to bring the children to you now? Are you feeling strong enough?"

Isabel wept into her hands. "What choice do I have? If I am to see them again this side of the grave, I must see them now."

Tears of pity wetted Adele's eyes. "My dear girl," she said, "don't dwell on these things. Save your strength, and you may yet recover." She lowered her voice. "We are all praying for you."

It meant more to hear those words from her than from all the bishops on earth. Adele was a worldly woman who did not pray from habit. Isabel reached out and grabbed hold of her hand. "Mother," she said.

Sibylla watched as the two women wept in each other's arms.

It was close to midnight when the children were taken away.

Isabel kissed them both, then watched as Edythe and Sibylla took them from the room and out of her sight forever. *Goodbye my little son, my daughter. I hope you will be happier than I was.*

When they had gone Adele brought Henri in. "I cannot keep Sibylla out for very long," she whispered to him. "You have very little time." She squeezed his hand, then slipped discreetly from the room.

They looked at one another across the distance of the ill-lit room. Then Henri rushed to her side, dropping to his knees beside the bed. "Isabel," he sobbed against her arm.

She kissed the top of his head and stroked his hair. "You are the only man who ever truly cared for me. How fitting that you should be here at the last...."

He tilted his chin to look up into her face. "I do not wish to live without you. I *cannot* live without you!"

She pulled him closer so that his head nestled on her breast. "My babies were born dead, and now I know Philippe does not love me. He swore he would not leave, yet all the while he was making plans for the crusade." The tears fled down her cheeks and splashed onto his face. "Oh, Henri, God is always taking things away from me, and now He is punishing me with death."

They clung together like a pair of children frightened of the dark. "If He takes you, I shall curse His name forever!" Henri vowed. "You must fight, Isabel! You must not die!"

Her eyelids fluttered. She felt weak and helpless. "It doesn't matter anymore," she said. "I've lost the need to live."

He stayed with Isabel until she slept and Adele came to lead him from the room. Outside in the corridor he fell to his knees and sobbed, beating his fists on the stone floor. Then at last, exhausted, he crawled away to a dark corner near the stairs, and vomited, and prayed to die.

Isabel slept and woke then slept again as the dark hours of the night passed and rain splashed on the courtyard stones beneath her window. She was conscious of movement in the room, of hushed voices and whispered prayers. Whenever she cried out for Philippe there were hands to soothe her and quiet promises spoken in her ear that he would soon return.

Isabel knew he would not come. She knew it with all the instincts left to her. It was too late now; death was very near. She wanted to cry out against it, to push it away. But it hovered close upon her body like a greedy lover.

There was such despair within her, a sense of so much foolishness and loss. It would have been a little solace to her now if she could hate Philippe, but instead she wanted him more than she ever had. *She loved him, that was the lesson of her life.* It was all she had ever learned—and it had brought her nothing.

Sully came back sometime close to dawn. This time Isabel did not refuse his office. She mumbled her offenses and meekly drank the blood of Christ, but she could not taste salvation, only the bitterness of hope that had been lost. She lay with her eyes shut, listening as the bishop spoke a blessing. *He was giving her to God.* Soon they would shut her up in stone and darkness. They would perform obsequies, and they would weep. And then they would forget.

All wasted, all in vain!

Isabel was angry and it gave her strength to fight against this pious ritual of death. She cursed wildly and called out foul praises to her absent husband. There was a gentle hand stroking her forehead and she pushed it away. Why didn't all these mourners simply go and leave her here to die?

Suddenly there was another face above her.

Philippe? She squinted up, trying to divine his features.

Geoffrey Plantagenet stood there instead, looking handsome and amused. He toyed with a length of her hair, caressing it. Isabel tried to say his name but could not, for he leaned close and pressed his lips to hers. Excitement, thick and hot, burned in her blood and spread through all her body.

Was this death? It felt more like passion.

His kiss was cold and took her breath away.

Isabel died in the early hours of March 15, 1190.
She was twenty years old.

ℱOR AN HOUR Philippe lay beside the body of his wife. He could not believe that she was dead.

He had wept and spent his futile passion, he had cried out for her to set him free. Yet she would never let him go, for she had sworn she would not.

You are mine until the grave makes ghosts of both of us.

He kissed her parted lips once more, then left the room.

Sibylla was waiting for him in the corridor. He nodded and passed by her, but she grabbed his sleeve and pulled him back. "I am told by your mother that you have dismissed me from the court."

He glared down at her. "That is true, my lady. The sight of you offends me."

Her laugh was hard-edged by malice. "I *offend* you because you cannot hide the truth about yourself from me. I have always known you are a devil, and by your recent actions you have proven it to all the world."

His fine mouth twisted in a sneer. "What are you saying?"

She screamed the words as if she wanted God Himself to hear. "You killed your wife! You killed my sister!"

Philippe grabbed her by the shoulders and shook her till she begged for him to stop. "Why do you keep saying that to me?" he shouted into her face. "I did nothing to harm her, NOTHING, do you understand?"

"I understand that you plotted to abandon her, even while you promised you would never do so," Sibylla sobbed.

He loosed his grip on her. "What are you talking about?"

"Your commitment to the crusade."

"How did you hear about it?" he asked warily.

She shook off his hands. "What difference does that make? *I heard.* So did Isabel. That is enough."

Philippe was beginning to understand. "...and you told her."

Sibylla looked up into his face and pronounced the words with mingled bitterness and triumph. "I didn't have to. She found this instead." From her sleeve Sibylla pulled the rolled parchment that Isabel had seen in the council room, and thrust it into Philippe's hand. "The betrayal was too much for her, and so she died."

Philippe's heart was beating faster. "Isabel died in childbirth," he scoffed.

"Yes," Sibylla conceded, "but her labor came weeks too soon and that only happened because of this!" She snatched the paper back from him.

Sweet Christ, could it be true?

He had killed her after all.

"I loved her too much to tell her I was leaving."

"Love?" she sneered, "That word is a travesty on your lips. Isabel knew you cared nothing for her! She begged to see you before she died, but you betrayed her in even that!"

"I came back to Paris as soon as mother's message was put into my hands!" he cried out in frustration.

She flew at him. "Yes, you came back to rape a dead woman!"

Philippe lunged at her and this time his hands were on her throat. "You jealous, prying little bitch! How dare you throw accusations in the face of a king?" He flung her against the wall and leaned down close to her. Their faces were nearly touching. "You are the one who doesn't know what love is, girl, so mind your tongue when you speak of such things to me!"

The strength of Philippe's fingers was brutal on her slender throat. Sibylla pushed hard against his chest, trying to free herself, but his grip was far too powerful to fight. Finally he took his hands away, but his eyes still held her with vehemence.

"You *are* a demon!" she panted.

"Think what you like," he growled, "but keep your distance from me."

She inched along the wall, away from him, the rough stones scraping at her back. "There is no power in all the world could command me to do otherwise!"

His voice was even colder than his eyes. "Good, then at last we understand one another."

"I hate you," she said, and turned her back on him.

Philippe wept into his folded arms all that night.

It tore his heart to think of what her last hours must have been. Thinking he had lied to her out of malice, when he had only kept the truth from her out of love.

But she would never know that now.

Sibylla was right, he had betrayed his wife. Isabel had died believing that he did not love her. She had been afraid, in pain; she had needed him and he had not been there. It was the most terrible thing he had ever done.

Forgive me, Isabel.

Philippe slept, the tears still wet upon his face.

Down the corridor, Edythe, with the help of Adele's servants, bathed the body of the dead queen, and prepared it for burial.

Sweet narcissus.

It was all around him. Even here—in the chancel of the uncompleted Notre Dame cathedral, below the master altar—Philippe could scent her perfume.

It was evening. A thousand candles cast trembling light across her face. Tomorrow the priests would shut her body up in stone and place it in the crypt below. But for tonight her beauty still belonged to him.

They had dressed Isabel in rubies and red silk at his command.

A circlet of blushing stones banded her forehead like a crown. Her hair was combed out to its full length, nearly reaching to the tips of her gold damask slippers. Between her hands rested a prayer book which she herself had made.

The banner of Hainault—a black leopard *rampant,* set within a field of gold—lay at her feet, together with a flag of French significance, inscribed by the Capetian badge of gold fleur-de-lis. Beside it lay her little silver seal, bearing its crude likeness of her face.

Philippe had ordered the St. Clotilde pearls, those which had caused so many ruinous tongues to wag, be buried with her. They had been stitched at the sides of her low-waisted chainse, encasing her hips like a girdle. The memory of the times she'd worn them, privately and for his pleasure, caused an ache in Philippe's groin.

But there was one relic Isabel would not take into the tomb.

With his own hand Philippe had removed the Druid ring and its chain from around her neck and placed it on his own, silently vowing he would wear it till his death. There was no better symbol of their love than this pagan ring he'd given Isabel on the first night she had come into his bed.

What prayer to say for her?

No words came to his mind save hot, excited words passed between them in dark or daylight. From his sleeve Philippe drew a sprig of mistletoe which he had taken from the grove of oaks and apples in the palace garden. He kissed it, then pressed the greenery between her stony breasts. That was epitaph enough. Philippe crossed himself, then turned abruptly on his heels and walked away.

Behind him the candle flames trembled a little at his going.

The maid is not dead, but sleepeth.

Sully's voice rolled in vibrant accents to the ceiling.

Outside, the citizens of Paris pressed close to listen as the bishop solemnized the burial of their queen.

Some wept, remembering her many gifts of money to the poor, while others whispered bits of curious gossip, and a few chuckling men made lewd comments behind their hands. All were waiting for the king and his nobles to come out and distribute silver coins in honor of the queen's passing.

Inside the cathedral Sully was preaching his sermon.

Frightened by the large assembly and wondering why his mother was not there to comfort him, Louis sobbed throughout the service, while Jacquie-Marie, who was old enough to understand, sat quietly, holding tightly to her father's hand.

Philippe stared at the flickering candles on the wall.

Then at last the final prayers were said and it was over.

Isabel's black marble tomb was sealed with lead and lowered amid a swirl of fragrant incense into the crypt beneath the altar. It was embraced on one side by her dead children's tiny monuments, on the other by Geoffrey's splendid tomb.

That night Edythe came to Philippe's room.

"Forgive me, my lord," she said, holding a henap out to him, "but I have brought something to help you sleep."

He reached out and took the cup from her. "It was kind of you to think of me."

Edythe averted her eyes as Philippe sat up in bed, the coverlet falling from his naked chest. "I hope I did not disturb you."

He was actually quite touched by her attentions. Sully, his uncles, Adele—none of them had shown much consideration for his feelings. Yet this plain-faced serving girl had limped up four long sets of stairs to bring him a warming drink.

Philippe brought the henap to his lips. The beverage was hot and pungent, laced with herbs. It was good. He drank till the cup was empty, then handed it back to her. She tried to smile at him but couldn't manage it. Instead her brown eyes looked out sadly from her pale face. Philippe reached to take hold of her hand.

"You've been crying, Edythe," he observed.

"My mistress was very dear to me."

"Of course." He was still holding her hand. It felt small and delicate in his grasp.

Edythe looked timidly into his face, her calm eyes level with his. "Count Baldwin will doubtless come to Paris when he hears the news of Isabel's death. Do you wish that I should return to Hainault with him?"

Philippe thought about that for a moment, then shook his head.

"I don't see why you should leave. You're very good with the children and now, with their mother gone, they need you more than ever. Also, I shall be away for a long time in the East, and it would ease my mind to know my son and daughter were being cared for by someone I can trust, and whom they are fond of."

Now the smile showed itself.

"You are very generous and kind, my lord. I shall care for the children as if they were my own."

Edythe's pledge was made with such sincerity that Philippe took her in his arms and kissed her from a sense of gratitude. It was a gentle kiss and she responded willingly, yet after a moment she pulled away from him and began to cry.

"What is wrong?" he asked.

There was a hesitation, and then her arms went around his shoulders and she laid her cheek against his chest. Her voice was an apology. "My lord, I am not beautiful, nor even pretty. My body is twisted; I am nothing. Yet since the first day I came to live in Paris I have loved you. I love you still."

Her innocent confession struck at Philippe's heart and he took her in his arms once more. His kisses grew more forceful, straying over her throat and shoulders. Then with one swift move he pulled her onto the bed beside him. Edythe did not resist as he drew the woollen shift over her shoulders and tossed it away to the edge of the bed.

Her nakedness did not inspire passion. She was thin, with barely any breasts at all. Edythe could not miss his look of disappointmer t. "I do not blame you for not wanting me," she said. "I am ugly and without grace, not fit for the bed of a king."

"I will be judge of that," Philippe said and reached for her. When she drew back a little he gave her an encouraging smile. "Don't be afraid. I will not hurt you."

"It's not that," she confessed with downcast eyes. "I've never had a man before."

He stripped the coverlet away and let her see him. "Then we both have an adventure before us. I've never had a virgin." He pulled her hands to his belly. "There," he said, settling himself between her fingers, "you see? It is nothing to fear."

Edythe explored his body with the artless enthusiasm of a novice. Her innocence aroused him to subdued passion, and when he took her it was with gentleness, not lust.

Later Philippe reached for the porringer that sat beside the bed and splashed a little water between her legs to wash away the blood. Then he settled back, with Edythe held closely in his arms. "Next time you won't feel any pain, I promise you," he said.

Pain? She had never felt so happy in all her life.

He was silent for a long while. Edythe could almost read his thoughts. She stroked his beard lovingly. "It will be very lonely for you without Isabel, won't it?" she asked.

It hurt him just to hear her name.

"You must be the only one on earth who cares what my feelings are," Philippe said sadly. His voice trembled on the edge of a sob. "Oh Edythe, I loved her so much!"

"I know," she whispered.

"And yet she died thinking I cared nothing for her."

Edythe closed her eyes against the memory. "She was mad with pain. She was not herself."

He tightened his arms around her waist. "Sibylla blames me for Isabel's death. My mother too. They look at me with malice in their eyes."

Edythe's hands found his and squeezed them. "You must try to put their accusations from your mind. You know the truth of it, and so did Isabel."

Philippe listened to the sound of rain splashing against the stones far beneath his window. It called up memories of passion in firelit rooms with Isabel in his arms. Then he pictured her as she was now: shut away in darkness, and locked in endless, unconditional sleep. He could almost hear her whispering beside him.

You are mine until the grave makes ghosts of both of us.

I will never let you go.

He started at the sound of Edythe's voice. "Please let me make you happy if I can, Philippe." She wavered a little as she spoke his name.

His head drooped to her shoulder. "Then remain here at the palace. Tend to my children and warm my bed." His voice went low. "You are a sweet, lovng girl Edythe, and I need you. I need you very much."

She was so grateful for his words she nearly wept.

Baldwin came to Paris with a heavy heart.

Philip d'Alsace was with him.

The two men were no longer friends, no longer allies, but in

Isabel's death they shared a grievous common loss. Now they stood together at her tomb with offerings of white narcissus flowers and candles brought from Lille, her birthplace.

Baldwin looked old; his face was grim. "This was *his* doing," he said wretchedly.

Flanders gave his brother-in-law a quick sideways glance. "There is little point in blaming Philippe. Isabel is dead. What more is there to say?"

"I shall always blame him. And *you*." Baldwin's voice rang with accusation. "It was you who arranged this marriage, Flanders. I never wanted it. If my daughter had married elsewhere she would be alive today."

Flanders knelt and said a hurried *pater noster,* then rose to wipe the dust from his braies. "Let be," he said and put a hand on Baldwin's shoulder. "This was no man's fault. It was God's will."

All of Baldwin's pain showed in his eyes as he stared back at Flanders. "This is *not* what God intended. No one can make me believe this is what God intended!" He looked ruefully at the black tomb which held his daughter and muttered, "She was mine for such a little while."

Flanders took up a single blossom and brought it close to his face. "I loved her too, Baldwin."

He tossed the flower aside and walked away.

Flanders had chosen to remain in Paris for a while.

He had important business with the king.

Like Philippe he was preparing to lead a large contingent of his knights to the East. Acre had been under siege by the crusaders for more than a year, as they struggled to recapture the port city from Saladin and his infidels. Flanders was anxious to play a part in the liberation of Acre. There was no cause on earth which he championed more. Like Richard of England, he was keen to be on his way.

But the details of planning seemed endless.

There was much business to be accomplished in the two months before the kings of Europe set out upon their grand and noble enterprise. Provisions had to be secured and inventoried, arms stored, petitions reviewed, land grants settled, maps drawn, loans allocated, taxes collected. There also remained the overwhelming task of transporting an estimated one hundred thousand crusaders, as well as several thousand retainers (servants, grooms, and prostitutes), to the East.

It was a massive, complicated venture.

King Richard had ordered the construction of a hundred ships at the time of his coronation the previous autumn. Following completion of the fleet shortly after Easter, the vessels had been dispatched from English ports to Marseilles where Richard's army would meet them after traveling overland.

Philippe Capet had not yet solved the problem of transportation for his men. France had no great shipwrights like those of England; the ships would have to be got elsewhere. It was to this purpose he sought Flanders' advice. The two men met daily at the Cité Palais for a week, discussing all possibilities.

It was finally decided that the French and Flemish armies would travel overland together as far as the port of Genoa. There they would arrange separate passage on ships rented from the wealthy bishop of the city. The Flemish would pay one third the cost of sea transport, while France paid the remaining two-thirds. After this had been agreed upon, Philippe determined to begin negotiations with the Bishop of Genoa at once.

Flanders said goodbye to Philippe and left Paris.

He was anxious to return to his lands and set the final seal upon his own preparations. On his return journey to Ghent, however, he decided to halt briefly at Mons. He had some business to settle with the Count of Hainault regarding the crusade.

Baldwin had taken the cross a year earlier, but he had since changed his mind. He no longer had the heart for this grand venture. Isabel's death had embittered him. He had no trust left. He wanted no further dealings with either his brother-in-law or the king of France. Nothing d'Alsace could say would moderate that opinion.

Flanders went away, dissatisfied.

The two men never met again.

* * *

"Weep for her, people of Hainault!

"The Queen of France has died in Paris, but nowhere is she mourned with such sincerity and deep lamentation as here in the land which gave her birth...

"She died early, and yet she was never young. Her wisdom was of the

world, and yet her soul was always innocent. The noble Baldwin sired her from an illustrious line. She had the blood of ancient royalty in her veins.

"Through the son she bore, the line of Charlemagne was mated to the lesser house of French kings. May the boy keep his mother's covenant with fame!

"As he grows, let all who speak of him—Louis VIII, future King of France—remember Isabel of Hainault...."

Gilbert of Mons
fragment of a requiem
May, 1190

* * *

ＣOUNCIL ROOM, the Cité Palais, June 1, 1190.

Philippe affixed his name to the document. Then he passed it along the table so that the others gathered there might do likewise.

Adele, her brother William, and Bishop Sully put their signatures beneath his. The king's clerk came forward to attach a lump of red wax to the parchment, then stood by as the king planted his seal squarely in the middle.

It was done.

The bishops and Adele would be regents in Philippe's absence.

The king embraced each one in their turn. Then his expression sobered and he looked almost stern. "I entrust into your hands the care of my realm, and the safety of my son and heir. May God look with favor upon you, and preserve me in my quest to serve His Holy purpose...."

Adele was stirred by sudden emotion. She embraced Philippe and kissed him, then whispered in his ear, "May God protect you, my son, and bring you back to reign over us for many years."

He squeezed her hand. "He will, for we do His business."

She smiled, but did not trust her voice to answer.

There were aspects of the crusade which hardly fell under the category of "God's business," although the king treated them with the same gravity as all things spiritual.

Certainly there would be whores enough in Syria, but he was appalled at the thought of his soldiers satisfying themselves on the bodies of pagan women. It was equally unthinkable that they abstain from pleasure. Therefore, with the same tidy practicality he'd handled all other details for the crusade, Philippe directed the selection of nearly four thousand prostitutes from the brothels of Paris and its neighboring counties.

For his own needs he chose a woman who had served him well on earlier occasions: Fabiana, his pretty southerner from the tawdry *Chaussée St.-Lazare*. Edythe, who had become his nightly companion since the death of his wife, had offered to accompany him, but Philippe preferred she stay in Paris to look after his children. He had grown fond of her; she was too sweet to be subjected to the discomforts of the journey and whatever terrors lay in wait for them at Acre.

This was going to be a grueling expedition.

It needed whores.

Having accomplished all his preparations, Philippe took himself to St. Denis for two days of prayer and fasting. On the third day he made confession and was given Absolution. The abbot of St. Denis put into his hands the ceremonial pilgrim's *scrip* and staff. Like his father before him, Philippe was truly a crusader now.

It was done, save for the going. And the goodbyes.

With a show of royal dignity which could not mask his true emotions, Philippe said farewell to his family. Jacquie-Marie's stubborn little chin trembled just a bit as he knelt to embrace her, but she would not allow herself to cry. Louis, who was frightened at the sight of his father dressed in full ceremonial armor, hid his face in the folds of Adele's skirt and sobbed loudly.

Philippe stood up and lifted the boy in his arms.

"Remember what I have told you in the past, my son," he said gently, "you are a prince who will someday be king, and kings must never let others see their tears." He kissed the boy's face and stroked his golden curls, barely able to hold back his own tears. "Goodbye, my little prince, my son," he whispered, and then handed the boy into Adele's open arms.

Philippe exchanged farewell kisses with his mother and with

Edythe, who stood at her side. Then he knelt solemnly and bowed his head for Sully's blessing. The old bishop's hand hovered above the crown which surmounted Philippe's helm. "May God strengthen and protect you, for you are His anointed upon the earth. Serve His purpose well, my son, and deliver the homeland of our savior Christ out of the hands of Infidels."

The king crossed himself piously and stood up. "God be with all of you till my return," he said. He gave a last glance around him at the great hall, vacant but for the little cluster of people who stood at his side. A chill settled in his blood. It was very possible he would not return.

Philippe shook off the feeling.

Without another word he took his leave.

There was one last thing he had to do. Before leading his magnificent host of mailed knights out of the city, Philippe went alone to the crypt at Notre Dame. He prayed for a little while before Geoffrey's tomb, then went to stand in front of Isabel's. It seemed odd leaving her behind; he sensed that even now she resented his going. The two of them were still bound by a spell he could not explain. And yet, for the first time since Isabel had come into his life, he felt strangely free.

Leaning close upon her tomb, Philippe unsheathed his sword, and opened up a vein in his hand. He watched as the blood dripped in tiny beads of deep red upon her effigy. *It was a fair exchange, his blood for hers.*

Then he lay down upon her sculpted marble image and wept.

Near the end of June, at Tours, Richard was invested with his pilgrim's insignia. But when he leaned upon the staff it snapped in two, and some onlookers whispered that this boded evil tidings for the Third Crusade.

With thirty thousand men following in his wake, Richard made his way across Berry and into Burgundy where his forces would meet with Philippe's army at Vézelay. There the two kings had planned to hold court for a few days and consult with one another, before starting off together with their combined entourages, toward Lyon.

Richard had never been so ecstatic. This was the adventure for which he had waited all of his life. He sang Provençal ballads and composed poems from the saddle. He exchanged ribald stories with his marshals, and described all the great deeds that he would accomplish in the East.

The King of France had proceeded south from Paris to Véze-lay, and arrived a few days ahead of Richard. Philippe set himself up in the palace of the Benedictine abbot, and immediately began a tireless dispensation of paperwork and other administrative chores.

It was here in this scenic hillside village, on an Easter Sunday more than forty years ago, that Bernard of Clairvaux, since made a saint, had preached another crusade; here that Louis Capet and his radiant queen had come forth in tears of joy to declare themselves as pilgrims. A sense of that glorious history still seemed to hang in the air. Many a man among this current group of crusaders stood in awe outside the abbey and thought about an ancestor who may have taken the cross in this same spot a generation ago.

The realization of it inspired every man.

Except Philippe. He had no time for pious reveries. He was busy with organizing the next stage of the journey; feeling irksome because Richard had not yet arrived. The French king's mood did not improve when one of the clerks came to his room on the second night at Vézelay with the news that Sibylla of Beaujeu had requested an audience.

Philippe looked up from his maps, scowling. "What does she want?"

The young man shook his head. "I do not know, Lord. But she claims to know you. She also says her business is urgent."

What new complaints had she raised against him since the last time they had met? Philippe thought about refusing her, and then just as suddenly changed his mind. "Very well, bring her in," he said, his mouth twitching with displeasure.

A few moments later the door opened and Sibylla entered with the clerk close at her side. "Leave us alone," Philippe directed. He waited a moment until the clerk had gone, then fixed his eyes on Sibylla. "Why have you come to see me?"

She was dressed all in yellow, chainse and surcoat, and there were flowers braided into her dark hair. There was a definite sense of haughtiness in her manner—*the same as all Flemish*, Philippe thought—and yet her attitude seemed a bit more subdued than usual. She looked about for a chair. "Is it permissible to sit?"

There was a stool beside him and Philippe kicked it across the floor to her. "I have much to do, Sibylla. Say whatever it is you came to say, and go."

His rudeness made her careless of her words, and though she had come to ask a favor of him, Sibylla snapped, "Is it not the business of kings to dispense courtesy as well as justice? They say Richard of England keeps embroidered silken cushions for the comfort of his female petitioners."

Philippe leaned back, arms folded across his chest, eyeing her with annoyance. "That sounds very much like Richard. No doubt he brings in minstrels to sing to them as well. For myself, I have no time for such pretty manners. I am a busy man. *What do you want?*"

She came a little closer. "I want your assurance that I shall not be forced to marry against my will."

He seemed genuinely surprised. "Forced to marry? What do you mean? I have said nothing of this."

Her fingers toyed nervously with the silver bracelet on her wrist. "When you dismissed me from the court at Paris, I returned immediately to Beaujeu. There I was greeted by a certain Burgundian knight, Gerard of Dijon, who proposed to make me his wife, despite whatever objections I might have." She had momentarily forgotten her dislike of him and reached out her hands pleadingly, "I do not wish to marry him or anyone! Please —one word from you and he will be forced to leave off his amorous pursuit. Do this, I beg you . . ."

He was curious. "Why do you have so great a dread of marrying this fellow? I know him; he seems well enough to me. What could a young widow better hope for than a goodly lord to fill her bed and administer her lands?"

Sibylla looked sadly up into his face. Why had she expected him to understand? "William was my husband," she declared, "and I will have no other. But I live in fear of being carried off by Lord Gerard."

Philippe's expression was unreadable; the strong, handsome features of his face set and brooding. He reached down to take hold of her hand. "Gerard is an honorable man, Sibylla. I don't think you need worry for your safety."

She jerked her hand away. Smug, condescending bastard! How

he delighted in humiliating her. "I see I shall have to manage on my own," she chided, "which is just as well, for I could never put my trust in any man so utterly devoid of chivalry!!"

Philippe grabbed her about the waist, pulling her into his arms in a rough embrace. "You sassy, impudent little bitch," he sneered, "if you knew anything of men you wouldn't give a damn for things as meaningless as chivalry or good manners!"

His beard chafed against her skin as he left a path of kisses on her throat. The feel of his lips both stirred and frightened her, and for a moment Sibylla lost all sense of who she was and who was holding her. She closed her eyes and the excitement grew.

Helpless and groping, her hands strayed over his shoulders and down his back. What a fine body he had, how strong he was!

The sound of his hoarse words in her ear brought Sibylla back fully to herself. "You need a man in your bed, girl. You've been too long without one."

Horrified at her own weakness, Sibylla struggled out of his embrace. Panting, one hand pressed tightly to her breast, she stumbled back away from him. "How dare you treat me in this way? I'm not some strumpet you can use at your pleasure and toss away again!"

Philippe's black eyes glittered with a look of passion and danger. "You were enjoying it."

"You tricked me. You only agreed to see me so you could take advantage of my innocence!"

He laughed. "You pretend to hate me, but I know differently. I've seen the expression in your eyes when you look at me. You've heard the stories and you'd love to see if they are true. Or perhaps Isabel piqued your interest with some stories of her own."

The passion she had experienced only a few moments ago soured into a feeling of disgust. Sibylla fled toward the door, and with her hand safely upon the latch she looked back over her shoulder at him. "Whatever you may think of me, I'm not my sister." She could still hear him laughing as she slammed the door.

For a long while Philippe sat looking at his maps, and yet his thoughts were elsewhere. Sibylla had taken his mind away from work. What a little tease she was: half-submitting, then rejecting.

He had no use for women of that kind. Still, there was something about her which intrigued him, something reminiscent of Isabel —although she looked almost nothing like her and was nowhere near as lovely. But her voice, the gestures, the expression in her eyes—it reminded him too keenly of his dead wife.

Sibylla. He couldn't take his mind from her. She'd felt good in his arms. She had the bedworthy figure of so many Flemish women: full breasts, delicate waist, and rounded hips. What pleasing sport to bed that savage little cat.

Philippe picked up a map of Syria and stared at it.

He twirled his pen between slim, nervous fingers.

Amid a fanfare of trumpets and gay colors, King Richard arrived in Vézelay. Philippe had already been there for a week, and he was growing restless. When at last a messenger came to tell him Richard and his army had been sighted only a few miles away, Philippe gladly mounted his horse and rode out to meet them.

What a spectacle it was! So many thousands of knights, all in their shimmering mail and long split surcoat, each crested with a white cross. King Richard, riding at the front and flanked by his bodyguard, was the most magnificent of all.

Philippe raised his arm, signaling a greeting.

"My friend," Richard's voice boomed out across the distance, "I bring you Christ's own army!"

The French king brought his horse closer, till he and Richard were within an arm's length of one another. "Welcome to Vézelay," Philippe said, holding out his hand to the resplendent man who faced him. Then with a tinge of irritability in his voice he added, "We have been waiting these many days."

A broad smile creased Richard's suntanned face. "I'm glad to see you show such eagerness to be on your way."

Philippe answered with a tight smile. "Now that we have begun this venture, I see no reason to waste time."

Laughing, Richard brushed aside Philippe's conservatism with a wave of his hand. He had waited for so long to start this journey, and now that he was finally on his way Richard was determined to enjoy every step of it. *This was an adventure!* Why did Philippe have to make a business out of everything?

Richard leaned forward in the saddle, his voice lowered to a tone of intimacy. "These last months have been busy ones, but also lonely. I've missed you, Philippe."

Their hands came together, the fingers lightly touching.

"And I, you."

Richard frowned. "You've lost weight. You look unwell, and very tired."

The sun was going down in flaming colors over Richard's shoulder, and Philippe squinted into the glare. "Like you, I have been occupied with constant preparations. I've also been in mourning for my wife."

Richard seemed embarrassed at his negligence to remark on Isabel's death. "Of course," he said and added, "you have my sympathy."

Philippe's mouth twisted in a cruel smile. "Really? You never liked her much." He jerked on the reins and turned his horse around to fall into line with Richard's. "Will you dine with me tonight?"

"I would like that," he answered, and slid his arm around Philippe's shoulder.

Philippe laughed. "Good," he said, "I'm very hungry."

That night as Richard's men set up their pavilions and sang and scuffled in the camp, the two kings lay together in Philippe's bed, their hands clasped together in a pledge of love.

They listened to the noise out beyond the window.

Philippe turned his head on the pillow to look at Richard. "I never saw anyone look so splendid as you did today, riding into camp. It was quite staggering to see you, glinting beneath the sun like a polished jewel. You nearly took my breath away."

Richard rolled on his side and wrapped his arms about Philippe's waist. "I'm so glad we're making this pilgrimage together. You can't know what it means to me."

Philippe kissed his lips. "I know." Then he drew back a little. "You don't worry what mischief John might cause while you're away?"

There was a brief hesitation before he answered, "No. Eleanor will see to his behavior. Also, John has signed a treaty with me, vowing his obedience and loyalty to the crown in my absence."

"A treaty." Philippe's voice was touched with cynicism.
He yawned into his fist.

Two days later, on July the fourth, the armies left Vézelay.

It took six days to reach Lyon. All along their southern progress, townspeople rushed to greet them. They lined the roads
and threw flowers in the path of the crusaders. They cheered
and sang praises to Almighty God.

Full of good spirits and bravado, Richard waved to the crowds,
holding up his hand as if to give them blessing. They screamed
for him, calling out, "Lion Heart, Lion Heart!" They surged forward in a mob, eager to touch him, and young women fainted if
he looked them in the face.

Philippe was beginning to hate Richard's popularity.

He cared nothing for the cheering crowds or screaming
women—such demonstrations were beneath his dignity—but he
resented being completely overshadowed by his friend, and it
galled him to see how Richard loved every bit of the attention.
God knew how conceited he would have become by the time they
reached Acre!

Philippe seethed with regret. Why hadn't he done as Isabel
had suggested—stayed at home, gained conquests for France in
Richard's absence? Then *she* would not have died so wretchedly,
and Philippe would not be questioning his wisdom in consenting
to this journey.

They weren't even out of France yet and he was already sorry.

The crusaders reached Lyon on July 10th.

Flanked by a small band of their personal bodyguard, the two
kings crossed the river ahead of their armies. They had planned
to spend the night on the far bank, since it would take the best
part of an afternoon for the entire host to cross over the one
small bridge which spanned the Rhône.

But when the troops began to cross, the bridge gave away.

Philippe's nerves, hard-pressed the past few days by heat and
mosquitos, gave way as well. He stood with Richard on the opposite bank and screamed foul oaths at the men who floundered in
the water.

Richard took the mishap well in hand, and ordered that small
boats be lashed together to form a temporary "floating" bridge.

He turned to Philippe. "It is going to take at least two days to get them all across. See that our pavilions are made ready for us at once."

"I'm not your lackey!" Philippe shouted back, indignant, "Go give your orders to someone else."

The matter was promptly given into other hands.

Frustrated, bedeviled by heat and flies, Philippe went off to seek shade beneath a grove of poplar trees. He pulled off his coat of heavy mail and lay down upon the ground, wearing only his braies and smock.

Soon he dozed.

Richard sought him out later in the day.

"I think it would be best for both of us, if we kept our disagreements private," he told Philippe. "Commanders should know better than to let their soldiers see them at odds."

Philippe propped himself on one elbow and glared up at Richard. "And one king should know better than to miscall another in the presence of so many witnesses."

Richard kicked at the grass and looked off into the sky, heaving a deep breath, knowing what he was going to say would not be well received. "Philippe, it's important that we understand each other. We knew this journey wouldn't be an easy one. What occured today was unfortunate, but there will probably be many incidents like it before we reach our destination. You have to learn to sacrifice for this endeavor, to take discomforts like a man..."

Philippe leapt to his feet. He was trembling, paled by rage. "You dare to call *my* manhood into question? This whole fiasco was your doing, Richard! I agreed to be a part of it for your sake; I let friendship blind me. Now because of that my wife is dead, and my children have been deprived of a father. You can't begin to understand how I have suffered, so don't talk to *me* of sacrifice!"

This was so useless. Richard hated arguments; they called up the memory of confrontations with his father. He brushed Philippe's shoulder lightly with his fingertips. "My friend," he said, "let's just forget it. It's too hot to fight." He gave a glance over his shoulder. "I have to get back, there's much to do. Why don't you take a swim in the river and cool off? You'll feel better."

Philippe began unfastening the laces of his smock and grumbled, "I'll take a bath. I don't know how to swim."

* * *

That evening as Philippe took a meal in his tent alone, he was interrupted by the sound of voices just outside. Presently, a soldier entered, holding a kicking female in his arms. "Forgive me my lord," he said, "but we caught this woman trying to sneak into your tent dressed in the garments of a priest." He pulled the cowel from her head and a cascade of long brown hair spilled out.

It was Sibylla.

Surprised, Philippe stood up and came toward her. "What are you doing here?" he asked.

"Tell him to put me down," she cried, struggling to free herself, "he's hurting me!"

"Release her," Philippe ordered, "and wait outside." When they were alone he turned to her. "By what authority do you travel with my army—and in disguise?"

She was out of breath and blushing, unable to meet his eyes.

"Why did you come, Sibylla?"

She could not deceive him any longer. "I had to see you once more before you went to Syria."

Philippe reseated himself. "More petitions? More demands?"

Her chin trembled. "Only one."

He wanted her to say the words. "What is it?"

Sibylla dropped to the floor in front of him and put her head against his knee. "I want to love you."

He urged her up and pulled the priest's robe from her shoulders.

She closed her eyes and heard him say her name.

Sibylla lay on the rich carpet with Philippe over her.

She had none of Isabel's skill as a lover, but she was hot and eager, and she wanted him. Philippe pushed her legs apart. She was sable colored, silky—small and neat as a virgin. It was hard to believe she'd ever had a man or given birth.

But her breasts were so like Isabel's. Round and full. Firm. So beautiful. When Philippe closed his eyes he could almost make himself believe it was Isabel who lay under him. He tried to keep the image of her in his mind. White skin. Gold hair. *Oh God . . .*

But in the end all that mattered was the feeling.

Philippe turned on his side and clasped Sibylla close against his chest. She was panting, soaked with sweat. Philippe pushed the hair back from her forehead. "You are very sweet," he said.

It was hard for her to talk, to think. She was confused, excited, thoroughly beside herself with joy. She kissed his face and said his name over and over.

His arm was tight about her hips. "I'm glad you followed me. Ever since that evening in Vézelay, I knew I had to have you."

Sibylla clutched at him, incited by panic. "I cannot bear to be separated from you now. Take me with you to the Holy Land."

That was a pleasant thought.

But Philippe rejected it a moment later. "It isn't wise," he told her. "The journey is arduous and dangerous. And what of your children? Would you be so willing to leave them behind?"

Sibylla could scarcely believe the words that came from her own mouth. "I don't care about my children, only you . . ."

He licked the sweat that beaded at her temple. "You will have me again, never fear. Go back to Paris, live there for a while, and wait for my return."

"Such a long time . . ." she wailed.

He sat up, pulling her with him. "We have at least two days more here, before my army can move on. Let us just enjoy them and not think of what comes after. I've had my fill of sadness in these past few months."

Sibylla was staring past him, hardly listening. "How could I have loved William? He was *nothing* beside you! You were right, I know little of men, even less of love. But you . . ." she reached to stroke the heavy flesh beneath his belly, "you have taught me what it is to be a woman."

He swept her hair up in the palm of his hand and bent to nibble at her neck. She smelled good, tasted good, made him forget about the crusade and all its problems. It was a shame he couldn't take her with him. . . .

His hand sought her sweet opening. It was as soft as mink and still moist from his leavings. "Ah it's wonderful between us, girl," he said, his breath hot upon her throat. "But there's so much more I want to teach you." He whispered something into her ear. When she blushed furiously he laughed and said, "Don't be embarrassed. We need hide nothing between us now."

Philippe bent to tease her nipple with his teeth. *Oh God, the feeling!* It seemed that all her senses—her entire being—was

centered in that nipple. She squeezed him between her fingers
and felt his strength grow.

"And did you also teach my sister?"

He laughed. "Isabel knew more ways of love than anyone else
on earth. It was she who taught me." He rolled Sibylla over on
her face. "This will hurt," he warned, "but it is glorious pain..."

"I am yours," she said.

Two days later, despite her entreaties, she parted with the
king. In care of the same monks who had sheltered her on the
trip to Lyon, Sibylla set out upon the road back to Paris.

In a document signed and witnessed to assure its validation,
Philippe granted her ownership of the royal residence at Gonesse, just outside Paris. There she would be safe from any eager
lords who sought to marry her against her will, Philippe explained.

Sibylla was grateful. She would live there with her children.

And anticipate the king's return.

ING RICHARD led his men south to Marseilles.
They arrived at the port city on the last day of July, but to
Richard's fury the harbor was empty. His ships had not come. He
waited a week, but in the end he had to hire new ones at a ruinous cost.

Meanwhile, following mountain roads carved out by Roman
legions twelve centuries before, the King of France led his own
army through the Alps and down into Italy. Philippe was trying
very hard to make the best of this expedition, to bear up like a
soldier-king under the rigors of travel.

But as each day passed he loathed the journey more.

At Genoa he collapsed with fever and could go no further.

Certain he was going to die, Philippe lay sobbing in a borrowed
bed at the bishop's palace, wondering why God had abandoned
him when he had risked all to the crusade. After a week it became obvious he would recover, but even then Philippe could not
be cheered. He was far too weak to travel. He was in a land he
hated. He despaired.

Richard arrived in Genoa in the middle of August.

He went at once to see his friend. Philippe was glad of his

company but lapsed back into melancholy at the news Richard brought to him. Their fellow king and crusader, Frederick Barbarossa, the Emperor of Germany, had been drowned unceremoniously in Asia Minor, and most of his army had been carried off by plague.

The news of this struck a tremor of superstition in Philippe's soul. It seemed to him that the enterprise was doomed now and could not be salvaged.

But Richard only laughed when Philippe told him that. "Soon you shall be strong enough to continue on your way to Sicily," he remarked, "and then these gloomy notions will disappear."

Philippe felt himself grow weaker at the thought of travel. "I don't see how I shall manage to endure a sea voyage in my condition."

"You could go overland."

Philippe gasped. "That would be even worse!"

Richard clapped him on the back. "There's only one other way to get to Sicily," he winked, laughing. "You'll have to swim..."

It was a joke of course, but a poor one, and the image of the old emperor—drowned and naked—lingered in Philippe's mind for a long time after Richard left.

Suddenly he had never felt so afraid.

The French put into port at Messina on the 16th of September.

Barely recovered from his illness, Philippe looked thin and very pale in the somber black velvet clothes he had chosen to wear. He seemed so unprepossessing that the group of nobles sent by King Tancred to meet him, mistook the far more splendidly outfitted Count of Flanders as the King of France.

Philippe was humiliated, but he took it with good grace.

Richard arrived a week later. As he and his retinue moved down the gangplank, there was no mistaking which man among them was the king. He was a gorgeous sight in shimmering blue samite bliaud and surcoat. His mantle was cloth of silver.

Philippe and Tancred were there to meet him.

Richard and Philippe embraced warmly. Their kisses, meant to be seen as a ceremonial exchange between two monarchs, were made of more than that. Tancred stood a little to the side and watched.

He was a quiet, cautious man. Ruthless, some said, for he had

seized the throne from its rightful claimant upon the death of
King William the Good of Sicily. Though Tancred was eager to
make allies out of these two powerful Western princes, there
were some difficulties inherent in the plan. Tancred was cur-
rently holding Richard's sister Joanna—the former queen of Sicily—as his hostage. Richard's main purpose in coming to Sicily
was to negotiate her release and claim her dowry.

The troubles began almost at once.

Sicily was a Norman state, but its population was a mixture of
Lombard, Greek, and Saracen, with the Normans as a powerful
but distinct minority. Both society and culture bore the stamp of
Eastern influence, which was in opposition to the stern code of
feudal rule.

Pilgrims from the West were not welcome in Sicily; the people
hated them. In the past, many crusaders had despoiled their
towns, looted their shrines, raped their women. Tancred cast a
wary eye on these visitors to his realm.

Out of kingly courtesy and because he wished to buy their
favor, he had made his palace available to Philippe, while a residence of equal dignity was provided for Richard on the outskirts
of Messina. But the two armies were relegated to a squalid en-
campment near the beach. Supplies were already dwindling, so
the men were forced to buy most everything: food, wine, even
fresh water—all at treacherously inflated prices.

The crusaders, some of them swaggering bullies, set upon the
merchants and townspeople with their swords. The Sicilians retaliated with a raid on the camp. Many of the crusaders were
killed in the skirmish.

Philippe was thoroughly disheartened by these events.

Blood and corpses. The army hadn't even reached Syria yet!

But Philippe was far too politic to meddle. His own men were
not punished for their misconduct; neither would he raise a
finger against the Sicilians who had provoked them to these
deeds. It was too large a problem to be dealt with. He preferred
to let it go.

Not so the combative Richard Plantagenet, who had decided
that justice would be done. As usual, his methods were extreme.
He had ordered a gallows erected at the edge of the crusader
camp, and each day executions took place for all to see. He punished both his own men and local troublemakers; he seemed to

see himself as the sole judge of conduct in the land. The towns-people gathered in throngs to watch the daily spectacles, cheering when the condemned was an English crusader, throwing stones when it was one of their own.

Philippe warned Richard that his acts would raise the whole of Sicily to a revolt against him but the Lionheart would not listen. He was not afraid of Tancred's army! Let there be war and he would take Messina overnight! Actually, he had given much thought to the conquest of Sicily, for he was angry at Tancred for continuing to withhold Joanna and her dowry from him.

But there were other motives. Stronger motives.

This was a rich place: everywhere Richard's keen eyes searched they looked on gold, jewels, treasure. He could take it as inevitably as a drop of sweat falls in the desert, and all of it would go to pay for his holy enterprise. Well, perhaps *some* of it—a few trinkets—he'd keep for himself; that was only as it should be; but all the rest would be used to support his army and the greater glory of his God.

Richard and Philippe had signed a compact at Vézelay, agreeing to divide all spoils of conquest between them. But Richard had decided that no matter how much booty was captured in Sicily, Philippe would get nothing, because *nothing* was just what he deserved.

What a poor showing the Capetian had made so far! He didn't behave like a soldier, let alone a king. He complained endlessly about the heat, the discomforts of travel, the bad quality of wine anywhere outside of France. What kind of crusader spent his days hunched over a desk, assiduously involved in paperwork, recording details of expenditures with all the dedication of a low-born clerk? And instead of spending his evenings in the company of men—as befitted a soldier—Philippe retired to his bed early each evening with the buxom whore he'd brought along with him from Paris. For all the worth Philippe Capet was contributing to this venture, he might just as well have stayed at home within the dismal confines of his palace on the Seine.

So thought Richard.

Philippe's opinions tended toward the opposite extreme.

Why did Richard have to be such a bully? He had outraged the populace with his overbearing manner and egotistical personality, made an enemy of Tancred, and diminished his own troops by killing them needlessly for acts they would never have committed had he been organized enough to see that they were properly fed and housed. It seemed to Philippe that Richard cared only to make himself feared. And wealthier.

He could not be trusted.

That night while Philippe appeased his frustrations with the obliging Fabiana, Richard and a few of his men sneaked into Messina through an unguarded entrance in the wall, then flung open the city gates to let in the English army. By dawn Richard's flags had been raised all across the battlements. He declared the city his—by right of conquest.

Philippe was furious. This act of war against the people of Messina was an unbridled and deliberate insult to himself and the French crusaders. He sought Richard out immediately and demanded that the fleur-de-lis be raised alongside the banner of England—for had not the two kings pledged at Vézelay that they would share all honors and all spoils of conquest?

Richard promptly replied with a litany of Philippe's failings, till at last, flushed with anger, the French king took to his mount and rode back to the Messina palace. There he stalked the floor of his bedroom, brooding over this latest humiliation suffered at the hands of his royal lover and rival.

He'd nearly decided to lead his army in an attack against King Richard's forces—probably he would have done so had not the Count of Flanders intervened. The cool-headed d'Alsace suggested that a meeting be arranged between the two kings, at which time all grievances should be discussed and another treaty drawn up to replace the one made at Vézelay.

Philippe agreed, but only because he didn't know what else to do. The idea of fighting Richard in the field had been a rash and momentary plan, but Philippe knew it to be folly.

He turned to Flanders. "Very well," he said, "arrange it."

Tancred had taken himself off to Palermo—and when he heard that Richard had captured the city of Messina he was instantly convinced to let both Joanna and her dowry go. If this mad Plantagenet lion could accomplish conquests in so little time, he was truly a man to be feared. Messina itself did not matter so much; it was a small sacrifice to keep the peace. But it was possible the English king had designs on the rest of Sicily as well.

So Tancred acted speedily and sent off a message to Messina.
Joanna and her wealth had been set free.

Richard was jubilant.

Meanwhile the kings of France and England met, as Flanders
had suggested, and in the end Tancred came too, for there was
much to be decided. A code of behavior and punishments for
members of the army was set down on paper, and for himself
Tancred agreed to initiate a practice of harsh punitive measures
for all his subjects who raided the crusader camp or did harm to
the pilgrims.

Prices were fixed; gambling and wanton theft banned. Richard
demanded and was given full payment of his sister's dowry, and
in return he promised not to attempt the capture of any other
towns in Sicily. For this pledge Tancred was exceedingly grateful,
for the conquest of Messina had raised fears in him of losing his
throne altogether.

There was even a bonus thrown in to please him. Richard
agreed to the betrothal of his ward and heir, little Arthur of
Brittany, to Tancred's youngest daughter. This was pleasant news
to Philippe's ears. Ever since his arrival in Sicily, he'd been
plagued by Tancred's ploy of trotting out his three ugly little girls
and trying to interest him in marrying one of them.

God be praised, that disgusting ritual had been set aside!

At the close of three days of meetings, the French flags were
set beside the English flags at the Messina gates. Philippe and
Richard renewed their friendship with a fresh vow of unity and
the kiss of peace. It seemed as though the discord between them
had been put to rest at last. Both men were happy, and Tancred
counted himself a victor too.

Philippe made plans to set sail for Acre within the week.

𝕴N PARIS all was business as usual.

The king was far away, but the government carried on without
him. During the ten years of his reign Philippe had organized
the daily functions of the state so efficiently that it required little
more than an able custodian to oversee them.

France had three.

Besides his regular duties as bishop and responsibilities in di-
recting the Notre Dame construction project, Sully now tended

to the commerce of the realm. He supervised the collection of all taxes within the royal *demesne*, saw to the payment of fines, and guarded the king's treasury with more care than he did his own.

William of Rheims was the chief magistrate in France during Philippe's absence. He took petitions and heard high-level appeals by local barons and other members of the nobility. The Bishop of Rheims also handled all matters pertaining to diplomacy between the kingdom of France and other countries, and was responsible for the dispatch of urgent letters to Philippe along various stops of his journey.

Dowager queen Adele had duties too. Philippe had elected her as the guardian of his children, but she was also expected to hold court daily, and deal with charters relating to the royal administration of letters, arts, medicine, and education.

For the first time in years, Adele was satisfied with her life.

She had power and purpose and a sweet young lover.

William le Breton was only twenty-four years old and he was a priest—the king's own chaplain—yet in many ways he was the most suitable companion Adele had ever found in her long search for the perfect lover.

She lay looking at him as he slept beside her one afternoon in mid-October. She'd known him for little more than eight months, and they had been lovers for nearly three. But sometimes, times such as now when everything was quiet and she was at peace, Adele felt that she had known him all of her life.

She put her face to his chest and kissed him awake.

They lay in each other's arm for a long while speaking only a few words at a time, watching the sunlight fade slowly from the room. "I should go," William said at last, bending to kiss her.

Her fingers played over his face. "Is there some urgent work you must attend to?"

"No," he admitted, "but I do feel guilty coming to you in dark and daylight both." He made a move to rise.

His innocence made her smile. "My sweet," she offered gently, "it matters not what time of day or season of the year. Your love is precious to me. I want as much of it as you can give."

William fell back onto her breast. What strange creatures women were, for they could compel with gentleness, and send a man to his damnation by doing nothing more than uncovering their breasts and bellies. And yet what man—be he priest or pagan—could deny himself such pleasure? It was a weakness born in every man and no threat of hell or promise of heaven could drive it out.

He'd had women much younger than she; even more beautiful, for she was nearing fifty now, and much of her beauty had faded. Yet William had never known a woman who could inflame a man with as little as a look, or a twitch of her long, elegant back.

She still had a wonderful body.

William stroked the smooth, curved angle of her hip and thigh.

Adele smiled up at him, pulling his hands to her breasts. "I wish you wouldn't leave now. I still want you."

What an appetite she had! It seemed to him no matter how many times he took her, she always wanted more. He tickled her nipple with his thumb. Then, in a voice that sounded almost grim, he said, "I wonder what the king would say if he could see us together."

Her laugh was vulgar, full of fun—as if she enjoyed imagining the scene. "My son has enough sins on his own head without condemning others," she replied. Then she saw the expression which came over his face. "I know what you are thinking: he is a king, he is a man—and that excuses everything."

"A man cannot help but be a man," he remarked.

She shifted over on her back, legs parted, her black thicket showing. "And neither can a woman help but be a woman. We are all, in our own way, just as God intended." She reached for him, and even her voice was tempting. "Stop judging. When you are here in my bed you are not a priest."

William was forced to smile at his own piety.

Of the two of them, she was the more honest.

Sibylla had come to stay at the Cité Palais for a while, to see her sister's children, and to enjoy the festival of St. Denis.

On the morning of her departure for Gonesse, Edythe took her aside. Sibylla thought she looked ill, care-worn. "Will you help me?" she asked.

Sibylla crooked an eyebrow in puzzlement. "What is wrong?"

Edythe shifted on her feet, unwilling to answer. Finally she looked down at the floor and asked, "Will you take me to live with you in the country?"

An odd request. Sibylla blinked, then frowned. "But your home is here, at the palace. Why should you wish to leave?"

Dismayed by her predicament, Edythe could no longer hold back the truth. "I am pregnant," she confessed.

It took a few moments for Sibylla to react. Then all at once a wave of misguided sympathy engulfed her. "Edythe," she gasped, "who has done this terrible thing to you? You must tell me, and I shall see that he is punished."

She had misunderstood, making the situation all the more awkward. "It is not the way you think. I was not forced."

Now Sibylla was truly puzzled.

Could plain, shy Edythe have a lover? It seemed unlikely.

"When is the child due?" she asked warily.

The voice quavered just a little. "Near the end of March."

Sibylla peered nervously down the corridor to see that there was no one to overhear their words. "But what has this to do with wanting to leave the palace?" Her pretty mouth twitched in irritation. "Can you not force this man to marry you?"

Edythe took a breath. "It is the king's child," she admitted.

The words washed over her, absurd and meaningless. Sibylla could barely find her voice. "The king's child?" she repeated, incredulous. "The *king's child?*" The breath was fluttering in her chest. "How can this be?"

"I am his mistress," Edythe answered simply.

All the reason fled Sibylla's mind.

"His mistress? *You?*" she bawled. "You might just as well expect me to believe the king would take a sow into his bed!" Her hand flung out and hit Edythe hard across the face. "How dare you presume to call yourself the mistress of a king, you stupid little cripple!"

Edythe was sniveling, touching her reddened cheek. "Why do you say these things to me?" she asked. "What has it to do with you if the king chooses to love me?"

Sibylla grabbed a handful of Edythe's hair and tugged it. "He doesn't love you!" she screamed into her face. "He is mine, he belongs to me!"

Adele appeared suddenly at the end of the corridor. Hurried footsteps brought her quickly to where they stood. "What is going on here?" she asked. She looked at Sibylla. "Why are you shouting at Edythe? What has she done to you?"

Sibylla laughed as tears splashed down her face. She pointed viciously at Edythe. "Ask her!" she gasped, out of breath, "ask her!"

Without another word Sibylla turned and fled down the stairs.

Adele stared after her, then looked back at Edythe. "What was that all about?" she asked sharply, and when there was no answer she went on, "Why have all the things been taken from your room? I went to look for you and saw that everything had been put into a satchel."

Edythe wiped away her tears. "I am leaving, Lady Adele."

"Leaving? But why?"

She had meant to go quietly with no one knowing. Now there was no way to hide the truth from Adele, and Edythe feared what her reaction might be.

"Why are you leaving?" Adele persisted. "My son's children adore you."

Edythe's throat was dry as she tried to swallow. "I am going to have a child."

Adele stepped back, momentarily surprised. "And is my son the father?" she asked.

"Of course. I have never been with any other man."

Adele relaxed, then nearly laughed. "Then there is no reason for you to leave." She patted Edythe's cheek. "Dear girl, if my son is to have another child it will be born here, at the palace, as befits the baby of a king."

Now Edythe began to cry, this time from relief. "Oh, madam, I was so afraid you would be angry."

"My son's blood is mine," Adele declared, "and any child of his body is my blood too." She put an arm about Edythe's waist. "Philippe will be delighted to return and find himself to be a father once again. Come now," she urged Edythe toward the corridor. "We shall put away your things, and let me hear no further talk of leaving."

"God bless you," Edythe wept.

Adele patted the girl's abdomen. "God bless this child," she said.

* * *

At Gonesse, Sibylla shut herself up in her room.

She lay naked in her bed, staring up at the ceiling. For days she refused to eat; to see anyone. She would not sleep. She told herself she had to think, to puzzle out what was happening to her, but she already knew the answer.

Love for Philippe was eating her alive.

Sibylla did not want to love him, but she could not help it. How easily she could understand Isabel's fascination for him now; the total submission of her will to his—for a woman would suffer anything to keep him in her bed.

But Edythe...how could she expect to satisfy Philippe?

She must be a fool!

But no, I am the fool. Had she really been so naïve as to believe Philippe had taken no woman to his bed, save her, since Isabel's death?

Sibylla wanted him; that was all she knew.

She turned her face to the wall and wept for her illusions.

Adele was looking after Edythe.

She had arranged for her to take another room, a larger one, opposite her own, one which had been vacant many years. Edythe was also provided with new clothes, and her duties were restricted to caring for Jacquie-Marie and Louis.

The children had been restless and moody since their mother's death; worse since Philippe's absence. They woke from bad dreams nearly every night. Usually Edythe could comfort them with gentle words. But sometimes, particularly in the case of Louis, the firm hand of a grandmother was needed.

One chilly evening in late October, Louis woke from a dream and could not be comforted. Adele came to sit with him and she remained by his side an hour or longer. But all the while the frightened child kept calling for his mother.

Adele told him stories, sang to him, then scolded him to go to sleep. She smoothed his long blond curls and kissed his forehead, then put him back into his bed. "Mommy," he whimpered, and closed his eyes.

Adele lit another candle for him and left the room.

Louis pulled the coverlet up close beneath his chin and bit his bottom lip to keep back the tears. Then a familiar smell of sweet flowers filled the room and he smiled.

"Mommy," he said again.

𝕿HE HEAT had gone, but so had the fair wind for Acre.

Philippe took his ships out a little way and then, only hours later, was forced to bring them back into port. Storms menaced the coast, sweeping into the straits, threatening to destroy the entire fleet.

Days passed as Philippe waited for the savage winds to calm, but as November neared it seemed apparent that he and his men would be denied safe passage till spring. He cursed the trivialities that had kept them in Sicily for so many weeks and now conspired to keep them here still longer. Worse yet, Philippe could think of nothing more dismal than spending Christmas in this half-pagan land.

Spring could not come soon enough for him.

Surprisingly, Richard was in no hurry to be on his way.

He was busy organizing a splendid holiday celebration at his villa, engaged in almost daily sight-seeing, and occupied with the business of governing "his" city. He also spent many hours in the company of Joanna, for he had not seen his much-loved sister for many years.

The English fleet, all one hundred of Richard's original ships, had amazingly reappeared after suffering many perilous adventures. Once leaving ports in England, they had been blown far out to sea and into the midst of a terrible storm. Every man had feared for his life, but then a miracle saved them all.

Richard listened with rapt attention as an account was given by Baldwin, Archbishop of Canterbury. "We called on the Lord in our distress, and presently the figure of Thomas Becket appeared to us, promising to quell the fury of the sea if every man aboard knelt down to beg forgiveness for the ugliness of his life. When all men did this the sea went flat, and our ships were hastened on their way."

From there the ships had sought safe harbor off the coast of Portugal, and after a stay of many weeks they sailed through the straits and onto the brilliant concourse of the Mediterranean.

Richard was greatly relieved that his fleet had been spared, and the story of Becket's miracle touched the deepest core of his fervent soul. Perhaps he'd allowed himself to drift too far from an awareness of spirituality these last months. So now, for many days, he took himself away from worldly concerns and brooded alone over matters of religion.

He wanted to accomplish great things in the Holy Land; wanted to do God's purpose. But he'd become shamefully negligent, reveling in bodily sin; thinking only of loot and treasure and how to get the best of Philippe Capet.

It was time for Richard to cleanse himself.

On an excursion to the rugged plains outside Calabria, Richard visited the monastery of Corazzo and it was here he met Joachim of Floris, the abbot. Joachim was an ascetic visionary who held some unorthodox opinions. He and Richard engaged one another in profound conversations regarding the coming of the Antichrist, whom both men believed would appear in the guise of a holy man.

Joachim was dogmatic as he instructed Richard in his duty.

"God means for you to play a part in the establishment of His earthly kingdom, and it is coming soon. The time is near when the dove of peace shall descend from God's own bosom, and dwell in the hearts of all men. But before that comes to pass there will be a bath of bloodshed such as the world has never seen before...."

Richard thought upon these things, trying to interpret them. Like so many men of zeal he saw the crusades as Christianity's only method of divesting power from the followers of Islam. The men who pledged themselves to Mohammed were his sworn enemies—the enemies of every Christian on earth: king, noble or commoner.

And Richard would conquer them; bring Islam to its knees.

He knew it now. *He knew it.*

In a public display of humility, Richard walked barefoot from Messina to his villa outside the city. There in the chapel he threw off his clothes and knelt naked before the priests, confessing the wickedness of his life. He begged for God's pardon and the strength to reform his ways. The people cheered.

Richard was a hero.

By comparison the King of France seemed mean-spirited and shabby. He stayed in the palace with his whore, rarely showing himself among the men; never giving charity or *largess* to his nobles or any of his counselors.

When Philippe heard the news of Richard's public penance a cynical expression crossed his face. The hypocrite! Only two nights ago they had lain together in Richard's bed; no longer friends but still lovers. Hot words. Hot flesh.

And now, intimidated by the approach of Christmas, Richard had suddenly decided to repent! *But Philippe was not fooled.* This was no mere routine of religious breast-beating. It was a politically motivated act, aimed at gaining public favor and showing up the King of France. How typical of Richard to grab all the attention for himself! The more Philippe thought on it, the greater his frustration and anger grew.

He paced the floor and brooded on misfortune.

At Acre the siege dragged on and the men lost hope.

Where were the great kings who had promised to deliver them? Where were the armies to relieve their dwindling numbers? The supplies of food and water to sustain them?

Where was God's pity for their dreadful circumstances?

Baldwin of Canterbury came with a host of priests, but they only criticized the sin and squalor of the camp and brought no word of comfort with them. Let the priests complain: they knew nothing of sacrifice! What other consolation could these poor, bedeviled soldiers find but the willing favors of prostitutes who shared their bodies for the meager reward of a piece of bread or half cup of wine?

There were some men whose example gave the others courage: men like Guy de Lusignan and his brother Geoffrey. But the soldiers had been waiting years for the mighty kings of Europe to give strength to the failing efforts at Acre, and still no help had come. If the men had known what petty bickerings kept the kings so long in Sicily, they would have been even more discouraged.

So they waited, losing heart each day. How could Acre ever be taken if the soldiers of Christ were not fed, and the kings would not come to help them? The crusaders slaked their hungers with whores, their own or Moslem—it made no difference anymore. Likewise, some of the Christian women deserted to the tents of Islam, because their own men had grown too poor to pay or feed them.

In the end war makes enemies of all, all.

At Richard's villa there was splendid Christmas feasting.

With Joanna's help he had arranged every detail of this magnificent banquet and the entertainment which was to follow. The former queen of Sicily, who shared her brother's taste for luxury, saw to it that nothing but gold ware was put before the guests; no napkins save those made of re-embroidered damask.

To this feasting Richard had invited the King of France and a goodly selection of nobles, both English and French. One of these was a new arrival to Messina, Count Henri of Champagne, who had not originally planned to join the crusade. He'd left Paris for Troyes shortly after Isabel's funeral, sick to his soul with grief, and determined to involve himself in nothing more than the administration of his estates. When plague had carried off his wife and son that summer, Henri had changed his mind and decided to pursue the king's army to the Holy Land after all. It was not the spirit of religion which burned in him, but a hunger for adventure in strange lands. He cared little if he never saw Champagne, or France, again. Now it was his manly portion he wanted: glory in battle, and the sweet sanctity of an enemy's blood on his hands.

But tonight there was glittering company and no talk of war.

Richard was in a joyous mood. He led the dancing and recited poetry; even sang when he was asked. Philippe sipped on wine that he did not like, and thought: *Richard would love to hold court forever here or anywhere, so long as he could flaunt his clothes, his wit, his conversation. . . .*

Joanna sat close by Philippe's side all the evening.

She was pleasant and attentive but he did not like her. He sensed that she was much like Richard in temperment. And although Philippe supposed that she was beautiful, he did not find her so (except for her breasts; they were twin charms of loveliness!).

As for the rest of her, she was a tall, strongly-built woman with Richard's same square jaw and blazing red-gold hair. She even carried the same fierce aspect in her blue eyes. But there was nothing of the soft and subtle femaleness, or mystery, that Philippe always craved in women.

Tonight, like Richard, Joanna was dressed in cloth of gold.

Philippe watched as they danced together; so well matched, so elegant. He'd never seen Richard so at ease with a woman before. Of course, he was looking at a mirror image of himself in female form. What other woman could possibly attract the Lionheart so much?

Philippe drank more and his thoughts ran on like the swift currents of a river. Richard was complicated. A poet with a lust for blood. Philippe was only now beginning to understand what a formidable enemy he could be. It was not going to be easy for the French king to win any glory for himself in the Holy Land with Richard so ready to take each shred of honor for himself. But there was more to it than that.

Philippe feared him.

Not the man, but the *image* of the man. As a soldier, Richard had no peer, yet his leadership was made of something more illusive and more dangerous than military genius. Magic, glamor; things that Philippe could never hope to match with his own cool-headed intelligence.

A man can fight anything except a legend.

Isabel had understood that. She had known, just as she had always known so much else. Why hadn't he listened to her? Why hadn't he stayed in France? Dismally he remembered her words:

Think of what you could accomplish in Richard's absence!

You could have Normandy, Anjou, the Aquitaine for yourself!

Jesus, why hadn't he listened? Philippe doused his flushed face with cool water. It was no good remembering things that could not be fixed. He had made his choice and, even though it had been the wrong one, there was nothing to be done about it now, save follow Richard to the Holy Land and try to snare some prestige and money for himself.

Suddenly Philippe felt a hand thrust into his. He looked up to see Joanna standing over him. She had a pretty smile. "Would you like to dance with me?" she asked.

Philippe had never learned to talk to women, especially women of exalted rank. And dance! In all his years with Isabel he had never learned to dance, though she had often wished to teach him. He smiled self-consciously at Joanna. "I'm afraid I wouldn't be of much use to you. I don't know how to dance."

She gave him an indulgent smile. "No matter. Then would you care to talk with me a while? You have seemed so quiet all this evening." Without waiting for his answer, Joanna sat down beside him once again.

"I'm not much in the mood for celebration," Philippe grumbled.

She braided her fingers with his and looked earnestly into his face. "I understand. I'm moody too, sometimes."

"You looked happy enough dancing with Richard."

Joanna's eyes sparkled at the mention of her brother's name. "He is such good company. He brings out my smile no matter what I am truly feeling."

Philippe frowned a little at her words. He felt uncomfortable, unsure of what to say to her. At last he gestured toward the necklace and earrings she was wearing. "Your jewelry is most becoming to you," he said.

She seemed to glow, as if he had given her the highest compliment possible. "I didn't think you had noticed anything about me," she said, holding to his hand a little tighter. "Although I have spent the entire evening looking at you." Her voice went huskier. "You are even more handsome than my brother said."

Philippe smiled weakly, nodded, but did not respond.

Joanna refused to relinquish his hand. She bent closer to him and when she did the rich spice scent of her perfume flared in his face. "My brother has big plans for me," she confided. "He hopes to find a great and powerful lord for me to marry. For my sake, I hope he chooses someone dazzlingly handsome, and a marvelous lover as well. . . ." Her gaze swept over him, interested.

Philippe eased his hand out of hers. "Richard has similar tastes in men, Joanna. I'm sure you can trust him to choose one who will please you in every way."

Instead of pretending to be shocked or offended, as so many women would have, Joanna laughed enjoyably, her gold loop earrings tinkling like a gypsy's as she did. "You know my brother very well it seems," she said, "and you must learn to know me better too."

Before Philippe could make an answer, she had leaned close to press a kiss to his lips. Then without another word she stood up and moved to the far end of the table. A moment later she was engaged in conversation with some of her other guests.

Several times that night he caught Joanna watching him.

The look of interest had not gone from her eyes.

Philippe stood at the window in Richard's bedroom, looking out at vague outlines in a dark landscape. At the edge of the courtyard lay a low stone wall, encasing the ghost of a garden. Beyond it the land fell away quickly toward sloping dunes that ended at the sea.

Across the room Richard was taking off his clothes. He looked up to see Philippe by the window. "What are you staring at?" he asked.

Philippe shook his head. "Nothing." But he continued at his place.

Richard came up behind him, encircling Philippe's waist with strong arms. The French king let his head droop back to rest upon his lover's shoulder. *Oh it was nice!* Despite all the mistrust and jealousy of the past months, with surely more to come, there was a fascination between the two men that they could not ignore.

"You didn't enjoy yourself tonight, did you?" Richard asked.

"I was thinking of home," Philippe admitted. "It barely seems like Christmas here."

Richard fingered a lock of Philippe's hair. "I saw you talking to Joanna. She's lovely, isn't she?"

Philippe pulled out of Richard's arms and turned to face him, his handsome features set in scowling. "Please don't pretend you just happened to notice. I know it was your idea to have her seated next to me."

"Is it so wrong to bring my sister and my friend together?"

The black eyes flashed a warning. "I don't want another wife, Richard, at least not yet. If I ever do, I will choose her. Don't push Joanna at me. If you want to find a husband for her you had better look elsewhere."

Richard seemed a trifle insulted. "Very well," he agreed, "I only thought you would be happy for the company of a beautiful woman like Joanna. She's extremely accomplished, educated, well-versed in music and the arts."

"No doubt," Philippe answered, indifferent.

"If you do decide to marry again, you couldn't find a more illustrious bride," Richard reminded his friend. "She is a Plantagenet after all...."

It was difficult for Philippe to keep from laughing. Sometimes Richard acted like a naïve fool! Capet folded his arms across his chest. "For what I want from a woman, a whore will do just as well as a Plantagenet," he declared.

Richard sat down heavily on the bed. He pulled a thick golden chain from his neck and flung it to the floor. "That's a very cynical thing to say," he grumbled. He leaned forward, his long arms dangling between his knees. "You could do worse than marry into my family, Philippe. Joanna is a jewel among women. For God's sake, man, she is the daughter and the sister of a king! Even your precious Isabel couldn't claim that."

Philippe pointed viciously at Richard. "I don't want to hear her name on your lips!" He began to pace back and forth nervously in front of the window, muttering. "You don't know what it is to love a woman like Isabel. You don't know what it is to love any woman!"

Richard's lips settled into a pout. "I didn't bring you here tonight so we could argue. We do enough of that during the day."

Angry, Philippe stripped the red cloak from his shoulders and tossed it at Richard's feet. "*Bring* me here? I am a king, not one of those pretty little Greek boys you keep around to draw your bath water and scent your penis with perfume! Christ Almighty you better choose your words more carefully when you speak to me!"

"I didn't mean for it to sound that way, and you know it..." Richard blustered. "Goddammit Philippe, why do you have to be so disagreeable?"

Philippe snatched up his cloak and settled it over his shoulders. He gave Richard a hateful look, then started toward the door. "Goodnight," he snapped.

Richard jumped up and followed him, jerking him around by the arm. "Don't leave," he pleaded.

There were tears of anger in Philippe's eyes and his voice was bitter. "Ever since we started out on this grand adventure of yours I have suffered dishonor and humiliation at your hands! I'm sick of it!"

"That is not true," Richard said, his eyes blazing with sincerity, "you read deception into every move I make."

"With good reason!"

Richard shook his head sadly. "I don't understand how you can feel so bitterly toward me. God knows we've been as close as any two men can be."

"That's no reason for trusting you," the French king snapped.

Richard captured Philippe in a tight embrace, falling upon his friend's neck with kisses. "All right, don't trust me then," he said, "but love me in any case."

Philippe's expression softened. He sighed and took Richard's face between his hands. "If only it could be that simple! I wish things could be the same as they once were, when Henry was alive. We loved and trusted one another in those days. But it is different now."

They were silent for a moment, then their lips met.

Their kisses were desperate, searching for solutions. At last, breathless, Richard pulled away. "To hell with all the differences," he muttered, "I've never wanted anyone as much as I want you."

Philippe left a path of kisses over Richard's brawny chest. "My love," he whispered.

Later while Philippe slept, Richard lay beside him listening as the wind ruffled the tapestries on the wall, and rain sounded on the stones outside. It was a lonely sound.

He brooded, waiting for sleep.

It was wonderful to feel so close to Philippe once again, fed and satisfied by the glut of passion, but it was only temporary.

They both knew that. Their relationship outside this bed was strained by doubt; by differences between them as men and as kings. Time would only intensify those differences and in the end it would make them enemies as well.

And so Richard brooded, on this matter and on other things.

He thought of the letter he'd received last week from Eleanor. Ever since the coronation his mother had been advising Richard to take a bride. He'd shown little interest and so Eleanor had begun a search herself. Now she'd found a girl whom she deemed suitable to his tastes, and hers.

Berengaria of Navarre was no stranger to him. Richard knew her well for he had spent much time at the royal court in Pamplona visiting her brother Sancho, who was his close friend. Berengaria was more plain than pretty, but she had gracious manners and a fine talent for music and dancing. If he must marry, Richard supposed he could do worse than marry her.

But it was not so easy as that. Eleanor was planning to fetch the girl to Messina in the spring, at which time an explanation of the impending marriage would have to be made to the King of France. Philippe still expected Richard to marry the ill-used Alais Capet, and he was likely to greet any change in those plans with grim antagonism.

For himself, Richard could hardly wait to be quit of that old agreement and it had nothing to do with preferring Berengaria. What shame for a man to be affianced to his father's concubine! Richard had felt the disgrace of that for many years. Let Philippe argue as he may: let him demand whatever excessive payment in gold or silver he would almost certainly expect. Richard was determined to be rid of Alais no matter what the cost.

Sleep was coming. He could feel it settle in his blood like a warming drink of wine. Beside him, captive to a dream, Philippe grunted and turned over on his stomach, his cheek pressed tightly against Richard's arm. How comfortable the feel of male flesh, so close to his own.

Richard closed his eyes and surrendered to the lure of sleep.

In the weeks that followed Christmas, Tancred waited.

Aware of the curious love-hate relationship between the two visiting kings, he was eager to exploit it to his own advantage. So far, he had been careful to play the part of accommodating host to both Philippe and Richard, but all the while he'd been observing them, determining who would make the more obliging ally.

Both had complained to him in secret of the other's faults.

Tancred even had a letter under Philippe's seal which bore the evil tidings of Richard as "a traitor who sought, under the guise of keeping peace in Messina, to take all Sicily for himself." Tancred had preserved the letter, keen to use it at some later date. Richard had been equally free with unflattering comments regarding the King of France, confiding to Tancred that Capet was a thoroughly selfish and untrustworthy man who wished to garner all the spoils of conquest, without ever dirtying his hands.

To both men Tancred lent a sympathetic ear, and waited.

At last, in February 1191, he saw his chance.

Richard had come to pass a few days with him in Catania. The weather was fair and warm. Desiring some sport, Richard arranged a mock tournament between some of his own men and a group of French knights who had accompanied them to Catania. It had been intended as a practice match, a friendly joust with wooden staves instead of lances, but the spirit of fun turned to one of fierce rivalry when Richard drew the celebrated William de Barres as an opponent.

They were old adversaries. William had beaten Richard in the lists on earlier occasions—and he had done something even worse. Once, as a prisoner in Richard's charge, de Barres had broken an oath not to attempt escape, and Richard had never forgiven him for that unchivalrous act.

Now under a bright Sicilian sun they were joined again.

Richard charged at de Barres three times, and each time the king's stave was broken by his rival's. To the shock of all who had assembled there, Richard flew into a violent rage and ordered his opponent out of his presence, even out of the country! Then, in a state of uncontrolled fury, the king of England stomped off the field, muttering vulgar oaths beneath his breath.

Tancred cannily choose that evening to show him the letter.

Richard held the proof of Philippe's treachery between unsteady fingers. *So it had come to this!* Pretending to be a friend, then calling him a traitor behind his back. The truth of it stabbed at Richard like a wound. All they had shared; all that had gone between them—yet Philippe could slander him as easily as he could a hated enemy. Richard wept. He had lost his friend, his lover.

As for Tancred, he had gained an ally, so he smiled.

"This letter is a forgery," Philippe said and tossed it to the floor.

Richard did not believe him, and because of this one episode, the remainder of their stay in Sicily was troubled. Humiliated at having had his written denunciation of the English king uncovered, Philippe seized upon the news of Richard's engagement to Berengaria to trot out the old grudge of his sister's long-delayed marriage to Richard.

How did he dare to put another woman in her place?

The matter was argued with vehemence on both sides and it

was finally decided that, as before, a mediator was needed. Once again the Count of Flanders employed his talents as a diplomat in order to bring about a settlement between the two quarreling kings.

After days of wrangling and refusals, the following agreement was made, set down and signed. *Philippe would relieve Richard of his betrothal pledge to Alais; in return the French king would be recompensed with the territories of Auvergne, Issoudun and Graçay; and an additional ten thousand silver Troyes marks.*

As simply as that, it was done.

Both kings were well satisfied with the Treaty of Messina and chose to feel they had gotten an advantage on the other. Actually it was Philippe who had cut the best deal for himself, Richard who had blundered. By ceding those lands back to Philippe (whose soldiers had captured them during the wars with Henry) he had provided the French king with a convenient, even tempting, corridor into the Aquitaine. Either Richard did not see the dangers inherent in such a settlement, or he had decided to ignore them.

In any case, he did not care. The final, mocking reminder of Henry Plantagenet had been swept away and Richard was free to marry Berengaria. He was almost happy.

Philippe had even greater cause for celebration.

Now, having resolved the troublesome matter of Alais, and extended the boundaries of his domain at the same time, he was anxious to leave Sicily. At once the king set about gathering his army and making preparations for a sea voyage.

He was hoping to leave for Acre by the end of March.

Fabiana was gamboling in her bath.

"I still cannot believe my fortune at being able to use water whenever I wish," she giggled, looking across at Philippe who was sitting on a stool before the fire.

He gave a glance over his shoulder. "Enjoy it now, for I fear there will be little of it once we leave here, until we are able to capture Acre." He looked back toward the fire. "God only knows when that will be."

She skimmed the tiny flecks of jasmine oil off the surface of the water and rubbed her breasts and shoulders with the fragrant residue. This was all such luxury to her: the bath, the clothes of silk and linen; wholesome food when she wished to eat. Had Fabiana not already loved the king for himself, she would have loved him for the things he gave her.

She stepped from the water and wrapped herself in a lambswool coverlet, then filled a cup with wine and took it to him, holding it out like an offering.

Philippe took the cup. "Sit with me," he said. Fabiana huddled against his knee, her face tilted to look up at him. She had asked the question many times, but now she felt impelled to ask it once again. "Shall I be with you there? Will you keep me beside you always?"

His fingers played in her dark hair. "As close as close is," he answered, looking somber, till all at once he smiled, "Surely you don't mean to mount the very walls of Acre with my army..."

She did not return the smile. "I am afraid of being separated from you and claimed by other men. How would I ever find you? No one would believe me if I told them I belonged to the king."

Philippe bent to kiss her forehead. She was like a child, so dependent on him in every way; never quite sure why she merited his attention, and yet afraid it might dissolve at any time. He tried to reassure her. "Don't worry about such things," he said, "for you have my protection. No man is going to take the mistress of a king."

That seemed to ease her fears. "You are so good to me," she said, kissing his knee. "No one was ever good to me before." Then she looked past him at the tray of food on the floor; eager for it, but awaiting his permission.

Philippe pushed the tray toward her. "Eat," he said.

She fed happily on almond cakes, on pastries made with beef and cheese, and while she ate Philippe stroked her breasts and the black waves of her hair which fell over them. She smelled so sweet, so fresh from her bath water, and her skin was soft to his touch. He gave her wine from his own cup and licked away the tiny drops which spilled on her chin.

Fabiana looked up at him, her dark eyes glowing. "Do I please you, my lord?" she asked. "I want so very much to please you..."

He stood up, his hand in hers, and pulled her toward the bed.

"You please me well, Fabiana," he said, the breath catching in his chest as he reached out to fondle her heavy breasts, "but surely you must know that by now."

Contented, she settled back and spread her legs for him.

Philippe liked the look of her wide, welcoming cunt fringed with thick black curls, and he filled her in an instant. She was a hot-blooded southerner who could not hide her pleasure, and in a moment she was gasping, cooing vulgar praises in his ear, her arms coiled about his neck as he pumped against her.

Christ, she felt so good to him.

Fabiana closed her eyes. He was wonderful. No other man had ever filled her so completely. He was her king, her lover; he was *everything*. Whenever he took her, she felt as though God Himself had put a blessing on her.

Philippe was working furiously, sweat dripping from his face. She may have had a thousand other men in her before, but now she was his and there would be no others. "You belong to me," he cried out, "do you understand? To *me*."

Later he held her in his arms. She was lightly dozing.

"I will be so glad to leave here," he told her, "your presence is the only thing that has made it bearable for me."

She smiled, pleased. Then her eyes went wide with imagining. "What will it be like at the holy place?"

Philippe bent to lick her breasts. "I don't know, but the news from there is bad. So many killed..." He rubbed his cheek against her nipples. "I'm afraid, Fabiana. Not for myself, but for my son and the safety of my realm should I not return."

He had never spoken to her of fears before and hearing him do so now made Fabiana want to cry. She kissed his lips over and over again, while her hands played lightly upon his beard. "You are a great king, my lord, the greatest king who ever lived! God will protect you."

He tightened his arms around her. "I need your prayers."

She smoothed the tangle of curls back from his forehead. "I pray for you each day and every night." Her cheeks colored just a little. "Do you suppose God listens to the prayers of a whore?"

Philippe rolled Fabiana on her back and rested on her. "Yes," he said, "I shouldn't be surprised if He does." He nuzzled at her breasts with his chin, and his beard scratched her flesh. "What of this?" he asked, his hands tight against her hips. "Does a whore answer the prayers of a king?"

She had never known a man who was so lusty. On most nights he took her several times; more. The knowledge that she satisfied him added pride to her desire. She could please him. *She could please the king.* They kissed with wet, open mouths and Fabiana felt him grow big against her belly.

She wrapped her legs around his back and held him.

Adele held the child in her arms and smiled down at Edythe.

"You've done well, my dear," the admiring grandmother declared, "he is handsome like his father, and healthy too." Then she handed the baby over to William le Breton for baptism and took up Edythe's hand, squeezing it. "Philippe will be so proud of him, and of you too."

Edythe felt a weary peace settle over her. She looked past Adele at the priest who held her son and said, "I give him over to your care until his father's return, good chaplain."

William made the sign of a cross in the air. "Then he shall be in God's care," he answered, "and God shall keep him well."

Aloud, he began to pray in Latin.

PHILIPPE sailed to Acre on a blue, untroubled sea.

The French put into port on April 20th. They were met by a rejoicing crowd of knights and soldiers who had gathered at the shore to meet them. For so long they had awaited these reinforcements from the West! Now at last here were twenty thousand strong and well-fed men come to relieve their dwindling numbers, and soon they would be joined by even more, when the fabled king Richard of England brought his troops to Acre.

Richard of England! How grand it would be when he came!

But for now Philippe of France was the hero of the day.

The soldiers flocked to him, falling to their knees to pay him tribute. He was a fine sight, tall and strong, and this day dressed in brave shades of green and gold.

A king to lead them! At last a king!

After Philippe had eaten and rested he asked to be taken on a tour of the camp. His escort was Conrad of Montferrat who, with King Guy of Jerusalem, was one of the acknowledged leaders of the crusade. By virtue of his success in rescuing Tyre from Saladin's forces, Conrad had won much fame and honor among the crusaders, as well as the title Lord of Tyre. Philippe liked him at once, and marked him down as a man to trust. He was surely a wiser and more politic leader than the foolish Guy de Lusignan, of whom Philippe had heard few complimentary remarks.

The two men rode to the edge of camp and looked back.

"You cannot imagine what your presence here will mean to the men," Conrad said, his voice pitched low as if in awe. "For such a long time they've been without decent food, without leadership, worst of all without hope. Now, with you and all you have brought with you, I have no doubt we shall take Acre before summer comes."

"If God wills," Philippe nodded solemnly. His gaze carried to the farthest reaches of the Christian settlement. It was a squalid sight. Most of the pavilions were patched and ragged, their bright colors dulled by exposure to the sun. The soldiers, although there were many of them, were thin and ill-equipped, almost to a man.

But there was worse.

Far to the west, at the fringe of the camp, a thousand bodies lay congealing beneath the sun. Philippe regarded the scene with disgust and covered his mouth to keep from choking. The stench of death hung in the air like an evil perfume.

"Why have those bodies been left unburied?" he asked.

Conrad shrugged. "It's not a pretty sight, I agree, but there is reason for it. Those men mutinied against their commanders and led a surprise raid on the Moslem camp. They were slain to the last man. Their actions were foolish, and they were deemed unfit for a Christian burial."

"That is ridiculous," Philippe sniffed contemptuously. "Put some men to work digging a trench, and see to it at once." Then he jerked on his horses' rein. "My tent should be ready by now," he said to Conrad. "After I have taken my dinner with the Duke of Burgundy and the Count of Flanders, I want you to bring the commanders to my tent for a meeting. You will be present also, of course. In a short time King Richard will join us here at Acre and we will begin the siege at once. We have much to do."

Conrad was an old campaigner and not easily impressed by other men. But he looked admiringly at Philippe. "I will do whatever you ask," he said. Then as they made their way back down the sandy rise into the midst of the camp, he added, "You are a young man to be so wise. I shall consider it an honor to serve you."

Philippe smiled his appreciation. Then he asked, "Tell me, my friend, are there many women in the camp?"

"Not any more," Conrad replied dismally. "Many have died of plague, and others went off to serve the Moslems when our food ran scarce."

"I have brought over three thousand women with me," Philippe declared, "but I will not unload them from the ships until provisions have been made ready for their arrival. Will you see to this for me?"

Conrad squinted handsomely into the setting sun. *Was he to be taken for a whoremaster?* For a moment he wavered, but then thought better of it and agreed. "What would you have me do?" he asked.

Again the smile. "I want them billeted in groups of no more than one hundred at equal distances throughout the camp. The women are to be paid a sum of two *deniers* at a time, no more, for their services. See to it that the men draw lots. I want no riots on my hands." He reached out and clapped his new companion heartily on the shoulder. "You will be glad at some later date I have chosen to entrust you with this matter."

Conrad was beginning to understand, and a broad smile creased his face. "The men will doubtless think kindly of me," he mused.

Philippe laughed.

"Of us both, my dear Conrad. And you shall have yet another reward. For your help in this matter I will give you first choice of all the common women, except, of course, those which I and the men in my retinue have taken for ourselves." He paused, grinning at Conrad's look of skepticism. "Don't worry. There are plenty of pretties left for you to choose from. You won't be disappointed."

Laughing, they made their way toward the king's tent.

The moon was a piece of gold trapped in a sapphire.

It was evening now, and cool at last.

Philippe stood just outside his tent, waiting for Flanders and listening to the sounds around him. It was almost peaceful; he felt good.

The mood of the camp was good too, and much improved since his arrival two weeks ago. Philippe had given the soldiers a sense of worthiness by putting them to work: digging trenches, erecting new tents, and filling in the great ditch which lay before the walls of Acre. Once that was accomplished (and it would be soon) huge siege machines would be deployed against the city. By that time Richard should have arrived.

Philippe didn't understand the delay.

Originally, Richard's plan had been to remain in Sicily only long enough to greet his visiting mother, and collect his fiancé. But that had been over one month ago, and still he had not reached Acre. Philippe was beginning to lose patience. He wanted to start the siege in earnest. But he had promised to wait for Richard and his army. It was important to use the full force of both armies in the attack if Acre was to be taken speedily.

The stubborn little garrison inside the city walls had held out bravely ever since Guy de Lusignan had begun the siege over two years ago. They were impoverished, helpless. Saladin's army, encamped on the other side of the crusader settlement, was unable to aid them in any way.

Philippe had no doubt the garrison could be overthrown. It was the walls which troubled him, walls built by earlier soldiers of the cross! Philippe's tent was pitched directly opposite the primary defense stronghold of the fortification, the "Accursed Tower" which he was determined to take once the fighting began. Meanwhile he saw to the building of his siege engines, and waited for Richard.

Despite the new sense of purpose among the soldiers, there were problems in the camp. Saladin's men made periodic raids on the outer reaches of the settlement, and it was not unusual for a man to be murdered in his sleep, his throat slashed to near decapitation by a Moslem scimitar. Philippe had strengthened his patrols, and because of this the killings diminished, but did not stop entirely.

But disease was an invader that could not be stopped.

Men died every day of everything from plague to heat stroke, and the corpses (however quickly they were buried) only spread more sickness among the soldiers. Once June came, and July, the brutal heat of middle summer would make the situation even worse. Conditions had improved, however, since the previous autumn, when hundreds died every day, including Queen Sibylla of Jerusalem, the wife of king Guy.

Philippe squinted into the twilight. There was an intensity to this barren desert landscape, a fierceness both beautiful and strange. It was a place of zealots, of poets and prophets; a land that gave rise to legends and heroes with rich-sounding names. Richard belonged here, but Philippe did not. His nature rebelled against the all-too-pervasive spirit of Oriental decadence; he was frightened of a lure of mystery he could not understand. It was an enigma. *Like Geoffrey. Like Isabel.*

At last Flanders came and took Philippe out of his contemplative mood, and he was glad. How much more at ease the French king was with talk of practical matters! He greeted Flanders with a nod, and then waved him inside the tent.

Philippe had put him in charge of seeing to it that the siege machines were built according to the proper specifications, but it was not this business which had brought him to the king's pavilion tonight. He flung himself into a camp chair and waited silently as Fabiana served wine to him and Philippe. When she had withdrawn, Flanders gulped a little of the drink, then looked straight at his host.

"I bring you bad news, I fear," he said, wiping drops of wine from his mouth with a trailing sleeve. "Word has just arrived in the camp from the captain of a Genoese galley that some of King Richard's fleet has been lost in a storm off the Greek islands." He paused, anticipating Philippe's question and before the king could ask it he continued, "Richard is known to be safe, though the ship bearing his fiancé and sister may have been lost."

Philippe looked down at his folded hands. "Where is Richard now?"

"At Rhodes. But there is talk he has been sending letters to the emperor on Cyprus."

Philippe frowned. Emperor Isaac Comnenus was no friend to the crusaders. In the past he had been accused of favoring Saladin's cause against the Latins from the West. He was also known to have seized both ships and supplies bound for the Christian camp at Acre. He was a typically corrupt Byzantine despot and it puzzled Philippe that Richard would wish to have any dealings with him.

"What do you think?" he asked.

Flanders' amber eyes were full of doubt. "I don't know. It's possible Richard is trying to make some sort of deal with Isaac, in order to facilitate safe passage here to Acre. You must have heard how many ships the emperor has despoiled for his own purposes."

Philippe gave a small, ironic laugh. "Richard fears no man on earth. If he is in communication with the emperor, I say they are both up to no good."

Flanders finished his wine and stood up. "Well, we won't know what it's all about till Richard gets here, and I hope it will be soon. You have brought new blood to this endeavor, and the men are anxious to begin the siege."

Philippe looked up, interested. "How soon will my three hundred *mangonels* be completed?"

Flanders stroked his beard thoughtfully. "By the end of this week, I should think."

"Good," Philippe said at once, "as soon as they are ready we shall begin the siege. We cannot wait indefinitely for Richard to arrive."

The Count of Flanders caught the implication in the king's words and sympathized with his opinion. "Indeed, you are taken by the soldiers to be their leader, as you should be. But when Richard comes..." His voice trailed off, but Philippe understood what he was saying.

He looked up as Flanders moved toward the edge of the tent.

"Are you going so soon?"

The count tossed a cloak about his shoulders. "I've been up since before dawn. The prospect of a night's sleep is very pleasing to me."

"Of course."

Philippe followed him outside. The two men stood together for a time—silent, looking off into a sky filled with stars. "What a queer place this is," the king mused, "and how strangely out of place I feel here."

Flanders' fine profile was blurred against the background of night, but the gleam of his eye showed for a moment. "You prefer politics to soldiering, I know."

There was a melancholy note in Philippe's voice. "I shall be very happy to return to France again. Paris seems so distant to me now, as if it were a memory."

"You shall see it soon enough my friend, never fear." He made the prospect sound easy, possible.

Philippe stared ahead into the darkness. "I only wish I knew that to be true."

Flanders put an arm about the king's shoulder. "We've had our many differences, Capet, but whatever matters have divided us I have always felt a father's love for you, and my respect runs just as deep—so I must speak my heart. You will do great things in the East, for God has brought you here to that purpose. But you must trust in Him." Flanders' voice softened almost to a whisper. "Be vigilant Philippe. Take care Richard does not get the best of you. In any case, you are the better man by far."

Philippe groped for Flanders' hand and found it.

Richard had been sea-sick, shipwrecked, and stricken with fever.

It had been a hard few weeks.

Part of his fleet had been driven by storms onto the coast of Cyprus, including the ship of Joanna and Berengaria. The two women had prudently refused to go ashore, though Isaac Comnenus had invited them to do so, for they were afraid of being taken hostage and held for ransom. It was just the sort of barbarous act for which the emperor was famous.

But what to do?

After two weeks, the stranded passengers had nearly exhausted their supply of fresh water. The women were dismayed; and just when they were about to give themselves up to the questionable hospitality of the emperor, Richard's flagship appeared like a tiny painted toy at the edge of the horizon.

At once Isaac gave up all thoughts of hostages and ransom.

The Cypriots had pillaged several shipwrecked English galleys, killing the soldiers or taking them as prisoners. Richard had heard of this and he was furious. Isaac had promised to allow the English safe passage to Syria. Now he was abetting all manner of offenses against them.

Richard brought his troops ashore and chased the emperor and his men into the mountains. In a few hours the crusaders had taken the city of Limassol for themselves and Richard had inherited a vast amount of booty. But he was still outraged at Isaac for his lies and treachery, and determined to conquer all of Cyprus before setting sail for Acre.

Actually, Richard had already claimed it by way of a public

proclamation, swearing clemency to all who accepted him as their new lord, and destruction to those who did not.

There was no resistance. The Greeks were terrified of him.

On May 12th at Limassol, Richard married Berengaria.

It was a spectacular if hastily arranged affair, made somewhat incongruous by the fact that the splendidly adorned Richard outshone the bride.

The royal couple spent their wedding night at Isaac's palace.

Berengaria pulled the coverlet around her shoulders and looked across the room at Richard. He had been standing at the window for an hour; silent, moody. What was he thinking? His attitude was so withdrawn he might have been alone in all the world.

Was he angry with her? If so, what had she done to displease him? Berengaria was puzzled and embarrassed. She had done what she believed a bride should to: undressed submissively and lain herself down upon the bed. From what little she knew of the marriage night ritual, the rest was *his* responsibility.

This silence was no good; finally she spoke. "Richard, have I done something to offend you? If so, tell me. My only wish is to please you."

He turned toward her. Even in the dimness she could see the lines of strain etched in his face.

"I'm sorry," he mumbled and his chin drooped toward his chest. "I don't know what to say."

Berengaria didn't want to cry but the tears were coming closer. His words had made her feel helpless and ashamed. It was her own fault that Richard was not attracted to her; she wasn't pretty or exciting enough to hold his interest. If only she had been born beautiful!

She began to sob into her hands.

Richard hurried to her side at once, making a move to embrace her. Then he drew back, intimidated by the delicacy of her throat and shoulders. Surely his powerful arms could crush such a fragile girl.

Berengaria saw his reluctance and took it for displeasure.

"You cannot even bring yourself to touch me!" she wept.

He reached to take her hand and held it gently, like a flower.

"You are a lovely girl Berengaria, be assured. I am proud to have you as my wife."

She stopped crying long enough to look at him. *How she loved to look at him.* A few deep breaths steadied her a little. "If that is true, why can't you treat me as your wife?"

"I shall, in time." He kissed her hand.

Berengaria tried to find a speck of love in his eyes but there was only blue and coldness. At last she looked away. "I shall feel a dreadful fraud tomorrow, when the bishop puts the crown upon my head and calls me queen," she said.

Richard considered that for a moment. *She was right.* It was unfitting for him to leave her just as he had found her. If they were to be king and queen together they must first be man and wife. He hastened to pull off his smock, then stooped to undo his laces.

"Here," he said.

Berengaria stared as he thrust his penis into her hands. What did he want her to do? Hesitantly her fingers closed around the smooth and hairless stem. She squeezed gently a few times, then began to stroke it awkwardly.

It was obvious she had never touched a man before and although that hardly surprised him, Richard was frustrated by her inexperience. At last, still limp, he pulled away from her.

"Never mind," he said, lacing up his braies, "just go to sleep. You have an early day tomorrow, Berengaria."

She stared back at him, unbelieving, and suddenly the tears rushed from her eyes. "I don't know what you expect of me or what you would have me do!" she wailed.

Richard silenced her with a chaste kiss. "We are both tired," he said. "We'll deal with this matter at some later date; there is no need to rush." He kissed her once again. "I'm going to my own room now. Goodnight, dear wife."

"Goodnight, Richard," she whispered, but she couldn't even raise her eyes to watch him as he left.

Sleepless, Richard paced his bedroom for a long while.

This business with Berengaria was not going to work! He could not pretend desire for her as a woman, and she certainly had no talents to satisfy his lust in any other way.

She was so very much in love with him; that was the worst of it.

Doubtless, she felt rejected and betrayed by his attitude of indifference. What a trial this was going to be! Eventually he would have to make a son in her. Richard wasn't sure it could be done.

Earlier this evening, flushed with good wine and food and his success against the emperor, Richard had been in a mood to consummate his marriage. But then the sight of Berengaria's frail, naked little body had spoiled it all, and left him feeling like an overpowering brute.

Well, tomorrow she would be crowned as his queen and perhaps that would satisfy her for a while. In any case he was too tired to think on it further. His mind was busy, conjuring up successes on the island, and after that there was the siege of Acre to contend with. He had no time or heart for troubles with his wife.

He was halfway to bed when Joanna came into his room.

Richard looked up, surprised, and smiled at her.

"I saw a light beneath the door," she said, "and wondered why you were not with Berengaria this night of all nights."

Richard couldn't take his eyes from her.

How beautiful she was, this daughter of Henry Plantagenet and Eleanor of Aquitaine! She had her father's brash, high-colored Angevin good looks—and all her mother's charm.

This was a woman who stood before him.

Joanna read the message in his eyes and came closer, her arms reaching for him. "Berengaria is a lovely girl," she purred as he took hold of her, "but I'm afraid you are too much of a man for such a genteel little virgin." Her full, painted mouth beckoned in a smile. "But not for me, dear brother. Surely you must realize that by now."

He did. All those months in Sicily during their time together, he had felt an itch of something more than a brother's interest in her. Now Joanna had finally given voice to it.

They were so alike, so much more fitted to one another than he and Berengaria. Still he held back, caught in sweet dilemma until Joanna kissed him full on the mouth. *Just this once; just tonight.* All the passion he hadn't been able to feel for his wife now burned in him for his vivacious sister.

He pulled the silver dishabille down over her shoulders, and brought his lips against her throat. The feel of her sweet white skin was thrilling.

"This is madness," he whispered in her ear, "this is sin..."
Her hands were already on his laces. "I know," she said.

𝕱 OR ALL who came to fight at Acre there was a worse enemy than Moslems. It was summer now, and the heat was everywhere, burning into the earth like the wrath of God. There was no shield from it until the sun went down, when chilly gusts blew off the surface of the sea.

It was early June, and the siege dragged on.

Philippe's *mangonels* had been battering the walls of Acre for almost three weeks. His siege engines were magnificently designed monsters which stood four or five storeys high. Yet the crafty defenders destroyed them at the rate of two or three per day. They did this by pouring great cauldrons of boiling *naphtha* over the walls and catching the machines on fire. For each one that was burned, it took the Franks at least four days of work to repair it. The French king needed more machines, more men — but it was June now and still Richard and his army had not come.

New arrivals in the camp told grand stories of the Lionheart's bold conquest of Cyprus; how, with the help of the Knights Templars he had swept Isaac Comnenus and his Cypriot Greeks from power, and declared himself king of the island. Much to the scorn of Philippe and his ally Conrad of Montferrat, Guy de Lusignan (from whom Conrad wished to take the throne of Jerusalem now that Queen Sibylla, the legal claimant, was dead) had sailed to Cyprus with a group of hand-picked men. He was eager to help Richard, for by doing so he would also help himself.

Guy worried about the closeness between Conrad and Philippe; feared he was being eclipsed. He wanted his *own* ally, and who was better suited to that purpose than the legendary Richard of England? Guy was an adventurer at heart, and Richard's prowess appealed to his own sense of chivalry.

He also hoped to profit from the friendship.

So Guy went to Cyprus and became Richard's lieutenant, while the remainder of the force waited at Acre and the French king dispatched envoys to the island every few days, entreating Richard to come at once to Acre. Christ, the city could have been taken weeks ago if Richard had done his duty! Instead he parleyed with princes and made himself a marriage, while Philippe did the work which they had pledged to accomplish together!

No wonder the French king was in such foul temper these days.

It was not all because of Richard, though much of it was; there were other matters to concern him, and one which touched very deeply at his heart. The Count of Flanders had fallen ill of a fever and for many days he lay in his tent too sick to speak. Like so many pilgrims, he had come to the East determined to win Acre back from the Infidels who held it, and now it seemed that he would never see it.

All that it was possible to do was done for him.

When it became apparent he would not leave his bed again, Philippe ordered that the count's sword be laid beside him, and golden spurs put on his feet as a symbol of his many great achievements in battle. The Bishop of Beauvais knelt at his side reciting from the Scriptures, while Philippe held Flanders' head against his chest.

Sweat stung the count's eyes, and his tongue was numbed by fever. It was only at the last he roused from his delirium. He looked up into Philippe's face, and smiled the calm and resolute smile of a dying man. He squeezed the king's hand and made a plea.

"When I am dead," he whispered, "see that my body is put into the common trench before the city walls. For then on Judgment Day, when all men are raised up, my lord Christ in heaven shall see that I died in the land which gave Him birth, and he will know I praised Him with the last words of my mouth."

Philippe could barely speak for sobbing. "You are the finest, the bravest man I ever knew!" he cried. "I cannot believe that God would take you from our midst before our purpose here has even been accomplished!"

All of the proud and worldly aspects so familiar in Flanders' character were gone now, for the visage of death humbles any man. His amber eyes lighted with a look of weary peace, and with a feeble hand he reached to wipe the tears from Philippe's face.

"God's will be done," he said. "Do not feel sad. I have seen death many times as a soldier. It is not at all terrible to me." His lips twitched for just a moment as if he wished to say more and then went slack. His head lolled to one side, and he was silent.

For a long time afterwards, as candles flickered tiny gleams of light over all the objects in the room and the bishop muttered his prayers aloud, Philippe sat holding the dead man in his arms. The sense of loss was sharp and very deep.

He loved this man. His personal bravery and glamor had dazzled Philippe as a youth, and even later when they had faced each other on a battlefield. This was the man who had been more of a father to him than Louis ever had—the man who had given him Isabel, then tried with all the powers of heaven and hell to take her back. Now he was dead and his flesh would stink like that of other men.

Philippe wept and could not be comforted.

On June 8th, 1191, Richard finally landed at Acre.

The reception which greeted him at the shore was so tremendous that even the inhabitants of Saladin's camp came out of their tents to observe it. There was trumpet fanfare and the singing of songs. Banners set their gay colors against the sky and fluttered in welcome.

That night in the camp there was dancing and more singing and wine was passed to every man and woman. The celebration lasted till the sun came up on the new morning, but the memory of it would live in the songs of trouvères for a dozen generations.

Philippe was glad for Richard's coming, of course; he'd waited for it long enough. But on that night, between the singing and the laughter, he watched Richard, watched him with an intensity born of caution. Tonight all was contentment and accord. But what about tomorrow, and all the days to follow? How much harmony would there be once Richard set himself at the head of the combined armies by way of his extraordinary legend and popularity? What honor could the King of France salvage then?

All of this anger was enfeebling him, making him feel hot and unwell. Philippe wiped a hand across his face and looked across at his splendid rival. Richard lounged upon his silken litter, gold tassels fluttering over his head from the canopy above. How vain he was, how full of confidence. And how he loved every shred of the attention paid to him! Then, as if he could read his friend's thoughts, Richard raised his cup in a glib toast and smiled.

Philippe smiled back. Devil, he thought.

It was nearly dawn when Philippe crept into his own tent and called out for Fabiana to come and undress him. She came at once to his call, her expression vague from interrupted sleep, and began to unfasten his clothes. She removed his mantle and bliaud, then his smock, frowning as her hand passed over his naked chest. "Your skin is very hot," she said.

"For you," he answered, and reached for her.

His hands found her breasts, stripping away the muslin shift which covered them. His fingers began to tremble. Was it the wine or simple lust that put this giddiness into his blood?

Philippe took a breath. "I wish I had not drunk so much," he mumbled and pressed his forehead to her shoulder.

Fabiana gasped and encircled his waist with her arms to steady him. "You are ill my lord!"

He pushed her hands aside and laughed, mocking her concern. "Not ill at all," he said and bent to kiss her. But as he did, her pretty face wavered before his eyes and then blurred till he could hardly see it. Suddenly the blood was pounding in his temples and he felt his breath grow tight in his chest.

"Fabiana," he cried, lurching forward.

She tried to catch him but he fell groaning at her feet.

Only a miracle sent from God could save Philippe Capet.

The physicians who attended at the bedside of the king turned to each other with glum faces. It was the Eastern sickness which they called *arnoldia*. Many men in the camp had been stricken with it. The symptoms were always the same: loss of hair and fingernails; peeling of the skin. But worse than that was the constant fever, which could keep a man raving for a week.

It was having its way with the French king, feeding him delirium and the devil. His mind seemed to be inflamed by visions of his dead wife and only the devil put such dreams into a man's mind. So they purified the sick man with holy water and muttered no end of prayers, but nothing seemed to help. It was in God's hands.

"Isabel," he cried and reached for her. "Isabel!"

How was it that the others could not see her? She was there.

Standing over him, fair as the new dawn. He had forgotten— oh, how could he have forgotten?—she was as beautiful as that. She was clothed all in grey silk, her full and rounded breasts visible beneath the sheer material. There were grey opals at her ears and throat, nearly hidden by pale hair which fell in tousled waves to her feet. He could almost touch it.

For ten days Philippe lay sweating and screaming in his bed. Fabiana never left his side; not once in those ten days. She did not care that the physicians sniggered at her dutiful attempts to nurse the king, that they saw her as just a worthless little whore. *She* was the one who loved him; *she* refused to let him die.

Her own comfort meant nothing. Fabiana only ate if food was brought to her. She slept on the floor at Philippe's feet; she relieved herself in the pewter pot beside the bed. Priests and physicians came and went from the pavilion those many days, but only Fabiana remained in loyal obstinacy. She washed the sweat from his body, and fed him water from a cup.

"Take me, oh God," she wept, "but spare the king."

Which king?

Richard had also fallen ill of *arnoldia*.

This was devastating news to the soldiers. So long as their two leaders were insensible with fever, the siege against Acre had to be postponed.

Now at this time Duke Leopold of Austria, vassal to the dead emperor Barbarossa, tried to install himself as the new leader of the crusade. But the soldiers only laughed at his pretensions and soon he was driven back into his tent in shame. It was true that Leopold did not like either of the two kings, but he particularly resented Richard. Indeed, with all his pride, accomplishments and beauty, the King of England was a man whom any man might hate.

So the soldiers waited, and the kings grew worse.

Inactivity bred rumors. There was talk that Richard wished to make a friend of his chivalrous enemy Saladin; that Saladin himself held Richard in the highest esteem. More than once while the king of England lay prone on his sickbed, the great Saracen leader sent him gifts of fruit and wine, chilled with mountain ice. While such courtesies were appreciated by Richard, other crusaders, especially the French, viewed the matter with grim suspicion.

And then one day, just as suddenly as he had been afflicted, Philippe recovered from his terrible illness. Weak but resolute, he vowed to take Acre at once, and assembled all his men before the walls.

The news was brought to Richard's tent by Hugh of Burgundy.

The King of England lay on his bed, conscious but miserable. As with Philippe, this strange fever had done awful things to him. Great quantities of his lush red-gold hair had fallen out, and his skin was peeling as if from an extreme case of sunburn. Richard was so ashamed of his appearance, he kept his face covered by a veil of mosquito netting.

There had never been much friendship between Richard and Duke Hugh. Once again Richard's personality and gifts invited jealousy. But despite feelings of envy, Hugh was drawn to the Plantagenet, as all men of lesser talents were. Certainly he preferred Richard to the cold and quarrelsome Philippe; and it had brought him here.

"What are you going go do?" he asked. "Capet means to humiliate you by taking Acre himself. If that happens all the world will see him as a greater warrior than yourself!" Hugh's round face was red with exasperation.

Richard gave a muffled laugh behind the veil. "That will never happen."

"Don't be so sure," Hugh blustered, "he has already gathered his men and ordered the assault to begin at dawn."

"Besides his own soldiers, who has joined him?"

The duke shrugged. "The Genoese, Pisans. Some of Leopold's Germans. Others."

Richard thrashed about in discomfort on his bed. Despite his concern for what Hugh had told him, he was anxious to have the interview at an end. Illness caused him to tire easily. He gripped the arm of one of his attendants and struggled to a sitting position. "That is a goodly contingent of men," he grumbled, "and what is the French king paying them?"

Hugh thought for a moment. "Three gold *bezants* for a month's service."

Richard slumped back on his bed in satisfaction. "Summon my lieutenants," he told Hugh "and have them pass the word throughout the camp that I shall guarantee a sum of four gold *bezants* to any man who will serve beneath my banner. Do this at once and then we shall see how far the King of France gets with his plan to destroy my reputation and authority."

Hugh did just as he was asked.

And the result was as Richard had intended. All of the men, save for the French knights and foot soldiers (who were bound by their oath to support Philippe Capet) switched their loyalties to the English king. Worse yet, Richard refused to allow any of his soldiers to take part in Philippe's planned attack on the city.

When he heard of this, Philippe's rage was so extreme that he nearly suffered a relapse of his illness. So it had finally come to this! Richard no longer bothered to hide his treachery but was content to flaunt it for all the world to see! What an utterly faithless friend he was. Obviously he cared far more for his own aggrandizement than for the success of the crusade.

Philippe had withstood enough humiliation.

He was determined now to take Acre on his own.

For seven days the French besieged the Accursed Tower.

These were brave attempts and worthy, too, for by now the walls of the citadel had been badly undermined by tunnelling and showers of stones. But it was still impossible to take the city, for each assault upon the wall was met by fierce counter-attacks as Saladin's *mamelukes* charged the rear of the crusader camp.

Time and again the French knights drove them back, but at such a cost! Hundreds of them died as a result of every Saracen raid. With no support from Richard's loyalists the French were alone and greatly outnumbered. After each assault Philippe was forced to pull his troops back, unsuccessful.

The final attack of that dreadful and bloody week took place on June 24th. Philippe had deployed his men in a crescent formation at the rear in order to repulse any Moslem attack, and led a group of his most valiant knights in a charge against the Accursed Tower. He did not seek to shield himself from danger, but stood together with his soldiers, pulling a crossbow like the rest of them, against defenders who mounted the walls of Acre to pour down stones and burning arrows on them.

Victory was so close; it was almost theirs!

But once again the efforts of the Franks were thwarted as the scaling ladders broke under the weight of men burdened by excessive armor. Many of the king's prize *mangonels* were destroyed by showers of boiling *naphtha,* and fell to the ground in piles of burning rubble.

Philippe would remember those images all his life.

At last the sun set on that horrible day. The Christian dead were too numerous to count. With breast or brain laid bare, they were strewn along the entire length of the wall. Smoke helped to obscure the ugliness, but the sweet stink of blood was everywhere.

Wearied to the point of illness and devastated by defeat, Philippe staggered back to his tent. He threw his aching body down on the bed and called out to Fabiana. She came at once, offering him a henap filled with wine. He drank it greedily, then lay back to let her unloose his mesh *hauberk* and *coif*.

Philippe barely moved as Fabiana undressed him and washed his body with a cool cloth. He grunted his thanks when she had finished and pulled her down beside him on the bed, stripping off her clothes. After a day of bloodshed and terror, this! Oh Jesus, what solace could be found in the soft body of a woman.

He was tired but her touch soon restored feeling to his numbed senses. Scarcely a word passed between them as he took her, and afterwards he fell asleep with his head on her shoulder. Fabiana lay on her back, holding him in her arms. She was sleepless and dizzy. Her flesh grew hotter and the pain expanded in her head.

She had been fighting illness for several days. Now she was in its grip and there was nothing to do but lie here, sweating in fear and fever with the sleeping king clasped tightly in her arms. She had done so much to bring him back to health, but there was nothing she could do to heal herself, except to pray. Did God heed the supplications of a whore?

Fabiana doubted it; she felt herself grow weaker.

Later, Philippe awoke to see her puking on the floor.

He carried her back to the bed and held her to him, gently, as he would a child, kissing the tears from her face. He had seen so much death these past days, heard so much weeping, and suddenly her life meant everything to him. He held her all that night; it was all she wanted.

As the sun rose over Galilee and shed its light westward across the hills toward Acre, Philippe carried Fabiana outside to see the dawn. There were tears in her eyes as she looked up into his face, yet she wasn't really crying. She pushed a small cloth pouch into his hand. The bag was filled with silver coins.

"For the cathedral of Paris," she said pitifully, "do you think Bishop Sully will take it from me?"

Before he could make an answer she had closed her eyes.

The sun was fully up. He held her lifeless body in his arms.

At Philippe's orders she was wrapped in linen and put into the trench with others who had died in the shadow of the Acre walls. He watched as it was done, lingering to say a prayer, then turned away.

W ITH THE FAILURE of the French to capture Acre after an entire week of siege, a doleful silence settled on the camp. Philippe remained closeted in his pavilion for many days, admitting no one into his presence. He passed the time brooding over disappointments, his diminished health, and the unlikelihood that he could mount another attack upon the city and take it before Richard was recovered from his illness.

It was imperative Philippe take Acre; time was running out.

Richard had already covered himself in enough glory at Sicily and Cyprus, and managed to make himself rich as the Sultan with all his conquests! Since coming to Acre he had been most of the time in sickbed, yet by his secret acts of treachery Richard had undermined all Philippe's hard-won respect and popularity.

But while Philippe sat alone with dark thoughts, Richard was planning his own attack against the walls of Acre. He was yet too weak to sit a horse or wear his armor, and he had himself carried about the camp in a litter, so that he might direct the operations of his men.

He sat beneath the shade of a leopardskin canopy, making notes on a roll of paper and reviewing what mistakes had already been made in attempts to capture Acre. He scoffed at the failed heroics of Philippe's men. No wonder the efforts of the French had come to nothing! The walls were far too stout to crumble from bombardment by the *mangonels* alone. Even tunnelling and sapping hadn't helped.

Richard's shrewd eye quickly solved the puzzle.

In order to allow a breach wide enough to accommodate his soldiers, individual stones from the wall would have to be loosened and removed. Once the crusaders were inside the city, it would be an easy task to gather up the starving garrison.

Richard needed men brave enough to mount the walls. It was a dangerous business because the defenders kept watch there night and day. But when he offered four gold *bezants* to anyone who would remove a single stone and bring it to the king as proof of the deed, hundreds of men volunteered. Within an hour of Richard's announcement, they were already at work.

Conrad of Montferrat lost no time in telling Philippe.

The news brought the French king from his tent, shouting for an audience with Richard. Philippe found him near the eastern edge of the camp, reclining on a litter and surrounded by cohorts. It enraged Philippe all the more to see that his cousin and vassal, Henri of Champagne, was among them. Only yesterday he'd come to the king, begging a loan. When Philippe had required he pledge the county of Champagne as security, Henri had struck an angry pose and gone off muttering oaths beneath his breath. Now he was here laughing with Richard, who had doubtless favored him with a gift of money just to spite Philippe.

It was intolerable.

Richard looked up to see Philippe approaching, and waved his arm. "Come drink with me," he shouted, "we shall toast our impending triumph!"

Philippe pushed past the others and stopped just in front of Richard. "Triumph?" he asked coldly.

"Of course," Richard laughed, holding out a cup of wine toward Philippe. "Acre shall be ours within a fortnight."

Philippe took the cup but did not drink from it.

The two men who had been lovers and now were not even friends stared at one another silently and with a measure of regret. Neither was at his most attractive: nearly hairless, skin peeling from their faces, eyes rheumy and dulled. It was not pleasant for either man to see the other so. After a moment, self-conscious, they looked away.

Philippe glowered down into his wine. "Our triumph..." Then he jerked his head up and faced Richard with accusing eyes. "When you have done everything possible to exclude me from it? When you have bribed every man within scent of your money purse to leave my service for yours? Triumph it well may be— but not mine!"

Richard was instantly angry. "Don't play these women's games of jealousy with me!" he shouted. "If you were truly a leader every man at Acre would know you for their lord. But instead you only wish to stay inside your tent and think up calumnies against me."

The French king stared back, unbelieving. "Until ten days ago I was too sick to leave my bed! If I kept to my tent, it was only for that reason."

"I too have been ill," Richard said, sounding self-righteous and patronizing, "and so I sympathize with you. But as kings and leaders we must put aside our problems and concern ourselves with a single goal: we must capture Acre!"

Capture Acre? What a liar Richard was! He lusted after his own successes; cared nothing if Philippe had a part in them. Treachery was everywhere! As he thought the words, he studied the expression on the face of his cousin Henri. Smugness. Satisfaction. Deceit.

Faithless friends, all of them.

Philippe turned the henap over and let the wine run into the sand. "I will not drink with you," he said to Richard, flinging the empty cup aside. "You speak easily of taking Acre, but where were you last week when it was within my grasp? Out of spite for me you withheld your army from the fighting, because you couldn't bear to see someone besides yourself covered in glory. Yet you presume to call *me* jealous? It is you, YOU are the one..."

Richard staggered to his feet, pushing aside the hands which reached to steady him. His blotched face was florid, and his lips were twisted in a sneer. "Jealous of someone as treacherous and niggardly as you? When that day comes I will throw myself off the topmost tower of that wall!"

Some of the men laughed. Others turned away, uneasy.

White-faced, Philippe stared back, seeing the death of their friendship. He felt such hate for Richard now, more than he'd ever known. It was as if there had never been anything but hate between them. Somewhere Henry Plantagenet must be laughing!

Philippe gazed off into the distance and made his decision. "Very well," he said, "take your victory if you can get it: but as you withheld your men, so shall I withhold mine. Lead a charge on Acre and you'll not find one French soldier at your side."

Richard's lips were set in a contemptuous pout. They were enemies after all, and Philippe was no more than the sly, cold-hearted bastard Richard had first conceived him to be, so many years ago. Mutual hatred for Henry Plantagenet had made them friends; that and sex. But the feelings of love and brotherhood had turned to stone, and now Richard realized that their aims had been very different all along.

His voice was sober, almost grim. "You will not fight beside me? That is your final word?"

Philippe looked at him and saw the death of Isabel, the humiliations at Messina, the betrayal here at Acre. "For the time being you may be sure of it," he said.

They stared at one another. Suddenly there was nothing left to say. Philippe turned his back and started walking slowly toward the camp.

After a night of brooding, Philippe changed his mind.

He made immediate plans for yet another assault upon the wall, hoping to beat out Richard's proposed attack by at least two days. Indeed, throughout the whole of July 2nd and 3rd, Philippe's men besieged the Accursed Tower with such demonic fury that it seemed the citadel must surely crumble.

It did not.

Once more the scaling ladders were hoisted on the walls, and once more the defenders burned them to ashes. Stones flew and men screamed; the stink of blood and burned flesh filled the air. Hot to take the victory out from under Richard's grasp, Philippe forgot his own safety and several times during the siege had to be dragged out of the way of an enemy firebolt.

But although they fought like madmen and mauled Acre badly in that siege, the Franks did not take the city. Once more they had to pull back without success. Philippe was deeply grieved by this lost opportunity. It was as if God Himself were playing favorites with the two kings: aiding Richard, while frustrating every attempt that Philippe made. Depressed, and feeling the onset of another illness, he hid himself away in his tent and wept.

He had made a terrible mistake in coming here. The entire endeavor had been a failure and a waste. It had cost him Isabel, his health, and Richard's friendship. There was nothing left. Nothing.

If only he had stayed in France.

How he missed Paris! It seemed so long ago that he had lain in his own bed, listening to the sounds of night traffic on the river. Philippe missed his children, his mother, Sully and the rest. But more than anything or anyone on earth, he yearned for Isabel.

Ironically it was only now that Philippe realized just how much her love had meant to him apart from sex. She had sweetened his life with her grace and beauty; made him happy in more ways than he could count. She had been his queen, his wife, his lover —perhaps she'd even been his friend. And yet Philippe had traded off her life and love for a part in this bitter episode.

Fool. *Fool.*

What the French crusaders had not been able to accomplish with their swords, King Richard's men achieved by removing stones. On July 8th a group of Richard's Poitevans crawled through the breach and were driven back by fierce blows struck by the defenders. But now it was only a matter of days before the breach could be widened to allow a full-scale attack.

The time for victory had come.

Seeing defeat for the garrison and unable to help, Saladin now sought to negotiate a hasty truce. For days he'd tried to distract the crusaders by ravaging the fields and vineyards around Acre and by circulating word that he was awaiting reinforcements from Egypt. But it did no good. The Christians were within an eyelash of capturing the city which they had besieged for so long. They would not negotiate, and they would not be stopped.

The Accursed Tower fell to the Knights of Christ on July 11th.

Neither of the kings were in the field when it happened. Philippe was sleeping and Richard was at his evening meal when a group of Pisans scaled the rubble and rushed into the city waving banners of the cross. Acre surrendered on the following day.

Philippe was willing to allow the six thousand Saracens left in the city to go free if they would abandon all they owned to the crusaders. But it was Richard who insisted on dictating the terms and they were harsh. After two years of siege and some hundred thousand Christian dead sacrificed in the attempt, the Lionheart was not about to sanction any mercies.

In the great hall of the Templars the articles of surrender were set down: *Release of the 1,500 prisoners held captive by Saladin; payment of 100,000 bezants each to Philippe and Richard; return of the True Cross.* Till these conditions were fulfilled (and the emirs of the city were given one month in which to accomplish them), the garrison of Acre and their families would stand as hostages to the word of their commanders.

Throughout the parley Philippe watched his fellow monarch with jaded interest. It was obvious that surrender and the spoils of it had not been enough for him. Richard wanted bloodshed. Philippe thought: he could run every prisoner through with his own sword and not feel a moment of regret.

He'd never known a man who was so in love with killing.

The flags of conquest flew above the city.

But in the days following the surrender of Acre it seemed that every man among the leaders of the crusade had a list of grievances. Conrad of Montferrat and Guy de Lusignan argued incessantly over who had what right to which throne. The Knights Templars and the Hospitallers pressed their claims to confiscated property. Duke Leopold, feeling cheated and ignored, revenged himself by ordering Richard's banner torn down and thrown into the dung pots. Not surprisingly, Richard retaliated by having Leopold's banner torn down and thrown into the dung pots. The duke never forgot that injury and later he gave Richard plenty of reason to regret the action.

Amid the peace there was no end of fighting.

Richard occupied the royal residence with his wife and sister, while Philippe established himself in the fortress belonging to the Templars. The kings sent letters back and forth by messenger, arguing over bits of conquest, trying to maneuver the other into a position of subservience. Philippe invoked the Treaty of Messina in order to claim half of Richard's haul on Cyprus. Richard countered with equal entitlements to half the territories in Flanders which the king of France had inherited through the death of Philip d'Alsace.

Philippe immediately withdrew his demands.

He was tired of squabbling—and he was ill again, this time with an attack of dysentery. Philippe knew that to remain for much longer in the East could mean his death, and because of this made a sudden decision to leave. He'd fought before the walls of Acre, he had sacrificed himself, fulfilled his obligations. He felt no shame in returning home to France.

There were problems, however.

Richard had vowed to spend another three years fighting in the Holy Land, and he expected all the other leaders of the crusade to make a similar commitment. His principal objective was to recapture Jerusalem. From what Philippe understood of the political and military complications inherent in such a plan, it could not be done. The Christians held Acre now. They should be satisfied with that.

Richard would not be satisfied.

How to tell him? Philippe was too ill to go to him in person and anyway he preferred not to look the impetuous Richard in the face with that announcement. Instead he delegated his cousin, the Bishop of Beauvais, and his vassal Hugh of Burgundy (a poor choice) to state his intentions to the King of England.

The news hardly surprised Richard, for he had expected it. The Capet had been flagging ever since they had left Tours a year ago! But he pretended great sorrow and chagrin to hear of Philippe's anticipated departure from Acre. He bowed his head, seeming to think on it a while before replying.

He used his most impressive voice. "I am sorry to learn that our cousin and friend Philippe of France has been indisposed once again by illness," he told the suppliants, "but I cannot lend my approval to his going, for by doing so he leaves undone the Great Work which he should have come prepared to accomplish."

His keen eyes traveled the distance between the two men. They were uncomfortable in their duty, ashamed they should have been the ones chosen to mouth their overlord's disgrace. Richard played silently with their embarrassment for a moment before he pronounced his own judgment on the matter.

"I grieve for Philippe's decision, for by yielding to his weakness, he has brought everlasting shame upon himself and his race." Richard managed a pained, pretended smile and hurried on. "However, if he fears for his health in staying here, I shall not be the one to stand in his way."

The bishop lowered his head in sad appreciation. "My king and cousin shall be glad to hear of your generous dispensation."

"Indeed it is generous," Richard answered with a tone of gravity, "for I could surely profit by having his counsel in the time ahead." He paused wickedly, one eyebrow arched. "I assume he has other reasons. For instance, if he has heard news, as I have, from the late-arriving galleys, it is no wonder he wishes to return to France."

"News?" Hugh's ruddy face went quizzical. "What news is that?"

Richard clasped his hands together in his lap and stared off toward the far wall, feigning an expression of pity. "The news of prince Louis's illness, of course. I have heard that for many weeks he has lain near death, convulsed by a strange and sudden illness."

The bishop's face grew pale and he began to tremble. "My lord knows nothing of this!" he exclaimed.

Richard's smile was cold, his voice without a trace of charity. "Then you had best to tell him, in order that he make his departure all the sooner."

The two men bowed and left. Richard smiled as he watched them go. Let Philippe Capet see what it was to have a lie turned back on him; let him discover what hate could be got from disappointed love!

Henri of Champagne was standing nearby, occupied with admiring Richard's exquisite collection of hunting birds. "Is it true?" he asked when they were alone. "Is Philippe's son really dying?"

Richard looked ponderously at the plate of fruits before him, fingering a honeyed apricot as he spoke. "I don't know; how could I? Do I have eyes to look across the sea?"

Revenge. Henri shrugged. He understood it well enough. He relinquished the falcon to its perch and strolled over to where the king sat, engrossed now in his eating. Henri barely suppressed a smile. With his colorful attire and head covered by fine bits of newly-grown hair, Richard looked rather like a huge, exotic bird himself!

Just as quickly Henri chased the unkind thought away. In the past few weeks spent in Richard's service, he had prospered more than in all the time he'd worked for his penurious cousin Philippe. And Richard was such lively good company; always entertaining, always gay. He had lifted the code of chivalry to an art, and a man of Henri's tastes admired that.

He poured himself some wine, then sniffed at it to guess its flavor. Cherry. Isabel's favorite. He looked across at Richard. "You hate Philippe very much, don't you?"

He finished eating and pushed the plate aside. "There was a time when I loved him. But I let love blind me to his true character. He is cold. Friendship and love mean nothing to him."

Henri tasted the wine. Deep and sweet. It was like drinking Isabel. He reached across and patted Richard's shoulder. "Then you should be glad that he is leaving. Now you are the undisputed master here, and shall have all you wish."

"Yes," Richard said and pushed himself up from the table. "I have great things to do here in the East. I must put all of my old grievances behind me." He made the smallest attempt to smile. "It is not good to dwell upon the past."

Henri drained the cup and set it down. "I know," he said.

By his decision to leave the Holy Land, Philippe Capet had lost the respect of nearly every man among the crusading force. The lone exception was Conrad of Montferrat, who had become his closest friend and frequent bedmate since the estrangement with Richard.

It was Conrad who assured him Richard's story of Louis's illness was a lie; Conrad who handled the cache of paperwork which had to be dealt with before the king left Acre. Philippe was glad of his help and his companionship.

There was a final meeting with Richard, for there were certain things to be decided, among them the question of who would hold title to the crown of Jerusalem. Richard and Philippe convened a court to hear the claims of both Conrad and Guy. At last a ruling was made in favor of both men. Guy de Lusignan would keep the title of king until his death, at which time Conrad would succeed. Guy's claim was based upon his marriage to the late queen Sibylla; Conrad's on the basis of his recent marriage to her eighteen-year-old half sister Isabella. Both Guy and Conrad were satisfied with the way the matter was disposed of.

And so it was over, except for a few incidental ceremonies.

Philippe was asked to swear upon a casket full of holy relics that he would do nothing to disturb Richard's lands in France nor make any attempt to seize his territorial domains. Richard knew from past experience how little an oath meant to the French king, yet there was nothing he could do but believe his word, and hope all would be well.

For his own part, Philippe turned over the entire contingent of his army to Richard. This included some ten thousand knights, and over twenty thousand infantry; also their horses, weapons, and grain stores. He was given one-third of his portion from the surrender settlement, which Richard advanced to him in gold (since he had yet to receive payment from the Moslems). The full amount was scheduled to be sent to Philippe in Paris before the close of the year. And that was it.

There was no formal parting, not even a goodbye.

On the last day of July 1191, Philippe and a small group of his personal bodyguard simply rode out of Acre by way of the north gate. Conrad of Montferrat traveled with them as far as Tyre, and Philippe lingered there a few days, to summon all his health and strength for the return voyage to Brindisi. From there he would make his way overland across Italy and France, homeward. Philippe hoped to reach Paris before Christmas.

Tyre was a relaxing interlude. Conrad and the king parted as friends, pledging to keep faith with one another. They both wished for Richard's downfall, and their minds were full of subtle methods of conspiracy. For himself, Philippe was already planning an invasion of the Aquitaine upon his return to France. But for now it was enough to simply dream of seeing Paris again.

He and Conrad exchanged fond kisses. "Goodbye my friend," the king said, "throughout my stay here, you were the only one to show me any loyalty."

Conrad nodded humbly. "I was happy to serve you in every way. You did much for me on my behalf." They kissed again.

It was August 5th as Philippe's entourage set sail from Tyre.

There were tears in the king's eyes as he watched the blurred line of the coast recede. His business in this terrible place was done!

END PART VI

Epilogue
Autumn, 1192

$\mathbb{R}$ICHARD lingered in the East for another fourteen months.
He won splendid victories at Arsûf and Jaffa and twice he was able to bring his armies within five miles of Jerusalem. But that was as close as they got. Richard stood atop a hill outside of the Holy city, his face covered by a shield. He had said that if he could not take Jerusalem, he did not wish to even glimpse it.

In the end he signed a covenant with Saladin which allowed the right of pilgrimage for Christians to come and worship at the church of the Holy Sepulchre. This was a profound achievement, but not the glorious victory Richard had envisioned.

He was sorely discouraged.

The army had lost heart. The same men who had fought so valiantly before the walls of Acre had since given themselves up to the riotous pleasures of debauchery. Why should they fight the Infidel when it was so much more satisfying to drink Saracen wine and taste the caresses of these mysterious Eastern women?

Desertions were commonplace. There was no honor anymore.

Richard grieved for the attitude of his men. They had fought so hard, sacrificed so much and now it seemed as though they didn't even remember what it had all been for. They clamored like children to take Jerusalem: it was *Holy Sepulchre or die!* For what was the use of fighting other battles in other cities when it was the holy place they had come to free? If Richard would not lead them there, then the soldiers were content to loll in the brothels and taverns of Acre and Ascalon.

Richard grew ill with his vexation. How could he make the men understand? The army was too small now, too weak to attempt capture of a city so well secured by the enemy as Jerusalem. A battle now would give the crusaders a worse defeat than they had known at the Horns of Hattin, when Guy de Lusignan had all but annihilated his army by his own foolishness. Disillusioned and heartsick, Richard made his pact with the ailing Saladin—and commenced preparations for a return to England.

His great adventure had come to an end.

Many things had come to pass since Philippe Capet had taken his leave more than a year before. Guy de Lusignan had retired to Cyprus to reign as king there, and Conrad of Montferrat had been named king of Jerusalem by acclamation. Then unexpectedly, Conrad was set upon and killed by a group of Moslem fanatics. The throne of Jerusalem was left empty, and young queen Isabella was a widow with the eight month makings of a child in her belly.

And that was how Henri of Champagne became king of Jerusalem.

Richard had sent him to Tyre to halt the rioting which had resulted from the news of Conrad's death, and Isabella fell in love with the handsome Champagnois on sight. She begged him to marry her and promised him the crown. Richard was consulted, gave consent, and so within a week of Conrad's murder, Count Henri and the pregnant widow were married. Isabella was young and beautiful and not without charm; it was an easy thing to be husband to her, as Conrad had discovered. Henri could not love her; his love lay cold beneath the stones of Notre Dame. But this other queen pleased him well, in herself, and all she brought to him.

So when Richard made his plans to leave Syria he delegated the newly-crowned Henri as his replacement. He was a worthy administrator and a great soldier; he would keep peace in the places which the Christians had won. Henri was a man of dignity and honor, a fine example to the troops who served him. But he was not Richard—no man was—and with the Lionheart's departure for England, the Third Crusade was ended.

Richard had lived more intensely these past two years than ever before in his career; it was for this kind of life he had been born. But he could no longer ignore the disturbing rumors from the West. Letters from Eleanor confirmed the dangers. There hads been minor skirmishes with the French on the Norman border, a few uprisings in the Aquitaine; so far she had been able to keep the incidents from getting out of hand. But recently an ominous and too-familiar cordiality had sprung up between Prince John and Philippe Capet. How serious the friendship was, Eleanor could not be sure, but she did not know how much longer she could contain it.

So Richard put his wife and sister on a ship bound for the coast of Italy and promised to join them in a few weeks. He could not have guessed it would be much, much longer.

In Paris, as the year 1192 drew to its close, Philippe passed the first anniversary of his return to the city. Christmas was quiet, spent in the company of Adele, Edythe and his children. How proud he was of the three children he had made; fatherhood was the greatest joy he knew. Jacquie-Marie was now a little beauty of eight, not so much younger than Isabel had been when he'd married her. She had spirit, and loved to play at boys' games more than her brother did.

Sweet little Louis! He had nearly died while Philippe was in the East, so Richard's cruel story had been true after all. Adele and Sully had brought holy relics from Chartres and St. Denis to heal the boy. Ironically, Louis had been cured of his fever on the very day his father's army struck the fatal blow against the walls of Acre.

Philippe was delighted with the son Edythe had born. Pierre was a darling baby who had his father's dark hair and coloring; a healthy child. Philippe only wished Louis was as robust. He had Isabel's delicacy and tendency to catch colds and fever. Only last month the boy had been bedridden for a week with illness. Philippe worried endlessly about him.

And there were other worries to contend with.

If rumors could be believed, Richard was on his way back to England. What had happened to the pledge of three years' service in the Holy Land? The vow to take Jerusalem? Philippe's appraisal of the whole crusade was cynical and bitter. While news of Richard's triumphs had made their way back to Europe, so had tales of his atrocities: the ruthless slaughter of children, the beheading of some three thousand Moslem hostages on the barren plain outside of Acre.

Now he was coming back, and the French king was not pleased. He had anticipated a longer period of time in which to frustrate the borders of the Angevin domains. The crafty Eleanor had blocked his every attempt to snatch a piece of land here and there from the Plantagenets. But if Richard was returning soon, Philippe was uncertain of what to do. Unwilling to forsake his plans of an armed invasion of Normandy, he was still too cautious to pursue it in the wake of Richard's arrival. Philippe did not want to risk a confrontation with his arch-enemy on the battlefield.

He feared Richard, even from afar. Ever since his homecoming, Philippe had allowed his natural pessimism to get the best of him. He took extreme care for his personal safety, going about with a full bodyguard of thirty men; keeping soldiers on watch outside his room at night. He had his food and wine tasted before every meal, and nearly always slept uneasily. These precautions were taken in order to thwart attempts by the assassins which Philippe was certain Richard would send from the East to poison him, or run his body through with a sword.

He was anxious, always nervous.

And then inexplicably, a miracle. In the early days of January, 1193—a letter came to the Cité Palais from Emperor Henry VI, Barbarossa's son and successor; it was in his own hand. Philippe's interest turned to eagerness as he read. The words seemed to leap off the paper at him. His breath went rapid and his hands shook in excitement.

It was a sign, an omen. God was on the side of France.

Cyprus was Richard's last safe harbor, and he dallied there a while with his good friend Guy de Lusignan before putting out to sea. Luck was not with him, for once again his fleet was scattered by a violent storm, and after being twice shipwrecked, the king's vessel was driven up onto the Dalmatian coast.

At this point Richard began to make his way overland disguised as an ordinary pilgrim, returning from the East. It was necessary for him to conceal his identity from the Byzantines whom he had so offended during his earlier stays on Sicily and Cyprus. Capture for the purpose of ransoming was a common threat to any monarch traveling without the protection of his army. Richard knew this and hid himself as best he could.

But it was futile for this tall, majestic man whose bearing and appearance proclaimed royalty, to attempt anonymity for very long. Richard got only as far as Vienna before his deception was uncovered. Immediately he was taken prisoner, and turned over to the custody of the Duke of Austria.

Leopold had not forgotten the incident of the dung pots.

He shut Richard up in a drafty fortress on the Danube and sent news of his illustrious captive to Ratisbon where Henry VI was holding Christmas court. The emperor's joy matched his cousin's. The King of England was no friend of his.

And so Richard was kept locked away while the duke and the emperor haggled over his custody with all the dignity of fishwives in a market stall. They both knew what prestige there was in holding such a valuable prisoner, and what reward could be gotten for his release. Another giddy prospect was the money which could be had from sources who did not wish to see Richard Plantagenet set free.

Henry pondered that, then wrote his letter to the French king.

The news of Richard's capture raced through Europe like a river and in it John could see the promise of his own liberation. So far, he had been very careful in his dealings with the king of France— hinting only in the vaguest terms that he might be willing to fall in with Philippe's conspiracy against the absent Richard. As long as his older brother could appear at any time to demand an accounting, he'd been afraid to commit himself to any scheme.

But now fortune was whispering in John's ear.

Richard might never return! He could die in prison or be held indefinitely by his vindictive captors. Even if a hefty ransom was agreed to, there was no guarantee it could be raised in a land impoverished by the measures which Richard had initiated to support his crusade.

So England was without a king—until another could be found.

By the end of February correspondence between John and Philippe had increased to three or four letters a week. The messages were filled with talk of friendship, but did not neglect discussion of Normandy and the retrieval of the Vexin. Finally John was invited to come to Paris.

He did not refuse.

* * *

Philippe was growing weary of Sibylla.

Two summers ago on the banks of the Rhône he had promised to make her his mistress when he came back from Syria, and two days after his arrival in Paris she was in his bed once more. From that time hardly a week passed without at least one meeting between them. The gossip of the marketplace was that the king spent more nights at Gonesse than at the Cité Palais.

Sibylla was no fit substitute for Isabel—no woman was—but she was the closest he could find. She had the same blood, the same breasts, the same brazen Flemish pride. Many were the times he had loathed Isabel for that pride, but the natural sweetness of her temperament had made even her worst moods bearable.

But Sibylla was a shrew.

She demanded without Isabel's grace, sulked without Isabel's charm. And although she claimed to be happy only when she was with Philippe, she inevitably spoiled their meetings with her temper and her incessant carping.

Her primary complaint was Edythe. How jealous she was of the lame serving girl who had borne a healthy son to the king! Sibylla knew that Edythe still lived at the Cité Palais, that she was the one Philippe lay with when he was not with her. How could he bed anyone so ugly? How could he possibly desire her?

Sibylla wanted a child by him. Philippe did not want one from her. Because of that he seldom left his seed in her. It was one thing for them to be lovers; he felt no shame in that. But to make a child with the sister of his dead wife was something that he could not conscience and God would not forgive.

Sibylla was equally unforgiving. "Why can't *I* come to live with you in Paris?" she asked him one night in early March as they lay together in bed.

It was cold; they could hear the wind blowing outside. Philippe pulled her closer into his arms and silenced her complaining with a kiss. "I've explained that to you a dozen times," he sighed. "It would look sluttish to have my dead wife's sister living under my roof."

She licked at the scars upon his chest, then smiled up at him. "You are king. A little gossip cannot touch you."

He grabbed her by the arm and shook her roughly. "Idiot! I

don't care about the mutterings of tavern bitches and bath house whores. But I cannot risk criticism from the Church; not now when I'm just about to move on Normandy."

Normandy, always Normandy!

"But I'm so lonely when you aren't with me," she wailed.

"Then you must teach yourself restraint," he said and bent to kiss her lips.

She settled in his arms and closed her eyes, trying to convince herself that he belonged to her, trying to banish the image of her sister. She and Philippe rarely spoke of Isabel, but the memory was always there—scented and mysterious—between them.

It was Isabel he really wanted; Sibylla knew that. It was *her* face he saw, *her* body that he fondled. He dreamed of a dead woman while Sibylla lay, warm and living in his arms! It was cruel, and it was her own fault. She gave him every chance to hurt her, because even that was better than not having him at all.

Sibylla reached to stroke his face. It was such a handsome face, though he had never quite managed to lose the haggard look he had brought back from the Holy Land. There was disillusionment in his expression, and something behind his eyes had already begun to look old. He was thinner too, and much of his hair was gone. But his body was stronger and more beautiful than before, laced with the scars of his achievements in the East.

"You're perfect," she murmured, "so perfect...."

Philippe took up a handful of her soft hair, examining its rich brown color that was striped with gold in candlelight. She was a sweet little trinket, but many times he wanted to be rid of her; it was a relationship fraught with difficulties. Sibylla was jealous, obsessive; a bitch. But she was the only woman who halfway reminded him of Isabel, and because of that, he needed her.

"Sibylla," he began, "you must try not to love me so much."

There was a note of apology in his voice but she would not let him finish. She kissed his throat over and over. "You might just as well ask me to open up my veins and let every drop of blood spill out."

He rolled Sibylla over on her back and sprawled over her. "I warned you," he whispered.

And she whispered back, "Someday you *will* love me, Philippe. I know you will."

No, not her; not anyone.

He felt the muscles in her belly leap as he pushed her thighs apart. Her sweet sable nest was already edged with tiny drops of wetness and he stroked it gently. He loved the look of hunger in her eyes, the tenseness in her face. Once she had been an arrogant little prude, but Philippe had made her a woman. And now she could never get enough of him. At this moment that was excitement enough.

"Sweet girl," he muttered, and pushed into her.

In England, John was telling everyone that Richard was dead.

He almost believed it himself. Certainly it *could* be true; and anyway, regardless of what the truth was, Richard was not there and that gave John the right to assume the crown. At least he felt justified in trying for it.

It was not going to be easy for Henry Plantagenet's last born son to consolidate his power, that was sure. There was Eleanor to contend with. She would support Richard with her final breath, so there was no hope for John in that quarter. The English clergy, who had supported John's side in a conflict with chancellor Longchamp two years ago, were firmly united on the side of Richard. So were the barons. Even William Marshal, who had once hated Richard, refused to declare John's accession lawful.

There was already a great rush to collect Richard's ransom.

John sat at Dover for a while, unsure of what to do, pondering his future. Then he crossed to Normandy to confront the barons. He came to the fortress of Alençon, ostensibly to discuss the matter of Richard's imprisonment, but instead he made a bold proposal to the men assembled there. If they would swear an oath of fealty to him, John said, he would protect them against the French king, who even now was preparing an invasion of Normandy.

He had expected cold refusals. Instead they laughed.

There was only one man they would recognize as Duke of Normandy and he now languished in a German jail. If Richard was dead, God would send them a sign, they said. But all the rumors coming out of Würzburg (where Richard had been moved) declared that the king was not only in good health but in good spirits—charming his jailers, and engaged in writing letters to his mother, urging her to raise the money for his ransom.

The barons stood firm. So long as Richard lived he was their duke. John was no more than the ruthless fool who had abandoned a loving father on his deathbed and now sought to rob his unfortunate brother of the crown.

He would get no help in his treachery from them.

In mid-March John came to Paris to ask Philippe's help.

There was no other course. The French king planned to invade Normandy no matter what John chose to do, so it seemed foolish not to fall in with him. Now that the barons had made their decision known, John was in no position to defend Normandy against Philippe and his soldiers.

Philippe welcomed the last of Henry's sons to the Cité Palais.

"How good it is to have you here at last," he said to John on the first evening after they had feasted alone together, and then settled back to take their wine. "Last autumn when I invited you to Paris you let your mother talk you out of coming." Philippe's smile was goadingly sarcastic. "How did you manage to convince her on this occasion?"

John felt uneasy. He didn't know Philippe very well, and it was hard to face those cold black eyes. "I always meant to come," he offered weakly, ignoring the haughty reference to Eleanor, "but I had to see what the barons of England and Normandy were willing to offer first."

"How well you phrase it," Philippe smiled. "And what did you discover?"

John looked dismally into his wine cup. A blurred, red face looked back at him, taunting of failure. It was humiliating to admit defeat to the powerful king of the Franks, but John shrugged at his own embarrassment and said, "Neither Normandy nor England will accept me as their lord so long as Richard lives."

Philippe tipped his cup to drink. The wine tasted sweet as it flowed over his tongue. He swallowed, then said decisively, "They should be made to believe that he is dead."

"That is no longer possible," John answered. "Bishop Walter of Coutances has been in contact with him, and so has Eleanor."

Irritated, Philippe drummed his fingers on the table. "And is there any chance of . . . an accident?"

John laughed. "He is too well guarded."

"Damn," Philippe muttered.

A hint of green flashed in John's eyes. "Do you really wish my brother dead? I thought you only wanted to extend his imprisonment as long as possible."

"Does it matter to either of us what happens, so long as he is kept from returning to England?" Philippe asked.

John looked away, ashamed to answer, for in his heart he agreed with Philippe. They drank in silence for a while, listening to the sound of wind stirring up ashes in the fire grate, and hounds growling over bones in the deepest recesses of the hall. John, who had the same taste for luxury as all of his brothers, looked around the vacant, echoing room and wondered how any man could bear to live in such a place. It was austere and ugly, stinking of mold from centuries of too much rain and river mist.

It was here, perhaps in this room, that young Henry Plantagenet had met Eleanor for the first time. John seemed to see it in his mind, as if it were a play and he was watching. But then another image took its place, and he saw a dying man upon a sickbed, weeping, his arms outstretched.

He closed his eyes and tried to think of happy things.

Philippe's voice startled him. "The emperor will no doubt try to extort a fabulous sum from me in return for keeping Richard as his continual prisoner." His voice went low and serious. "But I will have to pay it, there is no other way." Once more the always nervous fingers tapped against the edge of the table. "Do you know if a price for his ransom has been set? Has your mother told you anything? Or anyone?"

John's soft, girlish mouth was peevish. "No one will tell me anything," he complained. Then suddenly his whole expression turned lively with mischievous intent as he grinned, "Can you believe it? They don't trust my motives."

Philippe didn't smile. His gaze was unrelenting. "Can I?"

John swallowed his wine in gulps and fidgeted a little in his chair. Trust was on his mind too. Was Philippe really interested in helping him, or was this interview just a way of leading another Plantagenet into a trap?

Wine had made John bold enough to speak his mind. "I could ask the same of you," he said to Philippe. "I've known you for so long and yet so little. I don't know what to expect, or even if I can find it within myself to trust you."

So he was not a complete fool after all.

Philippe nodded gravely, and reached across the table to lay his hand close over John's. "Then know me better. Stay here with me in Paris for a while."

John peered uneasily into his wine. "As a friend? A conspirator?" He paused for a moment. "Or something else?"

Philippe leaned back, arms folded behind his head. "What does it matter, so long as we achieve our purpose?"

"Our purpose is to be rid of Richard."

"No, my friend," Philippe corrected, "our purpose is to *torment* Richard." He waited to see if John had understood his meaning. "I know your brother very well. He is vain. If he thought that you and I were lovers, it would give him something more to brood over while he sits in prison and waits for his throne to be pulled out from under him."

John thought on that, then stumbled drunkenly to his feet.

"You're right, you know," he said and took the hand Philippe held out to him. "Let's go to bed."

After all the details of their treason had been agreed upon, Philippe left John behind in Paris and went off with his army to besiege the city of Rouen. First, he captured several of the border castles on the Norman *march* (including the fortress of Gisors), then overran Aumale and Eu.

The Norman resistance was beginning to crumble.

The tide of victory turned at Rouen, when the citizens opened the gates to Philippe's army and bade them enter without fear of retaliation. It was a bluff thought up by Queen Eleanor (who had ordered it), but the French could not afford the challenge, lest a full army lay in ambush to capture them.

They would have to wait until another time to take Rouen.

Philippe emptied his wine casks into the river and withdrew.

No man needed an oracle to help him read the signs these days.

Prince John was living with his brother's sworn enemy at the Cité Palais, and Philippe was busy taking bits of the wild Normandy frontier for himself. He gave several of the captured fortresses to John as a "token of his love" but the *castellans* refused to surrender the property of their rightful duke. Furious at the insult, John took a troop of Philippe's soldiers north to have his way with those who had forbidden his claim.

Meanwhile throughout the whole of France and England thousands of pilgrims and fighting men were coming home from the crusade, and each one of them had a story to tell of Richard's splendid bravery. Such tales contrasted greatly with the ugly stories of duplicity and pettiness which Philippe had told upon his return, in order that he might blacken Richard's name.

But heroism won out in the end.

Opinion began to turn against the conspirators.

Emperor Henry VI had set the price of Richard's freedom at one hundred fifty thousand silver marks—and suddenly everyone in England was scurrying to help collect the money. It was awkward at first. With all the counties and estates Richard had given him, John controlled nearly one third of England's revenue. Without his cooperation it had seemed unlikely that such a vast amount of money could be got.

But Richard had more friends than he knew.

As the legend of his triumphs spread through villages and towns, the churches opened up their coffers willingly to share their wealth and poorfolk came with meager offerings to help in purchasing their king's release. These monies were given over to Hugh de Pudsey, the aging Bishop of Durham, who was Eleanor's own choice to serve as a treasurer for the ransom.

Slowly, but with steadiness, the money pile grew.

Back in Paris, Philippe was getting nervous.

Hastening to strengthen his ties to John, he proposed to give him Alais as a bride. What better way for the French king to prove his contempt for Richard than to give the rejected Alais to his brother? Philippe gave only minor consideration to the fact that John was still married to Hadwisa, and Alais was securely locked away in the fortress of Rouen, closely watched by Eleanor's guards.

Rumors of all this subversive strategy found their way back to Richard via the letters of his friends. He was hardly surprised. John, always so envious of his older brother's domains and titles, was a perfect candidate for deeds of treason. But however bitter Richard felt about this latest series of events, he could not find it in his heart to blame John. Though his younger brother may have had the personality to aspire to evil, he did not have the resourcefulness to implement it.

Only one man could devise such a criminous scheme.

John had merely been the most recent victim of Philippe's cold and ignominious charm. It flayed Richard to think of them together, hot with their passion and deceit. Oh, for the chance to face Philippe on a field of battle—to see the cowardly French monarch and his army put to rout!

But he would have to wait for that sweet satisfaction.

His only hope now was to separate John from Philippe. Richard knew his brother well enough to realize that he would not be swayed from his purpose by mere threats. Giddy with superficial power, he doubtless felt himself invulnerable to any warning words from Richard. John's conceit always blinded him to anything but the closest dangers. But Philippe was a subtle and suspicious man who could be bribed by the promise of an easy conquest.

Immediately Richard drew up a treaty which ceded a portion of eastern Normandy to the French king, together with the promise of twenty thousand silver marks to be paid upon his return from exile. Richard sent off the document with hopes that it would satisfy Philippe's ambition for a while. It was Capet's nature to prefer lands gotten by extortion to those won by combat in the field.

Meanwhile, Richard waited for news of his release.

In the past month, the emperor had improved the conditions of his imprisonment. Richard was allowed to hold court now, and meet with emissaries from England. It was better than the harsh confinement he'd been forced to endure under Leopold: a drafty cell and bad food. But whatever the conditions, he was still a captive.

Each night he dreamed of freedom, and vengeance on his enemies.

Laughter.

Philippe could hear it in his council room, all the way from the great hall. He frowned in irritation. It meant that John was drinking with members of the household bodyguard again. Recently it seemed to be his only interest; that and hawking.

Later John came swaggering in with a falcon on his arm.
"We're going hunting," he said, "do you want to come?"

Philippe gave a glance toward him, then bent once more to his
paperwork. "I'm busy, John," he grumbled. "Can't you find anything more profitable to occupy your time?"

The pleasant expression turned instantly sour. "Hunting *is* a
man's occupation."

The king shoved aside his papers with a grunt of aggravation.
"John, you should be in Normandy with the army instead of here
wasting time at court."

John struck a bored pose. He had heard *that* from Philippe
before. "Your cousin Robert of Dreux is there. He's more a soldier than I am. Why should *I* go?"

Philippe tapped his knuckles on the table. Talking to John was
sometimes no more rewarding than talking to a child. How like
Harry he was. Logic had no part in his thinking. "Listen, John,"
he said, "we need more than just the presence of an army there.
It is your responsibility to try and win the Norman barons to our
side."

"I've tried that," John complained, "but they don't like me."

The king's patience was growing feeble, but he tried hard to
keep his voice even. "Diplomacy is our insurance against war. We
can't risk another failure at Rouen, you know that! If Richard is
kept away much longer, the barons will have no other choice but
to accept you as their lord, and through that comes our chance to
win the rest of Richard's continental territories." His voice rose to
a sharp tone of reprimand. "So go and do what only you can do
for our cause: negotiate!"

John shook the bird loose and watched it rise to the ceiling,
and settle itself on a perch below the high window. *Lucky fowl to be
so free of all constraints.* John slumped to a stool. "Will you come
with me?" he asked.

Philippe got to his feet and came to stand behind him, hands
resting on John's shoulders. "We have to be careful. We must
preserve the appearance of caution. Pope Celestine has warned
us that an invasion of Richard's lands could bring the interdict
upon us or even excommunication. He may be bluffing but we
can't be sure. So much depends on what the emperor is willing to
do. Twice he's driven up the price of keeping Richard prisoner.

If I can see my way to paying him what he asks, we have no worries for a while."

John tilted his head back to look up at Philippe. "I know."

"Good." Philippe bent to kiss his cheek. "Just remember: we are *this* close to getting everything we want."

John sighed in admiration. Philippe was so practical, so smart! "When do you want me to leave?" he asked.

Philippe's arms went tight around his friend's shoulders. He managed a little laugh. "Stay the night here at least, for my sake."

They talked some more and drank a toast to pledge eternal fellowship. As they kissed, Philippe sucked the wine from John's mouth and swallowed it.

Two days later he smiled as John rode away to Normandy.

Philippe had not divulged the whole of his plot against Richard to the younger Plantagenet. There was more: a sweeping plan of conquest that could lift his own fortunes to the sphere of legend and end Angevin dominance forever.

Philippe was planning to invade England.

Two months ago he had concluded a crafty pact with Denmark's King Cnut. The alliance promised France free access to the shores of England from the Danish coast—ships, soldiers, and ten thousand silver marks—and all toward the purpose of invasion.

That was the prize.

The penalty was marriage to Cnut's sister, Ingeborg.

Philippe knew nothing of her, only what he had been told by the ambassadors from Cnut's court. They said she was beautiful (a probable exaggeration), well-educated, and blameless. She was close to twenty and had never been involved in a betrothal, which gave him a suspicion. But when Philippe was assured that she was blond, that, together with all the rest, convinced him.

Personally he was not anxious to take another wife. There was something vaguely unwholesome in making a vow when he still felt himself bound by vivid memory to Isabel. *He could never hope to have again what he'd had with her.* But the prize of this new marriage, the lure of triumph over Richard, was too strong to be ignored.

At the start of summer he went up to Amiens to meet his bride.

It was over almost before it had begun.

On August 14, 1193, Philippe married Ingeborg at the cathedral in Amiens—and by the following morning, after her coronation, he had changed his mind about the marriage. Without any explanation he ordered the ambassadors from Cnut's court to take the princess back to her own land.

He would not live with her as wife or queen.

William of Rheims begged his nephew to reconsider.

"You wanted this alliance very much," he reminded Philippe.

The king was pacing back and forth across the floor and nervously wiping the sweat from his face with trembling hands. He was pale, on the edge of illness. William had never seen him look so disturbed.

"To hell with the alliance!" Philippe shouted. "I will not sacrifice myself to a piece of paper. I am a *man*, uncle. I have a man's desires. And a treaty warms no bed at night."

"But surely," William argued, "she is much like any other of her sex. She is a pretty girl, and sweet tempered. Whatever she does not know I'm sure you could teach her."

Philippe turned his face away and would not answer.

Priests. What did they know of women?

The truth was that in person Ingeborg so repelled him he had not been able to consummate the marriage on the one night they had spent together. Well, thank God for that now, for it would be all the easier to obtain the annulment that he wanted.

"Annulment?" William sounded shocked when Philippe told him of the plan. "But Ingeborg has been crowned already and by my own hand! You cannot cast her off by some mere caprice. Philippe, you are courting troubles if you do this, for the Church will have some pretty things to say on such a matter."

"Don't be a fool," Philippe snorted. "The Church accepts annulment as easily as pigs take to mud. My own father after fifteen years of marriage to Eleanor and children by her, got free of her as quick as that." He snapped his fingers in William's face.

"That was different," William protested, "both of them favored the divorce, there was no injured party. But this poor girl

—one day a wife and queen, the next cast off? It is dishonorable. And she *is* your crowned queen by right of law."

"Crowned or uncrowned makes no difference," Philippe declared. "She cannot be my queen if she is not my wife. And I say that she is not."

And he would say no more.

Richard was freed in February, 1194.

His aging mother had traveled all the way to Mainz in order to be present when he was set free. She knew, more than anyone, what happiness he felt at the end of his confinement. Eleanor had not forgotten what it was like to be a prisoner.

England welcomed back their king with shouts of joy.

After he had seen to the security of his kingdom and reclaimed his crown, Richard prepared to cross over into France in middle May. The news of his coming was met with terror by all who had schemed for his destruction.

But no one was more terrified than John.

Uneasy with the news himself, Philippe had sent a message to John in Normandy, ending with these warning words: *Look to your own safety, for the devil is loose in the land.*

Indeed, John did not know where to turn.

He couldn't trust Philippe to protect him against his brother's fury. It seemed equally useless to appeal to Eleanor. She had always loved Richard best of all her sons. John was just the unloved youngest child made in his mother's womb at a time when she already hated Henry. The memory soured any affection she might have felt.

In the end John resolved to make his peace with Richard.

The two men were reunited at Lisieux in Normandy after almost four years of separation. John was timid and penitent, afraid to look his famous brother in the face. But Richard, who loved the act of forgiving, was happy to forgive John.

"I understand," he said. "Whatever you have done was not your fault. Philippe enticed you with his evil lies, and in the end he would have betrayed you just as he did me."

The significance of what he'd done had not hit him fully till that moment, listening to Richard's words of reconciliation. John hesitated, then stumbled forward and fell weeping at his brother's feet.

T̲HE BREACH between Philippe and Richard never healed.

They spent the next five years in a series of wars against one another. Philippe kept up his steady and determined raids on the borders of Normandy, but he was always beaten back in the end. The only gain he made against his rival in all that time was in August of 1195 when Richard allowed him to take back Alais from the tower of Rouen. Philippe swiftly arranged a marriage for her with the Count of Ponthieu, so that he might have a strategically placed ally to ward off threats from Normandy and Flanders.

Baldwin of Hainault had died earlier in the year; his wife a few months before him. Isabel's brother ruled in both Hainault and Flanders now, and he had made himself the ally of King Richard. In Boulogne a cousin of the Hainault family, Count Reginald, had also turned against Philippe and thrown in his lot with the English king.

Philippe's political fortunes were at their lowest ebb.

He was fighting a paper war with Pope Celestine over the Ingeborg situation. The Danish princess was still asserting her claims and demanding that they be recognized by both her husband and the Church. Philippe was equally willful, keeping Ingeborg imprisoned in a series of convents. He swore over and over that she was not his wife; that he would never live with her.

But the Church would not allow him a divorce.

Despite that, Philippe married for a third time in June, 1196, and took as his wife Agnes of Meran, the daughter of a petty noble from Bavaria. This was Philippe's bold way of putting a challenge to the pope. Now he would be forced to dissolve the union with Ingeborg.

For no man would dare to make the King of France a bigamist.

But the pope did dare. And the fight went on.

In mid-November Philippe came to Barbeaux in Melun to pray at the tomb of his father. From there he continued south to Fontainebleau to visit Edythe at the fine chateau which he had provided for her and their young son. She had left the Cité Palais when Philippe brought Agnes there to live, but Philippe sought her out whenever his travels took him anywhere near Fontainebleau.

More than any other woman since Isabel, he loved Edythe. She gave him the peace he needed and the tenderness he craved. Her love was genuine and perfect as a prayer—not motivated by any purpose other than love itself.

Edythe laid a wedge of pastry on a dish and handed it to him. "I baked this earlier today," she said.

He smiled as she set the food before him on the table, still so very much the serving girl, although she was now the mistress of her own home.

Philippe ate well while she sat at his elbow, admiring him with her eyes. What a treat it was to see her lover once again. She missed living with him, seeing him every day, though at least their separation made each meeting special now.

"I never get meals as good as this anymore," he told her as he sampled a fishcake. "Ever since mother went back to live in Champagne and took all our best cooks with her, the food at the palace has been dreadful."

Edythe leaned to his shoulder. "I miss Paris sometimes."

He turned to smile at her. "But not the palace surely; not that drafty place."

She gave a sniffing little laugh. "Oh, it is much more comfortable here. This is a lovely house." Her face sobered. "But I love it all the more because you gave it to me."

After he had finished eating he poured wine for both of them, and they sat on stools near the fire, warming themselves and drinking. "Oh, Edythe," he sighed, his voice a mingling of weariness and satisfaction, "you give me the only peace I know in life. All the rest is such a tangle now. Everyone is against me: my family, the bishops, even the pope himself." He twirled a loose lock of her soft brown hair between his nervous fingers. "All of this business about Ingeborg—ridiculous. I shouldn't have to fight to end a marriage which is no marriage. But because of this controversy I am blamed for every current ill: the droughts and famines, even the fires last year in Beauvais and Amiens."

Edythe tugged at his sleeve. "It is only vicious tongues and jealousy at work."

"Jealousy—yes," he agreed, "and revenge. I know for certain Sibylla has done all she can to turn every noble in Paris against me." His voice lowered to a near whisper. "How she hates me now!"

His cup was almost empty and Edythe rose to fill it up, before settling herself once more at his side. "She is unhappy because you married Agnes. She wanted to keep you all to herself."

He brushed away her gentle explanation with a wave of his hand. "It's foolish. She knew why I did it, why I *had* to do it. I thought that in the face of another marriage the pope would sanction my divorce from Ingeborg. But he didn't. Damn him to hell."

"Perhaps you should take Ingeborg back," she said hesitantly.

He gave her a look hard-edged by anger. "You should know better than to say such things to me, Edythe. I loathe that woman! I will never take her back!"

Edythe reached to stroke his beard with her fingertips. "I know. But I can't help feeling sorry for her. And for Sibylla too, though I have never really liked her. You see, my darling, I know how I'd feel without you."

He kissed her hand lovingly. "You could never be anything but what you are—my sweet and gentle girl." He raised his cup to her mouth and fed her a little wine from it, then kissed away the drops that remained on her lips. "You know," he said, "when Sully died last month I thought: that's it; I've lost the last true friend I have. They're all gone now: Harry, Geoffrey, Isabel. And Richard might as well be dead, for the friendship between us died years ago. Now Sully. All who cared for me are gone— except for you, sweet Edythe. I care for you more than you can know."

She raised her face to him. "And you are everything to me."

He tossed the cup aside and eagerly took her in his arms, and after several kisses Edythe could sense the passion racing in his blood. She closed her eyes and felt him lift her in his strong embrace and carry her from the room.

He had taught her everything she knew of love, how to free herself from the constraints of morality and plunge herself joyfully into passion. And although she had never known another man, she felt that no one else could bring such excitement to a woman's bed.

Afterwards she lay in his arms, sleepy and full of peace. Her cheek was on his chest and she could hear his heart beating. "I love you," she whispered.

His arms tightened around her. "I can forget almost everything when I'm with you, dear Edythe."

Except for Isabel.

Edythe left kisses on his chest where the scars were. "You still miss her, don't you?" she asked, reading his thoughts.

There were deeper scars which could not be seen. "Yes," he admitted ruefully. His embrace grew harder till Edythe winced in pain. "Oh God, why can't I be free of her? Why does her memory haunt me like a ghost that cannot be laid to rest?"

She struggled out of his embrace and sat up, looking down at him. She'd learned long ago to master whatever jealousy she felt, but there was quiet pain in her voice. "You don't *want* to be free of her, Philippe. Your grief for Isabel is the most precious thing you have and you will treasure it until the day you die."

You are mine until the grave makes ghosts of both of us.

He turned his face away so she could not see the tears.

Outside the town of Chartres, just a mile beyond the cathedral, Philippe stood in a little grove of yew trees, remembering another November.

He stared out toward the grey sky where the snow was falling.

It was cold and the world seemed empty but for him. When the wind rattled a branch behind him he jumped at the sound. After a moment he relaxed, but turned his head a bit, anticipating a presence that was not there and a sweet scent of narcissus that had faded long ago.

Philippe pushed at the snow with booted feet as the pale sky deepened to vaguer shades of smoke color. Then when the light was gone, he straddled his horse and rode away.

Alone in the empty grove there was a sudden hiss of wind.

$\mathfrak{I}$N APRIL of the year 1199, King Richard died in France from a battle wound and the crown of England passed to John.

There were those who believed it should have gone to the other claimant, Arthur of Brittany. But John murdered him or caused him to be murdered, and when the posthumous son of his brother Geoffrey was dead, there was no one to contest the throne which Henry had promised to John a decade before.

Richard's death was a stroke of magnificent luck for Philippe.

It meant unlimited potential gain against the Plantagenets, for

John was no fit warrior like his older brother; and indeed as years passed Philippe was able to confiscate more and more of the great Angevin domains in France. Normandy, the prize of all prizes, fell to the French in 1204.

And yet, Philippe's power continued to be threatened by the Ingeborg fiasco. Finally a new pope—Innocent III—pronounced the dreaded *interdict* upon all of Philippe's lands until the king was forced to put away Agnes of Meran, and acknowledge Ingeborg as his lawful wife. For a year Philippe refused. But when Agnes died in childbirth in 1201, he finally agreed to take back Ingeborg, on the condition that the pope legitimize the two children Agnes had borne to him.

And so it was done.

But once again Philippe reneged on his word, and it was not until 1213, a full twenty years after the marriage had been celebrated at Amiens, that he was at last persuaded to recognize the unhappy Ingeborg as his queen. She was given a manor house near Chantilly, and allowed to exercise minor rights as Philippe's consort. But he never bedded her; never treated her as a wife.

She outlived her unloving husband by thirteen years.

Fortified by forgiveness of both God and pope, Philippe turned his attentions toward the dangers of an invasion by his enemies. For several years a number of coalitions had arisen to threaten his power. Then in 1214 they all banned together against him: England, the Empire, Germany, certain French vassalages, and the counties of Flanders and Hainault.

At Bouvines, a little town just a few miles south of Isabel's birthplace, Philippe proved his might to the world by defeating his aggressors in the most splendid victory France had ever known. If any man alive had doubted Philippe to be master of Europe, they did not doubt it after the battle on that hot summer day.

At the head of his triumphant army, he came back to Paris.

Philippe led his bloodied troops through streets gone mad with celebrating, and took them into Notre Dame. There before the great altar, they all knelt to give thanks for this great victory.

Above their heads the bells thundered out *Te Deum* to the glory of God, and the honor of their king.

* * *

In July of the year 1223 the noble Philippe-Auguste, king of the Franks, fell ill of a fever and died at the abbey of Ste. Gabrielle in Mantes, after a reign of forty-three years. This man of great skill and courage, noble in his deeds, a winner of battles, greatly enriched the treasury and brought honor to France.

He enlarged the royal demesne by four times what he found it at the start of his reign. To its small area he added Vermandois, Artois, Amiens, Poitou, Anjou, Touraine, Maine, Alençon, Clermont, Valois, Ponthieu, and Normandy.

He gave generously of his monies to building and fortifying his beloved capital, and was a friend to the churches. During his reign France knew the rise of great cathedrals, including Notre Dame de Paris, which he loved. He was a builder of other things and put himself a fortress in the center of the city which he used to keep his treasury, called the Louvre; and he put the wall about the city of Paris to keep it free from enemy invaders.

As befits so great a monarch and illustrious a man, he was laid in burial at St. Denis beside the tombs of his ancestors, and amid the sound of cries and mourning from all the nobles in France.

At his death he has left us a worthy successor, a strong and mighty warrior-king who it may please God long to reign over us, Louis VIII, son of Philippe-Auguste and his first queen, who was Isabel de Hainault...

William le Breton
Preface to *The Philippid*
November 1, 1223

THE END

Glossary

Albigenses—An extremist and heretic religious sect of southern France.

Almoner—A small pouch, made of silk and decorated with beading or fringes, carried by men and women for distributing coins to the poor.

Arnoldia—The mysterious wasting illness suffered by men at Acre, including the two kings, during the Third Crusade. The symptoms were high fever, peeling skin, and vomiting. It also caused damage to the hair and fingernails.

Assize of Arms—A survey of equipment held by feudal tenants; generally, an assize came to mean any law which modified a law already in existence.

Bezant—Gold coin of Byzantium.

Blazon—A coat of arms, or its representation in heraldry.

Bliaud—A tunic-style garment worn to the knees or longer, usually belted and decorated with embroidery at the neck, wrists and hem. Worn most often by men, though women wore a more free-flowing variation.

Braies—Loose trousers worn by men, held together at the front by lacing.

Brunette—Wool dyed dark brown in color, used for the making of blankets or common clothes.

Cantel—Medieval vestment for the mass; also called a *cope*.

Castellan—The keeper of a castle, though not necessarily its lord.

Cendal—Also *sendal*. A fine, shimmery silk, often decorated with appliques.

Chainse—A long tunic with tight sleeves, worn by women, usually under their bliaud or pellison. Isabel wore hers alone, in the Flemish fashion.

Chambrette—A small room, usually a bedroom annex.

Chamois—Soft leather made from the hide of the animal of the same name. Most often used in making boots and gloves for the nobility or royalty.

587

Champagnois—The ruling house of Champagne; those representing it.

Chapter house—Place of assemblage for a religious order, usually attached to a cathedral. Guests could be housed here as well.

Chasuble—Long, sleeveless vestment worn by the priest at mass.

Chatelaine—A decorative chain worn at the waist, whereon a mistress of the house kept her keys.

Chemise—Loose garment worn by women, often made of silk or fine linen.

Chief Justiciar—A top-level judicial and political figure of state, particularly in Norman and Plantagenet England.

Circlet—A dainty and ornamental band worn by women of rank.

Coif—A skullcap worn beneath a knight's mesh hood; the hood itself.

Corselet—A breastplate or light form of body armor to cover the breast.

Courlieu—A private messenger in the service of a king or great lord.

Crespinette—A delicate net, usually ornamental, used to cover braided or upswept hair, worn by women of rank.

Curia Regis—A feudal council, most often convened by the king. In the case of Philippe's *curia*, it was composed equally of nobles and commoners.

Custos—A guardian or keeper; custodian. Does not imply the powers of a procurator.

Dalmatic—A bishop's outer vestment. Often worn by monarchs as well.

Damask—Rich patterned cloth, usually of linen or heavy silk.

Demesne—Generally, the realm or domain. In Philippe's case, the *royal demesne.*

Deniers—Silver coins or "pennies" used in England and France. Larger denominations were had by weighing deniers. A *sou* was 12 denier weight. A *livre* was one pound denier weight. Gold coins, rare in England and France, were worth about twenty-five silver denier.

Dishabille—A woman's loose, informal gown, made of silk or muslin.

Dot—Also *dotalicium.* A woman's marriage portion; her dowry.

Draughts—Board game for two or more players; a medieval version of checkers.

Duchy—Territory ruled by a duke or duchess, often held as an annexed portion to a king's domain.

Epiphany—Christian feast, celebrated January 6th, observing the manifestation of Christ's divinity to the Magi, and His baptism.

Esplanade—A flat, grassy area, open to public gatherings or for walking.

Ewerer—A servant who washed the hands of noble lords and their guests at table.

Fief—A feudal estate, often held by lower nobles in the name of the overlord or king.

Florin—A Spanish or Italian coin, usually made of gold.

Galleys—Large, slender ships, propelled by oars, used for navigating the Mediterranean Sea.

Galliard—Formal dance, stately in style.

Gigue—A long, slim, stringed instrument shaped like a figure eight. It was strummed for playing.

Gonne—Variant of *gown*. Often used to describe an ecclesiastical vestment.

Gothic—In architecture, the style which grew to popularity (particularly in France) during the 12th–15th centuries. It was characterized by high pointed arches, flying buttresses, rib vaulting. This allowed higher windows, and "Light" became an integral part of Gothic architecture, symbolizing God's presence and His love.

Grande Chartreuse—Celebrated Carthusian monastery founded in the 11th Century in southeast France, near Grenoble.

Grande Pont—Literally, "the big bridge" spanning the Seine.

Hauberk—A long tunic made of chain mail.

Henap—A cup or goblet for wine. Decorative types were also called *knight jugs*.

Herbal Posset—A drink of hot milk, curdled by wine and mixed with herbs, used as a relaxing sleep aid or a "cure-all."

Homage—The act of allegiance to a lord or king by his vassal, acknowledged by a ceremonial oath.

Illusion foods—Banquet foods molded into the shapes of animals and decorated by artificial coloring.

Interdict—Church law denying certain sacraments to offending individuals or nations. Pope Innocent proclaimed the Interdict against France when Philippe II refused to acknowledge Ingeborg of Denmark as his wife.

Jongleurs—Wandering musicians and story-tellers of northern France.

Knights Hospitallers—Members of a military religious order which grew out of the hospital established during the First Crusade in order to care for pilgrims in the Holy Land.

Knights Templars—Members of a military religious (Benedictine) order, they were called the Soldiers of Christ and noted for their loyalty, rigid code, and prowess in battle. After the Third Crusade they held Acre till 1291.

Lais—A form of medieval ballad, usually set to music. Marie de France was famous for these.

Largess—Generosity in giving money or gifts, a much-prized element of chivalry.

Lists—An enclosed area of land, prepared for public jousts and tournaments.

Livres—See *deniers*.

Mamelukes—Saladin's mounted soldiers. Originally they were slaves brought from Egypt, but became an elite military order.

Mangonels—Siege engines built to hurl stones in the manner of a catapult. They varied in size, but the ones used at Acre were very large.

Mantle—A long cape, often fur-trimmed.

Mark—Sum of money equal to two thirds of the English pound sterling.

Mayors of the Palace—Institution under the early Frankish kings. The "mayor" was actually a combination chancellor and *major domo*. Under the Carolingians, the mayors of the palace were the ancestors of Hugh Capet.

Michaelmas—Feast of the archangel Michael, celebrated September 29th.

Mitre—Tall, decorative peaked hat worn by bishops and archbishops.

Molle—A clay model, worked to scale.

Oath of Fealty—An oath of homage, but not restricted to matters of land-holding. Rather it was a promise of loyalty to any overlord. An oath of fealty to the Crown held sway over any other oath or pledge.

Oriflamme—The ancient banner of the Franks. It was usually of red silk or samite and embroidered with golden stars. The word quite literally means "gold and flame." This banner was still carried by the time of Philippe II but had been somewhat supplanted in significance by the Capetian device of the fleur-de-lis.

Paladin—A tournament champion; loosely, any competitor in such a match.

Palfrey—A small, gentle horse, usually ridden by women.

Parvis—The courtyard or space in front of a church or palais.

Pater Noster—Literally, "Our Father..." The Lord's prayer.

Patriarch—A bishop, holding the highest rank beneath the Pope. These served in Constantinople, Antioch, Jerusalem, and Alexandria.

Pellison—Thin cloak for men, usually worn over the bliaud; sometimes trimmed with fur. Women wore a more decorative version over their chainse, often belted, to show off the figure.

Pennon—Small, two-tailed flag; in the case of fashion, women's long sleeves which resembled the same.

Pentecôte—French form for *Pentecost*.

Petite Pont—Literally, "the little bridge" spanning the Seine, so-called not because of its size but because it handled less trade from the river.

Pilgrim's Scrip—A small bag or satchel; the symbolic knapsack for travelers to the Holy Land.

Pole-axe—Battle weapon consisting of an axe mounted on a long shaft.

Porringer—Shallow vessel with handle, used for wine and other liquids, also for soups.

Portières—Small tapestries, cut into panels, used to cover vacant doorways and keep out drafts.

Potage—Soup made with vegetables and herbs, mixed in a stock broth.

Provençal—Relating to the Romance language of Provence, especially the literary language of the troubadours.

Provost—Title attached to various ecclesiastical and secular offices, denoting authority. In the case of Gilbert of Mons, he was undoubtedly head of the church school.

Psalter—Small book containing psalms and drawings relating to them.

Pucelles—Daughters of petty nobles who worked as servants for royalty, usually in the role of a hand-maiden. They were unpaid, but treated better than regular servants, as fitted the rank of their originating household.

Queen of Love and Beauty—A symbolic title for the Lady who was elected to preside over tournament festivities.

Reliquary—A receptacle, usually small, for the storing of holy relics.

Romanesque—In architecture, a medieval style preceding Gothic, characterized by thick walls and heavy, wide vaulting.

Sacred Chrism—Oil used for anointing the kings of France, said to have been sent down from heaven on the wings of a dove for the baptism of Clovis, first of the Franks to be Christianized. The Chrism was kept at Rheims and said never to diminish. It was the most prized relic of the monarchy till the time of Louis XVI, when it was destroyed by the Revolutionaries.

Sacristy—A room inside a church or cathedral housing sacred vessels and vestments.

Salic Law—Named for the Salian Franks who instituted it, the code is actually little more than a collection of barbarian customs written down. There is no truth that it had anything to do with the royal succession, and in any case the Salic Law was no longer in force during the Capetian period. But it did forbid women to inherit property in France, and this tradition was carried into the time of Philippe II. Because of this it was likewise traditional that women could not rule, though there was no actual law against it in the 12th century.

Sallat—A salad.

Salle—Rooms or apartments.

Samite—A heavy and beautiful silk fabric, often interwoven with threads of gold or silver.

Scimitar—An oriental sword having a long curved blade.

Scrofula—A blood disease characterized by swelling of the lymph glands. It was said in medieval times that the touch of the French king could cure it.

Seignior—Lord of the manor; a titular ruler.

Seneschal—A title of courtesy, usually implying limited significance as an officer of the household. In the case of Geoffrey Plantagenet, of course, it implied a great deal more.

Serge—Worsted wool used to make blankets or thin coverlets like sheets.

Shift—A light chemise or slip worn by women as an undergarment.

Siege Engines—Machines, mainly stone-throwing catapults used to breach walls or fortresses. See *mangonels*.

Sirventes—Form of lyric verse written by the Provençal troubadours, satirizing political and social events. Bertran de Born was famous for his sirventes, many of which dealt with the struggles between Henry Plantagenet and his sons.

Sous—See *deniers*.

Spar—Long pole used for jousting in "mock" tournaments.

Surcoat—Long garment for men, sometimes worn over armor, usually decorated with embroidery of heraldic arms. Split at the side for riding. Women wore a fitted, more flattering version.

Suzerain—A feudal lord with authority over vassals who owe allegiance in return for use of his lands.

Tableau Vivant—A still-life drama; in the Middle Ages this was often accompanied by dissertations read by individual actors or a chorus.

Te Deum—Latin hymn, part of the mass; either the music of such, or its text, "We praise thee, O God..."

Tisane—A hot herbal beverage, praised for its medicinal purposes.

Tourdion—Fast-paced, formal dance.

Trouvères—Lyric poets of northern France, as compared to troubadours who were from the south, though their function was similar.

Vassal—Any individual owing allegiance to a higher feudal power or lord.